CONTENTS

AIR

FRAME

MICHAEL CRICHTON

Turbulence is just the beginning. . . .

"A taut, absorbing suspenser."

—*Booklist*

MONDAY

ABOARD TPA 545

5:18 a.m. Emily Jansen sighed in relief. The long flight was nearing an end. Morning sunlight streamed through the windows of the airplane. In her lap little Sarah squinted in the unaccustomed brightness as she noisily sucked the last of her bottle and pushed it away with tiny fists. "That was good, wasn't it?" Emily said. "Okay . . . up we go. . . ."

She raised the infant onto her shoulder, began to pat her back. The baby gave a gurgling belch, and her body relaxed.

In the next seat Tim Jansen yawned and rubbed his eyes. He had slept through the night, all the way from Hong Kong. Emily never slept on planes; she was too nervous.

"Morning," Tim said, looking at his watch. "Just a couple of hours more, hon. Any sign of breakfast?"

"Not yet," Emily said, shaking her head. They had taken TransPacific Airlines, a charter from Hong Kong. The money they saved would be useful when they set up housekeeping at the University of Colorado, where Tim was going to be an assistant professor. The flight had been pleasant enough—they were in the front of the plane—but the stewardesses seemed disorganized, the meals coming at odd times.

And even now, Emily was surprised by the casual behavior of the crew. They left the cockpit door open during the flight. The pilots strolled around the plane at night, kibitzing with the stewardesses. One was leaving right now, walking to the back. Of course they were probably stretching their legs. Stay alert, all of that. And certainly the fact that the crew was Chinese didn't trouble her. After a year in China she admired the efficiency and attention to detail of the Chinese. But somehow the whole flight just made her nervous.

Emily put Sarah back down in her lap. The baby stared at Tim and beamed.

"Hey, I should get this," Tim said. Fumbling in the bag under his seat, he brought out a video camera, trained it on his daughter. He waggled his free hand to get her attention. "Sarah . . . Sarah . . . Smile for Daddy. Smile."

Sarah smiled and made a gurgling sound.

"How does it feel to be going to America, Sarah? Ready to see where your parents are from?" Their daughter had been born seven months ago in Hunan, where Tim had studied Chinese medicine.

Emily saw the camera lens pointed at her. "And what about you, Mom?" Tim said. "Are you glad to be going home?"

"Oh, Tim," she said. "Please." She must look like hell, she thought. All those hours. She needed to comb her hair.

"Come on, Em. What are you thinking?"

She said, "Well, what I really want—what I have dreamed about for months—is a cheeseburger. With onions and tomatoes and lettuce and pickles and mayonnaise."

Tim turned the camera back to their daughter, who was tugging at her toes with one tiny fist. She pulled her foot into her mouth.

"Taste good?" Tim said, laughing. The camera shook as he laughed. "Is that breakfast for you, Sarah?"

Emily heard a low rumbling sound, almost a vibration, that seemed to come from the wing. She snapped her head around. "What was that?"

"Take it easy, Em," Tim said. "We're almost home."

But even as he spoke, the plane seemed to shudder, the nose of the plane turning down. Suddenly everything tilted at a crazy angle. Emily felt Sarah sliding forward off her lap. She clutched at her daughter. Now it felt like the plane was going *straight down,* and then suddenly it was going up, and her stomach was pressed into the seat. Her daughter was a lead weight against her.

Tim said, "What the—"

Abruptly she was lifted off the seat, her seat belt cutting into her thighs. She felt light and sick to her stomach. She saw Tim bounce out of his seat, his head slamming into the luggage compartments overhead, the camera flying past her face.

From the cockpit Emily heard buzzing alarms and a metallic voice that said, "Stall! Stall!" She glimpsed the arms of the pilots moving swiftly over the controls; they were shouting in Chinese. All over the aircraft people were screaming, hysterical. There was the sound of shattering glass.

Emily looked at Tim, but her husband wasn't in his seat anymore. Yellow oxygen masks were dropping, one swinging in front of her, but she could not reach for it, because she was clutching her baby.

She was pressed back into her seat as the plane descended steeply, an incredibly loud whining dive. Shoes and purses ricocheted across the cabin, clanging and banging; bodies thumped against seats, the floor.

Emily felt dizzy and faint. The alarms continued to sound. The passengers continued to scream. The plane was still in a dive.

Emily lowered her head, clutched her infant daughter to her chest, and for the first time in her life began to pray.

SOCAL APPROACH CONTROL

5:43 a.m. "Socal Approach, this is TransPacific 545. We have an emergency."

In the darkened building that housed Southern California Air Traffic Approach Control, senior controller Dave Marshall heard the pilot's call and glanced at his radar screen. TransPacific 545 was inbound from Hong Kong to Denver. The flight had been handed over to him from Oakland a few minutes earlier—a perfectly normal flight. Marshall touched the microphone at his cheek and said, "Go ahead, 545."

"Request priority clearance for landing in Los Angeles."

The pilot sounded calm. Marshall saw that TPA 545 was approaching the California coastline. Soon it would pass over Marina del Rey. It was still half an hour out of LAX.

Marshall said, "Okay, 545, say the nature of the emergency."

"We need ambulances on the ground," the pilot said. "I would say thirty or forty ambulances. Maybe more."

Marshall was stunned. "*Forty* ambulances?"

"Affirmative. We encountered severe turbulence during flight. We have injuries of passengers and flight crew."

Marshall spun in his chair, beckoned to his supervisor, Jane Levine. She picked up a headset, punched in, and listened.

Marshall said, "TransPacific, I copy your ground request. What is the nature of the injuries you are bringing in?"

"I am not sure."

Levine made a spinning gesture: Keep the pilot talking. Marshall said, "Can you give us an estimate?"

"I am sorry, no. An estimate is not possible."

"Is anyone unconscious?"

"No, I do not think so," the pilot answered. "But two are dead."

"Nice of him to tell us," Jane Levine said. "Let's not have anymore surprises. Is the aircraft all right?"

Marshall said, "TPA 545, what is your aircraft's condition?"

"We have damage to the passenger cabin," the pilot said. "Minor damage only."

"What is the condition of the flight deck?" Marshall said.

"Flight deck is operational. FDAU is nominal." That was the flight data acquisition unit, which tracked faults within the aircraft. If it said the plane was okay, it probably was.

"What is the condition of your flight crew?" Marshall asked.

"Captain and first officer in good condition. Two stewardesses are hurt. One is not conscious. The other one, I don't know."

Marshall was shaking his head. "He just told us nobody was unconscious."

"I'm not buying any of this," Levine said. She picked up the red phone. "Put a fire crew on level one alert. Get the ambulances. Have medical notify the Westside hospitals." She looked at her watch. "I'll call the L.A. FSDO. This'll make his damn day."

LAX

5:57 a.m. Daniel Greene was the duty officer at the Federal Aviation Administration's flight standards district office, half a mile from LAX. The local FSDOs—or fizdos, as they were called—supervised the flight operations of commercial carriers, checking everything from aircraft maintenance to pilot training. Greene had come in early to clear the paper off his desk; his secretary had quit the week before, and the office manager refused to replace her, citing orders from Washington to absorb attrition. So now Greene went to work, muttering. Congress was slashing the FAA budget, telling them to do more with less. But passenger traffic was up, and—

His red phone rang, the emergency line. He picked it up. It was a woman at traffic control.

"We've just been informed of an incident on an inbound foreign carrier," she said.

"Uh-huh." Greene reached for a notepad. "Go ahead."

"It's TransPacific flight 545, incoming from Hong Kong to Denver. Pilot's requested emergency landing at LAX. Says they encountered turbulence during flight."

"Is the plane airworthy?"

"They say it is," Levine said. "They've got injuries, and they've requested forty ambulances."

"Forty?"

"They've also got two stiffs."

"Great." Greene got up from his desk. "When's it due in?"

"Eighteen minutes. I've notified EMS and the fire crews."

"Fire crews? I thought you said the plane's okay."

"Who knows?" the woman said. "The pilot is not making much sense. Sounds like he might be in shock."

"Okay," Greene said. "I'm on my way."

He grabbed his badge and his cell phone and went out the door. As he passed Karen, the receptionist, he said, "Have we got anybody at the international terminal?"

"Kevin's there."

"Beep him," Greene said. "Tell him to get on TPA 545, inbound Hong Kong, landing in fifteen. Tell him to stay at the gate—and *don't let the flight crew leave.*"

GREENE roared down Sepulveda Boulevard toward the airport. Just before the highway ran beneath the runway, he looked up and saw the big TransPacific Airlines wide-body, identifiable by its bright yellow tail insignia, taxiing toward the gate. TransPacific was a Hong Kong–based charter carrier. Most of the problems the FAA had with foreign airlines occurred with low-budget charters. But TransPacific had an excellent reputation.

At least the bird was on the ground, Greene thought. And he couldn't see any structural damage to it. The wide-body was an N-22, built by Norton Aircraft in Burbank. The plane had been in revenue service five years, with an enviable dispatch and safety record.

Greene stepped on the gas and rushed into the tunnel, passing beneath the giant aircraft. He sprinted through the international building. Through the windows he saw the TransPacific jet pulled up to the gate and the ambulances lined up on the concrete below. The first of them was already driving out, its siren whining.

At the gate Greene flashed his badge and ran down the ramp. Passengers were disembarking, pale and frightened. Many limped, their clothes torn and bloody. On each side of the ramp paramedics clustered around the injured.

As he neared the plane, the nauseating odor of vomit grew

stronger. A stewardess stepped back as Greene slid past a mother clutching an infant and stepped into the plane.

He looked at the interior and stopped. "Oh, my God," he said softly. *"What happened to this plane?"*

GLENDALE, CALIFORNIA

6:00 a.m. "Mom? Who do you like better—Mickey Mouse or Minnie Mouse?"

Standing in the kitchen of her bungalow, still wearing her jogging shorts from her five-mile morning run, Casey Singleton finished making a tuna sandwich and put it into her daughter's lunchbox. Singleton was thirty-six years old, a vice president at Norton Aircraft in Burbank. Her daughter sat at the table, eating cereal.

"Well?" Allison said. "Who do you like better, Mickey Mouse or Minnie Mouse?" She was seven, and she ranked everything.

"I like them both," Casey said.

"But who do you like *better?*" Allison said, exasperated.

"Minnie."

"Me, too," she said, pushing the cereal carton away.

Casey put a banana and a thermos of juice in the lunchbox, closed the lid. "Finish eating, Allison. We have to get ready."

"What's quart?"

"Quart? It's a measure of liquid."

"No, Mom. Qua-urt," she said.

Casey looked over and saw that her daughter had picked up her new laminated plant ID badge, which had Casey's picture, her name, and then, in large blue letters, QA/IRT.

"It's my new job at the plant. I'm the quality-assurance rep on the incident review team."

"Are you still making airplanes?" Ever since the divorce, Allison had been extremely attentive to change. Even a minor alteration in Casey's hairstyle prompted repeated discussions.

"Yes, Allie," she said. "I'm still making airplanes. Everything's the same. I just got a promotion. Now get your shoes on. Your dad'll be picking you up any minute."

"No, he won't. Dad's always late. What's your promotion?"

Casey bent over and began pulling on her daughter's sneakers. "Well," she said, "I still work at QA, but I don't check the planes in the factory anymore. I check them after they leave the plant."

"To make sure they fly?"

"Yes, honey. We check them and fix any problems."

"They better fly," Allison said, "or else they'll crash!" She began to laugh. "They'll all fall out of the sky! And hit everybody in their houses, right while they're eating their cereal! That wouldn't be too good, would it, Mom?"

Casey laughed with her. "No, that wouldn't be good at all. People at the plant would be *very* upset." She finished tying the laces, swung her daughter's feet away. "Now where's your sweatshirt?"

"I don't need it. It's not even cold!"

"It may be cold later in the week. Get your sweatshirt, please."

She heard a horn honk outside, saw Jim's black Lexus in front of the house. Jim was behind the wheel, smoking a cigarette. He was wearing a jacket and tie. Perhaps he had a job interview, she thought.

Allison stomped around her room, banging drawers. She came back looking unhappy, the sweatshirt hanging from her backpack.

Casey opened the door, and they walked to the car in the hazy morning sunshine. Allison cried, "Hi, Daddy!" and broke into a run. Jim waved back with a boozy grin.

Casey walked over to Jim's window. "No smoking with Allison in the car, right? We had an agreement about it."

Jim stared at her. "Good morning to you, too." His voice was raspy. He looked hung over. "Do you see me smoking?"

"I'm just saying."

"And you've said it before, Katherine. A million times."

Casey sighed. She was determined not to fight in front of Allison. "Okay," she said, forcing a smile. "See you Sunday."

Their arrangement was that Allison stayed with Jim one week a month, leaving Monday and returning the following Sunday.

"Sunday at six." He nodded curtly. "Same as always."

She bent over. "Bye, Allie."

Allison said, "Bye, Mom," but her eyes were already distant, her voice cool; she had transferred her allegiance to her father even before her seat belt was fastened. Then Jim stepped on the gas, and the Lexus drove away, leaving Casey standing there on the sidewalk. The car rounded the corner and was gone.

Casey was turning to go back inside when her beeper went off with a squeal. She unclipped it from her shorts and read:

***JM IRT 0700 WR

She sighed. Three stars signaled an urgent message: John Marder, who ran the factory, was calling an IRT meeting for 7:00 a.m., a full hour before regular morning call. Something was up.

BURBANK AIRPORT

6:32 a.m. Rush hour traffic crept forward in the pale morning light. Casey twisted her rearview mirror and leaned over to check her makeup. With her short, dark hair, she was appealing in a tomboyish way—long-limbed and athletic. She played first base on the plant softball team. Men were comfortable around her; they treated her like a kid sister, which served her well at the plant.

In fact, Casey had had few problems there. She was the only daughter of an editor at the Detroit *News.* Her two older brothers were both engineers at Ford. Her mother died when she was an infant, so she had been raised in a household of men.

After she graduated from Southern Illinois in journalism, Casey had followed her brothers to Ford. But she found writing press releases uninteresting, so she got an M.B.A. Along the way she married Jim, a Ford engineer, and had a child.

But Allison's arrival had ended the marriage: Confronted by diapers and feeding schedules, Jim started drinking, staying out late. Eventually they separated. When Jim announced he was moving to the West Coast to work for Toyota, Casey decided to move out, too, so Allison could grow up seeing her father. California offered Casey a fresh start. She imagined herself driving a convertible, living in a sunny house near the beach, with palm trees outside her window. She imagined her daughter growing up tanned and healthy.

Instead, Casey lived in Glendale, an hour and a half inland. She had indeed bought a convertible, but she never put the top down. Casey worried about Allison's education in a school system where fifty languages were spoken. And she worried about the future, because the California economy was still depressed, jobs scarce. Jim had been out of work for two years now, since Toyota fired him for drinking. Casey had survived wave after wave of layoffs at Norton, where production had slumped thanks to the global recession.

She had never imagined she would work for an aircraft company, but she had found that her plainspoken, midwestern pragmatism was perfectly suited to the culture of engineers that dominated the company. Her attention to detail had served her well at Norton, where she had for the last year been a vice president of quality assurance.

She liked QA, though the division had a nearly impossible mission. Norton Aircraft was divided into two factions—production and engineering—which were perpetually at war. Quality assurance stood uneasily between the two. When a problem emerged, QA was expected to get to the bottom of it. That rarely endeared them to mechanics on the line or the engineers.

At the same time, QA was expected to deal with customer-support problems. Customers were often unhappy with decisions they themselves had made, blaming Norton if the galleys they had ordered were in the wrong place, or if there were too few toilets on the plane. It took patience and political skill to keep everybody happy and get the problems resolved. Casey, a born peacemaker, was especially good at this.

In return for walking a political tightrope, workers in QA had the run of the plant. As a vice president, Casey was involved in every aspect of the company's work. She had a lot of freedom and wide-ranging responsibility.

And now John Marder had just promoted her to liaison for the IRT. This was a position of considerable visibility—and it put her in line to head the division.

CASEY turned her Mustang convertible off the Golden State Freeway onto Empire Avenue, following the chain-link fence that marked the southern perimeter of Burbank Airport. She headed toward the commercial complexes—Rockwell, Lockheed, and Norton Aircraft. From a distance she could see the rows of hangars, each with the winged Norton logo painted above.

Her car phone rang.

"Casey? It's Norma. You know about the meeting?"

Norma was her secretary. "I'm on my way," she said. "What's going on?"

"Nobody knows anything," Norma said. "But it must be bad. Marder's been screaming at the engineering heads."

John Marder was the chief operating officer at Norton and had supervised the manufacture of the N-22 aircraft. He was a ruthless and occasionally reckless man, but he got results. Marder was also married to Charley Norton's only daughter. That made Marder the second most powerful man in the company after the president.

"What do you want me to do with your new assistant?" Norma said. "He's waiting in your office. You haven't forgotten?"

"Oh, right." The truth was, she had forgotten. Some nephew of the Norton family was working his way through the divisions. Marder had assigned the kid to Casey, which meant she'd have to baby-sit him for the next six weeks. "What's he like, Norma?"

"Well, he's not drooling."

"Norma."

"He's better than the last one."

"How much better?"

"I'm looking at his résumé," she said. "Yale law school and a year at GM. But he's been in marketing for the last three months, and he doesn't know anything about production. You're going to have to start him from the beginning."

"Right," Casey said, sighing. Marder would expect her to bring him to the meeting. "Have the kid meet me in front of administration in ten minutes. And make sure he doesn't get lost, okay?"

"You want me to walk him down?"

"Yeah, you better."

Casey hung up and glanced at her watch. Traffic was moving slowly. She drummed her fingers impatiently. What could the meeting be about? There might have been an accident or a crash.

She turned on the radio to see if it was on the news. She got a talk station, a caller saying, "—not fair to make kids wear uniforms to school. It's elitist and discriminatory—"

Casey pushed a button, changing the station. "—forcing their personal morality on us. I don't believe a fetus is a human—"

She pushed another button. "These media attacks are all coming from people who don't like free speech."

Where, she thought, is the *news?* Did an airplane crash or not?

She had a sudden image of her father, reading a big stack of newspapers from all over the country every Sunday after church, muttering to himself, "That's not the story; that's not the story!" as he dropped the pages in an untidy heap around his living-room chair. Of course, her father had been a print journalist back in the 1960s. It was a different world now. Now everything was on television. Television and the mindless chatter on the radio.

Up ahead she saw the main gate of the Norton plant. She clicked the radio off.

NORTON Aircraft was one of the great names of American aviation. The company had been started by aviation pioneer Charley Norton in 1935; during World War II it made the legendary B-22 bomber, the P-27 Skycat fighter, and the C-12 transport for the air force. In recent years Norton had weathered the hard times, and now it was one of just four companies that still built large aircraft for the global market. The others were Boeing in Seattle, McDonnell Douglas in Long Beach, and the European consortium Airbus in Toulouse, France.

Casey drove through acres of parking lots to gate 7, pausing at the barrier while security checked her badge. As always, she felt a lift driving into the plant. It wasn't a factory so much as a small city, covering sixteen square miles. It had its own hospital, newspaper, and police force; thirty thousand people worked here. Here they built the N-20, the narrow-body twinjet; the N-22, the wide-body; and the KC-22, the air force fuel tanker. She could see the principal assembly buildings, each more than a mile in length.

She headed for the glass administration building, in the center of the plant. Pulling into her parking space, she left the engine running. She saw a young man, looking collegiate in a sport coat and tie, khaki slacks, and penny loafers. The kid waved diffidently as she got out of the car.

"Bob Richman," he said. "I'm your new assistant." His handshake was polite, reserved. She couldn't remember which side of the Norton family he was from, but she recognized the type. Plenty of money, divorced parents, an indifferent record at good schools, and an unshakable sense of entitlement.

"Casey Singleton," she said. "Get in. We're late."

"Late," he said, climbing into the car. "It's not even seven."

"First shift starts at six," Casey said. "Most of us in QA work the factory schedule. Don't they do that at GM?"

"I wouldn't know," he said. "I was in legal."

"Spend any time on the floor?"

"As little as possible."

Casey sighed. It was going to be a long six weeks with this guy, she thought. "You've been over in marketing so far?"

"Yeah." He shrugged. "But selling isn't really my thing."

She drove south toward building 64, where the wide-body was built. Richman suppressed a yawn. "Boy, it's early. What are we rushing to?"

"The incident review team," she said. "Every time something happens to one of our planes, the IRT meets to figure out what happened and what we should do about it."

"How often do you meet?"

"Roughly every two months."

"That often," the kid said.

"Actually," Casey said, "two months is pretty infrequent. We have three thousand aircraft in revenue service around the world. With that many birds in the air, things happen. So every morning we hold a conference call with the service reps. They report everything that caused a dispatch delay the day before. Most of it's minor stuff: a lav door jammed; a cockpit light failed. But we track it in QA, do a trend analysis, and pass that on to product support."

"Uh-huh. . . ." He sounded bored.

"Then," Casey said, "once in a while we hit a problem that warrants an IRT. It has to be serious, something that affects flight safety. Apparently we've got one today. If Marder's pushed the meeting up to seven, you can bet it's not a bird strike."

"Marder?"

"John Marder, our chief operating officer."

She pulled over and parked in the shadow of building 64. The gray hangar loomed above, eight stories high, a mile long.

They walked through the side doors and entered an interior corridor that ran around the perimeter of the building. Casey led Richman through another door, onto the production floor.

"Jeez," Richman said.

The huge, partially assembled wide-body jets gleamed under halogen lights. Fifteen aircraft in various stages of construction were arranged in two long rows under the vaulted roof. Directly ahead of them mechanics were installing cargo doors in the fuselage sections. The barrels of the fuselage were surrounded by scaffolding. Beyond the fuselage stood a forest of assembly jigs—immense tools painted bright blue. Richman walked under one of the jigs and looked up, openmouthed. It was as wide as a house and six stories tall.

"Amazing," he said. He pointed upward. "Is that the wing?"

"The vertical stabilizer," Casey said.

"The what?"

"It's the tail, Bob. The wing is over there." She pointed across the floor. "It's two hundred feet long—almost as long as a football field."

Richman was turning around, looking in all directions. "Awesome," he said. "Why are they all lime green?"

"We coat the structural elements with epoxy to prevent corrosion. And the aluminum skins are covered so they don't get dinged during assembly. The skins are highly polished and very expensive. So we leave that coating on until they reach the paint shed."

"Sure doesn't look like GM," Richman said.

"That's right," Casey said. "Compared to these aircraft, cars are a joke. A Pontiac has five thousand parts; you can build one in sixteen hours. But these things"—she gestured to the aircraft looming above them—"have one million parts and a timespan of seventy-five days. No other manufactured product in the world has the complexity of a commercial aircraft. Nothing even comes close. And nothing is built to be as durable. You take a Pontiac and run it all day every day and see what happens. It'll fall apart in a few months. But we design our jets to fly for twenty years of trouble-free service, and we build them to twice the service life."

"Forty years?" Richman said, incredulous. "You build them to last forty years?"

Casey nodded. "We've still got lots of N-5s in service around the world, and we stopped building them in 1946."

"Wow," Richman said, swallowing.

They moved on.

"We call this the bird farm," Casey said. "The planes are so big, it's hard to get a sense of the scale." She pointed to one aircraft at their right, where small clusters of people worked at various positions, with portable lights shining up on the metal. "There are probably two hundred mechanics working on that plane—enough to run an entire automobile line. But this is just one position on our line, and we have fifteen positions in all. There are five thousand people in this building right now."

The kid was shaking his head. "It looks sort of empty."

"Unfortunately," Casey said, "it *is* sort of empty. The wide-body line's running at sixty percent capacity. We haven't got all the orders we want. The Pacific Rim's the growth sector, but with Japan in recession that market's not placing orders. And everybody else is flying planes longer. So business is very competitive."

She started up a flight of metal stairs, walking quickly. Richman followed her, footsteps clanging. They came to a landing, went up another flight. "I'm telling you this," she said, "so you'll understand the meeting we're going into. People here are proud of these planes. And they don't like it when something goes wrong."

They arrived at a catwalk high above the assembly floor and walked toward a glass-walled room that seemed to be suspended from the roof. They came to the door. Casey opened it.

"And this," she said, "is the war room."

WAR ROOM, BUILDING 64

7:01 a.m. She saw it freshly, through his eyes: a large conference room with gray carpeting, a round table, tubular metal chairs. The walls were covered with bulletin boards, maps, engineering charts. The far wall was glass and overlooked the assembly line.

Five men in ties and shirtsleeves were there, a secretary with a notepad, and John Marder, wearing a blue suit. In person, the COO was dark, intense, in his mid-forties, with slicked-back hair. He looked like a cobra about to strike.

Casey said, "This is my new assistant, Bob Richman."

Marder stood up and said, "Bob, welcome," and shook the kid's hand. He gave a rare smile. Apparently Marder, with his finely tuned sense of corporate politics, was ready to fawn over any Norton family member, even a nephew on loan.

Marder introduced Richman to the others at the table. "Doug Doherty, in charge of structure and mechanical . . ." He gestured to an overweight man of forty-five, with a bad complexion and thick glasses. Doherty spoke in a mournful monotone and could always be counted on to report that everything was bad and getting worse. He gave Richman a sad, thoughtful nod.

"Nguyen Van Trung, avionics . . ." Trung was thirty, trim and self-contained. Casey liked him. The avionics guys were involved with the aircraft computer programs. They represented the new wave at Norton: younger, better educated, better manners.

"Ken Burne, power plant . . ." Kenny was red-haired and freckled; his chin thrust forward, ready to fight. Notoriously profane and abusive, he was known for his quick temper.

"Ron Smith, electrical . . ." Bald and timid, nervously fingering pens in his pocket, Ron was extremely competent; it often seemed he carried the schematics for the aircraft around in his head. But he was painfully shy.

"Mike Lee, who represents the carrier . . ." A well-dressed Chinese man of fifty, gray hair cropped short, Mike was a former air force pilot, a retired one-star general. He was TransPacific's rep.

"And Barbara Ross, with the notepad." The IRT secretary was in her forties and overweight.

Marder waved the kid to a seat, and Casey sat down beside him. "First item," Marder said. "Casey is now liaising QA to the IRT, so she'll handle any press inquiries we get. Okay? Let's get started. Barbara?" The secretary handed around stapled packets of paper.

"TransPacific flight 545," Marder said. "An N-22, fuselage number 271. Flight originated at Kai Tak Hong Kong at 2200 hours yesterday. Uneventful takeoff, uneventful flight until approximately 0500 hours this morning, when the aircraft encountered what the pilot described as severe turbulence—"

There were groans throughout the room. "Turbulence!" The engineers shook their heads.

"Severe turbulence, producing extreme pitch excursions in flight," Marder continued. "The aircraft made an emergency landing at LAX, and medical units were on hand. Our preliminary report indicates fifty-six injured and three dead."

"That's very bad," Doug Doherty said in a sad monotone. "I suppose this means we've got the NTSB on our backs."

Casey leaned over to Richman and whispered, "National Transportation Safety Board usually gets involved when there are fatalities."

"Not in this case," Marder said. "This is a foreign carrier, and the incident occurred in international airspace. NTSB has its hands full with the Colombia crash. We think they'll pass."

"Turbulence," Kenny Burne snorted. "Any confirmation?"

"No," Marder said. "No other aircraft at that altitude and position reported weather problems."

"What about the passengers?" Casey asked. "Did the captain make an announcement? Was the seat-belt sign on?"

"Preliminary information suggests no announcement."

Richman was looking bewildered. Casey scribbled a note on her yellow pad, tilted it so he could read: "No turbulence."

Trung said, "Have we debriefed the pilot?"

"No," Marder said. "The flight crew caught a connecting flight out and left the country."

"Oh great," Kenny Burne said. "We got a damn hit-and-run."

"Hold on, now," Mike Lee said. "On behalf of the carrier, I think we have to recognize the flight crew acted responsibly. They have no liability here, but they face possible litigation from the authorities in Hong Kong. They went home to deal with it."

Casey wrote, "Flight crew unavailable."

"Do, uh, we know who the captain was?" Ron Smith asked.

"We do," Mike Lee said. He consulted a leather notebook. "His name is John Chang. Forty-five years old, six thousand hours' experience. Senior pilot for the N-22. Very skilled."

"Oh yeah?" Burne said. "And when was he last recertified?"

"Three months ago."

"Do we know how he was rated?" Casey asked.

"Outstanding," Lee said. "You can check your records."

Casey wrote, "Not human error (?)"

"Unless we get a pilot interview," Trung said, "we may have a problem. The incident occurred one hour prior to landing. The cockpit voice recorder only stores the last twenty-five minutes of conversation. So in this case the CVR is useless."

"True. But you still have the FDR."

Casey wrote, "Flight data recorder."

"Yes, we have the FDR," Trung said. But this clearly didn't assuage his concerns, and Casey knew why. Flight recorders were notoriously unreliable. In the media they were the mysterious black boxes that revealed all the secrets of a flight. But in reality they often didn't work.

Casey said, "What do we know about the aircraft?"

"Aircraft's brand-new," Marder said. "Three years' service. It's got four thousand hours and nine hundred cycles."

Casey wrote, "Cycles = takeoffs and landings."

"What about inspections?" Doherty asked gloomily.

"It had a C check in March. At LAX."

"So maintenance was probably good," Casey said.

"Correct," Marder said. "As a first cut, we can't attribute this to weather, human factors, or maintenance. So let's run the fault tree. Did anything about this aircraft cause behavior that looks like turbulence? Structural?"

"Oh sure," Doherty said miserably. "A slats deploy would do it. We'll function hydraulics on all the control surfaces."

"Avionics?"

Trung was scribbling notes. "I'm wondering why the autopilot didn't override the pilot. I'll know more from the FDR download."

"Electrical?"

"It's possible we got a slats deploy from a sneak circuit," Ron Smith said, shaking his head. "I mean, it's *possible*. . . ."

"Power plant?"

"Power plant could be involved," Burne said, running his hand through his red hair. "The thrust reversers could have deployed in flight. That'd make the plane nose over and roll. But if the reversers deployed, there'll be residual damage. We'll check."

Casey looked down at her pad. She had written:

Structural—slats deploy
Hydraulics—slats deploy
Avionics—autopilot
Electrical—sneak circuit
Power plant—thrust reversers

That was basically every system on the aircraft.

"You've got a lot of ground to cover," Marder said, standing and gathering his papers together. "Don't let me keep you."

Burne said, "We'll nail this in a month."

"We don't have a month," Marder said. "We have a week."

Cries around the table. "A week!"

Marder said, "Last Thursday our president, Hal Edgarton, received an LOI from the Beijing government to purchase fifty N-22s, with an option for another thirty. First delivery in eighteen months."

There was stunned silence. A big China sale had been rumored for months, but nobody at Norton really believed it.

"It's true," Marder said. "It's an eight-billion-dollar order. It's four years of full-capacity production. It'll put this company on solid financial footing into the twenty-first century. It'll fund development for the advanced N-XX wide-body. Hal and I agree: This sale means the difference between life and death for Norton."

Marder placed the papers in his briefcase and snapped it shut. "I fly to Beijing Sunday to join Hal and sign the letter of intent with the minister of transport. He's going to want to know what happened to flight 545. And I better be able to tell him, or he'll turn around and sign with Airbus. In which case everybody at this table is out of a job. The future of Norton Aircraft is riding on this investigation. So I don't want to hear anything but answers. And I want them inside a week. See you tomorrow."

He turned on his heel and walked out of the room.

ADMINISTRATION

9:12 a.m. Harold Edgarton, the newly appointed president of Norton Aircraft, was in his office on the tenth floor when John Marder walked in. Edgarton was a big man, an ex-fullback, with a ready smile and cold, watchful eyes. He had previously worked at Boeing and had been brought in three months earlier to improve Norton's marketing.

Edgarton frowned at Marder. “This is an awful mess,” he said. “How many died?”

“Three,” Marder said.

Edgarton shook his head. “Of all the times for this to happen. Did you brief the investigation team on how urgent this is?”

“I briefed them.”

“And you'll clear it up this week?”

“I'm chairing the group myself. I'll get it done,” Marder said.

“What about the press?” Edgarton was still worried. “I don't want media relations handling this one. Benson's a drunk; the reporters all hate him. And the engineers can't do it—”

“I've got it handled, Hal. I've arranged for Singleton to do the press.”

“Singleton? That QA woman?” Edgarton said. “She's pretty enough, but she comes off as a straight arrow.”

“Well, that's what we want, isn't it?” Marder said. “We want honest all-American, no-nonsense. And she's good on her feet.”

“She'd better be. I don't want this China deal undermined.”

“Nobody does, Hal.”

Edgarton looked at Marder thoughtfully for a moment. Then he said, “You better be real clear about that. Because if this deal doesn't close, a lot of people are going to get taken out. Not just me. A lot of other heads will roll.”

“I understand,” Marder said.

“You picked the woman. She's your call. The board knows it. If anything goes wrong with her or the IRT, you're out.”

“Nothing will go wrong,” Marder said. “It's under control.”

LAX MAINTENANCE HANGAR 21

9:48 a.m. The blue minivan raced toward the line of maintenance hangars at Los Angeles Airport. From the rear of the nearest hangar the yellow tail of the TransPacific wide-body protruded, its emblem shining in the sun.

The engineers began to talk excitedly when they saw the plane. The minivan rolled into the hangar and came to a stop beneath the wing; the engineers piled out. The RAMS team—recovery and maintenance services—was already at work, a half-dozen mechanics up on the wing, wearing harnesses, scrabbling on their hands and knees.

"Let's do it!" Burne shouted as he climbed a ladder to the wing. He made it sound like a battle cry. The other engineers followed.

Casey stepped out of the van with Richman. "They all go right to the wing," Richman said.

"That's right. The wing's the most important part of an aircraft and the most complicated structure. They'll look at it first, then inspect the rest of the exterior. This way."

"Where are we going?"

"Inside."

Casey walked to the nose and climbed a roll-in staircase to the forward cabin door, just behind the cockpit. As she came to the entrance, she smelled the nauseating odor of vomit.

"Jeez," Richman said behind her.

Casey went inside.

She knew the forward cabin would have the least damage, but even here some of the seat backs were broken. Armrests had torn free and swung into the aisles. Overhead luggage bins were cracked, the doors hanging open. Oxygen masks dangled from the ceiling, some missing. There was blood on the carpet.

Richman looked pale. "This happened from *turbulence?*"

"No," she said, "almost certainly not."

"Then why would the pilot—"

"We don't know yet," she said.

Casey went forward to the flight deck. The cockpit door was latched open, and the flight deck appeared normal. All the logs and paperwork were missing. A tiny infant's shoe was on the floor. Bending to look at it, she noticed a mass of crumpled black metal wedged beneath the cockpit door. A video camera. She pulled it free, and it broke apart in her hands, exposing a cracked cassette. She gave the camera to Richman.

"Keep this."

Casey headed aft, knowing it would be worse in the back. "There's no question: This aircraft underwent severe pitch oscillations. That's when the plane noses up and down," she explained.

"How do you know?" Richman said.

"Because that's what makes passengers vomit. And the seat backs are broken. Do you know how much force it takes to break an airplane seat? They're designed to withstand an impact of sixteen G's. People in this cabin bounced around like dice in a cup."

Passing a shattered midship galley, they came into the center cabin. Here damage was much worse. Many seats were broken. There was a broad swath of blood across the ceiling. The aisles were cluttered with debris—shoes, torn clothing, children's toys.

A cleanup crew in blue uniforms marked NORTON IRT was collecting the personal belongings, putting them into big plastic bags. Casey turned to a woman. "Have you found any cameras?"

"Five or six so far," the woman said. "Couple of video cameras. There's all sorts of stuff here."

Stepping carefully over the litter, Casey moved farther aft. She passed another divider and entered the aft cabin, near the tail.

Richman sucked in his breath.

It looked as if a giant hand had smashed the interior. Seats were crushed flat. Overhead bins hung down, almost touching the floor; ceiling panels had split apart, exposing wiring and silver insulation. There was blood everywhere. The aft lavs were ripped apart, mirrors shattered, stainless steel drawers hanging open.

She heard a cleanup woman say, "Strangest thing I ever saw."

Another woman said, "How'd it get here?"

"Damned if I know, honey."

Casey went over to the galley to see what they were talking about. The cleaning woman was holding a blue pilot's cap. It had a bloody footprint on the top.

Casey reached for it. "Where'd you find this?"

"Right here," the cleaning woman said. "Outside the aft galley. Long way from the cockpit, isn't it?"

"Yes." Casey turned the cap in her hands. Silver wings on the front, the yellow TransPacific medallion in the center. It was a pilot's cap, with a stripe for a captain, so it probably belonged to one of the backup crew—*if* this plane carried a backup crew. She didn't know that yet.

Richman pointed out the windows. "What're those guys doing on the wing?"

Casey looked through the windows at the engineers. "Inspecting the slats—the leading-edge control surfaces."

"And what do slats do?"

You're going to have to start him from the beginning.

Casey said, "You know anything about aerodynamics? No? Well, an aircraft flies because of the shape of the wing." The wing looked simple, she explained, but it was actually the most complicated component of the aircraft, and it took the longest to build. By comparison, the fuse—the fuselage—was simple, just a lot of round barrels riveted together. And the tail was just a fixed vertical vane with control surfaces. But a wing was a work of art: incredibly strong, capable of bearing the weight of the plane, precisely shaped to within a hundredth of an inch.

"The shape," Casey said, "is what's crucial: It's curved on top, flat on the bottom. That means air going across the top of the wing has to move faster, and because of Bernoulli's principle—"

"I went to law school," Richman reminded her.

"Bernoulli's principle says the faster a gas moves, the lower its pressure. So the pressure within a moving stream is less than the air surrounding it. Since air moves faster across the top of the wing, it creates a vacuum that sucks the wing upward. The wing is strong enough to support the fuselage, so the whole plane is lifted up. That's what makes a plane fly."

"Okay."

"Now, two factors determine how much lift is created—the speed the wing moves through the air, and the amount of curvature. The greater the curvature, the greater the lift. When the wing is moving fast, during flight, it doesn't need much curvature. It actually wants to be almost flat. But when the aircraft is moving slower, during takeoff and landing, the wing needs greater curvature to maintain lift. So at those times we increase the curvature by extending sections in the front and back—flaps at the back and slats at the leading edge."

"Slats are like flaps, but in the front?"

"Right. Smaller planes don't have them," Casey said. "But this aircraft weighs close to three quarters of a million pounds, fully loaded. You've got to have slats on a plane this size."

As they watched, the first of the slats moved outward, then tilted down. The men on the wing watched.

Richman said, "Why are the slats so important?"

"Because," Casey said, "one possible cause of turbulence is slat extension. Remember, at cruise speed the wing should be almost flat. If the slats extend, the plane may become unstable."

"And what would make the slats extend during flight?"

"Pilot error," Casey said. "That's the usual cause."

"But supposedly this plane had a very good pilot."

"Right. Supposedly."

"And if it wasn't pilot error?"

She hesitated. "There is a condition called uncommanded slats deployment. It means the slats extend all by themselves."

Richman frowned. "Can that happen?"

"It's been known to occur. We don't think it's possible on this aircraft, but our job is to check everything until we find out what happened. And right now we haven't got a clue."

FOUR men were squeezed into the cockpit, hunched over the controls. Trung, who was certified for the aircraft, sat in the captain's seat; Kenny Burne was in the first officer's seat on the right. Trung was functioning the control surfaces one after another—flaps, slats, elevators, rudder.

Casey stood outside the cockpit with Richman. She said, "You got anything, Van?"

"Nothing yet," Trung said.

Burne said, "This bird is cherry. Nothing wrong with it."

Richman said, "Then maybe turbulence caused it after all."

Burne said, "Who said that? Is that the kid?"

"Yes," Richman said.

"Straighten him out, Casey," Burne said over his shoulder.

"Turbulence," Casey said to Richman, "is a famous catchall for anything that goes wrong on the flight deck. Turbulence certainly occurs, and in the old days planes had some rough times. But these days turbulence bad enough to cause injuries is unusual."

"Because?"

"Radar, pal," Burne snapped. "Pilots can see weather formations ahead and avoid them. They've also got much better communications between aircraft. If a plane hits rough weather at your flight level two hundred miles ahead of you, you'll hear about it and get a course change. So the days of serious turbulence are over."

Richman was annoyed by Burne's tone. "I don't know," he said. "I've been on planes where turbulence got pretty rough—"

"Ever see anybody get *killed* on one of those planes?"

"Well, no."

"Seen injuries of any kind?"

"No," Richman said. "But surely it is possible that—"

"Possible?" Burne said. "You mean like in court, where anything is possible?"

"No, but—"

"You're a lawyer, right?"

"Yes, I am, but—"

"Well, you better get one thing straight right now. We're not doing law, here. Law is a bunch of bull. This is an *aircraft.* A *machine.* And either something happened to it or it didn't. It's not a matter of *opinion.*"

Richman winced but didn't back down. "Fine," he said, "but if it wasn't turbulence, there'll be evidence—"

"That's right," Burne said, "the seat-belt sign. Pilot hits turbulence, the first thing he does is flash the seat-belt sign and make an announcement. Everybody buckles up, and nobody gets hurt. This guy never made an announcement."

Dan Greene, the chubby operations inspector from the FSDO, came on board, puffing from the climb up the metal stairs. "Hey, guys, I got your certificate to ferry the plane to Burbank. I figured you want to take the bird to the plant."

"Yeah, we do," Casey said.

"Hey, Dan," Kenny Burne called, "nice job keeping the flight crew here."

"Look," Greene said, "I had my guy at the gate a minute after the plane arrived. The crew was already gone." He turned to Casey. "We sent the seriously injured to Westside hospitals. Here's the list."

Casey took the list. "How many are at Centinela?"

"Six or seven. Including a couple of stewardesses."

Casey said, "I'll talk to them. Van? How much longer?"

"Figure an hour, minimum."

"Okay," she said. "I'm going to take the car."

"And take Clarence Darrow with you," Burne said.

10:42 a.m. As they drove out of the airport in the van, Richman gave a long exhale. "Are they always so friendly?"

Casey shrugged. "They're engineers." She was thinking, What did he expect? He must have dealt with engineers at GM. "Emotionally, they're all thirteen years old. They have poor social skills, dress badly—but they're extremely intelligent and well trained, and they are very arrogant in their way. Outsiders are definitely not allowed to play."

"Especially lawyers."

"Anybody. They're like chess masters. They don't waste time with amateurs. And they're under a lot of pressure now."

"You're not an engineer?"

"Me? No. And I'm a woman. And I'm from QA. Three reasons why I don't count. Now Marder's made me IRT liaison to the press, which is another strike. The engineers all hate the press."

"Will there be press on this?"

"Probably not," she said. "It's a foreign carrier. And they don't have visuals. They won't pay any attention."

"But it seems so serious."

"Serious isn't a criterion," she said. "Last year there were twenty-five accidents involving substantial airframe damage. Twenty-three occurred overseas. Which ones do you remember?"

Richman frowned. "Wasn't there something in Atlanta?"

"That's right. A DC-9 in Atlanta. How many people were killed? None. How many were injured? None. Why do you remember it? Because there was film at eleven."

The van left the runway, went through the chain-link gate, and out onto the street. They turned onto Sepulveda and headed toward the rounded blue contours of the Centinela Hospital.

"Anyway," Casey said, "we have other things to worry about now." She handed Richman a tape recorder, clipped a microphone to his lapel, and told him what they were going to do.

CENTINELA HOSPITAL

12:06 p.m. "You want to know what happened?" the bearded man said in an irritable voice. His name was Bennett. He was forty years old, a clothing distributor. He had gone to Hong Kong to visit a factory. He went four times a year, and he always flew TransPacific. Now he was sitting up in bed in a curtained-off cubicle. His head and right arm were bandaged. "The plane almost crashed, that's what happened. Who are you people, anyway?"

Casey handed him her card, introduced herself again.

"Norton Aircraft? What do you have to do with it?"

"We build the airplane, Mr. Bennett."

"That piece of crap?" He threw the card back at her. "Get out of here, both of you. Go on, get out!"

Outside the curtained cubicle Casey looked at Richman. "I have a way with people," she said ruefully.

Casey went to the next cubicle. Behind the curtain was one of the flight attendants, a twenty-eight-year-old woman named Kay Liang. She had a large abrasion on her face and neck, the skin raw and red.

Sitting in a chair by the empty bed, she explained that she had remained in the hospital to stay with Sha Yan Hao, another stewardess, who was in the next cubicle.

"She is my cousin," she said. "I'm afraid she was hurt badly."

When Casey introduced herself, Kay Liang looked confused. "You're from the manufacturer? But a man was just here . . ."

"What man?"

"A Chinese man. He was here a few minutes ago."

"I don't know about that," Casey said, frowning. "But we'd like to ask you some questions."

"Of course." She folded her hands in her lap, composed.

"Where were you when this incident occurred?"

"In the midcabin galley, just behind business class." The flight attendants were preparing breakfast, she explained. It was about five a.m. "The plane began to climb. I know that because I was setting out drinks and they started to slide off the trolley. Then, almost immediately, there was a very steep descent."

She thought the descent lasted about ten seconds, but she wasn't sure. Then there was another climb, extremely steep, and then another steep descent. On the second descent she struck her head against the bulkhead.

"Did you lose consciousness?"

"No. But that was when I scraped my face." She gestured to her injury. Then, she said, she was knocked to the floor. "We could hear the cries of the passengers. We saw them in the aisles."

Afterward the plane became level again. She was able to get up and help the passengers. The situation was bad, she said, particularly aft. "Many injured and bleeding, in pain. The flight attendants were overwhelmed. Also, Miss Hao, my cousin, was not conscious. She had been in the aft galley. This upset the other stewardesses. And three passengers were dead."

"What did you do?" Casey asked.

"I went to the cockpit." She wanted to see if the flight crew was all right. "And I wanted to tell them the first officer had been injured in the aft galley."

"The first officer was in the aft galley?"

Kay Liang blinked. "Of the relief crew, yes."

"You had two crews on board?"

"Yes."

"When did the crews change?"

"Perhaps three hours earlier. During the night."

"What was the name of the injured first officer?" Casey asked.

She hesitated. "I . . . I am not sure. I had not flown with the relief crew before."

"I see. And when you went to the cockpit?"

"Captain Chang had the plane in control. The crew was shaken but not injured. Captain Chang told me that he had requested an emergency landing at Los Angeles."

"You've flown with Captain Chang before?"

"Yes. He is a very good captain. Excellent captain. I like him very much."

Protesting too much, Casey thought. The stewardess, previously calm, now appeared uneasy. She looked away.

"Did Captain Chang say anything else?" Casey asked.

"Yes. He said they had an uncommanded slats deployment."

Uh-oh, Casey thought, this was not going to make the engineers happy. But Casey was troubled by the stewardess's technical phrasing. She thought it unlikely that a flight attendant would know about uncommanded slats deployment. But perhaps she was just repeating what the captain had said.

"Did Captain Chang say why the slats deployed?"

"He just said uncommanded slats deployment."

"I see," Casey said. "And do you know where the slats control is located?"

"It is a lever in the center pillar, between the chairs."

That was correct, Casey thought. "Did he say anything else?"

"He was concerned about the autopilot. He said the autopilot kept trying to cut in, to take over the plane. He said 'I had to fight the autopilot for control.' "

"I see. And what was Captain Chang's manner at this time?"

"He was calm, as always. He is a very good captain."

The girl's eyes flickered nervously. She twisted her hands in her lap. Casey decided to wait for a moment. It was an old interrogator's trick: Let the subject break the silence.

"Captain Chang comes from a distinguished family of pilots," Kay Liang said, swallowing. "His father was a pilot during the war, and his son is a pilot as well."

"I see. . . ."

The flight attendant lapsed into silence again. There was a pause. She looked down at her hands, then back up. "So. Is there anything else I can tell you?"

OUTSIDE the cubicle, Richman said, "Isn't this the thing you said couldn't happen? Uncommanded slats deployment?"

"I didn't say it couldn't happen. I said I didn't believe it was possible on this aircraft. And if it did, it raises questions."

"And what about the autopilot?"

"Too early to tell," she said, and went into the next cubicle.

"IT MUST have been around six o'clock," Emily Jansen said. She was a slender woman of thirty, with a purple bruise on her cheek. An infant slept on her lap. Her husband lay in the bed behind her; a metal brace ran from his shoulders to his chin. She said his jaw was broken. "I had just fed the baby. I was talking to my husband. And then I heard a sound—a rumbling or a grinding, like a vibration. I thought it came from the wing."

Not good, Casey thought.

"So I looked out the window at the wing. I thought the sound might be coming from the engine, but the engine looked normal."

"Was the seat-belt sign on?"

"No. Never."

"Did the captain make an announcement?"

"No."

"This sound you described—how long did it last?"

"I would say ten or twelve seconds."

A classic description of a slats deployment, Casey thought.

"Okay," she said. "And then?"

"The plane tilted, then started going down."

Casey continued to make notes, but she no longer really listened. She was trying to put together the sequence of events, trying to decide how the engineers should proceed. There was no question that both witnesses were telling a story consistent with slats deployment in flight. First, rumbling for twelve seconds—exactly the time it took the slats to extend. Then a slight nose up, which would occur next. And then porpoising as the crew tried to stabilize the aircraft.

What a mess, she thought.

Emily Jansen was saying, "Since the cockpit door was open, I could hear all the alarms. There were warning sounds and voices in English that sounded recorded. It sounded like 'Fall . . . fall.' Something like that."

It was the stall alarm, Casey thought. And the audio reminder was saying, "Stall, stall." *Damn.*

She stayed with Emily Jansen a few minutes more, then went back outside.

In the corridor Richman said, "Does that rumbling sound mean the slats deployed?"

"It might," she said. She was tense, edgy. She wanted to get back to the aircraft and talk to the engineers.

From one of the curtained cubicles farther down the corridor she saw a stocky gray-haired figure emerge. She was surprised to see it was Mike Lee. What the heck was the carrier rep doing talking to passengers? Lee had no business being here.

She remembered what Kay Liang had said: *A man was just here. A Chinese man.* "Mike," she said. "I'm surprised to see you here."

"Why? You should give me a medal," Lee said. "A couple of the passengers were considering lawsuits. I talked them out of it."

"But you talked to the crew before we did. That's not right."

"What do you think, I fed them a story? They gave *me* the story. I'm sorry, Casey, but flight 545 had an uncommanded slats deploy. That means you've still got problems on the N-22."

WALKING BACK TO THE VAN, Richman said, "What did he mean, you've still got problems?"

Casey sighed. No point in holding back now. She said, "We've had some incidents of slats deployment on the N-22."

"You mean *this has happened before?*" Richman said.

"Not like this," she said. "We've never had serious injuries. But yes. We've had problems with slats."

As they drove back, Casey continued. "The first episode occurred four years ago, on a flight to San Juan. Slats extended in mid-flight. We thought it was an anomaly, but then there were two additional incidents within a couple of months. When we investigated, we found that in every case the slats had deployed during a period of flight-deck activity—right after a crew change or when they punched in coordinates for the next leg of the flight, or something like that. We finally realized the slats lever was getting knocked loose by the crews—banged by clipboards, caught on uniform sleeves—"

Richman was staring at her with the skeptical expression of a prosecuting attorney. "So the N-22 *does* have problems."

"It was a new aircraft, and all aircraft have problems when they're first introduced. You can't build a machine with a million parts and not have snags. The question is how to resolve them."

"How do you resolve them?"

"Whenever we discover a problem," Casey said, "we send the operators a service bulletin, which describes our recommended fix. In this case we recommended the carriers install a hinged metal cover that sits over the lever. That meant the captain had to flip up the cover before he could deploy the slats, but it solved the problem. As usual, some carriers made the fix; others didn't. So the FAA issued an airworthiness directive making it mandatory. That was four years ago. There's been only one incident since then, but that involved an Indonesian carrier who didn't install the cover. In this country the FAA requires carriers to comply, but abroad"—she shrugged—"the carriers do what they want."

"That's it? That's the whole history?"

"That's the whole history. Until now."

LAX MAINTENANCE HANGAR

1:22 p.m. "They said it was *what?*" Kenny Burne said, shouting from the cockpit of TransPacific 545.

"Uncommanded slats deployment," Richman said.

"Aw, what a crock," Burne said. He started climbing out of the seat. "Hey! Clarence Darrow, come in here. See that seat? That's the first officer's seat. Sit down there. Come on, Clarence."

Awkwardly, Richman squeezed between the other men in the cockpit and got into the first officer's chair, on the right.

"Okay," Burne said. "Comfy in there? Good. So here you are, all set to fly the plane. Now, to your left is the pedestal."

Burne pointed to a boxy structure protruding between the two seats. There were a half-dozen levers in slots on the pedestal. "Now, from right to left, flaps-slats, two throttles for the engines, spoilers, brakes, thrusters. Slats and flaps are controlled by that lever nearest you, the one with the metal cover over it. See it?"

"I see it," Richman said.

"Good. Flip up the cover and engage the slats."

"Engage the . . ."

"Pull the slats lever down," Burne said. "Grab it firmly, pull it up, then right, then down. Just like a gearshift on a car."

Richman closed his fingers around the handle. He pulled the lever up, across, and down. There was a distant hum.

"Good," Burne said. "Now, look at your display. See that amber 'slats extd' indicator? It's telling you the slats are coming out of the leading edge. Okay? Takes twelve seconds to fully extend. Now they're out, and the indicator is white and says, 'slats.' Okay, now retract the slats."

Richman reversed his actions, then closed the cover over the handle.

"That," Burne said, "is a commanded slats extension. Now let's perform an *uncommanded* slats extension."

"How do I do that?"

"Any way you can, pal. For starters, hit it with your hand."

Richman reached across the pedestal, brushing the lever with his left hand. But the cover protected it. Nothing happened.

"Come on, hit that sucker."

Richman swung his hand laterally back and forth, banging against the metal. He hit it harder each time, but the cover protected the handle. The slats lever remained up and locked.

"Maybe you could knock it with your elbow," Burne said. "Or tell you what, try this clipboard. Give it a good whack."

Richman struck the lever with the clipboard. Nothing.

"You want to keep trying?" Burne said. "Or are you starting to get the point? *It can't be done.* Not with that cover in place."

"Maybe the cover wasn't in place," Richman said.

"Hey," Burne said, "that's good thinking, Clarence. They're not supposed to be flying with the cover up, but who knows what they did. Go ahead and lift the cover up."

Richman lifted the cover up. The handle was now exposed.

"Okay, go to it."

Richman swung his clipboard at the handle, banging it hard, but the raised cover still acted as a protection. The clipboard hit the cover before it struck the handle. Several times, on impact, the cover dropped back down again.

"Okay," Richman said. "I get the point."

"It can't be done," Burne said. "It simply can't be done. An uncommanded slats deploy is impossible on this aircraft. Period."

From outside the cockpit Doherty said, "Are you guys finished screwing around? Because I want to go home."

AS THEY came out of the cockpit, Burne touched Casey on the shoulder and said, "See you a minute?" He led her back into the plane, out of earshot of the others. He leaned close to her. "What do you know about that kid?"

"He's a Norton relative," Casey said. "Marder assigned him to me."

"You check him out?"

"No," Casey said. "If Marder sent him, I assume he's fine."

"Well, I talked to my friends in marketing," Burne said. "They say he's a weasel. They say don't turn your back on him."

"Kenny—"

"I'm telling you, something's wrong with that kid, Casey. Check him out."

WITH a metallic whir from the power screwdrivers, the floor panels came away, revealing a maze of cables and boxes under the cockpit.

Ron Smith was directing the operation, running his hand over his bald head nervously. "That's fine," he said. "Now get the panel to the left."

"How many black boxes we got on this bird, Ron?" Doherty said.

"A hundred and fifty-two," Smith said. Anybody else, Casey knew, would have to thumb through a thick sheaf of schematics to answer. But Smith knew the electrical system by heart.

"What're we pulling?" Doherty said.

"Pull the CVR, the DFDR, and the QAR if they got one," Smith said.

"You don't know if there's a QAR?" Doherty said, teasing him.

"Optional," Smith said. "It's a customer install. I don't think they put one in. Usually it's in the tail, but I didn't find one."

Richman was looking puzzled again. "There's *a hundred and fifty-two* black boxes?" he asked.

"They're all over the aircraft," Smith said. "But we're only after the main ones now—the ten or twelve NVMs that count."

"NVMs?" Richman asked.

It was left to Casey to explain. The public perception of an aircraft was that in the midst of all the machinery were two magic black boxes, recording events in the flight. The CVR, the cockpit voice recorder, was essentially a very sturdy tape deck; it recorded the last half hour of cockpit conversation on a continuous loop of magnetic tape. Then there was the DFDR, the digital flight data recorder, which stored details of the behavior of the airplane. A commercial airliner was controlled by a network of extraordinarily sophisticated electronics, Casey explained—dozens of computer systems linked by hundreds of miles of wiring. There were computers for flight management, for navigation, for communication. Computers regulated the engines, the control surfaces, the cabin environment.

Each major computer system controlled a whole array of subsystems. "A modern DFDR records eighty separate flight parameters every second of the flight," she said.

"Every second? How big is this thing?" Richman said.

"It's right there," Casey said, pointing. Ron was pulling an orange-and-black-striped box from the radio rack. It was the size of a large shoe box. He replaced it with a new box for the ferry flight back to Burbank.

"And the other boxes? What about them?" Richman asked.

The other boxes existed, Casey said, to facilitate maintenance. Because the electronic systems of the aircraft were so complicated, it was necessary to monitor the behavior of each system in case of errors, or faults, during flight. Each system tracked its own performance, in what was called non-volatile memory. "That's NVM."

They would download eight NVM systems today: the flight management computer, which stored data on the flight plan and the pilot-entered way points; the digital engine controller, which managed fuel burn and power plant; the digital air data computer, which recorded airspeed, altitude, and overspeed warnings—

"Okay," Richman said. "I think I get the point."

"None of this would be necessary," Ron Smith said, "if we had the QAR."

"The quick access recorder," Casey explained. "It's another maintenance item. Maintenance crews need to come on board after the plane lands and get a fast readout of anything that went wrong on the last leg."

"Don't they ask the pilots?"

"Pilots will report problems, but with a complex aircraft there may be faults that never come to their attention. So the maintenance crews go to the QAR, which spits out data from the previous flight. They get a fast profile and do the repairs on the spot."

"But there's no quick access recorder on this plane?"

"Apparently not," she said. "It's not required."

"At least I can't find it," Ron said. "But it could be anywhere."

Casey looked out the door. The maintenance people had all climbed off the wing. Burne was finishing up his inspection of the engines. Trung was loading the DFDR into the van. It was time to go home.

As she started down the stairs, she noticed three Norton security vans parked in a corner of the hangar. There were about twenty security guards standing around the plane and in various parts of the hangar.

Richman noticed, too. "That's a lot of security."

"Yeah, well." Casey shrugged. "It's an important plane."

But she noticed that the guards all wore sidearms. Casey couldn't remember seeing armed guards before. A hangar at LAX was a secure facility. There wasn't any need for armed guards. Was there?

BUILDING 64

4:30 p.m. Casey was walking through the northeast corner of building 64, past the blue steel scaffolding—the tools—on which the wing was built. The tools rose twenty feet above the ground. Up on the platform eighty people were putting the wing together.

To the right she saw groups of men packing tools into large wooden crates. "What's all that?" Richman said.

"Looks like rotables," Casey said. "Spare tooling that we rotate into the line if something goes wrong with the first set. We built them to gear up for the China sale. The plan is to build the wings in our facility in Atlanta and ship them back here."

She noticed a figure in a shirt and tie, standing among the men working on the crates. It was Don Brull, the president of the United Auto Workers local. He saw Casey and started toward her. He made a flicking gesture with his hand; she knew what he wanted.

Casey said to Richman, "Give me a minute. I'll see you back at the office."

"Maybe you want me to stay and—"

"Bob," she said as Brull came closer, "get lost."

Reluctantly Richman headed back toward the office. He kept glancing over his shoulder as he walked away.

Brull shook Casey's hand. The UAW president was a short and solidly built man, an ex-boxer with a broken nose.

"What's going on, Don?" she said.

"We got some problems with this China sale," Brull said. "Problems with the offset."

"What about it?" she said, shrugging. "You know there's always offset with a big sale." In recent years airframe manufacturers had been obliged to send portions of the fabrication overseas to the countries ordering planes. A country that ordered fifty planes expected to get a piece of the action.

"I know," he said to her. "But in the past you guys sent part of the tail, maybe the nose. Just parts. But these tools we're crating up are for the wing. And the Teamsters on the loading dock are telling us these crates aren't going to Atlanta. They're going to Shanghai."

"I don't know the details of the agreement, but I doubt that—"

"The *wing,* Casey," he said. "That's core technology. You give the Chinese the wing, you give away the store. They don't need us anymore. They can build the planes on their own. Ten years from now nobody here has a job."

"Don," she said, "I'll check into this, but I can't believe the wing is part of the offset agreement."

"You're not listening, Casey. The local's got a problem with the China sale. *A big problem.*" He paused. "Understand?"

She did. The UAW workers on the floor had absolute control over production. They could slow down, sick out, create hundreds of other intractable problems. "I'll talk to Marder," she said. "I'm sure he doesn't want a problem on the line."

"Marder *is* the problem."

Casey sighed. Typical union misinformation, she thought. The China sale had been made by Hal Edgarton and the marketing team. Marder was just the COO. He ran the plant. He didn't have anything to do with sales. "I'll get back to you tomorrow, Don."

"That's fine," Brull said. "But I hear that if the 545 thing isn't cleared up fast, it could kill the China sale. Feelings are strong against the sale, Casey. Some of the guys are pretty hot about it. I was you, I'd take a week off."

"I can't do that. I'm right in the middle of the investigation."

Brull looked at her. "In that case," he said, putting his hand on her arm, "you take real good care, honey."

ADMINISTRATION

4:40 p.m. "No, no," Marder said, pacing in his office. "This is nonsense, Casey. There's no way we'd send the wing to Shanghai. That's crazy. That'd be the end of the company."

"But Brull said—"

"You know how rumors run through the plant. It isn't true. Those tools are going to Atlanta. They know this."

"Brull didn't sit in on the China negotiations."

"I'll speak to him," Marder said.

Casey said, "I'd like to see the offset agreement."

"And you will, as soon as it's final."

"What are we giving them?"

"Part of the nose, and the tail," Marder said. "Hell, we can't give them anything else; they're not competent to build it."

"Brull was talking about interfering with the IRT. To stop the China sale."

Marder frowned. "Did he threaten you?"

Casey shrugged. "He recommended a week's vacation."

Marder threw up his hands. "This is ridiculous. I'll talk to him tonight, straighten him out. Don't worry about this. Just stay focused on the job. I'll take care of this for you."

NORTON QA

4:53 p.m. Casey rode the elevator from the ninth floor down to her own offices, on the fourth. She replayed the meeting with Marder and decided he wasn't lying. His exasperation had been genuine. And it was true what Marder said—rumors flew through the plant all the time.

She walked down the corridor, past the photographs of famous Norton aircraft with celebrities posed in front: Franklin Delano Roosevelt beside the B-22 that carried him to Yalta; Errol Flynn, with smiling girls in the tropics, in front of an N-5; Henry Kissinger, on the N-12 that had taken him to China in 1972. The photographs were sepia-toned to convey a sense of age and the stability of the company.

She opened the doors to her offices—frosted glass, with raised lettering: QUALITY ASSURANCE DIVISION. She came into the bull pen, where the secretaries sat. Executive offices lined the walls.

Norma sat by the door, a heavyset woman of indeterminate age, with blue-rinse hair. Norma had been with the company as long as anyone could remember; she knew where all the bodies were buried. Within the company she was treated with a deference bordering on fear.

Casey said, "What've we got, Norma?"

"The usual panic. Telexes are flying." She handed a stack to Casey. "The fizer in Hong Kong phoned three times for you, but he's gone home now. Fizer in Vancouver was on the horn half an hour ago. You can probably still get him."

Casey nodded. It was not surprising that the flight service representatives would check in. The FSRs were Norton employees assigned to the carriers; the carriers would be worried.

"And let's see," Norma said. "The Washington office is all atwitter. They've heard this might be exploited on Airbus's behalf. What a surprise. Fizer in Düsseldorf wants a confirm it was pilot error. Fizer in Milan wants information. Fizer in Bombay heard engine failure. I straightened him out. And your daughter said to tell you she did not need her sweatshirt."

"Great."

Casey took the faxes back to her office. She found Richman sitting at her desk. He looked up and rose quickly from her chair. "Sorry."

Casey said, "Didn't Norma find you an office?"

"Yes. I have one," Richman said, walking around the desk. "I was just, ah, just wondering what you wanted me to do with this." He held up the video camera they had found on the plane.

"I'll take it."

He gave it to her. "So. What happens now?"

She dropped the stack of telexes on her desk. "I'd say you're through for the day," she said. "Be here tomorrow at seven."

He left, and she sat down in her chair. Everything seemed to be as she had left it. But she noticed that the second drawer on the desk was not quite closed. Had Richman been going through her desk?

Casey pulled the drawer open, revealing boxes of computer disks, stationery, a pair of scissors, some felt-tip pens in a tray. It all looked undisturbed. But still . . .

She heard Richman leave, then went back down the hall to Norma's desk. "That kid," she said, "was sitting behind my desk."

"Tell me. The little twerp asked me to get him coffee."

"I'm surprised marketing didn't straighten him out," Casey said. "They had him a couple of months."

"Matter of fact," Norma said, "I was talking to Jean over there. She says they hardly saw him. He was always on the road."

"On the road? A new kid? Where'd he go?"

"Jean didn't know. You want me to find out?"

"Yeah," Casey said, "I do."

BACK in her office, Casey pulled the videotape from the shattered camera. She set it to one side, then dialed Jim's number, hoping to talk to Allison. But she got the answering machine. She hung up and began thumbing through the telexes.

The only one that interested her was from the FSR in Hong Kong, which included the passenger manifest and crew list for flight 545. She glanced at the crew list. It had eighteen names, including seven flight crew. Such a large flight crew was not strictly necessary. The N-22 was designed to be flown by just a captain and first officer. But all the Asian carriers were expanding rapidly, and they generally carried larger crews for extra training hours.

Casey went on. The next telex was from the Vancouver FSR.

> FYI FLIGHT CREW TPA 545 DEADHEAD ON TPA 832, FROM LAX TO VANCOUVER. FIRST OFFICER LUE ZAN PING TAKEN OFF THE AIRCRAFT AT VANCOUVER. MEDICAL EMERGENCY DUE TO PREVIOUSLY UNRECOGNIZED HEAD INJURY. REMAINING CREW OF TPA 545 TRANSIT BACK TO HONG KONG TODAY.

So the first officer had been seriously injured after all. He must have been in the tail when the incident occurred—the man whose cap they had found.

Casey dictated a telex to the FSR in Vancouver, asking him to interview the first officer as soon as possible. She dictated another to the FSR in Hong Kong, suggesting an interview with Captain Chang on his return.

Norma buzzed her. "No luck on the kid," she said. "Travel didn't make Richman's arrangements. His trips were charged to a special company account, a set-aside for foreign, off-budget stuff." Norma sighed. "But I'm having lunch tomorrow with Evelyn in accounting. She'll give me everything."

"Okay, thanks, Norma." Casey went back to work.

GLENDALE

7:40 p.m. She was tired when she got home. The house seemed empty without Allison's lively chatter. Too tired to cook, Casey went into the kitchen and ate a cup of yogurt. Allison's colorful drawings were taped on the refrigerator door. Casey considered calling her, but it was right around her bedtime, and she didn't want to interrupt if Jim was putting her to sleep.

She also didn't want Jim to think she was checking up on him. That was a sore point—he always felt she was checking.

Casey went into the bathroom and turned on the shower. She heard the phone ring and went back into the kitchen to answer it. It was probably Jim. She picked up the receiver. "Hello, Jim—"

"Don't be stupid," a voice said. "You want trouble, you'll get it. Accidents happen. We're watching you *right now.*" *Click.*

Casey stood in the kitchen holding the phone in her hand. She had always thought of herself as levelheaded, but her heart was pounding. She forced herself to take a deep breath as she hung up the receiver. She knew these calls happened sometimes. She'd heard of other vice presidents getting threatening calls at night. But it had never happened to her, and she was surprised at how frightened she felt. She took another deep breath, tried to shrug it off. She was suddenly aware that she was alone in a house with all the blinds open.

She went around the living room, closing the blinds. Then she went to the front door, bolted it, and locked the security chain.

TUESDAY

GLENDALE

5:45 a.m. Casey awoke uneasily, before the alarm went off. She pulled on a bathrobe, walked to the kitchen to turn on the coffeemaker. She considered taking her five-mile run, but decided against it. There was no point in taking chances.

She poured a cup of coffee, sat in the living room. Everything looked different to her today. Yesterday her little bungalow felt cozy; today it felt small, defenseless, isolated. She was glad Allison was spending the week with Jim.

Casey had lived through periods of labor tension in the past; she knew that the threats usually came to nothing. But it was wise to be cautious. She dreaded going to the factory. She had to go, though.

She had her coffee and dressed. She got into her Mustang and drove to the plant. First shift had already started; the parking lots were full, acres and acres of cars. Casey pulled up to the security guard at gate 7. The guard waved her through, and she parked at her spot in administration.

Casey looked around at the huge gray buildings: building 64 to the south; building 57 to the east, where the twinjet was built; building 121, the paint shed; the maintenance hangars in a row off to the west, lit by the sun rising over the San Fernando Mountains. It was a familiar landscape; she'd spent five years here. But today she was uncomfortably aware of the vast dimensions, the emptiness of the place in early morning. She felt alone.

NORTON AIRCRAFT

6:34 a.m. Rob Wong, the young programmer at Norton digital information systems, turned from the video monitors and said, "Casey, we got the flight recorder data, but there's a problem."

She was not really surprised to hear it. Flight data recorders rarely performed correctly. In the press these failures were explained as the consequence of crash impacts. But within the aerospace industry everyone knew flight data recorders failed at a high rate, even when the aircraft didn't crash. The reason was that the FAA did not require they be checked before every flight. In practice they were usually function-checked about once a year.

"We're doing the best we can, Casey," Rob Wong said. "But the flight recorder data is anomalous."

"Meaning what?"

"It looks like the number three bus blew about twenty hours before the incident. The data's pretty bad. What about the QAR?"

"There isn't one," she said.

"Well, if you're really stuck, I'll take this data to flight simulations. They have some sophisticated programs there. They may be able to fill in the blanks faster and tell you what happened."

"How long? Marder's on my back."

"It could be a while, Casey. Sorry."

6:50 a.m. Casey met Richman outside building 64. They walked together in the early morning light toward the building.

Richman yawned. "We sure didn't keep these hours in marketing," he said.

"What did you do there?"

"Not much. Edgarton had the whole department doing a full court press on the China deal. Very hush-hush. They threw me a little legal work on the Iberian negotiation."

"Any travel?" she said.

Richman smirked. "Just personal. Since marketing had nothing for me to do, I went skiing."

"Sounds like fun." She realized he hadn't answered her question. By then they had walked into building 64. Casey noticed the workers were openly hostile, the atmosphere distinctly chilly.

"What's this?" Richman said. "We got rabies today?"

"Union thinks we're selling them out on China by shipping the wing to Shanghai. I asked Marder. He says no."

A Klaxon sounded, echoing through the building. Directly ahead the big yellow overhead crane cranked to life, and Casey saw the first of the huge crates containing the wing tooling rise five feet up into the air on thick cables. The crate was constructed of reinforced plywood. It was as broad as a house, and probably weighed five tons. A dozen workers walked alongside the crate like pallbearers, hands up, steadying the load as it moved toward one of the side doors and a waiting flatbed truck.

Casey glanced to her left, where other tools were being crated for shipment. The huge blue tools were first packed in foam, then braced internally, and then crated. She looked back at the crate, moving on the hoist ten yards from where they stood.

All the men standing by it were gone.

"Uh-oh," she said.

"What?" Richman said.

"Run!" she shouted. "It's going to break loose!" She shoved Richman to the right, toward the shelter of some scaffolding.

Behind her Casey heard the creak of rending plywood and a metallic twang as the first of the hoist cables snapped and the giant crate began to slide from its harness. They had just reached the fuselage scaffolding when she heard another twang and the crate smashed down onto the concrete floor. Slivers of plywood exploded in all directions, followed by a thunderous whomp as the crate toppled over on its side.

"What was *that?*" Richman said, turning to look back.

"That," she said, "is what we call a job action."

Men were running forward, hazy forms in the cloud of lingering dust. There were shouts and calls for help. The medic alarm sounded, ringing through the building. At the opposite side of the building she saw Doug Doherty, shaking his head mournfully.

Richman pulled a four-inch splinter of plywood from the back of his jacket. "Good Lord," he said.

"That was a warning," Casey said. "And they've also wrecked the tool. Now it'll have to be rebuilt. This means weeks of delay."

"This was a warning?" Richman said.

"To the IRT," she said. "A clear signal: Watch your backs; watch your heads. We'll see falling wrenches, all sorts of accidents, whenever we're on the floor. We'll have to be careful." She picked up her dropped briefcase. "Come on," she said to him. "We're late."

7:00 a.m. Chairs scraped as everyone pulled up to the conference table. "Okay," Marder said. "Let's get started. We're having some union activity aimed at stalling this investigation. Don't let it get to you. Keep your eye on the ball. First item: weather data."

The secretary passed sheets around the room. It was a report from the L.A. Traffic Control Center about conditions at the time of the accident.

"We still have satellite data coming, but I think the evidence speaks for itself," Marder said. "The three aircraft nearest in time and location to TransPacific report no weather except light chop. I'm ruling out turbulence as a cause of this accident."

There were nods around the table. No one disagreed.

"Anything else for the record?"

"Yes," Casey said. "Passenger and crew interviews agree the seat-belt sign was never illuminated."

"Okay. Then we're done with weather. Flight recorder?"

"Data's anomalous," Casey said. "They're working on it."

"Leading edge?"

"No problem we could see," Doherty said. "We'll have the aircraft here today, and I'll look at the drive tracks and latches. But so far, nothing."

"You test the control surfaces?"

"No problem."

"Instrumentation?"

"After we heard the passenger's story from Casey, we did ten extensions, trying to get a disagree. But everything's normal."

"What story? Casey? You got something from the interviews?"

"Yes," she said. "One passenger gave a report of a slight rumble coming from the wing, lasting ten to twelve seconds, followed by a slight nose up, then a dive, and then a series of violent pitch excursions."

Marder glared at her. "Are you telling me it's slats again?"

"I don't know," Casey said. "One of the flight attendants reported that the captain said he had an uncommanded slats deployment and that he'd had problems with the autopilot."

"Damn it! *And* problems with the autopilot?"

"The heck with him," Burne said. "This captain changes his story every five minutes. Tells traffic control he's got turbulence, tells the stewardess he's got slats. Fact is, we don't know what happened in that cockpit."

"Okay," Marder said. "So we need more data. What about the NVMs? Ron? The faults suggest anything?"

They turned to Ron Smith, who hunched lower in his seat as if trying to pull his head between his shoulders. He cleared his throat. "Uh, yeah, we have a slats disagree on the FDAU printout."

"So the slats *did* deploy."

"Well, actually—"

"And the plane started porpoising, beat the heck out of the passengers, and killed three. Is that what you're telling me?"

No one spoke.

"What is the *matter* with you people?" Marder said. "This problem was supposed to be fixed four years ago!"

"John, let's not get carried away." It was Trung, the avionics head. "We're overlooking an important factor—the autopilot."

Marder glared at him. "What about it?" he snapped.

"Even if the slats extend in cruise flight," Trung said quietly, "the autopilot will maintain perfect stability. The slats extend, the AP adjusts, the captain sees the warning and retracts them. Meanwhile the plane continues, no problem."

"Maybe he went out of autopilot."

"He must have. But why?"

"Maybe your autopilot's screwy," Marder said. "The stewardess said the captain had to fight the autopilot for control."

"And I'd expect that," Trung said. "Once the aircraft exceeds flight parameters, the autopilot actively attempts to take over."

"Did that show up on the fault records?"

"Yes. They indicate the autopilot tried to kick in. The captain kept overriding it, insisting on flying the plane himself."

"But this is an experienced captain."

"Which is why I think Kenny is right," Trung said. "We have no idea what took place in that cockpit."

They all turned to Mike Lee, the carrier representative. "How about it, Mike?" Marder said. "Can we get an interview or not?"

Lee sighed philosophically. "You know," he said, "the tendency is always to blame the guy who's not there. It's human nature. I've already explained to you why the flight crew left the country. Your own records confirm the captain is a first-rate pilot. It's possible he made an error. But given the history of problems with this aircraft—slats problems—I'd look first at the aircraft. And I'd look hard."

"I couldn't have said it better myself," Marder said. "Guys, you have your marching orders. Get on with it. I want *answers.*"

BUILDING 202/FSIM

7:59 a.m. "Flight 545? It's very disturbing. Very disturbing indeed." A silver-haired, courtly man from Munich, Felix Wallerstein ran the Norton flight simulator and pilot-training program with Germanic efficiency.

Casey said, "Why do you say 545 is disturbing?"

"Because how could it happen? It does not seem possible."

They walked with Richman through the large main room of building 202. The two flight simulators, one for each model in service, stood above them. They appeared to be truncated nose sections of the aircraft, held up by a spidery array of hydraulic lifts.

"Did you get the data from the flight recorder?" Casey asked. "Rob said you might be able to read it."

"I tried," Wallerstein said, "with no success. I hesitate to say it is useless, but— What about the QAR?"

"No QAR, Felix."

"Ah." Wallerstein sighed.

They came to the command console, a series of video screens and keyboards. Here the instructors sat while they monitored the pilots being trained in the simulators. Both simulators were being used.

Casey said, "Felix, we're concerned the slats extended in cruise flight. We've had problems with slats before."

"Yes, but that is long since fixed, Casey. And slats cannot explain such a terrible accident. Where people are killed? No, no. Not from slats. I will show you." He turned to one of the instructors at the console. "Who's flying the N-22 now?"

"Ingram. First officer from Northwest."

On the closed-circuit video screen Casey saw a man in his mid-thirties sitting in the pilot's seat of the simulator.

"And where is he now?" Felix said.

"He's over the mid-Atlantic, FL three-thirty, point eight Mach."

"Good," Felix said. "So he's at thirty-three thousand feet, eight-tenths the speed of sound. He's been there awhile, and everything seems to be fine. He's relaxed, maybe a little lazy. Deploy Mr. Ingram's slats."

"Yes, sir." The instructor reached over and pushed a button.

Felix turned to Casey. "Watch carefully, please."

On the video screen the pilot leaned forward, suddenly alert.

Felix pointed to the instructor's console and the array of screens. "You can see what he is seeing. His slats indicator is flashing, and he's noticed it. Meanwhile, you see the plane gives a slight nose up."

The hydraulics whirred, and the big cone of the simulator tilted upward a few degrees.

"Mr. Ingram now checks his slats lever, as he should. He finds it is up and locked, which is puzzling, since it means he has an uncommanded slats deploy."

The simulator remained tilted up.

"So Mr. Ingram is thinking it over. He has plenty of time. The aircraft is quite stable on autopilot. Let's see what he decides. Ah. He pulls the slats lever down, then up. He's trying to clear the warning. But that doesn't change anything. So. He now realizes he has a system problem. What will he do? . . . He changes the autopilot parameters. . . . He descends to a lower altitude and reduces his airspeed. . . . Absolutely correct. . . . He is at more favorable conditions of altitude and speed. He decides to try the slats lever again."

The instructor said, "Should I let him off the hook?"

"Why not?" Felix said. "I believe we have made the point."

The instructor punched a button. The simulator leveled.

"And so," Felix said to Casey, "Mr. Ingram is restored to normal flight. He makes a note of his problem for the maintenance crews, and he continues on his way to London."

"But he stayed in the autopilot. What if he went out of it?"

Felix shrugged, turned to the instructor. "Fail his autopilot."

An audible alarm sounded. On the video screen they saw the pilot look at the controls and take the stick in his hands. The alarm ended; the cockpit became silent. The pilot continued to hold the stick.

"Okay," Felix said. "Deploy his slats."

The instructor pushed a button. On the systems monitor in the training console the slats warning flashed. At the adjacent video screen Casey saw the pilot leaning forward, noticing the warning.

"Now," Felix said, "once again we see the aircraft nose up, but this time Mr. Ingram must control it himself. . . . So he brings the stick back . . . very slightly . . . and now he is stable."

He turned to Casey. "You see?" He shrugged. "It is very puzzling. Whatever happened to that TransPacific flight, it cannot be the slats. The autopilot will compensate and maintain control."

"So? What do you think happened?"

"Well, let us be frank. Flight characteristics of an N-22 are such that if slats deploy at cruise speed and the captain goes out of the autopilot, the aircraft is rather sensitive. When the nose goes up, the captain must *gently* bring it back again. If he corrects too strongly, the plane noses over. In that case he must pull up, but again, gently, or he is likely to overcorrect, so the plane would climb sharply, then nose down once more. And this is precisely the pattern that occurred on the TransPacific flight."

"You're saying it was pilot error," Casey said.

"Ordinarily I would think so, except the pilot was John Chang, a *superb* pilot. He's one of the five or six best captains I have ever trained on this aircraft. So whatever happened to flight 545, it cannot be pilot error. Not with John Chang in the chair. It has to be a problem with the aircraft, Casey. It *has* to be that aircraft."

9:15 a.m. As they walked back across the vast parking lot, Casey was lost in thought.

"So," Richman said after a while. "Where are we?"

"Nowhere."

No matter how Casey put the evidence together, that was the conclusion she came to. The pilot had said it was turbulence, but it wasn't turbulence. A passenger gave a story consistent with slats deployment, but slats deployment couldn't explain the terrible damage to the passengers. The stewardess said the captain fought the autopilot, which Trung said only an incompetent captain would do. Felix said the captain was superb. They were nowhere.

She heard the whine of a jet. Looking up, she saw a Norton wide-body silhouetted against the sun. As it passed over her, she saw the yellow TransPacific insignia on the tail. It was the ferry flight from LAX. The big jet landed gently, puffed smoke at the wheels, and headed toward maintenance hangar 5.

Her beeper went off. She unclipped it from her belt.

***N-22 ROTR BURST MIAMI TV NOW

"Oh no," she said. "Let's find a TV. We have trouble."

9:20 a.m. "This was the scene just moments ago at Miami International Airport when a Sunstar Airlines jet burst into flames after an engine exploded without warning, showering the crowded runway with a hail of shrapnel."

"Aw, bull!" Kenny Burne shouted. A half-dozen engineers were crowded around the TV set as Casey came into the room.

"Miraculously, none of the two hundred and seventy passengers on board were injured," continued a reporter. "The N-22 Norton wide-body was revving for takeoff when passengers noticed clouds of black smoke coming from the engine. Seconds later the plane was rocked by an explosion as the left starboard engine literally blew to pieces and was quickly engulfed in flames."

The screen didn't show that. It just showed an N-22 aircraft seen from a distance, with dense black smoke gushing from it.

"Left starboard engine," Burne snarled. "As opposed to the *right* starboard engine, you silly twit?"

The TV now showed close-ups of passengers milling around the terminal. There were quick cuts. A young boy of seven or eight said,

"All the people got excited because of the smoke." Then a teenage girl shook her head and said, "It was rully, rully scary. I just saw the smoke, and like, I was rully scared." "Did you think it was a bomb?" she was asked. "Absolutely," she said. "A terrorist bomb."

Kenny Burne spun on his heel, threw up his hands. "Do you believe this? They're asking kids what they *thought.* This is the news. 'What did you think?' 'Golly, I swallowed my Popsicle.' "

On the screen the TV program now showed an elderly woman who said, "Yes, I thought I was going to die." Then a middle-aged man: "My wife and I prayed. Our whole family knelt down on the runway and thanked the Lord." "Were you frightened?" an interviewer asked. "We thought we were going to die," the man said.

Burne was yelling again. "In a *car* you would have died! In a nightclub you would have died. But not in a Norton wide-body! We designed it so you'd escape with your miserable life!"

"Calm down," Casey said. "I want to hear this." She was listening intently, waiting to see how far they'd take the story.

A strikingly beautiful Hispanic woman in a beige Armani suit stood facing the camera, holding up a microphone. "While passengers now appear to be recovering from their ordeal, their fate was far from certain earlier this afternoon when a Norton wide-body blew up on the runway, flames shooting high into the sky . . ."

The TV again showed the earlier telephoto shot of the plane on the runway, with smoke billowing from under the wing. It looked about as dangerous as a doused campfire.

"Wait a minute!" Kenny said. "A Norton *wide-body* exploded? A Sunstar *engine* exploded." He pointed to the screen image. "That's a damned rotor burst, and the blade fragments broke through the cowling, which is what I told them would happen!"

Casey said, "You told them?"

"Yes," Kenny said. "Sunstar bought six engines from AeroCivicas last year. I was the Norton consultant on the deal. I borescoped the engines and found a load of damage—blade-notch breakouts and vane cracks. So I told Sunstar to reject them." Kenny was waving his hands. "But why pass up a bargain? Sunstar rebuilt them instead. I told them again, Junk 'em. But Sunstar put them on the planes. So now the rotor blows—big surprise—and the fragments cut into the wing, so that nonflammable hydraulic fluid is smoking. And it's *our* fault?"

He spun, pointing back to the screen.

". . . seriously frightening all two hundred and seventy passengers on board. Fortunately, there were no injuries."

"That's right," Burne said. "No penetration of the fuse, lady. No injury to anybody. The wing absorbed it—our wing!"

"We are waiting to speak to officials from the airline about this frightening tragedy. More later. Back to you, Ed."

Casey sighed, relieved.

"I can't believe this," Burne shouted. He turned and stomped out of the room, banging the door behind him.

"What's his problem?" Richman said.

"For once I'd say he's justified," Casey said. "The fact is, if there's an engine problem, it's not Norton's fault. We build airframes. We don't build engines, and we don't repair them. Our engines are supplied by other companies—GE, Pratt and Whitney, Rolls-Royce. We build the plane and then install the brand of engine the customer selects. Just the way you can put any one of several brands of tires on your car. But if Michelin makes a batch of bad tires and they blow out, that's not Ford's fault."

Richman was looking unconvinced.

"All we can do," Casey said, "is certify that our planes fly safely with the engines we install. But we can't force carriers to maintain those engines properly over the life of the aircraft. The engine blew because it wasn't correctly maintained. It should never have happened. But our wing is so well built it absorbed the flying fragments, protecting passengers in the cabin. We're actually heroes—but Norton stock will fall tomorrow."

"Well," Richman said, "at least the reporters didn't mention TransPacific."

Casey nodded. That had been her first concern. She wanted to know if the news reports would link the Miami rotor burst to the

TPA in-flight incident the day before. That hadn't happened—at least not yet. But sooner or later it would.

"We'll start getting calls now," she said. "The cat is out of the bag."

9:40 a.m. There were a dozen security guards standing outside hangar 5, where the TransPacific jet was being inspected. But this was standard procedure whenever a team from recovery and maintenance services entered the plant.

Within the hangar the TransPacific wide-body stood in the glare of halogen lights, nearly hidden behind a gridwork of roll-up scaffolding. Technicians swarmed over every part of the plane. Casey saw Kenny Burne working the engines, cursing his power-plant crew. They were doing fluorescent and conductivity tests.

Ron Smith and the electrical team were standing on a raised platform beneath the midship belly. Higher up she saw Van Trung through the cockpit windows, his crew testing the avionics.

And Doherty was out on the wing. His structure team had used a crane to remove one of the inboard slats.

"It looks like they're tearing the plane apart," Richman said.

A voice behind them said, "It's called destroying the evidence!"

Casey turned. Ted Rawley, one of the flight-test pilots, sauntered up. He was wearing cowboy boots, a western shirt, dark sunglasses. Like most of the test pilots, Teddy cultivated an air of dangerous glamour.

"This is our chief test pilot," Casey said. "Teddy Rawley."

Teddy punched Casey on the shoulder. "So. How you doing, kid? I called you the other day."

"I know," she said. "I've been busy."

"I'll bet you have," Teddy said. "I bet Marder's got the screws on. So. What've the engineers found? Wait a minute, let me guess. They found absolutely nothing, right? Their beautiful plane is *perfect.* Must be pilot error."

Casey said nothing. Richman looked uncomfortable.

"Hey," Teddy said, "don't be shy. I've heard it all before. Let's face it, the engineers design planes to be practically automatic. They just *hate* the idea that somebody might actually *fly* them. It's so untidy. Makes 'em crazy. And of course, if anything bad happens, it must be the pilot. Gotta be the pilot. Am I right?"

"Come on, Teddy," she said. "You know the statistics. The overwhelming majority of accidents are caused by—"

At that point Doug Doherty, crouched on the wing above them, leaned over and said, "Casey, bad news. You'll want to see this. I'm pretty sure I know what went wrong on flight 545."

SHE climbed the scaffolding, Richman following, and walked out on the wing. Doherty was crouched over the leading edge. The slats were now removed, exposing the innards of the wing structure.

She got down on her hands and knees next to him and looked.

The space for the slats was marked by a series of drive tracks—little rails, spaced three feet apart, that the slats slid out on, driven by hydraulic pistons. At the forward end of the rail was a rocker pin, which allowed the slats to tilt downward. At the back of the compartment she saw the folding pistons that drove the slats along the tracks. With the slats removed, the pistons were just metal arms poking out into space.

As always whenever she saw the innards of an aircraft, Casey had a sense of enormous complexity. "What is it?" she said.

"Here," Doug said. He bent over one of the protruding arms, pointing to a tiny metal flange at the back, curved into a hook. The part was not much larger than her thumb. Doherty reached down, pushed the flange back with his hand. It flicked forward again. "That's the locking pin for the slats. It's spring-loaded. When the slats retract, the pin snaps over, holds them in place."

"Yes?"

"Look at it," he said, shaking his head. "It's bent." He set a metal ruler against the pin, showing her that the metal was bent a few millimeters to the left. "And that's not all," he said. "Look at the action surface of the hinge. It's been worn."

He handed her a magnifying glass. Thirty feet above the ground, she leaned over the leading edge and peered at the part. There was wear, all right: She saw a ragged surface. But you would expect a certain amount of wear. "Doug," she said, "do you really think it's significant if this one pin is bad?"

"The slats could pop loose in flight. They wouldn't necessarily fully extend. They wouldn't have to. Remember, at cruise speed a slight extension would change the aerodynamics."

Casey frowned. "But why would the lock suddenly open?"

"Look at the other pins," Doherty said, pointing. "There's no wear on the action surface. I think this one was changed. Look at the next pin down. See the parts stamp at the base?"

She saw a tiny embossed figure, an H in a triangle, with a sequence of numbers: the manufacturer's symbol. "Yeah. . . ."

"Now look at this pin. See the difference? On this part the triangle is upside down. This is a counterfeit part, Casey."

For aircraft manufacturers counterfeiting was the single biggest problem they faced as they approached the twenty-first century. Media attention focused mostly on counterfeit consumer items, like watches, CDs, and computer software. But there was a booming business in counterfeit airplane parts. And unlike a phony Cartier watch, a phony airplane part could kill you.

"Okay," she said. "I'll check the maintenance records, find out where it came from."

The FAA required commercial carriers to keep extraordinarily detailed maintenance records. Every one of the aircraft's one million parts could be traced back to its origin. Given enough time, they could find out exactly where this part had come from.

She pointed to the locking pin. "Have you photographed it?"

"Oh sure. We're fully documented."

"Then pull it," she said. "I'll take it to metals. By the way, could this situation give you a slats-disagree warning?"

Doherty gave a rare smile. "Yes. And my guess is, it did. You got a nonstandard part, Casey, and it failed the aircraft."

COMING off the wing, Richman was chattering excitedly. "So is that it? It's a bad part? Is that what happened? It's solved?"

He was getting on her nerves. "One thing at a time," she said. "First of all, we have to find out where that part came from. Go back to the office. Tell Norma to make sure the maintenance records are coming from LAX. And have her telex the fizer in Hong Kong to ask for the carrier's records. Tell him the FAA requested them and we want to look at them first."

"Okay," Richman said.

He headed off toward the open doors of hangar 5, out into the sunlight. He walked with a sort of swagger, as if he were a person of importance in possession of valuable information.

But Casey wasn't sure that they knew anything at all.

At least not yet.

10:00 a.m. Casey came out of the hangar, blinking in the morning sun. She saw the union leader, Don Brull, getting out of his car over by building 121. She headed toward him.

"Hello, Casey," he said as he slammed the door. "I was wondering when you'd get back to me."

"I talked to Marder," she said. "He swears the wing isn't being offset to China."

Brull nodded. "He called me last night. Said the same thing." Brull didn't sound happy. "He's lying."

"No way," Casey said. "It'd be pretty reckless to—"

"Marder's reckless. You know that. You know what he's capable of. Those tools aren't being shipped to Atlanta, Casey. I've seen the bills of lading. They say Seoul, Korea."

"Korea?" she said, frowning.

"Yes. They'll send them to Korea, then transship to Shanghai."

"You have copies of the bills? I'd like to see them."

Brull sighed. "I can get them for you, Casey. But you're putting me in a very difficult situation here. The guys aren't going to let this sale happen. It's out of my hands."

"Don—"

"I always liked you, Casey," he said, "but you hang around here, I can't help you." And he walked away.

OUTSIDE HANGAR 5

10:04 a.m. The morning sun was shining. The plant around her was cheerfully busy, mechanics riding their bicycles from one building to another. There was no sense of threat or danger. But Casey knew what Brull had meant: She was now in no-man's-land. Anxious, she pulled out her cell phone to call Marder when she saw the heavyset figure of Jack Rogers coming toward her.

Jack covered aerospace for the *Telegraph-Star,* an Orange County paper. He was a good, solid reporter, a reminder of an earlier generation of print journalists who knew as much about their beat as the people they interviewed. He waved.

"Hi, Jack," she said. "What's up?"

"I came over," he said, "about that wing-tool accident this morning. The one the crane dropped."

"Tough break," she said.

"This is obviously a job action, Casey. My sources tell me the union's opposed to the China sale."

"I've heard that," she said, nodding.

"Because the wing's going to be offset to Shanghai?"

"Come on, Jack. You know I can't discuss the sale. No one can until the ink's dry."

"Okay," Rogers said. He took out his notepad. "It does seem like a crazy rumor. No company's ever offset the wing. It'd be suicide."

"Exactly," she said.

Rogers made a note, then glanced up from his pad. "Shame about the rotor burst in Miami."

"All I know is what I saw on television."

"You think it will affect the public perception of the N-22?"

"I don't see why. The problem was power plant, not airframe. My guess is, they're going to find it was a bad compressor disk."

"I wouldn't doubt it," he said. "And how about the TransPacific flight? Was that an engine problem, too?"

"TransPacific happened yesterday, Jack. We just started our investigation. I can't comment. It's much too early."

"Not too early for speculation to start," Rogers said. "I'd just like to set the record straight. Have you ruled out engines?"

"Jack," she said, "I can't comment."

He made another note. "I suppose you're looking at slats, too. Given the 22 has a history of slats problems . . ."

"Ancient history," she said. "We fixed the problem years ago."

"But now you've had two incidents in two days. Are you worried that the flying public will start to think the N-22 is a troubled aircraft?"

She could see the direction his story was going to take. He was telling her what he would write if she didn't comment. It was a standard, if minor, form of press blackmail.

"Jack," she said, "we've got three hundred N-22s in service around the world. The model has an outstanding safety record. To speculate on what happened yesterday would be irresponsible."

That did it. He took his pen away. "Okay. You want to go off?"

"Sure." She knew she could trust him. "Off the record, 545 underwent severe pitch oscillations. We think it porpoised. We don't know why. We're working on it as fast as we can."

"Will it affect the China sale?"

"I hope not."

"By the way, is that China sale firm? I keep hearing it's not."

She shrugged. "I honestly don't know."

"Has Marder talked to you about it?"

"Not to me personally," she said. Her reply was carefully worded; she hoped he wouldn't follow up on it. He didn't.

"Okay, Casey," he said. "I'll leave this alone, but what've you got? I need something I can use tonight."

"Off the record, I've got a good lead, but you can't source it. The engine that blew was one of six that Sunstar bought from AeroCivicas. Kenny Burne was our consultant. He borescoped the engines and found a lot of damage."

"What kind of damage?"

"Blade-notch breakouts and vane cracks. Kenny told them to reject the engines, but Sunstar rebuilt them and put them on the planes. When that engine blew, Kenny was furious. So you might get a name at Sunstar from Kenny. But we can't be the source. We have to do business with these people."

"I understand," Rogers said. "Thanks. And what about Marder? Everybody knows he and Hal Edgarton are at each other's throats. Marder expected to be named president, but the board passed him over. But they gave Edgarton a one-year contract, so he's got only twelve months to produce. And I hear Marder's undercutting Edgarton every way he can."

"I wouldn't know about that," she said. Casey had, of course, heard such rumors. It was no secret that Marder was bitterly disappointed about Edgarton's appointment. What Marder could do about it was another story. Most people thought that Marder had no choice except to go along with Edgarton's agenda, at least for the moment. Marder might be unhappy, but the company had a cash-flow problem. They needed billions of dollars if they hoped to develop the next generation of planes and stay in business.

So the situation was clear. The company needed the sale. And everybody knew it, including Marder.

Rogers said, "You haven't heard that Marder's undercutting Edgarton?"

"No comment," Casey said. "But off the record, it makes no sense. Everybody in the company wants this sale, Jack. Including Marder. Right now he's pushing us hard to solve 545 so the sale goes through."

"Okay," he said finally, closing his notepad. "Call me if you get a break on 545, okay, Casey?"

"Sure, Jack."

WALKING away from him, Casey realized she was exhausted by the effort of the interview. Talking to a reporter these days was like a chess match: You had to think several steps ahead; you had to imagine all the possible ways a reporter might distort your statement. The atmosphere was relentlessly adversarial. Modern journalism was intensely subjective—"interpretive"—and speculation was its lifeblood.

And Jack Rogers, she thought, was one of the better ones. The print reporters were all better. It was the television reporters you had to watch out for. They were the really dangerous ones.

Crossing the plant, she fished her cell phone out of her purse and called Marder. His assistant, Eileen, said he was in a meeting.

"I just left Jack Rogers," Casey said. "I think he's planning a story that says we're shipping the wing to China and there's trouble in the executive suite. Edgarton better talk to him."

"Edgarton isn't doing any press," Eileen said. "John will be back at six o'clock. You want to talk to him then?"

"I better, yes."

"I'll put you down," Eileen said.

PROOF TEST

10:19 a.m. It looked like an aviation junkyard: old fuselages, tails, and wing sections littered the landscape, raised up on rusty scaffolding. But the air was filled with the steady hum of compressors, and heavy tubing ran to the airplane parts, like intravenous lines to a patient. This was proof test, the domain of the infamous Amos Peters.

Casey saw him off to the right, a hunched figure in shirtsleeves and baggy pants, bent over a readout stand beneath an aft fuselage section of the Norton wide-body.

"Amos," she called, waving to him.

He turned, glanced at her. "Go away."

Amos was a legend at Norton. Reclusive and obstinate, he was nearly seventy, long past mandatory retirement age, yet he continued to work because he was vital to the company. His specialty was the arcane field of damage tolerance, or fatigue testing. And fatigue testing was of vastly greater importance than it was ten years ago.

Since deregulation, the carriers were flying aircraft longer than anybody ever expected. Three thousand aircraft in the domestic fleet were now more than twenty years old. That number would double in five years. Nobody really knew what would happen to all those aircraft as they continued to age.

Except Amos.

Day after day his test fixtures applied repetitive pressures to aging aircraft, stressing them to simulate takeoffs and landings, wind shear and turbulence so Amos could study how they cracked.

"Amos," she said, coming up to him, "it's me. Casey."

He blinked myopically. "Oh. Casey. Didn't recognize you." He squinted at her. "Doctor gave me a new prescription." He gestured for her to walk with him toward a small building.

No one at Norton could understand how Casey was able to get along with Amos, but they were neighbors. He lived alone with his pug dog, and she had taken to cooking him a meal every month or so. In return, Amos regaled her with stories of aircraft accidents he'd worked on, going back to the 1950s. Amos had an encyclopedic knowledge of airplanes. She had learned a tremendous amount from him, and he had become a sort of adviser.

"Want coffee?" He opened the door to the shed, and she smelled the sharp odor of burned grounds. His coffee was always terrible.

"Sounds great, Amos," she said.

He poured a cup for her and one for himself, then waved her to a battered chair facing his desk. The desk was piled high with thick reports and journals. He cleared a path through them so he could see her. "So. What is it, Casey—545?"

She nodded.

"Can't help you there. The plane's new. Fatigue's not a factor."

"There's a question about a part, Amos." She showed him the pin in a plastic bag.

"Hmm." He turned it over in his hands, held it up to the light. "This would be—don't tell me—this would be an anterior locking pin for the second inboard slat."

"That's right."

"Of course it's right." He frowned. "But this part's bad."

"I know. Doherty thinks it failed the aircraft. Could it?"

"Well . . ." Amos slurped his coffee, then stared at the ceiling, thinking. "No. I got a hundred bucks says it *didn't* fail the aircraft. But this is a very valuable lead."

"But why? You just said it didn't fail the aircraft."

"Casey, Casey." Amos shook his head. "*Think.* Were the other locking pins replaced?"

"No. Just this one."

"Why just this one?"

"I don't know," she said.

"Find out. Think it through. You have a problem with slats. That's a wing problem. Now you've found a part that's been replaced on the wing. Why? Was that wing damaged in the past? Were other parts replaced as well? Are there other bad parts on the wing? Is there residual damage to the wing?"

"Not that you can see."

"Forget what you can see, Casey," Amos said impatiently. "Look at the ship's record and the maintenance records. Trace this part and get a history of the wing. Because something else is wrong."

He stood, sighing.

"You understand the situation, don't you?" he went on. "To check that part, you'll have to start with the ship's record. That's in building 64. I wouldn't go there right now. At least not alone."

"Come on, Amos," she said, "I used to work on the floor. I'll be okay."

Amos was shaking his head. "You know how the guys think. If they can mess up the investigation, they will. Be very careful."

BUILDING 64

11:45 a.m. Building 64 contained a series of chain-link cages that housed parts for the line, and terminal workstations. The workstations were placed inside small partitions, each containing a microfiche reader, a parts terminal, and a main system terminal.

In a parts cage Casey bent over a microfiche reader, scrolling through the ship's record for fuselage 271, the original factory designation for the aircraft involved in the TPA accident.

Jerry Jenkins, the parts-flow control manager on the floor, stood beside her, nervously tapping his pen. "Find it yet?"

"Jerry," she said, "take it easy."

"I'm easy," he said, glancing around the floor. "I'm just thinking, you know, you could have done this between shifts."

"Jerry," she said, "we're in kind of a rush here."

He tapped his pen. "Everybody's pretty hot about the China sale. What do I tell the guys?"

"You tell the guys," she said, "that if we lose that China sale, then this line will shut down and everybody will be out of a job."

Jerry swallowed. "That true? Because I hear—"

"Jerry, let me look at the record, will you?"

The ship's record consisted of the mass of documentation—a million pieces of paper, one for every part on the aircraft—used to assemble the aircraft. Norton warehoused five thousand pounds of paper, running eighty feet of shelf space for each aircraft, in a vast building in Compton. All this was copied onto microfiche for access at these readers on the floor. But finding the paper for a single part was time-consuming, and—

Suddenly Casey was staring at a photocopy of a sheet of paper from Hoffman Metal Works, in Montclair, California. The slats locking pin was described in a code that matched the engineering drawings. A typed date of manufacture, a stamped date of delivery to the factory, and a date of installation, followed by two stamps—one signed by the mechanic who installed the part and a second by the QA inspector who approved the work.

"So," Jerry said. "That the OEM or what?"

"Yeah, it's the OEM." Hoffman was the original equipment manufacturer. The part had come direct from them.

Jerry was looking out through the chain link at the factory floor beyond. Nobody seemed to be paying any attention, but Casey knew that the two of them were being watched.

Jerry said, "You leaving now?"

"Yes, Jerry. I'm leaving now."

She headed across the floor, staying on the aisle that ran by the parts cages. Away from the overhead cranes. Glancing up at the overhead walkways to be sure nobody was up there. Nobody was.

What she had learned so far was clear: The original installed part on TPA 545 had come from a reputable supplier. The original part was good; the part Doherty found on the wing was bad.

So Amos was right.

Something had happened to that wing, causing it to be repaired sometime in the past. But what?

She still had more work to do.

And very little time to do it.

NORTON QA

12:30 p.m. If the part was bad, where had it come from? Casey needed maintenance records, and they hadn't arrived yet. Where was Richman? Back in her office, she flipped through a stack of telexes. All the FSRs were asking for information about the N-22. One from the flight service rep in Madrid was typical:

> PERSISTENT REPORTS VIA MY IBERIA CONTACT THAT DUE TO MIAMI INCIDENT JAA WILL DELAY CERTIFICATION OF N-22 AIRCRAFT, CITING "AIRWORTHINESS CONCERNS." PLS ADVISE.

She sighed. What the FSR was reporting was entirely predictable. The JAA was the Joint Aviation Authorities, the European equivalent of the FAA. For some time now the JAA had been making special efforts to force American manufacturers to use European jet engines. The Americans had resisted, so it was logical that the JAA would take advantage of the rotor burst in Miami to put greater pressure on Norton by withholding certification.

But in the end, it was a political problem, not her area. She went to the next telex, which was from the FSR in Vancouver:

FIRST OFFICER LUE ZAN PING UNDERWENT EMERGENCY SURGERY FOR SUBDURAL HEMATOMA AT 0400 HRS TODAY. F/O NOT AVAILABLE FOR QUESTIONS AT LEAST 48 HRS.

Casey wanted to know why the injured first officer was in the back of the plane and not in the cockpit. But it seemed an answer to that question would have to wait until the end of the week.

She came to the next telex and stared in astonishment. It was from Rick Rakoski, the FSR in Hong Kong:

RECEIVED YOUR REQUEST MAINTENANCE RECORDS FOR TPA FLIGHT 545, FUSE 271, AND PASSED IT ON TO THE CARRIER. IN RESPONSE TO FAA REQUEST, TRANSPACIFIC RELEASED ALL RECORDS FROM REPAIR STATION KAI TAK HK, SINGAPORE, MELBOURNE. UPLOADED TO NORTON ON-LINE SYSTEMS AS OF 2210 LOCAL TIME. STILL WORKING ON CREW INTERVIEWS.

A smart move by the carrier, she thought. Since they didn't want to grant crew interviews, they had decided to provide everything else in an apparent display of cooperation.

Norma came into her office. "Records from LAX are coming in now," she said. "And Hong Kong already delivered."

"I see that. Have you got the storage address?"

"Right here." Norma handed her a slip of paper, and Casey typed it into her terminal. A screen flashed up: the maintenance records for Hong Kong, Singapore, and Melbourne.

"All *right,*" Casey said. She went to work. After the better part of an hour she had a good picture of what had happened to the slats locking pin on the TransPacific aircraft.

On November 10 of the previous year, on a flight from Bombay to Melbourne, the aircraft experienced a problem with radio communications. The pilot made an unscheduled stop on the island of Java, in Indonesia. There the radio was repaired, and Javanese ground crews refueled the plane for the continuing flight to Melbourne.

After the aircraft landed in Melbourne, Australian ground crews noted that the right wing was damaged.

Thank you, Amos. The wing was damaged.

Mechanics in Melbourne noted that the fuel coupling was bent on the right wing and the adjacent slats locking pin was slightly damaged. This was thought to have been caused by ground personnel in Java during the previous fueling stop.

Slats locking pins were an infrequent change item, and Melbourne repair station did not have one in stock. Rather than delay the aircraft in Australia, the plane was allowed to continue to Singapore and change the part there. However, a sharp-eyed maintenance person in Singapore noticed that the paper on their replacement locking pin appeared suspect. Maintenance crews were uncertain whether the replacement pin was genuine or not.

Since the part already in place functioned normally, Singapore elected not to replace it, and the aircraft was sent on to Hong Kong, the home terminal for TransPacific, where a brand-new slats locking pin was installed on the aircraft.

Paper for the part appeared to be proper, but Casey knew it was fake. Right now the only question was the one Amos had posed: *Were other parts replaced as well?*

Sitting at her terminal, Casey scrolled through the maintenance summary records for Hong Kong Repair Station for November 13 to find what else had been done to the aircraft that day.

It was slow going, but eventually she found a list of work that had been done on the wing. There were three notations.

CHG RT LDLT FZ-7. Change the right landing light fuse 7.

CHG RT SLTS LK PIN. Change the right slats locking pin.

CK ASS EQ PKG. Check the associated equipment package. This was followed by the notation NRML, meaning normal.

The associated equipment package was a maintenance subgrouping of related parts that had to be checked whenever a faulty part was detected. Changing the slats locking pin had triggered a maintenance check of associated equipment. But which equipment?

She knew the associated equipment packages were specified by Norton. But she couldn't pull up the list on her office computer. To do that, she would have to go back to the terminal on the floor.

BUILDING 64

2:40 p.m. Building 64 was nearly deserted, the wide-body line seemingly abandoned between shifts. First shift ended at 2:30 p.m. Second shift started at 3:30. This was the time that Jerry Jenkins had said she should examine the records because there wouldn't be an audience. He was right. There was nobody around now.

Casey went directly to the parts cage, sat down at the terminal, and called up the database of associated maintenance packages. She keyed in RT SLATS LK PIN and got the answer she was looking for. The associated parts package consisted of the other five elements of the slats drive track: the track, the lever, the hydraulic actuator, the piston, the forward coupling.

The list instructed mechanics to check the nearby proximity sensor, its coupling, cover plate, and wiring. If Amos was right, they ought to look very carefully at that proximity sensor. It was located deep in the wing. Difficult to get to. Difficult to inspect.

She shut down the terminal and crossed the plant floor, heading for her office. She needed to call Ron Smith to tell him to check the sensor. She walked beneath deserted aircraft to the doors.

As she neared them, two men entered the hangar. They were silhouetted against the midday sunlight, but she could see that one wore a red-checked shirt. The other had on a baseball cap.

Casey looked around. She saw no one else. It would be another fifteen minutes before people started showing up.

The two men were walking toward her.

Casey turned and started to walk away from them, heading back the way she had come. She could handle this, she thought.

She walked faster. Her shoes clicked on the concrete. The sound seemed to echo through the building. Could she really be alone here? Of course not. There were several hundred people in the building. She just couldn't see them; they were inside the airplanes.

She glanced over her shoulder. The men were gaining on her.

She picked up her pace, almost starting to jog, unsteady in her low heels. And she suddenly thought, This is ridiculous. I'm an executive of Norton Aircraft and I am running through this plant *in the middle of the day.* She took a deep breath.

To her left was a parts staging area. Ordinarily there would be dozens of men inside, fetching parts kits, working the bins. But now the cage was empty. She looked over her shoulder. The men were fifty yards behind, and closing.

She knew that if she started to scream, a dozen mechanics would suddenly appear. The goons would slip away, vanishing behind tools and scaffolding, and she'd look like a fool. She'd never live it down. The girl who lost it on the floor.

Where were the fire alarms? The medic alert alarms? Hazardous materials alarms? She could hit one and say it was an accident. . . .

But she saw no alarms.

The men were now thirty yards behind. If they broke into a run, they'd reach her in seconds. But they were being cautious—apparently they, too, expected to see people at any moment.

On her right she saw a forest of blue beams—the big industrial jigs that held the fuselage barrels in place while they were riveted together. She turned, ducking among the beams. She passed staircases and hanging lamps. She heard the men behind her shout in surprise and start to follow. But by then she was moving fast in near darkness through the girders. She knew her way around here.

Behind her she heard the men grunt, heard them bang into the crossbeams, swearing.

She started to run, jumping over cables and boxes, and then suddenly she came out into a clearing: station 14. A plane stood on its landing gear, high above the floor. She looked up at the wide-body and saw the silhouette of someone inside. Someone in the window.

Finally! Casey climbed the stairs to the plane, her feet clanging on the steel steps. She went two stories up, then paused to look. High above, in the hanging gardens, she saw three burly mechanics in hard hats. They were only ten feet below the ceiling, working on the topmost hinge of the plane's rudder.

She looked down and saw the two men below break clear of the forest of blue jigs and start after her.

She continued up. She reached the aft door of the plane and ran inside. The unfinished wide-body was huge and empty, like the belly of a metal whale. Halfway down she saw a solitary Asian woman attaching silver insulation blankets to the walls. The woman looked at Casey timidly.

"Is anybody else working here?" she said.

The woman shook her head no.

Casey turned, ran back out the door. Below, she saw the men just one level down. She turned and ran up the stairs.

Into the hanging gardens.

The metal staircase had been ten feet wide when she started. Now it narrowed to two feet. And it was steeper, more like a ladder, surrounded by a dizzying crosswork of scaffolding. Power lines hung down like jungle vines. The staircase swayed beneath her feet. It turned abruptly at right angles every ten steps or so. Casey was now forty feet above the ground, looking down on the broad crown of the fuselage and up at the tail rising above her.

She was suddenly flooded with panic. Looking up at the men working on the rudder above, she shouted, "Hey! Hey!"

They ignored her.

Continuing upward, she saw why. They were wearing audiopads, black plastic cups like earmuffs, over their ears. They couldn't hear anything through them.

She climbed. Fifty feet above the floor, the stairs abruptly angled right, around the black horizontal surface of the elevators, protruding from the vertical tail. The elevators obscured her view of the men above. The stairs here were not constructed for running. They swayed wildly; her feet slipped. She clutched at the railing with sweaty hands. She continued upward. She could no longer see the floor below; it was obscured by the layers of scaffolding. She couldn't see if the second shift had arrived or not. As she went higher, she began to feel the thick, hot air trapped beneath the roof of building 64. She remembered what they called this perch: the sweatbox.

Working her way upward, she finally reached the elevators. As she continued above them, the stairs angled back now, close to the broad, flat, vertical surface of the tail, blocking her view of the men working on the other side. She saw the wooden beams of the ceiling above her. Only five more feet . . . one more turn of the stairs . . . coming around the rudder . . . and then she would be—

Casey looked back, hearing the clang of the two men still racing up the stairs toward her. She could feel the vibration of their footsteps. They were close. And she had nowhere to go.

Directly ahead of her the stairs ended in a metal platform, four feet square, set alongside the rudder. There was a railing around the platform and nothing beyond. She was sixty feet up in the air on a tiny platform astride the huge expanse of the wide-body tail.

She should never have started to climb, she thought.

Casey swung her foot over the platform railing. She reached for the scaffolding, gripped it. She swung her other leg over and began to climb down the outside of the scaffolding.

Almost immediately she realized her mistake. The scaffolding was constructed of X-angled girders. Wherever she grabbed, her hands slid down, jamming her fingers into the cross joint with searing pain. Her feet slipped along the angled surfaces. The scaffolding bars were sharp-edged, difficult to hold.

Looking to her left, she saw the two men on the small high platform—the man in the red shirt and the man in the baseball cap. They were staring at her, trying to decide what to do. She was about five feet below them on the outside of the girders, hanging on.

She saw one of the men pull on a pair of heavy work gloves.

She realized she had to get moving again. Carefully, she unhooked her arms and started down again. Five feet. Another five feet. Now the girders were shaking.

Looking up, she saw the man in the red shirt climbing down after her. He was strong and moved quickly.

The second man was climbing back down the stairs.

Casey went down. Her arms burned. Her breath came in ragged gasps. She felt the man above her, descending toward her. She looked up and saw his big orange work boots. Heavy crepe soles. In moments he would be stomping on her fingers.

As Casey continued to scramble down, something banged against her left shoulder. She looked back and saw a power cable dangling from the ceiling. It was about two inches thick, covered in gray plastic insulation. How much weight would it support?

Above her the man was descending.

She reached out, tugged at the cable. It held firm. She looked up, saw no junction boxes above her. She pulled the cable close, wrapping her arm around it. Then her legs. Just as the man's boots came down, she swung out on the cable.

And began to slide.

She tried to go hand over hand, but her arms were too weak. She slid, hands burning. She couldn't control it.

She went ten feet, another ten feet. She lost track. Her feet slammed into a junction box and she stopped, swinging in the air. She heard shouts from below. Looking down, she realized with a shock that she was only about seven or eight feet above the floor. Hands were reaching up to her. People shouting.

She let go and fell.

She was surprised how quickly she recovered, getting right to her feet, embarrassed, brushing herself off. "I'm fine," she kept saying to the people around her. "I'm fine. Really." The paramedics came over; she waved them away. "I'm fine."

By now the workers on the floor had seen her badge, seen the blue stripe, and were confused—why was an executive hanging from the gardens? They were hesitant, unsure what to do.

"Everything is fine. Just . . . go on with what you're doing."

The paramedics protested, but she pushed through the crowd, moving away, until suddenly Kenny Burne was at her side, his arm around her shoulder. "What on earth is going on?"

"Nothing," she said.

"This is no time to be on the floor, Casey. Remember?"

"Yeah, I remember," she said.

She let Kenny walk her out of the building into the afternoon sun.

The huge parking lot was now filled with cars for the second shift.

Kenny turned to her. "You want to be more careful, Casey."

"Yeah," she said. She looked down at her clothes. There was a big streak of grease running across her blouse and skirt.

"I have to go home to change."

"I better drive you," Burne said.

She didn't protest. "Thanks, Kenny," she said.

ADMINISTRATION

6:00 p.m. John Marder looked up from behind his desk. "I heard there was a little upset in building sixty-four. I don't want you on the floor alone, Casey. This is no time to take chances."

"I understand."

"Now." He shifted in his chair. "What's this about a reporter?"

"Jack Rogers is working on a story that might turn ugly," Casey said. "Union allegations we're sending the wing offshore. Leaked documents that allegedly say we're offsetting the wing. And he's relating the leaks to, ah, friction in the executive suite. Between you and Edgarton."

"That's ridiculous," Marder said, annoyed.

"I stalled him," Casey said. "But if we want to kill the story, we have to give him something better—an interview with Edgarton or an exclusive on the China sale. It's the only way."

"That's fine," Marder said. "But Hal won't do any press."

"Well, somebody needs to," Casey said. "Maybe you should."

"That could be difficult. Hal has instructed me to avoid the media until the sale is finalized. I have to be careful here. If I give Rogers something on deep background, he'll cover me?"

"Sure. He just needs something to file."

"All right. Then I'll talk to him." Marder scribbled a note. "By the way, how's Richman working out?"

"Fine," she said. "He's just inexperienced."

"He seems bright. Use him. Give him something to do. That was the problem with marketing. They didn't give him anything to do."

"Okay," she said.

AFTER Casey left, a side door opened. Richman walked in.

"You idiot," Marder said. "She almost got hurt in sixty-four this afternoon. Where the hell were you?"

"Well, I was—"

"Get this straight," Marder said. "I don't want *anything* to happen to Singleton, you understand me? We need her in one piece. She can't do this job from a hospital bed. I want you next to her at all times, pal, until we finish this thing."

"Got it, John."

QA

6:20 p.m. Casey went back down to her fourth-floor offices. Norma was still at her desk. "You got another stack on your desk, waiting for you. Oh, and I talked to Evelyn in accounting about Richman. His travel at marketing was billed to customer services in the program office—a slush fund. And the kid spent a fortune."

"How much?"

"Ready? Two hundred and eighty-four thousand dollars."

"Wow," Casey said. "Who approved the charges?"

"It's a production account. It's controlled by Marder." Norma shuffled papers on her desk. "Not much else here. . . . FAA's going to be late with the transcript of the CVR. There's a lot of Chinese spoken, and their translators are fighting about the meaning. The carrier's also doing their own translation, so . . ."

Casey sighed. "What else is new," she said. In incidents like this one the FAA generated a written transcript of the cockpit conversation, since the pilots' voices were owned by the carrier. But disputes over the translation were the rule on foreign flights.

"Did Allison call?"

"No, honey. Your only personal call was from Teddy Rawley."

Casey sighed. "Okay."

In her office she thumbed through the files on her desk. Most of it was paper on TransPacific 545: flight-path charts, transcriptions of air-traffic control voice recordings, weather reports, a sheaf of fault-record data. She was tired. She decided to take it home.

GLENDALE

10:45 p.m. He sat up in bed abruptly, turned, put his feet on the floor. "So. Listen babe," he said, not looking at her.

She stared at the muscles of his bare back. The ridge of his spine. The strong lines of his shoulders.

"It's great to see you," he said.

"Uh-huh," she said.

"But you know, big day tomorrow."

She would have preferred he stay. The truth was, she felt better having him here at night. But she knew he was going to go. He always did. She said, "I understand. It's okay, Teddy."

That made him turn back to her. He gave her his charming, crooked smile. "You're the best, Casey." He bent over and kissed her, a long kiss. She knew this was because she wasn't begging him to stay. She kissed him back, hand around his neck.

He pulled away again. "So. Anyway. I hear you toured the gardens between shifts."

"Yeah, I did."

"You don't want to get the wrong people ticked off."

"I know."

He grinned. "I'm sure you do." He kissed her cheek.

"Teddy," she said, "you want coffee before you go?"

He was pulling on his cowboy boots. "Uh, no, babe."

Not wanting to be left alone in the bed, she got up, too. She put on a big T-shirt, walked him to the door, kissed him briefly as he left. He touched her nose, grinned.

"Good night, Teddy," she said.

She locked the door, set the alarm.

She had been telling herself for months to end it—end what? a voice said—but she somehow never got around to saying the words. She was so busy at work; it was such an effort to meet people. Six months ago she had gone with Eileen, Marder's assistant, to a country-and-western bar in Studio City. The place was frequented by young movie people, Disney animators—a fun crowd, Eileen said. Casey found it agonizing. She wasn't beautiful, and she wasn't young. She didn't have the effortless glamour of the girls who glided through the room in tight jeans and crop tops.

The men were all too young for her, their smooth faces unformed. And she couldn't make small talk with them. She felt herself too serious for this setting. She had a job, a child; she was looking at forty.

It wasn't that she had no interest in meeting someone, but it was just so difficult. There was never enough time, never enough energy. In the end, she didn't bother.

So when Teddy would call, say he was in the neighborhood, she'd go unlock the door for him. That was how it had been for a year now.

She made tea and got back into bed. She propped herself up against the headboard, reached for the stack of papers, and began to review the records from the fault data recorders.

She started to thumb through the printout. There were ten pages of dense data, and she wasn't sure what all the readings represented. She flipped ahead to the DEU listing, which stored faults by each leg of the flight. She scanned them quickly, yawning, and then suddenly stopped.

DEU FAULT REVIEW
LEG 04 FAULTS 01
R/L SIB PROX SENS MISCOMPARE
8 APR 00:36
FLT 180 FC052606H
ALT 37000
A/S 320

She frowned. She could hardly believe what she was seeing.

A fault in the proximity sensor. Exactly what her check of maintenance records told her to look for.

More than two hours into the flight a proximity-sensor error was noted on the inboard electrical bus. The wing had many proximity sensors—little electronic pads that detected the presence of metal nearby. The sensors were needed to confirm that the slats and flaps were in the proper position on the wing.

According to this fault, a "miscompare" had occurred between sensors on the right and left sides. If the main electrical box in the fuselage had had a problem, faults would have been generated on both wings. But the right wing alone had generated the miscompare. She looked ahead to see if the fault repeated.

She didn't see anything at once, but it was difficult to assemble a picture of the flight from these bits and pieces. She needed the continuous data from the flight recorder. She'd call Rob Wong in the morning and see how he was coming with that.

Meanwhile . . . Casey yawned, settled lower on the pillows.

WEDNESDAY

GLENDALE

6:12 a.m. The telephone was ringing. Casey awoke, groggy, and rolled over, hearing the crunch of paper beneath her elbow. She looked down and saw the data sheets scattered all over the bed.

She picked up the phone. "Mom." Solemn, close to tears.

"Hi, Allie."

"*Mom.* Dad is making me wear the red dress, and I want to wear the blue one with the flowers."

Casey sighed. "What did you wear yesterday?"

"The blue one. But it's not dirty or *anything!*" This was an ongoing battle. Allison liked to wear the clothes she had worn the day before. Some innate, seven-year-old conservatism at work.

"Honey, you know I want you to wear clean clothes to school."

"But it *is* clean, Mom. And I hate the red dress."

Last month the red dress had been her favorite.

Casey sat up in bed, yawned, stared at the papers. Do I need this? She wondered why Jim didn't handle it. He didn't hold up his end. He wasn't firm with her in these childish power plays.

"Allison," she said to her daughter, "if your father says to wear the red dress, you do what he says. He's in charge now."

"But Mom—"

"That's it, Allison. No more discussion. The red dress."

"Oh, Mom . . ." She started to cry. "I *hate* you." She hung up.

Casey considered calling her daughter back, decided not to. She yawned, got out of bed, walked into the kitchen, and turned on the coffeemaker. Her fax machine was buzzing in the corner of the living room. She went over to look at it.

The paper coming out was a press release issued by a public relations firm in Washington. Although the firm had a neutral name—the Institute for Aviation Research—she knew it represented the European consortium that made Airbus. The release was formatted to look like a breaking wire-service story. The headline said:

JAA DELAYS CERTIFICATION OF N-22 WIDE-BODY JET
CITING CONTINUED AIRWORTHINESS CONCERNS

She sighed. It was going to be a long day.

WAR ROOM

7:00 a.m. Casey climbed the metal stairs to the war room. When she reached the catwalk, John Marder was there, pacing.

"You've seen this JAA thing?" He held up the fax.

"Yes, I have."

"It's nonsense, of course, but Edgarton's very upset. First, two N-22 incidents in two days, and now this. He's worried we're going to get creamed in the press. And he has no confidence that our media relations people will handle this right. And let's face it, the reporters won't want to talk to press flacks. They'll want an executive. So Hal wants all the inquiries on the JAA routed to you."

"To me?" she said. "Are you sure?"

"I also think," Marder said, "we ought to prepare a decent press package on the N-22. Something besides the usual PR baloney. Hal suggested you compile a comprehensive package to refute the JAA stuff—you know, service hours, safety record, dispatch reliability data. I told Hal you were busy and that this was an added burden. He's approved a two-grade bump in your IC."

Incentive compensation, the company's bonus package. A two-grade increase would mean a substantial amount of money.

"Okay," she said. It would be a lot of work, but—

"The point is," Marder said, "we've got a good response to this fax, and Hal wants to make sure we get it out. Can I count on you to help us?"

"Sure," Casey said.

"Good." And Marder went into the war room.

Richman was already in the room, looking preppy in a sport coat and tie. Casey slipped into a chair. Marder shifted into high gear, waving the JAA fax in the air, berating the engineers. "You've probably already seen that the JAA is playing games with us. Perfectly timed to jeopardize the China sale. But if you read the memo, you know that it's all about the engine in Miami and nothing about TransPacific. At least not yet."

Casey tried to pay attention, but she was distracted, calculating what the change in IC would mean. A two-grade bump was—she did the figures—something like a twenty percent raise. Twenty percent! She could send Allison to private school. They could vacation someplace nice, move to a bigger house—

Everyone at the table was staring at her.

Marder said, "Casey? The DFDR? The data?"

"Sorry," she said. "I talked to Rob this morning. The calibration's going slowly. He'll know more tomorrow."

"Okay. Structure?"

Doherty began in his unhappy monotone. "We found a bad locking pin on the number two inboard slat. It's counterfeit—"

"We'll verify it at flight test," Marder said, interrupting him. "Hydraulics?"

"Still testing, but so far they check out. Cables rigged to spec."

"Electrical?"

Ron said, "We've checked the principal wiring pathways. Nothing yet. But there's one funny thing. The DEU faults indicate a problem with proximity sensors in the wing. If the sensors failed, we might get a slats misread in the cockpit."

This was what Casey had noticed the night before. She made a note to ask Ron about it later.

Marder said, "Power plant?"

"We're still not sure the pilot deployed the thrust reversers," Kenny Burne said. "It'll be another day."

"Go until you can rule it out. Avionics?"

Trung said, "Avionics check out so far."

"This autopilot thing . . ."

"Haven't gotten to autopilot yet. We'll know by flight test."

"All right," Marder said. "If that covers it, don't let me keep you. I need answers." He held up the JAA fax. "This is the tip of the iceberg, people. So get me those answers!"

NEWSLINE/NEW YORK

1:54 p.m. In midtown Manhattan, in the twenty-third-floor offices of the weekly news show *Newsline,* Jennifer Malone was in the editing bay, reviewing tape of an interview with Charles Manson. Her assistant, Deborah, walked in, dropped a fax on her desk, and said casually, "Pacino dumped."

Jennifer hit her PAUSE button. "What?"

"Ten minutes ago. Al Pacino blew Marty off and walked."

"*What?* His picture opens this weekend, and he's slated for the full twelve." A twelve-minute segment on *Newsline,* the most watched news show on television, was the kind of publicity that money couldn't buy. "What happened?"

"Marty was chatting with him and mentioned that Pacino hadn't had a hit in four years. He got offended and walked."

Jennifer swore. Marty Reardon was a notoriously abrasive interviewer. He liked to embarrass interviewees, putting them on the spot with intensely personal questions, even if the questions weren't relevant to the story.

"Has Dick talked to Marty? Can we salvage this?" Dick Shenk was the executive producer. In three years he had skillfully built *Newsline* into a solid prime-time success. He was the only person with enough clout to handle a prima donna like Marty.

"Dick is still at lunch with Mr. Early." Shenk's lunches with Early, the network president, lasted late into the afternoon.

"So Dick doesn't know?"

"Not yet."

"Great." Jennifer glanced at her watch: it was 2:00 p.m. If Pacino had dumped, they had a twelve-minute hole to fill and less than seventy-two hours to do it. "What've we got in the can?"

"Nothing. Just that wheelchair Little League segment."

Jennifer groaned. "Dick will never go with that." She picked up the fax. It was a press release from some PR group, one of hundreds that every news show received each day. The headline read:

JAA DELAYS CERTIFICATION OF N-22 WIDE-BODY JET
CITING CONTINUED AIRWORTHINESS CONCERNS

"What's this?" she said, frowning.

"Hector thought there might be something in it."

"Why? What's the JAA?" Jennifer scanned the text; it was a lot of aerospace babble, dense and impenetrable. She thought, No visuals.

"Apparently it's the same plane that caught fire in Miami."

"Oh. Hector wants to do a safety segment? Good luck. Everybody's seen the tape of the burning plane already. And it wasn't that good to begin with." Jennifer tossed the fax aside.

JENNIFER Malone was twenty-nine years old, the youngest segment producer on *Newsline*. She had advanced quickly because she was good at her job and Dick Shenk liked her spunk. The fact that she was bright, beautiful, and an Ivy Leaguer did not hurt either.

The show had fifteen producers. Each was expected to deliver a story every two weeks. The average story took four weeks to build. After two weeks of research, producers met with Dick to get the go-ahead. Then they visited the locations, shot for background, and did the secondary interviews. The story was shaped by the producer and narrated by the on-air star, who flew in for a single day, did the stand-ups and the major interviews, then flew on to the next shoot, leaving the producer to cut the tape.

It was a system Jennifer liked. She had considerable power, and she liked working behind the scenes, her name unknown. She found the anonymity useful. Often, when she conducted interviews, the interviewees spoke freely, even though tape was rolling. At some point the interviewee would say, "When will I get to meet Marty Reardon?" She would solemnly answer that that hadn't been decided yet, and continue with her questions. And in the process nail the stupid bozo who thought she was just a dress rehearsal.

The fact was, she made the story. She didn't care if the stars got the credit. And anyway, there wasn't time to do it any other way. A media star like Marty Reardon was more heavily booked than the President. You couldn't expect a person like Marty to waste his valuable time doing spadework, stumbling over false leads, putting together a story. There just wasn't time.

This was television: There was never enough time.

JENNIFER looked again at her watch. Dick wouldn't return from lunch until three or three thirty. Marty Reardon was not going to apologize to Al Pacino. So when Dick came back from lunch, he was going to blow his top, then be desperate to fill the hole.

Jennifer had an hour to find him a new package.

She looked again at the fax on her desk. "N-22 WIDE-BODY JET . . . CONTINUED AIRWORTHINESS CONCERNS"

Wait a minute, she thought. *Continued* airworthiness concerns? Did that mean an ongoing safety problem? If so, there might be a story here. Not air safety—that had been done. But a specific aircraft with a problem? That was a product-safety story. Don't buy this product. Don't fly this airplane.

That might be very *very* effective, she thought.

She picked up the phone and dialed.

HANGAR 5

11:15 a.m. Casey and Richman found Ron Smith with his head in the forward accessory compartment, just back of the nosewheel.

"Ron," she said, "tell me about this fault list." She had brought the list with her, all ten pages. "There's four AUX readings here. Lines one, two, three, and COA. What do they service?"

Ron sighed. "AUX one is the auxiliary power generator, the turbine in the tail. AUX two and three are redundant lines in case the system gets an upgrade and needs them later. AUX COA is an auxiliary line for customer options. That's the line for customer add-ons, like a QAR, a quick access recorder, which this plane doesn't have."

"Okay," she said. "What about the proximity-sensor faults?"

"We're checking them now. We may turn up something. But look, the fault readings are snapshots of a moment in time. We need the DFDR data. You've got to get it for us, Casey."

"I've been pushing Rob Wong . . ."

"Push him harder," Smith said. "The flight recorder is the key."

CASEY'S cell phone rang. It was Norma.

"It's starting," she said. "You got calls from Jack Rogers, from Barry Jordan at the L.A. *Times,* and from the Washington *Post.* And a request for background material on the N-22 from *Newsline.*"

"That TV show? They doing a story?"

"I don't think so. It sounded like a fishing expedition."

"Okay," Casey said. "I'll call you back." She sat down in a corner of the hangar and took out her notepad. She began to write out a list of documents to be included in a press package. Summary of FAA certification procedures for new aircraft. Announcement of FAA certification of the N-22; Norma would have to dig that up from five years ago. The company's internal report on N-22 safety in flight from 1991 to the present—the record was outstanding. The one-sheet features summary on the plane—basic stats on speed and range, size and weight. That would cover the bases.

Richman was watching her. "What now?" he said.

She tore off the sheet, gave it to him. "Give this to Norma. Tell her to prepare a press packet and send it to whoever asks for it."

"Okay." Richman walked away, humming cheerfully.

Her phone rang. It was Jack Rogers. "I keep hearing the wing's being offset. I'm told Norton is shipping the tools to Korea, but they're going to be transshipped to Shanghai."

"Talk to Marder," Casey said, "before you do anything."

Rogers sighed. "Look, Casey. I don't want to sit on a story that I've got right. Help me out here. If I were to write that several high-level Norton sources deny the wing is going to China, I assume you wouldn't have a problem with that?"

"I wouldn't, no." A careful answer, but then it was a careful question.

NEWSLINE

2:25 p.m. Jennifer Malone dialed the number on the fax and asked for the contact, Ms. Weld.

"I understand there's a delay in European certification of the Norton aircraft, the N-22. What's the problem?"

"Well, in the past the Europeans accepted FAA certification of a new aircraft. But lately JAA has been questioning the U.S. certification process. They feel that the FAA is in bed with the American manufacturers and may have relaxed its standards."

"Really?" Perfect, Jennifer thought. Inept American bureaucracy. Dick Shenk loved those stories. "What's the evidence?"

"Well, the Europeans find the system unsatisfactory. For example, the FAA doesn't store certification documents. They allow the aircraft companies to do that. It seems entirely too cozy."

"Uh-huh." Jennifer wrote:

—FAA in bed with mfrs. Corrupt!

She called the FAA next and was put through to a man named Wilson. "I hear the JAA is refusing to validate the Norton N-22."

"Yes. They've been dragging their feet for a while now."

"The FAA has already certified the N-22?"

"Oh sure. You can't build an airplane in this country without FAA certification of the design and manufacturing process."

"And do you have the certification documents?"

"No. They're kept by the manufacturer. Norton has them."

Ah-ha, she thought. So it was true.

—Norton keeps certification, not FAA.
—Fox guarding chicken coop?

"And you're satisfied the certification process was proper?"

"Sure," Wilson said. "The plane was certified five years ago."

She called the information office for Airbus Industries in Washington and got put through to a marketing guy named Samuelson. He reluctantly confirmed that he had heard of the JAA confirmation delays. "But Norton's having a lot of problems," he said. "For example, I think the China sale is not as firm as they pretend it is."

This was the first she had heard of a China sale. She wrote:

—China sale N-22?

She said, "Uh-huh . . ."

"I mean, let's face it," Samuelson continued. "The Airbus A-340 is a superior plane in every way. It's newer than the Norton wide-body. Better range. We've been trying to explain this to the Chinese, and they are starting to understand our perspective. And of course safety concerns are part of their decision."

—C thinks airplane unsafe.

"Who would I talk to about that?" she said.

"Well, the Chinese are generally reluctant to discuss negotiations in progress," Samuelson said. "But I know a guy over at Commerce who may be able to help you. He's with the Ex-Im Bank, which provides long-term financing for overseas sales."

"What's his name?" she said.

HIS name was Robert Gordon. It took fifteen minutes for the operator at Commerce to find him. Jennifer doodled. Finally the secretary said, "I'm sorry, Mr. Gordon is in a meeting."

"I'm calling from *Newsline,*" she said.

"Oh." A pause. "Just a minute, please."

Jennifer smiled. It never failed.

Gordon came on, and she asked him about the JAA certification and the Norton sale to the People's Republic. "Is it true the sale is in jeopardy?"

"Every airplane sale is in jeopardy until it's concluded, Ms. Malone," Gordon said. "But as far as I know, the China sale is in good standing. I did hear a rumor that Norton is having trouble with JAA certification for Europe. The company's had an awful lot of problems. There was that thing in Miami yesterday."

She called Norton Aircraft for their version of the story. She said she wanted to talk to someone in management, not PR. She was put through to the president's office, then was transferred to some woman named Singleton. "How can I help you?" the woman said.

"I understand there's been a delay in European certification of the N-22. What's the problem with the plane?" Jennifer asked.

"No problem at all," Singleton said. "We've been flying the N-22 in this country for five years."

"Well, I've been hearing that this is an unsafe aircraft. You had an engine flameout on the runway at Miami yesterday. . . ."

"Actually, we had a rotor burst. That's being investigated now." The woman was speaking smoothly, calmly, as if it was the most normal thing in the world for an engine to blow up.

—Rotor burst!

"I see," Jennifer said. "But if it's true your plane has no problems, why is the JAA withholding certification?"

The woman at the other end paused. "I can only give you background on this," she said. "Off the record, Ms. Malone. The issue concerns power plant. In this country the plane flies with Pratt and Whitney engines. But the JAA is telling us that if we want to sell the plane in Europe, we're going to have to equip it with IAE engines."

"IAE?"

"A European consortium that makes engines. Like Airbus."

"Uh-huh," Jennifer said.

"Now allegedly," Singleton continued, "the JAA wants us to equip the aircraft with the IAE engine to meet European noise and emission standards, which are more stringent than those in the U.S. But the reality is we make airframes, not engines, and we believe the engine decision should be left up to the customer. So we consider this an unwarranted regulatory intrusion by the JAA. The issue has nothing to do with airworthiness."

Jennifer frowned. "You're saying it's a regulatory dispute?"

"Exactly. This is a trading bloc issue."

—Regulatory dispute!!!

Jennifer was listening to the tone of the woman's voice at the other end of the line, trying to sense the emotion. This woman sounded slightly bored, like a schoolteacher at the end of the day. She detected no tension, no hesitation, no hidden secrets.

She swore. No story. Jennifer thanked her and hung up.

Nothing. Period. The end.

She punched the intercom. "Deborah, this aircraft thing—"

"Are you watching?" her assistant said, squealing.

"Watching what?"

"CNN. It's unbelievable."

Jennifer grabbed her remote.

EL TORITO RESTAURANT

12:05 p.m. The El Torito offered acceptable food at a reasonable price and fifty-two kinds of beer. It was a local favorite of the engineers. The IRT members were all sitting at a table right off the bar. The waitress had taken their order and was leaving, when Doug Doherty pointed across the room. "*Look at that!*"

They all turned to stare at the television set mounted above the bar. The sound was down, but the image was unmistakable: the interior of a Norton wide-body jet, as seen by a badly shaking video camera. Passengers were literally flying through the air, bouncing off luggage racks, tumbling over the seats.

Kenny Burne got up and ran into the bar shouting, "Sound! Turn up the sound!" The horrifying images continued.

By the time Casey got into the bar, the video segment had ended. The television now showed a thin man with a mustache, wearing a carefully cut blue suit. She recognized Bradley King, an attorney who specialized in airline accidents.

"I think this footage speaks for itself," King was saying. "My client provided it to us, and it vividly portrays the terrible ordeal passengers were subjected to on this doomed flight. This aircraft went into an uncontrolled dive. It came within five hundred feet of crashing in the Pacific Ocean!"

"What?" Kenny Burne said. "It did *what?*"

"I can say with conviction that what occurred is a result of well-known design flaws on the N-22 jet," King went on. "I personally know pilots who refuse to fly the N-22 because it is so unsafe."

"Especially the ones on your payroll," Burne said.

On the television King was saying, "Yet Norton Aircraft has

known about these design flaws for years and has done nothing. Now three people are dead, two passengers paralyzed, the copilot in a coma as we speak. Altogether fifty-seven passengers required hospitalization. That's a disgrace to aviation."

The television was showing the CNN tape again, this time in slow motion, the bodies spiraling through the air. Watching it, Casey started to sweat. She felt dizzy and cold. She dropped quickly to a barstool, took a deep breath.

Now the television showed a bearded man with a scholarly air, standing near one of the runways at LAX. Aircraft were taxiing in the background. The man was Frederick Barker, a former FAA official who had testified in court against the company several times in recent years. The engineers all hated him.

Barker was saying, "Oh yes, I'm afraid there's no question about the problem." About what problem? she thought, but now the television cut to a photograph of the N-22. Beneath the photograph it said, UNSAFE? in huge red letters.

"Do you believe that bull?" Burne said.

Casey turned away, got off the barstool, took another deep breath.

She picked up her purse, got her cell phone out, and called the office. "Norma," she said, "call CNN and get a copy of the tape they just ran on the N-22. Now. Do it right now."

NEWSLINE

3:06 p.m. "Deborah!" Jennifer screamed, watching the tape. "Call CNN and get a copy of that Norton tape!" Jennifer watched, transfixed. It was the greatest piece of tape she'd ever seen. And the sound! Fabulous! People screaming in pure terror, and all these incredible crashing noises as people and bags smashed into the walls and ceilings. Fabulous! Unbelievable!

"Deborah!" she screamed again. "Deborah!"

She was so excited, she felt like she was going to jump out of her skin. She was dimly aware of the guy on-camera now, some weasel lawyer; it must be his tape. But she knew he would give it to *Newsline.* He'd want the exposure, which meant—they had a story! A little frill and build, and they were there!

Deborah came in, flushed, excited. Jennifer said, "Get me the clips on Norton Aircraft for the last five years. Do a Nexis search on the N-22, on a guy named Bradley King, and a guy named Frederick Barker. Download it all. I want it now!"

Twenty minutes later she had the outlines of the story and the background on the key figures. Clearly they should stay away from the ambulance chaser, Bradley King. But Barker, a former FAA official, would be useful.

And she noticed that Jack Rogers, the reporter for the Orange County *Telegraph-Star,* took a particularly critical view of Norton. She noted several recent stories under Rogers's byline.

Smiling, she called him at his newspaper. "I've been reading your pieces on Norton. They're excellent. I gather you think the company's got some problems with the airplanes?"

"Well, yes," Rogers said, "but they're also having union problems. The plant's in turmoil, and management's not leading. The union's angry about the China sale. Thinks it shouldn't happen."

"Will you talk about this on-camera?"

"Sure. I can't give sources, but I'll tell you what I know."

Of course he would, Jennifer thought. It was the dream of every print reporter to somehow get on television.

"My office will contact you."

She called Fred Barker in Los Angeles. He almost seemed to be expecting her call. "That's pretty dramatic videotape," she said.

"It's frightening," Barker said, "when an aircraft's slats deploy at nearly the speed of sound. That's what happened on the TransPacific flight. It's the ninth such incident for the aircraft."

"The *ninth?*"

"Oh yes. This is nothing new, Ms. Malone. At least three other deaths are attributable to Norton's shoddy design."

"You have a list?"

"Give me your fax number."

The list, when it arrived, was compelling. There were detailed accounts of eight slats deployment incidents between January 1992 and June 1994.

She picked up the phone and called Barker back. "Will you talk about these incidents on-camera?"

"I've testified in court about this on numerous occasions," Barker said. "I'll be happy to speak to you on the record."

"How can you be so sure this flight was a slats accident?"

"I have a source inside Norton," Barker said. "A disgruntled employee who is tired of all the lying. My source tells me it is slats and the company is covering up."

Jennifer got off the phone with Barker and pushed the intercom button. "Deborah!" she screamed. "Get me travel!"

JENNIFER closed the door to her office and sat quietly. She knew she had a story. A fabulous story. The question now was, What's the angle? How do you frame it?

Older producers on *Newsline* talked about context, which to them meant putting the story in a larger setting. Indicating what the story meant by reporting what had happened before or reporting similar things that had occurred. Jennifer had no interest in the past. She was one of the new generation that understood that gripping television was *now,* events happening *now,* a flow of images in a perpetual unending electronic present.

The past was dead and gone. Who cared what you ate yesterday? What you did yesterday? What was immediate and compelling was *now.* And television at its best was *now.*

So a good frame had nothing to do with the past. Fred Barker's damning list of prior incidents was actually a problem, because it drew attention to the fading, boring past. Jennifer would have to find a way around it—give it a mention and go on.

And she must sell it to Dick Shenk. She had to come up with an angle that would appeal to him, that would fit his view of the world. And that was no easy matter. Shenk was difficult to please.

To sell him this segment, she would have to proceed carefully.

ADMINISTRATION

1:04 p.m. Casey got into the elevator in administration, Richman following her. "I don't understand," he said. "Why is everybody so angry with that attorney, Bradley King?"

"Because he's lying," Casey said. "He knows the aircraft didn't come within five hundred feet of the Pacific Ocean. Everybody'd be dead if it did. The incident happened at thirty-seven thousand feet. At most the aircraft dropped three or four thousand feet. That's bad enough."

"Hasn't Norton settled out of court with him in the past?"

"Three times," she said.

Richman shrugged. "If you have a strong case, take him to trial."

"Yes," Casey said. "But trials are very expensive, and the publicity doesn't do us any good. It's cheaper to settle and just add the cost of King's greenmail to the price of our aircraft. In the end, every airline passenger pays a few dollars extra for their ticket in a hidden tax. The litigation tax."

The doors opened, and they came out on the fourth floor. She hurried down the corridor toward her department.

"Where are we going now?" Richman said.

"To get something important I forgot about. And you did, too."

CASEY came into the QA office with Richman. Norma was back from lunch. "Norma," she said, "have you seen a videotape around here? One of those little eight-millimeter things?"

"Yeah," Norma said. "You left it on your desk the other night. I put it away." She rummaged in her drawer, brought it out. She turned to Richman. "And you got two calls from Marder. He wants you to call him right away."

Richman hurried down the hall to his office. When he was gone, Norma said, "You know, he talks to Marder a lot."

"What're you saying?" Casey said. "He's reporting to Marder?"

"About three times a day."

Casey frowned. "Why?"

"Good question, honey. I think you're being set up."

"For what?"

"I have no idea," Norma said.

"Something about the China sale?"

Norma shrugged. "I don't know. But Marder is the best corporate infighter in the company, and he's good at covering his tracks. I'd be real careful around this kid." She leaned across her desk, lowered her voice. "When I got back from lunch," she said, "nobody was around. The kid keeps his briefcase in his office. So I had a look. Richman's copying everything in sight—memos on your desk, your phone logs. And I found his passport. He's been to Korea five times in the last two months."

"Korea?" Casey said.

"That's right, honey. Seoul. Went almost every week. Short trips. One, two days only. And there's more. I talked to the fizer in Seoul. He's an old beau of mine. Remember when Marder had that dental emergency last month and took three days off? He and Richman were together in Seoul. Fizer heard about it later and was annoyed to be kept out of the loop. Wasn't invited to any of the meetings they attended. Took it as a personal insult."

"What meetings?" Casey said.

"Nobody knows," Norma said. "But be careful around that kid."

CASEY was in her office going through telexes when Richman poked his head in. "What's next?" he asked cheerfully.

"Something's come up," Casey said. "I need you to go to the flight standards district office. See Dan Greene over there and get copies of the flight plan and the crew list for TPA 545."

"Don't we already have that?"

"No. We have the preliminaries. By now Dan will have the finals. I want them for the meeting tomorrow. The office is in El Segundo."

"El Segundo?" He hesitated. "That'll take me the rest of the day."

"I know, but it's important. Get going," she said.

NEWSLINE

4:45 p.m. In his office Dick Shenk listened to Jennifer, his fingers pressed together to make a steeple. From time to time he nodded slightly as she spoke.

She ran through the proposed segment, hitting all the beats: the Miami incident, the JAA certification story, the TransPacific flight, the jeopardized China sale. The former FAA expert who says the plane has a long history of uncorrected design problems. The aviation reporter who says the company is mismanaged. FAA is in bed with the company and won't force the issue. Now, at last, the truth comes out. The Europeans balk at certification, the Chinese have cold feet, the plane continues to kill passengers, just as critics said it would. And there's tape, riveting tape, showing the agonies passengers went through as several died. At the close it's obvious to all: the N-22 is a death trap.

She finished. There was a long moment of silence. Then Shenk said, "Not bad. What's the company's response?"

"Stonewall. The plane's safe; the critics are lying."

"Just what you'd expect," Shenk said, shaking his head. "But what can they offer as proof?"

"Not much," Jennifer said. "The Miami and TransPacific incidents are still under investigation."

"Ah." He nodded slowly. "I like it. I like it very much. It's compelling journalism—and it beats the hell out of *60 Minutes.* They did unsafe airplane parts last month. But we're talking about a whole unsafe aircraft! A death trap. *Perfect!*"

"I think so, too," she said, smiling broadly. He'd bought it!

"You got twelve minutes," he said. He spun in his chair, looked at the colored strips on the wall representing the segments in production where the talent was going to be. "And you got, uh, Marty. He's doing Bill Gates in Seattle on Thursday; we'll shuttle him to L.A. Friday. You'll have him six, seven hours."

"Okay."

He spun back. "You sure you can put it together in time?"

She started collecting her notes. "Trust me, Dick."

"Remember, Jennifer. Don't come back with a frigging *parts* story!"

VIDEO IMAGING SYSTEMS

4:30 p.m. The back room of Video Imaging Systems in Glendale was packed with row after row of humming computers. Scott Harmon led Casey into one of the editing bays. It was a medium-sized room with an editing console wrapped around three walls. Scott waved her to a seat alongside him at the console.

"What's the material?" he asked.

"Home video."

"Okay," he said. "We should have it up in a second."

A screen flickered, and she saw mountain peaks shrouded in fog. The camera panned to a young American man in his early thirties, walking up a road, carrying a small baby on his shoulders. In the background was a village, beige roofs, bamboo.

"Where's this?" Harmon said.

Casey shrugged. "Looks like China. Can you fast-forward?"

The images flicked quickly past. Casey glimpsed a small house, the front door open; a kitchen, black pots and pans; an open suitcase on a bed; a train station, a woman climbing onto the train; busy traffic in what looked like Hong Kong; an airport lounge at night, the young man holding the baby on his knees, the baby crying. Then a gate, tickets being taken by a flight attendant—

"Stop," she said.

He punched buttons, ran at normal speed. She watched as the woman, holding the baby, walked down the ramp to the aircraft. Then there was a cut, and the image showed the baby in the woman's lap. The camera panned to the woman giving a theatrical yawn. They were on the aircraft; the cabin was lit by night-lights; windows in the background were black. The steady whine of the jet engines.

Casey recognized the woman she had interviewed in the hospital. What was her name? She had it in her notes.

The next image showed daylight. The baby was sitting up, smiling. A hand came into the frame, wiggling to get the baby's attention. The man's voice said, "Sarah . . . Sarah . . . Smile for Daddy. Smile."

The baby smiled and made a gurgling sound.

The man's voice said, "How does it feel to be going to America, Sarah? Ready to see where your parents are from?"

The lens panned up to the woman holding the baby. The man said, "And what about you, Mom? Are you glad to be going home?"

"Oh, Tim," she said, turning her head away, "please."

"Come on, Em. What are you thinking?"

The woman said, "Well, what I really want—what I have dreamed about for months—is a cheeseburger. With onions and tomatoes and lettuce and pickles and mayonnaise."

Now the camera panned back down to the kid, who was tugging her foot into her mouth, slobbering over her toes.

"Taste good?" The man laughed. "Is that breakfast for you, Sarah?"

Abruptly the wife jerked her head around. "What was that?"

Casey said, "Stop the tape."

Harmon hit a key. The image froze on the wife's expression.

"Run it back five seconds," Casey said. "Okay. Now turn the sound up."

The baby sucked its toes, the slobbering so loud it almost sounded like a waterfall. The hum inside the cabin became a steady roar. "Taste good?" the man said, laughing very loudly, his voice distorted.

Casey tried to listen between the man's sentences, to hear the cabin sounds, the murmur of other voices, the clink of knives and forks from the galley. . . . And now something else. Another sound?

The wife's head jerked around. "What was that?"

Casey couldn't be sure. She strained to hear. Was there a low-pitched rumble or not? She said, "Can you put this through an audio filter?"

The husband said, "Take it easy, Em. We're almost home."

"Oh, my God," Harmon said, staring at the tape.

On the monitor everything seemed to be crazy angles. The baby slid forward on the mother's lap. She clutched it to her chest. The camera was shaking and twisting. Passengers in the background were yelling, grabbing the armrests as the plane went into a steep descent.

Then the camera twisted again, and everybody seemed to sink into the seats, the mother slumping down under the G-force, shoulders falling, baby crying. Then the man shouted, "What the hell?" and the camera flew up in the air.

The image began to spiral rapidly. When it became steady, Casey saw an armrest from below, fingers gripping it. The camera had fallen in the aisle and was shooting straight up. The screams continued.

The video image began to slide, gaining speed, moving past seat after seat. But it was going aft, she realized. The plane must be climbing again. Then the camera lifted into the air.

Weightless, she thought. The plane must have reached the end of the climb, and now it was nosing over again, before—

The image crashed down, twisting and tumbling rapidly. There was a thunk, and she glimpsed a blurred gaping mouth, teeth. Then it was moving again, back in the aisle, facing the rear of the plane. People were screaming, clutching at anything. The camera immediately began to slide again, this time forward. The plane was in a dive.

The camera slid faster and faster, banging into a midship bulkhead, spinning so it was now facing forward. It raced toward a body lying in the aisle. Then the camera flew into the air, tumbling crazily, and came down again.

There was a close view of something shiny, like a belt buckle, and then the camera was sliding forward once more, into the forward compartment, still going, twisting, racing forward to the cockpit.

The cockpit door was open. Casey had a brief glimpse of sky through the flight-deck windows, blue shoulders, and a cap, and then with a crash the camera came to rest, giving a steady view of a uniform gray field. After a moment Casey realized the camera had lodged beneath the cockpit door, right where she had found it, and it was taping the carpet. There was nothing more to see, but she could hear the alarms in the cockpit, the electronic warnings, and the voice reminders. "Stall . . . Stall." More electronic warnings, excited voices shouting in Chinese.

"Stop the tape," Casey said.

She ran through the tape once more, and then did it in slow motion. But even then much of the movement was an indistinguishable blur. She kept saying, "I can't see. I can't see what's happening."

Harmon, who had by now become accustomed to the sequence, said, "I can do an enhanced frame analysis for you. I can use the computers to interpolate frames where the movement is too fast."

"Okay," she said. "Do it."

"We can do more," he said. "We can send it out, and—"

She shook her head. "Under no circumstances does this tape leave this building," she said.

"Okay."

"I need you to run me two copies of this videotape," she said. "And make sure you run it all the way to the end."

5:25 p.m. Casey called Norma. "Who can translate Chinese for me?"

"Let me see," Norma said. "How about Ellen Fong in accounting? She used to work for the FAA as a translator."

"Isn't her husband in structure and mechanical with Doherty?"

"Yeah, but Ellen's discreet."

"You sure?"

"I know," Norma said in a certain tone.

WHEN Casey found her in the accounting department, Ellen Fong was getting ready to go home.

"Ellen," she said, "I need a favor. I need something translated."

"Sure." Ellen was a perpetually cheerful woman of forty, a mother of three. "But you can get a much better translator—"

"I'd rather you do it," Casey said. "This is confidential." She handed Ellen the tape. "I need the voices in the last nine minutes. And I'd prefer you not mention this to anybody."

Ellen looked at the tape in her hand. "When?"

"Tomorrow? Friday at the latest?"

"Done," Ellen Fong said.

5:55 p.m. Casey took the second copy of the tape to the Norton audio interpretation lab, in the back of building 24. NAIL was run by a former CIA guy from Omaha, a paranoid electronics genius named Jay Ziegler.

Norton had constructed NAIL to help the government agencies interpret cockpit voice-recorder tapes. Although the agencies had experienced staff to transcribe the tapes, they were less skilled at interpreting sounds inside the cockpit—the alarms and audio reminders that often went off. These sounds represented proprietary Norton systems, so Norton had built its own facility to analyze them.

The heavy soundproof door, as always, was locked. Casey pounded on it. A voice on the speaker said, "The password."

"It's Casey Singleton, Jay."

"Oh. All right, Singleton." There was a click, and the thick door was pushed open a crack. She saw Jay Ziegler, hair down to his shoulders, wearing dark sunglasses.

She squeezed past him into a darkened room. Ziegler immediately slammed the door shut, threw three bolts in succession.

"Jay, something's come up," she said.

She handed him the spool of magnetic tape. "This is one-inch mag, Singleton," he said. "We don't often see this at this station."

"Can you read it?"

Ziegler nodded. "Can read anything you throw at us." He put the tape on a horizontal drum and threaded it. On all the monitors in the room she saw oscilloscope squiggles, green lines jumping against black, as the tape began to play. "Uh . . . okay," Ziegler said. "We got high-eight audio track, Dolby D encoded. Got to be a home video camera. So what am I doing here?"

Casey said, "The last nine minutes were shot on flight 545. This camera recorded the whole incident. I want to know what you can tell me about unusual sounds in the moments prior—"

"Don't tell me," he said, holding up his hand. "I don't want to know. I want to take a clean look. Better that way."

"When can you have something?"

"Twenty hours. Tomorrow afternoon."

"Okay. And I'd appreciate if you'd keep this tape to yourself."

Ziegler looked at her blankly. "What tape?" he said.

QA

6:10 p.m. Casey went back to her desk. There were more telexes waiting for her, including one from the FSR in Vancouver:

> F/O ZAN PING AT VANC GEN HOSPITAL FOLLOWING COMPLICATIONS FROM SURGERY. REPORTED UNCONSCIOUS BUT STABLE. CARRIER REP MIKE LEE WAS AT THE HOSPITAL TODAY. I WILL TRY TO SEE F/O TOMORROW TO VERIFY HIS CONDITION.

"Norma," Casey called, "remind me to call Vancouver tomorrow morning."

"I'll make a note," she said. "By the way, you got this."

Norma handed Casey a fax. The single sheet appeared to be a page from an in-flight magazine. The top read: EMPLOYEE OF THE MONTH, followed by an inky, unreadable photograph. Underneath was a caption: "Captain John Zhen Chang, senior pilot for TransPacific Airlines, is our employee of the month. Captain Chang's father was a pilot, and John himself has flown for twenty years, seven with TransPacific. When not in the cockpit, Captain Chang enjoys biking and golf. Here he relaxes on the Lantan Island beach with his wife, Soon, and his children, Erica and Tom."

Casey frowned. "What's this, and where'd it come from?" There was a phone number at the top of the page but no name.

"A copy shop near the airport. They had no idea who sent it."

Casey stared at the photo. "It's from an in-flight magazine?"

"TransPacific's. But not from this month."

"I'd like to get a better look at this picture," Casey said.

"I figured," Norma said. "I'm working on getting back copies."

Casey went back to the other papers on her desk. One was a memo to her from T. Korman in product support:

> We have finalized the design of the N-22 virtual heads-up display (VHUD) for use by ground personnel. The CD-ROM player now clips to the belt, and the goggles have been reduced in weight. The VHUD allows personnel to scroll maintenance manuals, including diagrams and parts cutaways. Preliminary articles will be distributed for comments tomorrow.

This virtual heads-up display was part of Norton's ongoing effort to help the customers improve maintenance. Under financial pressure from deregulation, the airlines were cutting personnel, including maintenance personnel. Norton, like Boeing and Douglas, saw it as in their interest to help crews work more effectively. That was why the virtual heads-up display, which projected the repair manuals onto the inside of a set of glasses, was so important.

She went on. She saw the weekly summary of parts failures, compiled to enable the FAA to track parts problems. None of the failures in the previous week was serious—an engine compressor stalled; an engine EGT indicator failed; an oil filter clog light illuminated incorrectly; a fuel heat indicator went on erroneously.

Norma came back. "TransPacific's office is closed. I'll have to find that magazine tomorrow."

"Okay."

"Hon? Go home. And get some rest, will you?"

Casey sighed. "You're right, Norma."

GLENDALE

9:15 p.m. Her daughter had left a message saying she was having a sleepover at Amy's house and that Dad said it was all right. Casey wasn't happy about it. She thought her daughter shouldn't have sleepovers on school nights, but there was nothing she could do now. She got into bed, pulled her daughter's photograph on the bedside table over to look at it, and then turned to her work. She was going through the flight tapes of TPA 545, checking the waypoint coordinates for each leg against the written radio transcripts from Honolulu and Oakland Center, when the phone rang.

"Casey Singleton."

"Hello, Casey. John Marder here."

She sat up in bed. Marder never called her at home.

Marder cleared his throat. "I just got a call from Benson in PR. He's had a request from *Newsline* to film inside the plant. A producer on that program named Malone. Very pushy and full of herself. He told her to forget it."

"Uh-huh." That was standard; news crews were never allowed inside the plant.

"This Malone said *Newsline* was doing a story on the N-22, and she wanted to interview the president. He told her Hal was overseas and unavailable."

"Uh-huh." Casey was waiting.

"Then she suggested we reconsider her request, because the *Newsline* story was going to focus on flight safety concerns—two problems in two days, an engine problem and slats deployment, several passengers killed."

Casey sighed.

"She said she wanted to be fair, that it always looked bad if the company didn't respond to allegations. So if the president wasn't available to talk to *Newsline,* maybe some other highly placed spokesman would. They're running the story this weekend. So I'm seeing this twit in my office tomorrow at noon."

"On-camera?" Casey said.

"No, no. Background only, no cameras. But we'll cover the IRT investigation, so I think you'd better be there."

"Of course."

"It's that damn CNN tape. That's what started it all. But we're in it now, Casey. We have to handle this."

"I'll be there," she said.

THURSDAY

AIRPORT MARINA

6:30 a.m. Jennifer Malone awoke to the soft, insistent buzz of the bedside alarm. She turned it off and looked over at the California sunlight streaming through the windows.

She got up and went to her closet to choose the clothes she would wear. She was doing pretty straight types, so she picked jeans, a white T-shirt, and a navy jacket. She carried them into the bathroom, ran a shower. While she showered, she reviewed the coming day.

Barker first at nine. Next the reporter, Rogers. She'd start him at Burbank. At noon she'd talk to the Norton guy, try to scare him enough to give her access to the president.

And then . . . let's see. The ambulance chaser later in the day, briefly. Someone from the FAA on Friday, for balance. Someone from Norton on Friday, as well. Marty would do a stand-up outside Norton. The script wasn't prepared, but all she needed was the intro and the rest was voice-over. B-roll of passengers boarding, going to their doom. Takeoffs and landings, then some good crash shots.

And she was done. This segment was going to work, she thought as she stepped out of the shower.

QA

6:40 a.m. As Casey came into the QA offices, Norma glanced up at her, then pointed down the hall. Casey frowned.

Norma said, "He was here when I came in today. Been on the phone for an hour. Mr. Sleepyhead's suddenly not so sleepy."

Casey went down the hall. As she came to Richman's office, she heard him say, "Absolutely not. We are very confident of how this will turn out. No. No. I'm sure. Hasn't a clue. No idea."

Casey stuck her head in.

Richman was leaning back in his chair, his feet up on the desk, while he spoke on the phone. He seemed startled when he saw her. He put his hand over the phone. "I'll just be a minute here."

"Fine." She went back to her office, shuffled papers. She didn't want him around. Time for another errand, she thought.

"Good morning," he said as he came in. He was cheerful, big smile. "I got those FAA documents you wanted. They're on your desk."

"Thank you," she said. "Today I need you to go to TransPacific's main office. They're in downtown L.A. Norma will get you the address. I need you to pick up back issues of their in-flight magazine. Back at least a year."

"Gee," Richman said, "couldn't we have a messenger do that?"

"This is urgent," Casey said.

"But I'll miss the IRT."

"You're not needed at the IRT. And I want these magazines."

He gave a crooked smile. "You're not trying to get rid of me, are you, Casey?"

WAR ROOM

7:30 a.m. John Marder was late. He strode into the room with an irritable, distracted look and took a seat. "All right," he said. "Let's have it. Where are we on flight 545? Flight recorder?"

"Nothing yet," Casey said.

"We need that data. Make it happen, Casey. Structure?"

"Well, it's very difficult," Doherty said dolefully. "I worry about that bad locking pin. We ought to be more cautious—"

"Doug," Marder said, "I already told you. We'll check it at flight test. Now what about hydraulics?"

"Hydraulics are fine."

"Electrical?"

Ron said, "We've scheduled the cycle electrical test to run overnight. If there's a problem, we'll know in the morning."

"Any suspicions now?"

"Just those proximity sensors in the right wing. They appear normal. To really check them, we'd have to remove the sensors from the housings, take them out of the wing. That means—"

"Delaying everything," Marder said. "Forget it. Power plant?"

"Zip," Kenny Burne said. "Engines are fine. We got a counterfeit reverser cowl. But it wouldn't cause the accident."

"Okay. Power plant is eliminated. Avionics?"

Trung said, "Avionics check out within normal limits."

"What about the autopilot? The pilot fighting to override?"

"Autopilot is fine."

"I see." Marder looked around the room. "So we have nothing, is that right? Seventy-two hours into this investigation and we have no idea what happened to flight 545? Is that what you're telling me?"

There was silence around the table.

Marder swore, disgusted. He pounded the table. "Don't you people understand? I want this thing *solved!*"

SEPULVEDA BOULEVARD

10:10 a.m. Fred Barker was solving all her problems.

To start, Jennifer needed a walk-to-work shot for Marty's voice-over intro—"We talked to Frederick Barker, a former FAA official, now a controversial crusader for aircraft safety." Barker suggested a location on Sepulveda with a sweeping view of the south runways of Los Angeles International Airport. It was perfect. No other film crew had used it before.

Next she needed an at-work shot, again for voice-over—"Since leaving the FAA, Barker has worked tirelessly to bring defective aircraft designs to the public's attention." In his office Barker placed himself in front of a bookshelf of thick FAA documents, at a desk heaped high with technical-looking pamphlets.

Barker was good on-camera, too. He was dressed for the part: informal shirtsleeves and tie reminiscent of an engineer, an authoritative look. Yet he appeared relaxed; he didn't use jargon; his answers were short. Everything he did was smooth, with no awkwardness.

Of course Barker was experienced not only on television but in the courtroom. The only problem was that he didn't give her strong emotion—no shock, no outrage. On the contrary, his tone, his manner, his body language, suggested profound regret. It was unfortunate that this situation arose. It was unfortunate that steps hadn't been taken to correct the problem. It was unfortunate that authorities hadn't listened to him for all these years.

"There have been eight previous problems with slats on the airplane," he said. He held up a large model of the N-22 aircraft. "These are the slats," he said, pulling out a panel from the front of the wing. "The slats are only deployed for takeoff and landing. During flight they are tucked back in the wing. But on the Norton N-22, the slats have been known to extend by themselves during flight. It's a design error. The consequence is that the airplane noses upward, like this, threatening to stall." He paused, tilted the model up slightly. "If the pilot tries to restore the plane to level flight, the plane overcompensates and goes into a dive. Again the pilot corrects to come out of the dive. The plane climbs. Then dives. Then climbs again. That is what happened to flight 545. That is why people died."

This wasn't an interview; it was a skilled performance. But just because Barker was smooth and camera savvy, Jennifer wasn't going to let him get away without a little probing.

"Mr. Barker," she said, "you are a former FAA employee. . . ."

"I used to work for the FAA," Barker said, "but I left the agency because I disagreed with their hands-off attitude toward manufacturers. When they refused to respond, I left."

"You work for Bradley King, the attorney?"

"Any expert witness is reimbursed for time and expenses. I am funded by the nonprofit Institute for Aviation Research in Washington. My job is to promote safety in civil aviation. I do whatever I can to make the skies safe for travelers."

"Mr. Barker, come on. Aren't you an expert for hire?"

"I certainly have strong opinions about air safety. It's only natural that I'm hired by employers who share my concerns."

"Is the FAA doing a good job?"

"I'm afraid the FAA is doing a very poor job. American lives are needlessly put at risk. Frankly, it's time for a thorough overhaul. Otherwise I am afraid passengers will continue to die, as they did on that Norton aircraft. And in my opinion," he said, "what happened on that airplane is a disgrace."

The interview ended. While Jennifer's crew was packing up, Barker came over to her. "Who else are you seeing?"

"Jack Rogers is next, then someone from Norton." She consulted her notes. "A John Marder."

"Ah."

"What does that mean?"

"Well, Marder is a fast-talker. He'll give you a lot of double-talk about airworthiness directives. But the fact is that he was the program manager on the N-22. He supervised its development. He knows there's a problem. He's part of it."

OUTSIDE NORTON

11:10 a.m. After the practiced smoothness of Barker, the reporter, Jack Rogers, was a bit of a shock. In his lime-green sport coat and check-patterned tie, he looked like a spruced-up golf pro.

Jennifer said nothing at first. She just thanked Rogers for coming and positioned him in front of the chain-link fence, with Norton Aircraft in the background. She went over her questions with him. He gave tentative answers, excited, eager to please.

"Gee, it's hot," she said. She turned to the cameraman. "How we coming, George?"

"Almost there."

She turned back to Rogers. The sound guy unbuttoned Rogers's shirt, threaded the microphone up to his collar. As preparations continued, Rogers began to sweat. Jennifer called for the makeup girl to wipe him down. He seemed relieved. Then, pleading the heat, she convinced Rogers to remove his sport coat, sling it over his shoulder, and remove his tie. She said it would give him a working-journalist look. He gratefully agreed.

Jack Rogers answered her questions. He rambled, burying her in detail and background she didn't care about. He didn't seem to understand she was making an assembled piece, that the average shot would be less than three seconds.

Finally she began to worry that she couldn't use any of the interview. So she went to her usual procedure.

"That's all perfect," she said. "Now we need something punchy to close the piece. So I'll ask you a series of questions, and you answer them with one punchy sentence."

"Okay," Rogers said.

"Mr. Rogers, could the N-22 cost Norton the China sale?"

"Given the frequency of incidents involving—"

"I'm sorry, Jack," she said. "I just need a simple sentence, like, 'The N-22 might very well cost Norton the China sale.' "

"Oh. Okay." He swallowed. "The N-22 might very well cost Norton the China sale, in my opinion."

She sighed. It was dry. No emotional force. He might as well be talking about his phone bill. But she was running out of time.

"Excellent," Jennifer said. "Very good. Let's go on. Tell me, is Norton a troubled company?"

"Absolutely," he said, nodding and swallowing.

She sighed. "Jack."

"Oh. Sorry." He took a breath. Then, standing there, outside Norton Aircraft, with his jacket slung over his shoulder and his shirtsleeves rolled up, reporter Jack Rogers said, "I think there's no doubt that Norton Aircraft is a company in serious trouble."

Then he paused. He looked at her.

Jennifer smiled. "Thank you very much. You were great."

NORTON ADMINISTRATION

11:55 a.m. Casey came into John Marder's office a few minutes before noon and found him smoothing his tie, shooting his cuffs. "I thought we would sit here," he said, pointing to a coffee table with chairs in the corner of his office. "You all set for this?"

"I think so," Casey said.

The intercom buzzed. Eileen said, "Ms. Malone is here, Mr. Marder."

"Send her in," Marder said.

Casey was shocked by the woman who walked in. Jennifer Malone was a *kid,* hardly older than Richman. She couldn't be more than twenty-eight or twenty-nine, Casey thought. Malone was blond and quite pretty—in an uptight, New York sort of way. She had short bobbed hair, and she was dressed very casually: jeans and a white T-shirt, and a blue blazer with a weird collar. The trendy look.

Casey felt uncomfortable just looking at her. But now Marder had turned and was saying, "Ms. Malone, I'd like to introduce Casey Singleton, our quality-assurance specialist on the incident review team."

The blond kid smirked.

Casey shook her hand.

YOU got to be kidding, Jennifer Malone thought. This is a captain of industry? This jumpy guy with slicked-back hair and a bad suit? And who was this woman out of a Talbot's catalog? Singleton was taller than Jennifer, which Jennifer resented. She looked like an athlete, and she seemed to be in pretty good shape.

Jennifer felt disappointed. She had been preparing for this meeting all day, honing her arguments. But she had imagined a much more commanding adversary. Instead, she was back in high school, with the assistant principal and the timid librarian.

And this office! Small, with gray walls and cheap, utilitarian furniture. It had no character. It was just as well she wasn't filming here.

Marder led her to a seating arrangement to one side. He gestured grandly, as if he were taking her to a banquet. Since he gave her a choice of where to sit, she took a chair with her back to the window, so the sun would be in their eyes.

CASEY watched as Jennifer Malone set out her notes. "I'll be frank," Malone said. "We've gotten some damning material on the N-22 from critics. And on the way this company operates. But there are two sides to every story. We want to make sure we include your response to the criticism."

Marder said nothing, just nodded.

"To begin, we know what happened on the TransPacific flight. The slats came out—deployed?—in midair, and the airplane became unstable, went up and down, killing passengers. We also know the N-22 has a long history of slats problems, which neither the FAA nor the company has been willing to deal with. This despite nine separate incidents in recent years. We know that the FAA is so lax in its regulatory policies that it doesn't even require certification documents to be submitted. The FAA has allowed Norton to keep the certification documents here."

Jeez, Casey thought. She doesn't understand *anything.*

"Let me dispose of your last point first," Marder said. "The FAA doesn't have physical possession of certification documents from any manufacturer. Not Boeing, not Douglas, not Airbus, not us. The FAA can't store the documents, because they contain proprietary information. Some of our competitors would like nothing better than to obtain them. Airbus in particular has been lobbying for a change in FAA policy—for the reasons I've just explained. So I presume you got this idea about the FAA from someone at Airbus."

Casey saw Malone hesitate, glance down at her papers. It was true, Casey thought. Marder had nailed her source. Airbus had fed her that tidbit, probably through its publicity arm, the Institute for Aviation Research. Did Malone know it was an Airbus front?

"Now, Ms. Malone," Marder said, "you mentioned flight 545. First of all, we don't agree the accident was the result of slats deployment."

Uh-oh, Casey thought. Marder was going out on a limb. What he was saying wasn't true, and it might very well—

Marder said, "Although it's premature for me to discuss the findings of our inquiry, I believe you have been misinformed. I presume you've gotten this slats information from Fred Barker."

"We are talking to Mr. Barker, among others. . . ."

"Well, let's just say he adopts an advocacy position that is factually incorrect." He pointed to the papers Malone had spread out on the table. "I couldn't help noticing your list of slats incidents. Did you get that from Barker?"

Malone hesitated a fraction. "Yes."

"May I see it?"

"Sure." She handed the paper to Marder. He glanced at it.

Malone said, "Is it factually incorrect, Mr. Marder?"

"No, but it's incomplete and misleading. Do you know about airworthiness directives, Ms. Malone?"

"Airworthiness directives?"

Marder got up, went to his desk. "Every time there is an in-flight incident involving our aircraft, we review the incident thoroughly to find out what happened and why. If there's an aircraft problem, we issue a service bulletin. If the FAA feels compliance with our bulletin should be mandatory, it then issues an airworthiness directive. After the N-22 went into service, we discovered a slats problem. The FAA issued an airworthiness directive to change cockpit controls. The airlines had a year to comply. As you can see, the subsequent incidents all occurred in aircraft which had not yet made the change."

"Well, not quite—"

"Please let me finish. In December of 1992 we discovered a second issue. The cables running to the slats sometimes became slack. So we added a tension measurement device so ground crews could check more easily whether cable rigging was within spec. That solved it. By December everything was resolved."

"Clearly not, Mr. Marder," Malone said, pointing to the list. "You have more incidents in 1993 and in 1994."

"Only on foreign carriers. Foreign operators aren't under FAA jurisdiction, and they don't always make the changes."

Malone scanned the list. "So you knowingly allow carriers to fly unsafe airplanes? You just sit back and let it happen?"

Marder sucked in his breath. "Ms. Malone, we build airplanes, we don't operate them. If Air Indonesia or Pakistani Air won't follow the airworthiness directives, we can't force them to."

"All right. If all you do is build airplanes, let's talk about how well you do that," Malone said. "Looking at this list here, you had how many design changes on the slats? Eight?"

Casey thought, She doesn't understand. She's not listening.

"No. Two retrofits," Marder said.

"But there are eight incidents here. You'd agree to that."

"Yes," Marder said irritably, "but we're not talking about incidents, we're talking about ADs, and there are only two ADs." He was getting angry, his face flushed.

"I see," Malone said. "So. Norton had two design problems on the slats for this aircraft. Didn't you test this aircraft, Mr. Marder, before you sold it to unsuspecting customers?"

"Of course we tested it," Marder said through clenched teeth. "But you have to realize—"

"What I realize," Malone said, "is that people have died because of your design errors. That plane is a death trap."

"Oh for heaven's sake!" Marder threw up his hands and jumped out of his seat. "I can't believe this!"

IT WAS almost too easy, Jennifer thought. In fact, it *was* too easy. She was suspicious of Marder's histrionic outburst. During the interview she'd realized he wasn't the assistant principal. He was much smarter than that. And in control. And she suspected he was in control now, deliberately losing his temper. Why?

She didn't really care. Her goal from the beginning had been to blow these people out. To make them worried enough to pass her on to the president. Then her segment would attain a new credibility.

Things were going well.

CASEY HAD BEEN APPALLED BY Marder's explosion. Marder was famously bad tempered, but it was a major tactical error to blow up in front of a reporter. And now, still red-faced and huffing behind his desk, Marder said, "You explain it, Casey."

"Ms. Malone," Casey said, "everyone here is deeply committed to flight safety. And the N-22 has an excellent safety record. If something does go wrong with one of our planes—"

"Something *did* go wrong," Malone said evenly.

"Yes," Casey said. "I'm on the team investigating that incident. We are working around the clock to understand what happened."

"You mean why the slats extended? But you must know. It's happened so many times before."

"Listen," Marder said to Malone, "it wasn't the slats. We'll issue a preliminary report in the next twenty-four hours that will conclusively demonstrate that."

Casey thought, *What?* What was he saying?

"Really," Malone said softly.

"That's right," Marder said. "Casey Singleton's the press liaison on the IRT. We'll be getting back to you, Ms. Malone."

Malone seemed to realize that Marder was terminating the interview. She said, "But there's much more we need to go over, Mr. Marder. There is also the Miami rotor burst. And union opposition to the China sale. Given the seriousness of these charges, I think that you may want to consider our offer to give your president, Mr. Edgarton, an opportunity to respond."

"That's not going to happen," Marder said.

"It's for your own benefit," Malone said. "If we have to say that the president refused to talk to us, that sounds—"

"Look," Marder said, "let's cut the nonsense. Without TransPacific you have no story. And we are going to issue a preliminary report on TransPacific tomorrow. You'll be informed when. That's all we have for the moment, Ms. Malone. Thank you."

"I CAN'T believe that woman," Marder said after Malone had gone. "She isn't interested in the facts or the FAA. She isn't interested in how we build airplanes. She's just doing a hatchet job."

"John," Casey said, "about the preliminary finding—"

"Forget it," Marder snapped. "I'll deal with it. You go back to work. I'll talk to the tenth floor, arrange a few things."

"But John," Casey said, "you told her it wasn't the slats."

"It's my problem," Marder said. "You go back to work."

WHEN Casey was gone, Marder called Edgarton.

"My flight's in an hour," Edgarton said. "I'm going to Hong Kong to show my concern for the families of the deceased."

"Good idea, Hal," Marder said.

"Where are we on this press thing?"

"Well, it's as I suspected," Marder said. "*Newsline* is putting together a story that's extremely critical of the N-22."

"Can you stop it?"

"Absolutely. No question. We'll issue a preliminary report that it wasn't slats. Our preliminary will say the accident was caused by a counterfeit cowl on the thrust reversers."

"Is there a bad cowl on the plane?"

"Yes. But it didn't cause the accident."

"That's fine," Edgarton said. "A bad part is fine. Just so it's not a Norton problem."

"Right," Marder said.

"And Singleton's going to say that? You've briefed her?"

"Yes. And I'll go over it with her again later."

"Okay," Edgarton said. "She should be fully prepared. Just remember. You mess this up, you're dead."

1:04 p.m. Outside the administration building, Jennifer Malone got into her car more distressed than she cared to admit. She now felt it was unlikely the company would produce the president. And she was worried they might make Singleton their spokesperson.

The audience wanted to see beefy, arrogant captains of industry get their just deserts. An intelligent, earnest, attractive woman wouldn't play as well. Were they smart enough to know that?

And of course, Marty would attack her. That wouldn't look so good either. Just imagining them together gave Jennifer the shivers.

But beyond that, she was starting to worry that the entire segment was weak. Barker had been so convincing when she interviewed him; she had felt elated afterward. But if these ADs were for real, then the company was on solid ground. And she worried about Barker's record. If the FAA had the goods on him, then his credibility was shot.

The reporter, Jack Whatshisname, was disappointing. He didn't play well on-camera, and his material was thin. She needed vivid, persuasive visuals to demonstrate that the airplane was a death trap.

She didn't have them. So far all she had was the CNN tape, which was old news, and the Miami rotor burst. Smoke coming out from a wing. Big deal. Worst of all, if the company really was going to issue a preliminary finding that contradicted Barker—

Her cell phone rang.

"Speak to me," Dick Shenk said. "So? Where are we? Marty finishes with Bill Gates in two hours. Do I send him or not?"

Part of her wanted to say, "Forget it. The story's flaky. It's not coming together. I was dumb to think I could nail it in two days."

But she couldn't say no. She couldn't admit she had been wrong. He'd kill her if she backed off the story now.

"Yes, Dick. I want him."

"You'll have the piece for Saturday?"

"Yes, Dick."

"And it's not a parts story? Because I don't want sloppy seconds on *60 Minutes,* Jennifer. It better not be a parts story."

"It's not, Dick."

"I don't hear confidence," he said.

"I'm confident, Dick. I'm just tired."

"Okay. Marty leaves Seattle at four. He'll be at the hotel about eight. Have the shoot schedule ready when he arrives and fax me a copy at home. You've got him all tomorrow."

"Okay, Dick."

"Nail it, babe," he said, and hung up.

QA

2:10 p.m. Casey went into her office and shut the door. She picked up a photograph of her daughter and stared at it. In the picture Allison had just emerged from a neighbor's swimming pool. She stood with another girl her age, both of them in swimming suits, dripping water. Sleek young bodies, smiling gap-toothed faces, carefree and innocent.

Casey pushed the picture aside, turned to a large box on her desk. Opening it, she removed a black portable CD player. There were wires that ran to a strange pair of oversize goggles. And there was a funny coating on the inside of the lenses, sort of shimmery in the light. This, she knew, was the maintenance virtual heads-up display, the VHUD.

She pushed the goggles aside, looked at the papers on her desk. The CVR transcript of cockpit communications had finally come in. Also a copy of *TransPacific Flightlines.* A Post-it was on one page.

She flipped it open to the picture of John Chang, employee of the month. The picture was not what she had imagined from the fax. John Chang was a very fit man in his forties. His wife stood beside him, heavier, smiling. And the children, crouched at the parents' feet, were fully grown: a girl in her late teens and a boy in his early twenties. The son resembled his father, except he was a little more contemporary. He had extremely closely cropped hair, a tiny gold stud in his ear.

She looked at the caption, which ended: "Here he relaxes on the Lantan Island beach with his wife, Soon, and his children, Erica and Tom."

The scene was mundane and uninteresting. Why would anyone fax this to her? She looked at the date. January, three months ago.

Someone had had a copy of that magazine and had faxed it to Casey. Who? An employee of the airline? A passenger? Who?

And *why?* What was it supposed to tell her?

She came out of the office. "Where's Richman?"

Norma smiled. "I sent him over to media relations to see Benson. Pick up some standard press packets." She smiled, looked at her watch. "I'd say you've got an hour to do what you want."

3:05 p.m. "So. Singleton," Ziegler said, waving her to a seat in the audio lab. "I believe we found what you were looking for."

On the monitor in front of her she saw a freeze-frame of the smiling baby sitting on the mother's lap.

"You wanted the period just prior to the incident," Ziegler said. "I'll start with full audio and then cut in the filters. Ready?"

"Yes."

At high volume the baby's slobbering was like a bubbling brook. The hum inside the cabin was a constant roar. "Taste good?" the man's voice said to the baby, very loudly.

"Cutting in," Ziegler said. "High-end bypass."

The slobbering was diminished. What Casey heard now were background sounds—silverware clinking, fabric movement.

The man said, "Is—at—akfast?" His voice cut in and out. Then the screen became almost silent again, just a few distant noises.

"Now," Ziegler said, "it starts."

A counter appeared. The timer ran forward, red numerals flickering fast, counting tenths and hundredths of a second.

The wife jerked her head around. "What—wa—at?"

"Damn," Casey said. She could hear it now. A low rumble, a definite shuddering bass sound.

"It's been thinned by the bypass," Ziegler said. "Deep, low rumble. Down in the two- to five-hertz range. Almost a vibration."

No question, Casey thought. With the filters in place she could hear it—the low-pitched rumbling. Then it ended.

"Stop!" Casey said. The red numerals froze. The numbers were big on the screen—11:59:32. Nearly twelve seconds, she thought. The time it took for the slats to fully deploy.

Ziegler stopped the tape. "There's your data, Singleton. Unequivocal, I'd say."

"The slats deployed."

"Sure sounds like it. It's a fairly unique signature."

"Why?" Why would they deploy? Was it uncommanded, or had the pilot done it? Casey wished again for the flight data recorder. These questions could be answered in a few minutes if they just had the data from the FDR. But it was going very slowly.

"The next point of interest is the cockpit alarms," Ziegler was saying. "Once the camera jams in the door, I can listen to the audio and assemble a sequence of what the aircraft was telling the pilot. But that'll take me another day."

"Stay with it," she said. "I want everything you can give me."

Then her beeper went off. She pulled it off her belt, looked at it.

***JM ADMIN ASAP

John Marder wanted to see her. In his office. Now.

NORTON ADMINISTRATION

5:00 p.m. John Marder was in his calm mood—the dangerous one.

"Just a short interview," he said to her. "Fifteen minutes at most. You won't have time to go into specifics, but as the head of the IRT, you're in the perfect position to explain the company's commitment to safety. How carefully we review accidents. Our commitment to product support. Then you can explain that our preliminary report shows the accident was caused by a counterfeit thruster cowl, installed at a foreign repair station, so it could not have been a slats event. And blow *Newsline* out of the water."

"John," she said. "I just came from audio. There's no question—the slats deployed."

"Well, audio's circumstantial at best," Marder said. "Ziegler's a nut. We have to wait for the flight data recorder to know precisely what happened. Meanwhile, the IRT has made a preliminary finding which excludes slats."

As if hearing her own voice from a distance, she said, "John, I'm uncomfortable with this."

"We're talking about the future, Casey. The China sale will save the company. Cash flow, new aircraft, bright future. That's what we're talking about here. Thousands of jobs."

"I understand, John, but—"

"Let me ask you something, Casey. Do you think there's anything wrong with the N-22? Think it's a death trap?"

"Absolutely not."

"What about the company? Think it's a good company?"

"Of course."

He stared at her, shaking his head. He didn't say anything.

Casey stood there for a moment. It would be best if they could tell the truth and explain the flight. She began to think that somehow she might find a way to tell the truth—or enough of the truth—to make this work. There were enough loose ends, enough uncertainties, that she might pull them together to form a coherent story.

"All right, John," she said. "I'll do the interview."

"Excellent," Marder said, smiling and rubbing his hands together. "I knew you'd do the right thing, Casey. *Newsline* has scheduled a slot at four p.m. tomorrow."

DIGITAL DATA CENTER

6:15 p.m. She had not promised to say what Marder wanted her to say; she had only promised to do the interview. She had less than a day to make significant progress in the investigation.

There were still many dangling leads: The possible problem with the locking pin. The possible problem with the proximity sensor. The possible interview with the first officer in Vancouver. The videotape at Video Imaging. The translation Ellen Fong was doing. The fact that the slats had deployed but had been stowed immediately afterward—what exactly did that mean?

Still so much to check.

"I KNOW YOU NEED THE DATA," Rob Wong said, spinning in his chair in the digital-display room, in front of screens filled with data. "But what do you expect me to do?"

"Rob," Casey said. "The slats deployed. I have to know why—and what else happened on the flight. I can't figure it out without the flight recorder data."

"In that case," Wong said, "you better face the facts. We have to calibrate twenty-three hours of data. And it's taking us about two minutes a frame to recalibrate."

She frowned. "What are you telling me?"

"Two minutes a frame means it'll take us sixty-five weeks."

"That's more than a year! Rob, we need this *now.*"

"It just can't be done, Casey. You're going to have to work this without the FDR. I'm sorry. That's the way it is."

SHE called accounting. "Is Ellen Fong there?"

"She didn't come in today," a woman said. "She said she was working at home. Then she had to go to a formal dinner. Some charity thing with her husband."

"Tell her I called," Casey said.

She called Video Imaging in Glendale, the company that was working on the videotape for her. She asked for Scott Harmon. "Scott's gone for the day. He'll be in at nine tomorrow morning."

She called Steve Nieto, the fizer in Vancouver, and got his secretary. "Steve's not here," she said. "He had to leave early. But I know he wanted to talk to you. He said he had bad news."

Casey sighed. That seemed to be the only kind of news she was getting. "Tell him I called."

IN HANGAR 5 she saw the electrical crews rigging TPA 545 for the cycle electrical test, the CET. The entire aircraft had been raised onto heavy blue metal fixtures. The crews had slung black safety webbing beneath the underside of the aircraft, some twenty feet above the ground. All along the fuselage, doors and accessory panels were open, and electricians standing on the webbing were running cables from the junction boxes back to the main CET test console, a six-foot-square box that stood beneath the tail, to one side of the aircraft.

The CET apparatus sent electrical impulses to all parts of the aircraft's electrical system. In rapid succession every component was tested—everything from cabin lights to landing gear. The full test cycle ran two hours. It would be repeated many times throughout the night.

As she passed the console, she saw Teddy Rawley. He gave her a wave but didn't approach her. He was busy; undoubtedly he'd heard that flight test was scheduled two days from now, and he would want to be sure the electrical test was performed correctly.

Casey headed back to her office.

OUTSIDE, it was growing dark, the sky a deep blue. As she walked back toward administration, she saw Amos Peters shuffling toward his car, carrying a stack of papers under his arm.

"Hey, Casey," he said when he saw her. He dropped his papers onto the roof of his car, bent to unlock the door. "I hear they're putting the screws to you. You going to do the interview? You going to say what they want you to say?"

She shrugged. She was not surprised he knew. The whole plant probably knew by now. Everyone knew everything.

"Don't get high and mighty," Amos said. "These are television people. They're beneath pond scum on the evolutionary scale. Just lie. Hell with it."

"We'll see."

He sighed. "You're old enough to know how it works," he said. "You going home now?"

"Not for a while."

"I wouldn't be hanging around the plant at night, Casey. People are upset. Next few days, it'd be better to go home early. You know what I mean?"

"I'll bear it in mind."

"Do that, Casey. I mean it."

QA

7:20 p.m. Norma was gone. The QA office was deserted. The cleaning crews had already started in the back offices.

Casey went to her office, flicked on the lights, and stared at the stack of papers waiting on her desk. She sat down and tried not to be discouraged by the way things were going. She had twenty hours until the interview, and her leads were falling apart.

Just lie. Hell with it.

She sighed. Maybe Amos was right.

She stared at the papers, pushing aside the picture of John Chang and his smiling family. She didn't know what to do, except go through the papers. And check.

She again came to the charts of the flight plan and to the general declaration, outward-inward, that had been filed with it, which listed the crew:

John Zhen Chang, Captain	5/7/51	M
Leu Zan Ping, First Officer	3/11/59	M
Richard Yong, First Officer	9/9/61	M
Gerhard Reimann, First Officer	7/23/49	M
Thomas Chang, First Officer	6/29/70	M
Henri Marchand, Engineer	4/25/69	M
Robert Sheng, Engineer	6/13/62	M
Harriet Chang, Flight Attendant	5/12/77	F
Linda Ching, Flight Attendant	5/18/76	F
Nancy Morley, Flight Attendant	7/19/75	F
Kay Liang, Flight Attendant	6/4/72	F
John White, Flight Attendant	1/30/70	M
M. V. Chang, Flight Attendant	4/1/77	F
Sha Yan Hao, Flight Attendant	3/13/73	F
Y. Jiao, Flight Attendant	11/18/76	F
Harriet King, Flight Attendant	10/10/75	F

B. Choi, Flight Attendant	11/18/76	F
Yee Chang, Flight Attendant	1/8/74	F

She paused. Something was odd about this list, but she couldn't put her finger on it. Next she checked a transcript of communications from Southern California Air Traffic Approach Control to 545:

0543:23	TPA545	SOCAL APPROACH THIS IS TRANSPACIFIC FIVE FOUR FIVE WE HAVE AN EMERGENCY
0543:29	ATAC	GO AHEAD FIVE FOUR FIVE
0543:31	TPA545	REQUEST PRIORITY CLEARANCE FOR LANDING IN LOS ANGELES
0543:35	ATAC	OKAY FIVE FOUR FIVE SAY THE NATURE OF YOUR EMERGENCY
0544:05	TPA545	WE NEED AMBULANCES ON THE GROUND I WOULD SAY THIRTY OR FORTY AMBULANCES MAYBE MORE
0544:10	ATAC	FORTY AMBULANCES
0544:35	TPA545	AFFIRMATIVE WE ENCOUNTERED SEVERE TURBULENCE DURING FLIGHT WE HAVE INJURIES OF PASSENGERS AND FLIGHT CREW

Casey puzzled over the exchanges, because they suggested very erratic behavior by the pilot. For example, the TransPacific incident had occurred shortly after five in the morning. At that time the plane was still in radio contact with Honolulu. With so many injuries the captain could have reported an emergency to Honolulu.

But he hadn't done that. Why not? Instead, the pilot continued to Los Angeles. And he had waited until he was about to land before reporting an emergency. Why had he waited so long?

And why would he say the incident had been caused by turbulence? He knew that wasn't true. The captain had told the stewardess the slats deployed. And Casey knew, from Ziegler's audio, that the slats *had* deployed. So why lie to approach control?

Everyone agreed John Chang was a good pilot. Even the best pilots sometimes behaved oddly in a crisis. But there seemed to be a pattern here—almost a plan. She looked ahead:

0544:59	ATAC	TRANSPACIFIC I COPY YOUR GROUND REQUEST WHAT IS THE NATURE OF THE INJURIES YOU ARE BRINGING IN
0545:10	TPA545	I AM NOT SURE
0545:20	ATAC	CAN YOU GIVE US AN ESTIMATE
0545:30	TPA545	I AM SORRY NO AN ESTIMATE IS NOT POSSIBLE
0545:35	ATAC	IS ANYONE UNCONSCIOUS
0545:40	TPA545	NO I DO NOT THINK SO BUT TWO ARE DEAD
0545:51	ATAC	TPA FIVE FOUR FIVE WHAT IS YOUR AIRCRAFT'S CONDITION
0545:58	TPA545	WE HAVE DAMAGE TO THE PASSENGER CABIN MINOR DAMAGE ONLY

Casey thought, *Minor damage only?* That cabin had sustained millions of dollars of damage. Hadn't the captain gone back to look for himself? Did he not know the extent of the damage?

0546:12	ATAC	WHAT IS THE CONDITION OF THE FLIGHT DECK
0546:22	TPA545	FLIGHT DECK IS OPERATIONAL FDAU IS NOMINAL
0546:31	ATAC	WHAT IS THE CONDITION OF YOUR FLIGHT CREW
0546:38	TPA545	CAPTAIN AND FIRST OFFICER IN GOOD CONDITION

At that moment one of the first officers had been covered in blood. Again, did the pilot not know? Casey glanced at the rest of the transcript, then pushed it aside. She'd show it to Felix tomorrow and get his opinion. She went on, looking through the structure reports, the interior cabin reports, the relevant records for the counterfeit slats locking pin and the counterfeit thruster cowl. Steadily, patiently, she worked on into the night.

IT WAS after ten o'clock when she again turned to the faults printout from flight 545. She had been hoping she could skip this and use the flight recorder data instead. But now there was nothing to do but slog through it.

Yawning, tired, she stared at the columns of numbers on the first page. She didn't want to do this. She hadn't eaten dinner yet, and she knew she should eat. Then she saw the AUX readings:

AUX 1	00000000000
AUX 2	00000000000
AUX 3	00000000000
AUX COA	01000000000

She had questions about these AUX readings. Ron had said the first was the auxiliary power unit, the second and third were unused, and the fourth, AUX COA, was a customer-installed line. But there wasn't anything on those lines, Ron said, because a zero reading was the normal default reading. But if there was a one . . . then that would mean . . .

She ran her finger down the columns of numbers. There was a numeral one! AUX COA had registered a fault on the second leg of the flight. That meant the AUX COA line was being used by the aircraft.

But what was it used for?

She sucked in her breath. She hardly dared to hope.

Ron said that AUX COA was a line for customer options. The customer used it for add-ons, like a quick access recorder, installed to help maintenance crews. It recorded many of the same parameters as a regular flight data recorder. If a QAR was on this aircraft, it could solve all her problems.

But Ron insisted this plane didn't have a QAR.

He said he'd looked in the tail, which was where it was usually installed on an N-22, and it wasn't there. But it could be just about anyplace in the aircraft the operator wanted it—in the aft accessory compartment or the cargo hold or the radio rack beneath the cockpit. It could be anywhere.

Had Ron really looked?

She decided to check for herself.

She spent the next ten minutes thumbing through thick service repair manuals for the N-22 without any success. She couldn't find any mention of the QAR. But the manuals she kept in her office were not the latest versions.

That was when she noticed the heads-up display on her desk.

Wait a minute, she thought. She grabbed the goggles, slipped them on. She plugged them into the CD player. She looked in the cardboard box, found a silver CD-ROM platter, and slid it into the player. She pressed the power button.

The goggles glowed. She was staring at a page from the first maintenance manual, projected onto the inside of the goggles. The projected page appeared to float in space two feet in front of her. The page was transparent; she could see right through it.

Tom Korman, who had built the unit, liked to say that virtual reality was virtually useless except for a few specialized applications. One was maintenance. Busy people working in technical environments, people who had their hands full or covered in grease, didn't have the time or inclination to look through a thick manual. So virtual displays were perfect for those situations.

By pressing buttons on the CD player, Casey found that she could scroll through the manuals. After a moment of whirring, a page hung in the air before her:

N-22

QUICK ACCESS RECORDER (QAR)

RECOMMENDED LOCATIONS

Pressing more buttons, she scrolled through a sequence of diagrams showing in detail all the places where the QAR could be located. There were about thirty places in all.

Casey clipped the player onto her belt and headed for the door.

AIRPORT MARINA

10:20 p.m. Marty Reardon was still in Seattle.

His interview with Bill Gates had run long, and he'd missed his plane. He was coming down in the morning. Jennifer had to revise the schedule.

It was going to be a difficult day, she realized. She'd hoped to start at nine. Now she couldn't begin until ten at the earliest. That made the day's schedule too tight—no time for lunch, for traffic delays, for normal production screwups. And Marty would want to make the six-o'clock plane back to New York.

The problem was that by the time Marty finished with Singleton in Burbank, it would be rush hour. He'd never make his plane. He really should leave Burbank by two thirty. Which meant pushing Singleton up and holding off the lawyer. The lawyer would be flexible. He'd wait until midnight if they asked him to.

She'd talked with him earlier. King was a blowhard, but he was plausible in short bites. Five, ten seconds. Punchy. Worth doing.

That would work. In her mind she reviewed her pullouts. If the FAA guy was good, then Marty might run over with him. She'd move Singleton up to two o'clock. Singleton would be fast.

Then head back to LAX, finish with King. Marty'd leave at six, and Jennifer would have her tape. She'd edit the segment, then uplink to New York that night. She'd call in and get Dick's comments Saturday morning, revise it, and uplink it again about noon. That was plenty of time to make air.

She made a note to call Norton in the morning and tell them she needed to move Singleton up two hours.

She turned to the stack of faxed background documents Norton had sent her office for Deborah's research. Jennifer had never bothered to look at these, but she had nothing better to do now. She thumbed through them quickly, suddenly stopped.

She stared. "They've got to be kidding," she said.

HANGAR 5

10:30 p.m. At night the Norton plant appeared deserted, the parking lots nearly empty. But it was brightly lit. Security kept floodlights on all night. As Casey crossed from administration to hangar 5, she heard her footsteps clicking on the asphalt.

The big doors to hangar 5 were pulled down and locked. She saw Teddy Rawley standing outside, talking to one of the electrical team. She went over to the side door.

"Hey, babe," Teddy said. "Still here, huh?"

"Yeah." She started through the door.

The electrical guy said, "Nobody's allowed in. We're doing the CET now."

"It's okay," she said.

"I'm sorry, you can't," the guy said. "Ron Smith gave strict orders. Nobody's to go inside. If you touch anything—"

"I'll be careful," she said.

Teddy looked at her, walked over. "I know you will," he said, "but you're going to need this." He handed her a heavy flashlight, three feet long. "It's dark in there, remember?"

The electrical guy said, "And you can't turn the lights on. We can't have change in the ambient flux—"

"I understand," she said. The test equipment was sensitive; turning on the overhead fluorescents might change readings.

The electrician was still fretting. "Maybe I better call Ron."

"Call whoever you want," Casey said.

She went into the hangar. Teddy was right; it was dark inside. She felt, rather than saw, the large space around her. All the plane's doors and compartments were open, cabling hanging down everywhere. Beneath the tail the test box sat in a pool of faint blue light. The CET screen flickered as systems were activated in sequence. She saw the cockpit lights go on, then off. Then the forward cabin lights, brightly lit, thirty feet above her. Then darkness again. A moment later the beacon lights on the wingtips and the tail came on, sending hot white strobe flashes through the room. Then darkness again.

Casey turned on her flashlight and headed for the aft accessory compartment in the tail. Ron had said the QAR wasn't there, but she felt she had to check again. She climbed the broad stairs rolled up to the back of the plane, being careful not to touch the handrails; electrical test cables were taped there.

The aft accessory compartment, built into the upward slope of the tail, was directly above her head. The compartment doors were open. She shone her light in and saw a maze of semicircular pipes, white couplings, readout meters, rack slots, and black boxes. If there was a QAR in here as well, she might easily miss it; the QARs were only about eight inches square.

She paused to put on her goggles, and turned on the CD player. Immediately a diagram of the aft accessory compartment hung in space before her eyes. She could see through the diagram to the actual compartment behind. The rectangular block marking the QAR was outlined in red. In the actual compartment the space was taken up by an extra readout meter: hydraulic pressure for a flight-control system.

Ron was right. There was no QAR here.

Casey climbed back down the stairs and walked beneath the plane to the forward accessory compartment, just behind the nosewheel. It, too, was open. Standing on the ground, she shone her flashlight up into the compartment and flicked to the correct manual page. A new image hung in the air. It showed the QAR located in the right anterior electrical rack. The slot was empty.

It had to be somewhere inside the plane.

She headed off to the right, where a roll-up staircase led up thirty feet to the passenger door, just behind the cockpit. She heard her feet ring on the metal as she entered the aircraft.

It was dark. She shone her flashlight aft, the beam moving over the cabin. It looked worse than before. In many places her beam caught the dull silver of the insulation pads—the electrical crews had pulled the interior panels around the windows to get at junction boxes along the walls.

Behind her the cockpit suddenly glowed as the overhead map lights came on, then the row of video display screens. The printer on the pedestal buzzed, printing out a couple of test lines, then was silent. All the cockpit lights went out.

Immediately the forward galley lights just ahead of her came on; the illuminators for heating and microwaves flashed; the overheat and timer warnings beeped. Then everything went off. Silence. Dark again.

Casey was still standing just inside the door, fiddling with the CD player at her waist, when she thought she heard footsteps. It was difficult to tell. As the electrical systems cycled through, there was a continuous succession of soft buzzes and clicks. She listened hard.

Yes, she was sure of it now. Footsteps.

Someone was walking slowly, steadily, through the hangar.

Frightened, she leaned out the door and called loudly, "Teddy? Is that you?"

She listened. No more footsteps. Silence. The clicking of the relays.

Never mind, she decided. She was up here alone, and it was getting on her nerves. She was tired, imagining things.

She walked around the galley to the left side, where the display showed an additional electrical storage panel, down near the floor. The panel cover had already been removed. She looked at it through the transparent diagram. No QAR.

She moved toward the tail, to the aft interior storage compartment. This was a more likely place—a square service panel just to the left of the rear exit door.

She came to the door, which was open. She felt a cool breeze. Darkness outside. She couldn't see the ground, forty feet below. The service panel was already open. If the QAR was there, it would be in the lower-right corner. It wasn't there.

The wingtip lights came on, brilliant strobes flashing repeatedly. They cast harsh shadows in the interior, through the open door and the row of windows. Then off again.

Clink.

She froze. The sound had come from somewhere near the cockpit. It was a metallic sound, like a foot kicking a tool.

Someone was in the cabin.

She pulled the goggles off, leaving them hanging around her neck. Silently she slid to her right, crouching behind a row of seats as the footsteps came closer.

She held her breath.

The cabin lights came on, first in front, then midships, then aft. Then they went off again.

She gripped the flashlight. The weight felt comforting. She peered between the seats but could see nothing.

Then the landing lights came on, and in their reflected glare a row of hot ovals appeared on the ceiling, from the windows along both sides, and a shadow, blotting them out, one after another.

Someone walking down the aisle.

What could she do? She had the flashlight in her hand, but she had no illusions about her ability to defend herself.

The man was close now. She edged forward and saw him. He was almost to the rear of the plane, looking in every direction. She could not see his face, but she saw his red-checked shirt.

The landing lights went out. Darkness. She held her breath.

She heard the faint thunk of a relay from somewhere in the forward compartment. She knew it was electrical, but apparently the man did not. He grunted softly and moved forward.

She waited. After a while she thought she heard the sound of footsteps on the stairs, going down. Cautiously she came out from behind the seat. Time to get out of here, she thought. She moved to the open door, listening. The sound diminished.

A voice inside said, *Get out of here,* but she felt the goggles around her neck and hesitated. She ought to give the man time to leave the hangar. She decided to look in another compartment.

She pulled on the goggles, pressed the button on the unit, saw the next page.

The next compartment was nearby, just outside the rear door, where she was standing. She leaned out and, holding on with her right hand, found she could easily look into the panel box. The cover was open. There were three vertical rows of electrical buses, and at the bottom . . . yes, the quick access recorder.

It was green, with a white stripe around the top. Stenciled lettering: MAINT QAR 041/B MAINT. A metal box about eight inches square. Casey reached in, gripped the box, and pulled gently. With a metallic click it came free of the inner coupling. And she had it in her hand!

She was so excited, she did not hear the rush of footsteps behind her until it was too late. Strong hands shoved against her, and then her body fell through the door, into space. Falling. To the floor thirty feet below.

Too soon—much too soon—she felt a sharp pain on her cheek, and then her body landed, but something was wrong. She was no longer falling, but rising. Then falling again. It was like a giant hammock.

The webbing. She'd fallen into the safety webbing that hung beneath the plane. She scrambled to her feet, but it was difficult to balance. The webbing was slowly undulating.

Somewhere forward she heard footsteps clattering on the metal stairs. The man was coming.

She had to get out. She had to get off the webbing before he caught her. She moved toward the wing, then heard a cough from the far edge of the wing, somewhere off to her left.

Someone else was here. Down on the floor. Waiting.

Suddenly the hot strobe lights above the tail flickered rapidly. They were so bright they illuminated the entire hangar.

Now she could see who had coughed.

IT WAS Richman.

He wore a dark blue windbreaker and dark slacks. The lazy, collegiate manner was gone. He stood near the wing—tense, alert. He looked left and right carefully, scanning the floor.

Abruptly the strobe lights went out, plunging the hangar into darkness. Casey moved forward, hearing the webbing creak beneath her feet. Would Richman hear? Could he figure out where she was?

She came to the wing, stretching forward in darkness.

She grabbed it with her hand, moved outward to the edge. Sooner or later, she knew, the webbing would end. Her foot struck a thick cord; she bent down, felt knots.

She lay down on the webbing, gripped the edge, and rolled over the side. She did not know how far it was to the floor: Six feet? Ten? She released the webbing and fell.

She hit the ground standing, dropped to her knees. Sharp pain in her kneecap as she banged into concrete. She heard Richman cough. He was very close, off to her left. She got up and began to run toward the exit door. The landing lights came on again, harsh and strong. In their glare she saw Richman throw up his hands to cover his eyes.

She knew he would be blinded for a few seconds. Not long, but perhaps enough.

Where was the other man?

She ran.

She hit the wall of the hangar with a dull metallic thud. Someone behind her said, "Hey!" She moved along the wall, feeling for the door. Her hand touched wood, vertical runners, then the metal bar. The door latch. She pushed. Cool air. She was outside.

Teddy turned. "Hey, babe," he said, smiling. "How's it going?"

She fell to her knees, gasping for breath. Teddy and the electrical guy came running over. "What is it? What's the matter?"

They were standing over her, touching her, solicitous. She tried to catch her breath. She managed to gasp, "Call security."

The electrical guy ran to the phone. Teddy stayed with her. Then she remembered the QAR. She had a moment of panic. "Oh no," she said. "I dropped it."

"Dropped what?"

"That box. . . ." She turned, looking back at the hangar.

"You mean the one in your hand?" Teddy said.

She looked. The QAR was there, clutched so tightly her fingers were white.

FRIDAY

GLENDALE

6:30 a.m. Something was wrong. Casey sat up quickly.

Sunlight poured through her window onto the foot of the bed. She looked down at twin arcs of grease on the bedspread. She still had her shoes on. She still had her clothes on.

She was lying on top of the bedspread, fully dressed.

Groaning, she swung her feet to the floor. Everything hurt. She looked down at the bedside table. The clock said six thirty.

She reached behind the pillow, brought out the green metal box with a white stripe that she had stuck there last night—the QAR.

She suddenly remembered: the interview with Marty Reardon. "Jeez," she said. Quickly she got off the bed, groaning again.

She went into the bathroom and turned on the shower. She looked in the mirror. Her face was streaked with grime. There was a purple bruise that started by her ear and ran back behind her neck. She had bruises on her elbow, on her hip, on her knees.

She came out of the shower. She had only ten hours until her interview. Between now and then she had only one thing she wanted to do. Clear up flight 545.

NORTON/DDS

7:40 a.m. Rob Wong placed the green box on the table, attached a cable, pressed a key on his console. A small red light glowed on the QAR box.

"It's got power," Wong said. He sat back in his chair, looked at

Casey. "Keep your fingers crossed." He pushed a single key on the keyboard. His screen began to show columns of numbers. "Looks pretty good, Casey. This could be your lucky day."

He typed rapidly. On the monitor a wire-frame aircraft appeared and rapidly filled in, becoming solid, three-dimensional. A sky-blue background appeared. A silver aircraft, seen in profile, the landing gear down. Wong punched keys, moving the aircraft around. The airplane image began to move, going down the runway, the nose raising.

"You just took off," he said, grinning.

The aircraft was still rising. Wong hit a key, and a rectangle opened on the right side of the screen. A series of numbers appeared, changing quickly. "All the major stuff is here," he said. "Altitude, airspeed, heading, fuel, deltas on control surfaces—flaps, slats, ailerons, elevators, rudder. Everything you need. And the data's stable, Casey."

The aircraft was still climbing. "I figure you don't want to real-time this," he said. "You know when the accident occurred?"

"Yes," she said. "It was about nine forty into the flight."

"Nine forty elapsed? Coming up."

On the monitor the aircraft was level, the numbers on the right stable. Then a red light began to flash.

"Fault recording. It's, uh, slats disagree," said Wong.

Five seconds. Then the slats emerged from the leading edge.

"Slats extending," Wong said. Then, "Slats fully extended."

Casey said, "So there was a fault first, then the slats extended afterward? Uncommanded extension?"

"No. Commanded. Now, plane goes nose up and—uh-oh—exceeding buffet boundary. Now here's the stall warning, and—"

On the screen the airplane nosed over into a steep dive. Alarms began to beep, flashing on the screen. "The plane's exceeding the G-load envelope. Wow, look at him."

The airplane pulled out of the dive and began a steep climb. "He's going up at eighteen . . . twenty-one degrees."

On commercial flights, a standard rate of climb was three to five degrees. Ten degrees was steep, used only in takeoffs. At twenty-one degrees, passengers would feel as if the plane were going straight up.

More alarms. Then the plane went into a dive again.

"I can't believe this," Wong said. "These wild oscillations should kick in the autopilot." He pointed to the box of data to one side. "Yeah, there it is. The autopilot tries to take over. Pilot keeps punching it back to manual. That's crazy."

Another climb. Another dive.

In all, they watched aghast as the aircraft went through six cycles of dive and climb before it returned to stable flight.

"What happened?" she said.

"Autopilot took over. *Finally.*" Rob Wong gave a long sigh. "Well, I'd say you know what happened to this airplane, Casey. But I'm damned if I know why."

WAR ROOM

9:00 a.m. A cleaning crew was at work in the war room washing the big windows overlooking the factory floor. Doherty and Ron Smith were standing near the door, looking at a printout.

"What's going on?" Casey said.

"No IRT today," Doherty said. "Marder canceled it."

She said, "How come nobody told me that—"

"CET test last night was near perfect," Ron said. "We only got two repeated faults. We got a consistent fault on AUX COA around ten thirty; I don't know why."

He looked at her, waiting. He must have heard that she had been inside the hangar the night before at about that time. But she wasn't going to explain it to him. Not right now. She said, "And what about the wing proximity sensor?"

"That was the other fault," Smith said. "It faulted six times."

"And if that proximity sensor faulted during flight . . ."

"You'd get a slats disagree in the cockpit."

She turned to leave.

"Hey," Doherty said. "Where are you going?"

"I've got to look at some video."

As swiftly as the investigation had stalled the day before, she felt it coming together. The QAR had been the key.

As she walked to her car, she called Norma on her cell phone. "Norma, I need a route schedule for TransPacific."

"Got one right here," Norma said. "It came over with the FAA packet. What do you want to know?"

"Flight schedule to Honolulu."

"I'll check." A pause. "They don't go into Honolulu."

"That's all I need to know." It was as Casey had expected.

"Listen," Norma said, "Marder has called three times for you already. And Richman has been trying to—"

"Tell them you can't reach me." She hung up.

Driving in her car, she called Ellen Fong in accounting. The secretary said Ellen was working at home again today. Casey got the number and called her there.

"Ellen, it's Casey Singleton. Did you do the translation?"

"Yes." Ellen's voice was cool. Careful.

"Can you fax it to me?" Casey said.

"I think I should bring it to your office. Two o'clock?"

"Fine," Casey said.

The pieces of the puzzle were coming together. Fast.

SEPULVEDA BOULEVARD

10:45 a.m. Fred Barker was sweating. The air conditioner was turned off in his office, and now, under Marty Reardon's insistent questioning, sweat trickled down his cheeks, dampened his shirt.

"Mr. Barker," Marty said slowly, leaning forward. Marty was forty-five, handsome in a thin-lipped, sharp-eyed way. He had the air of a reluctant prosecutor who was giving the witness every possible break. "You've described problems with the Norton N-22. But the company says airworthiness directives were issued that fixed the problems. Are they right?"

"Well, we just had another incident, involving slats."

"Norton told us it wasn't slats. Are they lying?"

"They're doing what they always do. They come up with a complicated explanation that conceals the real problem. This accident is the result of failure to redress a long-term design flaw."

"How can you be so sure? Are you an engineer?"

"No."

"You have an aerospace degree?"

"No."

"Your major in college was music, wasn't it, Mr. Barker?"

"Well, yes, but, uh . . ."

Jennifer watched Marty's attack with mixed feelings. It was always fun to watch pompous experts get cut down to size. But Marty's attack on the former FAA official's credibility could devastate her entire segment.

"Do you have any scientific or engineering training at all?"

Barker tugged at his collar. "Well, I worked for the FAA. . . ."

"Did the FAA give you any *formal* training in aerodynamics, fluid dynamics, calculus, metallurgy, or structural analysis?"

"Not formally, no. But I have a lifetime of experience."

"Good. That's fine. Now, I notice those books behind you and on your desk." Reardon leaned forward. "This one here. It's called *Advanced Structural Integrity Methods for Airframe Durability and Damage Tolerance.* You understand this book?"

"Most of it, yes."

"For example"—Reardon pointed to the open page—"here on page 807, it says, 'Leevers and Radon introduced a biaxiality parameter B that relates the magnitude of the T stress as in equation five.' You see that? What is a biaxiality parameter?"

"Uh, well, it's rather difficult to explain briefly. . . ."

Jennifer realized she had to put a stop to this. Marty was doing his attack-dog routine, snarling at the smell of fear. She tapped Marty on the shoulder. "We're running late," she said.

Marty jumped up. "I'm sorry, Mr. Barker, we have to cut this short. We appreciate your time. You've been very helpful."

Barker appeared to be in shock. He mumbled something. The makeup girl came up to him with wipes in her hand.

Marty Reardon turned to Jennifer. In a low voice he said, "What are you doing?"

"Marty," she said, answering him in the same low tones, "the CNN tape is dynamite. The story's dynamite. The public's scared to get on airplanes. We're performing a public service."

"Not with this clown you're not," Reardon said. "He's a litigator's stooge. He doesn't know what he's talking about."

VIDEO IMAGING SYSTEMS

11:17 a.m. "Tape's coming up now," Scott Harmon said. He drummed his fingers on the console.

Casey shifted her body in the chair, feeling twinges of pain. She still had several hours before the interview. And she still couldn't decide how she would handle it.

The tape began to run. Harmon had tripled the frames, the image moving in a jerky slow motion. The change made the sequence appear even more horrifying. She watched in silence as the bodies tumbled, the camera spun and fell and finally came to rest at the cockpit door.

"Go back, as slow as you can," she said. "One frame at a time."

The images ran backward. The gray carpet. The blur as the camera jumped away from the door. The glint of light off the open cockpit door. The hot glare from the cockpit windows, the shoulders of the two pilots, captain on the left, first officer on the right. The captain reaching toward the pedestal.

"Stop."

She stared at the frame. The captain was reaching, no hat, the face of the first officer turned forward, away from him.

The captain reaching his hand out.

There it is, Casey thought. In living color.

But what was she going to do about it?

Nothing, she realized. There was nothing she could do. She had the information now, but she could not possibly release it and hold on to her job. But she was probably going to lose her job anyway. Marder and Edgarton had set her up to do the press. Whether she lied or she told the truth, she was in trouble.

"Okay," she said. "I've seen enough. Run another copy."

Harmon pressed a button on the console. He shifted in his chair, looking uncomfortable. "Ms. Singleton, I feel I have to mention something. The people who work here have seen this tape, and frankly, they're pretty upset."

"I can imagine," Casey said, sighing.

"They've all seen that guy on television, the attorney, who says you're covering up the real cause of the accident. One person in particular, Christine Barron, a woman in reception, thinks we should turn this tape over to the authorities or to the television stations. I mean, we're sitting on a bomb here. If there really is something wrong with this airplane and people died because of it . . ."

Casey's mind was working fast. There was no way to know how many copies of the tape had already been made. There was no way to contain or control events now. And she was tired of the intrigue—with the carrier, with the engineers, with the union, with Marder, with Richman. All these conflicting agendas, while she was caught in the middle, trying to hold it together.

And now the tape company!

She said, "The woman in reception—does she know your company has signed a nondisclosure agreement with us?"

"Yeah, but . . . she thinks her conscience takes precedence."

"I need to make a call," Casey said, "on a private line."

He took her to an office that wasn't being used. She made two telephone calls. When she came back, she said to Harmon, "The tape is Norton property. It is not to be released to anyone without our authorization. And you have signed a nondisclosure agreement with us. You signed it. You violate it, and you're out of business. Keep that in mind."

She took her copy of the tape and walked out of the room.

ADMINISTRATION

1:00 p.m. John Marder was sitting at his desk arranging the documents—props—for Casey to use in her interview. He wanted them complete, and he wanted them in order. First, the parts record for the counterfeit thruster cowl. Finding that part had been a stroke of luck. Pratt and Whitney would scream when they saw it: The famous eagle on their logo had been printed backward. More important, the presence of a counterfeit part could throw the entire story in that direction, and it would take the heat off—

His private phone rang. He picked it up. "Marder."

He heard the hissing crackle of a satellite phone. It was Hal Edgarton, calling from the company jet on his way to Hong Kong. Edgarton said, "Has it happened yet?"

"Not yet, Hal. Another hour."

"Call me as soon as it's over. And it better be good news."

BURBANK

1:15 p.m. Jennifer was fretting. It was never a good idea to leave Marty alone during a shoot: He was a restless, high-energy guy, and he needed constant attention. Someone had to hold his hand and fuss over him. Marty was like all the on-camera talent at *Newsline*—self-centered, vain, demanding.

She also knew that Marty was, at bottom, worried about appearances. He was afraid that when the Norton segment was cut, he'd be fronting a lame story. He didn't care about journalistic responsibility. He just cared about appearances.

And the proof, Jennifer knew, was in her hands. She had only been gone twenty minutes, but as her car rolled up to the location, she saw Marty pacing, head down. Troubled, unhappy.

She got out of the car. He came right over to her, started to make his complaint, started to say he thought they should bail on the segment, call Dick—

She cut him off. "Marty. Look at this."

She took the videotape she was carrying, gave it to the cameraman, and told him to play it back. The cameraman popped it into the camera while she went over to a small playback monitor. The tape began to play. It started with a baby on the mother's lap. Goo-goo. Ga-ga. Baby sucking her toes.

Marty looked at Jennifer. His dark eyebrows went up.

She said nothing. The tape continued. With the sun glare on the monitor it was hard to see details, but it was clear enough—bodies suddenly tumbling through the air. Marty sucked in his breath.

"Where did you get this?" he said, excited.

"Disgruntled employee of a video shop that does work for Norton Aircraft. A solid citizen. She called me."

"Unbelievable," Marty said, watching the tape. "Shocking."

"Isn't it fabulous?"

The tape continued. It was good. It was all good—even better than the CNN tape, more kinetic, more radical.

"Who else has this?" Marty said.

"Nobody."

"But your disgruntled employee may—"

"No," Jennifer said. "I promised we'd pay her legal bills, as long as she didn't give it to anybody else. She'll sit tight."

"So this is our exclusive. *Actual tape* from *inside* the aircraft."

"Right."

"Then we've got a fabulous segment here," Marty said.

Back from the dead! Jennifer thought, as she watched Marty go over to the fence and start to prepare for his stand-up. Saved!

MARTY ad-libbed his stand-up, and he did it well.

"Who's the company contact?" he asked when they were back in the car, heading toward the Norton gate.

"A woman named Singleton. A vice president, late thirties. She's on the investigation team."

Marty held out his hand. "Give me the file and the notes." He started to read through them. "Because you realize what we have to do now, don't you, Jennifer? That tape runs maybe four, four thirty. And you may show parts of it twice—I would. So you won't have much time for Fred Barker and the others. It's going to be the tape and the Norton spokesman. So we have to nail this woman. Cold."

Jennifer waited while Marty thumbed through the file.

"Wait just a minute here," he said. "Are you kidding me?"

"No," Jennifer said.

"This is dynamite," Reardon said. "Where'd you get it?"

"Norton sent it to me in a background package, by accident."

"Bad accident," Marty said. "Especially for Ms. Singleton."

WAR ROOM

2:15 p.m. Casey was crossing the plant when her cell phone rang. It was Steve Nieto, the fizer in Vancouver.

"Bad news," Nieto said. "I went to the hospital yesterday. He's dead. Cerebral edema. Mike Lee wasn't around, so they asked me if I could identify the body, and—"

"Steve," she said. "Not on a cell phone. Send me a telex. But don't send it here. Send it to flight test in Yuma."

"Really? Okay."

She hung up and entered hangar 4. She wanted to talk to Mary Ringer of the interior-artifacts analysis team about the pilot's hat they'd found. That hat was now critical to the story.

She had a sudden thought and called Norma. "Listen, I think I know where that fax came from about the in-flight magazine," Casey said. "Call Centinela Hospital. Ask for a stewardess named Kay Liang. And this is what I want you to ask her. Better write it down."

She spoke to Norma for several minutes, then hung up. Immediately, her cell phone rang again. "Casey Singleton."

Marder screamed, "Where are you, for crying out loud? You're supposed to be *here.* For the interview."

"The interview's at four o'clock."

"They moved it up. They're here now. It's *now,* Casey."

Which was how she found herself sitting in the war room with a makeup woman daubing at her face. The war room was full of people. There were guys setting up big lights on stands and taping sheets of cardboard to the ceiling. Other men were setting up microphones and cameras. Two chairs had been arranged at opposite sides of the table—one for her, one for the interviewer.

Casey was off-balance; everything was happening too fast. The makeup woman kept asking her to keep her head still, to close her eyes. Eileen, Marder's secretary, came over and thrust a manila folder into her hands. "John wanted you to have this."

Casey tried to look at the folder.

"Please," the makeup woman said, "look up for a minute."

Jennifer Malone, the producer, came over with a cheerful smile. "How's everything today, Ms. Singleton?"

"Fine, thanks," Casey said, still looking up for makeup.

"Barbara," Malone said to the makeup woman. "Make sure you get the, uh . . ." And she waved her hand toward Casey.

"Get the what?" Casey said.

"A touch-up," the makeup woman said. "Nothing."

Malone went away. "I'm going to give you a little under the eyes," the makeup woman said. "So you don't look so tired."

"Ms. Singleton?"

The makeup woman jumped back, and Casey saw Marty Reardon in front of her. He was in shirtsleeves and a tie. He had Kleenex around his collar. "Marty Reardon. Nice to meet you."

"Hi," she said, shaking his hand.

"Thanks for your help with this," Reardon said. "We'll try to make it as painless as possible. You know of course we're on tape. So if at any time you want to restate an answer, go ahead and do that. You can say exactly what you want to say."

"Okay."

"Primarily we'll be talking about the TransPacific flight. But I'm going to have to touch on some other matters as well. I have a tendency to jump around in my questions. Don't let that bother you. We're really here to understand the situation as best we can."

"Okay."

"I'll see you later, then." Reardon smiled and turned away.

The makeup woman moved in front of her again. "Look up."

She heard Malone call out, "How much more time, guys?"

Someone said, "Five minutes."

A man came over and said, "Ma'am? Can I give you this?" and he thrust a plastic box with a dangling wire into Casey's hands.

"What is it?" Casey said.

"Look right, please," the makeup woman said. "It's the radio mike. I'll help you with it in a minute."

Casey's cell phone rang, in her purse. She reached for it.

John Marder said, "Did you get the folder from Eileen?"

"Yes."

"Did you look at it?"

"Not yet," she said.

"The folder documents everything we talked about. Parts report on the reverser cowl, everything. It's all there."

"Uh-huh . . . Okay . . . I'm all set."

"Good, we're counting on you."

When makeup was finished, the woman took Casey into the bathroom and showed her how to thread the mike wire up under her blouse and clip it to her lapel. The woman hooked the radio box to the waistband of Casey's skirt and turned the power on.

"Remember," she said, "from now on, you're live."

"Okay," Casey said. She adjusted her clothes, and the makeup woman led her back into the war room. Casey felt like a gladiator being taken into the arena.

Inside the war room the lights were glaring. The room was very hot. She was led to her seat at the table. There were two cameras behind her, two facing her.

On the opposite side Reardon was attaching his own microphone without assistance, chatting with the cameraman. Then he slipped easily into his chair. He looked relaxed and casual.

"Nothing to worry about," he said. "Piece of cake."

"All right," Malone said. "Roll tape."

THE interview began with Marty Reardon smiling at her and gesturing to the room. "So. This is where it all happens. This is where the Norton specialists meet to analyze aircraft accidents."

Casey nodded. "Yes."

"And you're part of that team. Vice president of quality assurance. With the company five years."

"Yes."

"They call this room the war room, don't they? Maps, charts, battle plans, pressure under siege. Your company, Norton Aircraft, is under siege at the moment, isn't it?"

"I'm not sure what you're referring to," Casey said.

Reardon's eyebrows went up. "The JAA, Europe's Joint Aviation Authority, is refusing to certify one of your aircraft, the N-22, because they say it's unsafe."

"Actually, the plane's already certified but—"

"And you're about to sell fifty N-22s to China. But now the Chinese, too, are said to be concerned about its safety."

Casey said, "I'm not aware of any Chinese concerns."

"But you are aware," Reardon said, "of the reason behind these safety concerns—earlier this week, a serious accident involving an N-22 aircraft, TransPacific flight 545. An accident over the Pacific Ocean. Three people died. How many injured?"

"I believe fifty-six," she said. She knew it sounded awful.

"Fifty-six injured," Reardon intoned. "Broken necks. Broken limbs. Concussions. Brain damage. Two people paralyzed. . . ."

She said, "Everyone at Norton feels great concern for air safety. That's why we test our airframes to three times the life—"

"Doesn't the company have an obligation to fix the design of an aircraft which it *knows* to be unsafe?" Reardon said.

"What do you mean?"

"What I mean is that what happened to flight 545 has happened before. On other N-22s. Isn't that true?"

"No," Casey said firmly. This was the moment, she thought. She was stepping off the cliff.

"No?" Reardon's eyebrows shot up. "Then perhaps you can explain this." He held up a sheet of paper. "This is a list of slats episodes on the N-22, going back to 1992, right after the plane was introduced. Eight episodes. TransPacific is the ninth."

"That's not accurate."

"Well, tell me why."

Casey went through, as briefly as she could, the way airworthiness directives worked. She explained why they had been issued for the N-22. How the problem had been solved except for foreign carriers that had failed to comply.

Reardon listened with continuously raised eyebrows, as if he had never heard such an outlandish thing before. "So in your view," he said, "the company has followed the rules. By issuing these air directives, which are supposed to fix the problem."

"No," Casey said. "The company *has* fixed the problem."

"Has it? We're told slats deployment is the reason people died on flight 545."

"That's incorrect." She was now dancing on a tightrope. If he asked her, Did the slats deploy? she would be in trouble.

"The people who told us the slats deployed are wrong?"

She decided to go further. "Yes, they're wrong."

"Fred Barker, former FAA investigator, is wrong."

"Yes."

"The JAA is wrong."

This called for a complicated answer, she thought. How could she put it briefly? "They're wrong to say the aircraft is unsafe."

"So in your opinion," Reardon said, "there is absolutely no substance to these criticisms of the N-22."

"That's correct. It is an excellent aircraft."

"A safe, well-designed aircraft. You'd fly in it."

"Absolutely."

"So what was your reaction when you saw the tape on television from flight 545?"

Casey was ready. “All of us here knew it was a tragic accident. When I saw the tape, I felt very sad for the people involved.”

“You felt sad. Didn’t it shake your conviction about the aircraft? Make you question the N-22?”

“No. The N-22 has a superb safety record. One of the best in the industry.”

Reardon smirked.

“Mr. Reardon,” she said, “let me ask you. Last year forty-three thousand Americans died in automobile accidents. Do you know how many died in domestic commercial transports? Fifty. Do you know how many died the year before that? Sixteen. Fewer than were killed on bicycles.”

“And how many of those died on the N-22?” Reardon asked, eyes narrowed, trying to recover.

“None,” Casey said.

“So your point is, Ms. Singleton . . .”

“That television exaggerates the real dangers involved. That tape will make people afraid to fly. And for no good reason.”

“You think the tape shouldn’t have been shown?”

“I didn’t say that. I said that those tapes create an inaccurate perception of the danger of air travel.”

“In your view, should such tapes be suppressed?”

“No,” Casey said.

“Has Norton Aircraft ever suppressed any tapes?”

Uh-oh, she thought. She was trying to figure out how many people knew of the tape. A lot, she decided: Ellen Fong, Ziegler, the people at Video Imaging. Maybe a dozen people—

“Ms. Singleton,” Reardon said, “are you personally aware of any other tape of this accident?”

Just lie, Amos had said.

“Yes,” she said. “I know of another tape. It was found on the aircraft and is being used in our investigation. We didn’t feel it appropriate to release it until our investigation is completed.”

“You weren’t covering up the plane’s well-known defects?”

“No.”

"Well, Ms. Singleton, *Newsline* obtained a copy of that tape from a conscience-stricken Norton employee who felt that the company *was* covering up. Who felt the tape should be made public."

Casey held herself rigid. She didn't move.

"Are you surprised?" Reardon smirked, enjoying the moment.

Now. "Have you yourself actually seen this tape, Mr. Reardon?"

"Oh yes," Reardon said solemnly. "It's painful to watch. A terrible, damning record of what happened on the N-22."

"You've seen it all the way through?"

"Of course. So have my associates in New York."

So it had already gone to New York, she thought.

"Ms. Singleton, if there was a problem with the airplane—a serious problem the company knew about—would you tell us?"

"But there is no problem."

"Isn't there? If the N-22 is really as safe as you say, Ms. Singleton, then how do you explain this?" And he handed her a sheet of paper.

She took it, glanced at the paper. "Oh, my Lord," she said.

REARDON had his media moment. He had gotten her unguarded, off-balance reaction. She knew it would look bad. She knew there was no way for her to recover from it, no matter what.

The paper was the cover sheet of a report done three years ago:

NORTON AIRCRAFT INTERNAL REVIEW ACTION COMMITTEE
EXECUTIVE SUMMARY
UNSTABLE FLIGHT CHARACTERISTICS OF N-22 AIRCRAFT

Casey knew that there was nothing improper about the study, nothing improper in its findings. But everything about it, even the name—"Unstable Flight Characteristics"—appeared damning.

And this was an internal company report, she thought. It should never have been released. It was three years old—not that many people would even remember it. How had Reardon gotten it?

She glanced at the top of the page, saw a fax number and the name of the sending station: NORTON QA. It had come from her own office. How? Richman, she thought grimly.

Richman had placed this report in the press packet on her desk. And Casey had told Norma to fax it to *Newsline.*

How had Richman known about it?

Marder. Marder knew all about the study. He had been program manager on the N-22; he'd ordered it. And now he had arranged for it to be released while she was on television, because—

"Ms. Singleton? Do you recognize this report?"

"Yes, I do," she said.

Reardon handed her three other sheets, the rest of the executive summary. "In fact, you were the chairman of a *secret committee* inside Norton that investigated flight instabilities of the N-22. Isn't that right?"

"It wasn't a secret," she said. "It's the kind of study we frequently conduct on operational aspects of our aircraft."

"By your own admission, it's a study of flight instabilities."

"Look," she said, "this study is a good thing. After the first slats incident four years ago, there was a question about whether the aircraft had unstable handling characteristics in certain configurations. We didn't avoid that question. We addressed it head-on, to see if it was true. And we concluded—"

"Let me read," Reardon said, "from your own report. 'The aircraft has demonstrated marked sensitivity to manual handling during attitude change.' "

"Yes, but if you'll read the rest of the sentence, you will—"

Reardon cut in. " 'Pilots have reported the aircraft cannot be controlled.' These are statements from *your* report."

"I thought you said you wanted to hear what I had to say." She was starting to get angry. She knew it showed, and didn't care.

Reardon leaned back in his chair, spread his hands. The picture of reason. "By all means, Ms. Singleton."

"Then let me put your quotes in context. All modern aircraft have to hold a very precise attitude, or position in the air. The most efficient position is slightly nose up. Computers hold the aircraft in this position during ordinary flight. None of this is unusual."

"Not unusual? Flight *instabilities?*" Reardon said sarcastically.

She struggled to control her temper. "You read a sentence before," she said. "Let me finish it. 'The aircraft has demonstrated marked sensitivity to manual handling during attitude change, *but this sensitivity is entirely within design parameters and presents no difficulty to properly certified pilots.'* That's the rest."

"But you've admitted there is sensitive handling. Isn't that just another word for instability?"

"No," Casey said. "Sensitive does not mean unstable."

"You have nothing to hide?"

"No," she said.

"We're told your accident team already has a preliminary finding on the probable cause. Is that not true?"

"We're close," she said.

"Close. . . . Ms. Singleton, do you have a finding or not?"

Casey stared at Reardon. The question hung in the air.

"I'm very sorry," a cameraman said. "But we have to reload."

Reardon looked as if he had been slapped. But almost immediately he recovered. "To be continued," he said, smiling at Casey. He was relaxed; he knew he had beaten her. He got up from his chair, turned his back to her. The big lights clicked off; the room seemed suddenly almost dark.

Casey got up, too. She pulled the radio mike off her waist. With the lights off, she saw Richman heading for the door. Casey hurried after him.

SHE caught him in the hallway, grabbed him by the arm, spun him around. "You s.o.b."

"Hey," Richman said, "take it easy." He smiled, nodded past her shoulder. Looking back, she saw the soundman and one of the cameramen coming out into the hallway.

Furious, Casey pushed Richman backward, shoving him through the door to the women's room. She pushed him back against the row of sinks. "I don't know what on earth you think you're doing, but you released that report, and I'm going to—"

"You're going to do nothing," Richman said, his voice suddenly cold. He threw her hands off him. "You still don't get it, do you? It's over, Casey. You just blew the China sale. You're *finished.*"

She stared. He was strong, confident—a different person.

"Edgarton's finished. The China sale's finished. And you're finished." He smiled. "Just the way John said it would happen."

Marder, she thought. Marder was behind it. "If the China sale goes, Marder will go, too. Edgarton will see to that."

Richman was shaking his head pityingly. "Edgarton's in Hong Kong. He'll never know what hit him. By noon Sunday, Marder'll be the new president of Norton Aircraft. It'll take him ten minutes with the board. Because we've made a much bigger deal with Korea. A hundred and ten aircraft firm and an option on thirty-five more. Sixteen billion dollars. The board will be thrilled."

"Korea," Casey said. "But why would—"

"Because he gave them the wing," Richman said. "And in return they're more than happy to buy a hundred and ten aircraft. They don't care about sensationalistic American press."

"He's giving them the *wing?* That'll kill the company."

"Global economy," Richman said. "Get with the program. The minute the deal's announced, Norton stock'll go through the roof. All we needed was somebody to publicly trash the N-22. And you just did that for us."

Casey sighed. Her shoulders dropped.

"So I suggest," Richman said, "that you ask me, very politely, what you should do next. Because your only choice now is to follow orders. Do as you're told, be a good girl, and maybe John will give you severance. Say, three months."

Her mind raced. She could see no way out. *Newsline* would run the story. Marder's plan would succeed. She was defeated.

"I'm waiting," Richman said. "Ask politely."

She looked at his smooth face. He was enjoying this. And in a moment of fury she suddenly saw another possibility.

"You have to face facts, here," Richman was saying. "It's over. There's nothing you can do."

"Watch me," she said. And she walked out of the room.

WAR ROOM

3:15 p.m. Casey slipped into her seat. The soundman came over and clipped the radio pack to her waistband. She saw Richman slip into the room, a faint smile on his face. He was confident there was nothing she could do. Marder had made a huge deal; he was shipping the wing; he was gutting the company.

Reardon dropped into his seat opposite her, adjusted his tie. Then Malone came over and whispered in Reardon's ear. Reardon said, "Really?" Then he nodded several times. Finally he said, "Got it." He began to shuffle his papers.

Malone said, "Guys? We ready? Roll tape."

This is it, Casey thought. She took a deep breath.

Reardon smiled. "Your incident review team has been working around the clock on an incident involving flight 545. And now we hear you have a finding. You know what happened."

She had to do this very very carefully. Because the truth was, she didn't know; she just had a very strong suspicion. They still had to put the sequence together, to verify that things had happened in a certain order. "We are close to a finding," she said.

"Needless to say, we're eager to hear."

"We will announce it tomorrow," Casey said.

Behind the lights, she saw Richman's startled reaction.

"If you know now, why wait?" Reardon asked.

"Because this was a serious accident, as you yourself said. There's already been a great deal of unwarranted speculation from many sources. Norton Aircraft feels it is important to act responsibly. Before we say anything publicly, we have to confirm our findings at flight test, using the same aircraft that was involved in the accident."

"When will you flight test?"

Casey had her answer ready. "Tomorrow morning. We've scheduled it for five a.m. We'll hold a press conference at noon."

"Noon," Reardon said. His expression was bland, but she knew he was working it out. Noon in L.A. was 3:00 p.m. in New York. Plenty of time to make the evening news in both New York and Los Angeles. Norton's preliminary finding would be widely reported. And *Newsline,* which aired at 10:00 p.m. Saturday night, would be out of date. It might even be embarrassing.

Reardon sighed. "We want to be fair to you."

"Naturally," Casey said.

4:15 p.m. "Who cares?" Marder said when Richman came to tell him. "It doesn't make any difference what she does now."

"But if she's scheduling a flight test—"

"So what? Flight test will only make the story worse. She has no idea what caused the accident. And she has no idea what will happen if she takes that plane up. They probably can't reproduce the event. And there may be problems nobody knows about."

"Like what?"

"That aircraft may have undetected structural damage. Anything can happen." Marder made a dismissive wave. "This changes nothing. Hal's friends on the board will drop him when they hear about a sixteen-billion-dollar deal. They've all got stock. They know what the announcement will do to their shares. I'm the next president of this company, and nobody can do a thing to stop it."

"I don't know," Richman said. "Singleton may be planning something. She's pretty smart, John."

"Not smart enough," Marder said.

4:20 p.m. The cameras were packed up; the electrical boxes and camera cases removed. But in the war room the negotiations dragged on. Ed Fuller, the lanky head of legal, was there; so was Teddy Rawley, the pilot; and two engineers who worked on flight test, to answer any technical questions that arose.

For *Newsline,* Jennifer Malone now did all of the talking. She began by saying that since *Newsline* was doing an entire segment on the Norton N-22, it was in their interest to film the flight test.

Casey said that presented no problem. Flight tests were documented with dozens of video cameras, mounted both inside and outside the plane. The *Newsline* people could watch the entire test on monitors on the ground. They could have the film afterward.

No, Malone said, that wouldn't be sufficient. *Newsline*'s crews had to actually be on the plane.

Ed Fuller broke in to explain liability. "You realize, of course, that there is inherent danger in flight test. It's simply inescapable."

Malone said that *Newsline* would accept any risk.

Ed Fuller said he would have to draw up waivers, but there wasn't time for *Newsline*'s lawyers to approve them.

Malone said she could get approval in an hour.

Fuller shifted ground. He said if Norton was going to let *Newsline* see the flight test, he wanted to be sure that the results were accurately reported. He said he wanted to approve the edited film.

Malone said that journalistic ethics forbade that.

They went back and forth. Finally Malone said she would include unedited comment on the outcome of the flight by a Norton spokesperson. This would be taken from the press conference.

"We have another problem," Fuller said. "You characterized the tape you obtained today as having been obtained from a Norton employee. The receptionist, Christine Barron, is not a Norton Aircraft employee. She is not, in fact, an employee of Video Imaging. She is a temp from an agency."

"What's the point here?"

"We want you to state the facts accurately—that you obtained the tape from sources outside the company."

Malone shrugged. "Okay," she said.

Fuller slid a piece of paper across the table. "This brief document conveys that understanding. Sign it."

Malone started to sign it, and paused. "Two crews on the aircraft during the flight test. Is that our agreement?"

"No. Your crews will watch the test on the ground."

"That won't work for us."

Teddy Rawley cleared his throat. "I don't think you understand the situation, Ms. Malone. You can't be walking around filming inside the airplane during a flight test. Everybody on board has to be strapped into a four-point harness. It can get pretty hairy up there."

"I have to be able to say our cameras are on board."

In the end, Casey hammered out a compromise. *Newsline* would be allowed to position two locked-down cameras in the plane to cover the test flight. They would take the feed directly from these cameras. In addition, they would be allowed to use footage from other cameras mounted in the interior.

Malone pushed the paper back to Fuller. "Deal," she said.

Reardon was looking fretfully at his watch as he left with Malone to shoot a stand-up outside building 64, where the assembly line was located. Casey was alone with Rawley and Fuller in the war room.

Fuller sighed. "I hope we've made the right decision, Casey. I did what you asked when you called from the video company."

"Yes, Ed," she said. "You were perfect."

"But I saw the tape," he said. "It's dreadful. I'm afraid that whatever the flight test shows, that tape will be the only thing anybody remembers."

Casey said, "If anybody ever sees it. I think they won't."

Fuller sighed. "I hope you're right. High stakes."

"Yes," she said, "high stakes."

Teddy said, "I watched that woman. She thinks she's going to get on the plane tomorrow."

"Yeah, probably."

"And you, too, right?" Teddy said.

"Maybe," Casey said.

OUTSIDE BUILDING 64

4:55 p.m. "No aircraft company in history," Reardon said, "has ever permitted a television crew on a flight test. But so important is this test to the future of Norton Aircraft that they have agreed to allow our crews to film. So today, for the first time, we will be seeing footage of the actual plane involved in flight 545, the

Norton N-22 aircraft. Critics say it's a death trap. The company says it's safe. The flight test will prove who's right."

"That should do it," Jennifer said.

"How do you want to handle the wrap?" Reardon asked.

"You've got to cover it both ways, Marty."

Reardon looked down at his feet, took a breath. "As the aircraft lands, the team is muted. Norton is devastated. The deadly controversy over the N-22 continues to rage." He looked up. "Enough?"

She said, "You better give me an on-camera about the controversy continues to rage. We can close with that."

"Good idea." Marty stood erect, set his jaw, faced the camera. "And yet the bitter controversy over the N-22 will not die. Here, in this building where the aircraft is made, workers are confident that it is a safe, reliable aircraft. But critics of the N-22 remain unconvinced. Will there be another harvest of death in the skies? Only time will tell. This is Martin Reardon, for *Newsline,* Burbank, California." He blinked.

"Great, Marty."

He was already unclipping his mike, removing his radio pack. "I'm out of here," he said, and sprinted to the waiting car.

Jennifer turned to her crew. "Pack up. We're off to Arizona."

SATURDAY

NORTON TEST FACILITY, YUMA, ARIZONA

4:45 a.m. A thin streak of red was starting to appear behind the flat range of the Gila mountains to the east. The air was very cold; Casey could see her breath. She zipped up her windbreaker, trying to stay warm.

On the runway, lights shone up at the wide-body as the flight test team finished installing the video cameras. Men were on the wings, around the engines, by the landing gear.

The *Newsline* crew was busy filming. Malone stood alongside Casey, watching them. "Damn, it's cold," she said.

Casey led Malone into a low Spanish-style bungalow beside the tower. A room inside was filled with monitors, each displaying the feed from a single camera. Most of the cameras were focused on specific parts. The room had a technical, industrial feeling.

Casey pointed around the room. "There's the cockpit. High mount, looking down. Cockpit, facing back at the pilot. You see Rawley there, in the chair. The interior cabin, looking aft. Interior cabin, looking forward. Looking out on right wing. The left wing."

Malone was frowning. "I thought it would be more, you know, glitzy." She looked unhappy. "These angles on the cabin, who will be in there during the flight?"

"Nobody."

"You mean the seats will be empty? That isn't very compelling. There should be people in the seats. Can't I go on board?"

"It's a dangerous flight. The airframe was badly stressed by the accident. We don't know what will happen."

Malone snorted. "Oh, come on. There aren't any lawyers here."

Casey just looked at her. She was a foolish kid who knew nothing about the world, who was just interested in a *look,* who lived for appearances. Casey knew she should refuse.

Instead, she heard herself say, "You won't like it."

"I'm going on," Malone said. She looked at Casey, her expression an open challenge. "So. How about you?"

Casey didn't have an answer, at least not an answer that would work for television. Not an answer that would *play.* And suddenly the days of strain, the effort to try and solve the incident made her furious.

"Okay," Casey said. "Let's go."

JENNIFER shivered. It was cold inside the airplane, and she was faintly shocked when she recognized, in places, the damage that she had seen on the videotape. There were still bloody footprints on the ceiling, broken luggage bins, dented fiberglass panels, and a lingering odor. She wondered if she had made a mistake, but by then Singleton was gesturing for her to take a seat.

Jennifer sat beside Singleton in the center cabin and waited as one of the Norton technicians, a man in coveralls, tightened the harness around her. Wide canvas straps came over each shoulder; another strap went across her thighs. The man pulled them tight.

"Jeez," Jennifer said. "Does it have to be that tight?"

"Ma'am, you need it as tight as you can stand it. Now here's your release." He showed her. "Pull that now."

She pulled. The straps sprang away from her body.

"And just do it up again yourself if you don't mind."

Jennifer put the contraption back together. It wasn't difficult. These people made such a fuss about nothing.

Alongside her, Singleton was calmly putting her harness on.

"I believe you ladies are prepared," the man said. "You have a pleasant flight." He turned and went out the door.

The intercom clicked. "Prepare to close." The doors were closed, clicked shut. *Thunk.* The air was still cold. Jennifer shivered in her harness.

She heard the whine of the jet engines as they started up, a low moan at first, then rising in pitch. The intercom clicked. She heard the pilot say, "Tower, this is Norton zero one. Request clearance for takeoff."

Click. "Cleared runway three. Contact ground point six three when off the runway."

Click. "Roger."

Then the plane began to roll forward, the engines increasing from a whine to a full deep roar. Jennifer felt the thump of the wheels going over the cracks in the runway. And then suddenly they lifted off, the plane going up, the sky blue out the windows. Airborne.

Click. "Okay, ladies, we are going to proceed to flight level three seven zero—that's thirty-seven thousand feet—and we are going to circle there between Yuma station and Carstairs, Nevada, for the duration of this excursion. If you look to your left, you will see our chase plane coming alongside."

Jennifer looked out and saw a silver jet fighter, glinting in the morning light. It was very close to their aircraft, close enough for them to see the pilot wave. Then suddenly it slid backward.

Click. "Uh, you won't see much more of him; he'll be staying high, behind us. Right now we are coming up on twelve thousand feet. It'll be another few minutes to cruise altitude. We will stabilize at point eight Mach, eighty percent of the speed of sound. That's the usual cruise speed for commercial aircraft. Everybody comfy?"

Jennifer said, "Can you hear us?"

"I can hear you and see you. And you can see me."

A monitor in the cabin in front of them came on. Jennifer saw the pilot's shoulder, his head, the controls arrayed in front of him.

Now they were high enough that full sunlight streamed in through the windows. Because she was sitting in the center of the cabin, Jennifer could not see the ground out the windows.

She looked at Singleton. Singleton smiled.

CLICK. "Ah, okay, we are now at flight level three seven zero, Doppler clear, no turbulence, a beautiful day. Would you ladies please unbuckle your harnesses and come to the cockpit."

What? Jennifer thought. "I thought we couldn't walk around."

"It's okay right now," Singleton said, taking off her harness.

Jennifer climbed out of hers and walked with Singleton up to the cockpit. She felt the vibration of the airplane beneath her feet. The door to the cockpit was open. She saw Rawley, with a second man he didn't introduce and a third who was working with some instrumentation. Jennifer stood with Singleton, looking into the cockpit.

"Now Ms. Malone," Teddy Rawley said. "You interviewed Mr. Barker. What did he say was the cause of the accident?"

"He said the slats deployed."

"Uh-huh. Okay, please watch carefully. This is the flaps-slats handle here. We are at cruise speed, cruise altitude. I am now going to deploy the slats." He reached his hand forward to the thing between the seats and pushed the lever down.

Jennifer heard a faint rumble that lasted a few seconds. Nothing else. The nose tilted, steadied.

"Slats are extended." Rawley pointed to the instrument panel. "We have just duplicated the exact conditions that Mr. Barker insists caused the death of three people on this very same aircraft. And as you see, nothing happened. Maybe you'd like to walk over and look at the wings, see what actually happens when the slats extend. It's kind of neat."

Rawley pressed a button. "Ah, Norton station, this is zero one. Can I have a monitor check?" He listened a moment. "Okay, fine. Ms. Malone, move forward so your friends can see you on that camera up there." He pointed to the ceiling. "Give 'em a wave."

Jennifer waved. She was feeling more foolish by the minute. The flight test was starting to seem like a trap. The footage would make Barker look like a fool. It would make the whole segment look ridiculous. It would make—

"We can do this all day, if you like," Rawley was saying. "That's the point. No problem deploying the slats at cruise speed on the N-22. Plane can handle it fine." He pulled the lever down again. The rumbling occurred again. The nose went up slightly. Exactly as before.

"Now," Rawley said, "we've got the chase plane getting views for you showing the slats extending, so you'll have exterior angles showing all the action. Okay? Slats retracting."

She watched impatiently. "Well," she said, "if the slats didn't cause this accident, what did?"

Singleton spoke now. "How long has it been, Teddy?"

"We've been up for twenty-three minutes. Could happen any minute now."

"What could happen?" Jennifer said.

"The first part of the sequence," Singleton said, "that caused the accident. On this aircraft we believe the initiating event was an erroneous fault reading caused by a bad part."

Jennifer said, "A *bad part?*" She felt her shoulders drop.

They waited. Five minutes went by. Nothing happened. Jennifer kept glancing at her watch. "What exactly are we waiting for?"

"Patience," Singleton said.

Then there was an electronic ping, and she saw amber words flash on the instrument panel. It said, SLATS DISAGREE.

"There it is," Rawley said.

"There what is?"

"An indication that the flight data acquisition unit believes the slats are not where they're supposed to be. As you see, the slats lever is up, so the slats should be stowed. And we know they are. But the airplane is picking up a reading that they are not stowed. In this case we know the warning is coming from a bad proximity sensor in the right wing. The proximity sensor should read the presence of the retracted slat. But this sensor's been damaged."

Jennifer was shaking her head. "Proximity sensor . . . I'm not following you. What does this have to do with flight 545?"

Singleton said, "The cockpit on 545 got a warning that something was wrong with the slats. Warnings like that happen fairly frequently. The pilot doesn't know whether something is really wrong or whether the sensor is just acting up. So the pilot tries to clear the warning; he runs out the slats and retracts them."

"But deploying the slats didn't cause the accident."

"No. We've just demonstrated that."

"What did?"

Rawley said, "Ladies, if you will please take your seats, we will now attempt to reproduce the event."

In the center passenger cabin Casey pulled the harness straps over her shoulders and cinched them tight. She looked over at Malone, who was sweating, her face pale.

"Tighter," Casey said. She reached over, grabbed Malone's waist strap, and pulled hard.

Malone grunted. "Hey!"

"I don't much like you," Casey said, "but I don't want your little rear end getting hurt on my watch."

Casey took out a white paper bag and shoved it under Malone's thigh. "And I don't want you throwing up on me," she said.

Malone's eyes were flicking back and forth. Sweat beaded her forehead. "Listen," she said, "maybe we should call this off."

"Change the channel? Too late now," Casey said.

Click. "All right, ladies, we are initiating the sequence." *Click.* "Chase alpha, this is zero one, initiating pitch oscillations now."

Click. "Roger zero one. We have you. Initiate on your mark."

Click. "Here we go, fellas. Mark."

Casey watched on the side monitor, which showed Teddy in the cockpit. His movements were calm, assured, his voice relaxed.

Click. "I have received my slats-disagree warning, and I am extending slats to clear it. Slats extended. I am now out of the autopilot. Nose is up, speed decreases. I have a stall. . . ."

Casey heard the harsh electronic alarm sounding again and again. Then the recorded warning, "Stall . . . Stall . . ."

Click. "Bringing the nose down to avoid stall condition."

The plane nosed over and began to dive.

It was as if they were going straight down.

Outside, the scream of the engines became a shriek. Casey's body was pressing hard against the harness straps. Sitting beside her, Jennifer Malone began to scream, her mouth open, a single unvarying scream that merged with the scream of the engines.

Casey felt dizzy. Five . . . six . . . seven . . . eight seconds . . . How long had the initial descent been?

Bit by bit the plane began to level, to come out of the dive. The scream of the engines faded, changed to a lower register. Casey felt her body grow heavy, then heavier still, then amazingly heavy, her cheeks sagging, her arms pressed down to the armrests. The G-forces. Casey now weighed two hundred and fifty pounds. She sank lower in the seat, pressed by a giant hand. Beside her, Jennifer had stopped screaming and now was making a continuous low groan.

The sensation of weight decreased as the plane started to climb again. At first the climb was reasonable, then uncomfortable—then it seemed to be straight up. The engines were screaming. Jennifer was screaming. And suddenly Casey felt the pit of her stomach begin to rise, followed by nausea. She saw the monitor lift up for a moment, held in place by the straps. They were weightless at the peak of the climb. Jennifer threw her hand over her mouth. The plane was going over . . . then down again.

Click. "Second pitch oscillation."

Another steep dive. The weight again.

Sinking. Pressing. Deep into the chair.

Casey couldn't move. She couldn't turn her head.

Then they were climbing again, steeper than before, the shriek of the engines loud in her ears. She felt Jennifer reach for her, shouting, "Stop it! Stop it! *Stop it!*"

The plane was coming to the top of the rise. Her stomach lifting, a sickening sensation. Jennifer's hand clapped to her mouth.

The plane going over. Another dive.

Jennifer vomited explosively into the bag. Afterward she turned to Casey, her face green, weak, contorted. "Stop it, please . . ."

The plane had started to nose over again. Going down.

Casey looked at her. "Don't you want to reproduce the full event for your cameras? Great visuals. Two more cycles to go."

"No! *No.* . . ."

The plane was diving steeply now. Still looking at Jennifer, Casey said, "Teddy! Teddy, take your hands off the controls!"

Jennifer's eyes widened, horrified.

Click. "Roger. Taking my hands off now."

Immediately the plane leveled out, smoothly, gently.

Jennifer wiped her lips. She stared. "What happened?"

"The autopilot is flying the plane."

Malone collapsed back in her seat, put her head back, closed her eyes. "I don't understand," she said.

"To end the incident on flight 545, all the pilot had to do was take his hands off the column. If he had taken his hands away, it would have ended immediately."

Jennifer sighed. "Then why didn't he?"

Casey didn't answer her. She turned to the monitor. "Teddy," she said, "let's go back."

YUMA TEST STATION

9:45 a.m. Back on the ground, Casey went through the main room of the flight-test station and into the pilots room. It was an old wood-paneled lounge from the days when Norton still made military aircraft. A lumpy green couch, a couple of metal flight chairs, a scratched Formica table.

Casey looked through the window at the *Newsline* crew walking around flight 545, filming it as it sat on the runway. The crew seemed lost, not certain what to do. They seemed to be waiting.

Casey opened the manila folder she had brought with her and looked through the sheets of paper inside. The color Xeroxes she asked Norma to make had turned out rather well, and the telexes were satisfactory. Everything was in order.

She went to the television, which she had ordered brought out here. She pushed a tape into the deck. While she waited for Malone, she remembered the motion-sickness patches on her arm. She rolled up her sleeve and pulled off the four circular bandages. The patches were why she had not vomited on the plane. She had known what she was in for. Malone had not.

Casey had no sympathy for the young woman. She just wanted to be finished. This would be the last step. This would end it.

The only person at Norton who really knew what she was doing was Ed Fuller. Fuller had understood immediately when Casey had called him from Video Imaging. He recognized the implications of releasing the tape to *Newsline.* He saw what it would do to them, how they might be boxed in. Flight test had done that. It had closed the box and locked it.

Five minutes later Jennifer Malone came in, slamming the door behind her. She was wearing a pair of flight-test coveralls. Her face was washed, her hair pulled back. And she was angry.

"I don't know what you think you proved up there," she said. "You had your fun. Taped the show. Scared me silly. But our story isn't changed. Your plane's a death trap. By the time we air our story, you won't be able to sell your crummy little airplane on *Mars*. We're going to bury you."

Casey did not speak. She let Malone rant a while longer, and then she said, "Actually, you're not going to do that. The only thing you can do is report what actually happened on flight 545."

"You wait," Malone said, hissing. "You just wait."

Casey sighed. "Did you ever wonder how a secretary at a video house in Glendale knew you were doing a story on Norton? Had your cell phone number and knew to call you?"

Malone was silent.

"Did you ever wonder," Casey said, "how Norton's attorney could have found out so quickly you had the tape? And then have gotten a sworn statement from the receptionist about it?"

Malone frowned. "What is this?"

"Ever wonder why Ed Fuller insisted you sign a document saying you didn't obtain the tape from a Norton employee?"

"It's obvious. The tape's damaging. He doesn't want the company to be blamed."

"Blamed by whom?"

"By . . . I don't know. The public."

"You better sit down," Casey said. She opened the file.

Slowly Malone sat. "Wait a minute," she said. "You're saying that secretary didn't call me about the tape? Then who called?"

Casey said nothing, just looked at her.

"It was *you?* You *wanted* me to have that tape?"

Casey smiled. She handed Malone the first sheet of paper. "This is a parts inspection record, stamped off by the FAA yesterday, for the number two inboard slats proximity sensor on flight 545. The part is noted to be cracked, defective. The crack is old."

"I'm not doing a parts story," Malone said.

"No," Casey said, "you're not. Because what flight test showed you today is that any competent pilot could have handled the slats warning initiated by the bad part. All the pilot had to do is leave the plane in autopilot. But on flight 545 he didn't."

Malone said, "We've already checked that. The captain of 545 was an outstanding pilot."

Casey passed her the next piece of paper. "This is the crew manifest submitted to the FAA with the flight plan on the date of departure of flight 545."

John Zhen Chang, Captain	5/7/51	M
Leu Zan Ping, First Officer	3/11/59	M
Richard Yong, First Officer	9/9/61	M
Gerhard Reimann, First Officer	7/23/49	M
Thomas Chang, First Officer	6/29/70	M
Henri Marchand, Engineer	4/25/69	M
Robert Sheng, Engineer	6/13/62	M

"And this is the crew manifest we got from TransPacific the day after the incident."

John Zhen Chang, Captain	5/7/51
Leu Zan Ping, First Officer	3/11/59
Richard Yong, First Officer	9/9/61
Gerhard Reimann, First Officer	7/23/49
Henri Marchand, Engineer	4/25/69
Thomas Chang, Engineer	6/29/70
Robert Sheng, Engineer	6/13/62

Malone scanned both lists. "They're the same."

"No. In one Thomas Chang is listed as a first officer. In the second list he appears as an engineer."

Malone said, "A clerical error."

Casey shook her head. "No." She passed over another sheet.

"This is a page from the TransPacific in-flight magazine, showing Captain John Chang and his family. It was sent to us by a TransPacific flight attendant who wanted us to know the real story. You will notice his children are Erica and Thomas Chang. Thomas Chang is the pilot's son. He was among the flight crew of flight 545."

Jennifer frowned.

"The Changs are a family of pilots. Thomas Chang is a pilot, qualified on several commuter aircraft. He is not type certified to fly the N-22."

"I don't believe this," Malone said.

"At the time of the incident," Casey continued, "the captain, John Chang, had left the cockpit. He was aft when the accident occurred, and severely injured. He underwent brain surgery two days ago. The hospital thought it was the first officer, but his identity has now been confirmed as John Zhen Chang."

Casey handed her a memo from Steve Nieto, the fizer in Vancouver, confirming the identification.

"Chang wasn't in the cockpit," Casey went on. "He was in the back of the plane. His hat was found there. So someone else was in the captain's chair when the incident occurred."

Casey turned on the television, started the tape. "These are the concluding moments of the videotape you obtained from the receptionist. You see the camera falling toward the front of the plane, twisting to eventually lodge in the cockpit door. But before it does . . . here!" She froze the frame. "You can see the flight deck. See that the pilot has extremely short hair. Look at the magazine picture. Thomas Chang has close-cropped hair."

Malone was shaking her head. "That visual is not good enough. You have a three-quarter profile. It doesn't say anything."

"Thomas Chang has a small stud in his ear. You can see it in this magazine photo. And on the video you can see the same stud."

Casey pushed another piece of paper across to her.

"This is a translation of the Chinese voice communications in the cockpit as recorded on your tape. Much is unintelligible due to the cockpit alarms, but the relevant passage is marked."

0544:59	ALM	STALL STALL STALL
0545:00	F/O	WHAT (UNINTELLIGIBLE) YOU
0545:01	CPTN	AM (UNINTELLIGIBLE) CORRECT THE
0545:02	ALM	STALL STALL STALL
0545:03	F/O	TOM RELEASE THE (UNINTELLIGIBLE)
0545:04	CPTN	WHAT DO (UNINTELLIGIBLE) IT

0545:11 F/O TOMMY (UNINTELLIGIBLE) WHEN (UNINTELLIGIBLE) MUST (UNINTELLIGIBLE)

Casey took the paper back. "That's not for you to keep or refer to publicly. But it corroborates the videotape in your possession."

Malone said in a stunned voice, "*He let his kid fly the plane?*"

"Yes," Casey said. "As a result, fifty-six people were injured and four people died—including John Chang himself. We believe that the aircraft was on autopilot and Chang left his son momentarily in charge. When the disagree warning occurred, the son extended the slats to clear it. But he panicked, overcorrected, and porpoised. Eventually, we believe, Thomas Chang was knocked unconscious by the severe movements of the airplane and the autopilot took over."

Malone said, "On a commercial flight some guy lets his kid fly the plane? *That's* the story?"

"Yes," Casey said. "And you have the tape that proves it. You have seen this shot of the cockpit. I have now informed you of what that shot represents. We have provided you with corroborating evidence. We have also demonstrated in flight test that there is nothing wrong with the aircraft itself. You are undeniably in possession of the facts, Ms. Malone. If *Newsline* does not report these facts, which you are now aware of, and if it makes any suggestion whatsoever that there is anything wrong with the N-22 aircraft based on this incident, we will sue you for reckless disregard and malicious intent. Ed Fuller is very conservative, but he thinks we will certainly win. Now, would you like Mr. Fuller to call Mr. Shenk and explain the situation, or would you prefer to do it yourself?"

"Where's a phone?" Malone asked.

10:05 a.m. Dick Shenk swore. "I got a hole in the show the size of Afghanistan and you're telling me you've got a *bad parts* story? Is that what you're telling me, Jennifer? Because I'm not going to run with that. I'll get murdered."

"Dick, it doesn't really play that way. It's a family tragedy—the guy loves his son; the son didn't know what he was doing—"

"But I can't *use* it. He's Chinese. I can't *go near* it."

"The kid killed four people and injured fifty-six—"

"What difference does that make? I'm very disappointed in you, Jennifer," he said. "Very disappointed."

"I didn't cause the accident," she said. "I'm reporting the story."

"You're reporting your ineptitude," Shenk said. "You messed up, Jennifer. You had a hot story, a story I wanted, about a lousy American product, and two days later you come back with some nonsense about a whack. And maintenance. And *bad parts.*"

"Dick—"

"I warned you, I didn't want bad parts." And he hung up.

GLENDALE

11:00 p.m. *Newsline*'s closing credits were running when Casey's phone rang. An unfamiliar, gruff voice said, "Casey, Hal Edgarton here. I'm in Hong Kong, and I've just been told that *Newsline* did not run a Norton story tonight."

"That's right, sir."

"I'm very pleased. Whatever you did, it was obviously effective," Edgarton said. "I'm leaving for Beijing in a few hours to sign the sales agreement. John Marder was supposed to meet me there, but I'm told that, for some reason, he hasn't left California."

"I don't know anything about that," she said.

"We'll be making some changes at Norton in the next few days. Meanwhile, I wanted to congratulate you, Casey. You've been under a lot of pressure. You've done an outstanding job."

"Thank you, sir."

"My secretary will call to arrange lunch when I get back," he said. "Keep up the good work."

Edgarton hung up, and then there were other calls. From Mike Lee, congratulating her, then from Doherty and Burne and Ron Smith. And Norma, who said, "Honey, I'm proud of you."

Finally she took her phone off the hook and went to bed.

SUNDAY

GLENDALE

5:45 p.m. It was a clear evening. Casey was standing outside her bungalow when she saw headlights in the darkening night swing around the corner and come up the street toward her. She walked to the curb as a car came to a stop. The door flew open.

"Mom!" Her daughter jumped into her arms, wrapping her legs around her. "Oh, Mom, I *missed* you!"

"Me, too, honey," she said. "Me, too."

Jim got out of the car, handed Casey the backpack. In the near darkness she couldn't really see his face. "Good night," he said to her.

"Good night, Jim," she said.

Her daughter took her hand. They started back inside. It was growing dark, and the air was cool. When Casey looked up, she saw the straight contrail of a passenger jet. It was so high, it was still in daylight, a thin white streak across the darkening sky.

Copyright Telegraph-Star, Inc.

NORTON SELLS 50 WIDE-BODY JETS TO CHINA

TAILS TO BE MANUFACTURED IN SHANGHAI

UNION LEADERS CRITICIZE LOSS OF JOBS

By: Jack Rogers

Norton Aircraft today announced an eight-billion-dollar sale of fifty N-22 wide-body jets to the People's Republic of China. Norton president Harold Edgarton said the agreement signed yesterday in Beijing calls for delivery of the jets over the next four years. The agreement also "offsets" fabrication work to China, requiring the N-22 tails to be constructed in Shanghai.

The sale represents a coup for the beleaguered Burbank manufacturer and a bitter defeat for Airbus, which had lobbied heavily, both in Beijing and Washington, for the sale.

News of the offset agreement produced anger in some quarters. UAW Local 1214 president Don Brull criticized the offset agreement, noting, "We're losing thousands of jobs every year. Norton is exporting the jobs of American workers in order to make foreign sales. I don't think that's good for our future."

When asked about the alleged job loss, Edgarton stated that "offsets are a fact of life in our industry and have been for many years. The fact is, if we don't make the agreement, Boeing or Airbus will."

Edgarton also noted that China had signed an option for thirty additional jets. The Shanghai factory will begin its work in January of next year.

News of the sale ends industry speculation that much publicized recent incidents involving the N-22 might terminate the Chinese purchase. Edgarton noted, "The N-22 is a proven aircraft with an excellent safety record. I think the Chinese sale is a tribute to that record."

DOCUMENT ID: C\LEX 40\DL\NORTON

AIRBUS CONSIDERS KOREAN PARTNERSHIP

Songking Industries, the industrial conglomerate based in Seoul, has announced they are negotiating with Airbus Industrie of Toulouse to manufacture major subassembly components of the new A-340B stretch derivative. Recent speculation has centered on Songking's efforts to establish an aerospace presence in world markets, now that long-rumored secret negotiations with Norton Aircraft in Burbank have apparently broken down.

The JAA today accepted certification of the Norton N-22 wide-body commercial aircraft. A JAA spokesman said there was "no substance" to rumors that certification had been delayed for political reasons.

MARDER TAKES CONSULTING POST

In a surprise move, John Marder, 46, has left Norton Aircraft to head The Aviation Institute, an aerospace consulting firm with close ties to European carriers. Marder assumes his new position effective immediately.

RICHMAN ARRESTED IN SINGAPORE

A youthful member of the Norton clan was arrested today by police in Singapore on charges of narcotics possession. Bob Richman, 28, is being held by authorities awaiting arraignment. If convicted under the nation's draconian drug laws, he faces the death penalty.

SINGLETON HEADS DIVISION

Harold Edgarton today named Katherine C. Singleton as the new head of Norton Aircraft's media relations division. Singleton was formerly a vice president for quality assurance at Norton, which is headquartered in Burbank.

MALONE TO JOIN *HARD COPY* STAFF

Veteran news producer Jennifer Malone, 29, ends four years with *Newsline* to join the staff of *Hard Copy*, it was announced today. Malone's departure was described as resulting from a contract dispute. Malone said, "*Hard Copy* is what's happening now, and I am just thrilled to be part of it."

Es

Diane Chamberlain

The
cape
ARTIST

She thought she was home free.

Afraid of losing her child, Susanna Miller created a whole new life for herself: new name, new looks, new identity.

But then she stumbled on a dangerous secret. And now everything she's fought for could be destroyed—including the child she loves.

Home free? Not yet. . . .

Chapter 1

THE cloud was back.

Not in the sky. The evening sky over Boulder was a vivid violet-blue, broken only by a jagged line of gold as the sun fell behind the Rockies. Yet, as Susanna made her way through the cemetery, Tyler in her arms, she felt the cloud over her shoulder, keeping pace with her.

She had endured the cloud's dark shadow eleven months earlier, when Tyler was born with a damaged heart. It had pained her own heart, seeing her son suffer, knowing she might lose him. She'd spent day after day in the intensive care nursery, touching his tiny hands through the restricting holes in his plastic bassinet. Talking to him. Singing to him. He was stoic, her little baby. She saw the determination in his face. He was not a quitter. He had not inherited her propensity for giving up. She hoped she'd learned from his bravery.

Tyler's heart was healthy now. "Nearly good as new," the surgeon had said. It was the best heart she could imagine. Her son had a gentle, affectionate nature and a laugh that, until recently, had always brought tears to her eyes. With all he'd been through, the fact that he could laugh with such abandon renewed her faith.

And Tyler had learned patience. Even while being carried around the cemetery for the past hour, he had not once protested the seemingly fruitless journey. He hung on to her with one arm around her neck, clutching his stuffed monkey as Susanna moved among the headstones, stopping to read each one. Not names; she didn't care about names. But every date on the smaller headstones merited her scrutiny. The sort of stone the parents of an infant might select.

Tyler finally made a sound of impatience, a whimper. With a sigh she leaned over to set him down in the grass, and he crawled to the nearest headstone and hoisted himself up by it, dancing up and down. She stood up and stretched. As the warm breeze wrapped her long skirt around her legs, she looked toward the foothills above Chatauqua Park. She could see Linc's house from here, and she felt tears fill her eyes. She wished she could tell him her plan. But that wouldn't be fair to Linc. Not that the plan itself was fair.

She was going to keep her child, but in the process she would lose the man who had been her strength and support for the past two years. For far longer than that, to be honest. How would she get by without him? She was not the sort of person who did things entirely on her own. She'd never possessed that sort of courage. But she would have to find it now. If she did indeed lose custody of Tyler to Jim and Peggy, she would have to put her plan in action and, in doing so, never see Linc Sebastian again.

It was so dark by the time she found the small, cold marker that she could barely read the words carved into the stone. "August 16, 1968–September 14, 1968." Perfect. She read the name. "Kimberly Stratton." Susanna sank to her knees to copy the information onto a notepad. She started to her feet again, but something held her down. Why did this baby die? Less than a month old. She thought of Tyler as a newborn, wounded and fighting. How had that mother felt? And who was Susanna to take this baby's name? This baby's life? She felt suddenly weighed down with responsibility. "I'll try to do right by you," she said. "I'll try to be worthy of your name."

She gathered Tyler and his monkey into her arms and stood up slowly. His downy blond hair brushed lightly against her chin. The cloud settled around her shoulders again, but she ignored it. She had escaped that cloud once before. She would escape from it again.

"ALL RISE."

Susanna got to her feet as Judge Browning entered the courtroom and took his seat behind the bench. When she sat down again, she was barely breathing. The judge looked like Santa Claus, his full beard snowy beneath his ruddy cheeks, but he had shown no inclination toward jolliness these past few days.

He shuffled the papers on his desk, seemingly unaware of the tension in the room as everyone awaited his decision. When he glanced up, Susanna saw the courtroom through his eyes, and if she hadn't already guessed his decision, she did then. For a week now, he'd looked out from his bench at the cast of characters in front of him. At the table on his left sat a small wiry-haired female attorney, Ann Prescott, and Susanna, her anxious, pale, overworked, poorly paid, divorced client. The client who had spent the month after the breakup of her marriage in a psychiatric ward, threatening to kill herself—and her unborn baby. Ann had brought in the psychiatrist from the hospital to testify that Susanna was well now, that she was a good mother. But that ploy had backfired, only serving to remind everyone of Susanna's stint as a psychiatric patient.

At the table on Judge Browning's right sat a dapper silver-haired attorney and his client, James Miller, an attorney himself and Susanna's ex-husband. Handsome, sharply dressed without overdoing it, sincerity in his blue eyes.

Seated directly behind Jim was his new wife. Not any wife, but Peggy Myerson, another attorney. She was also beautifully dressed. Her smooth dark hair swept her shoulders as she smiled confidently at her husband, as if they'd known they would win from the start.

Susanna could not look at Peggy for long. She always felt small and simple around her. Peggy was a woman with whom she could never hope to compete.

And what else did the judge see in this courtroom? Behind Jim and his lawyer and Peggy, Judge Browning would see Peggy's older brother, Ron, the surgeon who had saved Tyler's life, and Peggy's parents and Jim's sister and mother, all waiting anxiously to hear the fate of the little boy they already thought of as theirs.

The judge would see only one person seated behind Susanna, Linc Sebastian, a man known to the community as a convicted murderer turned disc jockey. Linc was the host of a weekly, nationally syndicated radio program, and he was something of a cult figure, one of Boulder's folk heroes. He'd taken out his earring for this week in court, but his blond hair still brushed his collar, and one look at him told you he had chosen a lifestyle outside the norm. "A man with a questionable past," Jim's lawyer had said in describing him. No one could argue with that.

Judge Browning cleared his throat, and Susanna wrapped her arms across her chest to wait out the inevitable. The judge lifted a single sheet of paper from his desk as though he might read from it, but instead, his Santa Claus eyes moved from person to person in the courtroom as he began to speak. "This court awards custody of Tyler James Miller to his father, James Miller," he said simply.

Susanna heard Peggy's squeal of joy and Jim's laughter. She tightened her grip on her arms. She heard someone on the other side of the room whisper "Congratulations" to Jim.

"Susanna Miller will be allowed visitation every other weekend and one night each week," the judge continued. "And she is forbidden to have any member of the opposite sex spend the night during those times she has visitation with her son."

Her cheeks burned, as if the judge had slapped her. In those horrible moments when she'd imagined this scene, she'd sobbed, but there were no tears now, only a numbness, a disbelief. They were going to take her baby away from her.

"They simply had too much in their favor, Susanna. I'm sorry," Ann said. "Let me go see what the plans are." Susanna could not even acknowledge her as Ann left the table.

"Sue?" Susanna turned to find Linc standing next to her. She stood up, and Linc drew her into an embrace. It was a quick hug, nothing more than that, as if he did not want to make a public display of the fact that he was that close to her. She knew he thought of himself as a major factor in her losing custody of Tyler, but she doubted her relationship with him had made that much difference. As Ann said, Jim and Peggy had too much in their favor.

They had the combined income of two attorneys, which was far more than she could ever hope to achieve as a secretary in a bank. They lived in a big, elegant house in a beautiful neighborhood called Wonderland. Never mind that Susanna had selected that house. Never mind that the week after she and Jim had moved into it, she'd come home early from a conference to find Jim sharing their bed with Peggy. So Susanna was in the little rental apartment, while Jim and Peggy sprawled out in "their" five-bedroom house with an elaborate swing set in the backyard for "their" son.

It had been her word against Jim's regarding the abortion, and Jim had scoffed at her accusation from his seat on the witness stand. "I'm pro-life," Jim had said, his blue eyes flashing in self-righteous fervor. "I would never suggest that any woman have an abortion, let alone a woman carrying my own child."

She'd been too ashamed to admit to any of her friends, other than Linc, that Jim had wanted her to get an abortion. But Linc did not testify. Ann thought it would "invite too many questions." So Jim's only challenger was Susanna herself, and no one seemed to pay much attention to anything she had to say.

Ann returned. "They said you can keep him tonight. They'll pick him up tomorrow around two. Is that okay?"

Susanna looked helplessly at her attorney. "What choice do I have?" she asked.

Ann shook her head. "None, Susanna. I'm sorry."

"Come on." Linc tugged at her shoulder. "Let's get Tyler and enjoy tonight with him," he said.

Susanna was dimly aware of the festive atmosphere on the other side of the courtroom as she left with Linc, and she turned her head away. She didn't want to see their joy.

Linc held her hand in the car, letting go of her only to turn the steering wheel. She sensed him looking at her from time to time, but kept her own eyes on the road. The silence between them felt alien.

"Would you mind very much getting him?" Susanna asked as they parked in front of Tyler's day-care center. She couldn't bear

Margaret Draper's questions today. Margaret would be outraged to hear Susanna was losing Tyler, and Susanna had enough rage of her own to deal with.

"Sure." Linc got out of the car, and she watched him walk up the sidewalk and into Tyler's day-care center. He had on gray pants, a pin-striped shirt, a tie, too. Every day this week. He'd tried hard, but he only looked as if he'd accidentally put on another man's clothes. His effort touched her, though. It made her love him even more, and that only made what she had to do harder.

After a minute Linc emerged, Tyler in his arms, and the legs of the little boy's stuffed monkey flopped up and down in rhythm with Linc's stride. Susanna got out of the car, hungry to get her son into her own arms. She then settled into the passenger seat with Tyler and his monkey on her lap. He curled against her contentedly, and the warmth of him against her body thawed the tears that had been frozen inside her. They spilled over her cheeks.

Linc got in behind the steering wheel and saw that she was crying. "Oh, Sue." He leaned over to hold her. "It's not fair."

She couldn't speak. If she spoke, she would say too much.

Linc pulled back from her and brushed his hand over her wet cheek. "I want to stay over tonight," he said, "but I guess that's against the rules."

She tried to pull herself together again. The judge had unwittingly made this easier for her. She hadn't been sure how she would keep Linc away tonight. "I know," she said. "I wish you could, but I think I need to be alone with Tyler tonight."

Linc looked at her in surprise. It was not like her to cut him out. She usually despised being alone, but that was going to have to change. It was true that Susanna Miller would never cut herself off from the company of others, but tonight Susanna Miller would die.

"Susanna," Linc said, "I love Tyler. I'd like the chance to be with him tonight. With both of you."

He'd been there from the moment Tyler drew his first, labored breath. He'd been with her through the entire pregnancy. She'd leaned on him for everything. That she would cut him out of her grieving tonight would make no sense to him. She thought of letting him come over for a few hours, but that would be impossible. She had too much to do tonight. "I'm sorry, Linc. I'm not feeling well. I'm going to give Tyler his dinner, tuck him in, tell him a story. And then crawl into bed. Please don't make this harder on me."

He sat back, defeated. "All right." He started the car, and neither of them spoke as they drove to her apartment. She knew he was hurt, but she would have to hurt him now to spare him later.

At the apartment, Linc changed Tyler's diaper while Susanna checked her answering machine. There were a few messages from her co-workers at the bank, anxious to know the judge's decision. She would not be returning those calls.

When she came into the living room, Linc was setting Tyler down on the floor next to a salad bowl filled with plastic blocks. He kissed the top of Tyler's head, then walked with Susanna to the front door, where he stopped and rested his hand on her shoulder. "Are you regretting . . ." Linc hesitated. "I mean, maybe we shouldn't have continued seeing each other when the custody thing came up."

"I couldn't have gotten through this without you," she said. "I don't regret us being together at all."

He leaned over to kiss her good-bye, and the reality of what she was about to do washed over her. She closed her arms around him, holding on to him. This was the last time she would see him. "You've been my best friend for so long," she whispered.

"And I always will be."

"No matter what?"

"No matter what."

She was as close as she'd come to telling him about her decision. She had to get him out the door before the words spilled from her mouth. "You've got to go," she said. "I love you."

He looked alarmed. "You don't sound like yourself, Susanna."

She read his thoughts, saw the worry in his eyes. He thought she might do something really crazy. Kill both herself and Tyler. She nearly smiled at his misperception. She was over that now. That sort of depression could not get its grip on her again.

"I'm all right," she said.

"Do you want me to be with you tomorrow?"

She shook her head. "I think I'd better do it alone. Besides, tomorrow's Wednesday. You have to tape your show." She leaned forward to kiss him. "I love you, Linc," she said.

"I love you, too. I'm going to call you later, all right?"

"All right." She wished he wouldn't, but she couldn't possibly tell him not to.

She shut the door quickly behind him and immediately went into action. She fed Tyler and got him into bed, read him a story. Then she positioned herself in front of the bathroom mirror, scissors in hand. She had worn her blond hair long all her life. She'd loved the way people stared at her hair, the way they wanted to touch it. She knew it made her look far younger than twenty-nine.

Her hand shook as she raised the scissors. Not yet. She'd do everything else first. But she got the bottle of dye she'd been saving for weeks from her bathroom cabinet. Copper Glow, the color was called. Susanna read and reread the directions. She'd never dyed her hair before. She was a true blonde, a pale blonde. Her features belonged with blond hair. Nearly invisible eyebrows and eyelashes. Delicate white skin. Pale blue eyes that Tyler had inherited. She looked in the mirror and tried to imagine her face with darker hair. It wasn't going to work. No one with auburn hair would have such pale eyebrows. It said right on the package not to use the dye on eyebrows, but she was already breaking more laws than she could count. She would break that one as well.

She walked into her bedroom and pulled out a thick envelope from under the mattress. It held the copy of Kimberly Stratton's birth certificate she'd sent for and eight thousand dollars she'd withdrawn from her savings account, as well as the copies of Tyler's medical records she'd requested. She divided up the money between her purse, her duffel bag, and Tyler's diaper bag.

She made several peanut butter and jelly sandwiches for herself and packed some bananas, baby oatmeal, formula, crackers, and juice boxes for Tyler. She put their clothing in the duffel bag.

She had done everything but cut and dye her hair by the time Linc called at eleven thirty. She was feeling wired and restless, but she tried instead to sound tired on the phone, yawning loudly, muffling her voice. She hated this dishonesty with the person who knew her better than anyone else.

"Are you getting depressed again?" Linc asked.

"No. Really, I'm fine. Just wiped out from this whole fiasco." She looked at herself in her dresser mirror, trying to imagine how she would look with her new identity. She would be a different person in the morning. A stronger person. More independent. Gutsy and self-reliant. She would have to be.

Linc was talking quietly, completely unsuspecting, and suddenly she could stand it no longer. "Linc? Is it too late to request a certain song for your show Sunday night?"

"No. What would you like to hear?"

" 'Suzanne.' " It was one of her favorite songs, and Linc often sang it to her.

"I should have guessed," Linc said.

"Please make a note to do it."

"I won't forget."

"I'm serious, Linc. Write it down. Do you have a pen?"

"Uh, hang on. Yeah, I've got one."

"Write down, 'Susanna wants to hear me play "Suzanne" for her on Sunday night.' "

She heard him sigh. "I never knew you were so demanding."

"Now tape it to your bathroom mirror."

Linc laughed. "What's with you, Suze?"

"Nothing. Just promise me you'll tape it to the mirror in your bathroom before you go to bed tonight, okay?"

"If you say so."

She drew the conversation to a quick close, afraid she might be tempted to give him even grander hints. Then she returned to the bathroom. She raised the scissors to her hair. And with the first cut she knew there was no turning back. She was going to kill Susanna Miller. She was bringing Kimberly Stratton back to life.

LINC MADE HIMSELF A CUP OF coffee and sat in front of the wall of windows in his living room, looking out at the lights spread over Boulder like a blanket of glitter. He could see nearly all the way to Susanna's apartment. He took a swallow of coffee. Why didn't she want him around tonight? It seemed crazy. She hated being alone. Okay, so tonight was different from any other night. Tonight was her last night as custodial parent of her son. But until now Susanna had treated him as though he were Tyler's father, and he'd slipped happily into that role. But apparently, she did not think of him that way at all. Maybe she blamed him for the custody verdict.

He'd talked with her lawyer about how much his involvement with Susanna might figure in whether or not she retained custody. Not much, Ann had assured him. That struck him as an understatement. Having a relationship with a man who'd served four years in prison for murder hardly helped her case.

Linc got up, stepping over Sam, the big black dog that was asleep at his feet, and walked into the kitchen. He poured himself a second cup of coffee and carried it to his studio. As he pulled out the Leonard Cohen CD with "Suzanne" on it to record for his show the following day, his eye fell on the framed photograph standing on the table next to the mixing board. It had been a gift from Susanna for his last birthday, an enlargement of a picture of the two of them as children. Susanna was sitting on the swing in his backyard, and Linc was standing behind her. She was six, a slender child with long white braids. Linc, at twelve, looked like he might be the older brother of the girl. Her protector. He had fancied himself that back then, although he had never quite known how to go about protecting her. He only knew that she needed it.

Linc and his mother had moved next door to the Wood family a few months before that picture had been taken, shortly after his father's sudden death from a stroke. Soon after they'd moved in, Linc's mother was in the kitchen when he caught her staring out the window at a small blond waif playing hopscotch by herself in the driveway next door.

"That little one looks like she'll break in two if you breathe on her," his mother said, and for weeks Linc couldn't look at Susanna without picturing the seedball of a dandelion, delicate and fragile.

Sometimes if Susanna's parents were going out, they'd ask Linc to baby-sit her. That was how he came to know what life was like in the Wood household. Susanna's father was mean. Downright cruel.

"You behave while we're out," he'd say to Susanna, "or you know what'll happen, don't you?" She'd nod, and her father would come back with "Say it. What will happen?" And he'd grip her by the arm until she answered, in a voice as pale as her hair, "I'll get the belt."

Susanna had liked Linc to read to her when he baby-sat, although she had very few books of her own. She liked to draw as well, and he thought she was pretty creative. Once, she drew a picture of a lion, and he suggested they hang it on her refrigerator, but she said her parents wouldn't allow it.

Linc had seen Susanna's bruises, and her mother's as well. The smell of booze in the Woods' house seemed inescapable. And sometimes in the summer, when everyone had their windows open, he and his mother could hear the battle being waged next door. His mother called the police a few times, but Susanna's father always managed to get out of whatever charge was leveled against him, and Mrs. Wood would never stick up for Susanna. That tore Linc's mother apart. She started inviting Susanna to their house after school. She'd buy the girl books and let her hang her pictures on their kitchen walls. Susanna was a different child at his house. He liked thinking that his home had become her haven. So he grew up with a special feeling for his neighbor, a bit fatherly, a bit brotherly.

When Linc formed a band during high school, Susanna would sit on the mildewy sofa in his garage and listen to them practice. She might do her homework, or sketch the guys or the instruments or whatever caught her eye. She grew into an excellent artist. Whenever her school needed a poster designed, it was Susanna they called on. She won a couple of contests, and she was planning to enter a statewide competition when her father was killed. She dropped out of school then, and her interest in art died with her father.

Back then, the age difference had been so great that it never occurred to Linc to think of Susanna as a potential girlfriend. He hadn't even realized how startlingly beautiful she was until a new guy joined the band and was unable to take his eyes off the leggy, long-haired blonde idly sketching in the corner. Linc began thinking about her differently after that. Then prison happened to him. And Jim happened to her.

That little one looks like she'll break in two if you breathe on her. Linc still thought that was an accurate description of Susanna. Yet she'd been strong enough to say no to Jim when he wanted her to have an abortion. Strong enough to give birth and to stay by Tyler's side through those horrific medical treatments. Yet he worried about how easily Susanna could be broken in two.

It wasn't fair. Susanna was determined to give Tyler the sort of safe, happy home she had never enjoyed. She was a good mother. The best. Now she'd been told she wasn't good enough.

Sam appeared in the studio and walked over to rest his head on Linc's knee. "You're right, fella." Linc stood up. "It's time for bed."

In his bedroom, he saw the note she'd had him write earlier. He saw no point in taping it to his bathroom mirror, now that he'd already added the record to his list, but she had been so insistent. So he walked into the bathroom to tape her words to the mirror.

Chapter 2

IT WAS still dark when Susanna got Tyler dressed in the morning. The first bus didn't leave for Denver until five fifty. She hadn't slept all night, but she'd forced herself to lie in bed anyway, planning her morning over and over in her head. Now, as she changed Tyler from his pajamas to his overalls, tied his shoes, and poured juice into his bottle, she knew the routine as if she'd done it ten times already.

She slowed down only long enough to groan at her image in the mirror. She looked like an auburn-haired, pale-eyed scarecrow. She'd cut her hair to chin length and given herself bangs. She would never find a job as a hairstylist, that much was certain. She'd put the lopped-off hair and the empty dye bottle into a garbage bag to take with her. She didn't want to leave any clues behind.

She glanced at Tyler's crib. It would have to be replaced, along with the high chair and the car seat and— *Don't think about it.* She couldn't afford to get overwhelmed right now.

She gathered the duffel bag, the diaper bag, her purse, and her son. In the foyer downstairs, she set up the stroller and lowered Tyler into it. Then she opened the foyer door and walked outside.

At the bus stop, there were five other people—four men and a woman—all of them dressed for work. She should have thought of that. She stood out in her jeans and denim jacket, pushing a baby. She wished she were invisible. The first leg of her trip would be entirely too traceable. But what choice did she have?

The bus arrived, and she lifted her sleeping son into her arms, collapsing the stroller. She climbed up the steps with her cargo.

"Going to Denver?" the driver asked.

"That's right." She smiled at him with such confidence that she was surprised to see her hand shake when she handed him the fare. She walked toward the rear of the bus. The fewer boarding passengers who walked past her, the better. But her fellow travelers seemed uninterested in her, and for that she was grateful. The baby seemed content to sleep in her arms.

She was doing the right thing. From the moment she'd thought of leaving, she hadn't wavered in her decision. The next few days would be rough, filled with uncertainty, but she and Tyler would be together and they'd be okay. The only thing that could derail her determination would be thoughts of Linc, and she made a conscious effort to keep them at bay.

She didn't get off the bus until it reached its last stop—the terminal in Denver. Her plan was to take the first bus heading out of town, no matter where it was going, as long as it was far away, someplace where no one would think of looking for her. For ninety-eight dollars she bought a ticket on an eight-ten bus headed for St. Louis, Missouri. Missouri might have been on another planet, for all she knew, and that made it appealing. But the bus would arrive at four fifty the following morning. She and Tyler would be dumped in a strange city practically in the middle of the night.

She settled onto one of the plastic seats to wait for her bus and sorted through her wallet, removing anything with the name "Susanna Miller" on it. She threw her driver's license, checks, and credit card into the garbage bag she'd brought. She didn't allow herself to look at the picture of Linc before dropping it in. She carried the garbage bag over to the nearest trash can and pushed it through the swinging door in the lid, then returned to her seat.

A woman sat a few seats away from her, knitting. She caught Susanna's eye and smiled. "He's precious," she said, nodding at Tyler. "What's his name?"

"Cody," she answered quickly. That had been Linc's suggestion for the baby's name. She'd selected Tyler in the eleventh hour.

The bus to St. Louis was finally ready for boarding, and Susanna was relieved that she and Tyler would have two seats to themselves. She closed her eyes, but as she started to doze, she was jerked awake by a dream: Two policemen were stomping down the length of the bus to wrest her son from her arms.

Susanna shook her head to wake herself completely and hugged Tyler tight. No one was even looking for her, she told herself. At least not yet. But if the police did board the bus, what exactly could she do? What could she say?

I'm Kimberly Stratton, she practiced. *This is my little boy, Cody. He's eleven months.* Hard to fudge on that one. Anyone who knew kids would be able to guess Tyler's age.

"Tyler," she whispered, "what are we doing?"

When Tyler finally woke up, he was filled with his usual morning energy. She wondered how she would ever be able to contain him on this long trip. She gave him his bottle, then fed him a banana. When he'd had his fill, he climbed up to his feet to peer at the woman sitting behind them, who played peekaboo with him. After a while Susanna made Tyler sit down. She used to enjoy the attention strangers paid to her son, but now it felt threatening.

Tyler was not happy. "Mamamama," he said.

She reached into the diaper bag for his monkey. Would Jim know the difference between the "mamamama" that meant "mama" and the "mamamama" that meant "monkey"? Would Peggy? She doubted it. Peggy would probably think he was calling her mama. *Sorry, Peg. He's mine, not yours.* She smoothed her hand over his blond hair. He settled against her, his monkey curled in one of his arms, his thumb locked into his mouth. Susanna closed her eyes and breathed in his warm scent. She couldn't get enough of it.

Before she could stop herself, she pictured Linc waking up that morning. By now he'd probably tried to call her. Would he panic when he got no answer, thinking she was lying there, dead from an overdose or— *Cut the drama.*

The escape artist, he'd called her, because she always tried to escape from any difficult situation instead of facing it head-on. Well, she'd outdone herself this time.

Tyler whimpered at her side. She knew he was yearning to get up and climb all over her, all over the seats of the bus.

"I'm sorry, Ty— Cody." She hugged him close. "We'll have a few rough days, honey," she whispered. "Then we can settle down in our new life."

That new life had to start now, she thought. She was Kim Stratton. And she would never call her son Tyler again.

"PEGGY in Wonderland!"

Peggy stood back from the door to let Nancy Curry into the house. "That's me," she said. She did feel a little as though she lived in a fairy tale these days.

"What a great house!" Nancy gave her a hug, then leaned back to study her. "You look terrific," she said.

"And you look like California agreed with you." She hadn't seen

Nancy in a couple of years. They had been best friends at one time, but Nancy had moved to Santa Barbara right before Peggy started seeing Jim. Peggy had been thrilled to hear that her old friend was returning to Boulder, where Nancy and her husband would both be teaching at one of the middle schools.

"This is for you." Nancy handed a wrapped gift to Peggy.

"Thanks." Peggy took the package and ushered Nancy into the living room.

"Wow, what a view!" Nancy said, looking out at the mountains. Then she turned around to face Peggy, warmth in her eyes. "Oh, Peg," she said, "you deserve this."

"Thanks," she said again. "Somebody's definitely been smiling down on me these last few years, that's for sure." She looked at her watch. Another couple of hours until Tyler arrived, and her stomach was tied in knots. "Do you have time for a cup of coffee?"

"Sure, but do *you?* What time do you get the baby?"

"Jim's picking him up at two. I've done everything I can to get ready," she said. "Now I just have to sit around here and be nervous. It would help if you'd sit with me."

She showed Nancy the pale yellow nursery while the coffee was brewing. "We already had the crib and some toys, since we've had Tyler here every once in a while. He's really a good baby." Peggy felt herself tearing up. "He's been through so much, and he's a little trouper, you know?" She handed Nancy a picture of Tyler from the white-enameled dresser. "He's about eight months there," she said.

"Oh, he's adorable." Nancy grinned at the picture, then pulled a teddy bear out of the crib. "This is one lucky little kid."

Peggy stroked the stuffed bear. "He was in terrible shape when he was born. Part of his aorta—the part closest to the heart—was too narrow." She had not seen Tyler then, but she'd heard about his condition from her brother. "For a while they didn't think he'd make it. He needed to have the narrow section of his aorta removed and a synthetic graft inserted. Ron did the surgery." That her brother had saved Tyler's life seemed like a good omen.

"Does he need any more treatment?"

"Just checkups. Yearly echocardiograms to make sure everything's working all right. But he should be fine."

They walked to the kitchen, and Peggy poured them coffee. Sitting at the table, she opened Nancy's gift, a small silver-topped photograph album.

"Perfect!" she said, leaning over to give Nancy a kiss on the cheek. "Come back in a week and it will be full."

"I plan to." Nancy blew on her coffee. "I want to meet this husband of yours. I've heard he's handsome as sin."

Peggy laughed. "I'd have to agree. He's good-looking, intelligent, and a great lawyer," she said.

Peggy was her husband's best admirer. Jim had grown up in a family of six children raised on a factory worker's salary. He was one hundred percent self-made and proud of it. "Jim was at the top of our law school class." She added with a smile, "Or maybe second. I'm not sure which of us ended up in first place." She rested the photograph album on the table. "My parents love him," she said, wishing she could add that her brother liked Jim as much as her parents did, but Ron had not yet warmed up to her new husband. She worried that Ron might think Jim's less than affluent background had attracted him to a woman who'd never wanted for anything. There'd been wealth in her family for generations, although her parents were philanthropists, firm believers in sharing with those who had less. That's why she'd elected to work for Legal Aid instead of some posh law firm. And that's why Ron occasionally treated babies whose families could not ordinarily afford the best.

She suddenly broke into a grin. "Can you believe I'm going to get to be a mother, after all?" Three years earlier Phil Rudy had broken off his engagement to Peggy after she had a hysterectomy. Phil had wanted a woman who could give him children. Jim, on the other hand, didn't seem to care.

"Did Jim's ex-wife lose custody because she was unfit?" Nancy asked gingerly.

"Well, I would never say Susanna was unfit, exactly, but there are definite problems. She's single, with zero family support. She works at Rocky Mountain National Bank, so he's in day care all day."

"My sister, Julie, is a teller in the North Street branch."

"She must know Susanna, then, because that's where she works." Peggy studied the reflection of the overhead light in her coffee. "Susanna's made some poor choices in her life, and I feel sorry for her. But that's not a good enough reason to allow her to keep Tyler when we can give him so much more."

"You don't make much money in a bank," Nancy agreed.

"Money's only a small part of it, though," Peggy said quickly. She would never fight a woman for her child based on finances alone. Besides, Susanna was not in bad shape financially. Jim was generous with child support, and he was buying her out of the house. Eventually Susanna would have her share. "Susanna's not terribly stable. After she and Jim split up, she spent a month in a psychiatric ward because she threatened to kill herself. And it's the boyfriend that worries me most. He's Linc Sebastian. Do you know who he is?"

Nancy frowned. "Is he on the radio or something?"

Peggy nodded. "He has a syndicated show called *Songs for the Asking.* Old folk-rock sort of music. But he's an ex-con."

"You're kidding? What was he in for?"

Peggy leaned forward. She couldn't help herself. The story was so lurid that it never failed to get a rise out of an audience. "Murder," she said. "And guess who he murdered?"

Nancy shook her head.

"Susanna's father. It happened when Susanna was sixteen and Linc was twenty-two. He lived next door to Susanna's family, and he was over there one day and her parents were apparently inebriated, which I gather was typical, and a fight broke out. Linc claimed that the father started knocking the mother and Susanna around and that the mother was actually knocked unconscious, and Linc got the father's gun and killed him to stop him from beating them up. The mother, on the other hand, said that what really happened was that Susanna's father suspected Linc of having a sexual relationship with his daughter, and so he started berating him, telling him to get out of the house. That's when Linc shot him."

"Holy cow, Peg."

"The jury was never sure whether Linc killed the father in self-defense or if he was protecting Susanna and the mother. That's why he got such a light sentence. But Jim feels pretty certain that Susanna and Linc have been lovers all along. Even while he and Susanna were married." Peggy shuddered. The whole situation made her skin crawl. "She denied it vehemently, but as soon as she and Jim split up, she moved into Linc's house." Peggy looked at the clock above the stove: twenty-five to two.

She remembered well the hurt look in Jim's eyes when he first told her about his marriage. He'd made a mistake in marrying Susanna, he'd said. He was a bright, ambitious man married to a woman with few aspirations.

"The main reason they broke up was simply that Jim outgrew her," Peggy said. "He was spending his days with all these bright law students and going home to Susanna at night. He and I became good friends, going out to lunch and studying together, and he'd confided in me how unhappy he was. After school we went our separate ways. Then one day we bumped into each other and went to lunch. His marriage was worse than ever. He told me about Linc, that he'd asked Susanna not to see him anymore, but she said he was an important friend. This guy who killed her father, right?"

Nancy made a sound of disgust.

"Then she got pregnant. Jim was really upset."

"I don't blame him," Nancy said. She added quietly, "Are you sure Jim's the father?"

Peggy drew in a long breath. This was something she'd wondered about herself. "Not one hundred percent," she said. "But we've decided it doesn't matter one way or another. Tyler's still ours."

She was skipping something in the telling. She always skipped it because it was the one thing that shamed her—she'd started sleeping with Jim when he was still married. Peggy would never forget the look on Susanna's face when she walked into the bedroom and found them together. She'd heard so many negative things about Susanna that she had not been prepared for her to look so vulnerable, so hurt. She'd been trying to rid her mind of that image ever since.

The phone rang, and she jumped to her feet to answer it. When she got off, she was smiling. "Jim's on his way to pick up Tyler."

Nancy stood up. "Well, I'm not going to stay any longer. Don't want to intrude on your family reunion. Give me a call when you're ready to show off your son, okay?"

"I will," Peggy said. "And thanks again for the album."

She watched Nancy drive off, then sat in a chair in the living room and, although she'd read it four times already, opened the book on one-year-olds. Peggy's eyes darted from the book to her watch to the window to her watch again. At three o'clock she had the ominous feeling that something was wrong.

At four o'clock she saw Jim pull into the driveway, get out of the car, and walk toward the house, his arms empty. She rushed outside. "What happened?" she asked.

"Susanna's not there." Jim looked tired and perplexed. He put his arm around her. "I've been trying to call Linc Sebastian to see if he knows anything," he said as they walked toward the house. "But I got his voice mail. I think he tapes his shows on Wednesday, so he's probably there but not picking up his phone."

He pushed open the front door and headed for the kitchen.

Peggy followed him. "I think we should call the police."

"Let me try Linc again first." Jim dialed the number from memory. "Maybe she misunderstood me. Maybe she thought I said Thursday at two. Or maybe Thursday at ten. Or—"

"You said tomorrow at two. I was standing right there."

They waited for Linc to answer.

"What if he's taken off, too?" Peggy asked. "What if—"

"Sh." Jim held up his hand. "Linc? This is Jim Miller. Do you know where Susanna is?"

Peggy wished she could hear Linc's answer.

"No, she's not," Jim said. "I went over to pick Tyler up at two, and she wasn't there. Her car was, though."

"Ask him if she knew it was today at—"

Jim hushed her again with his hand. "I thought of that," he said into the phone, "but I waited over an hour, and she didn't show up. Could she have the time wrong or something?"

"What is he saying?" Peggy couldn't stand it any longer.

Jim cupped his hand over the receiver. "He says she knew I was going to pick him up today." He removed his hand from the receiver. "What, Linc? . . . I'll be there in twenty minutes."

Jim hung up the phone. "Linc sounds worried himself."

"Oh, God," Peggy said. "If she did anything to Tyler, I'll—"

"Hold on, Peg. No point in borrowing trouble."

"You're going over there?"

"Yes." Jim reached for his car keys on the counter. "He has a key to her apartment, so he'll meet me over there in twenty minutes, and we can make sure nothing's wrong."

"I'm coming, too." She grabbed her sweater, and he didn't object as she followed him out to the car.

Neither of them spoke on the ride to Susanna's apartment complex on the other side of town. When they reached the apartment, they parked on the street. Linc pulled up in his van as they were getting out of the car. He looked more like himself than he had in court. The small loop earring was in his ear again, and he was dressed in jeans and a long-sleeved, dark green jersey.

They followed him through the front door of the complex and up the stairs to a long dark hallway that smelled of mildew. Peggy realized she was holding her breath as she watched Linc unlock the door. He poked his head inside. "Susanna?"

The living room was small but neat and uncluttered, and Peggy felt relief. She realized she'd been expecting to find Susanna and Tyler lying in a pool of blood.

"You two stay here," Linc said. Jim started to protest, but Peggy took her husband's arm and nodded toward the sofa. Linc scared her a little, and she thought they should go along with whatever he said. She sat down on the sofa, but Jim paced back and forth.

"There's got to be a simple explanation for this," Jim said. "I can't believe that Susanna would have the brains or the gumption to defy a court order."

Peggy bit her lip to keep from speaking. For the first time she was wondering if Jim had ever really known his ex-wife.

IN THE master bedroom, there was nothing out of order. The bathroom, too, looked clean and orderly, and Linc felt a relief he did not want to give a name to. He hadn't really expected Susanna to harm herself. She was not the same person she'd been when Jim left her. But where was she, then?

Tyler's room was on the other side of the hall, and the first thing that greeted Linc was the large, colorful mural of Noah's Ark she'd painted on the wall across from the crib. He stood in the middle of the small room and turned slowly in a circle. Nothing missing or out of the ordinary, as far as he could see. Except . . . He frowned at the bare changing table. Susanna usually put Tyler's diaper bag there. That didn't mean much, he told himself. He checked the crib. Tyler's monkey was gone, too, but that made sense. Wherever Tyler was, he'd have his monkey with him. It would have been more ominous to find the monkey alone in the crib.

Back in Susanna's bedroom, he checked her closet, where she kept her old duffel bag. It was not there.

Susanna, he thought, incredulous. You didn't.

"Linc?" Peggy called. "Have you found anything?"

"No," he called back. Walking past the bathroom again, he noticed a small reddish brown smear on the countertop. Blood? He stared at it. Hair dye. He knew that's what it was. He took a few sheets of toilet paper, wet them, wiped the stain away, and slipped the paper into his pocket. Starting right then, he began looking not so much for clues to her disappearance as for clues she might have left behind that someone else might find. There was a pain in his heart, but it was born of understanding. He went back to the living room, keeping his face expressionless.

"There's no sign of her," he said. "I don't see Tyler's diaper bag or his monkey, but otherwise everything seems to be in place."

"I told you we should have gotten him last night," Jim said to his wife.

"You were right," Peggy said. "I just thought she should have one last night with him. I never thought she'd—"

"Is she at your place?" Jim looked at Linc with hatred.

"Sure," he said. "She's at my place, and I'm snooping around here for my health."

Jim scowled at him. "I want to look around myself, and then I'm getting the police on the phone," he said. He walked out of the room, calling over his shoulder, "And you don't go anywhere."

Linc could barely tolerate Jim's pomposity. But he managed to swallow his annoyance as he sat down next to Peggy. He was still stunned by the realization that Susanna had taken off without telling him. He hadn't thought she was that gutsy.

"When was the last time you talked to her?" Jim asked Linc as he walked back into the room.

"I spoke to her last night."

"What did the police say?" Peggy said to Jim.

"They're sending someone over here." Jim turned to Linc again. "Did she say anything about going away?"

"Not a word."

Jim raised his eyebrows, as if he didn't believe him. "No hint?" he asked. "Nothing? What sort of mood was she in?"

"Oh, she was in a great mood. She couldn't wait to give her baby away."

"Cut the sarcasm, all right?" Jim said. "You'd better get used to answering questions, because I have the feeling you're going to be getting plenty of them."

"She was down," Linc said. "Quiet. Exactly what you'd expect from a mother who has to give up the child she loves."

"Linc," Peggy pleaded, "the judge made the right decision. I'm sorry you don't see it that way, but it was the only sane decision anyone could possibly make."

"Spare me." Linc stood up and walked to the window. He saw a police car pull up outside, and let out a long sigh. Jim was probably right: He was going to have to face a torrent of questions. He was suddenly glad that Susanna had left him none of the answers.

There was just one officer, which seemed to distress Peggy and Jim. He was middle-aged, gray-haired, well seasoned, and unexcitable, and he doubted that Susanna was really missing.

"In cases like this," he said, standing in the middle of Susanna's living room, "when someone's been gone just a few hours, they usually turn up visiting their sister down the street."

"She has no sister down the street," Jim said in annoyance. "She has no family, period."

Linc tried to play along with the officer's casual demeanor, but he knew better. Susanna had a long history of running away. Even as a child, she'd escape to the little room above his family's garage. He'd find her there, give her a lecture about not running away from her problems, and take her home. This time was different, though. He didn't have a clue where to look for her, and he knew she'd planned it that way.

The police officer told them to contact him again if Susanna remained missing for twenty-four hours. Linc let Jim and Peggy out of the apartment the same time the policeman left, but he remained behind. He looked through the rooms one last time, deciding to take Susanna's photograph albums home with him. If Susanna did indeed remain missing, he didn't want all those pictures of Tyler to end up with Jim.

It wasn't until he was driving home that the hurt and betrayal overwhelmed him.

Why didn't you tell me, Suze? He pounded the steering wheel with his fist. *How could you just walk out like that?*

He felt numb that night as he walked his dog, Sam, down a winding street in his neighborhood, numb as he stared out at Boulder from his living room. But when he went into the bathroom to get ready for bed, he saw the paper taped to his mirror: "Susanna wants to hear me play 'Suzanne' for her Sunday night."

Suddenly he understood her words. His show reached listeners all across the United States every Sunday night. No matter where Susanna was, she would be able to hear him. Reading her words again, he wasn't certain if he should laugh or cry.

Chapter 3

THE bus smelled like the inside of a locker room by the time it reached St. Louis. People were sleeping in their seats, but Kim Stratton was awake. It was not quite five in the morning.

Her body was stiff as she worked her way down the tight aisle of the bus carrying Cody and the diaper bag. Her other belongings were in the belly of the bus, and once on the sidewalk, she waited for them to be unloaded. When she had everything she owned with her, she put Cody in his stroller and moved into the terminal.

She bought a cup of coffee and a stale doughnut for herself and gave some formula to Cody. Then she bought a newspaper, sat down in a corner, and opened it to the used-car ads. She was allotting fifteen hundred dollars to a car, and she'd decided it was safest to buy from an individual to avoid having to fill out a lot of paperwork. There were several cars that fell into that price range, and she circled two of them.

She worked on the crossword puzzle and read about most of the news in St. Louis to try to keep herself awake until eight o'clock, when she thought it would be late enough to call about the cars. She fed Cody some oatmeal and a banana, then made her calls from a pay phone and found the car she wanted: a 1985 dark blue Toyota Celica with only seventy-five thousand miles on it.

She took a taxi to the owner's address. The driver helped her unload her belongings, piling them on the sidewalk, and Kim paid him before settling Cody in the stroller. Her duffel bag slung over her shoulder, she pushed the stroller up to the front door of the house. She rang the bell, hoping she didn't look as desperate as she felt.

A woman opened the door and smiled. "Are you one of the people who called about the car?" she asked.

One of the people? It suddenly occurred to her that the car might already be sold. "Yes," she said. "Do you still have it?"

"Uh-huh." The woman reached behind her to pick up the keys from a table, then walked out the door and led Kim around the side of the house. The car sat at the end of the driveway, next to a garage. At least on the outside it was in great shape—no dents.

Kim took the car for a test drive, with the woman holding Cody in her lap. It drove well, at least as well as her car back in Boulder.

"I'd like to buy it," she said to the woman after pulling back into the driveway.

"Great! It's sixteen-fifty, firm."

"That's fine." Kim didn't want to haggle. She stepped out of the car, then got her wallet from her duffel bag and counted out sixteen hundred-dollar bills and a fifty. Her hands were shaking, not because she was handing over so much money, but because she knew she must seem like a suspicious sort of character to the car's owner. Here she'd shown up early in the morning, alone, with luggage and a baby in tow. What if her face and Cody's had been splashed across the country on TV on one of those most wanted–type shows?

But the woman seemed concerned only with selling her car. She pulled out the certificate of title from the glove compartment and began filling it out. When she had finished, Kim asked, "Where's the nearest store where I could buy a car seat?"

"There's a Kmart close by. Go about a mile, and it's on your left."

She thanked the woman, then got back into the car—her car—and pulled out of the driveway.

At the Kmart and the grocery store next to it, she bought more formula, juice, bananas, baby food, animal crackers, and a car seat. Before even setting up the car seat, though, she gave Cody his bottle. She sat with him in the back seat, rocking him and talking to him, apologizing for uprooting him. Soothed by the food and her words, he was soon sound asleep. She buckled him into the car seat, then looked up at the sky. The sun was to her left, so that had to be east. Pulling out of the parking lot, she headed in that direction.

She stopped four times that first day on the road. She was not in a rush. There was nowhere she had to be. And each time she got back in the car, she headed east, as far from Boulder as the highway could take her.

At six o'clock she decided to pull over for the night. They were outside Henderson, Kentucky, and she found a motel along the road. After she'd registered, she walked over with Cody to the restaurant next door and shared a plate of pasta for dinner.

Back in the motel room, she lay down next to her exhausted son, wishing she'd thought to pack a few of his favorite books. She sang him a couple of songs instead: "Froggie Went a-Courtin' " and "The Old Woman Who Swallowed a Fly," songs Linc liked to sing to him. Then she sang "The Name Game," using Cody as the name—*"Cody, Cody, Fo Fody . . ."*—until the little boy could barely stop giggling. She wanted him to get used to his new name.

Toward the end of her pregnancy she and Linc had often sat up late at his house with the baby-name book. She'd been feeling stronger about herself then, buoyed by Linc's strength and caring. They hadn't been sleeping together then—that didn't begin until Cody was a few months old—but their friendship had been deep and abiding nonetheless.

Linc had loved the name Cody. But she hadn't been able to get the name Tyler out of her head. Her son was nearly six months old when she finally realized why she'd given him that name: Jim had once said he liked it.

"Still trying to please Jim," Linc admonished her.

Kim stared at the ceiling above her motel-room bed. She did not want to think about Linc. Imagining how he'd felt when he discovered her disappearance this morning was the only thing that could destroy her resolve. She could not allow that to happen.

Kim closed her eyes. She would never be able to touch Linc again. Never make love to him or hold him. Never pick up the phone to hear his voice on the other end, joking with her, making her laugh. Telling her he loved her.

She would be able to listen to him, though. Sunday night. On the radio. At least she could still have that much of him.

THE pace Kim set was slow and easy. It was impossible to rush when you had no idea where you were going. It wasn't until late Friday night that she began to feel the inescapable awareness of her homelessness. She could head east only a little longer. Sometime tomorrow she was going to run out of country. She'd keep going until she ran out of road, and then she'd plant herself wherever she'd landed.

How was she going to support herself? She couldn't get a job in a bank; that would be the first place anyone would look for her. Maybe she could get a secretarial position, but then she'd need day care, and she was nowhere near ready to let Cody out of her sight. Or she could take in word-processing jobs. She was a great typist. She could work at home—wherever home turned out to be. She hoped it would not be the back seat of the Toyota. If things were ever that bad for her, she would take Cody back. She had no right to him if she couldn't provide for him any better than that.

From behind the steering wheel of the car Saturday morning, she knew she was hitting civilization in a major way. The traffic was wild, and before she knew it, she'd been dumped onto the Capital Beltway—the fast, frightening highway that looped around Washington, D.C. She'd heard that if you were trying to hide, a big city would be your best bet, but the thought chilled her, so she took the first exit east she could find, Route 50.

It was nearly time for lunch, and Cody was assertive in letting her know it. She sang "The Name Game" for what seemed like the zillionth time, but he was having none of it. It was food or nothing.

She pulled off the road at Annapolis. Annapolis was the capital of Maryland, she was quite certain, yet she found herself in a quaint little town. The streets were narrow, and she felt as if she'd stepped back in time. She drove, enchanted, until she came to water, and an enormous dock filled with boats and activity. There were sidewalk cafés and benches overlooking the water.

There was a parking lot, and she managed to pull into a space as someone was leaving. The sun was warm and bright as she lowered Cody into the stroller. Her first stop was to get something to eat. She bought take-out fish and chips for herself and a container of strawberry yogurt for Cody. As she walked toward one of the benches, she passed a mural painted on a windowless brick wall. She stepped back to look at it, captivated.

A tall ship, white sails billowing, was set against a midnight-blue sky dotted with stars and a full moon. The artist's name, Adam Soria, was painted below the white-capped sea. Until Cody started his I-am-terminally-hungry wailing, she could not tear herself away.

A sense of calm surrounded her as she sat on a bench by the water to feed her hungry son. This beautiful little town was a capital city? There were plenty of people around, to be sure, but no one seemed rushed or harried. Seagulls swooped over the water, and the air was filled with the sound of lapping water and the scent of brine.

"Oh, Cody," she said. "Does this feel like the end of the road to you?" Her excitement was edged with trepidation. Once she actually stopped traveling, she would have time to think about what she'd done—and what she'd lost in the process.

When they finished eating, Kim spotted a newspaper-vending machine, dug a quarter from her purse, and bought a paper. She turned to the classified ads. One apartment for rent claimed to have a view of the Naval Academy and the Severn River, and that was enough to intrigue her. It was partly furnished, and rented for four hundred and fifty dollars a month.

She asked a passerby for directions and began walking with Cody in the stroller. She found Maryland Street, which was lined with antique shops and bookstores. Soon the shops gave way to small homes and a church, and she spotted a large house graced by a towering maple tree. An APARTMENT FOR RENT sign beckoned. She checked the address. Apparently, the apartment was in the house.

A wide front porch was graced by four rocking chairs and a glider. "Hey, Cody," she said, "I think this is it." She carried Cody onto the porch and knocked on the door. A woman opened it.

"Hi." The woman smiled. "Are you here for an appointment?"

"No. I'm sorry," Kim said. "I guess I should have called. I'm interested in the apartment you have for rent."

"Oh!" The woman laughed. "Forgive me. I'm a massage therapist, and I thought you were a new client of mine." She shook her head. "So you're here about the apartment?"

Kim nodded.

The woman looked hesitantly at Cody. "I'm not sure about a baby," she said, but she reached out to stroke the back of her fingers down Cody's cheek, and the little boy smiled. Kim had the feeling the battle was over before it had even begun.

"It's just the two of you?"

"Yes. My husband and I are divorcing, and he got the house." She knew immediately that she'd spoken the magic words.

"Oh, I know what *that's* like," the woman said. "Come in. My name is Ellen King. I live on the ground floor, and I just turned the upstairs into two apartments. Neither is rented out yet. This was the house my husband and I lived in until *our* divorce."

"Oh," Kim said. "My name's Kim Stratton, and this is Cody. That's great you could keep the house." She stepped into the foyer and started up the stairs behind Ellen King.

"Well, it's pretty tight. But I think with the rent from the upstairs, I'll make it." There were two doors at the top of the stairs. Ellen unlocked the door to the left of the small landing.

As soon as Kim stepped inside, she knew she wanted the apartment. The rooms had all the charm of an older home, yet despite their obvious age, they were clean and fresh and sunny. The living room was spacious and furnished with a couch and two chairs. At the opposite end of the room stood an old oak table and four chairs. The kitchen was tiny but usable, and the bedroom held a full-sized bed, a dresser, and just enough extra space for a crib. She could see the Severn River in the distance from several windows.

"I would really love to live here," she said.

Ellen nodded. "Great," she said. "Come downstairs, and I'll get the paperwork. I'll need some credit references."

"Oh," Kim said, flustered. She should have expected as much. "Everything was in my husband's name."

Ellen wrinkled her nose. "Nothing like adding insult to injury," she said. "I learned my lesson there. If I get married again, I'm keeping everything in my own name." She looked thoughtful. "Let's approach this from a different angle, then. Where do you work?"

"I'm not working at the moment." Kim laughed nervously. "I must sound really pathetic. But I plan to take in word-processing jobs and work at home so I can be with Cody."

Ellen looked disappointed. "I really can't rent to you if you have no income."

"Well, I get child support," she lied. "And I can give you two months' rent right now. If I'm not making enough to handle the rent by the end of next month, you can kick me out."

"All right," Ellen said. "We'll try it out."

"Thank you so much. I can understand your reluctance, but it'll work out. Honest." She followed her new landlady down the stairs.

"Where did you and your husband live?" Ellen asked.

"New Jersey." What was the capital of New Jersey? "Near Trenton," she added. She thought about the Missouri plates on her car and hoped they would go unnoticed.

"What brought you down here?"

"Oh, I have some family in Maryland. But I really don't want to lean on them. I want to make it on my own."

"I know the feeling." Ellen led her into her living room. Kim could see into the next room, where a massage table was draped in sheets. Ellen handed a lease to Kim, who read and signed it, then counted out nine hundred dollars for Ellen, who handed her a set of keys. Kim thanked her and walked down the steps with Cody.

Once Kim was back on the street, she let it all sink in. She was going to live in Annapolis. She'd made her decision in a split second based on the quaintness of the streets and the smell of the air. She hoped there would be enough word-processing work to let her pay the rent when the two months were up.

She looked up at the house again, at the windows of her apartment, then at the windows to the right. She hoped it was a while before Ellen was able to rent out that other apartment. She didn't want to have to answer another person's questions, at least not yet.

She found her way back to her car and took herself shopping, buying only what she needed and buying cheap. She bought a crib and a small portable playpen, sheets and towels, pots and pans, and dishes. She would need to buy a fairly good computer and printer if she wanted to earn a living doing word processing, but she splurged on her final purchase—a radio. When she heard Linc's voice the following night, she wanted to hear it clearly.

The next day, Sunday, was filled with grocery shopping and a toy- and clothes-buying spree at a local garage sale. But Kim knew all her activity was a preamble to that evening, when she would be able to hear Linc's show from eight to ten. The thought of hearing his voice again was overwhelming. It pervaded her thinking. It intruded on her newfound sense of peace as she settled Cody into his crib and, later, as she sat in her new living room looking out at the river.

At eight o'clock the strains of Paul Simon's "Song for the Asking" filled the room. Linc always opened his show with that song, and the pain of hearing the familiar simple, haunting music was more than she had expected. She didn't bother to fight the tears that had been close to the surface all day long. When he had taped this show on Wednesday, as he always did, she doubted that anyone had realized she was missing. Would Linc have tried to call her? What on earth did he think when he realized she was gone? *Don't be angry with me, Linc.*

"Good evening," Linc said once the song had ended. "Tonight we're going to focus on Joni Mitchell." He was his usual soft-spoken, untroubled self. He gave a little history, then played Joni Mitchell, interspersed with a few other songs, including "Suzanne." When she heard the first line, Kim nearly laughed out loud. *"Suzanne takes you down to her place near the river."* Prophetic, she thought. She'd had no idea when she'd requested the song that she would be living in just such a place by the time she heard it. But her smile faded as Linc's show continued and reality sank in.

Forever. You've left him forever. You are completely alone with a baby to raise, and you'll never meet another person in your entire life with whom you can be completely honest about who you are. You've never made it on your own before. What makes you think you can do it now?

Jim had destroyed whatever faith she'd had in herself. She could hear him telling her that going back to school as an art major made no sense. "How do you know you even have any talent?" he asked her. "I've never seen you draw a single thing."

He was right. All her artwork had been destroyed, and after her father died, she seemed to have lost all motivation. But the interest was still there.

"And besides, it makes a lot more sense financially for me to go to law school before you go back to school yourself," he said. "Even if you could get a job as an artist, there's no money in it." He told her to stick with banking. She'd have a chance for growth in banking. For promotions.

Kim stood up. There was a half hour left of Linc's show, but she turned the radio off. She'd thought it would comfort her to hear him. But this had been torture, not comfort.

What have I done? The tiniest seed of regret edged its way into her mind. She walked into her bedroom and leaned over Cody's crib. He was lying on his side, his monkey nestled under his arm, and the regret melted instantly away. She had her child with her. He was young; he would never remember the confusion and heartache of the past few days. He would only remember the life she made for him from this day forward. She would make it a good life.

PEGGY grabbed Jim's arm as soon as he came in the door Monday evening. "I've been trying to reach you all day," she said. "I got loads of information this morning."

"I'm sorry." He kissed her. "I was in court all morning and in meetings all afternoon. Let me change out of my suit, and you can tell me what you found out."

She watched him climb the stairs to their bedroom, then walked into the kitchen to gather the brochures and booklets and notes from the table. She carried them into the living room and sat down on the sofa to wait for him.

It had been a painful few days. She didn't dare screen her phone calls in case someone was calling with news about Susanna or Tyler, but that meant taking dozens of calls from well-meaning friends, wanting to know how she was doing as a new mother. She told them what had happened and that she didn't have time to talk just then. Trying to find Tyler had become her full-time job. She'd provided information about Susanna and Tyler to the missing children's hot line, and she'd pushed the police to obtain search warrants for Susanna's bank records. She'd collected photos and made posters.

Jim finally came downstairs and sat next to her on the sofa.

"First of all," Peggy said, "I spoke with Bill Anderson, the private investigator Detective Rausch suggested."

Jim frowned. "I thought we were going to let the police see what they could come up with first."

"I know, but I just wanted to see what he had to say about the situation, in case we need him later." What she really wanted was to hire him right that minute, but she knew Jim didn't think it necessary. "He says we should have a press conference immediately, get as much media attention as possible. And we should offer a cash reward to anyone with information leading to Tyler's safe recovery."

"Did he suggest an amount?"

"Not really, except that it should be substantial. I was thinking twenty thousand."

Jim's eyes widened. "I was thinking more like ten."

She'd guessed as much. She and Jim rarely saw eye to eye on money. "Someone might be more willing to take a risk for twenty than they would for ten," she said, and pulled a thick booklet from a pile in her lap. "The National Center for Missing and Exploited Children sent this. It describes what we need to do, step by step."

Jim smiled. "We're already doing everything we can, hon."

"There's a lot more we can do," she said. "We need to badger people. The police, this national center." She held up the booklet.

"I spoke with a case manager there. He said that they send out these little postcards with pictures of children and their abductors to thousands of households. They get a really good response."

"And can they do that for Tyler?"

"In the future maybe," she said. "They have a big backup, and of course, the kids who have been taken by nonfamily members get priority. But we can be a little pushier than we have been." She set the booklet aside. "I also spoke with Detective Rausch. Susanna is now classified as a felon. They have a warrant for her arrest."

"This is getting ugly," Jim said.

"Yes, it's ugly. But what she did is serious. The police aren't going to bother with her if we act as though it's no big deal. Bill—the P.I.—suggested we alert doctors and hospitals, since Tyler's surgical scar and medical problem are very recognizable. But it's expensive to send out those sorts of announcements."

"Well, do they work?"

"Ron says it will work if it hits the right doctor at the right moment." Actually, her brother had said that most doctors would end up filing the flyer away or throwing it in the trash. "I also called that TV show *Missing Persons.*"

Jim laughed.

"Don't laugh. This is the sort of thing they handle. It's just that they're not planning a show about parental kidnappings for a while. But I left them my name and number." She prayed they would never need it. Surely this would all be resolved soon. "I really like Detective Rausch," she continued. "He understands that a custody violation is every bit as serious as a kidnapping. The FBI won't get involved unless there's evidence that Susanna crossed state lines. And even then, Detective Rausch said, they're not thrilled about putting time into a parental kidnapping case. But now that Susanna's a felon, if they do figure out that she crossed state lines, the FBI will go after her for unlawful flight to avoid prosecution."

"I think it's Sebastian they should be going after," Jim said. "I'm sure he knows more than he's saying."

"Rausch talked to him today but didn't get anywhere with him."

"Linc's an old pro at being interviewed by the police," Jim scoffed. "What about tapping his phone?"

"It's too expensive. The taps have to be manned twenty-four hours a day. But they are getting a search warrant so they can look at his phone records and faxes. And they can check his bank records to see if he took out a lot of money to help her get away. Also, they've checked Susanna's bank records. She withdrew eight thousand dollars over the last few weeks, bit by bit."

"Phew. Still, that won't get her too far for too long."

Peggy laughed. Susanna could probably last a lot longer on eight thousand dollars than either of them could.

She'd reached the end of her stack of information. With a sigh she leaned her head against Jim's shoulder. "Does it surprise you that Susanna did this?" she asked. "You always said she lacked ambition. Get-up-and-go. But this took quite a bit of get-up-and-go, I'd say."

"Well, I don't know about that," Jim said. "If you ask me, this fiasco is simply the work of an unstable mind, and that she definitely has. I have to admit, though, that I never thought of her as much of a fighter." He stretched. "Why don't we have some dinner? We can talk more about this later. Maybe in bed?" He looked hopeful.

She felt torn between guilt and annoyance. Nothing like losing your baby to kill desire. She didn't know how he could even think about sex with everything else going on.

She looked down at the pile of information on her lap. "Jim, I feel like I'm doing this all on my own."

"Oh, I'm sorry, Peg." He put his arm around her. "It's just that you've got this time off, and I'm working like a dog."

He was right. She had the time to do this. He didn't. She simply didn't like the sense of being alone in the battle. "What I would really like," Peggy said, "is your permission to hire the P.I."

Jim sighed. "If you honestly think it would help, go ahead."

She smiled. "Thank you." She leaned forward to kiss him and tried to let her lips linger on his, but all she could think about was making the call to Bill Anderson.

Chapter 4

BILL Anderson leaned forward on the sofa, notepad on his knee, and Linc noticed that the private investigator was keeping one wary eye on Sam. The dog, now lying at Linc's feet, had let out a wise and knowing growl when Anderson walked in the door, and Linc had had a hard time keeping a straight face.

"So," Anderson said, "when was the last time you saw her?"

Everyone's favorite question. "I've already answered—"

"For the police. But not for me. So bear with me, all right?"

Linc sighed and gave in. "I last saw her in my car after the judge's decision. We picked up Tyler from day care, and I drove them home. We spoke again on the phone that night. She sounded all right. She didn't say anything about leaving."

"Had she ever mentioned to you places she might like to visit?"

"Contrary to what her ex-husband might have told you," Linc answered, "Susanna is not stupid. She wouldn't try to hide out someplace she'd told people she wanted to go."

From behind the closed kitchen doors he could smell the aroma of the chicken soup his friends Grace Talbot and Valerie Diehl were making. He'd found the women waiting on his doorstep when he got home from teaching his class in American folk music at the university that afternoon. They were going to nurse him "back to mental health," they insisted. But as soon as Anderson's car pulled up, Linc had shoved his friends into the kitchen and told them to stay there. He didn't want Anderson badgering them, too.

"Any family you know of?" Bill asked. "What about her mother? Do you know where she is?"

"She hasn't seen her mother since she was a teenager." Linc scratched the dog behind his ears. "Susanna would never turn to her for help." His own mother would have been a more likely choice, but she had died two years earlier.

"What special skills does Susanna have?"

"She's great with children. She's a terrific mother."

"Yeah, yeah." Bill waved a bored hand through the air. "Tell it to the judge."

"She's artistic. She's smart. She can type like a bat outta hell. She's good with numbers, with money."

"Yeah. I spoke to her supervisor at the bank," Bill said. "Besides you and her co-workers, did she have other friends around here?"

"Just Grace Talbot and Valerie Diehl."

Bill flipped through his notes. "Let's see. Talbot works in the library at the university, and Diehl teaches psychology, right?"

"Right." Linc stood up. "I don't know what more I can tell you."

Bill Anderson stood up himself. "If you honestly don't know where she is and whether she's safe or whatever, I would think you'd want her found," he said.

"Look," Linc said, "I'm not hiding anything from you. Susanna was smart enough to leave me in the dark, too." And he had not yet forgiven her for it.

He and Sam walked Anderson to the door and watched as the investigator negotiated the long, winding driveway in his aging Mercedes. He went into the kitchen, where Grace was setting bowls of soup on the table and Valerie was pulling dinner rolls from the oven.

"Smells great," Linc said as he sat down. The soup was very thick, more of a stew, and he suddenly realized he was hungry. "He might want to talk with you two," he said after they had eaten a bit. "I told him you were friends of hers."

"Let him," Grace said. "I doubt we'd be able to help him much." Grace was the head of the American-studies section of the university library. Linc had met her when he'd donated part of his American music collection to the library, and their friendship had been quick to develop. She was outspoken, loud-voiced. It was hard to believe she was a librarian. Valerie, on the other hand, was quiet and analytical.

"I think you should go out with Val and me tonight," Grace said. "We can do a movie. Okay?"

He shook his head. "No. I have to tape the show tomorrow, and I haven't put it together. I haven't even checked my faxes yet." Most of the musical requests for his show came in by fax these days.

"Do you think Susanna can hear the show?" Valerie asked.

"Yeah, actually, I do." He swallowed a spoonful of soup. "Before she left, she asked me if I'd play 'Suzanne' for her, so she must have been thinking she would hear it wherever she was. I've been trying to come up with some way to get a message to her through the show, but the cops and this P.I. are going to be listening pretty carefully. They seem certain I'm in on her escape somehow."

"Why don't you play 'Suzanne' for her every week, then?" Valerie said. "She'll know it's your way of keeping in touch."

"Every week." He groaned. "I don't want to think about her being gone that long."

"So you're hoping they find her, huh?" Grace asked.

He rested his spoon in his empty bowl. "I want her back," he said, "but not if she doesn't want to be here." It still hurt to think that she could leave him with such ease.

He helped the women clean up after dinner, then disappeared into his studio to read his faxes, while they watched TV in his family room. He felt like he was being baby-sat, but it didn't bother him. Suddenly Grace knocked on his studio door.

"Hurry!" she said. "It's a press conference."

He walked into the family room to see Jim and Peggy on the television, ashen-faced in the lights of the cameras. He sat down on the floor next to Grace.

Jim was saying, "We have reason to believe that Susanna Miller has kidnapped our son, Tyler."

Linc clenched his teeth. Until now no one had introduced the concept of Susanna having kidnapped Tyler.

"Tyler has a serious heart condition," Jim continued, "and we are extremely concerned that he be returned home to get the medical care he needs. Susanna Miller has a history of mental illness."

Linc pounded his hand on his knee. "What crap," he said.

"Please," Jim continued. "We are offering a twenty-thousand-dollar reward to anyone who can give us information leading to the safe return of Susanna and Tyler Miller."

A photograph of Susanna and Tyler appeared on the screen, along with an 800 number. The picture was one Linc had taken of the two of them at the park. The photograph had been sitting on top of the television in her apartment. The police must have taken it, and he was glad he'd thought to rescue her photograph albums.

He muted the sound on the TV when the newscaster moved on to his next story. Linc's face felt hot. "Mental illness. She was depressed, you bastard," he said to the TV. "She never would have been in that hospital if it hadn't been for you."

"Get it out," Valerie said. She was always one for encouraging people to express their emotions.

"He makes her sound deranged," Linc said. "I just hope Susanna's far enough away that she can't see Peggy and Jim begging for the safe return of 'their' baby on TV." He shook his head. "She shouldn't have run away. It's her natural response to a problem. As a kid, I'd always find her and drag her home. And then her father would beat her up." At least until that last time, when Linc put an end to the beatings. But he didn't want to get into that now. Grace and Valerie knew he'd killed Susanna's father. Everyone knew it, but no one, not even these two close friends, ever dared to question him about it.

When Grace and Valerie got up to go home, he didn't bother walking them to the door. Instead, he lay down on the floor and watched the muted TV until he fell asleep.

ELLEN and one of her massage clients were talking on the front porch, and Kim was trapped in her apartment. She sat on the sofa staring out at the maple tree. She was gutless. Why didn't she simply walk past the two women, nod hello, get in her car, and drive to the computer store, as she'd been planning to do? It wasn't Ellen she feared but the stranger with her. She trusted no one.

Everyone looked suspicious to her lately. She'd taken at least one long walk every day since her arrival, pushing Cody in his stroller, trying not to look as uneasy as she felt, but all eyes in town seemed to be trained on her and her son. She had not thought about how unbearably lonely self-imposed isolation could be.

Cody looked up at her, annoyance in his face. She didn't blame him. She'd put his sweater on and then made him sit in it for ten minutes in the too warm apartment.

"We'll give them five more minutes, Cody," she said. "Then we'll go anyhow. What's the worst that could happen?"

The worst that could happen was entirely too easy to imagine. Maybe Ellen's client down there was not a client at all, but a private investigator no doubt hired by Jim to help locate her. It would be clever of him to hire a woman.

She'd kept busy the past few days, afraid to allow herself too much idle time for thinking. She'd gotten a phone, a new driver's license, new plates for her car, and a checking account. Kim Stratton existed now. She practiced her new signature and stared at the driver's license for hours, studying the picture of the fair-skinned copper-haired stranger next to the stranger's name. She thought again of the baby in the grave back in Boulder. She'd stolen that baby's life, and she felt a keen responsibility to make it a life worth living.

Her attention was drawn back to the maple tree outside her window. As a squirrel hopped onto a branch, only a couple of feet from where she was sitting, Kim was jarred by a sudden memory. She'd been seven or eight years old, peeking into her parents' bedroom from behind their slightly open door. Her father was standing by the window. A cigarette dangled from his lips, and as usual, an open bottle of whiskey rested on his night table.

Susanna watched as he carefully removed the screen. Only then did she see a fat gray squirrel on one of the branches of a tree outside. Her father never took his eyes off it as he opened his night-table drawer and pulled out a gun. At first she had thought it was a toy. She watched as he raised the gun and pointed it at the squirrel.

It's a toy, she told herself. It has to be. She closed her eyes, and the sudden explosion made her yelp, but her father didn't seem to hear her. When she opened her eyes, the squirrel had disappeared, as had any remaining shred of trust in her father.

That was the first time she ran away, hiding in the little room above Linc's mother's garage. For weeks afterward she avoided the part of the yard where the squirrel would have fallen. That way she could pretend it had found its way to safety.

A sudden burst of laughter, and Kim knew that Ellen and her client were finally inside the house. Ellen's door closed with a click.

"We're on our way, Cody-boy," Kim said.

In the car, she checked the directions Ellen had given her. Computer Wizard, the store was called. "Best prices on computers," Ellen had said. The night before, Kim had counted her money. She had forty-eight hundred left, and the computer and printer were going to take an enormous bite out of that. After today about eighteen hundred would be all that stood between her and starvation. She would have to find work quickly.

Stopping for a red light at a busy intersection, Kim noticed another of the murals on the side of a bank building, only this one was unfinished, a work in progress. The painting was of a whimsical snow-covered village.

Besides the painting of the tall ship with the billowing sails, she had noticed several other murals during her walks through town. All had been painted by the same artist, Adam Soria, and were identifiable by their clear intense colors. Her favorite was a jungle scene with white birds in flight against a deep green backdrop of trees.

She'd studied the murals with fascination, admiring the artist's skill and thinking how rewarding it would be to have such a huge and public canvas on which to paint.

Computer Wizard was an enormous building standing alone in an expansive parking lot. Kim put Cody in the stroller and walked across the lot. The salesman who greeted her at the door was no older than twenty. He reminded her of Jim when he was younger—

perfectly groomed, bright-eyed, and ready to set the world on fire.

"I'd like to buy a personal computer," she said.

It was as if she'd pushed a button. He was off and running, talking about megabytes and memory and CD-ROMs. When he paused for breath, she threw herself on his mercy. "I don't know about any of that stuff," she said. "You'll have to tell me what I need."

He showed her computer after computer, even letting her play with a graphics program. As she changed fonts, she got an idea for a brochure she could use to advertise her word-processing business. She finally settled on one of the computers. It had everything she wanted and then some.

"I love it," she said. "But I really can't afford it."

"Hmm," the salesman said. "Well, I think you're in luck."

He was so slick that she doubted the veracity of anything he told her. He walked toward the register. She followed him, pushing Cody, who was now asleep in the stroller. On the counter stood a computer like the one she'd been using, but this one had a large red label stuck on the monitor. The price was hundreds lower.

"This is the same model," he said. "But someone bought it and returned it, for one reason or another. We can't sell it as new." He winked at her, as though that was their little secret. "It's a real bargain. Plus, the guy left a ton of software on it."

He turned it on. There was the word-processing program she was accustomed to using, as well as some games and a screen saver.

"It's nice," she said, "but why would the person bring it back? Something must be wrong with it."

"Oh, there could be a zillion reasons why someone would bring a computer back, none of them having to do with the quality of the product. In fact, I'm pretty sure this computer was just a loaner. When one of our customers brought in his own computer for repairs, we loaned him this one."

She didn't believe a word out of his mouth, but she wanted this computer. "Okay, then," she said. "I'll need a printer, too."

The salesman helped her pick out a printer, along with a simple graphics program and some paper.

It wasn't until all her purchases had been loaded into her car that she noticed the large art-supply store across the street. She stared at it, wondering if she were being given some sort of sign. First there were the murals, now a huge art store. Maybe it was time for her to start drawing again.

She spent nearly an hour walking the aisles of the store. When she finally walked out the front door, she was carrying a sketch pad and a pencil set, the first she'd owned since she was sixteen.

She waited until Cody was in bed that evening before setting up the computer on the oak table in the dining area of her living room. She'd never gotten a computer up and running on her own before, and she was proud of herself. Everything worked as it was supposed to. Not only had the previous owner loaded some software on the computer, but he'd left a file on it as well—a list of names and addresses, with curious information.

> Katherine Nabors, 448 Labrador Lane, Annapolis, 47, 2 children, 2 adults. September 27, 8:30 a.m., home.
>
> Sellers, Sellers, and Wittaker, 5588 Duke of Gloucester Street, Annapolis, every damn day of the year. Use October 17, 2 p.m. (so all will be there).
>
> Ryan Geary, 770 Pioneer Way, Annapolis, 51, elderly couple. November 13, 9 p.m.

There was another page and a half of similar cryptic listings of individuals and businesses. Kim couldn't bring herself to delete them—they might still be needed by their creator.

She called the store, but her salesman had already left for the night. She told the woman who answered the phone about the file on her computer, but the woman sounded as if she didn't want to be bothered. "I'm sure if the file was important, the person who had the computer would have made a copy. It's your computer now. Go ahead and erase it."

Kim hung up with a grimace. The store had made its sale. What did they care if some poor soul desperately needed this list of names? She copied the names to a floppy disk before erasing them from the hard drive, then slipped the disk into her top dresser drawer so it wouldn't get mixed up with her own work.

Over the next couple of days Kim taught herself the graphics program for her computer. She designed and printed business cards and matching brochures, hoping that the eye-catching composition would make up for her slim credentials. She got a directory of businesses from the chamber of commerce and stuffed envelopes labeled with the addresses of one hundred businesses in town. She bought stamps and on Sunday dropped the stack of envelopes filled with her brochures and business cards into the mailbox outside the post office. She'd done her best. Now she'd just have to wait.

Walking back home with Cody in his stroller, she came to a house entirely surrounded by yellow police tape. Apparently, there'd been a fire. The porch was blackened, and the ragged-looking opening where the front door had been was covered by plastic sheeting. Above the porch the roof appeared to be on the verge of collapse.

"What happened here?" Kim asked two women who stood in the street in front of the house.

"They think it was a bomb," one woman said. "The gal who lives here opened an Express Mail package that someone left on her porch, and it blew up in her face and killed her."

Kim's already shaky sense of security grew instantly more precarious. "Annapolis seemed so safe to me," she said.

"Oh, it's a perfectly safe town," the other woman reassured her. "This sort of thing never happens here."

"No place is safe," the first woman said. "You just can't get away from crime and violence."

Maybe not, Kim thought, but she could get away from this neighborhood. She said good-bye to the women and continued in the direction of home.

AFTER dinner that night Kim moved the radio to the shelf behind her bed and tuned it to the station that carried Linc's show. Then she sat on the bed with her sketch pad and pencils and, while waiting for the show, filled an entire hour—and several pages of her sketchbook—with drawings of the objects that made up her new life.

When Simon and Garfunkel began singing "Song for the Asking," she got beneath the covers. Then Linc began to speak, and Kim listened for any trace of emotion in his voice. Did he know she was listening? There was no way to tell. At least not until the very end of his show, when he once again played "Suzanne."

Oh, Linc.

THERE was only one woman in the small square waiting room at Legal Aid, and Peggy glanced at the next name on her list. "Bonnie Higgins?" she asked from the doorway.

The woman had the swollen features and red eyes of someone who'd been crying a great deal, and she gave a slight nod at the mention of her name.

"Please come in," Peggy said. She led the woman down the hallway to her office and, once there, took a seat behind her desk. "I'm Peggy Miller," she said.

The woman did not speak, and Peggy wondered if either of them had the energy for this appointment. It was her first day at work since Tyler's disappearance. If things had gone according to plan, she would have been off for another two months. But there seemed little point in sitting at home. She could at least work part-time to keep herself busy.

The receptionist had given Bonnie the lengthy Legal Aid questionnaire to fill out. Peggy took it from her and began leafing through the pages. "You're interested in a divorce?"

"Well, no, not really." Bonnie's eyes filled with tears. "But my husband is. He says he feels trapped and wants to be free."

"Your children are four and five," Peggy said, reading from the form. "Has your husband said anything about custody?"

"He hasn't said a word about the kids," Bonnie said.

"Do you think he's seeing someone else?"

"He says no. I don't know when he'd have time. He's pretty much always working."

Peggy looked over the rest of the form and began questioning

Bonnie about the family's financial situation, telling her what she needed to do to protect her assets. Peggy promised that she would help Bonnie fight for fifty percent of everything.

"But he says I don't deserve half of everything, because he's the one who's been bringing home the money all these years."

"While you've been raising the children and managing the household, right?"

Bonnie nodded, a small hopeful smile on her lips. "Right."

At the interview's end Peggy walked Bonnie to the door. "Call me if anything comes up before our next meeting," she said, shaking the woman's hand.

At noon she left the office. She was anxious to get home. When she turned onto her street, she saw several cars in front of her house. Ron's car was there, and she thought the blue one belonged to Bill Anderson. Jim's car was in the driveway.

In the house, Peggy found Jim, Ron, and Bill Anderson sitting at the kitchen table, laughing, drinking beer. "Is this a celebration?" she asked. "Did something happen?"

Jim looked contrite. "No, hon," he said. "At least, not what you're hoping for. But Bill does have some news."

"What?" Peggy sat down next to Ron. "What did you find out?"

The private investigator ran a hand over his chin. "Well, to begin with, Susanna Miller was on a bus to St. Louis, Missouri, the morning of the day she disappeared."

Peggy leaned toward him. "Tell me everything. How do you know that? Tyler was with her, wasn't he?"

"I've been talking to the ticket people and drivers at the bus terminal in Denver, as well as the drivers on the routes near Susanna's apartment. I told them there's a good chance she altered her looks. A wig, maybe. Or dyed hair. A bus driver for one of the routes near her house recognized her and the baby from a picture. He said the woman looked very different, but they stood out anyhow. Usually he picks up the same people on that route day after day, people commuting to Denver for work. He picked her up around five thirty in the morning and let her off at the terminal in Denver."

Peggy squeezed her brother's hand. "Then what?"

"The driver wasn't the greatest at descriptions," Bill said, "but he did say that her hair was a lot darker and a lot shorter. I had a computer-generated picture made up of what she might look like now." He pulled the picture out of a folder on the table.

"Oh, no," Peggy said, dismayed. She doubted she would ever recognize the woman in the picture as Susanna. "No wonder we haven't gotten any calls from the photographs we've been showing on TV. She looks like a totally different person."

"Bill said we can get this altered picture on the news, though, and show it in St. Louis, too," Jim said.

"What were you saying about St. Louis?" She looked at Bill.

"Right," Bill said. "At the Denver bus terminal one of the drivers said she and Tyler had definitely been on his bus to St. Louis. Said the baby was really good. Hardly cried at all."

"Maybe he was sick," Peggy said. "And she's carting him all over the country."

"Peggy, he's not going to break." Ron sounded impatient. "He's fixed, all right? He needs good checkups. Maybe an echo every now and again, just to know everything's working as it should be. That's all. You won't be doing him any good if you get to be his mother and you coddle him like he's some delicate flower."

Peggy didn't respond. She felt betrayed by her brother's attitude. She turned to Bill. "Is she still in St. Louis?"

"I don't know. No one there recognized her, but that's a much bigger and busier terminal. I'm working on it, though."

"So this means the FBI can get involved now, doesn't it?" she asked.

"That's right," Bill said. "She's a felon. They can get her for unlawful flight to avoid prosecution."

Ron made a sound of disapproval. "Sounds like overkill to me," he said almost under his breath.

"Now"—Bill sat back in his chair—"send me any videos of Tyler and whatever other pictures you have lying around. I'm going to get them to that TV show *Missing Persons.*"

"I already called them," Peggy said. "They told me it would be months before they'd be doing a show on parental kidnappings."

"That's true, but when they start planning that show, they'll choose the case they have the most material for." Bill flipped through his notepad. "We're keeping tabs on the health insurance company, too. If Susanna tries to use her insurance, either for Tyler or herself, we should be able to track her down. The insurance company knows to notify us if they get a claim from her or a change of address or anything."

"He's due for his inoculations soon," Peggy said. She had marked the date on her calendar.

"Isn't it likely, though, that she'd assume we've alerted the insurance carrier?" Jim asked.

"Yes, but maybe she'll get desperate."

"Or, God forbid, she might skip his inoculations," Peggy said. "Or maybe she won't even remember to get them."

Ron made that disapproving sound in his throat again. "There's one other thing you should know, Peg," he said. "Bill had asked Della in my office to pull Tyler's medical records, and she found a note in his file. Apparently, Susanna had requested—and received—a copy of all of Tyler's records a couple of weeks before she took off."

"She'd been planning it that long?"

"Uh-huh." Ron nodded. "And I have to hand it to her. I'm not sure I would have had the presence of mind to remember those records before I split."

"Ron," she said, "whose side are you on?"

"Tyler's," Ron answered quickly, and Peggy knew he'd given this whole matter a good deal of thought.

Ron stood up. "I've got to go."

Peggy stood up, too. She walked her brother to the door in silence, then turned to him. "You know, Ron, I don't think you can relate to what's going on with Tyler and Susanna and Jim and me. I have a stepson out there somewhere, and I have no idea what's happening to him. I have no idea if I'll ever get to see him again." She didn't want to cry. Much as she adored Ron, he'd always had a way of provoking her tears.

He reached out and pulled her into a hug. "I feel certain that Tyler is safe," he said quietly. "I don't think you want to hear that, though. You don't want to hear that I think Susanna is a perfectly fine mother. She never missed an appointment with me. She did everything she was told to do to take care of Tyler."

Peggy nodded woodenly as she let go of him. They said good-bye, and she turned to walk slowly back to the kitchen. She knew she should be heartened by his assessment of Susanna's ability to care well for Tyler, but he was right. She didn't want to hear it.

Chapter 5

KIM and Cody had spent the morning at a playground a few blocks from their apartment. When they returned to the house, there was a piece of mail waiting for Kim. Ellen had left it on the table in the foyer, and Kim nearly walked past it before she noticed her name on the cream-colored envelope. "Kimberly Stratton." She stared at the envelope before picking it up. Mail for her? Here?

It was a squarish envelope with a typewritten label. She carried it upstairs to her apartment. She put Cody down for his nap, then sat on the sofa to open the envelope. Inside was a formal invitation: "You are cordially invited to a showing of Adam Soria's work at the Cherise Gallery, October 3, 7:00 p.m."

The mural painter. How on earth? She studied the card, then peered inside the envelope, as if she might find a clue as to why she'd received the invitation. Maybe Ellen knew someone at the gallery and asked them to invite the new kid on the block.

Kim set the invitation aside, pulled out her sketchbook, and began working on a sketch she'd started of the house across the street. She'd gotten a couple of books from the library on drawing, and the techniques were coming back to her. She reminded herself that there was no one around now to tell her she had no talent. No one could take this sketchbook away from her. She was finding it hard to concentrate, though. The invitation kept creeping back into her mind. She decided she would go to the show the following night.

After Cody awakened from his nap, they went outside. Ellen came out the front door of the house, the mesh bag she used for groceries hanging over her shoulder. "Guess what?" she said. "You two are going to have a new neighbor. Her name is Lucy O'Connor. She's sixtyish, I'd say. Divorced, so that makes three of us, huh? She writes articles for parenting magazines, works at home, and says babies are right up her alley."

Kim forced a smile. "Sounds perfect. When is she moving in?"

"Tomorrow night. You can meet her then."

"Oh, I'm going out tomorrow night. To an art show." She waited for Ellen to say "Oh, so you got the invitation!" but Ellen didn't even seem to hear her.

"Well, you can meet her when you come home," Ellen said. She started down the stairs, then turned to study her quizzically. "You know, I might be able to find a baby-sitter if you want to get out without Cody sometime."

"No, thanks," Kim said. She didn't plan on being separated from her son anytime soon. She wondered, though, if it would be inappropriate to show up at an art show with a baby in tow.

It was dark by seven o'clock the following evening when Kim drove to the gallery. She found a parking space a block away. Even from that distance she could hear the noise from the gallery as she got out of her car. She decided against trying to maneuver the stroller through a crowd of people and carried Cody in her arms instead.

She began walking toward the commotion. A few people were outside the gallery itself. She stepped between them and walked through the open front door.

The bright lights and press of people nearly took her breath away. She was definitely the only person carrying a child, and she was not as formally dressed as most people. Her fifty-cent garage-sale skirt had seemed appropriate before she left the apartment, but now she felt dowdy. Some of the women looked as if they belonged in a nightclub.

A few people, plastic cups of wine in their hands, glanced at her. A tall black woman, her hair braided and beaded, emerged from the throng, shaking hands, touching shoulders, talking quickly and loudly. She looked as though she was in charge.

"Excuse me." Kim tightened her hold on Cody. "Is it all right if I bring my son in? I'll hold him."

"You will *not* hold him." The woman laughed. "Because I'm gonna hold him." She snatched the baby, monkey and all, from her arms so quickly that Kim felt a second of panic.

"I'm Cherise, honey," the woman said. "And you're . . ."

"Kim."

Cherise waved at someone leaving the gallery, then returned her attention to the little boy in her arms, who was fascinated by her long, dangling beaded earrings.

"Don't pull her earring, Cody." Kim reached out to brush his hand away.

The woman didn't seem to share her concern. "Cody," she repeated. "He's just like my sister's little boy. Well, not the same color, but he's the same age. Just about a year, right?"

"Close to it," Kim said.

"And just as handsome as my nephew, aren't you?"

Kim found herself smiling at the gallery owner's electric chatter and easy hospitality. "I'm relatively new here," she said. "I've been admiring Adam Soria's murals all over town."

"Oh, yes, aren't they something? He's a genius, that man. Of course, all this is his old work." She waved her bangle-studded wrist toward one of the walls of paintings. "I was just about to show these pieces when the accident happened. It's taken Adam till now to feel ready to do it. Do you realize he hasn't done a single new piece in the six months since it happened? We have to get him working again, don't you think?"

"Absolutely," Kim agreed. She had no idea what the gallery owner was talking about, and she wasn't about to ask. She reached for her son. "Let me take him off your hands."

"He does get heavy, doesn't he?" Cherise handed the baby over to her. "Hey! There's Adam." Cherise nudged her forward. "Come on, girl. You need to meet the artist himself."

She saw him from the back first. He was of average height, average weight, with short salt-and-pepper hair. His arm hung loosely around the shoulders of a dark-haired woman. They were talking with another couple.

"Adam!" Cherise said. "I want to introduce you to a couple of admirers."

He turned to face them. Unlike everyone else in the gallery. Adam Soria had not dressed for the occasion. He wore jeans and a gray cardigan over a pale blue shirt. His short beard and mustache were graying, like his hair, although he looked to be only in his mid-thirties. He had warm brown eyes, but there was a tiredness in his smile, as though he had to force it. He dropped his arm from the woman's shoulders to shake Kim's hand.

"I'm Kim," she said. "And this is Cody."

"What a doll!" The woman's large dark eyes lit up at the sight of Cody. She looked young, probably no more than twenty-five. "I'm Jessie," she said to Kim. "Adam's sister. May I?" She reached out her arms to Cody, who did the same in response. It was frightening how easily he went to strangers.

"Oh, I'm in love!" Jessie settled the little boy into her arms and made Cody's ragged stuffed monkey dance on Adam's shoulder, eliciting a giggle from the little boy and a slightly more animated smile from the artist.

"Kim's been admiring your murals, sugar," Cherise said to Adam. "She's just moved here from— Whoops!" She looked toward the door as a new stream of people filed into the gallery. "Gotta run."

Kim smiled at Adam as Cherise rushed off.

"I've seen you walking Cody in a stroller, right?" Jessie said.

Nothing like being noticeable. "Right. This is a wonderful town for walking. That's how I stumbled across the murals. They're beautiful."

"Thank you," Adam said.

"I always wanted to paint." That sounded stupid, but she wasn't sure what else to say. "I was going to be an art major in college but had to drop out."

"Where did you move from?" Jessie asked.

"New Jersey."

"What brought you to Annapolis?"

"Oh, I have some family nearby. And it's pretty here. I like being near the water."

"Are you working around here?" Jessie asked.

What was with the third degree? "I'm just starting my own business. Word processing out of my house."

"Really?" Jessie asked. "Do you use a word processor or a computer or—"

"Jessie." Adam laughed. "Give her a chance to catch her breath between questions, all right?" He looked at Kim. "My sister's the curious type."

"Sorry." Jessie smiled. She pointed toward one corner of the gallery. "Can I take Cody over to see the ice sculpture?"

Kim looked where she was pointing, and noticed the huge ice statue of a dolphin on the table in the corner. "Sure," she said bravely. He would only be a few yards away from her.

She watched as Jessie carried Cody through the press of people, then directed her attention to the painting in front of her. It was another jungle scene, similar to the mural she liked best. "Acrylics?" she said. It had to be for him to get those vibrant opaque colors.

"Uh-huh," he said.

She wanted to tell him how much she'd enjoyed his murals, and hunted for words that wouldn't make her sound completely ignorant. "There's a strength in your paintings," she said. "They're hard to ignore. It's the colors, and I don't know . . ." She cocked her head to study the exotic white bird nestled in the green jungle. "It's your style. You really have a style all your own."

"Thanks. It's probably because I paint what I dream."

She looked over to see Cody reach out to touch the dolphin's icy nose. "You paint what you dream?" she repeated.

"I used to. I used to sketch my dreams every morning. Then I'd paint my favorites." He reported this without enthusiasm.

"No wonder they're so unique. You're not painting what everyone else sees. Just what you see."

"Hmm." He actually seemed to perk up at that, as though he liked her analysis. Then he followed her eyes to the dolphin. Jessie was talking with a woman who was making the monkey's hand touch Cody's nose over and over again.

"He's all right." Adam touched Kim's arm lightly, kindly. "Jessie's oozing with maternal instincts."

"Adam!" A woman in a red-sequined dress approached them. "These are wonderful. You shouldn't have kept them locked away for so long."

Kim felt intrusive. "I'd better go get Cody," she said, but Adam caught her elbow in his hand and held it firmly.

"Don't go," he said. It was a plea of such unmistakable sincerity that she didn't budge.

"When do we get to see something new?" the woman asked.

"One of these days." That forced smile again.

"Don't make it too long, please." The woman winked at him and slipped back into the crowd.

Adam turned to Kim. "I would have introduced you, but I can't remember her name." Then he asked quickly, "So, which is your favorite of the murals?"

"Actually, the jungle scene on Duke of Gloucester Street."

"The dream was even better," he said. "I don't think I ever quite captured the feeling of it."

"When will the mural on the bank be finished?"

"Probably never." He rubbed his short beard with his hand. "I stopped working on it six months ago, when my dreams died."

She wasn't sure what to say. There'd been an accident, Cherise had said. What had happened?

"What sort of painting do *you* do?" he asked her.

"None." She smiled. "My dreams died thirteen years ago."

"Thirteen years, huh? Now that's discouraging."

Kim looked over at the ice dolphin, but she couldn't spot Jessie and Cody. She stood up on her toes, her heart kicking into high gear. Nowhere. "Excuse me," she said. "I—"

"Over there." Adam pointed. Jessie was sitting on a countertop talking with a man standing near her. Cody was on her lap.

"Oh," Kim said, relieved. "I should go free your sister."

"A little separation anxiety?" Adam asked. "I can appreciate that. It was nice talking to you, Kim. Hope you get back to painting one of these days."

"You, too," she said. "And I'm very glad I had a chance to meet you." She slipped away to get her son.

She was relieved to get Cody back in her arms again, but he was getting antsy, and she decided she would have to come back some other day to see the rest of Adam Soria's paintings.

By the time she got home, Cody was asleep. There were lights burning in the other upstairs apartment. She walked up the stairs with Cody in tow and listened for a moment. There were no sounds coming from the other apartment, but the landing felt different somehow, heavy with the presence of the new tenant, yet another stranger to whom she would have to explain her existence.

THE following morning Kim took Cody for a walk near the city dock. She was pushing the stroller past a row of shops, when Adam Soria suddenly stepped out of a small pharmacy on the corner.

"Hey," he said, his smile of recognition slow. "Hello again."

"Hi." She stopped walking. "That was fun last night."

He made a sound in his throat as if he were not quite certain he agreed with her. He was about to say something when Jessie walked out of the pharmacy and came to stand next to him. "Hello." Jessie smiled and stooped to greet Cody. "Hello again, little guy."

"Mamama." Cody giggled and held his monkey out to Jessie.

"He doesn't offer his monkey to just anyone," Kim said.

Jessie looked up at her. "Out on one of your walks?"

"Yes. I'll get them in while I can. I hope I'll get some work soon, and then I won't have time to walk."

"Word processing, right?" Jessie stood up.

"Right. You have a good memory."

Cody let out a long yawn. "You tired, Cody?" Jessie asked him. "Did your mom keep you up too late last night?"

"I think I did," Kim said. "Plus, it's past nap time. We'd better get home."

"All right," Jessie said. She waved at Cody. "Bye-bye, Cody."

"Nice seeing you again," Adam said. He and Jessie began walking up the street, while Kim hung back to zip Cody's jacket. Then she noticed that Jessie and Adam had stopped, glancing over their shoulders at her. Suddenly Adam walked back to her.

"Since you're new in town," he said, "would you and Cody like to join us for dinner tonight?"

Surprised, she couldn't answer right away. Adam and Jessie were obviously well established in Annapolis. They possessed a gallery full of friends. Why were they being so nice to her? She wanted to say yes, her hunger for company at war with her better judgment.

"Come on," Adam coaxed. "What else do you have to do tonight?"

She smiled, thinking of her little apartment and the entertainment it offered: the computer and her sketchbook. "Not much," she admitted.

"All right, then." He gave her the name and address of a restaurant, and she agreed to meet them there at seven thirty.

KIM had finished dressing Cody to go out that night, when a knock came at her apartment door. The sound was so unfamiliar that she jumped. She put Cody into the playpen in the middle of the living room and opened the door to find an attractive gray-haired woman on her landing.

"Hello," she boomed in a voice that held no timidity. She stuck out a hand. "I'm your new neighbor—Lucy O'Connor."

Kim shook her hand. "Kim Stratton," she said.

Lucy peered into the room. "Oh, there's the little one Ellen told me about." She marched into the apartment and over to the little boy. She lifted him out of the playpen, got down on the floor with him, and began scooting one of his toy trucks across the floor.

"Duk, duk!" Cody squealed. He was entranced with Lucy, as he was with everyone, and Kim watched the scene with a brand-new seed of paranoia growing in her head. If Jim were really smart, he could do no better than to hire a grandmotherly private investigator to move in next door to her.

"He reminds me of my little grandson," Lucy said. She ran the truck up Cody's leg. "He has your eyes. Such a pretty light blue." She looked up at Kim. "Ellen told me you're newly divorced. Must be terrible with such a little one."

Kim nodded. "It's hard, but I think we're better off without him than we were with him."

"Oh, one of *those.* He helps out with child support, I hope."

Kim hesitated. What was the best answer? She'd told Ellen she received child support. "A little," she said.

"It's never enough, is it? Does he live nearby? Does Cody get to see his papa ever?"

Kim was anxious for a change of topic. "Not too often." She made a show of looking at her watch. "I hate to tear him away, Lucy, but we have to meet some people for dinner."

"How lovely for you." With some effort Lucy was back on her feet again. "Ellen said you work at home?"

"I plan to. I'm hoping to take in word-processing jobs."

"Well, that will be wonderful. I work at home, too, so maybe we can take a coffee break together once in a while."

"Sure," Kim said, but she didn't know about that. Lucy seemed a bit too intrusive. Overbearing.

"And if you ever need someone to watch Cody, you just let me know, okay?"

Kim nodded, but once she'd closed her door on her new neighbor, she shook her head. "Don't hold your breath," she said.

THE restaurant was a small Italian eatery with a relaxed atmosphere. Adam and Jessie were already sitting across from one another at a table. Adam had his back to the door, but Jessie spotted Kim and waved, a smile on her face.

Kim left Cody's stroller by the coatrack, then walked toward the table. She sat down next to Jessie, and the waitress brought a high chair for Cody to the end of the table.

"Did you walk here?" Adam asked.

"Yes. I don't live that far. On Maryland Street. I'm renting an apartment in a big house near the Naval Academy."

"I bet I know the house," Jessie said. "Isn't the woman who owns it a massage therapist?"

"Right. Ellen King."

"Is that who Cherise goes to?" Adam asked his sister.

"Yes."

"Ah." Kim smiled. "That's got to be the connection, then. I didn't understand why I got an invitation to your show last night. I mean, I don't know anyone in Annapolis except Ellen. But if Ellen knows Cherise, I bet she asked Cherise to invite me."

"That's probably it," Jessie said.

Kim unwrapped a breadstick for Cody. "Cherise seems nice."

"One of those people who never met a stranger," Adam said. "She has an eye for art, though, and she's really been my champion. Always after me to get back to painting again."

"Do you think you ever will?" she ventured.

He shrugged. "All depends on my dreams. I've never been able to have much control over them."

"They'll come back, Adam," Jessie said reassuringly.

He looked at Kim. "What happened six months ago was that my wife and two children were killed in a car accident."

"Oh, no." She was stunned he would reveal something that personal so quickly, so openly, and she felt a painful rush of sympathy.

"I'm terribly sorry," she said. "I can't even imagine . . ." Her voice trailed off. She did not know what to say.

"I just wanted to tell you what happened so you'd understand why I was monopolizing you last night," Adam said. "I wanted to apologize. I didn't give you a chance to meet anyone else."

"It didn't bother me at all." She'd spent the evening talking with the star of the show and he was apologizing to her?

"I used you," he said. "There were so many people there who know about the accident and that I'm not working anymore. I really had no desire to answer their questions and listen to them try to persuade me to get back to work. I welcomed the opportunity to talk to someone who didn't know a thing about me."

"Glad I could serve some purpose," she said with a smile.

"You did," Jessie said, and there were tears in her eyes. "We were both dreading last night. We've discovered that we can't talk too easily about what happened in public. We tend to fall apart."

"Of course you do," Kim said.

"About the same time as the accident," Jessie continued, "I split up with the man I'd been living with for five years. And I was going to school, but all of a sudden I couldn't concentrate. So I dropped out. I was working on my master's degree in engineering. Now Adam and I are both trying to put the pieces back together."

Kim felt overwhelmed by their openness and frightened by her desire to be open in return. "Well, it's great that you have each other," she said.

The waitress appeared at their table and took their orders. "So, let's switch the topic to you," Jessie said when the waitress walked away. "Tell us your life story."

Kim laughed, and she hoped that neither of them picked up the nervousness in the sound. "Well," she began, "I was born and raised in Los Angeles." Nice, big, anonymous city. She had been born in Boulder. Never lived anyplace else. "I loved art, growing up. I was planning to major in art when I started college, but then I dropped out to put my husband through school." No harm in being honest about that part, she thought. Nobody was going to be looking for her based on the fact that she had once hoped to major in art.

"Ouch," Jessie said.

"Worse than ouch," Kim said. "Then he decided he wanted to be a doctor. So I worked to put him through medical school."

"What kind of work were you doing?" Adam asked.

She'd told Ellen she'd worked in a bank, but she wouldn't make that mistake again. "Receptionist for some nondescript business in L.A.," she said. "After he got out of medical school, he met someone better educated than me."

"Oh, man. I bet you wanted to kill him," Adam said.

"I'd considered it." She smiled. "But I was pregnant at the time and didn't want to give birth in prison."

"You were pregnant and he went out on you?" Jessie asked.

"Yeah." She grinned. She liked this. They were definitely on her side. She had to be careful where she took her tale in terms of truth and lies, though. Already she'd forgotten to add in the part about living in New Jersey.

"Did he ask for a divorce?" Jessie asked.

"No. I did. I was so angry. He'd cost me all those years when I could have been getting an education myself. Plus, I knew he was still seeing Babette, and I—"

"Babette?" Jessie laughed. "That was her name?"

"That's the name I gave her." Peggy was no Babette, but it didn't matter. Kim was on a roll. "Anyhow, I knew I could never trust him again. I didn't even *like* him anymore."

"Who could blame you?" Adam said. "He doesn't sound particularly likable."

"What about Cody?" Jessie asked. "Didn't your husband—What was his name?"

She had not thought of a name for him. "Ted," she christened him. "And no, he wasn't very interested in Cody." She wanted to tell them the truth. She wanted to tell them what a creep Ted had turned out to be. What a traitor. But she couldn't.

"He pays child support, I hope," Adam said.

"No. If I took child support from him, I'd have to let him visit.

And I don't want that." She would have to change the stories she'd told Lucy and Ellen.

"Well, it must help that he lives out west," Jessie said.

"Actually, we were living in New Jersey at the time we split up."

"Really?" Adam asked. "Where in New Jersey?"

"Sort of between Trenton and Princeton," she answered vaguely.

"Dana—that was my wife—was from Passaic."

"Oh." She nodded, hoping she shouldn't be making more of a connection than she seemed to be.

The waitress delivered their salads, and Kim cut a wedge of tomato on her bread plate and set it in front of Cody.

"So you're all on your own with Cody?" Jessie asked. "That must be hard."

"That's why I hope I get some word-processing jobs soon."

Adam looked at his sister. "We can probably help out with that, huh, Jess?"

Jessie nodded. "Sure. Betty always has too much typing to do, and maybe Noel's worn out his latest typist by now."

"I sent brochures to a lot of the businesses around town," Kim said.

"Great," Adam said. "And Jess and I will put in a good word for you. Get you some work."

Kim felt her eyes burning. Her nose was probably turning red. "That's really nice of you." She was embarrassed by her reaction to their warmth.

After dinner they walked her home, telling her it was not too far out of their way.

"Do you live together?" Kim asked.

"I've been renting the house next to Adam for the last five years," Jessie explained. Jessie was pushing Cody's stroller. The talk was light and easy, and Kim could not believe the level of comfort she felt with them. She was *too* comfortable. It would be easy to slip up and reveal something she should never reveal.

And that was why, when they reached her house, she said good night without inviting them in.

Chapter 6

KIM sat with Cody on the floor of the porch, helping him play with his garage-sale blocks, taking them apart, putting them back together again. The weather was clear and warm, the sky a perfect blue. Classical music poured through Ellen's open window.

In two days it would be Cody's—Tyler's—birthday, but she wouldn't dare celebrate on that day. She had not thought through the ramifications of changing Tyler into Cody, not the way she'd considered her own change in identity. What would she do when she needed to produce a birth certificate for her son? As far as the world knew, Cody Stratton had never been born.

The front door opened behind her, and Lucy stepped onto the porch, a mug in her hand. She was wearing dark palazzo pants, a white sweater, and a necklace made of huge green beads.

"What a beautiful day!" She sat down on the glider and took a sip from her mug. Cody crawled over to her and pulled himself up by hanging on to her knees.

"Hi, sweetheart," she greeted the little boy. Then to Kim, "Does he walk yet?"

"Almost."

"Oh, yes." Lucy watched him balance next to her legs. "He's almost there, isn't he?" She set her mug on the floor, then lifted Cody onto her lap and let him play with her necklace.

"Do you have children of your own?" Kim asked.

"Five. And eight grandchildren."

"Wow. Do they all live around here?"

"Well, I raised all my kids here in Annapolis, but only a couple of them still live here. Two are in California, and one's in Florida."

"Do you happen to know of a good pediatrician?" she asked. It was nearly time for Cody's inoculations and checkup. He'd also need an echocardiogram soon, but she'd deal with that later.

"Oh, sure," Lucy said. "I used to take my kids to Dr. Sweeney over in West Annapolis. His son's taken over his practice, and he's supposed to be just as good."

"Thanks." Kim wondered how she would deal with Cody's medical records. Every sheet in those records had the name "Tyler Miller" printed on it, not to mention the names of the doctors who had treated him and the hospitals where he had been a patient. She had a sudden disconcerting thought. Could doctors around the country have been alerted to look for a year-old male child who'd had surgery for coarctation of the aorta?

Ellen's radio switched from music to the news, and Kim heard the newscaster announce that there were still no leads in that bombing at the house she'd walked past the previous week.

"Did you hear about that woman who was killed by a bomb at her house?" Kim asked.

"I did," Lucy replied. "They said it was an Express Mail package. Someone left it on her porch and rang the bell."

Kim was imagining the horror of being blown apart, when she noticed a man on the sidewalk walking in their direction. She followed him anxiously with her eyes, until she realized he was Adam Soria.

"Good morning!" He stopped at the bottom of the porch steps, holding a bag in the air. "Would you ladies care to join me for some bagels and cream cheese?"

"Lucy, this is Adam Soria," Kim said. "He's the artist who paints the murals around town. Have you noticed them?"

"Oh, of course!" Lucy said. "My, you're very talented."

Adam bowed slightly. "Thank you." He turned to Kim. "And besides breakfast, I've brought you some work."

"Work?"

"Yeah. You know, that activity people perform to earn money?" He pulled a scrap of paper out of his pocket. "Kitty Russo's a friend of ours who works for an engineering firm. The woman who usually does their typing has a new baby and is taking a break, so Kitty was happy to hear about you."

Kim reached out to take the scrap of paper, trying to hide her disbelief. "Fantastic," she said. "Thank you so much."

"So how about it?" he asked again. "Bagels, anyone?"

"I'd love one," Kim said.

"No, thanks," Lucy said as she set Cody down on the floor and got to her feet. "It was nice meeting you, Adam." She picked up her mug and headed into the house. "You two have a good breakfast."

"Thanks," Kim said. She looked at Adam. "Why don't you come up to my apartment? I'll make some coffee."

"Great idea." He followed Kim and Cody up the stairs.

In the apartment, Kim started the coffee. As Adam set the bagels on a plate, he spotted one of her brochures on the kitchen counter. "This is nice. Did you design it?"

"Yes."

"Very nice work. Do you do mostly graphics?"

She laughed. "I don't 'do' mostly anything," she said. "I taught myself how to use a graphics program for the brochure. And I sketch a little. That's about it."

"Really? Let me see your sketches," he said.

She wrinkled her nose. "Do I have to?"

He smiled. "Uh-huh."

She pulled the sketchbook from the magazine rack in the living room, knowing she wanted his appraisal of her drawings despite her hesitation. She'd been drawing every day, but she felt as if she were working in a vacuum. There was no feedback. She had no idea if she was any good or not.

Adam went through the sketchbook page by page. "Not bad," he said when he reached her first drawing of the house across the street. He turned the page and saw her sketch of the sofa with its downy cushions. "You seem to be improving on every page."

"I got some books out of the library. I haven't really done any drawing since high school, so I'm afraid I'm stuck at that level."

"You don't seem stuck at all." He turned to one of her numerous sketches of Cody. "Wow," he said, and she couldn't help but beam. "People are your forte. I can't believe you didn't keep up with this. You're very talented."

"Thank you. I planned to, but . . . I sort of lost steam when my father died. I was seventeen," she lied, but only by a year.

"How did he die?"

She thought quickly. "Cirrhosis of the liver, from alcohol." Almost certainly her father would have killed himself with his drinking if Linc hadn't beaten him to it with a gun.

"That stuff ruins a lot of lives," Adam said bitterly.

"Well, it was more than my father dying, really. My husband wasn't very supportive."

"Oh, that's right. The doctor you put through school?"

She had almost forgotten that she'd made Jim into a doctor. A doctor named Ted. "Right," she said.

"You know, it's never too late to get back to it," Adam said. "Why don't you let me give you a lesson or two? I'm not painting myself. I might as well help someone else do it."

"Maybe," she said hesitantly. She was afraid of committing to anything anymore without thinking through the consequences.

She put Cody down for his nap, then poured them each a cup of coffee and cut the bagels. "Shall we take these down to the porch? I can leave the window open so I can hear Cody."

"Good idea." He took one of the mugs from her and led the way down the stairs. They settled on the porch, Kim on the glider, Adam in the rocker. He was telling her more about Kitty Russo, the woman who needed typing help, when Kim held up a hand to stop him, cocking her head to listen. Had she heard a noise upstairs?

Silence. "Sorry," she said. "Didn't mean to interrupt you."

"You're hypervigilant," Adam said. "Always on the lookout, as if you're expecting something terrible to happen. You startle easily. I noticed it at the gallery and the other night at dinner."

She looked down at her cup so he couldn't read her eyes. "I think you're imagining things."

"Maybe," he admitted. "I've been hypervigilant myself since the accident. It's not that I actually expect someone to leap out of the shadows at me, but I don't trust the world anymore. I don't trust it to be the same tomorrow as it is today. Things can change so quickly." He stared out at the street.

"It was Molly's tenth birthday," he said. "We'd had a little party. Just Dana and Molly and Liam—my son, who was five—and Jessie and Noel, her boyfriend. After the party we all planned to go to a bike store to pick out a bike for Molly. There were too many of us to fit in one car, so Dana took Liam and Molly, and Jessie, Noel, and I followed in my car. Dana pulled into an intersection on a green light, but a drunk from the other direction ran the red at full speed. He bulldozed Dana's car and smashed it against the side of a truck. The three of them were killed instantly." He looked down into his cup, and Kim wondered what horrors he saw reflected there.

"What happened to the driver who hit them?" she asked.

Adam snorted. "Essentially nothing. Not in the accident and not in court. He got off with a slap on the wrist."

"That's not fair."

"An understatement. I would like to personally lay him down in the street and run my car back and forth over him until he . . ." Adam looked up, his cheeks red. "Sorry," he said.

"Don't be. I don't blame you a bit. As a matter of fact, I'd hold him down for you while you ran over him."

Adam smiled. "So now I start over."

"I think you're supposed to let yourself grieve for a while."

"Let myself? My self isn't giving me any choice in the matter."

She wished she could tell him the extent to which she was starting over. She'd lost Linc. Lost her friends in Boulder. Nearly lost Cody, first to heart disease, then to Jim and Peggy. It was not the same thing, of course, but she felt a bond with Adam. She wanted to share back. Be careful, she told herself.

"When Cody was born," she said softly, "he had a heart condition. They thought he would die. A pediatric cardiac surgeon saved his life. But for those few days when he was so sick, I was in terrible shape. I imagined his death over and over again. I know it's not the same as what you've gone through. I can only imagine what it's been like for you. The one thing I don't think I could survive is losing him. He seems so vulnerable to me. If I'm hypervigilant, that's why. I'm always afraid something might happen. I hate loving someone that much. I would do anything for him."

He set his coffee cup on the floor. "I know what you mean. I'd about gotten over feeling afraid for the kids all the time. Liam broke his arm, and he bounced right back. I began to take their resiliency for granted. Then suddenly *wham*—they're gone."

Kim winced.

Adam let out a sigh and stood up, bringing the conversation to a close. "Well, I didn't mean to get into all of that."

She stood up, too. "I'm so glad you stopped over. And thanks for the bagels. Not to mention the job."

"You're very welcome." He started down the stairs. "Jessie says hi, by the way. She's excited because Victoria's pregnant."

"Victoria?"

"Her cat. Jess is so thrilled, you'd think she's pregnant herself."

Kim remembered Jessie's affection toward Cody. "She seems like she's cut out to be a mother."

Adam opened his mouth as though he were about to say something, but then he changed his mind.

"What happened with her boyfriend, Noel?" Kim asked.

"Nice guy, but he drinks too much," Adam said.

"Oh." Kim nodded. "Say no more."

AFTER she put Cody to bed that night, Kim turned on the radio on the shelf behind her bed and crawled under the covers to wait. Linc was her one source of pain, and she'd made a decision this week. She would not allow herself to think of him except on Sunday nights. Otherwise those thoughts would take over her life.

Immediately after "Song for the Asking," Linc played a recording of Pete Seeger singing "Froggie Went a-Courtin'," and Kim knew that was his birthday present to Cody. Or rather, to Tyler.

Linc sang that song to him often. She must be the first person in the universe to listen to "Froggie Went a-Courtin' " with tears in her eyes. Her mind began to drift.

When Linc got out of prison, Susanna had been overjoyed by his freedom. She'd always blamed herself for his incarceration. Though she had married Jim before Linc's release, she'd wanted to nurture her old friendship. But Jim had been dead set against it.

So she saw Linc on the sly. She encouraged him when he was looking for a job in radio, listened to the trials and tribulations of his relationships with other women, and called him when she was troubled about something and Jim was not around.

When Jim realized she was seeing Linc, he assumed there was more between them than friendship. "Your father was right!" he'd yelled. "You've probably been sleeping with him all along!"

Only later did she realize that Jim was looking for an excuse to leave their marriage.

The beginning of the end came when she attended a bank conference in Denver. She checked into the hotel on a Friday evening, locked herself in her room, and pulled out a home pregnancy test she'd bought earlier that day. Her period was ten days late, and she was hopeful and excited. She was not surprised when the test bore out her suspicions.

She thought of calling Jim but decided against it. She wanted to celebrate with him by her side, not alone in a hotel room an hour from home. Besides, this weekend was to be their first together in their new house. She could zip home, spend the night with her husband, and return to Denver before the meetings began in the morning. Within minutes she was on the road back to Boulder.

When she got home, the living-room lights were dim and soft music played on the stereo. She called Jim's name, but there was no response, and she started up the stairs.

As she opened the door to the bedroom, she was greeted with gasps of surprise and a flurry of sheets covering flesh. Susanna stared at her husband and the woman in her bed, unable to speak. She was finally able to step out of the room and close the door.

Walking numbly down the stairs, she wondered how she had failed him. She had not been good enough for him. Not pretty or smart enough.

She drove to Linc's house, where he held her and let her cry. What he wouldn't let her do was blame or belittle herself.

"Jim's done enough of that," Linc said. "You don't need to do it to yourself."

Jim came over the following day—he'd had no problem figuring out where she'd gone. He wanted to end their marriage. He was sorry; he hadn't wanted her to find out that way. He went on and on about financial details while she pretended to listen.

When he finally paused for breath, she told him about the pregnancy, and he reacted with anger. She would have to have an abortion, he said.

He began badgering her about it, calling her several times a day at Linc's to try to persuade her, and she slipped deeper and deeper into a pit of despair. Permanent escape began to sound like a wonderful idea, but when she confided that thought to Linc, he called Valerie, who arranged to have her hospitalized. In the hospital, Susanna decided she could not have an abortion. Her father was dead, her mother was as good as dead, and she no longer had a husband. She wanted her child above all else, and it was concern for her baby that finally got her well.

Linc went to her doctor's appointments with her. He was there for her first sonogram, and he never missed any childbirth classes. He was with her through labor and during those frantic moments in the delivery room when it became obvious that something was terribly wrong. But it was when she saw Linc weeping over her baby's tiny gray body that, in her mind, he became Tyler's father. Jim was nothing to her after that. As though they shared her feelings, everyone at the hospital treated Linc as if he were Tyler's father—the nurses, the social worker. After all, Jim was nowhere to be found.

Tyler was four months old when she and Linc became lovers. She'd been sleeping in his guest room for over a year by then, and one night he simply came into her room, took her by the hand, and walked her back to his own bedroom. And there he made love to her, and it felt so rational, so simply right, that she wondered why they had put it off for so long. The commitment between them had been forged a long, long time ago, and they both knew it.

Now Linc's slow, soft voice floated from the radio behind Kim's head. It sounded so close, she pretended he was lying next to her. Eyes closed, she reached out and touched the pillow, imagining she was stroking Linc's cheek, touching his lips. She rolled away from the pillow with a sense of defeat. How could she go on this way, living for Sunday nights, when all the while she knew that the morning would reveal the truth? Her lover would be gone, leaving in his place only the impersonal hum of a stranger's voice on the radio.

BONNIE Higgins stood up as soon as she saw Peggy at the door of the waiting room of the Legal Aid office.

"Everything's changed," she said as she followed Peggy back to her office. "I found out he's been having an affair."

"Oh, I'm sorry," Peggy said, although she was not surprised.

"It's been going on for years." Bonnie still looked stunned by the news. "It's his secretary." She sat down in front of Peggy's desk.

"How did you find out?" Peggy made some notes on a legal pad.

"She called me and told me all about it. She asked me to please let him go. 'Don't make it so hard on him,' she said."

"Has he denied it?"

"No. He told me everything. He's feeling guilty."

"Okay." Peggy leaned forward. "This changes your case, but only slightly. We'd better get to work on a property settlement."

She spent another forty-five minutes with Bonnie, then left the Legal Aid office. She was going to have lunch with Ron today. After picking up some submarine sandwiches, she headed for his office. He was waiting for her when she arrived.

"Hi, sis." He kissed her cheek and sat down behind his desk.

She took a seat and handed him his sub and a can of root beer.

"How are you doing?" Ron popped the top on his root beer.

"All right," she said, unwrapping her sandwich. "This whole

thing with Tyler is dragging on way too long, though. Three and a half weeks already." She peered uninterestedly inside her turkey sub. She really wasn't hungry. "Tyler's birthday was two days ago, you know. He's a year old now."

His birthday had been a sad day for her, made even sadder by the fact that Jim had not remembered the date until she reminded him.

"A year already, huh?" Ron said. "Doesn't seem that long ago that I did his surgery."

"I was thinking," Peggy said. "We should probably send some information about Tyler to general practitioners around the country, in addition to the cardiologists. Susanna will have to take him to a doctor at some point."

Ron had already helped Bill Anderson put together a medical report on Tyler, which they'd sent to hospitals and pediatric cardiologists around the country. He sighed. "I'm not going to write another report, Peggy. You can use the one I already wrote if you think it's so important."

She was disturbed by his tone of voice. "I wasn't suggesting a new report. But . . . I guess I don't understand you, Ron. Why wouldn't you want to do everything possible to find Tyler?"

"Peggy"—he swallowed a bite of his sandwich—"when I listen to you talk about all this supposed danger Tyler is in with his mother, I just . . . I can't be party to that sort of hysteria."

"Hysteria?" She was incredulous. "Are you saying you think Tyler is better off with Susanna than he would be with us?"

"If 'better off' means having anything money can buy and the attention of two parents, then of course he's better off with you and Jim. But if it means being loved and well cared for, then I see no difference which parent he's with."

"The court—"

"I don't care what the court said. Susanna didn't lose custody because she was an unfit mother. She lost because she lacked the resources to fight you and Jim."

"Oh, Ron, that's simply not so. Money had very little to do with it. Other things came into play, and you know it. What about Linc

Sebastian? Do you like the idea of Tyler spending time with someone like that?"

"Linc served his time. He paid for what he did. And I think he genuinely cared about Tyler. Linc was at the hospital for Tyler's emergency surgery. Not you. Not Jim."

Peggy bristled. "We weren't there because we knew it would make things more complicated if we—"

"Peggy," Ron interrupted, "listen to me. Jim became interested in Tyler when *you* became interested in Tyler."

"You've never liked Jim," she said. "You've always hated lawyers."

Ron laughed. "You're a lawyer, and I love you."

"I don't feel very loved at the moment."

"You're missing my point," Ron said. "You're a wonderful person. So is Jim. So is Susanna. So is Linc Sebastian, as far as I know. There's no right or wrong here, just a lot of pain."

"What do you mean, no right or wrong? Susanna broke the *law,* Ron. She kidnapped a baby. She's a criminal."

"You and Jim made her into a criminal when you pressed criminal charges. You turned a frightened mother into a felon."

"We *had* to make her a felon," Peggy argued, "to get the authorities to take the case seriously."

Ron leaned toward her. "How would you have felt in Susanna's position? You get pregnant, then discover your husband is sleeping with another woman."

Peggy winced. Ron was the one person to whom she'd confessed that miserable incident in Jim's bedroom. "I never should have told you," she said.

"So you find your husband with another woman," Ron continued, "and then you have to give up your new home to her. Not only that, but—surprise!—the other woman wants your baby, too."

"That's not fair. You're making me sound like a villain."

"No one's a villain. But just because you are not able to have a baby yourself doesn't mean you're entitled to someone else's."

Peggy stared at her brother in wounded silence. Then she

rewrapped her sandwich, picked up her purse, and started for the door. "I thought I'd only lost my stepson," she said, her throat tight, "but I see now that I've lost my brother, too."

"You haven't lost me," Ron said. "All I'm saying is that I can't, in good conscience, join you in bashing Susanna any longer."

Chapter 7

I LOVE this early autumn smell." Ellen sat down in one of the porch rockers and smiled at Kim and Lucy. "It's one of those comforting smells from childhood, you know?"

"Yes," Lucy said. "It's just like where I grew up in Pennsylvania."

"I guess you didn't have this sort of smell as a kid in L.A., huh Kim?" Ellen asked.

"No." Kim leaned over to fix the cuff on Cody's jeans. "It's the smell of smog that comforts me."

They laughed, and Kim chuckled herself, pleased with the ease she was beginning to feel with her two neighbors as she settled into Kim Stratton's life. As she created Kim Stratton's life. She'd learned to deal with Lucy's many questions by saying whatever popped into her head, and Lucy did not seem to notice the inconsistencies in her answers. People accepted whatever you told them, Kim was discovering, as long as they had no reason to doubt your story.

She and Cody had drifted into a routine that let her hope her new world might hold promise and not pain. Early mornings were spent over coffee on the porch with Lucy. Ellen usually had clients in the morning, so it was rare for her to be able to join them. This morning, though, Ellen's first client had canceled, and since Kim had proclaimed this to be Cody's birthday, she had joined in the celebration. They ate doughnuts, and Cody unwrapped a pull toy—a wooden basset hound—from Lucy and a mobile of stars and planets from Ellen.

After coffee Kim usually took Cody for a walk through town or to a nearby park, where she could push him on the swing. She loved to see the healthy glow from the fall air on his cheeks.

She had a fairly substantial amount of work now. Kitty Russo was keeping her busy, and she'd received a paycheck when she turned in the last of the typing on Friday. It was a good start.

Cody pulled himself up to his feet, one hand on the glider, and Kim showed him how he could walk by holding on to the glider with one hand. She studied her son. In a few hours she was taking him to the pediatrician Lucy had recommended, and she was not looking forward to it. She'd tackled Cody's medical records over the weekend—a stack two inches thick—pulling out the information that looked important and typing it into a fresh document. On the sheets with blood work, she whited out the name of the lab as well as Tyler's name and typed "Cody Stratton" over it, along with the fictionalized name of a lab in Trenton, New Jersey. She took her work to a nearby copy shop and made two copies. Then she stayed up half the night wondering whether or not doctors would be on the lookout for a year-old boy with a telltale scar on his chest.

"I've got another cancellation this afternoon," Ellen said. "Maybe I'll call Cherise Johnson and see if she wants to come in. She's got a flexible schedule."

Kim looked up at the mention of Cherise's name. "I keep forgetting to thank you for asking Cherise to invite me to her gallery when I first got here," she said.

Ellen looked puzzled.

"Remember when Cherise had a showing of Adam Soria's paintings at her gallery and she sent me an invitation? I didn't know a soul in town at the time, so I assumed you mentioned me to her and that's why she invited me."

"Hmm." Ellen leaned back in the rocker. "I might have mentioned to her that someone moved in upstairs, but I don't think

I went into more detail than that. I'm glad she asked you anyhow."

"Me, too," Kim said. "That's where I met Adam and Jessie."

"Ah, yes . . . Adam," Lucy said. "So tell us, Kim, is he your boyfriend?"

Kim looked at her in surprise. "Adam?" she asked as if the question were ridiculous—which it was. "He's just a friend."

"Well," Lucy said, "let's find me a friend that handsome."

Kim hadn't thought of Adam as handsome. She hadn't evaluated his looks one way or the other. Suddenly, through the open upstairs window, she heard her telephone ringing. Setting down her mug, she went into the house, taking the stairs two at a time.

"This is Noel Wagner," an unfamiliar male voice said. "I'm a friend of Jessie Soria's."

Kim remembered the name. Jessie's old boyfriend. "Yes?"

"Do you feel like typing the great American novel?"

"I beg your pardon?"

He laughed. "I've been working on a book," he said. "But I write in longhand. Do you think you could type it for me?"

"I'd be happy to. I charge two dollars a page, double-spaced."

"Sounds good to me," he said. "I'm in no rush for it. I'll drop by a couple hundred pages to start you off."

"I don't mind picking them up if you live close by."

"Well, that'd be great," he said. "I've been living in an apartment above Kelly's Music Shop ever since Jessie kicked me out. Do you know where that is?"

"Yes. Is sometime between three and four all right?" She could stop by on the way back from the doctor's.

"I'll be here," Noel said.

Kim was grinning as she hung up the phone. She immediately picked up the receiver again and dialed Jessie's number. "Thank you," she said when Jessie answered. "Noel just called, and I'm going to be doing some typing for him."

"Great," Jessie said. "He's a good writer. Alcoholics make good writers." There was an edge of bitterness to her voice. "But his handwriting isn't very legible. He's been through a couple of typists already. Their optometrists ordered them to give him up as a client."

Kim laughed. "Listen," she said impulsively, "I'd like you and Adam to come to dinner tonight. As a thank-you for all you've done for me. And besides, it's Cody's first birthday."

"Is it really?" Jessie asked. "Well, we'll definitely have to come, then. I'll check with Adam and get back to you."

THE doctor's office was packed. Seeing the crowd in the waiting room helped Kim relax. Cody would be one patient among many. He would not stand out from the crowd.

After a long wait a young nurse ushered them into an examining room. She instructed Kim to undress Cody, then left them. A few minutes later the doctor walked into the room and shook her hand. "I'm Dr. Sweeney," he said. "And this is Cody?" Kim could see that the doctor was already fascinated by the scar on Cody's rib cage.

"What's this?" He ran one finger lightly over the smooth skin, and Cody giggled.

Kim licked her lips. They were very dry. "He was born with coarctation of the aorta," she said, "which was corrected by surgery. I brought those records with me in case you wanted to see them."

"Yes, I'd like to." Dr. Sweeney sat down and began leafing through the records. Midway through, he frowned, deep lines forming across his forehead, and Kim read all sorts of things into that frown. Her muscles tightened. She was ready to bolt for the door. She vowed that if they made it through this appointment, she would come up with a plan of escape from Annapolis that she could put into place at a moment's notice.

"Who was the surgeon?" Dr. Sweeney asked.

"Dr. Farnhager." The fabricated name popped out of her mouth. It was so silly, she almost laughed. "He's in L.A."

"I used to practice in L.A. What hospital was he affiliated with?" Dr. Sweeney asked. "I don't remember his name."

"I'm not sure how long he's been practicing there." She struggled to convey an air of indifference in her voice. "But he has an excellent reputation. We were lucky to get him."

L.A. If anyone ever requested a time line of where she'd been living when, she'd be in deep trouble.

She had not answered Dr. Sweeney's question, but he seemed finished with his interrogation. At least for the moment.

He examined Cody. His manner was very quiet, and Kim squirmed in the silence. She shouldn't have written her correct address on the forms she'd filled out in the waiting room. The police would probably be waiting for her when she got home.

"You can go ahead and get him dressed," Dr. Sweeney said after giving him his shots. "He seems hale and hearty. I'll give you the name of a cardiologist who can do the echocardiogram on him, but I don't think you need to rush."

She dressed Cody, paid for the appointment with a hastily written check, and breathed a sigh of relief when she and Cody were back in the car. That doctor had been entirely too uncommunicative, she thought as she drove toward Noel's apartment. Had he been merely thinking about his tennis game, or was he plotting a call to the police? He might be staring right this minute at a flyer or the back of a milk carton with a picture of her and Cody on it.

She needed an escape plan, she thought again. She would keep a fat black felt-tipped marker in her glove compartment to alter her license plate. And she should keep a good amount of cash in the apartment. That way, if she had to leave in a hurry, she wouldn't lose everything. What she would take with her would depend on how much time she had. Under the best of circumstances she could take the computer and printer out to her car under the cover of darkness. At the very least, she would take the playpen and the stroller.

She found the music shop and grabbed a parking spot in front of the store. She got Cody out of the back seat and climbed the stairs at the rear of the building. Noel greeted her and Cody at the door, looking every bit the hard-drinking novelist. His brown hair was uncombed, and she could smell the subtle scent of alcohol as she walked past him into the living room. The sound of a flute wafted up through the floorboards from the shop below.

"You must have music here all day long," she said.

"Yes, I do. They give lessons. I look forward to the flute, actually. Every Monday at three. But the beginning violin lessons . . ." He shuddered. "Well, I have earplugs."

She laughed as Noel began stacking sheets of yellow paper into a pile. On a desk in the corner Kim spotted a picture of Noel and Jessie, caught in a grinning embrace. Jessie looked so happy that for a moment Kim did not recognize her. She guessed it had been a while since Jessie had grinned with such abandon.

Noel noticed her looking at the picture. "Jessie doesn't call me often anymore, but it seems she wants to help you out."

"She and Adam have been very kind to me."

"Yeah. They're good people," Noel said. "Screwed up by the accident, though. They sort of went off the deep end. I wish they'd get on with their lives." He looked at her appraisingly. "I'm glad to see that Jessie's made a friend who has nothing to do with what happened. Maybe she's finally moving on."

He loved Jessie, still. That was apparent.

"Here we are." Noel fit the thick pile of paper into a cardboard box. "I'll carry this down for you," he said.

They walked down to her car. Kim buckled Cody into his car seat, then took the box from Noel and put it on the passenger seat.

"Call if you have trouble reading it." He grinned.

"I will," she said, and drove away. She made one more stop—to pick up chicken and an ice-cream cake for Cody's birthday dinner—then drove home. There were no police waiting for her at her apartment, and she felt silly for worrying. The doctor's visit was behind her, Cody was taken care of, and she had a bundle of work to do. She was glad she'd invited Jessie and Adam over to celebrate.

Jessie was carrying a wrapped gift, and Adam, a bottle of sparkling cider, when they arrived. "To toast the employed one," Adam said. "Told you we'd find you work." He surprised her by kissing her cheek as he walked into the apartment, as though they were old friends, and she was warmed by the gesture.

Jessie seemed more interested in Cody. "How's the birthday boy?" she asked, picking him up from the playpen.

"I'm not sure what I would have done if I hadn't met you two," Kim said. "I haven't heard anything back on the brochures I'd sent."

"Those things take time," Adam said. "People file them away until they need them. You'll get some calls."

"Noel can keep you going for a long time," Jessie said, bouncing Cody on her hip. "He's prolific. He lives for his writing."

Kim heard the bitterness again. "He seems to miss you," she said.

Jessie shrugged. "He could have me or the booze, not both."

Kim nodded. Fair enough.

"What word-processing program do you use?" Jessie walked over to her computer, now perched on the coffee table. Kim had moved it to clear the dining-room table for her dinner guests.

"WordPerfect," she said.

Jessie bent over to lightly touch the keys. "What else do you keep on it? Do you have any games? Myst or anything?"

"No. Sorry," Kim said. She'd removed the games the day after setting up the computer. "I'm afraid I'd never get any work done if I had games on it."

"You're more disciplined than I am." Jessie gave Cody a big kiss on the cheek and lowered him carefully into the playpen again. "What can we do to help?" she asked.

Kim put Jessie to work with the lettuce and the salad bowl, and Adam with the potatoes and the peeler, while she cut up the chicken. The three of them chatted as they worked together, and Kim felt lighthearted. She was actually having fun. She'd nearly forgotten about the possibility of the police showing up at her door.

Adam spotted the sketchbook next to the computer. "May I show Jessie your sketches?" he asked.

She nodded. Adam brought the book into the kitchen and leafed through the pages, with Jessie peering over his shoulder.

"They're really good, Kim." Jessie sounded surprised.

"When are you going to let me give you a lesson?" Adam asked. "Come on. You'd be doing me a favor."

How could she turn him down when he worded it that way? "All right," she agreed. "Whenever you say."

"Good." He closed the book. "You'll come to my studio, which is in my house. But till then, keep your sketchbook under your bed, and as soon as you wake up in the morning—before you even get out of bed—sketch what you've dreamed."

"I don't remember my dreams." It was a lie, but her dreams were every bit as negative and frightening as his.

"You will," he said. "Just give it a try."

Dinner was ready quickly, and the four of them sat down at the table, Cody next to Kim in his high chair.

"To Cody." Jessie raised her glass of sparkling cider in the air. "On his very first birthday."

Adam raised his glass as well. "And to Kim," he said. "The only one of us who's working these days."

Kim took a sip from her glass, glad they'd brought cider instead of wine. "Do you two drink alcohol?" she asked.

"Not anymore," Adam said. "I stopped drinking after the accident when I saw what havoc it could wreak on the unsuspecting."

"And I couldn't handle seeing Noel drink every day," Jessie said.

"Both my parents were alcoholics," Kim confided. "They were sloppy drunks. Mean drunks. They turned me off to alcohol."

"We were made for each other," Adam said, and there was something in his eyes that told her he was beginning to feel that was the truth. A well of conflict sprang up inside her. She liked Adam, but she could not imagine loving him. He was not Linc.

Yet there was such warmth in Adam's eyes. Such tenderness. Jessie saw it, too. Kim noticed her studying her brother's face, and she did not seem to like what she saw.

When dinner was finished, Jessie stood up abruptly and carried her empty plate to the sink. "We should go soon, Adam."

He looked at Jessie in surprise. "It's early," he said.

"You have to have dessert," Kim said.

"And Cody has to open his presents," Adam added.

Jessie let out a sigh. "All right," she said. "Sorry. I felt worn out all of a sudden."

Kim saw the worried look on Adam's face as Jessie cleared away his plate. She rose to get the gifts, suddenly feeling the need to hurry the festivities along.

Though he'd never had a birthday before, Cody seemed to know what was expected of him. He happily tore the wrapping off his presents. Kim gave him a couple of toys she'd found at a garage sale, while Jessie and Adam's gift was a beautifully illustrated book about animals. Then Kim brought out the ice-cream cake, a candle burning in the center of the icing. The three of them sang "Happy Birthday," then helped Cody blow out the flame.

"Ice-cream cake," Jessie said as Kim cut the first piece. "Molly's favorite. Remember, Adam?"

Adam nodded, and as if Jessie had popped a pin in him, he deflated. The smile he'd been wearing most of the evening was gone. "We had it at her birthday party the night of the accident," he said.

"Oh." Kim drew back. "I guess this was a bad choice."

"Don't worry about it," Adam said. "It looks great."

The mood of the evening, though, had lost its charm. Jessie didn't eat any of the cake. She took it on her plate, but Kim knew it would not be touched. Jessie again pleaded fatigue immediately after Adam had finished his piece.

"Stay if you like, Adam," she said. "But I'm leaving."

Adam looked clearly torn, and so was Kim. He had grown more attractive to her in the last hour, yet she was not at all certain what she wanted from him. She was too needy for her own good, she thought, unable to separate desire from loneliness.

Jessie brushed a hand over Cody's head as she passed his high chair on the way to the door. She was serious about going, and going *now.* She seemed almost panicky as she waited at the door, one hand on the knob, for Adam's decision.

"I'll come with you, Jess," he said, looking apologetically at Kim. He stood up.

Kim walked with him to the door. "Thanks for coming," she said. "And Cody thanks both of you for the wonderful book."

"It was a great dinner," Adam said. "I'll call you, and we can set up a time to—"

"Adam?" There was a plea in Jessie's voice.

"All right, Jess." He put his arm around his sister.

Kim watched them walk onto the landing, Adam holding tight to his sister's shoulders, and when they started down the stairs, Kim did not miss the unmistakable relief in Jessie's eyes.

"WE NEED music," Adam said as he walked toward the stereo in the corner of his studio. "Loosening-up music."

Kim stared at the empty canvas on the easel in front of her. Although this was the third night she'd painted in Adam's studio, it would be her first time painting on canvas, and she felt paralyzed, afraid of making a mistake.

"You *can't* make a mistake," Adam said as soulful piano music filled the air. He took her hand, moved it to the palette, and dipped her brush into a blob of pale blue. He swept her arm across the canvas, leaving a long blue streak. She gasped, then laughed.

"Now you don't have to worry about wrecking a pristine canvas," he said. "So have at it."

She stared at the blue streak. The first night she'd painted in Adam's studio, she'd felt awkward. She found herself holding back, afraid to show him her best for fear of his pronouncing it poor. Adam, though, encouraged her to stretch, to challenge herself, and soon she was doing her best and better.

The color and angle of the blue streak looked suddenly familiar to her. It reminded her of the sky above the house across the street. She began to paint the house from memory, trying not to be intimidated by Adam's glances in her direction.

She might not be falling in love with Adam himself, but she *was* falling in love with his house and his studio. Adam lived in a small two-story white house, the mirror image of Jessie's next door. Inside, the house was decorated in the same strong opaque shades that marked his paintings. Dotting the walls and covering tabletops and shelves were photographs and paintings of the family he'd lost. Dana had been attractive and slender, with a pretty, engaging smile. Her hair was a deep red, framing her face in soft waves.

A painting of Molly and Liam hung above the fireplace. Kim recognized it immediately as an Adam Soria painting, with its vivid green background and the white clothes of the children. She wondered how Adam could tolerate having it there in his home, an exquisite reminder of what he had lost. She felt dishonest and intrusive, being witness to the things Adam held dearest. He did not think to hide anything from her, while she hid everything from him.

The studio was in what had once been an attic. It had odd wall angles and a pitched ceiling, but every surface was painted white, and the effect was bright and inviting.

Cody slept in Liam's old bed while Kim painted. The room was still a little boy's room, and she'd worried that it would pain Adam to have another child in it. But it seemed, instead, to please him.

As a matter of fact, Adam seemed happy in general these past few days. There was laughter in his studio. More than once, though, she'd felt his eyes on her instead of on her work, and she knew she'd soon have to sort out her own feelings about him. All she knew now was that she needed his company. She wondered how she'd ever thought she could survive living in isolation.

A door slammed shut downstairs.

"Sounds like Jessie's here," Adam said.

They heard footsteps on the stairs, and Jessie appeared in the doorway to the studio. She looked tired. "Hi," she said, her voice flat. "I brought some pizza if anybody wants some."

Adam looked at Kim. "Hungry?"

She nodded. "Pizza sounds good."

Adam carried her brush to the sink, while she covered the paint palette with plastic wrap.

Jessie had come over every night she'd been there, and Kim began to see her as their chaperone. Any potential for intimacy between Adam and herself seemed cut short with Jessie's arrival, and Kim wondered if that was her plan.

In the living room, Jessie had set plates and the pizza on the coffee table and poured them each a glass of Coke. The television was on, the news a white noise in the background.

"Are you okay tonight, Jess?" Adam asked his sister.

"Sleepy." Jessie swallowed a bite of pizza.

Suddenly Adam leaned toward the TV. "That's right near here," he said. He turned up the sound with the remote.

A young female reporter stood in front of a blackened office building. There'd been an explosion in the building that afternoon, she said. An attorney was killed, along with a receptionist and her two small children, who happened to be with her at the time.

"What caused it?" Kim asked.

"It was a bomb," Jessie said. "I heard about it on the car radio when I went to get the pizza."

"Wasn't there another bombing around here recently?" Adam asked.

"Yes," Kim said. "I walked past the house where it happened. A woman was killed when she opened an Express Mail package someone left on her porch."

Adam squinted at the image of the building on the television. "It's that law firm down on Duke of Gloucester Street, isn't it? Sellers, Sellers, and Wittaker?"

The name was familiar. Maybe she'd sent them one of her brochures. "I've heard of them somewhere," she said.

"You've probably walked right by the building," Jessie said.

That wasn't it, Kim thought. Maybe someone had mentioned the law firm to her. It didn't matter. Her attention was drawn to the image on the screen, a picture of the receptionist and her husband as they cuddled their two small children.

Adam abruptly hit the OFF button on the remote. "Can't watch it," he said. His face was white, his jaw set, and the old pain she'd seen in his eyes when she'd first met him had returned.

"Are you okay, Adam?" Jessie asked. Her own eyes were red.

"Well, I'm in better shape tonight than that guy in the picture."

"Why the hell did she have her kids with her in an office building?" Jessie asked.

"Maybe she'd just picked them up from day care," Kim suggested. "Was it another Express Mail package?"

"Yeah," Jessie said. "That's what I heard on the car radio."

Adam shoved the pizza box away, as if he couldn't bear the smell any longer. "I think I've gotta turn in," he said, standing up. "Sorry, Kim." He tried unsuccesfully to smile and turned toward the stairs.

Impulsively Kim got to her feet and put her arms around him, keenly aware of Jessie's presence in the room. Maybe it was Jessie's comforting he needed right now? She let go of him and saw that Jessie's brown eyes were indeed glued to her brother's face. She should leave. This was a family pain she'd stumbled into.

She walked upstairs to Liam's old room. While she was getting Cody out of bed, she heard the door to Adam's room close, then heard it open as Jessie softly followed her brother inside. Downstairs, Adam's house was quiet and dark, and Kim closed the front door quietly behind her as she left.

When she arrived home, she lowered her son into his crib, then got into her own bed. There was something discomforting gnawing at the edge of her mind, but she couldn't quite get a grasp on it. Then it hit her.

She got out of bed and rummaged in her lingerie drawer for the disk containing the file the previous owner had left on her computer. She turned on the computer, inserted the disk, called up the information, and there it was: "Sellers, Sellers, and Wittaker, 5588 Duke of Gloucester Street, Annapolis, every damn day of the year. Use October 17, 2 p.m. (so all will be there)."

October 17. Today's date. And when had the bomb gone off? Hadn't the reporter said two o'clock?

Her hands were shaking as she looked at the previous name on the list. "Katherine Nabors, 448 Labrador Lane, Annapolis, 47, 2 children, 2 adults. September 27, 8:30 a.m., home."

Labrador Lane. She was certain that was the name of the street where the previous bombing had occurred. But the name of the victim of that explosion couldn't be Katherine Nabors. It simply couldn't be.

There were eight other people and businesses on the list. Kim printed the file in its entirety, set it on her desk, and tried to put it out of her mind so she could fall asleep. It wasn't so much those names that haunted her as she drifted off, though, as the white-jawed pain in Adam's face.

The following morning she went to the library and sorted through back issues of the local newspaper until she found the edition for September 28. The article she dreaded finding leaped out at her from the front page: WOMAN KILLED IN EXPLOSION. There was a picture of the house, and the caption read "Katherine Nabors, 47, killed by a bomb left in a package outside her front door."

The room began to spin, and Kim closed her eyes. By some bizarre twist of fate she had a hit list on her hands. But why these people? Why a housewife and a law firm? And what was the meaning of the "2 children, 2 adults," the "every damn day of the year"? Who were the others on the list? How could she warn them? She could hardly go to the police. There would be far too many questions and far too much explaining to do, and that would put a quick end to her low profile. But she couldn't simply ignore the information either.

The next name on the list was that of a man. "Ryan Geary, 770 Pioneer Way, Annapolis, 51, elderly couple. November 13, 9 p.m."

November 13. She had nearly a month to figure out what to do. Maybe she could write anonymously to the newspaper. Would the authorities be able to trace a letter? The television images of that young mother and her children filled her head. If only she'd made the connection before, maybe she could have prevented the tragedy.

She checked out a few books for Cody and then drove to the city dock to eat a take-out lunch by the water. Usually an hour by the water calmed her, but this afternoon nothing could ease her anxiety. She ended up throwing away most of her lunch, then began pushing the stroller aimlessly around town. She was not anxious to go home to her computer.

By the time she finally turned into her street, it was nearly five, and she'd lost a day of work. She would have to call Adam to tell him she wouldn't be over for her lesson, because she had to catch up on her typing. But he was already there, sitting on the top porch step. She was immediately flooded with the desire to tell him about the computer and the list of names. She wanted to tell him everything and knew she could tell him nothing.

"Hi," she said as she lifted Cody out of the stroller.

"I've been waiting for you," he said. "Let me take that." He collapsed the stroller with the quick action of a man who had raised two children through the stroller stage. Then he looked her squarely in the eye. "I'm sorry about last night," he said.

"Don't apologize. I know that news report upset you."

"Well," he said, "you're very understanding."

She knew instantly that something was different about Adam. There was a new tenderness in his smile, and he did not seem to want to take his eyes from her face. As they went into the house, she knew, as surely as if he'd told her, that he was falling in love with her. She didn't know whether to be flattered or afraid.

Once they were in her apartment, she heated Cody's dinner, then settled the little boy in his high chair and sat next to him. "I was going to call you," she said to Adam. "I have to work tonight, so I was going to cancel our lesson."

"I was going to cancel our lesson, too." Adam sat down at the minuscule kitchen table. "I was going to cancel because I wanted to see you tonight, but not over a canvas and paints. And not with Jessie around."

She winced at his openness, his willingness to be vulnerable when she was allowing herself to be anything but. She slipped a spoonful of carrots into Cody's mouth before responding.

"Adam," she said finally, deciding to be as frank as she was able, "I think I'd better tell you that I'm in love with someone."

He raised his eyebrows in surprise. "Ah," he said, as if that explained everything.

"I mean . . ." She fed Cody another spoonful. "It's confusing. Hard to explain. I doubt very much that I'll ever see him again. I left him behind when I moved here and our relationship is over. But he's still . . . in my heart. You need to know that."

"You mean— Are you talking about your ex-husband?"

"No. Someone else."

"What was the problem? Was he married?"

"No. Nothing like that. We both just knew it wasn't meant to be." Her chest tightened with the lie.

"Well, I'm glad you told me." Adam picked up a napkin and wiped a carrot spill from the edge of Cody's high-chair tray. "And it's all right. I don't think my feelings are very trustworthy these days anyhow. All I know is that I think about you a lot. And when I do, I feel very . . . happy." He smiled. "But Jessie says it's too soon to trust what I'm feeling for you."

"I think she's right," Kim said. "I don't think either of us is ready to get involved right now."

"Well, listen," Adam said with a sigh, "how about I make you dinner?" It was obvious he had no intention of leaving, and Kim gave up on the idea of getting any work done that night. It was a relief, actually, to have an excuse to avoid the computer. With its unsavory past life, it suddenly felt like a tainted presence.

She gave Cody a bath and put him to bed. By the time she returned to the kitchen, Adam had created a dinner of black beans, rice, frozen green beans, and chopped tomatoes, the stark contrast of colors looking like one of his paintings.

After dinner Adam tuned her radio to a station that played one slow, sensuous song after another. She danced with him, aware of his need to hold and be held, and she gave in to it. She, too, was hungry for closeness, and when he tipped her head back to kiss her, she responded in spite of herself.

"I want to stay over," Adam said into her hair.

Her head was on his shoulder, and she closed her eyes with the effort of choosing her answer. She wanted Adam to stay. He felt so warm in her arms. So solid. But she was afraid of hurting him.

"I'd like you to stay," she said, "but—"

"I know. You've been honest about the other guy. I'm not asking you to feel something for me that you don't."

They danced a while longer, then moved to the bedroom, where Cody was sleeping soundly in his crib. Kim trusted Adam. His kisses were tender and sweet, his touch warm and exciting. His hunger for her was matched by her own for him as they began to make love. But then she thought of Linc, and once his face was in front of her, she couldn't rid herself of it. Adam's gentle, skillful movements were lost on her, and soon she was in tears. She was glad it was too dark for Adam to see her misery.

ADAM was already awake when she opened her eyes in the morning, and he was watching her. "Where's your sketchbook?" he asked. "You need to sketch your dreams."

She groaned. "I told you, I don't remember my dreams."

"Before you go to sleep at night, you should tell yourself that you *will* remember them." He stroked her hair back from her forehead, and she felt affection in his touch.

"All right," she said. "I'll try it tonight."

She looked over at the crib, where Cody was still sound asleep, a splash of sunshine shimmering on his blanket. Then she looked at Adam and felt a smile form, unsolicited, on her lips. To her surprise she was not at all unhappy to wake up with him beside her.

KIM spent the entire day at the computer. Every once in a while, the TV images of the bombing swept into her mind, and panic rose in her chest. She brushed the thoughts away, telling herself she had time to figure out what to do, but those images kept barreling their way into consciousness each time she let down her guard.

She put Cody to bed around seven that evening and was sitting at the computer when she heard the slamming of a car door. She looked out the window to see a police car parked at the curb and a male police officer walking up to the house.

She jumped up and switched off the overhead light. She thought she could feel the vibrations of his steps on the floor of the porch, but she did not hear him ring the bell to be let in. She tiptoed to her door and pressed her ear against the wood.

The front door creaked open, and she heard the man's heavy footsteps on the stairs. She would hold very still. Pretend she was not here. How did he know? The doctor? A private investigator? Had someone been watching her every move?

The knock came, and although she'd been expecting it, she jumped. It was a soft knock, muffled, and only when it came again did Kim realize the officer was knocking on Lucy's door, not her own. She heard Lucy open her door and a mumbled exchange of greetings. Lucy's door shut again. She had let him in.

Had Lucy figured out who she was? Had she turned her in? Would it be a matter of minutes before the officer left Lucy's apartment and knocked on Kim's door, for real this time?

She'd taken two thousand dollars out of her bank account the day before so she'd be ready to leave at a moment's notice. Was this the moment? Did she have the time to pack up a few things and leave quietly before the police officer knocked on her door?

Paralysis set in as she tried to think through her limited options, and she jerked back to attention when she heard Lucy's door open again. She waited stiffly for the knock on her own door, but instead, the footsteps thudded on the stairs once again. The front door opened and closed. A moment later a car engine coughed to life.

She leaned back against the door, breathing hard. Was he getting some backup? Or might he have been seeing Lucy about something totally, blessedly unrelated to Kim Stratton?

Thirty minutes passed before she could move. She turned off the computer. Mechanically she packed her duffel bag and filled some garbage bags with things to take with her. The thought of leaving was suddenly appealing. She'd gotten herself in too deep here. She knew terrible, incriminating information she did not want to know. She was involved with a man she seemed destined to hurt. It would be so easy to pile up her car with her belongings and drive away.

In her bedroom, she leaned over the side of the crib to look at her sleeping son. He'd adjusted so beautifully to the move, and he seemed to love his little world: the apartment, the park, the wonderful long walks around town. How could she uproot him again so soon? She'd wanted more for her child than she'd ever had for herself, and she was well on her way to giving him less.

You always run away from your problems, Linc had told her more than once. *You're always looking for an easy way out.*

She hadn't wanted Kim to be that way. She turned the garbage bags upside down on the bed and shook out their contents. Susanna Miller had been the escape artist; Kim Stratton would have to be stronger than that.

Chapter 8

IT WAS Sunday evening and Kim had just gotten Cody to bed when she heard Simon and Garfunkel's "Song for the Asking" on the radio. She turned off the light and got under the covers.

"Welcome to *Songs for the Asking,*" Linc said. As usual, his voice brought tears to her eyes. *I miss you, Linc.* She listened to the music, willing the songs to go quickly so she could hear his voice in between them. She pictured him sitting in his studio, taping this show, shuffling the CDs. She saw him leaning back in his chair, drinking coffee from the mug she'd given him for his last birthday.

Too soon there was an instant of silence from the radio, and then Leonard Cohen's voice filled the air. *"Suzanne takes you down . . ."* The end of the show.

When it was over, she sat on the sofa writing a letter to Linc in her head. It was filled with innuendo, with esoteric meaning only he would understand. It made her laugh out loud, and somewhere around the third or fourth paragraph she knew she was going to actually write the letter. On paper. And mail it. No, fax it, from some other town. He received hundreds of faxed requests for music. Anyone sifting through his mail to see if she were in contact with him would never be able to separate her requests from the others. She would make sure of that. But Linc would be able to. He would know.

She sat down at the computer and looked out the window toward the dark river.

"Dear Linc Sebastian, I'm writing from my place near the river," she began to type, an allusion to a line from the song "Suzanne." "I would appreciate it if you would play the following for me." She listed several songs he would recognize as her favorites. Then she signed the letter "S.T.U. Downe," alluding to the first line from "Suzanne."

She slept well that night, content that in a few hours her words would find their way into Linc's hands.

"WHEW!" Peggy looked at Nancy across the ruins of the Currys' family room.

Nancy put her hands on her hips. "Glad that's over."

Peggy sank into the chair closest to the front door. "So that's what life is like with kids in the house." She'd spent the afternoon helping Nancy with a birthday party for her twelve-year-old daughter, Renee, with twenty wild and giggly preadolescent girls. Even with the last of the girls out of the house, Peggy's ears still rang from the din. She was truly exhausted. But it had been fun.

"Renee's adorable," she said. She smiled and cocked her head at Nancy. "Do you think girls are easier to raise than boys?"

"No way."

"Well, I hope I get the chance to find out." It had been five weeks since she'd last seen Tyler.

"You will," Nancy said. "You've got to."

"Nothing's worked so far," Peggy said with a sigh. "All the legal channels seem to be failing us."

"You know . . ." Nancy looked pensive. Her voice drifted off.

"Know what?" Peggy asked.

"Oh, I'm just confused about something."

"About what?"

Nancy looked at her. "Well, I feel awkward talking to you about it, but I was talking to my sister the other day. Remember? She worked with Susanna? Well, her take on the whole situation is so different from yours. Julie said that everyone liked Susanna at the bank. They thought she was really nice and a very good mother."

Peggy's defenses sprang to life. "They're her friends," she said. "Of course they'd think that."

"She *did* say that Susanna was pretty unassertive, though. A very passive sort of person. Certainly not the type to take the law into her own hands. She said no one at the bank could believe she'd leave like that, but they all seem to think she did the right thing. Julie said that when their supervisor told them Susanna had taken off, there was this stunned silence and then everyone started cheering."

"They cheered?" Peggy was incredulous.

Nancy nodded.

Peggy could tell that Nancy had more to say. "What else?" she asked.

"Well, it's Julie's opinion that Jim held himself above everyone at the bank. He never came to any of the bank parties or picnics or anything."

Peggy shook her head. "He was probably too busy. Law school was incredibly demanding, and his job is even worse."

Nancy nodded, as if that explained everything, but Peggy knew in her heart that Jim *did* tend to see himself as superior. It annoyed her sometimes, especially when he'd tell her she was wasting her skills working with the "sort of clients" she saw at Legal Aid.

"He can seem a little haughty sometimes," she admitted, "but it's because he worked so hard to get where he is." She smiled. "You still haven't met him. I don't want your feelings about him tainted by other people before you've gotten to know him yourself."

"Oh, I know," Nancy said quickly. "And don't worry. I'll keep an open mind. According to Julie, Susanna thought Jim was pretty great herself, at least until they broke up." Nancy leaned over to pick up a piece of crumpled wrapping paper. "Everybody at the bank, though, is under the impression that you were having an affair with Jim while he was still married to Susanna. I told Julie that was off the wall. It really got my back up. I hate people to think of you as a home wrecker."

Peggy glanced at Nancy. "I *was* seeing Jim for a while before he officially ended things with Susanna," she said quietly.

"Oh, Peg." Nancy grimaced, disappointment in her face. "I wanted it to be a rumor. Something Susanna was making up."

Nancy's husband, Gary, suddenly walked in the front door, back from taking some of Renee's friends home. "I was hoping you two would have this place cleaned up by now," he said, a smile on his bearded face. He sat down, oblivious to the tension in the room.

Nancy's eyes were still on Peggy. She was probably viewing things from Susanna's perspective for the first time, Peggy thought. And now with Gary in the room there was little Peggy could say to change the direction of her thinking.

"Nance, I'd better be going." Peggy got up from the chair, a pocket of shame burning in her chest.

Nancy stood up to walk her to the door. "Thanks for helping out. I couldn't have gotten through today without you."

Peggy felt a desperate need to clear the air. "Seriously," she said, "let's get together sometime soon. The four of us."

Nancy touched her arm in what Peggy hoped was a gesture of understanding. "We'd love to," she said.

Peggy walked out to her car, remembering the last time she'd mentioned going out with Nancy and Gary to Jim. The first thing Jim had asked her was what sort of work the Currys did, and he had not seemed impressed that they were both teachers. "We wouldn't have much in common with them," he'd said. She wondered now if he'd been referring to interests or income.

FORTY-TWO faxes had arrived during the night. Linc opened the shades, wincing against the Boulder sunshine, then sat down with a cup of coffee and began reading the faxes, chuckling over some of them, jotting requests on a notepad. A woman from Cleveland wanted him to do a profile of Donovan. Good idea. He made a note, then flipped to the next fax.

"I'm writing from my place near the river."

Did he know this person? Seemed like an odd way to start. He glanced at the name. "S.T.U. Downe." Weird. He read on.

"I would appreciate it if you would play some of my favorite songs on your next show: 'Desperado,' 'Circle Around the Sun,' 'Fire and Rain,' and 'Suzanne.' "

He looked out the window. Then he turned to the fax again with a fresh eye. "I'm writing from my place near the river. . . . S.T.U. Downe." Susanna. It had to be.

The return line at the top of the fax listed a 301 area code. He picked up the phone from the table and dialed the operator. Area code 301 was in Maryland.

"And how about the 598 exchange?" he asked.

"Rockville," the operator said.

He hung up the phone and stared at the fax. Rockville. He'd been there once. It was near Washington, D.C. Not too far from the Potomac River. Was that the river Susanna was referring to? He doubted it. She wouldn't put as much effort as she had into disappearing and then fax him from the very town in which she was living. But at least he now knew what part of the world she was in.

Linc spent that afternoon carefully selecting music for the show he would tape the following day. He was not going to play the songs Susanna had requested, at least not at the beginning of the show. Instead, he was going to send her a message. He deliberated for hours over what he would say to her, poring over tapes and CDs. He would have to reach far outside the type of music he usually played, and he would probably take some flak for it, but he didn't care.

KIM arrived for her lesson at seven. After settling Cody in Liam's bed, she went upstairs to the studio, where Adam was squeezing paint onto the palette.

She felt things weighing on her tonight and had a hard time concentrating on her painting. She'd been watching the news and reading the paper, hoping that the police would find the person who had planted the bombs and save her from having to do something about the information in her possession. The list of names haunted her. She had the unwanted power of being able to predict who was going to die. One more week, she'd told herself. If the police had not found the killer by then, she would have no choice but to find some way to help them out.

After the lesson Adam put a sheet of plastic wrap over the palette, then put his arms around her and pressed his lips against her temple. "Stay here tonight, Kim," he said. "Stay with me."

She had not intended to spend the night. Her memory of the last time, when visions of Linc had clouded her head, was still keen. She would have to keep Linc from creeping into her mind tonight. Over and over again she'd imagined him reading the fax she'd sent. He would either know it was from her, or he'd overlook it in the stack of requests. By now he had done one or the other, and there was nothing she could do to change that outcome.

"Can we watch the late news if I stay tonight?" she asked Adam.

"The news?" He looked surprised.

"I'm curious about the bombings. I keep watching to see if they've gotten any clues. They haven't mentioned anything about it in days. It's like they're not even trying to solve the mystery."

"Oh, I'm sure they are. The cops often know more than they say publicly, in case the bomber's following the news. They're probably setting a trap for him right now."

She hoped he was right. They watched the news, and the only allusion to the bombing was the mention of a memorial service for the secretary's children. Seeing pictures of those children reinforced Kim's gloom, and she was glad she'd agreed to stay the night.

Very early the following morning she opened her eyes to see Adam propped up against his pillow, drawing in a sketchbook. She didn't want to disturb him, and she feigned sleep when he got out of bed and walked into the bathroom. Curious, she leafed through his sketchbook, which he'd left on his side of the bed. She recoiled from the first several pages, filled with images of hollow-eyed people, wolves with their teeth bared, and tongues of fire. The last few pictures, though, were different: trees, flowers, dolphins, ships, a woman fishing from a dock, a small town viewed from the air.

Adam walked back into the room as she was studying one of the sketches. She looked at him. "I hope you don't mind," she said, nodding toward the book. "I couldn't resist."

He shrugged. "I saw yours," he said. "Fair is fair."

"The beginning, though." She shook her head in sympathy. "What terrible nightmares you were having."

Adam smiled and walked over to the bed. "Ah, yes. But you, my sweet thing"—he leaned over to kiss her—"have completely changed my dreams."

KIM was working on Noel's book later that morning when someone knocked on her door. She jumped, a small well of panic rising in her chest. Ever since seeing the police car in front of the house, she had not been able to react calmly to the phone ringing or to an unseen visitor at the door.

"Who is it?" she called out.

"Jessie."

Relieved, she got up and opened the door. Jessie walked into the living room. "I was nearby and wondered if you might be taking a lunch break soon."

Kim looked at her watch and only then realized how hungry she was. "Sure."

"Great." Jessie smiled, but it was a guarded smile. "We could walk down to the deli or—"

"Let's eat here," Kim said, heading into the kitchen. "I've got tuna salad. Peanut butter and jelly. Or"—she picked up a can with a wry smile—"mini ravioli. Cody's favorite."

"Tuna sounds good," Jessie said. Cody crawled across the floor and lifted himself to a standing position by hanging on to her pant leg. She picked up the little boy and pressed her lips tenderly to his cheek. Kim was touched by the gesture.

She dumped the can of tuna into a bowl. "You know, Jessie," she said, "I got the feeling when I met Noel that he misses you a lot. He still has pictures of you around his apartment."

"I know he does. I miss him, too, but he wouldn't acknowledge that he had a problem and . . ." Jessie shrugged.

"I understand," Kim said quickly. The last thing she wanted to do was talk someone into a relationship with a drinker. She finished making the tuna salad and put it on the table, along with a few slices of bread and a couple of plates. Then she microwaved some ravioli and lifted Cody into his high chair.

"Anyhow," Jessie said, "I didn't come here to talk about Noel."

"Ah." Kim sat down next to Cody. "You have an agenda."

Jessie took a slice of bread and spooned tuna salad onto it. "I like you, Kim," she said. "And if Adam were ready to get involved with someone, I'd be really happy it was you." She placed a second slice of bread on top of the tuna. "But he's *not* ready. It's too soon. He lost his entire family. He hasn't had time to get over it yet, and I'm afraid he's jumping into something with you just so he can stop feeling the pain." She looked at Kim. "I understand him wanting to do that. I'd like to find an escape from the pain myself. But we need to feel it for a while."

Kim fed Cody a piece of ravioli. "I've been honest with him, Jessie," she said. "I've told him I'm not ready for a relationship either. Right now we're just a comfort for each other."

Jessie began to cry. "I know I'm being selfish. Until you came along, Adam and I were both wallowing in grief. It was awful, but at least we were doing it together. Now he's happier because you're around, and I'm still wallowing, all by myself."

"You must have been very close to Dana and the children."

"Molly and Liam were everything to me." She pulled a tissue from the box on the kitchen counter. "I don't think I'm the marrying type. I may never have children. Molly and Liam felt like the closest I might ever get to having kids of my own."

"There'll be other guys for you," Kim said. "There'll be children." She knew her argument was weak, even offensive. Molly and Liam were no more replaceable than Tyler Miller would have been had she lost him to Jim.

"It would have helped if the guy who killed them had to pay for what he did." Jessie tore at the tissue in her hands. Her face was red, and there was anger in her eyes. "This way there's no justice. No resolution."

"I know," Kim said. "I think Adam feels the same way."

"He *used* to feel that way," Jessie said bitterly. "At least until you came along. Now everything's just peachy."

"No. Everything's not peachy," Kim argued. "It's just that Adam's learning to—"

"Look, quit trying to fix my brother, okay? He needs to get better at his own pace."

Kim was surprised by the hostility in her voice. "I'm not trying to—"

Jessie held up her hands to stop Kim's words. "I know you're not intentionally doing anything to help or harm, but it's happening anyway." She stood up and took a step from the table.

"Aren't you going to eat?" Kim asked.

"I'm sorry." Jessie started for the door, and Kim felt distressed by the turn the conversation had taken. Jessie was jealous, all right, but not of the attention Adam was paying to Kim. She was jealous of her brother's ability to get on with his life.

Kim followed Jessie to the door. "I know this has been an awful year for both of you," she said, "but it's not fair for you to try to hold Adam back this way."

"Don't tell me what's fair," Jessie said. "Nothing, absolutely nothing, about life is fair. Maybe you haven't figured that out yet, Kim. You have this great little boy and a comfortable life. You don't know how quickly all of that can change."

Kim opened her mouth to argue that point but wisely closed it again. "Maybe not," she said quietly. "Maybe I don't."

Shutting the door after Jessie left, she leaned against it, eyes closed and her knees shaking from the confrontation. She knew more than Jessie could ever guess about life's unfairness.

IT WAS chilly the next morning when Kim put Cody in the stroller and started walking toward the park. The leaves seemed to have deepened to richer golds and reds overnight, and she felt as though she and Cody were moving through a tunnel of color as they approached the playground. The stroller made a crackling sound as she pushed it through the layer of fallen leaves.

After half an hour of pushing Cody on the swing, she left the park and started walking toward town and the bank. She'd gotten a check from Noel the day before, and she couldn't cash it soon enough.

As she neared the bank building, she noticed something different about the unfinished mural painted on its outside brick wall. At first she thought it was just the clean, bright October sunshine, but then she saw that the enchanting little snow-covered village depicted in the mural now had children skating on a frozen pond surrounded by pine trees laced with snow.

Best of all, though, the artist himself stood on a ladder at the far side of the mural, a huge paintbrush in his hand. Kim stopped, a smile spreading across her face.

"Hooray," she said under her breath. She quietly sat down on a bench a few feet away, then whispered to Cody, "Adam's painting. See the pretty church? See the children on the pond?"

When one of Cody's squeals caused Adam to turn around, he smiled and climbed down the ladder to walk toward them. "How long have you been sitting here?" he asked.

"Just long enough to feel overjoyed. How wonderful to see you working."

Adam sat down next to her. "Great weather for this," he said. "My favorite time to paint. And the dreams were there this morning. They've been there for a few days." He grinned at her. "My dream last night was about you, actually. I think that means I should paint you."

She groaned. "Try to find some other meaning in it, okay?"

An elderly woman walked by and let out a gasp of pleasure when she saw the mural. Then she noticed Adam sitting on the bench. "I've been praying every day to see you back at that wall again, Mr. Soria," she said.

"Thanks." Adam waved at her. "I can use all the prayers I can get." Once the woman had passed, he returned his attention to Kim. "Want to go to a movie with Jessie and me tonight?"

She wondered if Jessie would want to go out with them, given the conversation they had had the day before. "I don't think I'd better." She nodded toward Cody.

"Look," Adam said, "I've got a list of baby-sitters a yard long. We used them for Molly and Liam, so they're tried and true. Let me call one of them for you."

"No." She wrapped her arm lightly around her son.

Adam frowned. "It would be good for you to have some non-maternal time, Kim. Good for both of you."

She couldn't shake the feeling that leaving Cody with someone else for a few hours made her a bad mother. But Adam was right. Even the best mothers left their kids with sitters from time to time.

"All right," she agreed.

Adam glanced at his mural. "You going to watch for a while?"

"If that's okay with you."

"Be my guest."

She watched him work with a mixture of envy and admiration. There was something about the vast canvas that appealed to her, that made her arm ache with longing to sweep paint across that wide brick wall.

KIM left Cody at Adam's house that night with a baby-sitter while she and Adam and Jessie went to the movies. There were actually periods of time during the evening when Kim didn't think about Cody at all, but she declined Jessie's suggestion to get something to eat after the movie, and Adam supported her need to get home.

"It's mama's first night out." Adam hugged Kim's shoulders as they left the theater. "She needs to make it short."

Jessie didn't argue. Although she was quieter than usual, she did not seem to harbor any ill feelings toward Kim.

Kim felt ridiculous about her anxiety once they arrived at Adam's house. The sitter reported that Cody had slept through the entire evening. Kim checked on him and found him sound asleep, curled up with his monkey in Liam's bed. Jessie, though cheerful, seemed determined to foil any attempts at intimacy between her brother and Kim for that night, so Kim went home around eleven.

The following night Adam stayed at Kim's apartment. They spent the evening playing board games and watching a movie on TV. They spent Sunday together as well, Adam showing her sights around Annapolis she hadn't yet taken the time to explore. As evening approached, though, and Adam gave no indication of going home, Kim finally had to tell him she needed some time alone.

After Adam left, she lay in her bed waiting for the start of Linc's show, trying to form an image of him in her mind. Her memory of his face was beginning to blur.

"Song for the Asking" came on the radio. But before Linc even bothered to greet his listeners, he played the Everly Brothers' "Wake Up Little Susie."

"I'm awake, Linc," Kim said as she sat up straight in bed. She was impatient as she waited out the rest of the song. She knew he was playing it for her. He never played the Everly Brothers.

"Good evening, everyone. Got a lot of requests this week from all over the country," Linc said in his slow, easy radio voice. "Requests from Leslie Potters . . . and James Abbott . . . and S.T.U. Downe."

Kim grinned to herself. He rarely read the names of his requesters. He was letting her know. Not only had he received her fax, he was saying, he had understood it, and he knew she was listening right now.

"Some songs for Ms. Downe," he said, and he opened with "Philadelphia" by Bruce Springsteen. She hadn't requested "Philadelphia," and he didn't ordinarily play Springsteen. He had to be trying to communicate something to her.

She grabbed her sketch pad from under the bed and wrote down the song title. Next he played Simon and Garfunkel's "At the Zoo." Frowning, she wrote it down.

Then "The Lion Sleeps Tonight," and she thought she was beginning to understand. Was there a zoo in Philadelphia? When he played "Saturday Night's All Right for Fighting," she laughed out loud. Did he mean next Saturday? What time?

Then he played "Five O'Clock World" by the Vogues.

"Yes!" She laughed.

Linc finally spoke again. "Those were all for Ms. Downe," he said. "And now we'll move on to Leslie Potters's selections." Those songs were more typical of *Songs for the Asking:* old Joan Baez and Tim Hardin and Tom Paxton. Linc's listeners had to be wondering why S.T.U. Downe had ever tuned in to the Linc Sebastian show in the first place.

She looked at her pad. Unless she was reading him wrong, Linc was asking her to meet him on Saturday at five o'clock at the lion enclosure at the Philadelphia Zoo. She had a tiny fear that it might be a setup. Maybe they'd bargained with him. If they thought he was aiding and abetting her, could they threaten him with jail time again if he didn't cooperate to help them find her? Or maybe Linc himself was convinced that she'd done a terrible thing and he would have the cops waiting for her at the lion enclosure. But he would never betray her. If there were anyone in the world she could still trust, it was Linc. Tomorrow she would buy a map of Philadelphia.

Chapter 9

PEGGY hated Sundays. She hated weekends, actually, because she couldn't talk to the man who was working on Tyler's case at the National Center for Missing and Exploited Children. She couldn't talk to the police or to Bill Anderson, either; that is, she wasn't supposed to. She did call Bill the day before, though, to ask him if he'd checked Susanna's health insurance records again.

Bill didn't appreciate being bothered on a Saturday, and he let her know it. She backed down with an apology. The last thing she wanted to do was alienate any of the people who were helping them find Tyler, but she was disgusted with herself for her weakness. She was changing, and the change was not for the better. Her entire life she'd been strong and capable, someone who took action, who righted wrongs. Now she'd been reduced to a timid, ineffectual woman who waited around for others to solve her problems.

Jim took her to an afternoon movie "to get her mind off things." She did not understand how Jim could simply block the situation from his thoughts. He turned everything over to the authorities, put his trust in them, and then concentrated on his day-to-day workload. Peggy, on the other hand, was fairly useless the two days a week she was spending at Legal Aid. She wondered if she could still call herself a good lawyer.

When they got home from the movie, she turned on the radio and began making dinner, while Jim did some work. As she was sautéing chicken breasts, she decided there was something strange about Linc's show tonight. True, she'd only been listening to Linc's program since Tyler's disappearance, but he usually had a theme, some featured musician or type of music. Tonight's music was a mishmash, some of it rock and roll instead of the old and mellow folk-type songs he usually played. And he played "Wake Up Little Susie." And a little later, "Fire and Rain," with the line *"Suzanne, the plans they made put an end to you,"* and that's when she turned off the burner under the chicken and ran upstairs to Jim's study.

"Turn on Linc's show," she said. "He's up to something."

"What do you mean?" Jim sat back from his computer as Peggy tuned his radio to the show. Linc was playing a song by Peter, Paul, and Mary.

"He's been playing songs with 'Susan' in them," she said. "And he's playing a different type of music than he usually plays."

Jim seemed unimpressed. "This sounds exactly like the sort of song I'd expect to hear on his show."

"Well, this one, yes. But before, he was playing . . ." Her mind went blank. "I don't know, but believe me, this show is different." She sank into the armchair in the corner of the study. "Jim, he's up to something. I think he's in touch with her somehow. He's communicating with her."

"Hon." With a sigh Jim rolled his chair over to hers and took her hands in his. "I think you're reading too much into it. But if it will make you feel better, tomorrow we can call Bill Anderson, and he can try talking to Linc again."

Tears of frustration burned her eyes. "He'll just deny he knows anything, as usual."

Jim leaned forward to kiss her. "You know what we need?" he asked. "I think we need a vacation. Where would you like to go? This thing with Tyler has become our total focus."

"Of course it's our total focus," she said. "A member of our family is missing. How are we supposed to think about anything else?"

Jim nodded. "But worrying about it all the time is hurting us," he said. "I think we need a break."

Peggy pulled away from him and sat back stiffly in the chair. "Then take a vacation by yourself," she said angrily. "I'll let you know when I find your son."

Jim's jaw dropped open in surprise, and she immediately regretted her words. "I'm sorry," she said. "But I can't think about a vacation until we have something to celebrate. All right?"

He nodded and touched her cheek. "All right," he said. "It's just that . . . sometimes I feel as though my son isn't the only person who's missing. My wife is gone, too."

She winced. "Oh, Jim. Forgive me. I know I haven't been very . . . attentive to you lately." She had become not only a negligent lawyer and a helpless mother but a lousy wife as well. "Dinner's almost ready. You want to come down?"

"Sure." He rolled back to his computer. "I'll be down in a sec."

ON WEDNESDAY night, driving to Adam's house for her painting session, Kim took a detour. She wanted to drive past the home of Ryan Geary, the next victim on the list. She needed to believe that the man and his home were real, not some fictitious name and address on her computer.

The house was real, all right. It was set in a large tree-filled yard and separated from its neighbors by a patch of woods on either side. It was big enough to hold any number of people.

Kim finally had a plan of sorts. She would wait until November 6, exactly one week before the bombing was to occur. If she'd heard nothing on the news about the capture of the killer by then, she'd send the information on the list to the police. But she'd drive to a town a few hours away to mail it. Then she'd sit back and hope that the police would hunt for the killer instead of the messenger.

Kim stopped at a Chinese restaurant a few blocks from Adam's house and picked up some lo mein. Once at Adam's, she tucked Cody into Liam's bed while Adam and Jessie set the kitchen table. Adam was in a good mood—cheerful, hungry, and excited about a dream he'd had the night before.

"My colors are back," he said as he dug into the lo mein. "Everything's vivid again."

"The bank mural looks wonderful," Kim said. "It's almost finished, isn't it?"

"Finished it today, actually," Adam said. "Now I'm starting to think about something new. The Waterfront Museum has been after me to paint a mural on one of the walls of its entryway for years, and I've already gotten a few ideas."

Jessie had been running her fork idly through her noodles. "Do you think you should start another painting right away?" she asked. "Maybe you should take a break first."

"I'm on a roll, Jess." He squeezed his sister's hand reassuringly. "Everything's under control."

Kim and Adam talked about his dream from the night before as Jessie continued toying with her food. She helped them do the dishes, then excused herself and went home.

Upstairs in the studio, Kim worked on her painting, while Adam experimented with colors, hunting for the shades in his dream. "Does Jessie seem depressed to you?" Kim asked as they worked.

"No, she doesn't seem depressed." Adam didn't take his eyes from his canvas. "She *is* depressed."

"Well, maybe she needs some professional help."

"She saw a psychiatrist for a while. We both did. Jessie still gets into a funk now and then, but believe me, she's much better than she was. And I am much, *much* better." He sidestepped toward her and planted a kiss of gratitude on her neck, then returned to his canvas. He changed the subject. "Would you like to go to Washington with me on Saturday? There's an exhibit at the National Gallery I'd like to see."

She bit her lip. She would have to tell him about Philadelphia sooner than she'd wanted to. "Oh, Adam, I'm sorry," she said, "but I have to go out of town for the weekend."

"You do? Where are you going?"

It would be better if Adam didn't know where she was. But she couldn't lie to him any more than she had to. "Philadelphia," she said. "I'm visiting a friend there."

"Oh." Adam glanced over at her. "Is this friend, by any chance, the man who's 'still in your heart'?"

She hesitated long enough to let him know he was right. "There's a possibility that he'll be there." It was, after all, only a possibility.

Adam nodded without speaking and returned to his work. They painted quietly for twenty minutes or so before Adam set down his brush and left the room. When he didn't return after a quarter of an hour, she knew he was more upset than he'd let on. She covered her palette, then walked downstairs.

He was sitting in the dark living room. "I'm sorry if my plans upset you," she said as she sat down in the chair nearest his.

He drew in a long breath. "Well," he said, "I guess we made it pretty clear right from the start we weren't viewing our relationship as something serious. At least we said that. I'm not sure I meant it, though. I realize that now. I don't like the idea of you seeing him."

She nodded. "I don't blame you. I'd feel the same way. And I'm not certain that I *will* see him. But I have to if I can. We left too many things unfinished."

"This is some sort of closure, then?"

She sighed. "Adam, I don't know what it is. I can't make promises to you or to him. Not right now."

"So," Adam said, "my choice is to either end my relationship with you or accept the fact that you'll be sleeping with someone else this weekend, huh?"

His words brought tears to her eyes. She remembered how it felt to care about someone when you knew they were sleeping with someone else. She stood up and walked behind him. Putting her arms around his neck, she kissed the top of his head. "I don't even know if I'll be seeing him, much less anything else," she said. "I'm sorry, Adam. I'm trying to be honest."

He squeezed her hand. "I know. I wish you'd be conniving and deceitful instead. It would make things much easier." He slipped out of the circle of her arms and stood. "Back to work, all right?"

She nodded uncertainly. The conversation was over.

She followed him up the stairs to the studio. They worked together for another hour or so. But when it came time to decide if she should stay over or not, he didn't suggest it and she didn't ask.

PEGGY leaned back in her seat at the tiny Russian Café and tried to relax. She had called Linc Sunday night after his show, and he had reluctantly agreed to have lunch with her. Now, as she sat across from him, she pushed a menu toward him. "Let's order first, okay?" she said, although she was not in the least hungry.

He ordered the goulash, and she did the same. "Look, Linc," she said after the waitress had left, "are you in contact with Susanna?"

"No, Peggy, I'm not. I've told you and your people that a hundred times."

"Then why were you playing those Susanna songs on Sunday?"

"Pardon? Susanna songs?"

" 'Suzanne,' 'Wake Up Little Susie.' Those songs."

"Did I? It wasn't intentional, Peggy. I admit she's on my mind a lot. I was probably driven to play them by my subconscious."

Peggy felt her lower lip begin to tremble, but she was determined not to cry. "Linc, I want my baby back," she said. "Jim's and mine. I want him safe and sound, here with us. I doubt very much Susanna will use Jim's health insurance anymore, so that means she has no coverage for Tyler. And very little money. How can she possibly be getting him decent care?"

"Peggy, I know you sincerely care about Tyler, but he is not, no matter what the courts say, your baby."

She gritted her teeth. She was certain he knew more than he was telling her. "Look," she said, "you don't have to admit to me that you know where Susanna and Tyler are. I just want you to see that Tyler's welfare is in danger as long as he's with her."

"I don't agree."

She rolled her eyes. "The fact that she took off with him doesn't show the best judgment, does it?"

"It shows how desperately frightened she was about losing her child. Sort of like how frightened you are." He leaned toward her. His blue eyes were so intense that she had to force herself to hold his gaze. "You know how you feel?" he asked. "Well, trust me, she felt ten times worse about losing him. She gave birth to him. She carried him around in her body for nine months."

"There are plenty of birth mothers who carry their babies for nine months and still don't care a whit about them."

"That isn't true of Susanna, and I think you know it."

Peggy looked down at her hands. "Do we have to be enemies?" she asked quietly. "Is there any way we can work together on this?"

"I don't see how. You think she's a terrible mother and I think she's a terrific mother, and never the twain shall meet."

"Terrific mothers don't cut their children off from the people who love them and from good medical care. Her running away only proves how unstable she still is. She's poorly educated, a high school dropout. A very dependent person. It makes sense that someone so totally reliant on her husband would—"

"Peggy, just shut up, all right?" Linc interrupted her. He waited while their bowls of goulash were set in front of them, then began again. "You have bought into Jim's propaganda. Yes, it's true that

Susanna was a high school dropout. Her father was dead, she had no support whatsoever from her mother, who was an alcoholic, and she couldn't continue to live at home. So yes, she dropped out. She lived with my mother, she worked as a waitress to make money, and she studied like the devil to get her GED and go to—"

"Her father was dead because her boyfriend—*you,* in case you've forgotten—murdered him," Peggy said. "You left that part out. And I know both her parents were alcoholics. I'm supposed to want Tyler to be with a woman who was raised in that environment?"

"I wasn't her boyfriend," Linc said. "I was her neighbor. She can't help what her parents were, and she doesn't even drink. And being raised the way she was only made her want to be a better mother for Tyler." He lowered his voice. "Yes, I killed her father. I killed him to stop him from hurting his wife and his daughter. And I've never been able to muster up regret for what I did. He was a terrible, cruel, and abusive husband and father and human being."

She was fascinated by his candor, but this was going nowhere. "Look," she said, "it's ridiculous to argue about all of this. What we have to figure out now is—"

"I'm not done," Linc said. He swallowed some goulash. "So Susanna got her GED and went to college. But she dropped out because Jim asked her to support him as he finished school himself. He never told it to you that way, I bet. Susanna was planning to go back to school, but then Jim wanted to go to law school, so they still needed her income. Her turn would come later, he told her. So she worked in that bank, which she hated. When Jim finally started working, they could afford a house. Susanna spent weeks looking and found a terrific house. She was so excited about it. And to make things even better, she discovered she was pregnant."

"But things were not good between her and Jim at that point. She must have known—"

"Known what? Jim wasn't telling her anything about being unhappy. In fact, she thought that things were going to be great. He had a super job; she'd finally be able to go back to school; a baby was coming. Life looked like it was going to be perfect. Until that day she came home early from a business trip and discovered Jim in bed with some lawyer."

"Keep your voice—"

"And *that* was who he planned to live with. He'd let Susanna find the house, let her fantasize, while all the time he was setting his trap for you."

Peggy looked down at her untouched lunch, her insides churning. "I guess trying to get together with you was a mistake." She reached for her purse. She would put a twenty on the table and leave. But Linc grabbed her wrist.

"Look, you asked me here," he said, "and you're going to hear me out. I know you think Jim wants Tyler just as much as you do. But guess what? Susanna wasn't making it up when she said Jim wanted Tyler aborted."

"I don't believe that for an instant. Not an instant."

"Believe it. Susanna called me in tears the night after they fought about it. He'd gotten her the names of doctors and offered to pay for it. He even suggested a few low-tech ways she might take care of the problem herself."

"If Jim had ever wanted Tyler aborted, which I don't believe, it was only because he thought he might be yours."

Linc stared at her, wide-eyed. "Oh, Lord," he said. "That's rich. Tyler is not mine. Susanna and I never—not ever—had sex until quite a while after Tyler was born. Not when we were next-door neighbors. Not when she was married to Jim."

He sounded so sincere that she almost believed him. "Whether you were lovers or not is a separate issue," she said. "The fact is that Jim loves Tyler, and he—"

"I can't speak for how Jim feels now, but I'm telling you, Peggy, he didn't want that baby until he realized you wanted a child and couldn't have one. Then all of a sudden it was 'Are you taking care of yourself, Susanna? Taking your vitamins?' "

"That's an ugly accusation."

He laughed. "You bet it is. You're a catch, Peggy, one in a million for someone like Jim. He'd stand on his head in the middle of traffic if that's what he had to do to hold on to you. Making his ex-wife look like an unfit mother is nothing."

"Forgive me, Linc, but I'm having trouble believing the word of a convicted murderer over that of my husband."

He smiled at her. "You know, Peggy, I don't dislike you." His voice suddenly softened. "Actually, I admire you. You work for Legal Aid when you could be making a ton of money privately. And I know you love Tyler and you're genuinely worried about him."

A lump rose in her throat. "Is he okay? You don't have to tell me where he is, but is he all right?"

He shook his head. "I don't know where he is. Susanna left me as much in the dark as she left you. But I can just about guarantee you that Tyler's safe and happy."

It was unbearable, the kindness in his voice. She did not want tenderness from him. She wanted to slough off all he had told her, and return to her former disregard for him. She looked down at her lunch, then at his. His bowl was nearly as full as her own. "We didn't do too well with the goulash," she said.

"We weren't here to eat."

She nodded. It was the first thing they'd agreed on. With some fear in her heart she thought it might not be the last.

ALTHOUGH Peggy hadn't planned to tell Jim about her lunch with Linc, too much needed clearing up for her to keep it to herself. She managed to wait until they had finished dinner and were sitting in the living room reading the paper.

"I had lunch with Linc today," she said. "I was still thinking about that weird show he did, and I needed to pick his brain."

Jim set the paper down on his knees. "I wish you'd told me you were going to do that. I already had one wife seeing Linc Sebastian behind my back."

"Linc denies he and Susanna were lovers prior to Tyler's birth."

"Did you expect him to admit it?"

"He said that you wanted Tyler aborted. That you gave Susanna the names of physicians and offered to pay for it."

Jim sighed. "Well, I might have said something about it right in the beginning."

She was taken aback. "But you denied that you'd ever suggested abortion to her."

"I never *suggested* it. We were just weighing the options."

"And you gave her a list of doctors?"

"I don't know where Sebastian got that from. It didn't go that far. Susanna didn't want an abortion, and that was her choice."

"Linc said that Susanna thought your marriage was fine at the time she . . . found out about us."

Jim scoffed. "It was over, as far as I was concerned."

"But you never told her that? That you were feeling that way—"

"What is this third degree? I swear, Linc Sebastian can twist a woman's head around until it's upside down. I can't believe you let him get to you like this. And I'm really ticked off that you'd see him behind my back. I already lost one wife to him. I'd just as soon not lose another."

For a startled moment she wondered if this was how Susanna had felt, defending an innocent relationship with Linc to a jealous husband. "You haven't asked me if he said anything about knowing where Tyler is," she said.

"I haven't had a chance. You're badgering me with all these questions about things I thought we resolved long ago."

"Well, he said he doesn't know where Tyler is, and I think I believe him."

"So what does that mean? You and Linc are buddies now?"

"Of course not. I'm just saying that he might be telling the truth about not knowing anything."

Jim sighed. "Whatever you say."

"Sometimes I feel as though it's far more important to me than it is to you to get Tyler back."

"Are you kidding? I can't wait to get him back. Maybe then you'll feel like making love again."

"Jim."

"Sorry." He folded the newspaper and set it on the end table, then stood up and walked over to her. He bent low to kiss her forehead. "I'm sorry. Really."

She hesitated for a moment before putting her arms around his neck. She couldn't blame him. She did have a one-track mind these days. If she didn't keep her marriage healthy, Tyler wouldn't have a mother and father to come home to.

"Let's go upstairs," she said. "I promise, no more talk about Linc or Tyler or anything except you and me."

IT WAS four forty-five when Kim and Cody reached the lion enclosure at the Philadelphia Zoo. A busload of elementary-school children were laughing and screaming in the area in front of the enclosure. Kim hunted for Linc in the sea of children. Two frazzled-looking women were trying to maintain some sort of order with their charges, but other than the two of them and Kim, there was no one over four feet tall in front of the enclosure.

From out of nowhere a police officer appeared in the crowd and began talking to one of the chaperones. Kim turned so that her back was to him.

After a few minutes she glanced around. The police officer was still chatting with one of the chaperones, and they were both laughing. Kim looked more closely at his uniform. He was not a cop, after all. Just a security guard. She shook her head at her paranoia.

It was nearly five when she felt someone's arms wrap around her from behind. She started for a second, then let herself sink back against that familiar embrace.

He kissed her cheek. "I've missed you," he said.

She turned to face him, wrapping her arms around his neck. She tried to speak, but the words wouldn't come.

"I almost didn't recognize you." He touched her hair. "It's kinda cute." He kissed her tenderly, then bent down to Cody. "Hey, Ty." He lifted the little boy out of the stroller. "I think you've put on about ten pounds." He kissed his cheek.

"His name is Cody," she said.

Linc's eyes widened. He grinned. "Well, if you had to change it,

I'm glad that's what you changed it to. And who has Susanna become?"

"I don't think I should tell you," she said. "I think the less you know, the better off you'll be."

He studied her face a moment, then nodded. "All right," he said.

She glanced around them. The children were moving on to the next exhibit, and she felt exposed without their noise and activity forming a shield around them. "Could anyone have followed you here?" she asked.

He shook his head. "No one knew I was going anywhere, and I took a circuitous route to get here. I've been all over the country. It was kind of fun."

"It gets old quickly," she said.

His smile disappeared, and he shifted Cody to his other arm. "Just tell me this," Linc said. "Are you on the run? I mean, moving from place to place? I can't stand to think of you doing that."

"I've settled down somewhere. People think I'm someone else. I have work. Except for missing you, I'm okay."

Linc looked away, and she knew he did not quite share her joy over her having a new life that didn't include him. "There's a hotel near here," he said. "I thought we could get a room."

"Good." She was tired from the drive, and she wanted to be someplace where she could curl up with him in safety.

They drove to a Holiday Inn, anonymous and utilitarian, but the room was spacious, with huge windows and a view of the city. She carried Cody's bottle and the can of formula into the bathroom, while Linc flopped down on the bed.

"I have no interest in going out to eat. Do you?" he called to her.

"None whatsoever."

"Let's just do room service," Linc said when she returned. He reached for the bottle in her hand. Cody snuggled up next to him to drink his formula as Linc smoothed his hand over Cody's head. The two of them looked so content and comfortable together that Kim felt guilty about keeping them apart.

"I have something in my backpack for his birthday," Linc said.

"I'll give it to him when he's finished with his bottle." He picked up the room-service menu from the night table. "Are you hungry?"

"Famished."

They ordered their dinner, and while they waited for the food to be delivered, Cody opened Linc's gift. It was a large plastic activity box, with doors that opened, drawers that pulled out, and a half-dozen other working parts guaranteed to keep small hands occupied for a long time.

Kim laughed when she saw it. "Smart man," she said. "That ought to keep him busy."

Their food came, and they sat on the bed as they ate fried chicken and baked potatoes. They kept their conversation light.

"Did I miss any of the clues you sent me in your show?" Kim asked. She ticked off the song titles she could remember.

"Nope. Sounds like you got them all." Linc spooned sour cream on his potato. "You wouldn't believe the complaints I got about that show. My listeners thought I'd gone off my rocker."

"Well, even if you lost one or two, I hope it was worth it."

He touched her knee. "Absolutely," he said.

When they finished dinner, Kim took Cody into the bathroom and gave him a quick bath, then held his hands to walk him back into the main room, where his pajamas were waiting.

"Hey, Cody." Linc reached out his arms. "Come here, fella." He motioned for Kim to let go of Cody's hands. She did so gently, and Cody took one wobbly step toward Linc, then another.

Linc leaned low. "Come on, Cody, you can do it!"

Kim watched as her naked son toddled over to the man who was, in all ways but one, his father. Linc grabbed him just as he was about to fall and lifted him high in the air. "What a champ!" Linc said. Cody giggled from his lofty position. "He did it!" Linc lowered the little boy and nuzzled his neck.

"Yes, fans, Cody . . . Miller?" Linc looked at Kim quizzically, and she shrugged. "Cody whoever the heck he is has broken the record in the free-form upright toddle. That little wobble at the finish line will cost him with the judges, but what style this kid has."

Cody didn't need to understand what Linc was saying. Linc's rapid-fire delivery made him laugh anyway.

"Toddlers around the world are watching, Cody," Linc said. "What do you have to say to them?" He held an imaginary microphone in front of the little boy, but wiped out by his fit of giggles, Cody simply collapsed against Linc's chest. Linc suddenly sobered and pressed his lips to the top of the baby's head.

When he looked up at Kim, she said quietly, "That was his first time." She stepped back into the bathroom. She didn't know if Linc was close to tears, but she was, and she didn't want to cry in front of him.

When she came out, Cody was already in his pajamas and in the crib. The room was dark except for one light. Linc sat on the bed, his back against the headboard. Kim tucked Cody's monkey next to him under the covers and rubbed his back. Then she closed the drapes and sat down cross-legged in front of Linc. Taking his hands in her own, she looked deeply into his eyes.

Linc sighed. "Where do we begin?" he asked.

"Are they still looking for me?" she asked.

"Oh, yes." He nodded. "They'll be looking for you until they find you. *If* they find you." He squeezed her hands. "Jim and Peggy have hired a private investigator. Plus, they have the National Center for Missing and Exploited Children working on it."

"How close are they to figuring out where I am?" she asked.

"I don't know. The don't keep me informed. I *do* know that the FBI's involved, though."

"The FBI!" Somehow that made her feel hopeless.

"They've questioned me ad nauseam, and I guess I have to thank you for not telling me anything, although, I swear, Suze, I thought I was going to go out of my head at first. I was so angry with you."

"I'm sorry. I didn't know how else to—"

"And you were right. If you'd let me in on it, I would have tried to stop you and I would have had a harder time talking to the cops. This way I didn't have to lie."

"Do you think they're going to find me?" she asked.

"I don't know. I've been impressed with the means they have. You should know they've alerted doctors around the country to be on the lookout for a child with Cody's condition."

"I was afraid of that. But we've been to a doctor, and that went all right."

"Did you use your insurance? They can trace you that way."

"No. I knew that would be a bad move."

Linc sighed. "The National Center Peggy's working with sends out these postcards with pictures of missing children on them. They can send them to just about every household in the country, and I've heard they're really effective."

"Have they sent one out with Cody's picture on it?"

"Not that I know of," Linc said. "Peggy keeps badgering them to, though. She's a real squeaky wheel."

"You sound as though it's only a matter of time till I'm found."

Linc was very quiet. "Please consider coming home with me."

"And give Cody up?" She felt a wave of anger. "No."

"You can't run away from your problems for the rest of your life," Linc said.

"Have you forgotten what happened the last time you said those words to me?" He lowered his eyes, and she knew that he understood exactly what she was talking about.

"That was half your life ago," he said quietly. "This is totally different." He leaned back against the headboard. "I know I'm being selfish. My motivation's simple: I want you back home with me again."

"I want to be back, too," she said, "but I'm not willing to give up my son, not even for you."

"All right." Linc shook his head as if clearing it of the conversation. "Let's not talk about it anymore tonight. We don't have much time together. I don't want to spend it arguing with you."

"Me neither."

"Come here, then." He reached toward her as he stretched out on the bed. She lay down next to him, resting her hand lightly on his side. Neither of them said a word. He stroked her cheek.

"I'm afraid to kiss you or touch you," she said finally. "I'm afraid if I do, I won't be able to leave you again."

"That's what I'm counting on."

She drew away from him. "Don't," she said.

"All right. I'm sorry," He kissed her. His lips were so warm, so familiar. She drew out the kiss, making it last. She wouldn't let herself think about tomorrow or the day after. The memory of tonight might have to last her an eternity. Linc seemed to feel the same way, because he lingered over every inch of her body, touching her softly with his hands and his mouth. His movements were slow and measured, as they'd always been. She succeeded in blocking thoughts of the future from her mind until all the longing she'd felt for him this past month and a half exploded inside her. Despite the exquisite pleasure of the moment, she found herself sobbing.

"Don't think," he said. "Don't think about anything." He held her tightly, waiting for her tears to stop. For a while it seemed as if they never would.

She must have tired herself out, though, because when next she opened her eyes, the room felt different, and she knew there'd been a shift in time. She must have fallen asleep. She rolled onto her back and looked at the dimly lit ceiling.

"I took your photo albums from your apartment," Linc said. "I didn't want Jim to have them."

"Thank you." She'd thought about how carelessly those albums would have been treated in Jim's hands.

"I loved seeing the few remaining sketches you did of my old band," Linc said. "Haven't seen them in a while."

She remembered the summer nights she'd spent in his garage, sitting on the lumpy old sofa, sketching the band while Linc and his friends played music and joked. She'd treasured the warmth and security she felt in his house, and she'd hated going home, never knowing if her father would be a mean or weepy drunk that night.

"Your house was my oasis," she said.

"I know."

Unbidden, the memory of the night her father was killed slipped into her head. “Sometimes I think about what happened that night,” she said, “and I realize I’ve told the story the way you said it happened for so long that I’ve almost come to believe it’s the truth.” It wasn’t that far from the truth anyway. Just a little twisting, a little distortion of the facts.

“Well, it’s all behind us.”

“I just regret that you had to do time.”

“Shh. Water under the bridge.”

She pulled closer to him. She didn’t want to fall asleep again and waste this time with him, but she was sinking down. Dreamlike images floated in and out of her head, and she comforted herself with the fact that, at least for tonight, she would be sleeping with the man she loved.

Chapter 10

LINC woke up to find her still asleep, looking very young, like the delicate little girl he’d loved as a sister before he’d loved her as anything else. He got out of bed, opened the drapes, and looked out at a still quiet, still dark Philadelphia.

She’d brought up the night her father was killed, opening a whole world of memories for him. And they all began with him posing for her in her bedroom.

“Fully clothed,” she’d assured him. He’d agreed, and he would sit for hours in her bedroom—when her parents were out—while she sketched him. Then she’d gotten those books on figure drawing from the library, and she wanted to draw “more of him.” He posed as she wanted him to, although he knew it was asking for trouble. He could still picture her bedroom clearly, the bed in one corner, a desk against the wall next to it. She'd lock the bedroom door; then he'd sit or lie on the bed, while she sat in the desk chair, the sketchbook on her lap. Taped to the walls were her sketches of his band, mostly in black and white. She was very proud of them and was about to enter them in a statewide competition, along with the work in one of the sketchbooks resting on her desk. She'd already won a local competition with what she called the Garage Band Series. Winning the state would guarantee her scholarships for college.

She wore a serious look on her face as she sketched him, and he felt guilty for the fantasies running through his twenty-two-year-old male mind. His feelings for her had been undergoing a dramatic shift. He'd stopped thinking of her as the needy, gawky little girl next door. Instead, she had suddenly become a talented, beautiful young woman in his eyes.

One evening, as she sat drawing him, she looked up from her pad, a small smile on her lips. "I think I want you to make love to me," she said. He could see his own longing mirrored in the pale blue of her eyes.

But he shook his head. "You're too young," he said.

She set the sketch pad on her desk and moved over to the bed. She kept her eyes on his as she pulled her T-shirt over her head. There was no way he could stop himself. Her lips were on his; she lifted his hands to her breasts.

"I love you, Linc," she said, and he offered the words back to her without hesitation and with all his heart.

They were so lost in each other that night that they didn't hear Susanna's father come home. Not until he began pounding on her bedroom door did they realize he was there. Linc and Susanna flew out of the bed and began pulling on their clothes.

"Open this damn door!" her father snarled.

"Oh, my God," Susanna said. "He'll kill us. We've got to get out of here." She began trying to open the window, but it was stubborn and she could only lift it a few inches.

For a moment Linc thought she was right. Escape seemed like the only solution. But he knew better. Maybe they could escape for a few hours or a day, but eventually they would have to face Susanna's father and his wrath.

Linc grabbed her hands. "You can't always run away from your problems, Susanna," he said. "You'll only be putting off the inevitable. We have to face him. I'll tell him it was my fault."

She looked unconvinced. There was terror in her eyes.

"I won't let him hurt you," he promised. He stepped to the door and unlocked it.

Susanna's father burst into the room. He grabbed his daughter by the hair like a rag doll, cursing at her, spitting his foul whiskey breath into the air. "Who brought you up to be a whore?" he boomed. "Who raised you to be a slut?"

"Leave her alone!" Linc lunged at him, and Susanna's father let go of her to take a punch at him. Though he was very drunk, he managed to land a punch on Linc's shoulder. He raised his fist to strike again, but then suddenly spotted the open sketchbook on Susanna's desk. "What the hell's this?"

Susanna tried to grab it, but he was too fast for her.

"Is this the kind of drawing you've been doing?" He tore the top sketch of Linc in half, then started shredding the ones below. "Sixteen years old and a whore already." He poked one finger in the air toward Linc. "You're going to jail, boy," he said. "And your girlfriend there's going to reform school if I let her live."

Susanna's Garage Band Series was in one of the other sketchbooks on the desk, and Linc didn't know whether to try to grab them or not. Just then he heard footsteps in the hall.

"What the hell's going on in here?" Susanna's mother appeared at the door, every bit as drunk as her husband. "Paul! What are you doing to her pictures?" She reached for the sketchbook in his hands. "You shouldn't—"

Paul Wood knocked his wife off her feet with one sweep of his arm, and she landed against the radiator, her eyes closed. Linc was not at all certain she was still alive.

He pulled Susanna behind him to get her out of harm's way. She was trembling with fear, but when her father reached for one of the band pictures on the wall, she darted out from Linc's protection.

"Daddy, please, not those! They're for the competition!"

In an instant the picture was down and torn, then the next.

Susanna frantically tried to save the other drawings. She clawed at her father's hands as he shredded them, but nothing could stop the big man's destruction. Finally Susanna ducked beneath his arm and ran out of the room.

Linc was glad to see her go, but he was too busy dodging her father's punches to say a word.

In a few seconds, though, Susanna was back. She stood in the doorway. "Dad!" she called out. "Get away from Linc, or I'll shoot!"

Only then did Linc see the gun she had in her hands.

"Gimme that!" Paul Wood lunged at his daughter. He plowed into her, and the gun flew from her grasp across the room. In an instant Linc grabbed it. Before he had even a moment to think, he aimed at her father's back and pulled the trigger.

The next few minutes seemed to happen in slow motion. Paul Wood flung his arms out to his sides, his blood spraying across his daughter's white T-shirt. He fell toward her, landing hard on the floor, face first.

Susanna stared at Linc across the broad expanse of her father's body. Blood was pooling on the floor around her bare feet. With his stomach churning, Linc realized the bullet must have pierced the man's heart. He felt his own blood drain from his face, and he sat down on the edge of Susanna's bed.

He looked at her, and when he spoke, he was surprised by the calmness in his voice. "It happened like this," he said. "Your father came home drunk. He started beating you and your mother up. I knew where he kept his gun, right?" He remembered her telling him about the time her father killed the squirrel.

Susanna nodded.

"I got the gun. He threw your mother down and then went for you, and that's when I killed him. I killed him to stop him from hurting you and your mother."

"Yes," Susanna agreed. "That's what happened." She glanced at the shreds of paper at Linc's feet. There was no expression whatsoever on her face. "What about the drawings?" she asked.

Linc got slowly to his feet and put the scraps of paper into the bottom drawer of her desk. There would be no evidence of his nudity; there was no witness to their lovemaking. He and Susanna were neighbors. Friends. Nothing more.

His knees shook, and he sat down on the bed again.

She let out a small cry and pressed her fist to her mouth. "All my work," she said.

It was only later that he would feel the irony of that moment. Her father lay dead at her feet, her mother lay unconscious on the other side of the room, and the only loss she felt was for her drawings.

"We need to call the police," he said.

She nodded, her face expressionless. She turned, her feet leaving bloody footprints as she walked down the hall toward the kitchen. He did not move until the police came to take him away.

A PALE sun cast its soft glow on the buildings of Philadelphia, and Linc suddenly became aware of the chill in the air. He turned and went back to bed.

Susanna. He'd thought he'd be able to bring her back with him. Persuade her somehow. But he could see that wasn't going to happen. She was settled, she'd said. She was doing okay. He wanted that for her. Wanted her to be happy, to be safe. He was selfish to want her to be happy only with him.

He lay on his back, wide-awake and filled with frustration. He had never thought that he loved her more than she loved him, but right now he wondered. At least until she opened her eyes and gave him a startled smile at finding him next to her. She pulled him closer then and began to cry.

"Can we stay here longer?" she asked. "Do you have to go back today? Can we stay a few more nights? Please?"

"I have to go back," he said, putting his arm around her. He feared being gone too long. They'd suspect he was with her. Much as he wanted her back, he would not lead them to her.

Cody began talking to himself, that little soliloquy that could go on for half an hour. It made Linc smile to hear it.

"Can I ask your advice about something?" Susanna said.

"Of course."

"Well, something weird happened." She told Linc about buying the computer secondhand and how she had discovered the file on it left by the previous owner. "I called the store I bought it from," she said, "but they didn't seem to care. So I made a copy of the file, erased it from the hard drive, and forgot about it. Then a few weeks later I heard about a bombing at a law firm in the town where I'm living. I recognized the name as being in the file. I looked at the file again. It was a list of . . ." She lifted the blankets and started to get up. "Here, I'll show you."

He watched her walk across the room to the table and bring two folded sheets of paper back to the bed with her. She held them out so he could see them.

"Oh!" She suddenly lowered the papers facedown. "You'd see the name of my town."

"Let me see," he said. Unwise though it might be, he desperately wanted to know where she was living.

She hesitated only a moment longer before raising the papers again. "See?" she said. "It's a hit list. This woman was killed in an explosion. And this law firm was bombed, too. Both of them on these exact dates."

Annapolis. All the addresses were in Annapolis. "Wait a minute," he said. "You're saying this is a list of people that the previous owner of the computer somehow knew would die?"

She nodded. "Not just die. Be killed. This first woman opened an Express Mail package with a bomb in it. Then someone at the law firm opened an Express Mail package, and it, too, had a bomb in it."

Cody's babbling was getting louder, working its way toward his angry I-want-to-get-up sounds.

"That's insane," Linc said. "It's probably some sort of coinci—"

"It's not, Linc. How can it be a coincidence that on these dates and at these times, two separate bombings occurred, killing the people on this list? As you can see, the next date is November thirteenth, and I can't just sit by and let this guy get blown up. I've been trying to figure out what I should do. My best bet is to—"

"This sounds way too dangerous," Linc interrupted. "I think you need to forget it. Pretend you never saw this list."

"But I *have* seen it."

She was right. He'd never be able to turn his back on something like this. He couldn't ask her to do so either. "Is there any way the person who had the computer before you could know you have it? I mean, could you be in danger?"

"I don't think so. The salesperson at the store didn't even write down my name when I called back."

"This is bad news." He didn't like the dilemma she was in. "Maybe you could send the information to the police without any explanation. Or better yet, *I'll* send it from Boulder.

"No." She gave her head a violent shake. "If you sent the information to the police and they somehow traced it to you, how would you explain it? With your record they'd never believe anything you said, and you'd be back in prison again."

The thought of prison was enough to make him back down. "All right," he said. "But let's do it this way. You leave this copy of the list with me. If you can't figure out a safe way to get the information to the authorities, let me know. Fax me again and sign it S.T.U. Downe. And I'll take care of it."

Cody started to cry. As Susanna went to get his bottle and a can of formula, Linc looked at the list again. Annapolis. He suddenly wished he didn't know where she lived. It made it harder somehow, imagining her with a new life in a new place.

After Susanna leaned over the crib to give Cody his bottle, she climbed under the covers again.

"Tell me about your life in Annapolis," Linc said.

She told him about her apartment and Ellen and Lucy. "I expected to keep to myself," she said, "but I've made some friends in spite of myself. I'm self-employed, doing word processing. I've gotten a few jobs through friends. And—you'll love this—I'm taking painting lessons from an artist who paints murals around town."

"Really? I'm proud of you," he said, but he could hardly bear the sudden jealousy burning in his chest. Exactly how complete was this new life of hers? "Is there a man there?" he asked.

She hesitated. "The artist," she said. "Please don't be angry or upset, Linc. I didn't know if I'd ever see you again. And I'm not in love with Adam, not that way, but he is a good friend."

"I'm not angry." He couldn't speak for a minute, and she waited out his silence. She knew him well enough to do that, he thought. Knew him better than any woman could. And now she was happily keeping company with an artist in Annapolis in her brand-new life. "I'm amazed you even took the time to come see me," he said.

She sat up, eyes blazing. "Linc, I *love* you. I listen to your show every Sunday night. I cry when I hear your voice. I miss you. I want to be with you. But I can't be with you and have Cody, too." She touched his arm. "And besides, I've told the artist about you. That you're still very important to me. He understands I can't get serious right now. And the same is true for him. His wife and two kids were wiped out by a drunk driver seven months ago. So we're two lonely, miserable people. Please don't be upset. Please—"

"All right." He raised his hand to stop her. He didn't want to hear any more.

She lay down next to him again, her arms across his chest. "I don't want to end our time together on this note."

Neither did he. He wanted to hold her, though. Hold her and tell her he loved her. Tell her he admired her for being able to start over. When he returned to Boulder, he would have to find a way to start over himself.

IT WAS afternoon when Kim got on the road. She reached Annapolis after nightfall, and the house was dark when she pulled up out front. Ellen's car wasn't in the driveway, nor was Lucy's at the curb.

There was an almost wintry nip in the air as she unbuckled Cody from his car seat. The little boy was tired, and she carried him and her suitcase up the walk to the house. She couldn't manage both Cody and the luggage on the stairs, so she left the suitcase on the porch. She'd get Cody into bed first.

At the top of the stairs, she started to put her key in the lock but stopped short when she saw that the door was not completely closed. She stared at it for a minute. She distinctly recalled closing the door and locking it behind her when she left on Saturday. She hugged Cody tighter, trying to still her trembling. Had the private investigator finally caught up with her? The FBI?

There was no way she could make herself walk into the apartment. Instead, she grabbed the railing and ran down the stairs as fast as she was able to. She forgot about her suitcase on the porch, quickly loaded Cody into the car, and drove two blocks to the nearest pay phone. She dialed Adam's number.

"Adam, it's Kim," she said when he answered. "I think someone's broken into my apartment. The door's unlocked, and I'm afraid to go in by myself. I'm calling from a pay phone."

"Did you call the police?"

"No, I—"

"I'll call them and be right over."

"No!" She panicked, leaning toward the phone. "I mean, please don't. Please just come over yourself."

He hesitated. "All right. I'll be there in a few minutes."

She hung up in relief, trying to ignore the little wave of guilt she felt over turning to Adam for help when she'd spent the night before with Linc.

By the time Adam arrived, she was sitting on the front steps with Cody, shivering in the cold, and although Cody was dressed warmly enough, he was fussy, annoyed at being carted around when he belonged asleep in his crib.

Adam looked up at the darkened windows of her apartment. "You stay down here while I make sure the coast's clear," he said, starting up the porch steps. She walked into the house with him and waited at the bottom of the stairs while he went up to her apartment.

After a minute he leaned his head out the door. "All clear."

She walked up the stairs, her son in her arms. Adam had turned on the lights, and Kim put Cody in his crib. Then she began to look around the apartment. "Nothing's out of place," she said.

"Did you leave your computer on?" Adam was standing in front of the computer. The screen saver was on.

"No." She stared at the screen. "I'm certain I didn't."

The floppy disks were out of their storage case and scattered across the tabletop. "And I didn't leave these out either. Just a minute." She walked into her bedroom and opened the lingerie drawer. The disk containing the hit list was still there, under her bras. *You could be in danger,* Linc had said.

"What's that?" Adam said when she returned with the disk.

Her hands were shaking. "I have to tell you something," she said. She sat down at the computer; then for the second time in two days she repeated the story of how she'd come to own the computer, and described the information she'd found on it.

The color drained from Adam's face as he listened to her. When she had finished, he said, "That bombing we saw on TV, that law firm—that's on the disk?"

"And that woman, too." She slipped the disk into the drive, and the list of names appeared on the screen. Adam stood behind her. "This first woman was killed on this date." She pointed to the screen. "And here's Sellers, Sellers, and Wittaker. And, as you can see, there's a man scheduled for November thirteenth."

"Good God." Adam looked even more shaken by the information than she had been. "Kim, how long have you known this?" There was a reprimand in his voice. "Why haven't you called the police?"

She stared at the screen, unsure how to answer him.

"Kim?" His voice was gentler now. His face was puzzled but kind, and lined with worry. She bit her lip, then took his hand. They walked over to the sofa and sat down.

She knew she was going to tell him everything. She was exhausted from keeping it in. "Please, please, don't tell anyone what I'm going to tell you. Not even Jessie. Promise me?"

"I promise."

"I can't call the police, because . . . I have to avoid the police."

He looked puzzled. "Have you committed a crime?"

"Some people would say I have. You see, my ex-husband and his wife were given custody of Cody. So I left with him before I had to turn him over to them."

"But why on earth would you lose custody? You're such a good mother to him."

His words made her smile but only for a second. "Because they're rich and live in a great house," she said. "I should know. I picked it out thinking my husband and I would be living there."

"Did your husband have an affair with this woman?"

She liked the way he said "this woman," as if the words tasted sour in his mouth. "Yes. And her brother was the doctor who performed heart surgery on Cody. That added to their argument about being able to take better care of Cody than I could." She couldn't tell him about Linc and her father. It was too complicated, and she didn't want Adam to think the court had made the right decision.

"I'm stunned," Adam said. "I thought I knew you and now I— Is Kim Stratton your real name?"

She shook her head.

"You poor thing," he said. "Are they looking for you?"

"Yes. Some sort of organization that hunts for missing children is looking for me. Plus the police, the FBI, and a private investigator."

"Kim, how do you know all this?"

She hesitated. "The friend I saw this weekend told me."

"Oh." Adam's lips tightened. "The man in your heart. I don't like him much."

She smiled. "He's not crazy about you either."

"You told him about me?"

"I'm honest to a fault." She nodded toward the computer. "So anyhow, I realize I have to get this information to the police, but I want to do it without them tracing it to me."

"Give me the disk," Adam offered quickly. "I'll figure out a way to get it to them without implicating you."

She gnawed at her lower lip. "How would you do it, though?"

"I'm not sure, but I'll think of something."

"All right." She popped the disk out of the computer, then handed it to him. "But they need to know right away," she said. "The next bombing is only a little more than a week away."

"It'll be in their hands tomorrow. I promise."

She looked around the room and shivered. "Creepy, imagining someone being in here. I feel violated."

He nodded. "Come home with me. You and Cody. You'll be safe there." He reached out to tenderly touch her cheek.

She couldn't look him in the eye. A few hours before, Linc had touched her the same way. She could not stay with Adam tonight, not after spending the previous night with Linc. She was about to answer him when she heard Lucy's unmistakable footsteps on the stairs. "Thanks," she said. "But I'll be all right. Lucy's home."

"Are you going to tell her what happened?"

She shook her head. "No. I don't need someone else asking me why I didn't call the police."

"Good. The fewer people who know, the better." Adam stood up. "Well, look, you have a safe night tonight. I'll come over tomorrow and put a dead bolt on this door for you, okay?"

She nodded. "I'd appreciate it."

After Adam left, Kim lay awake in bed for an hour before finally getting up and pushing an end table in front of her apartment door. Even then she couldn't sleep.

ADAM arrived in the morning with a bag of bagels and a dead-bolt lock. Kim was working on Noel's novel but put it aside when Adam told her he had good news. "It's taken care of," he said.

"You mean, the police have the disk? How did you do it?"

He set the bagels on the kitchen counter. "I felt like I was in a movie," he said. "First I copied the information to another disk so there'd be no fingerprints. Then I typed a note explaining it, and I put the disk and the note in an envelope marked 'Urgent.' I drove around last night until I found a police car—parked at the all-night doughnut shop, of course—and put the envelope on the windshield. I parked a half a block away and watched the cop come out of the shop and open the envelope. It's in their hands now."

She threw her arms around him. "Oh, thank you," she said. "I'm so relieved."

While Adam worked on the door, Kim began typing the next chapter in Noel's book. But she was unable to concentrate. She wished now that she hadn't left the list with Linc. What if he tried to get it to the police himself? She hadn't really thought about fingerprints. Linc's would be easily traceable.

She closed the file containing Noel's book and opened a new document. "Dear Mr. Sebastian," she typed. "Thanks for playing my favorites for me, but you don't have to worry about that other list I sent you. The artist has taken care of it. Still, I do hope you'll play something special for me from time to time. S.T.U. Downe."

LINC was reading a paper when the fax arrived. He studied the brief message, his eyes instantly drawn to the middle two lines—"you don't have to worry about that other list I sent you. The artist has taken care of it."

He knew he should be pleased and relieved, but he was not. The artist was taking care of entirely too much, it seemed.

He remembered what she'd told him about the artist's family: They'd been killed by a drunk driver, wiped out in an instant. He should pretend that's what had happened to her. Then he could grieve, assign her and Cody to a warmly remembered part of his past, and move on. He would send her no messages in this week's show. He would not even play "Suzanne." What was the point?

The list of names and addresses she'd given him was tacked on the bulletin board above his desk. Linc removed it from the board and carried it into the kitchen, where he poured himself a bowl of cereal and a cup of coffee. Then he sat down to eat, the list on the table in front of him. Very bizarre, that list. Halfway through his breakfast, he reached for the phone and dialed his friend Grace's number at the university library.

"Have a minute?" he asked when he'd gotten her on the line.

"For you," she answered.

"Okay. Let's say you knew of a bunch of people who had been killed. Murdered. On the surface they seem to have nothing in common, but you suspect there must be something that unites them. Some reason they've been singled out for murder. Assuming they did have something in common, how would you find out what it is?"

"Linc, what have you gotten yourself mixed up with now?"

"This is hypothetical, Grace."

"Oh, right. If you say so. Okay, so you think something unites these people. Do you have addresses for them? Do they all live in the same neighborhood or work in the same office or go to the same university?"

"I have no idea," Linc said.

"Well, then I would start by looking at the news coverage of their murders to see if you can tie them together that way. Or you could check the newspaper abstracts using the names of the victims to see if there might be any other articles on them."

"But what if the people live far away?"

"You'd want to check the local papers in the area where they live. What city are you talking about?"

"Annapolis, Maryland."

"Hmm," Grace said. "You couldn't check that from here. You'd have to— Look, I know a librarian at the Naval Academy in Annapolis. If you call him and use my name, he'd probably help you with it, as long as he's got the time. Hypothetically, of course."

"Thanks, Grace."

She gave him the name and number of the librarian.

When he got off the phone, he called the librarian in Annapolis. The librarian sounded dour and uncooperative until Linc mentioned Grace's name. Then he perked up and was unabashedly friendly. Linc gave him a few of the individuals on the list, along with the dates written next to their names.

"How soon do you need this information?" the librarian asked.

"Whenever you can get to it," Linc said.

"I'll see what I can do."

Chapter 11

KIM was anxious to get to Adam's house. For the first time she'd had a dream she could use. She'd gotten out of bed that morning and sketched quickly and quietly, listening to Cody as he babbled to himself in his crib.

When she arrived at the house that night, she told Adam, "I had a dream last night."

He grinned at her. "I told you it would happen."

"It took place in a park," she said. "It had all these rays of sunlight coming through the trees. And there was a group of children playing in a circle on the ground." The dream was still vivid in her mind. "I don't know if I can paint the children, though."

"Save them for last," Adam said. "Although I have complete faith in your ability, especially when it comes to painting people."

Kim put Cody to bed, then joined Adam in his studio. He was well into his painting—a treelined road leading to a lake dotted with sailboats—and she was inspired to get to work on her own. The minutes ticked by unnoticed as she transferred her dream of the night before from her mind to the canvas.

"The dream artists," Adam said after a while, glancing at her work. "You are getting damn good."

"Thanks." Kim took a step back to look at her canvas. For the first time she thought she truly deserved his compliment.

"You know why you suddenly had a great dream, don't you?" Adam asked. "You feel freer, now that you've told me everything. You have nothing to hide from me anymore."

"Maybe," she said. It did help that Adam knew the truth about her. He seemed to have taken the news in and then tucked it away, where it could do her no harm. She knew it tied her to him, though, and that frightened her. She must never make an enemy of him.

There was another reason she felt freer: The list was finally in the hands of the police. She would not have said she felt totally free, though. Anyone who looked over her shoulder several times a day—wondering if the man keeping pace with her across the street might be a private investigator—and who kept her duffel bag still packed and ready to go at a moment's notice could not claim to be free.

Adam walked over to a cupboard to get a rag. On his way back to his canvas, he stopped behind her, putting his arms around her waist. "I think you have to stay here tonight," he said.

She remembered that Linc had held her this way at the Philadelphia Zoo. She brushed the thought quickly from her mind.

"I love the idea of waking up with you, now that you're dreaming." Adam nuzzled her ear. "Both our heads will be packed with dreams, and we'll grab our sketchbooks in the morning and fill page after page after page."

"All right," she said with a smile.

Later that night Kim climbed into Adam's bed, with its dark sheets and light feather comforter. Adam was in the bathroom, and she could hear him singing. She tucked her sketchbook beneath the bed, lay down, and closed her eyes.

Like magic, an idea came to her for the painting she was working on. She sat up, retrieved the sketchbook, and grabbed her pencil from the top of the night table. She'd barely gotten a few lines on paper before the point of her pencil snapped off.

Leaning across the bed, she opened the drawer to Adam's night table in search of another pencil, then drew back with a yelp. Poking out from beneath a few sheets of paper was the unmistakable steely gray nose of a gun. Kim stared at it, instantly transported back to her parents' bedroom and her father's night table. She closed the drawer gingerly as Adam came into the room. He leaned over to kiss her, then stood back with a frown. "What's wrong?"

"I opened your night-table drawer and saw a gun," she said.

He looked briefly surprised. "Oh, jeez, I forgot it was there," he said. "Let me get rid of it right now." Handling the gun with entirely too much ease, he put it away in the closet.

She was still shaken. She wished the gun were out of the house entirely. Better yet, she wished Adam didn't own it. She shuddered. "I hate guns. Why do you have it?"

He let out a long sigh. "Do I have to say?"

"If you want me to sleep easy tonight, yes."

He lay down and took her with him, his arms around her shoulders. "I bought it shortly after the accident because, frankly . . . I was considering killing myself."

She put her arm across his chest. "Oh," she said. "I'm very glad you didn't."

"Yes, so am I. I didn't do it because of Jessie. She was so despondent, I knew I couldn't do that to her. She knows I own the gun, but she doesn't know I'd ever considered using it on myself, and I'd appreciate it if you never told her."

"I won't."

"So now we know each other's secrets, huh?" he said.

"Mine's a little heavier than yours."

"Well"—he raised himself up on his elbow and gently ran his hand over her cheek—"your secret is safe with me."

THE next day Lucy came over to visit Kim. As they sat on the sofa talking, the phone rang, and Kim rose to answer it. "Hello?" she said into the phone.

"Ms. Stratton? This is Barb Kotter from Kotter Enterprises. We received your brochure regarding word processing."

"Oh, yes," Kim said.

"Well, we're in a bit of a bind," the woman said. "We have an urgent job, and the person who usually does our word processing for us is ill. Is there a chance you could come over for a quick interview? I know it's nearly five, but—"

"Yes. I can do that." She glanced at Cody. He was sitting on the living-room floor playing with the activity box Linc had given him.

She wanted to ask if she could bring her baby along, but thought better of it. She had a feeling people didn't bring their children to interviews at Kotter Enterprises.

"Oh, that would be wonderful," the woman said. "I can only be here another hour, though. Can you make it before then?"

"Yes."

Kim wrote down the address and got off the phone, wondering if she had time to change into a skirt. "I have a job interview," she said to Lucy. "Right now. They're in a bind."

Lucy stood up. "Let me watch Cody for you," she offered.

Kim looked down at her son. He was opening and closing the little red door on Linc's activity box, oblivious to her dilemma. She chewed her lip.

Lucy let out an exasperated sound. "Come on, Kim," she said. "Cody and I will be fine."

"You're sure you don't mind? I shouldn't be long."

"You run and get dressed," Lucy said. "Hurry up now."

KOTTER Enterprises was located on the third story of an office building near the water. The building was clean and modern, but it seemed deserted, and Kim found herself glancing over her shoulder as she made her way to Barb Kotter's office.

Barb Kotter asked Kim a few perfunctory questions, looked greatly relieved, and handed her a pile of work to be returned in two days. Kim would have to put everything else on hold, but she knew she could get the work done. And then she'd have a new client, as well as a good reference.

She saw the police car the second she turned onto her street. It was parked in front of Ellen's house. There were lights on in Ellen's first story, as well as in her apartment and Lucy's. *Cody and I will be fine,* Lucy had promised. Had she called the cops the second Kim was out the door?

She had to get to her son. Her heart in her throat, she parked behind the police car and ran up the front walk and onto the porch. Racing up the stairs, she reached the landing as the officer emerged from Lucy's apartment. Lucy stood behind him, Cody in her arms.

"Here's Mommy now," the policeman said.

Kim was trembling as she reached for Cody, and Lucy relinquished her hold on the little boy without protest.

"Is something wrong?" Kim looked from Lucy to the policeman.

The policeman laughed. "Wherever I go, people think there's something wrong."

"Not a thing, honey. This is Frank Raglan. Frank, this is Kim Stratton."

Kim couldn't answer. She was so nervous, her teeth were chattering, and she wrapped her arms tightly around her son.

"I'll be in touch, Lucy." Frank headed down the stairs.

Lucy smiled after him, then turned to Kim. "You get in here and tell me about your interview. It must have been terrible. You're white as a sheet. Do you want a cup of tea?"

Kim followed her into the apartment and sank into a chair. "I just . . . When I saw the police car in front of the house, I thought that something might have happened to Cody."

Lucy set a pot of water on the stove and shook her head. "You are the most overanxious mother I've ever seen," she said. "Relax."

"But what's going on? Why were the police here?"

Lucy sat down with a sigh. "Frank and I are . . . involved."

"Oh." Kim had not expected that.

"He's the reason I left my marriage. I had a terrible marriage, a loveless, dishonest sort of existence. But I stuck it out because, well, in my generation that's what you were supposed to do. You just accepted it. And I did, for thirty-six years, until I met Frank. Suddenly a man treated me like I was a human being. I'd forgotten what it felt like to be taken seriously by someone on a personal level. I realized then that I'd been a doormat, both for my husband and my kids. Frank gave me the strength to do something about it. So I left." Lucy's eyes lit up. "He's good-looking, though, don't you think? Did you see how blue his eyes are?"

Kim hadn't noticed, but she nodded all the same. She felt a little giddy. The cops didn't have a clue as to who she was. Her paranoia had been entirely unfounded. And as Lucy went on and on about her boyfriend and his blue eyes, she listened in numb relief.

"SOME mornings I wake up and think it's all a bad dream." Bonnie Higgins wiped her eyes with a ragged tissue.

Peggy reached across the desk to hand her another. Her concentration was worse than usual today. Bill Anderson had called earlier to tell her that *Missing Persons* was moving its parental kidnapping show up by several months. "This Wednesday night, to be exact," Bill had said. In a few days Tyler and Susanna's pictures would be splashed across the country. Someone was bound to recognize them. Yet that realization didn't give her much of a thrill.

"I mean, how do you explain it?" Bonnie asked. "First everything seems fine. Then all of a sudden he wants out. I find out he's been seeing his secretary. And now he says he wants the kids."

Peggy forced her attention back to her client, who could not stop crying. Her husband was now fighting actively for their two children. Bonnie said he'd even threatened to steal them.

Peggy felt close to tears herself. A threatened kidnapping hit a little too close to home. There was no way she would let what had happened to her happen to her client. "Your husband is not getting the children, legally or otherwise," she said firmly. "Has he done anything that might indicate he's planning to take off? Has he quit his job, for example? Closed out a bank account? Sold a car?"

"Not that I know of."

"Good," Peggy said. "You need to let your kids' preschool know that their father has threatened kidnapping. And we're going to modify your custody order. We'll restrict visitation and say he can't take the children out of Boulder." She spent another half hour with Bonnie. By the time Peggy left Legal Aid, she was drained.

She drove to Ron's office. She had called her brother that morning, telling him she couldn't bear the silence between them any longer. When he suggested they take a walk together after work, she'd readily agreed.

Peggy walked into the waiting room as Ron emerged from the

rear of his office, already dressed in his sweats. "Hi, sis." He gave her a kiss. "It's good to see you."

"You, too." She hugged him. She wanted this to be a healing visit, and she was determined to keep the conversation off Tyler. She missed Ron too badly to risk alienating him again.

His office was close to Cuyamaca Park, and they set out in that direction. They talked about Ron's work, the plans for his vacation, and the movies he'd seen recently.

"Enough about me," Ron said finally. "How are things going in the search for Tyler?"

She hesitated. "I wasn't going to talk about him. You made it pretty clear you'd rather not discuss the situation with me."

"So what's new at Legal Aid?" He changed the topic.

Again she hesitated. The only case occupying her mind was Bonnie's, and she wasn't certain she could safely discuss that case with him. "Well," she said, "I saw a woman this afternoon whose case really gets to me. But I don't know if I should talk to you about it, because it reminds me of what we're going through with Tyler."

"You don't have to censor what you say to me," Ron said.

"It started out as a simple divorce case," Peggy began as they walked uphill. "The woman's husband told her he wanted a divorce. Then she found out he'd been having an affair with his secretary. Now he says he's going after the kids, and he's alluded to the fact that if she puts up a fight, he'll kidnap them and—"

"Let me get this straight," Ron said. "You're relating to this case because the husband might kidnap his kids?"

"Yes." She hated the tone of his voice and braced herself for whatever he might say next.

"This sounds very familiar to me. Her husband had an affair, and now he's threatening to get custody of the children. Your sympathies are with *her,* but your client is to *her* children as Susanna is to Tyler. The betrayed wife about to lose custody of her children to her cheating husband and his new girlfriend."

She was appalled. "There is no comparison. No analogy. This guy's girlfriend is a tramp."

"What makes her a tramp and you not? The fact that you're an attorney and she's a mere secretary?"

"Why do you always have to attack me?" she asked, her voice rising. "It's as if you're waiting for a chance to jump down my throat."

"I just find it hard to listen to you compare yourself to your betrayed client."

"I wasn't talking about the infidelity part of—" She stopped walking, trying to rid herself of the trapped feeling that was closing in on her. "That's what it's all about, isn't it?" she said. "You've been angry with me ever since I told you I'd slept with Jim. I never should have told you. You're never going to let me forget it."

"I was disappointed in you, yes. I've never given you grief about the affair, because I didn't want to come off as your judgmental big brother. But when you start comparing yourself to this client of yours, when you can't even see that she is Susanna and not you, then I can't keep my mouth shut any longer. How would you feel if your client told you she'd come home and found her husband and his girlfriend together in her bed?"

"I'd feel outraged, but that's totally different. Her husband's a self-centered, arrogant bastard."

"Oh. Jim's a nice guy, so that makes it all right."

Peggy was exasperated. "Look, I'm ashamed of what I did. I convinced myself it was all right, because Jim said it was. I was upset when Susanna came home early, but I didn't really feel sorry for her, because Jim always said she . . ." Her voice trailed off. She let out her breath and sat down on a large rock. "I don't know what I think anymore. I'm confused." She looked up at her brother. "I had lunch with Linc Sebastian the other day. He said some things that shook me up. I shouldn't listen to him, but he sounded so sincere."

Ron nodded. "I think Linc *is* sincere," he said. "He doesn't care enough about what people think of him to bother lying to them."

Peggy let his words sink in. She knew they were the truth. "So now I'm mixed up. There's a part of me that wishes Linc did know where Susanna was. I wish he were slipping her money. Even if we never find her, I'd rather know that she's out there with good insurance and plenty of money for Tyler than for her to have to struggle to take care of him."

Ron's smile was slow to form. "That's the Peggy I know and love," he said, his voice gentle. "Welcome back, sis. I've known that deep down you've had Tyler's best interests at heart. Take a few steps back from this mess so you can see it clearly. Then follow your head and heart, all right?"

"I'm not sure that would make any difference," she said.

Ron leaned over to help her up. "I think it will make all the difference in the world," he said.

PEGGY thought about Ron's words as she made dinner that night. He was right. She hated to admit it, but she was no better than the secretary Bonnie's husband was shacking up with, and she didn't like herself very much. Still, there was something freeing about approaching the problem with a fresh eye, but she knew, as she sat down at the table with her husband, that she would have to tread softly in presenting her thoughts to him.

Jim was extremely busy at work, she knew. Even now, as he sat at the table, he kept glancing at his watch and jotting notes on a pad resting next to his plate.

"I'll have to go back to the office after dinner," he said.

"I was hoping we could talk a little. I have a question about Tyler's medical care."

"What about it?"

"Let's say the *Missing Persons* show doesn't work out and we still don't know where Tyler is," she said. "Could Susanna still use your insurance for him without letting you know where she is?"

"It would be great if she tried," Jim said. "We could probably catch her that way."

"But the most important thing is for Tyler to have good medical care, right? And if Susanna could use your insurance for him, she could get him the best, but she'd have to be assured we wouldn't try to track her down or—"

"Have you lost your mind?" Jim slipped the notepad into his

shirt pocket. "If Susanna wants my insurance for him, then Susanna can damn well bring him home," he said, his face reddening. It was obvious he was finished with the conversation. "I've got to go. I'm not sure what time I'll make it home," he said as he picked up his briefcase from the counter. "I'll give you a call."

She sat at the table for a long time after he left. Finally she got to her feet and walked into Jim's study. She opened the filing cabinet and pulled out the file on their health insurance. She wasn't certain what she was looking for. The claim forms and information booklet didn't tell her much. She was putting the papers back in the file when her fingers caught on a slip of paper.

The handwriting was unmistakably Jim's: "S—Here's the list of some Boulder M.D.'s who perform abortions. I'd appreciate it if you'd get it done before your second trimester, since the price goes up after that." There followed a list of six doctors, along with their phone numbers and addresses.

Peggy stared at the list. Hadn't Jim said he'd never given Susanna the names of doctors? What else had he lied to her about? She tried to quiet her thoughts, but it was no use.

She dialed Ron's number. When he answered, she asked, "Can I come over? I think I have some decisions to make."

LINC whisked through the stack of faxes, hunting for anything that might be from S.T.U. Downe. Nothing. So what did he expect? He was supposed to be getting on with his life, yet every day he went over his faxes with a fine-tooth comb. They were of the usual "please play this for me" variety except for several pages that were copies of newspaper articles. He found a cover letter accompanying them and saw that it was from the librarian in Annapolis.

> Attached are articles from *The Capital,* the Annapolis daily newspaper, relating to the people on the list. I found the information by checking the dates on the list. As you can see, there is one possible connection between these people. I hope this is helpful to you. Give my best to Grace.

Linc read the first article, then the second. By the time he'd finished the third, he understood the connection. And if he was right, Susanna was in grave danger. Dropping the faxes to the floor, he pulled the phone book from his desk drawer. Within minutes he had reservations on the next flight to Washington.

Chapter 12

KIM awoke Wednesday morning to the patter of rain against Adam's bedroom window. She rolled over to see him sitting up against the headboard, sketching furiously—a vegetable garden with winding vines and huge squashes and a dozen or so sunflowers edging one side. A dream, no doubt.

"I'm going to skip working on the mural today," he said. "I want to get started on this painting."

"It's raining out anyway." She suddenly remembered what day it was: November thirteenth—the next date on the hit list. She still had seen no mention of the list either in the paper or on the news. "Today was supposed to be the day for that next guy on the list."

"Oh, right." Adam stopped sketching and kissed her cheek. "Don't worry about it. I'm sure it's all been taken care of."

"I hope so. You'd think there would have been something on the news, though, wouldn't you?"

"Trust me, Kim. The cops could not possibly ignore the letter I wrote." He started to draw again.

"I'd better get up," she said. "I have a ton of work to do today. Are we still on for painting together tonight?"

"You bet."

She got dressed and made breakfast for herself and Cody. Adam was still propped up in his bed by the time she peeked into his room to say good-bye. "I'll see you tonight," she said.

She spent the day at her computer, stopping only long enough to take Cody for a walk. She returned to Adam's at seven that night, and he greeted her with a quick kiss. "Hi," he said. "Come see."

She followed him upstairs to his studio, where the sketch he'd made that morning had been transformed into a canvas filled with intense Soria colors.

"I love it." She stood back to take it in.

"I've had a great day," he said. "Don't mind me if I ignore you, all right?"

She didn't mind a bit. She settled Cody in Liam's bed and had just returned to the studio when the doorbell rang.

"Oh, I forgot." Adam looked distracted. "That's probably Cherise. She said she'd stop by to pick up a painting for the gallery."

"I can give it to her."

"Would you? It's ready to go. It's wrapped and standing by the front door." He looked at her gratefully. "Thanks, Kim."

"You're welcome." She went downstairs and opened the door.

Cherise stood in the porch light, a wide grin on her face. "Hey, lady! Where's the man?" She stepped into the room.

"Upstairs in his studio. Engrossed in a new painting."

"Oh, that is music to my ears. Cherise looked down at the wrapped painting at Kim's side. "I gotta see this one right now, though. Do you mind?"

"Of course not."

Cherise unwrapped the painting. "Oh, this is a beauty." She stood back to look at it. "This is a Soria, all right. I'm so glad he's painting again." She cocked her head at Kim. "And you're painting, too, Jessie told me. When are you going to have something for me to hang in my gallery?"

Kim laughed. "I hope you're not holding your breath. I'm no Adam Soria. Besides, I don't have much time to paint. I've gotten a few word-processing jobs. They're keeping me busy."

"Well, at least you're bringing in some money," Cherise said. "I'll tell you, the quicker Adam can turn out more paintings like that one"—she pointed to the canvas—"the quicker he can make himself a living again. People love his work. Tourists come by asking where they can see paintings done by the mural painter. I show them what I have, and I swear they'd buy a painting right that second. But Adam's so weird about it. He won't give me permission to make a sale for him. Always likes to come down and meet the people buying his work. A couple months ago a couple came in and wanted to buy that one with the leaves. You know the one I mean?"

Kim nodded. It was one of her favorites.

"But I couldn't reach Adam, couldn't reach him, kept trying and they finally had to leave. Frustrating! I told him, 'Adam, you need to carry a pager.' Turns out he was at Computer Wizard, returning a loaner computer. I asked him, is that as important as selling a painting? I said, if you're going to run around—"

Kim did not hear another word out of Cherise's mouth.

"Can I disturb him?" Cherise finally asked. "I want to see what he's working on."

"Go ahead up," Kim said. "I don't think he'll mind."

Cherise went upstairs, and Kim sat down. She felt sick.

It can't be. It had to be a coincidence. Probably hundreds of people borrowed computers from Computer Wizard. But wouldn't Adam have mentioned that he'd been one of them when she told him about her computer? Wouldn't he have nodded knowingly when she talked about it being a loaner?

The invitation. She nearly groaned out loud. She'd thought Ellen had been behind that unexpected invitation to Adam's show, but Ellen had denied knowing about it. Had Adam somehow discovered that she'd bought his computer? Had he befriended her in an attempt to get his file back? Was it Adam who had ransacked her apartment? Surely he couldn't be responsible for the explosions. For murder. She thought of the gun in his night-table drawer, and nausea washed over her. Thank God, the police had the disk.

No. The police did not have the disk. Not if Adam was the killer. He had been so quick to ask her to let him take the list to the police, so quick to suggest she not send it herself. The pieces of the puzzle fit together with sickening ease. Adam had betrayed her. She thought of how kind he'd been to her, how loving. What a joke!

Her head spun. It *didn't* fit together. It didn't make sense. Why would Adam want to hurt people? He was a kindhearted person. How could he have sat in his living room and calmly watched the horrific aftermath of that bombing at Sellers, Sellers, and Wittaker if he'd had anything to do with it? With a sinking heart she remembered that he hadn't. *I can't watch this,* he'd said. Then he'd turned the television off.

She walked over to where she'd left her purse and dug out a copy of the list. What were these people to him?

In addition to the names of the individuals, there was one other company besides Sellers, Sellers, and Wittaker on the list: Weirs and Taft, targeted for January. It sounded like another law firm. Kim pulled the phone book from the shelf next to the phone and turned to the yellow pages. She looked under lawyers, and what she saw made her gasp. Two full-page ads—one for Sellers, Sellers, and Wittaker, the other for Weirs and Taft. The Sellers ad proclaimed a specialization in "criminal traffic offenses and DWI." Weirs and Taft promised "experienced and thorough defense of DWI offenses." They defended drunk drivers. Was that the connection? She checked some of the other names to see if they, too, were attorneys, but none of them appeared to be.

She looked at the name targeted to be a victim tonight. "Ryan Geary." Nine o'clock, it read next to his name. She should call the police. Better yet, she should drive to the police station and hand them the list. Maybe she could get away with it. Lucy's friend Frank hadn't thought her suspicious. But there had to be a less risky way for her to keep Ryan Geary safe tonight. She heard Cherise's footsteps on the stairs and quickly put away the phone book.

"Can't wait till he's done with that one," she said. "And yours has real promise, girlfriend. You get upstairs and finish it."

Kim nodded. After she walked Cherise to the door, she climbed the stairs to the studio, knowing that the man up there was not the same man she had left a half hour ago. He'd suddenly become a monster in her eyes, a monster she'd decided she would stay with every minute that night. She would not let him out of her sight. She would not give him the chance to harm anyone.

"Hi." Adam gave her a distracted smile. He was painting some of the greenery in front of a picket fence.

She looked at the sunflower-filled garden taking shape on the canvas. That painting could not be the work of a man about to kill someone. Whatever demons had driven him to those earlier bombings were gone now. They had to be.

She tried to get back to work on her own painting, but the brush trembled in her hand. Tomorrow she would have to find a way to contact the police, as well as a way to back out of her relationship with Adam. But how could she? He knew far too much about her.

She was so preoccupied with her own thoughts that it was a while before she realized that Adam was anxious himself. He kept checking his watch and looking out the window.

"You seem a little uptight tonight," she ventured finally.

"Do I?" He sounded completely innocent. "I guess I have a lot on my mind. I've been so focused on painting today that I haven't had much time to get anything else done." He looked at his watch again, and she glanced at her own. It was nearly eight thirty.

"Let's get Jessie over here," Adam suggested suddenly. "I'm in the mood to whip up something to eat. How does spaghetti sound?" He was already reaching for the phone.

"Sure," she said. She was surprised by the suggestion, but it sounded like a great idea. They would get Jessie over here and eat and talk until late, and Ryan Geary would be safe.

She continued painting as Adam dialed Jessie's number. With the phone held to his ear, he tapped the table with his fingers. He drew in a few deep breaths and blew them out through his mouth. She had never seen that agitation in him before.

Abruptly Adam hung up the phone. "I just remembered we don't have any tomato sauce," he said. "I'll run out and get some."

"No. That's silly. Why don't we just order a pizza?"

But he was already heading down the stairs. She set down her brush and followed. She had the sickening thought that he had not called Jessie at all. He'd called the Geary residence to make sure that Ryan was home.

"I'll go with you."

"No," he said sharply. "I won't be long." He brushed his lips over her cheek and was gone.

She looked at her watch: twenty of nine. In her mind she suddenly saw the TV images of the children killed in the Sellers, Sellers, and Wittaker office. Did Ryan Geary have children?

"You have no choice," she said out loud. She had to call the police. Downstairs, she had the phone in her hand when it startled her by ringing. She stared at the receiver, uncertain what to do, and the answering machine picked up before she could decide. Suddenly Noel's voice filled the air.

"Hey, Adam, did you happen to catch that *Missing Persons* show tonight? I'm certain Kim Stratton and her little boy were on it. Her real name's Susanna somebody, and she's from Colorado. You might want to give her a heads up. She's a good lady, not to mention a good typist." Noel laughed. "I need her to stick around."

Kim closed her eyes, one hand gripping the counter. She was trapped. They'd shown her picture, told her story on TV. Who'd seen it? Who'd be the one to turn her in?

No time to waste. She lifted the receiver again and dialed. No reason she had to identify herself. She'd make the call, race home, and if the coast looked clear, she could get her money and her duffel bag before she disappeared again. She could be far away by the time anyone realized Kim Stratton was missing.

"Is this an emergency?" the dispatcher asked when she answered the call.

"Yes," Kim said. "Someone is planting a bomb to go off at nine o'clock at"—her hands trembled as she flattened the list on the counter—"Two oh seven North Plain Street."

"What is your name?" the dispatcher asked.

"Just trust me," Kim said. "The person responsible for the explosions that have killed people around Annapolis is about to strike again." She hung up before the woman could ask more questions.

She ran up to Liam's bedroom, where she literally snatched her sleeping son out of the bed and carried him downstairs. She grabbed their jackets and raced out to her car. She buckled Cody into his car seat, then drove away as quickly as she dared, trying to plan what she would do. Had Lucy or Ellen seen the show? Could she get in and out of her apartment without either of them noticing her?

She was nearly there when an unsettling thought crossed her mind. That North Plain Street address she'd given the 911 dispatcher wasn't right. She pulled the car over to the side of the road and yanked the list from her purse. Switching on the overhead light, she scanned the names. "Ryan Geary. Pioneer Way."

No. How could she have done that? In her nervousness she'd given the dispatcher the next address on the list.

She looked at her watch: ten to nine. There was no time to drive to her apartment and call the police from there. She made a left turn at the next corner and headed toward Pioneer Way.

In the Geary neighborhood, she pulled up to a man walking a dog and rolled down her window. "Call the police," she said. "Tell them to go to Seven seventy Pioneer Way. It's an emergency. Hurry!" As she drove away, she could see him in her rearview mirror, running in the opposite direction down the sidewalk.

The Geary house looked as she remembered it, with woods on either side of its broad lot. The front porch light was on, along with lights in the second-story windows. Kim spotted Adam's car in front of the wooded lot to the left of the house, but Adam himself was nowhere in sight. She parked her own car behind his.

Then she spotted him, crouching in the woods, not far from the street. He did not seem to notice her.

She got out of her car and locked it quickly. She hated leaving Cody alone but had no option. He would be safer in the car than he would be with her. As quietly as she could, she slipped into the trees, nearly tripping over their roots in the darkness and cringing at the rustle of leaves under her feet.

Adam started as she neared him, and spun around. "Kim!" His face was lit only by the light coming from the house, but she saw the shock in his eyes.

"I know what you're doing, Adam," she said, her voice shaking. "I can't let you do this. I called the police."

In the darkness she could detect anger in his features. "You shouldn't have done that," he said. "I told you I'd take care of it."

"Where is it?" she asked. "Where's the bomb?" Her eyes searched the ground around him for the package.

"I don't have time to explain it to you. You have to get out of here." He turned back to the house, and a terrible thought passed through her mind: Maybe he'd already planted the bomb.

"Adam, did you—" Her attention was suddenly drawn to the street, where a taxi swerved to a stop in front of the woods. Kim did a double take when a man emerged from the back seat.

"Linc?" she said softly. Then loudly, "Linc! Over here!"

"Shush!" Adam suddenly turned on her. "Shut up, Kim!"

Linc had started toward the house but turned at the sound of their voices. He ran through the trees and was quickly at her side. "What are you doing here?" he asked her. Then he noticed Adam. "Has he already left the bomb?" he asked Kim.

"I don't know." She shook her head. "How did you know—"

"I know all the people on the list were convicted of drunk driving and—"

"Oh." Kim's hand flew to her mouth. "That's it!" she said. "I should have—"

Adam suddenly turned on them both. "Look, neither of you knows what's going on, and you've got to get out of here!" He looked toward the woods on the other side of the house. "There!" he said, and sprang forward, starting to run through the trees, but Linc was too quick for him. He lunged at Adam and tackled him to the ground. Adam went down hard, and Kim heard him groan.

"The police are on their way," she told Linc.

"Then get out of here before they come, Susanna," Linc said. "They don't have to know you were involved in any of this."

Already she could hear the faint sound of a siren in the distance. She tried to think. Maybe she still had time to escape. But how would Linc ever be able to explain his involvement in this mess?

She looked down at Adam. There was blood on his forehead. He tried to get up but winced and fell back, his eyes narrow with pain. He grabbed Kim's hand. "It's not me," he said softly. "It's Jessie. I think she's going around to the rear of the house."

In a horrified instant Kim understood. She looked toward the street, but the siren was still distant. The police would never arrive in time. "Stay with him," she said to Linc.

She ran out of the woods, cutting through the side yard to reach the rear of the house. The small back porch was dark, but the moonlight illuminated a wide, grassy yard, interrupted by a swing set. Kim stopped short when she came face to face with Jessie, who was emerging from the woods, an Express Mail package in her arms.

"Jessie, don't do it. Put the box down. Or give it to me." Kim reached out trembling arms. "Please, forget the vendetta."

"A vendetta." Jessie looked very calm, and a small smile played at her lips. "Good word," she said. "And I admit that's what it is. Revenge, pure and simple. It feels great." She started toward the house again, but Kim darted in front of her.

"If you leave the package, I'm going to warn the people who live here not to open it," Kim said. "So why bother?"

"You won't warn anyone," Jessie said calmly. She raised her right hand, and for the first time Kim saw the gun. It looked like the gun from Adam's night table, and it was pointing directly at her.

The wail of the siren was closer now, but Jessie did not seem to hear it. Kim pointed to the swing set. "Do you see the swings, Jessie?" she asked. "Children live here. They could get hurt."

Jessie flinched, and Kim knew she'd hit a nerve. "Liam and Molly were innocent victims," she said. "But so were those children at the law office."

"Please don't talk about them."

"And the children in this house are innocent, too," Kim said. "Just as innocent as Molly and—"

"Stop it!" Jessie said, and suddenly dropped to her knees. "I never meant for those kids to get hurt." She was crying. "Their mother should never have brought them in to work with her."

"I know," Kim said. She heard car doors slamming in front of the house, more sirens. Any minute it would all be over. "I know you would never intentionally hurt any children," she continued. "And I'm sure you don't want to hurt the children who live here either."

Jessie was sobbing. The gun shook with the trembling of her body.

"Please put the gun down, Jessie," Kim said.

To her surprise Jessie obeyed and set the gun on the ground next to her. Kim took a step forward, but Jessie immediately stopped her.

"Stay back!" she warned.

Kim stopped walking, horrified to see that Jessie had slipped her hand into the lid of the box.

"Jessie, no!" Kim took another step closer.

"I just wanted Molly back," Jessie said, a catch in her voice. "That's all I wanted." Her hand still in the box, she quickly lay down on top of it. Before Kim could even think of reacting, the world exploded with a burst of light and noise. Kim heard herself scream as she fell backward, and a searing pain cut across her forehead. In an instant all was black.

THERE were more police officers at the hospital than there were doctors and nurses. At least it seemed that way to Kim. Two of the officers had been questioning her for the last hour. She had not bothered to lie. The jig was up, and she knew it. She would not be running away again.

Linc was sitting close to her on the hard vinyl couch in the waiting room, and Cody was asleep on her lap. The three of them formed an inseparable unit. For a little while longer anyway.

Kim had completely lost track of the time. All she knew was that a child-protection worker was on her way to the hospital and, unless a miracle occurred, would take Cody from her.

Kim had come to the hospital by ambulance, Linc had told her, but she had no memory of the trip, nor did she remember the doctor's stitching the cut above her eye. She'd been in shock, Linc said. As far as she was concerned, she was still in shock. She couldn't string two coherent thoughts together. "I still don't get it," she said to Linc. "How did you know where I was?"

He explained, for the third or fourth time, how he had learned about the connection between the victims through the librarian at the Naval Academy, how he'd figured out that "the artist," whose family had been killed by a drunk driver, was probably behind the deadly explosions. "I knew that Adam would not have taken the information to the police, and since I had the addresses on the list, I thought I could intercept Adam myself."

"Why didn't you just call the police?"

"Why do you think?" he asked. "I was afraid I'd be leading them straight to you."

Another police officer, a dark-haired woman, came to the door of the waiting room. "Mr. Soria would like to talk to you now," she said to Kim.

Kim shifted Cody to Linc's arms. She followed the policewoman down the hall to a treatment room. Adam was propped up in a hospital bed, a bandage around his head and a smear of blood on the shoulder of the blue hospital gown. He looked pale and sick, and her heart went out to him.

"I'm so sorry about Jessie, Adam," she said, taking his hand and sitting down in the chair next to his bed. "I'm sorry for everything."

"I need to tell you . . . to try to explain," he said slowly. His voice was hoarse, and she had to lean close to hear him.

"Are you all right?" Kim asked. "Is it just your head?"

"Ribs. Two of them broken. That boyfriend of yours packs a wallop." He tried to smile but didn't come close to succeeding. "I want you to know some things."

"I think I know everything," she said. "Jessie was targeting drunk drivers. The people on the list—the 'one adult' or 'elderly couple'—they were the people who had been killed in accidents, right?"

"There's more." Adam closed his eyes. It was a few seconds before he could speak. "Molly was Jessie's daughter," he said finally.

His words didn't register. "Molly was what?" she asked.

He looked directly at her. "Jessie got pregnant when she was fifteen. She knew she couldn't raise a child. Since Dana and I were already married, we decided to adopt her baby so that Jessie could always be close to her."

"Oh, my God," Kim said. "No wonder Jessie felt such a bond with your children."

"Molly was everything to Jessie," Adam said. "She and I were both nearly insane with fury when that driver got off so easily after the accident. We started thinking about all the drunk drivers who were still out there, free to kill again. Jessie joked about taking them out one by one. At least I thought she was joking. I realized after the break-in at your apartment, when you told me about the information on the computer, that she'd actually gone through with it. I didn't want to believe it, but—"

"I still don't understand," she interrupted. "I thought you owned the computer before me."

"Uh-uh. It was Jessie's. She used a loaner while hers was being repaired. One morning she asked if I could take it back to Computer Wizard for her and pick up her repaired computer. I said I would do it that night, but then my schedule changed, and I was able to take it that afternoon. I didn't realize there was information on it that Jessie wanted deleted before it was returned. She was furious with me when I told her I'd taken it back." He looked into space, as if remembering that scene. "I never understood why, until someone broke into your apartment and you told me what you'd found on the computer." He returned his gaze to Kim. "Jessie had called Computer Wizard to see if she could get the computer back, and they told her it had already been sold but that the person who bought it had called to tell them someone had left a file on the disk. The salesman thought it would be okay to give Jessie your address, since you seemed concerned about getting the information to its rightful owner."

"So was it Jessie who sent me the invitation to your show?"

"Yes. She followed you around for a few days, I guess, and knew that you were interested in the murals." He stopped for a few seconds, then continued. "Those kids at the law firm. I can't tell you how upset I was when I realized Jessie was behind that . . . catastrophe. And I wanted to tell you. We were in your apartment and you were telling me all about your life and your running away and I was lying to you through my teeth."

"You said you'd go to the police with the disk."

"I went to Jessie's house that night when she was asleep and checked out her basement. It looked like an explosives factory down there. Then I couldn't deny it to myself any longer. But I couldn't turn her in, Kim. She's—she *was* my sister and all I had left. So I talked to her instead of to the police, and she promised me there'd be no more bombings. When I called her last night, though, and got no answer, I was afraid. I thought I could head her off." His eyes filled with tears. "But it didn't work out that way."

"Maybe if I hadn't been there, you could have stopped her," Kim said. "But I thought you were the person behind—"

"I know, and I can't blame you for that. Or for any of this." Adam stroked the back of her hand. "What will happen to you and Cody?"

"Well, Cody will go to my ex-husband and his wife." Her tears started, and it was a minute before she could continue. "As for me, I've been told I'm a felon. I suppose they lock felons up. Right now I don't really care." She shrugged her shoulders. "When I think about my life without Cody, I just . . . I don't see the point."

"Don't talk that way," Adam said. "You sound like Jessie."

Kim tried to wipe her tears away with her fingers, but new ones quickly took their place. "I feel like it's my fault," she said. "If I hadn't interfered last night, if I hadn't tried to stop her, Jessie'd be alive."

"Yes, but someone else wouldn't be," Adam said. "There were five people in that house. You did what you had to do, Kim. You saved at least one life, probably more."

Kim bit her lip. "And Jessie saved mine, you know."

Adam nodded. "Yes. They told me. They said you were so close to the bomb that you would have been badly injured if she hadn't covered it with her body."

Linc poked his head in the door, Cody still in his arms. "The social worker's here, Susanna."

"I'll be right there." She turned back to Adam. "I have to go."

Adam smiled at her. "Susanna, huh? So how is Susanna different from Kim?"

She sighed. "Kim is brave and independent and gutsy. Susanna is weak and needy. But right now they're both the same person." She glanced at the door leading to the hallway. "Both of them are terrified of walking out that door."

"They've both been the same person all along, Kim," Adam said. "And don't you forget it."

AT FIRST Susanna did not understand. She was standing in the emergency-room hallway, numbly waiting to be handcuffed, or whatever they would have to do to her to take her to the police station, when the policewoman brought her the news.

"You're free," the policewoman said. Susanna stared at her blankly. "It happens a lot once a child's been located and taken into custody," the woman continued. "The custodial parent is really only interested in getting his or her child back."

Susanna knew she should be elated by that news, yet she had no room in her for joy just then. "And Cody?" she whispered.

The social worker who'd questioned her earlier appeared next to the policewoman. "Tyler will be in protective custody overnight," she said. "Colorado's sending a child-protection worker out here in the morning, and she'll take Tyler back with her. You can be on the same plane, if you like," she added.

Susanna guessed the authorities were confident she'd be unable to kidnap Cody when she was thirty thousand feet above the ground.

She was sick most of the night, and Linc sat up with her in the hotel room, holding her. "Why couldn't he have stayed with me overnight?" she said to him. "He doesn't know what's going on. He'll wake up in the morning surrounded by strangers."

Linc did not have to answer for her to know the reason she was not with Cody tonight: They were afraid she'd take off with him again. And the truth was, she might have tried.

IN THE morning Susanna visited Adam in the hospital. He was understandably subdued, and she was not much better.

"Jessie said I was using you to hide from my grief," he said. "She was right in a way. It was easier to be with you than to be with people who'd known Dana, who kept reminding me of Dana and the kids." He gave her a half smile. "That doesn't mean I didn't enjoy our time together, Kim. I truly did."

"I'm worried about you," Susanna said. "I'd like to stay in touch with you, if that's all right."

"I hope you will," he said.

She rested her hand on his. "You have a lot of friends here. People who care about you. I know they remind you of all you've lost, but you need them now. Don't cut yourself off from them, Adam."

He motioned her closer to him. "I want you to remember something," he said hoarsely. "Remember that even if Cody is living with his father and stepmother, at least he's alive and healthy. You can always have a future with him."

She began weeping then, not for herself and Cody, but for Adam and the emptiness that awaited him once he left the hospital. "I'll miss you," she said.

Adam gave her a weak smile. "You'll be Boulder, Colorado's, dream artist," he said. "Every town should have one."

CODY looked pale and sleepy when Mary Michaels, the social worker, handed him to Susanna as they waited for the plane. Susanna held him close to her as she tried not to cry. Her crying would only upset her son, and he seemed upset enough as it was.

She sat between Linc and the social worker on the plane. In her lap Cody clutched her arm in one hand, his monkey in the other. His sudden lapse into insecurity broke her heart.

She looked past Mary Michaels at the clouds outside the window, wishing the flight would go on forever. Her throat was tight. "Will Jim and Peggy meet the plane?" she asked.

"I think so," Mary answered.

The plane bounced a few times as it landed on the runway. It lumbered toward the gate, and as soon as it came to a stop, passengers filled the aisle, opening overhead compartments. Susanna did not even bother to unfasten her seat belt. Neither did Linc, and Mary seemed to know better than to rush them.

The four of them were the last to deplane. Linc kept his arm around Susanna's shoulders as they entered the waiting area. Susanna expected to see Jim and Peggy with outstretched arms and joyful smiles, but the room was filled with strangers. Cody started crying, and Susanna tried to comfort him. Her outward calm could not fool her baby. He knew she was falling apart inside.

Mary led them to the side of the waiting area, then scanned the crowd one more time. "Let me call the office," she said. She looked at Susanna. "If you want to hold Tyler, you'll have to come with me to the phone booth."

Susanna followed her obediently. Mary was in the phone booth a long time, and when she finally emerged, she was shaking her head. "I've been told to bring Tyler to Child Protective Services. I guess the parents will be meeting him there. Let me take him now," she said to Susanna.

The social worker reached for Cody, but Susanna turned away. Linc gently touched Susanna's arm. "Let him go, Sue. The easier you are about it, the less anxious he'll be."

She knew he was right. She drew in a breath. "Go with Mrs. Michaels, Cody," she said, her voice as bright as she could make it. "That's it. And here's your monkey to take with you."

"What a good big boy." Mary turned to Susanna. "I know this is hard," she said. "Worse than hard. You're a good mom. I'll be sure they know that."

Susanna nodded woodenly. She watched Mary walk away. She could no longer see Cody in the social worker's arms. Only the legs of his monkey were visible as they bounced against Mary's side.

Susanna took a step after them, but Linc caught her shoulder. Without a word he turned her toward him, and she buried herself in his arms. The two of them stood in silence.

She felt a soft touch on her back. "Susanna?" It was a woman's voice.

Pulling away from Linc, Susanna came face to face with Peggy. Instinctively she recoiled.

"You're too late," Linc said to Peggy. "The social worker already took him away. Why weren't you here to pick him up?"

Peggy didn't even acknowledge him. "Susanna," she repeated, and Susanna noticed the red in her eyes. "Please," Peggy said. "Can we sit down?"

Susanna's legs were rubbery as she and Linc followed Peggy to a nearby grouping of seats. Peggy sat down and looked directly at Susanna. "Jim and I are separating," she said.

Susanna frowned, unable to register the meaning of the word. "Separating?" she said.

"It was my decision," Peggy continued. "So much has changed since you left. I've come to realize Jim and I have different values."

Susanna shook her head. "But Cody . . . Tyler . . ."

Peggy's eyes glistened. "On his own as a single father, Jim is no longer interested in custody," she said.

Susanna glanced at Linc, not certain she'd heard Peggy correctly. "He doesn't want custody of Tyler?"

"No," Peggy said. "That's why he dropped the charges. And that's why Tyler's going into foster care instead of home with Jim and me. They need to evaluate the situation to make sure he'd be safe with you before letting you have him back." She leaned forward to cover Susanna's hand with her own. "And I know he is. I know he's safe with you, Susanna. I know you were railroaded. I was duped. I thought Jim was someone he wasn't."

Susanna opened her mouth, but no words came out. This was too fast. She didn't know if she could trust what was happening.

"I wanted Tyler," Peggy said, "but I didn't want to get him that way."

"How long will this evaluation take?" Linc asked.

"I'm not sure, but his stay in the foster home will be very brief, I promise you that," Peggy said. Her hand was still on top of Susanna's, and it felt warm and reassuring. "You come to my office at Legal Aid first thing in the morning, Susanna, and I'll help you do whatever you have to do to get Tyler back."

"Is there a chance Jim might change his mind about custody?" Susanna gave voice to her fear, and Peggy smiled ruefully in return.

"If he does," she said, "I'll represent you for free."

SUSANNA spent the night at Linc's house. They sat on the sofa watching the moon and stars over Boulder, and she felt as though she'd come home. She wished she could talk to Cody and explain to him that they only had to endure a short period of separation before they'd be together once again. But she and he would survive this. In the morning she would borrow Linc's car and go to Legal Aid and begin the process of getting him back. Ironic though it was, she knew she had an ally in Peggy.

The next morning she woke up early, a vivid dream still in her head. She'd dreamed the town of Boulder was covered with a pristine blanket of snow. She wanted to wake Linc to tell him about the dream, but he looked so peaceful, she thought better of it.

She ate a bowl of cereal alone in Linc's breakfast nook, and only then did she realize that the snow had been more than a dream. Looking out the window, she could see Boulder spread out far below her, clean and sparkling in a layer of white.

After breakfast she wrote Linc a note to let him know she was on her way to Legal Aid. She drove to a nearby grocery store and bought a bouquet of mixed flowers. Then she returned to the car and headed in the direction of the cemetery.

There were no other cars in the cemetery parking lot, and the snow had already melted from the macadam. She got out of the car and started across the frosty grass, remembering the last time she'd been there, back when Cody could only crawl. When Cody was Tyler and his future was as uncertain as her own.

A layer of powdery snow dusted the gravestones, making them all look alike. She thought it would take a while to find the stone she was looking for, but to her surprise she walked straight to it.

Crouching next to the grave, she laid the bouquet of flowers in front of the small stone marker. "I'm giving you back your name, Kimberly," she said. "Thank you for letting me borrow it."

She stayed a moment by the grave, then slowly rose to her feet and began walking toward her car. Halfway to the parking lot, she turned around. Kimberly Stratton's small headstone stood out from the rest, marked by the splash of color from the flowers in front of it. The scene gave her a sense of satisfaction, and she continued to walk to her car with a lighter heart.

There was an emptiness in the car without Cody in the back seat, but Susanna felt undeniably optimistic as she drove to Legal Aid. Optimistic, yet determined to be kind to the woman who had wanted to take her son from her. She remembered the pain in Peggy's eyes the day before. Susanna knew all about that pain, and she would do nothing to add to it. Peggy was no different from her—no better or worse—and she and Peggy were equals when it came to strength and courage. She'd had the guts to try to keep her son. Peggy'd had the guts to lose him.

Susanna turned one corner and then another. She'd had to ask Peggy for directions to her office, yet now she didn't seem to need them. She had the odd sense of knowing exactly where she was going, and as she neared the broad, windowless south side of the Legal Aid building, she thought she knew the reason why. It was the perfect canvas for a mural.

Reebok

Weeding out the Tears

A Mother's Story of Love, Loss and Renewal

Jeanne White

with Susan Dworkin

When Jeanne White found out that her son was infected with a virus that would one day claim his life, she wept. What else could a mother do?

The disease, however, was only one of Ryan White's enemies. He would face others just as cruel: suspicion, ignorance, hatred. And there was a great deal his mother could do about that.

Prologue

Dear Lord, please let me do Ryan proud. . . .

MY SON, Ryan, was buried on April 11, 1990. The trees had already begun to bud, but there was no spring in Indiana that day. The clouds hung gray and heavy. A sudden hailstorm chilled everyone, pounding like bullets on the big black cars and the pavement. All the papers carried pictures of the large crowd of fifteen hundred people who actually managed to come inside the Second Presbyterian Church in Indianapolis, and the hundreds more who kept a vigil outside, and the pallbearers—including Phil Donahue; Elton John; Howie Long of the Los Angeles Raiders; my brother, Thomas Hale, and brother-in-law, Leo Joseph; and Ryan's best friend, John Huffman. I still remember that some stray ray of sunshine glittered on Elton's black sequined cap.

I was in shock. I couldn't accept that my little boy was gone. The truth is, through everything, I had never really believed Ryan would die. From the moment just before Christmas, 1984, when I was told that he had contracted AIDS from the factor needed to control his hemophilia, to the moment he died at the age of eighteen, I had always felt sure he would be healed, that he would survive long enough for a cure to be found. Not wanting to appear faithless, I had never planned his funeral. That was why, when the time came, I was so utterly dependent on others to make the arrangements.

In that open coffin Ryan looked so thin and young. It was as though the illness had taken him back from being an eighteen-year-old and made him seem like a small child again. We dressed him the way he would have wanted—pop-star style—with his sharp, reflective sunglasses, in his favorite red shirt and his faded jean jacket.

The Second Presbyterian Church in Indianapolis had been selected—actually by Elton John—because it was so spacious, with place enough for Ryan's many friends from Hamilton Heights High School in Arcadia, which had canceled classes so the children could attend. The church was a big, beautiful building of pale brown stone, with a rose window in the front and a broad lawn all around and perfectly trimmed evergreens hugging the walls. In the large auditorium off to the back, the celebrities and the media who had flocked to Ryan's cause could gather, away from the general public. Tons of famous, important people seated themselves in the sanctuary. Truthfully, I'm not sure that I was sufficiently gracious to them, because I felt so dazed, exhausted and unable to concentrate.

My daughter, Andrea—then sixteen years old—reined in her tears with an iron self-control that she had learned from close acquaintance with discrimination and suffering. Beautiful, blond, strong and athletic, she had withstood public rejection better than some others in our family. My mother nearly collapsed from it. My father, a salt-of-the-earth heartlander, never quite recovered from the moment in church when an old friend refused to hold Ryan's hand during an Easter prayer. My sister and her husband had come up from Birmingham with their three daughters; my brother and his wife stood nearby with their four children. The family members formed a wall of strength around me and Andrea, as they always had.

Michael Jackson—who had been a buddy and a comfort to Ryan—came and stood beside me. When it got really hard for me, he was there to lean on. Michael's people and Elton John's people had worried that some fans might come, not to pay their last respects to Ryan, but to see the celebrities, possibly behaving as though they were at a rock concert instead of a funeral. We were all pleased that nobody did that.

On the cover of the funeral program were Jesus' words from John's Gospel: *"I am the resurrection and the life; he who believes in me, though he die, yet shall he live, and whoever lives and believes in me shall never die."* Also on the cover was Ryan's picture, and under it the words that had so greatly comforted all of us who mourned for him: "I know I'm goin' to a Better Place."

President George Bush's wife, Barbara, was there. Many of the folks we had come to know through the television movie about Ryan came as well, among them Lukas Haas, who played Ryan; Judith Light, who played me; Linda Otto, the producer.

Governor Evan Bayh, who had called Ryan "an American hero," ordered flags in Indiana flown at half-mast. And the state's former health commissioner, Dr. Woodrow M. Myers, Jr., told a reporter, "Instead of living his short life in peace and harmony with those around him, Ryan, his mother and his sister were forced to confront the angry venom of fear from neighbors, strangers and public officials who preferred to remain comfortable, cloaked in their mutual ignorance." Dr. Myers had always seen our family's struggle in the context of a greater American struggle for freedom from fear.

Outside, folks stood patiently in the rain, even after all the seats were filled. One of them was our neighbor Roy Ginder. Roy was a mechanic and auto-body expert who had helped Ryan class up the red Ford Mustang that Michael Jackson had given him and that he loved more than anything in this world. It was sitting on the front lawn of our home in Cicero, among wreaths of flowers—a fitting memorial to a car-crazy kid.

Some of the people who couldn't get inside the church gathered under the wide gray sky and sang "Amazing Grace" for my boy. Inside, the Hamilton Heights High choir wept as they sang "That's What Friends Are For."

Elton John sent a wreath of roses—dozens and dozens of red roses in the shape of a heart, with a border of baby's breath. Its red ribbon said, "Dear Ryan, You will always be with me. You have touched so many people. Thank you. I love you. Elton." When we set all the flowers out at the gravesite, we took some of the roses and wrote Ryan's name in them. I have one; I'll keep it always.

All along the thirty-five-mile funeral route to Cicero people were standing or stopped in their vehicles. Folks stood in front of the fast-food places with their hands over their hearts, leaned out the windows of office buildings and waved good-bye to Ryan. Phil Donahue, riding in the funeral procession, saw one of the state troopers assigned to traffic control standing in the middle of an intersection, saluting. The sight put a lump in his throat; tears rolled down his face. It was Phil who would become my most treasured guide and adviser in setting up the Ryan White Foundation for AIDS Education and shaping Ryan's legacy.

The Reverend Bud Probasco, whom Ryan had personally selected to lead the service, told how we had not received the miracle cure we had hoped for, but that "God gave us a miracle in Ryan. He healed the wounded spirit and made it whole.

"Many of you here are very successful," he continued. "Your lives are filled with glamour and fame. Yet you brought Ryan and his cause into your lives and aided him in his mission and showed us how to do the same. Ryan was successful, too, in getting all of us involved. He helped us believe that with God's help, nothing is impossible—even for a kid." The minister quoted Ryan himself, urging everyone to "make AIDS a disease—not a dirty word."

At the front of the church Elton sat at a grand piano that held a picture of Ryan, the one with the spiky haircut and big smile that I loved best. Elton sang a hymn and played his song "Skyline Pigeon." It brought me an image of Ryan's spirit "turned loose" from his fate, flying "off to distant lands."

I remember every single thing about that funeral: the inspiring words, the grief, the beautiful singing. And yet in a strange way I felt that I wasn't even present. I felt like I was floating above the funeral, a witness to some bizarre dream. It seemed impossible that all this commotion was about my smart, funny kid with the blond cowlick. I saw him thundering along on his tricycle down the street from Grandma's house. I saw him lining up his Matchbox cars for a big race on the kitchen floor. I saw him healthy. Before AIDS.

Elton John playing "Skyline Pigeon" at Ryan's funeral. My favorite picture of Ryan (at left) is on the piano.

"Turn me loose from your hands
Let me fly to distant lands
Over green fields, trees and
  mountains
Flowers and forest fountains
Home along the lanes of the skyway"

You think you're prepared, but you cannot know the loss until it happens. A blank emptiness comes into your life, sort of like a fog. You lose focus. I felt that Ryan's absence was temporary, as though he was just away. I wandered around the house looking for my child, looking for his eighteen years. If somebody spoke to me, I could hardly hear; that was how loud the grieving roared in my head.

I kept thinking, Why are all the people who made him so miserable—the school officials and teachers and bigoted parents, the hate-radio hosts, the people who shot at our house and sent us pornographic letters—still out there enjoying pleasant, uneventful lives? It made no sense to me. I couldn't piece it all together.

I sat in Ryan's room and looked at old pictures, played old videotapes. I read and reread the wonderful letters I had received. It seemed to me that the history of our times was in those letters.

A country that had treated AIDS with ignorance and superstition had learned to accept and, to some extent, deal with the disease. A letter from President Bush said that my Ryan had had a part in that. "With his good nature, and clear-sightedness," the President wrote, Ryan had "helped to educate our nation." There was a letter from Donald Almquist, CEO of Delco Electronics, where I had worked for almost twenty-five years before ending my factory days in a storm of slander and ridicule: "Ryan seemed almost invincible. He will always represent courage in the face of ignorance."

One letter from Hal Wingo, assistant managing editor of *People* magazine, which had always given Ryan so much support, haunted me: "God knew what He was doing by making you Ryan's mother. You can live the rest of your life in the absolute certainty that you were chosen for this purpose and that you gave him the most important things he needed to face his situation with all the strength and dignity he always demonstrated."

If that was true—if God had put me here to be Ryan's mom—what was I to do with my life now that Ryan was gone?

I knew with all my heart that Ryan was in a better place. What I could not find was *my* place. How would I know my task? How would I recognize my direction now?

BY THE TIME RYAN PASSED away, eighty-one thousand people had died from AIDS and a million more were HIV-positive in our country alone, yet no legislation had yet been passed to help AIDS victims. Because there was so much news coverage about Ryan during the weeks surrounding his death, a bill cosponsored by Senators Ted Kennedy and Orrin Hatch finally received the media attention it deserved.

The Ryan White CARE Act would provide home health care for AIDS sufferers, allowing them to stay out of the hospital, close to those who loved them until the last possible minute. It would also help with such things as transportation to the clinics where their drugs were dispensed, and underwrite the cost of drugs, portable IV equipment, hospital beds and other gadgetry.

Senator Kennedy called to ask me to come personally to Washington to help lobby for its passage.

I said, “No, I can’t. I’m not smart enough. I would just mess up everything.” It was only a few days after Ryan’s funeral. I was drained, empty, angry. If I went to Washington, I might just break down and create a scene. I felt I wasn’t in control of myself.

The Senator tried to encourage me. He told me I needn’t be afraid, that I would just be a mom talking to people who happened to be U.S. Senators about what it was like to lose a child to AIDS. He said, “We have twenty-three Senators we’d like you to approach, Mrs. White.” That about scared me to death. I continued to say no.

Senator Hatch called me the next day and also tried to reassure me. They would brief me, he said, tell me everything I needed to know. Politics was just people, plain people after all.

Senator Hatch’s confident words lingered in my mind.

“You’re strong, Mrs. White. I know you can do it.”

Ryan’s words echoed in my memory.

“I’m not afraid of dying,” he had said on one of Phil Donahue’s programs. “It’s how you live your life that counts.”

If he wasn’t afraid of dying, then how could I be afraid of twenty-three Senators?

So finally I said okay.

I went to Washington, and one by one I met with the Senators. I said to them, "I am here to ask you to support my boy's bill. I don't know anything about politics, but I know what it is to lose a child. And there are other people out there just like me, losing their children, losing everything . . . and we have to help them."

At last the bill got to the floor and was passed by huge margins in both the House and the Senate.

I believe now that that trip to Washington to help the lobbying effort on the Ryan White CARE Act (CARE stands for Comprehensive AIDS Resource Emergency) was the most transforming thing I ever did. As I walked the long, stony corridors of the Senate Office Building, I could feel my steps growing more determined, my voice growing stronger. All I had wanted to do was grieve and feel sorry for myself, but now I didn't totally possess my own life. My son had given me a new work, made me by his suffering and courage a new woman.

All through that time in Washington I kept praying, Dear Lord, please help me do Ryan proud.

I looked back at where I had started—a shy, chunky kid in Kokomo, playing house with her mom, expecting nothing but an ordinary little life—and I couldn't believe how far I had come.

Chapter 1
We All Get Tested in This Life

I SOMETIMES wonder how a person manages in this tricky, hard world without a family. Life has taught me that if you lose your family, you've lost everything. And if you have a family to love you and stand by you, no matter how much you lose, you're always a winner in the end.

My mother, Gloria Hale, was born and raised in Kokomo, Indiana. Her grandparents had been farmers in Germany. Mom's father died when she was only nine. That left Grandma Helen with nine children—six girls and three boys—to raise pretty much on her own.

They had a house and a yard, but beyond that, not much more than the bare necessities of life. Mom says they had oatmeal for breakfast, lunch and dinner, and they each received one pair of shoes a year. The church would help out sometimes by donating used clothing. Mom remembers her mother tearing apart old coats and making them over to fit her kids. The big kids took care of the little ones. The little ones did what chores they could. Those old enough to work brought every dollar back to the family.

No matter that they were poor, Grandma Helen never turned away from a beggar's outstretched hand. During the Depression, when there were so many down-and-out people on the road looking for work, she would invite any stranger into her house for toast and coffee. She was never afraid. She told my mom, "When a stranger comes to the door, even if it's someone who seems not right in the head, you should help that person because you never know if he or she might not be a messenger of the Lord, or even the Lord himself."

As a child, I felt a little disappointed that Grandma Helen didn't live close by. I wanted a grandma like the kids across the street had, who came over with presents on holidays, but as I matured, I realized that what Grandma Helen had given us was a lot more important than presents. She had given us an ideal of family on which we could model our own.

THE story in our family is that Dad fell in love with Mom just from looking at her. Mom was working at a restaurant called the White Hut. Dad—Thomas Edward Hale—worked at Kroger's Market, a big chain of supermarkets out our way. He had had to quit school at sixteen to go to work when his dad died. He had lunch at the White Hut one day when they were serving peanut butter cream pie. All the customers were raising hell because the pie was sour. Mom asked Dad if he had any problem with the pie. He had no idea what she was talking about. He had been staring at her so intently that he had just gobbled up the awful pie without even tasting it.

My folks married when they were scarcely twenty years old and started life together in a ramshackle apartment on Jasper Street in Kokomo. First I was born, then my sister, Janet, then my brother, Tommy Joe. Mom stayed home and took care of us, except when she worked canning tomatoes at the Libby's factory. It was seasonal work—ten weeks, just long enough for her to earn the money for our school clothes.

Dad rose through the ranks at Kroger's and stayed there for forty-three years, until he retired. A loyal union man and an Eisenhower Democrat, he was the shop steward at the grocery and soon became the produce manager. He was famous for his displays. He would make incredible arrangements of fruits and vegetables. Millions of mushrooms. Towers of oranges. Popcorn cascading over pyramids of soda cans! Dad's displays won prizes from the Kroger's chain. They kept offering to make him manager, but he always turned down the job, preferring a little less responsibility and more time and freedom to do some of the things he loved.

Dad was co-founder of the Kokomo Bass Anglers Club and wrote articles for their magazine. As long as I can remember, we'd take picnics and go fishing. For a couple of years we had a tiny trailer up at Bruce Lake.

A lot of times Dad would go out by himself—leave in the evening and stay out on the lake all night. I was fascinated.

"What happens out there, Dad? Why do you love it so?"

"It's the feel of the wind," he said. "It's the quiet. It's watching the night sky full of shooting stars. Makes you know there's got to be a better Being behind all this."

I idolized my mother, too. It seemed to me she did everything that a good mom should—she made great chicken and noodles, did lovely handwork, gave out excellent advice and always had a few dollars in her pocket that she had earned herself. She was a Brownie

Scout leader, then a Girl Scout leader. If somebody asked her to help out—even if it was just kitchen cleanup—she would do it willingly, without ever seeking attention or recognition.

Although money was tight, we never lacked for anything we wanted. We might have to save up for it, but eventually we got it. We all had a clear sense of how hard our parents worked and how they shared everything with us. So we shared back.

Every supper we had meat, potatoes, vegetable and a dessert. The rule was that you couldn't eat dessert until after supper. Mom made an exception for me because I liked chocolate pudding on my fried potatoes. So she'd give me a scoop ahead of time, and I would gobble it up while my brother and sister made faces and my father covered his eyes. We always could have more if we wanted, before Mom and Dad did. On the other hand, if there was something we knew Dad liked and we saw there wasn't enough, we automatically left him seconds without even thinking twice about it. We always said a prayer before dinner.

When I look back on the family system now, it seems like a collection of small things—sharing, making allowances for this preference and that peculiarity, not taking blessings for granted. It's those small habits from home that prepare you for the world.

My very favorite game as a little girl was playing house with my mother. She'd be ironing, and I would pretend I was the neighbor, "Mrs. Jones," come to visit. We'd talk about our tea parties, our children, all the things that neighbors talked about in what now appears to be totally bygone days. I couldn't wait to grow up and become "Mrs. Jones"—for that fantasy of motherhood and homemaking to become my real life.

WE MOVED to the house on Fisher Street when I was around seven years old. It was our first house, a small model in a suburban development. I remember just loving it and thinking we must be rich now that we were moving there. The house cost $8600. The down payment was $600.

Everybody there was the same as us. Same age kids, same financial situation, same race, same religion, same politics. There were no Communists, no K.K.K. members, no criminals or homosexuals. Dad and Mom even swear there were no adulterers, but I believe that about as much as I believe the rest. Anyone "different" must have been in deep hiding. That was just the way things were in the suburbs of Kokomo, Indiana, in the '50s.

When I was in fourth grade, Mom began to think there might be something wrong with me. I wasn't eating much, but I was gaining weight. The doctor said it was nothing, but it got worse in the fifth grade. And the sixth and the seventh. I was getting to be a big, heavy girl in a family of slender people, just at the time when I was becoming interested in boys.

Finally Mom got me to Dr. Craig, who took one look at me and said, "This girl's got thyroid problems."

They put me in the hospital and finally figured out how to regulate my thyroid. The puffiness and the dryness went away. My weight became my personal problem, not some mysterious disorder.

My energy returned, but my shape still conditioned my self-image. I felt bad because I was squat and chunky, and I did everything I could to make people like me in spite of that. I was famous for being a pushover.

I wanted to be a teacher, but I didn't think I was smart enough to go to college. Besides, at eighteen I was determined to go to work, get married and have the happy-homemaker life I had played at as a little girl. So—to my eternal regret—I never went beyond high school. Instead, I put in my application at Delco.

Now a subsidiary of GM Hughes Electronics Corporation, Delco produced automobile engines and audio electronics, including car radios. The plant stretched for miles and employed thousands of people. At Delco you could be assured of a good paycheck and just about the best insurance coverage available to any working person in the United States.

I worked as a parts stuffer—putting transistors and capacitators into car radios. There were about forty people on the line, all women. First you had to wrap the little three-legged transistors—carefully, since they had real sharp edges. You couldn't wear gloves to protect your hands, because you wouldn't be able to feel the thing to wrap it right. You also had to make sure the legs weren't touching. Then you stuffed the transistors and several capacitors into the radio.

You would do the same thing over and over and over—eight hundred, a thousand sets a day. A bell would ring every twenty seconds, and you would have to pass the radio on. You had three spares, which didn't have your work done on them yet, so if the lady in front of you got behind, you could always grab a spare and not have to waste a second waiting for her. The whole line had a quota. There was a buzzer for your break and another that told you to go back to your seat. At the end of the day you'd have one minute to clean up. Then the buzzer would ring to clock out. The buzzer controlled your life.

The line is a thing of the past now. Today machines do the work, and they're computerized. But only twenty years ago it was all done by hand. Rough as it was on the fingers, it was rougher still on the brain. Your mind really went stale on the line.

During my first ten years mostly women worked on the line. The men were the stockroom boys, the group leaders, the foremen. They worked hard, but they didn't have to live by the buzzer; they could socialize and talk on the job. Then suddenly, around 1975, the whole plant changed. Women started to be group leaders, stock watchers. They started getting the real trade jobs, too—some were even electricians.

It was a funny feeling to be in the middle of that change. I had heard vaguely about women's libbers, but I certainly didn't consider myself one of them. I was the most nonpolitical person in the world. I never voted, and I don't think I knew who was representing me in Congress. And here my whole life was being transformed by some faraway new political movement.

I became a parts changer, a job I loved. When there was something wrong with a radio, the parts changer had to change all the parts that were defective or badly installed. So you had to know how to tear down the radio and reassemble the whole thing from scratch. It was the first time I had ever had a job that required intelligence and remotely suited my abilities.

Like most of the women at Delco, I thought of my job as temporary. I said to myself, You make good money, and that's fine for now, but when you get married and have children, you'll quit. It never occurred to me that I wouldn't leave for twenty-three years.

At Delco a guy named Wayne White started paying attention to me. Wayne and I had been in the same grade at school, but I really didn't see him again until he returned from serving in the army in Germany and became a group leader at Delco.

He asked me if I wanted to go out for a Coke sometime, and we ended up having a regular date. He was good-looking, short, with blue-green eyes, and dark hair that he styled real nice. He looked great in jeans. He didn't smoke or drink at the time, which I really liked, and he had a neat sense of humor.

I really don't think I was *crazy-crazy* about him, but I did like him, and I was twenty-one. My friends were getting married, and I was ready to move out of my folks' house and have my own family.

We went together for about three months and then got married. Three years later, when I became pregnant, I was so excited.

I WAS a big woman and healthy, and I was sure I wouldn't have any trouble, but when my time came, something went wrong. I was in labor for almost twenty-three hours. And after I delivered Ryan, on December 6, 1971, the pain didn't stop. I kept calling the nurse. She told me to stop acting like a big baby. They brought Ryan to me. I wanted that little boy more than anything, but I was in so much pain I asked the nurse to take him away.

The lady next to me, who had two other kids, told me, "You're not supposed to be hurting so bad. Or to bleed like that."

The doctor came and pushed on my stomach. Blood clots came out. It was horrible; blood was everywhere. I lost consciousness. A specialist arrived.

They sent helicopters all over Indiana for Rh-negative blood for me. Thirteen pints. I can remember looking around the room and seeing Mom and Dad, Wayne and the minister. I thought I wasn't going to make it. I saw the tunnel that they talk about, and the light, but I never entered the tunnel. I'd sort of dream about my little baby boy and think, You can't die. You have this baby now. You have to make it. For him. That's what kept me fighting.

When I was finally out of danger, they brought Ryan back to me. He was a cute little thing with a lot of hair. They took him away again to be circumcised, and I waited for them to bring him back to me, but they didn't.

"Where's my baby?"

"He's still bleeding from the circumcision, Jeanne. We've tried everything to get the bleeding stopped."

After three days Ryan was still bleeding. Wayne and my folks took him to a hematologist at Methodist Hospital in Indianapolis. I was still too sick to get out of bed. When the hematologist called, he pulled no punches. He said, "Your son has severe hemophilia. That means his blood does not clot. You will have to be very cautious. He will never be able to play contact sports. He will never be able to have any major surgeries. If he is in a car accident, the chances of him surviving are almost zero because he will bleed faster than they can ever put blood into him."

Then he said in a deadpan voice, "Hemophiliacs used to have to have blood transfusions one after another. They would often die or be crippled by the time they were teens. Now we are fortunate to have a clotting factor, which is just being approved by the Food and Drug Administration. However, it has to be given in the hospital, so your son will require a lot of hospital stays."

I remember trying to take it all in.

How could this have happened? My little son had been born with a disease occurring only in boys and caused by a deformed gene carried by their mothers. It had a history of affecting the sons of European royalty. My mom and my grandma tested negative for the gene; I tested positive. The gene just showed up out of the blue.

It looked like my little Ryan had simply been unlucky. In this he was exactly like about twenty thousand other American men.

When they tell you that something is terribly wrong with your child, it takes a while to be able to think clearly about it.

Sure, I had wanted a perfectly healthy child. Everybody does. But all through life things come out not perfect. Even if people are born perfect, they eventually may not have perfect lives. So you have to say to yourself, It's the person inside that counts. If I ever felt disappointed in Ryan, I was ashamed of myself and smashed down that unworthy feeling.

Look at all the people who can't have kids at all, I said to myself. Think how much luckier you are than them!

When we got through our initial panic and hysteria, we sat down with the doctors. They told us that factor VIII, the clotting factor, would help to make Ryan's hemophilia a controllable chronic disorder. It was expensive—$350 per shot. Ryan received up to two a week. Thank heaven we had the company insurance.

The great danger was not only that the child would cut himself but that he would bruise himself. Any bump could trigger a bleed internally, in a joint, that would cause terrible pain and swelling. There was nothing to be done except to treat the pain and wait for the blood to dissipate. Meanwhile, every bleed would cause ugly bruises. Parents of hemophiliacs are sometimes suspected of child abuse for that reason.

I learned quickly that stories from other sufferers were often every bit as important as advice from your doctor. My family and I developed the habit of gathering intelligence in waiting rooms, at fund-raisers, on line at pharmacies.

One day a woman came to visit me with her hemophiliac son, who was seven or eight at the time. One of his legs was an inch shorter than the other because of so many hemorrhages in the knee, but he was a good-looking, cheerful boy, and the sight of him filled me with hope that Ryan would grow strong despite the disease.

My visitor said, "Every case is different. You'll just have to see what he can do and what he can't. You'll learn by experience."

She was right. I quickly learned that handling this thing was very much a matter of attitude. I wanted Ryan to think, Yes, I've got a problem, but it's not going to ruin my life. I told him, "Now, Ryan, when you start to feel a tingling sensation and you think you're getting a bleed, you come and tell Mom and we'll get you to the hospital and give you some factor, and then it won't hurt so much."

OF COURSE, the doctors had advised me not to have another baby, and I had tried not to get pregnant, but when I found I *was* pregnant again, deep down I was thrilled. For some reason I just knew the baby was going to be a girl. Also, I had faith that the Lord wouldn't give me another hemophiliac. Wayne was furious at the news. I had told him at work so he couldn't make a scene.

Andrea was born on October 15, 1973. She arrived in maybe an hour and a half. No bleeding. No problems. What a beautiful baby—healthy and robust, with lots of hair! Right after she was born, I had my tubes tied. I was so grateful to God for this blessing and afraid to test the generosity of fate any further.

I can remember Mom bringing two-year-old Ryan to the hospital. They wouldn't let such a little child come up to the wards, so I looked down from my third-floor window. He was standing on the hospital grounds waving up at me with this big grin on his face. I said to myself, Jeanne, your boy was born in the era of factor VIII; your second child is a healthy girl; you are the luckiest woman in the world.

WHEN he was four or five months old—he wasn't even crawling yet—Ryan climbed up over the side of the crib. We found him sitting on the floor laughing. By nine months he was walking. Before you knew it, he was potty trained. I realized I had a real smart kid.

Maybe because he had to limit his physical activity so much, Ryan became a really fascinated reader. He loved Dr. Seuss and the Berenstain Bears. When he was ten years old, his grandparents asked him what he wanted for Christmas, and he said, "A subscription to *Time* magazine."

We accepted him as our smart kid. He always knew just a little bit more than the rest of us.

Ryan frequently had to go to the hospital, and whenever he did, I stayed with him. At Riley Children's Hospital, a division of the Indiana University Medical Center in Indianapolis, they always let parents stay, but at other hospitals the nurses hated that.

"It's hospital policy. Parents can't stay."

"Dr. Fields said I could stay."

"He didn't leave any orders."

"That must have been an oversight. I'm staying anyway."

"Mrs. White!"

"Please don't be mad at me. That's just the way it is."

Our trips to the emergency room were like a recurring nightmare of ignorance and incompetence. Once, Ryan hit his head and needed stitches. The emergency-room personnel gave him factor VIII and sent him home with his head all wrapped up with gauze. He didn't want to sleep in his own bed after that, so we took him into ours.

I woke in the night feeling wet, and turned on the light. The whole bed—me, Wayne, Ryan—we were all covered in blood. If Ryan had been in his own bed that night, he would have bled to death. From then on I knew that he could never just be treated and discharged. Any injury would require a hospital stay.

One Christmas Eve, when he was about five, we were at Mom and Dad's, and Ryan started to run a high fever. The doctor said to take him to the emergency room, but before he arrived to supervise, the nurses had given Ryan a shot to lower his temperature.

"Wait a minute!" I cried. "You shouldn't be doing that! This boy's a hemophiliac. He needs the factor before getting a shot."

"Don't worry, Ms. White. We used a very small needle."

They sent him home. His hip hemorrhaged and swelled up like a giant boil. He was in agony for three days.

The experience of living with Ryan's hemophilia put me in conflict with my own natural personality. I was a shy woman, a docile person, used to taking orders, taking care, making things nice. And here these ignorant, obstinate medical people were turning me into an aggressive, pushy mother who could create a big stink right out in public. I was quickly learning that there was going to be nobody to speak out for my child but me. Doctors and nurses are not gods.

It was bad enough that there were nurses who wouldn't listen to me; some of them wouldn't even listen to the child. When Ryan was about six, he had a hemorrhage in his kidneys and couldn't urinate. It was terrible. He was crying, miserable. He kept saying he was going to vomit, but this grumpy hospital nurse kept telling him he was not going to do any such thing. I asked her to let me take him to the bathroom, but she refused and said he had to come with her to the examining room. When she went to pick him up, Ryan vomited all over her. Then something released in his kidneys, and he urinated everywhere. She was fit to be tied.

"Now I've got to go change my uniform!" she hollered.

I was so happy that he was peeing again, I think I actually laughed. I thought, Lady, your uniform is the least of my worries.

I made my share of mistakes, too, and I remember every single one of them with the same aching guilt that I felt at the time. Ryan was always a collector, even as a little kid. His Matchbox cars were his treasure. He always took six or eight to bed with him. Every night I would go in and get all the cars out of his bed after he went to sleep. One night I missed one. He rolled over on it, and the next morning his whole neck had hemorrhaged. I wept and berated myself. Guilt left me sleepless.

Until Ryan was three, if he had a bleeding episode, I had to take him to the hospital so they could give him the factor in an IV. Then it became possible for him to receive it in the doctor's office. We went on Mondays and Thursdays to get it so he would be okay over the weekend. Wayne never came with us. When Ryan was five, the doctors suggested that I try giving the factor myself. It took three months of training, but I learned. It would have made our lives a lot easier if Wayne had learned, too, but he just didn't want to be involved with Ryan's illness.

WE KEPT the factor in our refrigerator. I'd pick up eight to twelve boxes at a time from the hospital and mix it up as needed. If Ryan was going to stay overnight someplace, we'd give him some as a prophylactic in case something happened. My dad was the most cautious one in our family when it came to the factor. He had heard a rumor from someone at the hospital or someone at the pharmacy that the more you took, the less effective it would become in time.

"I don't like that factor," Dad said with a suspicious frown. "You're giving him too much of that stuff."

I didn't see that we had an alternative.

Ryan eventually began to take care of himself quite a bit. He learned what he could do and could not do. But he wanted to do it all. We were leery about him riding a bike and made him wear kneepads. Once he learned, he tossed them away.

He tried Little League. I'd tell the coaches what to do if something happened. But during practice one day he was hit in the mouth by a fly ball and started bleeding. The coach handled it fine. He called me, and I got Ryan some of the factor. After that, however, Ryan didn't want to play anymore. He had matured enough to know fear. He missed baseball—not the game so much as the social aspects of being part of the team—but he knew he couldn't play it.

Ryan could always tell when a bleed was coming on. His skin tingled. And then slowly the vessels underneath would start swelling with blood. As soon as he felt that, we could give him the factor and the bleed would stop. But as he got older, he set his own agenda. If he thought the bleed and its treatment would keep him from doing something he really wanted to do, he wouldn't tell me about it. I'd get mad because then it would get really bad and he'd have to go to the hospital, and it would take two or three or four days for the swelling to dissipate.

He was always supposed to wear Ace bandages when he had a bleed. Often he ignored that rule. The doctors would say, "He needs to be on crutches for the next three or four days." But Ryan wouldn't use the crutches. He didn't like kids saying, "What's wrong with you now?"

He got used to being in the hospital two or three times a month, to receive the factor after a minor scrape or bruise. Riley became his home away from home.

"I saw this kid who was burned, Mom—his whole face and chest and arms. He was in such pain. . . . I saw this kid with cancer. He's getting chemotherapy, and he has no hair and vomits all the time. . . . I saw these kids who are so retarded they have to wear diapers, and they're in their teens."

"Oh, honey, I hate for you to see so much suffering."

"It's okay, Mom. I'm just glad all that's wrong with me is my hemophilia."

I DO believe that evil befalls folks who do evil, that what goes around comes around, but I never felt that Ryan's disease was a punishment. No, this illness felt to me much more like a test. We all get tested in this life. God gives you tests to see how you can handle them. I always thought, I'm going to handle this, Lord. You will see.

Chapter 2
"Let's just pretend I don't have it."

AN ILLNESS belongs to everybody in the family. Even if you're not the main caregiver, if you never change a bandage or carry a bedpan or drive a suffering child to the hospital, that illness will invade your life. Better to face it and do battle with it directly than try to avoid it. That's the only chance you have of winning the battle.

I often think that if my husband had shared in caring for Ryan, the illness wouldn't have seemed such a threat to him and would not have depressed him so.

THE center of our social life was the euchre club—six or eight couples who would gather each week to play cards and have a few laughs. One of the guys who played euchre with us was always trying to get Wayne to go out drinking with him. After Ryan was born, he succeeded.

Wayne had never been a drinker, but now when I saw him acting kind of silly, I'd ask myself, *Is he drunk?* When he was, he'd sometimes get mean. For example, he'd humiliate me because of my weight. If I ate something, he'd say—in front of everybody—"You don't need that!" I'd feel myself turning scarlet and run to the kitchen to hide.

I felt if I could only get Wayne away from his drinking buddies, the growing sickness in our marriage would go into remission. We had a wonderful time on vacation to Florida when Ryan was five and Andrea was three. Then as soon as we came home, Wayne was out every night again, and most of the time he'd come home drunk.

Wayne had never struck me when he was sober. Now he occasionally gave me a swat. One night he shoved me, so that I fell between two stools. He stood there laughing while I floundered, trying to get up. When I finally regained my footing, I punched him in the stomach. He staggered back.

"You're not going to start beating me up," I said. "It will not happen." I shoved him away and shut myself in the bedroom. He never raised a hand to me again.

When Ryan was five, Wayne announced that he and a drinking buddy were taking their boys fishing. I was pleased; I thought that would be fun for the kids. But it turned out not to be a fishing trip like the ones we used to have up at Lake Bruce with Dad. This was one of those trips where the men sit around the campfire boozing and the boys watch.

On the way home Wayne was so smashed that he drove into some guy's fence. When the guy came out of his house yelling, Wayne fled to our house and ran right into the wall of the garage. With Ryan in the car! I went crazy.

"Look at you. You're smashed! You could have killed Ryan!"

"Aw, leave me alone."

"You're a drunk, Wayne. You've got to get help."

"I am not a drunk. I am fine. I can take it or leave it."

Andrea, age four, and Ryan, age six

"You've got a problem."

"*You've* got the problem, Jeanne. Why don't you go on a diet?"

That really got to me. The biggest hang-up in my life has always been my weight. I responded to Wayne's counterattack by going on a killer diet.

Everybody thought I looked terrific at one hundred forty pounds.

At one hundred and sixteen, everybody thought I looked sick. It turned out I was. I had a burning feeling in my lungs; it was impossible to inhale. They put me in the hospital, convinced that I had lung cancer, although I had never smoked. Finally they put me in the Indiana University Medical Center and ran some more tests.

Wayne came to see me. He was drunk and upset about some bill he thought I had not paid. Nothing I could say would stop him calling me names and yelling. The hospital staff stood gaping; the lady in the bed next to me was horrified. For the first time, I saw Wayne through the eyes of other people, and I thought, Jeanne, you are not going to live like this. You have a good job, two wonderful kids, a supportive family. There is no reason to go on subjecting yourself to this kind of abuse. Your children deserve a home like you had. A loving home. I made myself a promise that if I got out of the hospital and didn't have lung cancer, I was going to divorce Wayne White.

THE tests came back. I didn't have cancer; I had a lymph node infection called sarcoidosis. It's serious. Some folks die from it, but if you're lucky, as I was, you get rid of it with rest and antibiotics.

I had Wayne served with divorce papers while he was at work. As with the announcement of my second pregnancy, I was scared of his reaction. I also dared to hope he might be happy about the separation. Instead, he begged me to stay with him. He said he would stop drinking, go to church again—anything I wanted. I think he panicked at the idea of losing the security of a home and kids and a wife.

He said, "I'll stay with my mom for a few days, and then we'll see, okay?"

"Sure," I answered, but I knew there was no way I was going back with him.

WHEN I became ill, a man named Steve Ford had taken over my job. After I returned and took back my old job, we became friends and eventually started dating.

Steve was quite a bit older than I. He was a group leader and a UAW representative. He had been married several times but had no children. Maybe we shouldn't have married, but each of us needed something from the other right then. I wanted a father for my children, and he wanted a family.

Wayne and I were divorced in September, and I married Steve on September 30. We built a house in Windfall, where Steve's folks and his brother and sister lived. I loved those people. They were a great family. I loved the woods at the back of the yard, too, and the feeling of space under the wide Indiana sky. I canned corn and peas and green beans that we had grown in our own garden. I even put up beef stew and chili.

WHEN I married Steve, Ryan was seven and Andrea was five. She adored her big brother, and he played with her all the time. He could bounce her, chase her, put rice pudding in her hair, and she'd just giggle and coo. He showed her how to build whole towns out of Lego, how to put each little plane neatly away in its little hangar, each little car in its little box.

To our dismay Andrea showed absolutely no inclination to put anything away herself, and when she was about four years old, she abandoned her dolls and the pretty dresses I'd made her in favor of T-shirts and jeans, and went out to play in the mud. She was a real tomboy. She could run as fast and throw as far as any kid on our block.

One day right after Steve and I were married, we heard that Delco was offering afternoon roller-skating at the local rink. It was close by, so we figured we'd take the kids after work. The very first time Andrea went out on that floor, she could skate. She went around a couple of times with Ryan guiding her, and then *whoosh!* she took off. Ryan, Steve and I stood there amazed, watching her race around that rink shouting, "Look at me!" as she passed us in a blur of blond hair and rosy cheeks.

"Can I have lessons, Mom?" she pleaded. "Can I?"

A local teacher named Rick Gunning, who had just started a skating club, said he would be delighted to take her on. The club had about eight members, and Andrea was the youngest. She improved very fast. In no time flat she could do a set spin and then come up. After her first year of skating, she qualified for a state meet. My mom made her a costume with a big butterfly on it. She placed third. I just about fainted with pride.

Steve loved the skating. On Sundays he'd take both kids to the rink and skate with them himself. He said we should spare no expense to train Andrea and outfit her.

We heard about a terrific teacher in Alexandria named Jim Harmer, whose skating club members came from all over the Midwest and often made it to the national competitions. When Andrea joined Harmer's club, she met other skaters her own age, and I was real pleased by that. But the schedule was hectic. She practiced every night after school and Saturday mornings from 6:00 a.m. until noon. There were times when we'd stay in Alexandria all day Saturday, get back at eight o'clock at night, have supper, fall into bed and go back and spend all day Sunday.

In her first year with Jim Harmer, Andrea won the state meet in the primary division. Then she placed third in the regionals, which meant that she qualified to go to the nationals. And she had only been skating for *two years!*

All the other skaters were nervous wrecks before a meet, psyching themselves up with motivational tapes. Not Andrea. She said, "If I do good, I do good. If I don't, I don't." She had a highly developed sense of reality.

Andrea's favorite event was freestyle—although she also competed in figures, dance and pairs. She had a seven-jump combination—axel, loop, double mapes, loop, double mapes, uller, double flip—that was just terrific. She had a wonderful "broken ankle" (where she'd spin on the sides of her wheels) and inverted spin. If she hit those moves, she was unbeatable.

A friend of mine from high school, Susan Slaughter, made Andrea's basic costumes, and then I added the glitter. Sequins, bugle beads, and aurora stones that give off all the colors of the rainbow. Each tiny stone had to be attached separately. It was hard on the fingers but worth the effort to see your child shining.

I loved getting to know the other mothers and kids in the skating club. We had great times together, and they remained my friends through everything. We even shared rooms at nationals to cut costs.

In 1983 Steve and I divorced very amicably. Our marriage may not have worked, but it had warmth and respect and fun and a lot of comfort. For my beautiful little towheaded daughter it was the best thing I ever did—because it gave her a real father. Steve was crazy about Andrea. Even after we were divorced, he always went to see her at nationals.

I moved back to Kokomo, to a little house on Webster Street, to be near my mom and dad.

Andrea's new skating teachers were Larry Dorset and his wife, Karen Mejia. In 1984 Andrea made it to nationals in three events. She placed fourth in juvenile girls singles, made the finals in pairs with her partner Darren Merkle, and was runner-up for the Harmer Trophy, the Indiana Skater of the Year award. Maybe Andrea grew to champion level in reaction to Ryan's not being able to do anything athletic. I don't know. I never thought about the psychology. I just felt that skating was something she could do naturally, and if she was motivated to compete, then I was determined to encourage her.

At nationals we met a boy named Mike Underwood, a terrific skater from Chicago. He and Andrea hit it off and decided they'd like to compete as partners. For several months we drove to Chicago every weekend. Ryan came with me a few times to watch his sister and Mike practice, but he seemed listless, distracted. So I began to leave him with my folks, and when I returned from my long drive, I'd find him lying around, not doing anything. It wasn't like him.

One weekend Andrea and I were driving home, and we hit a terrible rainstorm. I squinted through the beating wipers, trying to see the edges of the road and not lose sight of the car crawling along ahead of me. "Andrea, hon, if we get home, this is going to have to stop. I can hardly handle this schedule anymore. Ryan's not feeling good, and I have no idea how he's doing. What if we had an accident in a storm like this and Ryan was left all alone?"

"I understand, Mom."

We made it back to Kokomo. I drove straight to my mother's house. Ryan was very sick.

HE'D get a little better; then he'd get sick again. He ran fevers. Then they'd go away. He woke up in the middle of the night sweating. He had diarrhea. His lymph nodes were swollen. The baffled doctors gave him antibiotics, trying to figure out what was wrong.

In November 1984 Ryan went to the annual screening clinic for local hemophiliacs. The clinics were important in assessing whether the factor was working as it should, but Ryan hated them because they were so boring. Blood tests. Dental exams. Questions. At this clinic he tested positive for hepatitis B. The doctors asked if he had been sick a lot during the past year, and I said yes, thinking it must have been the hepatitis.

We were told that we were going to be receiving a new, heat-treated factor that would be a lot safer than the old stuff. The label on the new factor said something about a less than one percent chance of AIDS. We had heard of AIDS in homosexuals, of course, but the only hemophiliacs we had heard of who had contracted the terrifying new disease were older men who had received blood transfusions before factor VIII became available. The factor itself had never been questioned in this regard.

At the end of that clinic visit I had both heat-treated and non–heat-treated factors in my refrigerator. Nobody told us to stop using the non–heat-treated variety. Just a few days later Ryan got sick.

ON DECEMBER 6, 1984, Ryan turned thirteen years old. The next day he got off the school bus, came into the house and said, "Mom, I can't figure out what's wrong. I can't even get off the school bus without being tired. We had to run a lap today, and I couldn't do it, and the teacher got real upset with me."

That weekend he ran a fever of one hundred and four. Our doctors said to give him Tylenol, but the fever wouldn't go down. On Monday morning they put him in the local hospital. X rays showed pneumonia in both lungs. They gave him antibiotics. The attendants pounded his chest and his back. It hurt so bad he couldn't stand it.

"Ryan, you've got to cough that stuff up out of your chest," they said. "You're not trying to get better."

And he said to me, "Mom, there's nothing to cough up. Why can't they understand that?"

Dr. Fields walked me down the hall. I had known him for years, and I could tell he was frightened. "The antibiotics aren't working," he said. "We're going to transfer him to Riley—in an ambulance, because he needs oxygen."

I kept hearing my dad's voice saying, *I don't like that factor. You're giving him too much of that stuff.* I kept hearing the voice of the attendant at the hemophilia clinic: *The new, heat-treated factor is much safer than the old kind.* Suddenly I turned to the head nurse. "Did the doctors say anything about AIDS?"

Her face registered shock. "No, they didn't say anything like that."

I put the nurse's reaction out of my mind and went with Mom and Andrea to Riley Children's Hospital, in Indianapolis. Ryan was in emergency with so many specialists around him that Andrea and I could barely see him. He looked worn-out. He couldn't breathe without the oxygen. His eyes brimmed with questions: *What's wrong with me, Mom? What's going on? Tell me. Help me.*

All I could say was, "You rest, hon. You're going to be all right."

The doctor who talked to me was a man I had never met—Martin Kleiman, an expert on infectious diseases in children.

"Ryan doesn't have bacterial pneumonia," he said. "We know because the antibiotics would have worked on that. We have to find out what kind of pneumonia he has. And for that we need to do a lung biopsy. We need your signed consent because there is a possibility of complications during the procedure."

I signed the papers.

I know now that Dr. Kleiman had considered AIDS the minute Dr. Fields described Ryan's case on the phone. Ryan's hemophilia made him suspect it. He had seen a lot of children with pneumonia caused by *Pneumocystis carinii,* a microbe that lives as a parasite in the body. Usually it doesn't cause any trouble, but when the immune system is compromised either because of disease or drugs used to treat disease, it can cause a kind of viral pneumonia characterized by a hard, dry cough and an eventual breakdown of lung function. You can tell when somebody's immune system has deteriorated, because there is a huge decline in the number of T lymphocyte cells in the person's blood. These are the cells that we learned about in high school biology as the white antibodies that naturally fight infection. Dr. Kleiman's experience with pneumocystis was in children who had had chemotherapy or leukemia that destroyed their T cells. But when he heard Ryan's history, he thought of the dreaded new disease, AIDS.

I waited with Andrea for the biopsy to be over. In a couple of hours Dr. Kleiman returned. "It looks like Ryan's got a viral pneumonia. We're sending the specimen to Denver."

At about two in the morning on December 18 Dr. Kleiman told us that the biopsy revealed that Ryan had pneumocystis.

That meant he had full-blown AIDS.

I COULD not imagine losing my child. I could not believe that he really had AIDS and would die. I thought, This is so new, maybe they don't quite know what they are dealing with. I'll make them run the tests over, and maybe the results will come out differently.

I had no basis on which to comprehend the disease. My family and I were living with words we had never heard before: autoimmunity, opportunistic. One treatment for pneumocystis was Septra, a sulfa drug administered by painful shots in the leg. Ryan had an allergic reaction to it and nearly died.

He had tubes in his feet, his legs, his chest, his nose, his mouth. They stuck another tube down in his lungs to suction him out. It was like watching some medieval torture—except that a mom doesn't just watch; she *feels*.

They put him on a respirator, a machine I associated with people in comas who would never recover. They told me he would be on the respirator for only a day or two. Three days later he was still on it. One tube created a bad sore in the corner of his mouth. It looked terrible because the hemophilia caused it to bleed under the skin. They kept him pretty well sedated, but he was awake enough to mumble things into my ear and to write me notes asking to be suctioned out because he couldn't breathe.

Dr. Kleiman consulted everybody he could think of: the Centers for Disease Control in Atlanta (CDC), the National Institutes of

Health (NIH), medical centers in Canada. He gave Ryan a drug called pentamidine. It began to clear out my boy's lungs.

On December 22 they started removing the tubes. On the morning of the twenty-fourth they took Ryan off the respirator. He still had a tube in his throat, and if he moved, it would make him cough and choke. So he tried not to move.

Years later, when my father had a heart attack and they put a similar tube down his throat, I remember Ryan leaning over him, saying, "Grandpa, don't move, because if you do, it makes you cough."

AT THAT time there was no blood test available to determine the presence of AIDS. So the CDC, which was trying to give support to physicians making diagnoses in the field, provided Riley with serology testing so everyone around the patient—family members and medical professionals—could be tested for the presence of the virus. Dr. Kleiman gave me a questionnaire from a group of infection-control people doing a family contacts study. It had a long list of questions, from the most mundane—Do you often share drinking glasses and eating utensils with family members?—to the most intimate: Do you have multiple sexual partners? Of which gender? And on and on.

I was terrified. *We're all going to get it!* I thought. I imagined Andrea and Mom and Dad with those tubes in their lungs. "We're a real affectionate family," I cried hysterically. "We hug. We kiss. We share drinks, use each other's towels!"

"No family member has ever come down with AIDS from ordinary household contact," they said. "You have nothing to worry about."

Both Dr. Kleiman and I knew immediately that Ryan had contracted AIDS from his factor. It sat in my refrigerator, a death sentence in a small blue-and-white box. I later learned that the pharmaceutical companies needed such a huge volume of blood to make it that they couldn't depend on donations. They had to pay people for their blood. Naturally, some IV drug users availed themselves of this chance to make a little fast money for the next fix. All the blood would be mixed in a big container; then the container would be spun in a centrifuge to separate the clotting factor.

What nobody realized was that *one* infected donor could contaminate the whole batch of factor. Ryan got at least two shots a week, and if he had a bleed, he might get a shot a day for a month. So he was probably infected not once but thousands of times.

Once I understood the procedure, I thought, There's no way any hemophiliac could escape getting AIDS. In the years since, I have heard of mild hemophiliacs who had only one shot of the factor in their entire lives and who are HIV infected.

RYAN was completely isolated. You couldn't go in to see him without wearing a gown and gloves. Laura Krich, a wonderful young nurse, always volunteered to take care of Ryan if she was on duty. As far as I could see, the hospital staff was well informed.

One day, however, Andrea and I were in the little snack area. A physician whom we had met was sitting nearby, talking to a nurse.

"I absolutely refuse to go in that kid's room," the nurse said, "and you are not going to make me."

It took me some minutes to realize she was talking about Ryan.

The next hint of paranoia came when two of Ryan's teachers paid him a visit. They brought a lot of cards and letters from his classmates and asked what was wrong with him.

"They say he has AIDS," I said, "but I think they'll find it's something else. Ryan will be very pleased to see you. You can take the cards and letters and go on in to see him yourself."

"No, that's all right," they said.

I said, "No, really, it's okay. All you have to do is put on the gown and gloves, and you can go on in and see him."

They had this pained look on their faces. They said, "That's okay. We'll just leave the cards and letters here."

I thought, My goodness, they're *scared* of him. Maybe I shouldn't have told them.

People ask me all the time why we went public, and I tell them that we never *went* public; we just didn't know not to tell the truth. I didn't know that people would think only gay men and IV drug users got AIDS and that Ryan would have to be one or the other to be infected. I thought that all I had to do was tell people he got it from his factor and they would believe me.

I SAID to myself, Jeanne, what you have to do now is believe. This is the first time for you to prove your faith, to show the Lord that you believe in his healing.

I kept having this vision that Ryan was going to wake up and be well, and all the doctors and nurses would come and say, "Gee, Mrs. White, it's just unbelievable, but somehow Ryan is cured."

ALL through the days before Christmas I sat in the lobby with the other mothers of hospitalized children, keeping watch, sleeping in the waiting room. The Reverend Harold Williams from our church came a couple of times every week. Wayne visited. So did Steve, my brother Tommy and his wife, Deb, and Mom and Dad. Andrea was allowed into intensive care to see Ryan only once a day for ten minutes. She sat on my lap and hugged me and held my hand. She understood that I was at my wits' end.

We kept a picture of Jesus on Ryan's wall. Nancy Trent and her husband, Bob, who attended our church, brought Ryan a guardian-angel night-light. Each night Ryan and I would pray together: "Thank You, Lord, for another day." When I left, I'd make sure that his guardian angel was lit. It got to mean so much, that little statue. One night Ryan woke and found that a nurse had shut it off.

"Never do that!" he yelled, really agitated. "My mom does that! She shuts it off when she comes in. That way I know she's here."

Shortly before Christmas the social worker at Riley helped us get a room at Ronald McDonald House, where there would be a decent bed, a decent meal. But once I got Andrea set, I couldn't stand being away from Ryan, and I went back to the waiting room. I felt helpless. I kept thinking, This is not happening. I was eating myself up, trying to figure out how to tell my boy about his disease. One of the doctors warned me to tell him soon.

Ryan's case was bound to attract media attention because it was the first to prove that the disease could be caught from the factor. It would be terrible if he heard the news from the TV.

When I saw Ryan on Christmas Eve morning, he looked a thousand times better. Although he still had the heart monitor, the tubes were out. He smiled at me. I thought, Maybe now I'll tell him. Then I thought, No. After Christmas. When he has his new computer and is looking forward to going home.

On Christmas morning I went over to the I.U. Med Center to get breakfast and suddenly heard myself being paged. It was my mother. She was terribly upset. "I don't know how to tell you this, Jeanne, but you've been robbed. We went over to your house to get the Christmas presents, and it felt cold in there, and it turned out somebody had broken the window and climbed in and stolen them all."

They had taken the computer I had bought for Ryan and the VCR I'd bought for Andrea so she could study her skating tapes. They took the tapes, too. My precious memories of my little girl's earliest skating meets, all gone. In the midst of this terrible crisis my kids' Christmas had been stolen.

The family of another child in the hospital heard about the robbery. The aunt and the grandma went out and found an open drugstore and bought my kids a whole bunch of presents: a Care Bear and paint sets, coloring books, crayons, whatever they could find. Sometimes strangers are so sweet and good and kind it just fills up your heart.

On the day after Christmas, Ryan felt better than he had in weeks. Reverend Williams and Andrea were in the room when I told him about his disease.

"Ryan, you know you've been really sick."

Ryan said, "Yes."

"They say you have AIDS."

I saw no panic on his face. "Does Laura know?" he asked.

"Laura, your nurse? She knows."

I guess that meant a lot to him, realizing that Laura would take care of him even though he had such a dread disease.

"Let's just pretend I don't have it," he said.

"Well, Ryan, we can't really do that, because we have to take precautions to keep you from getting sick."

"That's not what he means, Mom," Andrea said.

Ryan explained, "I just don't want that every time somebody comes in the room, they're thinking like, Oh, poor Ryan, he's dying."

Here I was, trying to be supportive and explain things to him, and he understood everything and was explaining it to me.

WHEN somebody tells you that somebody you love is going to die, the first thing you think is, There's no way I can live without that person. I love that person so much. But the truth is, you have to go on. It's just too easy to say, "I can't do it."

They told me Ryan had three to six months to live. But in my heart I believed I was going to get a miracle. As the months and then the years went by, I thought the miracle would surely come.

Later, when Ryan's life ended, I asked, "God, why didn't I get a miracle? Wouldn't it have been great to show the world your miraculous power by healing this boy?"

Now I have the feeling that when I get to heaven, God's going to say, "You know what? You had a miracle. Ryan was only supposed to live three to six months, and he lived five and half years."

Chapter 3
The Strength to Never Ask Why

I WAS mad at everybody, but I didn't know who to blame. They had given Ryan a drug that was supposed to help hemophiliacs live normal lives, and now they were telling us this drug had given him a disease that was going to kill him. How fair was that?

I kept asking, "Why Ryan? Why our family? Why?"

But Ryan never asked, "Why me?"

In the hospital he had had a vision.

"I've got to talk to you a minute, Mom. Close the door."

"What is it, hon?"

"Last night the Lord came and spoke to me."

"What? Well, what did He say?"

"He told me I had nothing to fear—that I was going to be taken care of."

"Now, Ryan, are you sure it wasn't a doctor or a nurse dressed in a white gown?"

"No, Mom."

"Well, what did He look like?"

"He sure didn't look like that picture of Jesus on the wall. From now on," he continued, "every night I'm going to thank the Lord for another day."

"All right, hon, that's exactly what we'll do."

And so we did. Every night we sat together before he went to sleep and thanked God for another day.

I had heard stories about people talking to the Lord, and I don't know whether I ever believed them, but when Ryan told me about his vision, I believed. I saw this inner peace in him after that. What makes somebody accept what is happening to them and able to deal with it the way Ryan did, especially when he had a mother who was overwhelmed by the unfairness of it all? For Ryan to have the strength to never ask why, well, I think only God gives that to you.

AFTER Christmas, little by little, he began to get better. It's almost impossible to explain the joy I felt at every little milepost—every tube that came out of his body, every spoonful of lime Jell-O he kept down. When he was first diagnosed, Ryan had gotten down to fifty-seven pounds. Now, when he gained an ounce, even part of an ounce, I was wild with happiness. I wanted to cheer. I had thought that I might not ever see him breathing on his own again . . . and here it was, January 24, 1985, and he was leaving the hospital, inhaling the cold winter wind and laughing.

By the time Ryan came home, I was going broke. Never in my life had I expected to receive a nickel of charity from any source, but I was trapped between my need to care for Ryan and my pride, and my pride had to be sacrificed. Fortunately, Riley Hospital had a special endowment that provided up to six weeks of missed paychecks for parents who needed to stay off work to be with their children. That was a life saver. Also, my friends at Delco had taken up a collection for us after the robbery, to help pay for nonmedical expenses like house payments and car payments and gas and food. And luckily, Wayne never missed one child-support payment.

Ryan still weighed less than sixty pounds when he came home. Dr. Kleiman insisted that I do anything in my power to get him to eat. He didn't care if Ryan ate fast food and Twinkies, as long as he ate. Most of the time, food just flushed right through him, but he did seem to be able to keep down little bits of food better than whole meals. So I cooked all the time, anything he wanted. If he craved something—Denny's beef stew, hot chocolate from the Waffle House—I'd take him anytime, day or night, to get it.

The news that Ryan had AIDS had quickly spread through Kokomo. The first negative reaction we got was when a restaurant owner destroyed our dishes and our silverware. Ryan was upset, but I told him the man was probably just an ignorant person who didn't understand that AIDS could not transmitted by sharing utensils. I was too happy to be upset. Because Ryan was miraculously gaining weight, ounce by ounce, and feeling a lot better. Maybe they're wrong, I dared think. Maybe Ryan is going to beat this thing.

Folks in the hospital had told me that AMFAR (the American Foundation for Aids Research) had the best, latest information about AIDS. I hesitated calling them at first, because I knew many people at AMFAR were homosexual. But I needed to pick their brains, absorb their knowledge. Whether or not it suited me, that meant talking to the gay community.

Terry Beirn at AMFAR had heard about Ryan's case. He and Mike Callan and others there were so kind and so helpful that my prejudice simply evaporated. Once you have AIDS, you're just like everybody else with AIDS; you're all fighting to stay alive. Terry and Mike told me about new drugs, warned me about side effects, comforted me when I felt desperate. I trusted them completely. They became my closest friends and allies in the battle to save Ryan's life.

AS WINTER ended, Ryan began asking to visit school. I put him off. I thought, He's doing so well. Do I really want him around other kids' germs? But Ryan kept at me.

So finally I called the principal, Mr. Colby, and told him Ryan was feeling better and wanted to come visit his friends. Mr. Colby was real nice and said to call back after spring break.

We took a vacation and went down to see my sister and her family in Alabama. It was great the way Janet and Leo made us all comfortable. We sorely needed some time in the sun and couldn't have afforded any other kind of break.

During that vacation Ryan swung on a rope across the river; he rode his bike again. You could feel the happiness bubbling up in him as his health returned. I felt much easier in my mind about having him visit school. When we arrived home, I called the principal again.

"Can we arrange this visit now, Mr. Colby?"

"You need to talk to the board of health, Mrs. White. They're considering putting a quarantine sign on your front door. The school system has to abide by their rules. . . ."

I could hear that he was having a real hard time talking to me. Folks sounded no less nervous at the local board of health. They had already dropped the quarantine idea, but they were waiting for guidelines from the state board of health. They were afraid of a lawsuit if they let Ryan go to school, and afraid of a lawsuit if they didn't.

Late in July, 1985, I received a phone call from Channel 8 TV. They asked me whether I'd heard that the school board had decided not to readmit Ryan.

I was so shocked, I broke down and wept. I had thought with all the doctors saying it was fine and more people being educated about AIDS, they'd say okay. My naïveté—and my total absorption in getting Ryan well—kept me from realizing the truth, which was that from the day those teachers visited Riley and reacted with terror, Western School District was determined not to let Ryan return.

The phone started ringing off the hook. The local news. The national news. "What are you going to do, Mrs. White?" "Are you going to sue?" "Are you going to court?" *Good Morning America.* The *Today* show. *CBS Morning News.*

"I don't know what I'm going to do."

"Can you come to New York and be on our show tomorrow?"

That was the beginning of a media siege. After the stunning revelation that Rock Hudson had AIDS, the whole dumbfounded country was engaged in this issue. How many more famous people were secretly gay and hiding their illness? Ryan was trying to hide nothing, so he was a natural for television interviews, newspaper and magazine articles. The media seemed to understand something that nobody in Kokomo, including me, had figured out: This was an important story because it represented the tip of a deadly iceberg. We were having a plague. Not just *them,* but *us.*

Two important people strongly supported Ryan's desire to go to school. The first was Dr. Woodrow M. Myers, Jr., the state health commissioner. A tall African American born in Indiana, he had been educated at Stanford and Harvard and, despite prejudice, had risen to the top ranks of the medical establishment. Dr. Myers was in San Francisco during the first terrible outbreak of AIDS, and he had seen the havoc and hysteria that could be caused when health authorities were unprepared for a new disease. He didn't want that to happen in Indiana. He authorized a statewide information campaign to assure the public that nobody could give anybody AIDS by breathing the same air or touching the same doorknob or using the same toilet. You couldn't get AIDS from saliva or sweat or kissing or tears. You could get it only from having unprotected sex with an infected person or from direct blood contact.

The other person who supported Ryan was a lawyer, Charles Vaughan. We had met him during an unsuccessful suit against the blood companies by six hemophilia families whose loved ones had contracted AIDS from infected factor. The suit was thrown out because in Indiana you can't sue the blood suppliers. But Mr. Vaughan invited us to his office and explained that we could use legal means to get Ryan back in school. He was prepared to represent us on a pro bono basis.

I thought, There's no way we can win. And even if we do, Ryan could die before he ever gets to attend classes.

Ryan didn't see it that way. He was as determined as I was indecisive. Some kid made a joke about him at school ("What do faggots eat? Ryan White bread."), and his friend Chris was suspended for three days for hitting the kid. Ryan hated that—having other people fight his battles. He wanted to fight himself.

"Come on, Mom, let's take them to court."

"I've got to weigh this thing out, hon."

"I want to go to school."

"They'll make fun of you. They'll say awful things to you. Can you handle that?"

He regarded me with patience and heaved a sigh. Had I forgotten that he was already handling hemophilia and AIDS?

"I can handle anything, Mom."

Mr. Vaughan grinned at me across his big desk and said with confidence, "I guess Ryan is my client now, Mrs. White."

THE legal battle lasted for about a year. It felt like a century. It aged me; it exhausted me; it strengthened me. When it was over, I was not the same person I had been when it began.

On July 30, 1985, Western School Corporation denied Ryan the right to return to school.

On August 3 the Indiana State Board of Health issued guidelines under which Ryan could have been admitted.

On August 8 we sued in federal court to get him admitted.

On August 12 one hundred and seventeen Kokomo parents threatened a civil suit if Ryan was allowed in.

On August 15 about fifty teachers voted to support the decision to keep Ryan out.

The next day a federal judge ruled that we had to exhaust administrative appeals (for example, to the department of education) before the case could be heard in federal court.

When classes began on August 26, Ryan was linked to them from home by a computer telephone hookup.

On November 25 the Indiana Department of Education hearing officer ruled that Ryan must be admitted to school.

On December 17 the Western School Board voted to appeal.

On February 6, 1986, the Indiana Department of Education Appeals Board ruled that there was nothing to prevent Ryan from attending class if he was cleared by the county health officer.

On February 13 the Howard County health officer certified that Ryan was fit to attend class.

On February 21 Ryan returned to school. Out of 360 students, 151 stayed home and 7 transferred to other schools. That very day, a group that called itself the Concerned Citizens of Kokomo received a restraining order that kept Ryan out of school. So no sooner did he get back in than he was out again.

On April 9 Ryan's case was argued before the higher court.

On April 10 the restraining order was dissolved, and Ryan went back to school. Twenty-seven kids went home rather than stay in the same building. Meanwhile, the parents appealed the court's ruling.

On April 30 a judge vacated the parents' arguments and upheld the earlier decision.

On July 18 the Indiana Court of Appeals dismissed the appeal of parents who did not want Ryan to attend school.

On August 21 the Howard County Health Department examined Ryan and declared him fit to go to class.

On August 25 he began eighth grade at Western Middle School.

Every minute of the short time he was there was hell.

Somebody broke into his locker and scrawled homophobic obscenities all over his school folders. Nobody wanted to sit next to him in class. When he walked down the hall, the kids would flatten themselves against the walls and yell, "There he goes! The AIDS kid! Stay back!" or they'd run up and touch him, then touch other kids and say, "Now *you've* got it."

And it wasn't just school. The spite and malice surrounding us in the community were beyond belief. People accused Ryan of spitting on vegetables in the supermarket. They said that when angered, he would bite people, that he urinated on the walls in public places. They said I was a front for the gay community, a slut who slept with bisexual men and brought the disease home to my son. I still remember the hate mail, the letters that called me a whore, the articles asking why we didn't do the decent thing and go off to a desert island. (The evangelist Jerry Falwell suggested just that—a leper colony–type exile, where AIDS patients could be kept in isolation.)

We got dozens of letters from the religious right, telling us that AIDS was God's punishment on my son. Frankly, up to that time I thought I *was* a member of the religious right, so I dismissed these letter writers as nutcases and didn't pay them any mind.

People I had known forever stopped speaking to me and didn't want their kids associating with mine. People who supported me were attacked. Chris MacNeil of the Kokomo *Tribune* covered our story when other reporters refused to enter our home. He got death threats. Marcia Blacklidge, a friend of our family, was ostracized by women at her gym who didn't want to sit in the hot tub with her.

The folks at our church wanted to do the charitable thing and help a family in trouble, but lots of them were on the side of the school board and the Concerned Citizens group, and they wanted to make sure we didn't use their money for legal fees. So they gave me gift certificates! For the gas station! For Kroger's Market! And then, when I'd go shopping, some people would stare boldly into my shopping cart to see if I was buying something too extravagant.

Our family was asked to sit alone in the middle of a pew in the back of the church. One Christmas I was thrilled to hear some of our parishioners singing carols outside our door. I invited them in for hot chocolate. They were afraid to enter the house. They would pray for Ryan. That was the way people prefaced their testaments of sympathy—and their rejection. "We pray for Ryan; he is in our prayers. But . . ." It was a big "but."

I told my kids, "You cannot worry about what other people think.

You must do what is necessary and right and go on with your life."

But one day, stinging from the pain of rejection, Ryan had made me promise that at his funeral the Reverend Bud Probasco would lead the service instead of our regular minister. Reverend Probasco had been the assistant minister at our church, then moved on to another pulpit in Pendleton, Indiana. He visited Ryan several times, and they had a good relationship. I thought, Well, so be it. It's Ryan's life, and he should be able to choose the preacher he wants praying over him at the end.

Somebody shot at our house. We found the bullet hole in our picture window. Andrea was too terrified to sleep. I felt sick with confusion. I prayed for a way we could somehow leave this mess.

IN ONE thing I was lucky, though. Ryan's doctor, Dr. Martin Kleiman, was a fairly conservative physician. He didn't jump at the news of every exciting possible drug as we did, but in his quiet, gentle way he was very persistent. He acquired AZT for Ryan even though Ryan wasn't yet sixteen, the required age for a prescription. One day I called AMFAR, and Mike Callan asked me how much AZT Ryan was getting. When I told him, he was shocked. "Cut that dosage in half," he insisted. "Too much can cause liver damage."

I was so afraid of offending Dr. Kleiman that I cut the dosage without telling him. Six months later he told me, "We have to cut down Ryan's dosage of AZT because there are reports of side effects." When I admitted that I had already done that, he smiled and wasn't mad at all. He knew that in those early days of AIDS there was what he called "a very useful grapevine" that brought information to patients long before it reached practitioners.

Dr. Kleiman's protocol was to make my boy feel as well as he could, to treat his symptoms in a way that would keep him out of the hospital if at all possible. This meant keeping him off intravenous, not rushing to put him on a feeding tube. Dr. Kleiman believed that nothing doctors could do for Ryan would help him as much as one more day of living like a well boy. He never prescribed any treatment that he would not have prescribed for his own child, and he let Ryan do things that Ryan was clearly too sick to do. He knew Ryan would be less sick if he did them.

Ryan learned a lot about doctoring from being Dr. Kleiman's patient and from reading *Time* magazine. I'll never forget one incident that occurred about a year after Ryan was diagnosed. Mom and Dad had come to stay with him while I was at work. Dad had gone out for lunch with my brother. When he returned, he looked kind of pale. He was sweating on a cold day.

"I feel kind of funny," Dad said. "Think I'll go lie down."

"Grandpa, listen," Ryan said, "you can't lie down. You have to go right to the hospital. You're having a heart attack."

Dad went to the hospital and ended up with a quadruple bypass.

Dr. Kleiman and Ryan talked in the privacy of the hospital, in those deep night hours when the day is turned upside down and they were awake and everybody else was sleeping. I suppose their friendship stood in somewhat for the father-son relationship that Ryan so sorely missed. Ryan was a very smart boy, a dedicated student. He needed somebody who represented the well-educated world to talk to him, and Dr. Kleiman was the man on the spot.

NOTHING shocked me so greatly as the hostility from the families of the twelve other hemophiliacs in our community. As soon as I understood how the factor was made, the blood bought from anyone who would give it, I knew that they all were in terrible danger.

"Don't you see?" I kept saying. "The gay community is already being blamed for causing this disease. Soon hemophiliacs will be blamed as well. They're going to start unknowingly giving it to their wives and their children. This has to be discussed now!"

But it was too painful for them to face the fact of AIDS. It was too complicated to explain to an ignorant, jittery public what hemophilia was exactly, that "hemo" wasn't "homo." The lawyer for the Hemophilia Association spent more than an hour on the phone with me, trying to convince me that the members could not afford to be associated with AIDS. "This is a hemophilia organization," he said, "not an AIDS organization."

I couldn't believe it. There was a hemophilia clinic at the mall, where they were passing out brochures and information. They didn't want me to come anywhere near it.

In 1985, when the clinics started testing hemophiliacs, they found that more than 80 percent of them had AIDS.

EVERY day throughout the conflict between Ryan and the school board, and then the Concerned Citizens group, I considered giving up. I was at the end of my strength, ready to listen to those who told me to withdraw. I was not prepared to sacrifice Ryan and Andrea and my mom, who was close to a nervous breakdown, in order to continue with my crusade. That's it, I thought. *You've got to give up.*

And I would have, too—except for something that happened in the winter of 1986.

In February, after Ryan had been certified fit to attend class and a Howard County judge refused to issue an injunction to prevent it, the school district lacked money to go on fighting. So the parents organized on their own. They hired a lawyer and had a meeting.

What the Concerned Citizens of Kokomo planned to do was have me declared an unfit mother, have Ryan taken away from me and placed in foster care, and then have his foster parents keep him out of school until he died. All the reasoning behind this scheme had been worked out. I would be declared "unfit" because I was trying to send a child with AIDS to school, thereby exposing him to all kinds of bacteria that he would not be able to fight off because of his disease, which would ultimately kill him. It wouldn't be a problem to get this ruling from the child welfare authorities, because they, too, were "concerned citizens" and would support the parents group. No less than three families were already lined up as prospective foster parents for Ryan. (What these folks were going to do with Andrea, I do not know.) According to the reports that came to me, their lawyer advised that this plan seemed horribly cruel, and that just the attempt would create adverse publicity for their cause. They dropped the idea.

But proof of how powerful and well connected these people were was demonstrated on February 21, the very day that Ryan went back to school. That afternoon, with phenomenal speed, a local judge issued a restraining order to keep Ryan out. The crowd in the courtroom burst into wild cheers and whooped and hollered as though the Hoosiers had just won the national championship.

The story of the parents meeting and the delirious joy when Ryan was defeated did something to me. I felt like I had entered a new psychological state. I wasn't fighting for Ryan's education anymore; I wasn't even fighting for his right to go to school. I was fighting hatred, plain and simple. Some sort of lead thing got into my gut, and I realized that my strong son was absolutely right when he said, "We're going to educate these people one way or another, Mom, or die trying."

Chapter 4
Guardian Angels

IT TOOK a long time before I felt like I was on solid ground with the media people. They intimidated me. If I found a reporter I trusted—and I found a few, thank heaven—I stuck with that person. But one thing I knew going in, and it stood me in good stead. "Always tell the absolute truth. Never lie," I said to Ryan. "Never. If you tell the truth, people will recognize it."

He took that advice. He never changed his story. He never changed himself. He was the same boy on-camera and off. And that is a rare thing indeed in this two-faced world.

THE media arrive on your doorstep. They ring your phone off the hook. They demand. They plead. They're pitiful. They're imperial. Sometimes they threaten; other times they love you to death. They are the biggest asset you can have and the biggest pain in the butt.

I hated dealing with the media. But at the same time I thought if we did a few interviews, it would educate people in Kokomo and lessen their fear of Ryan. He knew that if he wanted to go back to school, he was going to have to make it happen, and talking to the press was the only way.

People said I forced him to make these appearances. That is a lie. I never made Ryan do anything. However, if he said he'd do it, I told him he couldn't change his mind. He had to stick to his commitment.

Ryan became the love of the nation, while I became the "wicked mother." "I feel sorry for the kid," said one typical letter, "but I bet his mother loves all this publicity. I bet she's not turning down the money she's getting from TV and magazines. I think she should offer Kokomo an apology, not vice versa."

I suppose I should have blown off such attacks, but to be perfectly truthful, I never could. I cared what people thought. When I saw myself on TV, I thought, Boy, I look mean. I look hard. I think I looked that way because I didn't know who to trust or what to say. I was scared. My own anger welling up inside scared me worst of all. You get so sick of trying to explain yourself and trying to make people understand, that you just want to scream. Every time I got to one of those moments, I would pray, Lord, help me not to say anything I'll be sorry for later.

The greatest thing about the media people was that they weren't afraid to be with Ryan. They replaced the kids who wouldn't play with him, the teachers who wouldn't educate him. Taro Yamasaki, a photographer from *People*, did a photo essay on him and gained his trust and friendship. So did Daliepe Menta, an Indian photographer from *Picture Week* and *Time* who enchanted Ryan with tales of his worldwide travels. Carrie Jackson, then a reporter with Channel 13, became a close friend.

These folks were Ryan's home school; they brought the world back into his isolated, lonely life. Most important, they made him feel worthwhile because they thought he was doing something important by going public about AIDS.

One casualty of the media blitz was my daughter. Andrea was hearing all these terrible things about her mother and her brother, and the reporters were always popping in the door, peeking in the windows, sticking microphones in her face. She became absolutely phobic about the press.

When Ryan returned to school in February 1986 (before the Concerned Citizens got him thrown out again), there was a tremendous media crush. Reporters arrived as early as three or four in the morning to find a place up front. I asked my ex-husband, Steve Ford, to escort Ryan and Andrea to school, and he accepted immediately.

Steve looked so strong and confident walking those kids to school. I kept thinking, How do I get that way? How can I learn to stand up to people like that?

AIDS was such a mystery back then that every idea seemed worth a try, and we heard a new one just about every day. Heat the blood. Exchange the blood. Give the patient smallpox to jump-start his immune system. Feed him this; soak him in that. While I was busy investigating one remedy, the media would announce another.

Dr. Kleiman said, "These cures are wacko, Jeanne." I nodded respectfully, but half the time I went right home and started calling all over the country to find out more about them. Our garage gradually filled to the ceiling with potions from all over the world: every kind of vitamin, cases of ginseng, garlic, mineral baths, milk shakes. People sent them out of the goodness of their hearts, without ever asking for money.

We also had all these ministers calling and wanting to pray over Ryan, saying they could heal him.

At first I let them come, even those who seemed obviously insane. I kept hearing Grandma Helen's caution about the beggar at the door who might be Jesus, and I was determined not to overlook anything or anyone who might have the answer. I didn't care how my boy was cured; I just didn't want him to die.

The preachers would enter the house. They would pray. They would pull on Ryan's legs, stretch his back, then wait for the disease to depart from his body. Ryan's faith in all this deteriorated quickly.

After three or four months he looked at me with weary eyes and said, "Enough, Mom, please. No more. If the Lord's going to heal me, He's going to heal me."

"I am so sorry, hon. I just didn't want to give up hope."

"I know, Mom."

What would I have done without that boy's tenderness and understanding? Ryan was more worried about me than about himself.

DURING the time when I was trying to get my son into school in Kokomo and survive the hostility of the townspeople there, the loneliness of my situation made me miserable. But then, because of Ryan's exposure in the media, something happened. Perfect strangers took our cause to heart and became a new community in spirit for us to depend on.

We received get-well cards and balloons and flowers. A lot of mail came from men with AIDS and from their families. Parents wanted to commiserate, to pool their strength with mine, just to talk. Young people wrote constantly to Ryan. Very often he heard from children with disabilities or their well siblings.

Sometimes folks would send us money. "Here's $20, Mrs. White. Take yourself and the kids out to dinner." Or "Here's $25. Buy Andrea and Ryan something special." In February 1987 some kids from the Catholic Youth Organization had a talent show at Our Lady of Lourdes School in Utica, New York, called *Tryin' for Ryan,* and they raised $1500, which helped us enormously. I was overwhelmed that kids should be so incredibly generous.

Here I was always trying to figure out how I was going to have gas money or milk money, saving pennies, and somehow people understood. They understood about the phone bill, the electric bill, the mortgage payments, the bank penalty on a bounced check, the tank of gas that it takes to get to the hospital, the regular everyday stuff that no insurance covers. I tried to write thank-you notes to every single one, but no note could adequately express my gratitude.

Right there in Indiana we had another important group of friends working on behalf of our cause. Led by Dr. Myers, the state health commissioner, they operated at the grassroots level to make folks in Indiana understand AIDS and how to prevent it. They sent nurse educators to schools and public meetings across the state. (Unfortunately, Western Middle School turned down offers for a nurse educator to come and talk about Ryan and AIDS.)

They explained that because of the long incubation period—the lag time between contracting the disease and showing symptoms—it was impossible to know who had AIDS. Therefore it was essential to adopt "universal precautions," a standardized way of treating bodily fluids that would be taught to everybody from cops to athletic coaches. It was kind of like basic hygiene—washing your hands after you go to the bathroom—except that this was a new, more intimate hygiene dealing with blood, semen and vaginal secretions.

Their mission took them to the Indiana State Legislature. That must have been some job to get those dignified lawmakers to talk about secretions! But the law that was written as a result was a monument to the American democratic process, and it helped Indiana face down the great plague of our time.

They called it the Ryan White Law.

I have since heard about the terrible pressures that were exerted against Dr. Myers and others who supported Ryan's right to go to school and who championed a new way of looking at AIDS. They had to fight the prejudices of people who were perfectly ready to shun members of *any* group showing a high incidence of HIV infection: Haitians, hemophiliacs, intravenous drug users, members of the gay community. I do not have words to explain how courageous I think these people were, and I know there were hundreds more who just fought quietly and kept on fighting until the fight was won.

WHENEVER I would boil over in anger at the people who were trying to keep Ryan out of school, it was Ryan himself who would calm me down. "Mom, they're just trying to protect their own kids the way you're trying to protect me," he'd say. "We can't be angry. We have to understand them and try to teach them."

So I tried to do that. I held on to the belief that folks would change, that they'd gradually learn about AIDS the way we had. Our hearts filled up with the certain feeling that we were right, and that meant there was no room in our hearts for anger.

MY CHILDREN hated Kokomo.

We had won our court case by the middle of April, 1986. Ryan was back in school. Still, the bitterness and anger against us in our town never went away. The kids were shunned and insulted daily. "Get us out of here, Mom," they pleaded. "Please find us another place to live."

I sat at my kitchen table at night, going over bills, trying to see a way to rescue my family. I was flat broke. When Ryan would take sick and I couldn't get to work, I had no income.

Andrea's skating life was all but destroyed by the lack of money and time. Skates cost about $500 a pair. Steve had bought her last pair. Now she had outgrown them.

I got her new ones by borrowing from my family and paying off the balance week by week. But Andrea understood that it was a tremendous effort. She was missing so much practice because of Ryan's illness that girls she had beaten in years past were placing ahead of her at the meets. She fought back tears and said, "I'm going to quit skating, Mom. We can't afford it anymore. There's no point in going on. . . ."

I couldn't even keep one young roller skater properly equipped. How was I going to get enough money to move out of Kokomo?

DURING that difficult spring Ryan's story received a lot of media attention, and we were invited to New York City to participate in a big fund-raising benefit for AIDS research. It would be cohosted by Calvin Klein and Elizabeth Taylor. Of course I said yes.

I eagerly anticipated meeting Elizabeth Taylor. To me she was the biggest star ever. But when Ryan appeared on ABC's *Good Morning America* and was asked which celebrities he was looking forward to meeting at the benefit, he said, "Elton John. Definitely Elton John."

To be perfectly honest, I had hardly heard of Elton John. I knew he was a singer. I could recognize his name, but I couldn't match it with a face. A singer-songwriter who sometimes sported a pink ponytail or golden sneakers seemed like no big deal to me.

As it turned out, Elton didn't come. He had jet lag. Ryan was terribly disappointed. I told him, "Honey, you mustn't get caught up with these celebrities. They're not like *real* friends. They may hang around for a bit, but that's all."

At the benefit, photographers bugged Ryan to pose with this celebrity and that celebrity. "Smile! Big smile! One more time!" I could see he was exhausted. I stood behind him so he could lean on me. Terry Beirn held on to him when he walked. I was hoping to get Elizabeth Taylor's autograph and have a picture taken with her that I could show to my family back home, but before I even had a chance to speak to her, she was gone.

Even though I was disappointed, I still loved the benefit. It was the first thing we had done that had nothing to do with our court battles. This was something that was helping in the fight against AIDS itself. The experience gave Ryan a new sense of personal security because he realized people were proud to be around him. And now he had something to do, a cause, a sense of being part of a movement. I think that helped him live longer.

The next morning we were on our way to the airport in a limo, and suddenly the phone rang. Who could it be? Who would know we were in this limo at this moment?

It was Elton John. He had tracked down the service that was taking us to the airport and then convinced them to give him the phone number of our car. He was calling because he had heard Ryan mention him on TV and wanted to apologize for missing the benefit. He told Ryan he would call again to set up some good time when we could come and see him perform. And to my astonishment he did! In the autumn he invited the kids and me to join him for three days in Texas, where he was giving a concert.

We didn't get to go, because Ryan landed in the hospital, but when he got out, Elton John brought us to California.

He toured us around Disneyland, and we flew in his private jet to his concerts in San Diego and Oakland. Andrea and Ryan adored him. When Ryan became exhausted and couldn't walk another step, Elton got hold of a wheelchair and raced him around with such energy that it seemed more like a ride at an amusement park.

In a serious moment Elton turned to me and asked, "What do you need, Jeanne? Not tickets to concerts, not sweatshirts and balloons. What do you need to make your life easier?"

I laughed. In the midst of all this fun it was almost impossible to recall my little practical Indiana needs. What could I tell this kind man? That I needed to leave my hometown. That I needed our story to die down and disappear so my parents and my kids wouldn't have to face hostility and despair every single day? My "needs" were so great that I couldn't begin to explain them. So I just said, "Oh, well, I don't need much of anything, Elton. We're okay."

I completely forgot that conversation. Then, sometime after we got home, out of the blue, Elton John sent me a check. I set it out in front of me on the kitchen table and wept all over it.

I paid my four past-due mortgage installments and brought my account up to date. I paid my bills. I bought a dishwasher. And a clothes dryer. And a television. And a one-year-old Chevy van. Now I needn't worry about Ryan impatiently waiting for me at Riley Hospital because I was delayed while the '81 diesel was towed yet again. The sense of security—knowing that when I put the key in the ignition, the engine would turn over—was wonderful. A vanload of worry slipped off my back. Elton John was just what I had told Ryan celebrities could never be—a *real* friend.

ANOTHER wonderful friend we made at that time was Greg Louganis. He just suddenly called one day and invited us to the U.S. Diving Championships in Indianapolis. Greg gave Ryan the medal he won at that meet—the 38th National Title medal—and later he developed a unique relationship with each one of us.

To Andrea he became a kind of back-seat coach. He encouraged her to hang in at roller-skating. He even flew to Michigan to watch

Ryan with Michael Jackson.

With Olympic diver Greg Louganis.

My husband, Roy, and me, with Phil Donahue.

"I thought of them as Ryan's guardian angels."

February 21, 1986, Ryan's first day back at Western Middle School. Behind him is another angel, his stepfather, Steve Ford.

her skate in the regional championships in 1990. And for me Greg served as a precious friend, guide and protector. He helped us when some people decided to make Ryan's story into a television movie, warning that just because we had sold the rights didn't mean we had sold the movie.

We received a check for $25,000 for the rights to the film. For two weeks I didn't cash it. I was too busy *looking* at it. I felt like maybe, just maybe, this money could get us out of Kokomo.

WE WENT looking in a lovely lakeside development in Cicero—a little community of about four thousand people in the next county south. The last house we looked at was a Cape Cod with a real country feeling. A lake. Woods. Birds swooping around, waiting to be fed. A yard that begged for a garden. In the summer, when the leaves were on the trees, you couldn't see your neighbor. I felt as though we could regain our private lives here.

We moved to Cicero on May 15, 1987. It was a great day.

Because I didn't want to seem to be sneaking into Cicero, I called the high school and the local health department. I was scared. Would we face more of the same bigotry? Would we suffer the same isolation in our new home as we had in the old one? The first time somebody rang my bell, I was afraid to answer the door. It turned out to be Mary Baker and Betsy Stewart, my neighbors, welcoming me to Cicero. Betsy's husband, Gil, who was active in the Kiwanis, had helped the state board of health to institute a community-wide AIDS education program. And from then on, everything was uphill.

Hamilton Heights High School gave Ryan his first chance to live as a normal teenager. When he was feeling okay, he went to games, to proms. People talked to him in the halls. He sat on the telephone with his new friends for hours. He even got a job at the local skateboard shop.

Andrea found a whole new gang of buddies, too. They went boating on the lake; they hung out at the Dairy Queen. Our lives had stabilized so much that I could now go back to work and Andrea could go back to skating. She performed in the opening ceremonies of the Pan Am Games in 1987. I was sewing on sequins again. The sparkle returned.

In the winter of 1987, then Governor Robert Orr presented Ryan with a Sagamore of the Wabash award for citizens who have accomplished something special for Indiana. The convocation was held at Hamilton Heights High, which then received the first ever Spirit of the Heartland award for welcoming Ryan with such warmth. I had finally found a safe place for my children.

MICHAEL Jackson invited us to spend a day at his magical Neverland Ranch north of Santa Barbara. Twenty-seven hundred acres, with a zoo, an amusement park with a Ferris wheel and merry-go-round and bumper cars, and a movie house that stocked only happy films. Music came out of the gardens.

I think that one reason Michael is so popular is that he's in touch with the part of ourselves we usually keep secret and treasure most—the fantasy part. At the pool he noticed Ryan leafing through his favorite car magazine, *Mustang Monthly.* That glimpse into Ryan's dreamworld was all he needed.

Shortly after we came home, a car salesman from Noblesville called and said, "Ryan White? We've got a red Mustang here for you. It's from Michael Jackson."

Phil Donahue had seen Ryan on the children's program *3-2-1 Contact,* in a show called "I have AIDS," and he was impressed with the possibilities of educating America's children on a grand scale. He asked Ryan to do a live show before an audience of kids, to answer questions and talk kid to kid about his disease. Because of the respect Phil showed him, Ryan began to understand that he was a national figure whose task it was to help his country overcome the plague of AIDS. He began to plan the rest of his life, and his death, with that in mind.

I KNOW that each of the celebrities who developed close relationships with Ryan did so because he moved them and inspired them. Like the media, they were starved for sincerity, and Ryan was the real article. His suffering was real. His joy and his appreciation of everything they did for him—every toy and T-shirt they sent, every concert and dinner they brought him to—were genuine.

Each of these people gave something of their personal magic to make his burden lighter. I soon stopped thinking of them as celebrities. I thought of them as Ryan's guardian angels.

Chapter 5
The Sparkle

A CHILD who knows he's going to die wants everything right away. That's natural. He wants to experience every single thing that he can, even if it's dangerous: driving a fast car, traveling everywhere, meeting everybody. Ryan would sit in his room—filled with miniature figures, action heroes, model cars and planes, comic books and autographed photos of rock stars and athletes, images and symbols of all the powerful, active, high-tech lives he could lead—and the small figures would fill him with bigger and bigger dreams. That's all he had really, those dreams. He put all his strength of mind into touching as many of them as he could in his short time.

MUCH as Ryan enjoyed Hamilton Heights High, he couldn't get to class much during the 1989–90 school year. When he could go, he drove his Mustang. It was the pride of his life, that car that Michael got him.

Kids who didn't know him would sometimes joke that he wasn't old enough to drive—because he looked so young. The disease had hit him just before puberty started, so he never grew much or got hair on his body. If he went to McDonalds, he had to sit on a pillow.

Very often he'd wake up full of energy in the morning, take his shower, get dressed, eat a bite of breakfast—and then be too exhausted to go to school.

His nights were hard. Frequently he just couldn't get comfortable, or he'd be too cold to sleep, or he'd run a high fever. I'd get up at six thirty and go in and see if he was sleeping all right. If he was, then I'd have an hour or so. I'd let the dogs out, clean my kitchen, wash the floor. Then I'd get his factor and his AZT and his antibiotics ready before he woke up.

If Ryan was well enough to attend school, I tried to work the shift that started at 5:48 a.m. and got me off at 2:00 p.m., because then I could make it home just about the time he did. I could work a full week, except for every other Friday, when we went to Riley Hospital for gamma globulin. Sometimes he was sick, and I couldn't work at all. Then I would fall back on the money that kindhearted folks had sent us, which I had banked for just such a time.

Many people have asked me if I ever considered giving up this sporadic time-on, time-off system and just quitting my job. The answer is never. I knew an awful lot of folks suffering from AIDS who had been forced to go on welfare because of the colossal expense of this disease. Delco's insurance plan was such that I never had to do that. We might have needed help, but we weren't completely down and out—and that meant everything to me.

I never hired homemakers or nurses either. Having a nurse would make our pretty yellow house feel like an extension of the hospital. Ryan would never feel that he wasn't sick. Andrea would never be able to escape from her brother's illness. The semblance of a "normal" life—with a bustling kitchen and phones ringing and the TV blaring—was what I wanted for Ryan.

He helped as much as he could. He did his own wash, kept his room clean, changed his sheets. He took care of his own grooming completely. Ryan was always finicky about his hair and picky about his clothes. The more he was out of school, the more he wanted to look just like all the other kids.

If he couldn't get to school, he'd go down to the basement, where

Ryan and me at home

In class with his best friend, Heather McNew

Tug-of-war with our mutt, Wally, the best dog ever

"The semblance of a normal life was what I wanted for Ryan."

A quiet moment in his own space

we kept his car magazines. I'd join him, and he'd tell me about some new thing he was going to do to his car, and I'd say, "Yes, hon, that sounds grand," when, truthfully, I didn't have the faintest idea what he was talking about. Or sometimes he'd just go out and drive around. That would revive him and lift his spirits.

At one point during 1988 Ryan developed a stomach infection. He was in the hospital for close to two months, retching and vomiting everything he ate. He didn't want a feeding tube, but at last Dr. Kleiman told him he simply had to have it or he would starve to death. He had several diabetic seizures during that time. They made him temporarily blind. He nearly died. He recovered, but after those two months in the hospital there was a new weariness about Ryan and a grave, deliberate kind of maturity.

The nightmare of AIDS is that it brings you one powerful infection after another. The patient is sick and then gets well, and no sooner does he get well than he gets sick again.

It is the same for your hopes. They go out like candles, and then they flare up again, and then they die down. Again.

EDUCATING the public about AIDS became Ryan's life, his career. Between bouts of illness he spoke at Boys Town in Nebraska, at the National Education Association in New Orleans, and in Washington, D.C., before the President's Commission on AIDS. He also made a series of extremely effective public-service announcements. He was plagued with infections, but he did the PSAs anyway.

The first one aired in November 1989. There he was, with his direct, honest gaze, talking to kids:

> "Hello, I'm Ryan White. You know, as much as we've talked to you about AIDS, a lot of you still aren't listening. Today is World AIDS Day, so please listen. I didn't have a choice when I got AIDS. You do. If someone's feeding you a line, trying to get you to have sex or do drugs, before you do something stupid, pick up the phone and call the Indiana AIDS hot line. Let's work together to beat AIDS."

In September 1989 we went to the Emmy awards ceremony. Our show, *I Have Aids—a Teenager's Story: a 3-2-1 Contact Extra,* produced by Al Hyslop and Susan Schwartz Lynn for PBS and the Children's Television Workshop, was up against *Free to Be . . . a Family,* produced by Marlo Thomas and Christopher Cerf and Robert Dalrymple for ABC in association with Gostelradio (Soviet TV). We lost to Marlo's show, but we felt like we were losing to friends who had the same values and the same agenda that we had: to make this world safer for children.

Ryan looked kind of beat sitting there in the glare of those celebrity lights, and Phil Donahue saw that.

"How you doing, buddy?"

"Okay, Phil. Just fine."

"How about you and me skipping out of here and getting some burgers?"

"Great!"

So off they went to have fast food while the rest of us did our Emmy thing. That was pure Phil—that ability to get past all the glamour and the glitz and see what a real kid really needed.

In the fall of 1989 Ryan developed worsening liver dysfunction and hernia trouble that interfered with urination. It got so bad he needed an operation to repair it, and because of his hemophilia this usually simple procedure was life-threatening. In preparation for it Ryan needed so much factor that the bill for the month was $19,000.

At last we checked into Riley. Ryan was all prepped, ready to go as soon as the results of some last-minute blood work came back. We waited and waited, wondering what was taking them so long. Finally Dr. Kleiman reported that Ryan's blood-platelet count was so low that surgery could not be safely performed.

I knew we were in serious trouble then. If they couldn't operate on his hernia, that meant they couldn't do any more for him. Before, Ryan had been sick and then he'd get better. Now he wasn't getting better.

Andrea couldn't accept that. "Ryan will get better," she said. "You listen to me, Mom. Ryan will get better."

For the first time, Ryan himself began to feel as though his time was running out. *People* magazine called, wanting to buy the exclusive rights to be with our family if it looked like he wasn't going to make it.

"I can't allow you to sell those rights," I told Ryan. "It'll feel like selling your life, and I want you to keep fighting. . . . I don't want people to think you've given up."

"It's about time we stopped worrying what other people think, Mom," he said gently.

"No, Ryan. . . ."

He smiled and held my hand and went ahead and sold the rights. He was thinking like a man, trying to take care of his sister and his mom, and buying himself an insurance policy.

Hopelessness was hitting us for the first time. I saw it in Ryan, and he saw it in me. He needed a tremendous infusion of protein to keep up his strength. Dr. Kleiman suggested that we bypass his wrecked digestive system with a feeding tube again. Ryan absolutely refused. I know now that he was so sick by then that Dr. Kleiman was reluctant to do anything that would cause him more pain. So he allowed us to go home from Riley with gallons of this horrible protein drink and orders that Ryan had to take it seven times a day.

How Ryan hated that stuff! I tried mixing it with orange juice, with milk, anything to get him to drink it, but when he saw me coming with it, he'd just snarl. So now I became the enemy, chasing him around the house with a spoon.

"I'm so tired of being sick," he said.

I was tired, too. I wouldn't be honest if I didn't say that. It is the hardest thing for me to live with now, the memory of those moments when I became so depressed from seeing him suffer that I didn't think I could stand it one more minute. I kept praying, "Please come out with a cure before the time runs out," but I knew in my heart that the time had already run out. You feel that as a mom, you should be able to carry the world for your children. How shall I ever forgive myself for those few moments when the world grew too heavy?

IT WAS MARCH 1990, AND WE had been invited to Los Angeles for a big Oscar party sponsored by Athletes and Entertainers for Kids. President and Mrs. Ronald Reagan were going to be there, and Ryan wanted very much to go. At the party Mrs. Reagan did not let go of his hand the whole time they were together. She knew how bad he was. She whispered to me, "He's not doing well. I can tell." A mom can always tell.

The next morning Ryan didn't feel well enough to go out. His face had swelled up, and he had a wispy, wet cough.

We flew back to Indiana in the middle of the night on March 29 and checked right into Riley. Ryan had a severe respiratory infection. For the first three days they gave him oxygen. He was different this time, more frightened. He didn't want me to leave the room. Then he took a terrible turn for the worse and was moved to intensive care. I don't know how the media found out that Ryan was probably facing his last battle, but in no time it was on the news.

Elton came right away. He had a press conference scheduled about a new album, and his people wanted him to just look in on us and return immediately to L.A. But when he talked to Dr. Kleiman and realized how serious it was, he just held my hand and said, "I'm not leaving. I'm going to be here for you."

Every single day, from early in the morning to late at night, that man was at the hospital. He talked to the doctors, to my poor, frightened mother and father. He distracted Andrea with jokes and stories. Whatever I needed, he made sure I got. During that last week and a half my leaning torch was Elton John.

The press began arriving with trucks and equipment, needing information, parking spaces, hotel accommodations, fax machines, electrical cables, food. And some of them weren't so polite in their dealings with the hospital and the citizens of Indianapolis.

Not content to receive the news that was being given out by our friend Carrie Jackson Van Dyke, who had taken leave from her job to serve as family spokesperson, they would sneak into the hospital, try any trick to get up to see this dying kid. People kept trying to photograph him, too—not just the press but regular people with their own little cameras, the hospital staff even. Elton had to hire a security service to guard Ryan and, incidentally, the celebrities who were coming to see him.

RYAN fell into a coma. I kept waiting for him to wake up. I called to him, sat by his bedside and told him that I loved him over and over and over again. But he didn't hear me.

Then Elton got it into his head that music might revive Ryan, so he went out and bought a stereo, along with a whole slew of Bruce Springsteen and Michael Jackson tapes.

"Why didn't you bring any of yours?" I asked.

"Oh, Ryan likes Bruce and Michael," he answered. "He doesn't want to listen to me."

It tickled me so, this big star suddenly getting all bashful about pushing his own songs. Believe me, Ryan would have wanted to hear Elton John.

I sat by my boy's bedside and held his hand, which had grown so swollen. When I thought I would faint, Elton hugged me. When I cried, he cried with me.

Elton said, "You know, when he wakes up, I want this room to be *decorated.* The kids at all these schools have sent so many beautiful banners wishing him well. Let's hang them."

The hospital staff must have thought we were insane. Here's this comatose kid, on life support, with a half-crazy mother calling his name, trying to talk to him while he sleeps. He probably can't hear a thing, but Elton buys him music. He can't see a thing, but Elton gets hold of one of the doctors, and the two of them are standing precariously on chairs, hanging decorative posters and banners on the walls above the screens and the wires and the bleeping monitors.

I stood there watching Ryan's thin body. I knew there was nothing more anybody could do. Before he drifted into unconsciousness, he had told me, "If you think there's a chance, Mom, go for it." We did. Until the last second we went for everything we could.

I leaned down close to him and whispered, "It's okay, son. You can let go."

Then he died. For a few minutes they got his heart going again by mechanical means. He would die again; I knew that perfectly well.

"If you want, you can tell them no more," Elton said. "It's up to you, Jeanne."

I talked to my parents, to Andrea. Then I told the doctors, "No more."

Marty Kleiman, who had taken care of Ryan from the beginning, who had helped him live for almost six years when other physicians had predicted that he would die in six months, went out and made the announcement that my boy had passed away in his sleep, without pain.

The sparkle was gone.

I REMEMBER Carrie Jackson Van Dyke once asked me, "How do you live, Jeanne, day to day, knowing that your son is going to die?"

And I had answered, "We don't think about death in this house. We don't have time for it. If you allow it into your life, it will eat you up. You have to go on with your life, making the most of every day and every hour."

Chapter 6
One Piece at a Time

NO MATTER how much time passes, death is so hard to accept. Most of the time I believe I'll see Ryan again. That's what keeps me going, that I really believe this. But I still want somebody to tell me, definitely, that this is the way it's going to be. Sometimes I feel like I can't wait until I die, because I'm so sure I'm going to know something after I die that I can't know for certain now.

I have the hardest time when I visit Ryan's grave. I can plant it, clean it, laugh over the stuff that kids have left there, and I'm fine, but if I try to talk to Ryan, the tears just start flowing.

There's so many things you want to say, and you just can't . . . and you just can't bear it. I look at the beautiful stone, and I feel a terrible emptiness in my heart.

IN THE wake of Ryan's death I felt that I was in pieces, a dilapidated old wreck, like one of those cars that my neighbor Roy Ginder used to rebuild in his driveway. I had worn an old, ill-fitting dress to the funeral. Most of the stuff in my closet was like that. Andrea watched me sitting around the house, looking just a mess, and she suggested gently that I start paying some attention to my appearance again and go out and get some new stuff to wear. It seemed an impossible task.

I think now that I could never have healed myself. If the pieces of my life eventually did get back together, it was because of the love and concern and strength of other people—members of my family patiently waiting for their powerless time to end, and perfect strangers just reaching out.

I received sixty thousand letters. Sixty thousand. Phil Donahue took some of them back to New York with him. He called me from there, all excited.

"Jeanne, almost all of this mail is from kids! Ryan's a hero, an idol, to them. We've got to do something. I think it's important to answer these letters."

"I can't now. I just can't. . . . I haven't got the strength."

"I understand. I'm going to get you some help. We'll set up an account and get you an assistant."

"Please, Phil, I don't think I can do this."

"I know you're hurting. I know you're grieving. But this boy of yours left a legacy, Jeanne, and you've got to stay involved, for his sake."

Phil Donahue had always possessed a sense of history about the AIDS crisis and Ryan's role in it. His talk show was the one that ran the earliest program on AIDS, back in 1982. He believed that the disease was going to be stopped only if young people could be made aware of the danger it posed. He focused on kids. He had tremendous support for this way of thinking from his late father-in-law, Danny Thomas, who had started St. Jude Children's Research Hospital in Memphis, the leading institution in the country for children with catastrophic diseases, and from his wife, Marlo, who devoted much of her career as an actress and producer to creating great shows for kids.

In an effort to help me with the masses of mail, Marlo Thomas contacted somebody who had worked on the St. Jude's telethon and asked her to recommend a person in the Cicero area. The networking led her to a pretty, blue-eyed woman named Shelley Henson.

Shelley was just like me, a mom juggling a million obligations. She had incredible stamina and an open mind, the two most important qualifications for the job. She adjusted quietly and quickly.

We set up an office in the basement of my house, and Shelley worked there every day, but it seemed like we weren't getting anywhere. The letters just kept coming. Two high school friends of Ryan's spent the summer helping us. We had little hearts made up that said, "Ryan White thanks you from the heart. 1971–1990." We sent out thousands.

PHIL wanted me to start a foundation to teach young people about AIDS. He offered the help of his lawyers to set up the necessary legal and financial underpinnings. Their efforts came none too soon.

One day a man from Boston called and told Shelley that some folks had come to him asking for money for the Ryan White Foundation. He had given them $5000. Then they showed up again a few months later, wanting more. He wanted to know whether we had ever received the money.

Well, of course we hadn't. The poor man—and heaven only knows how many others—had been ripped off by a horrid scheme to take advantage of his kind heart and Ryan's good reputation.

The folks at the Atlanta office of Coca-Cola were more suspicious. Coca-Cola had always been very generous to Ryan's cause, and they would have known if there was a Ryan White Foundation, so when two men and a woman walked into their Atlanta office and said they represented us and wanted a grant of $10,000, the Coke folks went into another room and called me, and the would-be swindlers were caught red-handed.

Then someone called from California and told us Ryan's picture had shown up on some awful AIDS baseball cards. This company was printing the cards, using well-known faces without permission and selling them as novelty items. Ryan's picture was packed with a condom! I couldn't believe it. The company said that all the money from the sale of these cards was going to "an AIDS foundation," but when we called to inquire which one, we never got an answer.

We needed a foundation to protect ourselves against all these scams, and to protect the use of Ryan's name for bona fide purposes. Our earliest executive director, Karen Engledow, established a connection with the Junior League of Indianapolis. These hard-working, charitable women devote themselves to good works, particularly those affecting young people. They provided a large initial grant and dedicated volunteers.

Meanwhile, the mail kept coming. Requests for pictures and tapes of Ryan, for information about AIDS written in language that teens and preteens could understand. And since people couldn't have Ryan—to make an appearance, to kick off a fund-raising drive, to participate in a panel—they wanted me. I had a choice: either ignore them and return to private life, or pull myself together and try to be the leader everybody seemed to want me to be.

Phil Donahue said I really didn't have a choice, and eventually his confidence got to me. I tried to reassure Andrea that AIDS education would just be a job, that I would leave it at the office when I came home. I don't think she believed me for a minute, but she smiled and said, "Well, okay, Mom, if you think you can do that."

FROM the moment Ryan became a media subject, folks had called us—for advice, for consolation, with ideas for cures. But after he died, people would call every single day, at all hours, desperate just to talk. I had already lost my child, and those who waited for the same fate to befall their loved ones felt that I could somehow help *them.* Even if I changed the number or made it unlisted, they found me anyway.

I don't think Americans understand to this day the slaughter that occurred in hemophiliac families. One little girl said she was calling for her aunt, who was losing both of her brothers to AIDS—and both of her sons. A mother was watching three hemophiliac sons die. Another woman, in Seattle, told me that her three sons and two nephews were all HIV-positive. These people would expect me to have all the answers. And, of course, I didn't have any.

Everybody wanted to know how long: How long do I have to live? How long does he or she have to live? I had been the same. You keep asking how long, because if they have a year or two, you can dare to hope for a cure, but if they have only a month, maybe you should call the family and arrange the funeral. We try to make logical arrangements even in the presence of illogical tragedy.

With hindsight I understood that many of these people were looking to me for something I would have given anything to possess back in Kokomo—a group of folks in the same boat to take counsel with. I had expected that group to be other parents of hemophiliacs. However, the hemophiliac families in my area were terrified that I would identify them, so they shunned me. The sister of a friend of mine, whose two sons were hemophiliacs, left town. I understood her flight, but I couldn't understand why she never called me, and I felt abandoned.

After Ryan died, she got in touch. She said that she was really sorry she hadn't been there for me when Ryan was sick. "When the trouble began," she said, "I just had to get out."

One of the reasons I always talked to the people who called me in the spring and summer of 1990 was that I knew how much help that unhappy woman and I could have been to each other in the spring and summer of 1985. It was a piece of me that had always been missing—the piece that involved an understanding community. As usual, it was provided by what I call "my public sector."

A YEAR AFTER RYAN'S DEATH Phil did an anniversary show in his memory, and another on the fifth anniversary. That one featured forty kids, now young adults, who had been members of the audience in the first show Phil ever did with Ryan.

Because of shows like those and other AIDS-related events, I met a number of AIDS mothers, some of whom affected me in important ways. One was Louise Ray, who made contact after seeing us on TV. She and her husband, Clifford, lived in Arcadia, Florida, and had three hemophiliac sons—Ricky, Randy and Robbie—and one daughter, Candy. The family had been receiving death threats.

One night Louise called and said, "Well, they did it."

"What?"

"They burned our house down."

I was shocked.

"We have nothing now," she said. "Nothing."

The Rays moved to Sarasota, where the school accepted the children. In the years before Ryan's death, he and the Ray children did many benefits and media appearances together, and a recent bill to recompense hemophiliac families is named for Ricky, who has died.

Quite a number of the HIV children I met in those days are gone now. If I need to talk, there are—sadly—plenty of bereaved parents with whom I can share my feelings. But it's ironic that those who became my confidants were people I met on talk shows or at public fund-raising events—not people from my hometown. So when Ryan and I were voted Man and Woman of the Year by the readers of the Indianapolis *Star* in 1991, I considered it one of the most touching events that ever happened. How Ryan would have loved knowing that he was a hero among his own neighbors.

MATT Frewer came to see us a few weeks after Ryan died. The hilarious actor who had played Coke's Max Headroom had befriended Ryan and quietly, without any fanfare, had supported and encouraged us for years. He asked me whether I had thought about what sort of monument I wanted for my son. I hadn't thought anything about it. "Whatever you decide you want," he said,

"I'd like to take care of it." With this sensitive, generous gesture Matt wanted to guarantee that I would not have to hesitate in creating the monument Ryan deserved.

I thought very hard about all the mail we had received when planning that monument. It seemed as though folks wanted a piece of Ryan, as though his memory gave them strength. I wanted the stone to be a way of meeting him for all those who never had the chance to do that when he was alive. For the rest of us in the AIDS community I wanted the monument to serve history. A hundred years down the road, when this nightmare is just an old story, I want people to be able to look at the monument and remember Ryan's story and honor his cause.

The monument man had a piece of stone six feet eight inches high, in tones of gray and white and black. I thought, Yes! This is what Ryan would have wanted. He had always wished to be tall.

On the base are the words that Bill Shaw of *People* magazine had ascribed to Ryan: PATIENCE, TOLERANCE, FAITH, LOVE, FORGIVENESS, WISDOM, SPIRIT. On the front the stone carver created a cross with Ryan's picture in the center, and above it a bird flying away, like the skyline pigeon in Elton's song. I wanted the words to Elton's "Candle in the Wind," and the words to Michael's "Man in the Mirror," the words about making a difference, making it "right," that were so meaningful to Ryan. When Michael came to our house after the funeral, he and Andrea sat in the red Mustang and Michael turned the key. "Man in the Mirror" came on. It was the last song Ryan had listened to in that car.

Reverend Probasco's funeral tribute went on the stone, as did Dr. Kleiman's words said right after Ryan died, to the effect that he had passed away without pain. It seemed terribly important to many people to be reassured of that. We also added Governor Evan Bayh's comment that Ryan would be remembered more for what he taught us about living than for the disease that afflicted him.

When I told the monument man I wanted a cartoon on the stone, too, he looked at me as though I was crazy. He didn't realize I meant Jim Boardman's Pulitzer prizewinning cartoon of Ryan being hugged by Saint Peter in "a place where no one is afraid to hug." It summed up in one moving image Ryan's struggle and his victory.

Finally, I thought, since all these kids were always asking for Ryan's autograph, I would have his signature carved on the stone so that they could visit the grave and bring paper and rub over it and take a piece of Ryan back home with them.

That gravestone in the Cicero cemetery has been a magnet for young people. They leave gifts and notes—a teddy bear, a candy cane at Christmas. On his nineteenth birthday we found a bottle of Budweiser on the grave with a note that said, "This Bud's for you, Ryan." A girl named Shannon comes from Chicago every year and cleans up the gravesite of all winter debris. The sweetness of that pilgrimage overwhelms me.

Then sometimes something happens that makes you realize that hatred still festers in a few hearts. I was watering the flowers on Ryan's grave this past spring, and a big red truck pulled out of a lot nearby. The driver leaned out of the cab and yelled, "Bitch!" Like I was his enemy. Like that boy in the ground and his mom watering flowers on his grave had done him an evil turn.

One year some boys knocked over Ryan's headstone, and one of them was brought to me by his minister to ask my forgiveness. Of course I forgave him, but while he was there in my house, I asked him, "Why? Why would you go in the dead of night and turn over a stone that was marked with words like patience, tolerance, faith, love? Why?"

This child said, "I didn't like the attention Ryan got."

It was unbelievable. He was jealous of Ryan! As though Ryan would not have given all the world to *not* have had that attention.

"Would you like to change places with him?" I asked this boy.

"No," he said.

IN THE early summer of 1991, I made the fateful decision to quit Delco, take the buyout they were offering, and go to work as head of the newly formed Ryan White Foundation.

The worst part for me was the speaking engagements. Talking before an audience made me a nervous wreck. I would try to arrive at the site of my appearance early in the morning, even though the speech was at night. I couldn't eat, because I was afraid I would have to go to the bathroom in the middle of the speech. I would rehearse it out loud. I would end up not saying what I had been working on. Trying to stick to a prepared speech was getting me all messed up. I thought, The only thing I can do is just tell my story. If I tell my own story, then I won't get messed up. I know my story better than anybody.

It took me close to two years before I became really comfortable. The pattern was usually very similar from one place to another. I would start out with a video to remind everybody of what Ryan had gone through. Then I would talk about what had happened to us and why it was so important for parents and children to talk frankly about sex and sexually transmitted diseases, even if that offended their sensibilities. Then there would be questions.

Before each address I'd say a prayer. "Dear Lord, please help me do my very best. Ryan, please be by my side and help me, too." I would say it repeatedly, over and over, like a chant, and wait for this feeling to rise up inside me, a kind of psychic security blanket. And then when the spirit and the purpose had filled me up, I would go out there and make my speech.

As long as I have the prayer and the feeling, I'm okay. It comes from Ryan, I know. It is all that I need.

ONE of the most delightful events I attended during that period was a fund-raising fair for the Wisconsin Hemophilia Association in March 1991. It was a real hoot. The place was full of colorful swamis and palm readers offering to tell your fortune for $5.00. One of them looked at my hand and said that the last broken piece of Jeanne White was about to be repaired, that I was going to meet a man.

"Oh, boy, that's all I need." I laughed. "A man in my life!"

Exactly one year later I fell in love.

Chapter 7
"Don't ask me until I know I can say yes."

I WAS so tossed and prodded and pushed after Ryan's death that I all but lost contact with some of my closest neighbors. Roy Ginder, for example, who had been so kind to my son. Roy was as much of a nut about cars as Ryan, and helped him add all kinds of things to his Mustang: new tires, hubcaps painted the exact red of the car body, ground effects—gadgets that lower the actual body of the car without moving the suspension, like air foils on racing cars.

"Mr. Ginder is just totally the greatest guy, Mom," Ryan had said after one of their grease-monkey sessions.

The last I remembered seeing Roy was when we were about to take our last trip to California, shortly before Ryan got so sick and I had so much to worry about. Then, about a year after Ryan's death, I heard that he and his wife had separated. She had moved out. He stayed with the kids. According to folks who knew them, the Ginder household was pretty hectic after the mom departed.

I chanced to meet Roy during this difficult time because Andrea and I were thinking of giving Ryan's Mustang to the Children's Museum in Indianapolis, and no sooner had we made that decision than somebody backed into the car. All that careful, artistic work, scratched and dented—it was a real shame.

I went over to Roy's body shop with my mom and asked if he could repair the damage. He was a big, thick, strong man, with light brown hair and pale blue eyes. His uniform was covered with grease and grime; his face and hands were smeared. When he said yes, I knew the Mustang would soon be as good as new.

I do remember looking back in through the body-shop door as

we left, and thinking, Well now, that is really a cute guy. But I never thought about him again after he fixed the car . . . until somebody told me he and his wife were getting a divorce.

I SENT him a Christmas card.

It wasn't a personal thing. Shelley was sending cards from me and the newly forming Ryan White Foundation. We sent out hundreds that year. I didn't think anything about it, but Roy did. When his daughter showed him that card, he asked her, "Do you think Mrs. White is going out with anybody?" Shawn, then a sophomore, said she would ask Andrea, a senior, at school.

Andrea came home one day and said, "Mom, do you remember Roy Ginder?"

"Yes."

"Well, his daughter, Shawn, says he wanted to know if you're dating anybody, and if you're not, would you go out with him?"

"Well . . ."

"Go for it, Mom."

Andrea turned and left me there in my kitchen. I don't think she really thought I would do it, but she was tickled to death at my confusion and enjoying her role as message carrier.

It took about three months from the time I sent the Christmas card for all these messages to get delivered. By that time Roy's mother and grandmother had moved in with him, and he had things at home a little bit more under control. I suppose he would have gotten around to calling me one day, but as fate would have it, I ended up calling him first—to invite him to a foundation event. He said he'd be happy to come.

At the end of the evening he took me to the door and said good night. Not a handshake, nothing.

I thought, Too bad, Jeanne. He had a rotten time. You'll never hear from him again.

Then he said, "I really enjoyed myself tonight. I'd like to see you again."

I thought, *Yesss!*

On our next date we went to the movies. I remember it—*Fried Green Tomatoes*—but I don't think I watched much of it. I was too busy worrying: Why doesn't he hold my hand? Why doesn't he try to kiss me? Maybe he really doesn't like me. Then I remembered what Ryan had said: *Mr. Ginder is a super guy, Mom.* So I grabbed Roy's hand and leaned over and gave him a little kiss on the cheek. I couldn't believe I did that. Afterward we went back to my house.

"What is the matter with you, Roy Ginder? I can't believe I had to kiss you first."

"Well, it wasn't 'cause I didn't want to. I was just kind of nervous. I didn't want you to think I was being too forward."

"Oh, for heaven's sakes . . ."

And he put his big arms around me, and all the childish tension between us just melted away, and that was that.

What appealed to me so much about Roy was his honesty, his down-to-earth attitude and his trusting nature. I couldn't ever understand how his ex-wife had let him go. As the weeks went by, I found that I was crazy about him, thrilled to hear his drawling tenor voice on the phone, excited to hear the sound of his old truck in my driveway. I began to get scared. This is moving too fast, I thought.

Then Andrea came home from school one day, all upset. She had heard from Shawn that Roy was thinking about asking me to marry him, and she had serious doubts about the whole thing. She liked Roy but thought our courtship was too sudden. And I think she was really annoyed that Roy's daughter "knew" more than she did.

I told Andrea there was nothing to know yet, and I would never take one step without telling her first. But now I was kind of prewarned. When Roy called me that night and said he had something really important he wanted to ask me, I said, "Don't ask me until I know I can say yes."

The thing about being alone is that it has certain advantages, and one of them is personal freedom. I had started earning a good living as a speaker and educator, and for the first time in my life I could buy what I liked. I loved that I could just decorate a house to suit my tastes alone. I didn't have to ask some man what he thought.

I was also worried about finances and the future. I felt like everything we had was because of Ryan. We had a really nice house now. Phil had once done a show with kids whose divorced or widowed parents had remarried. They reported that everything their parents had went to the new stepparents. I swore that would never happen to my Andrea. It was us three that had battled the world during Ryan's illness—just us three, nobody else. If Andrea wanted to sell the house after I was gone, that was her business. I needed to feel secure in the knowledge that she would have what was rightfully hers.

Roy and I talked about it. He understood exactly how I felt, and we made our arrangements accordingly.

In order to acquaint Roy more fully with my life, I asked him if he would come to Washington with me to lobby on the Ryan White CARE Act. I wanted to see how Roy reacted when faced with being around political people.

We went to a party in one of those beautiful Georgetown houses with lovely antiques and lots of history. I was proud to show Roy off to people I had worked with over the years. These were folks who knew my struggles. They were positive about my work, and they had respect for me. One of the lawyers got into a discussion with Roy about antique cars; another filled him in on the political background of the Ryan White CARE Act. It was a wonderful evening.

We walked outside into the calm evening. I took Roy's arm.

"Boy," he said. "Just to think all this was about a bill named for Ryan. It's just now dawning on me how important it is. You have got the best friends in the whole world." He hugged me. I knew he was real proud.

"Roy, did you know that lawyer you were talking to was gay?"

"You've got to be kidding."

"And that other guy, the one who collects cars . . . Actually, honey, most of the people you met at the party tonight were gay."

"Say it ain't so!" He laughed. People who've been brought up the way Roy was, and the way I was, too, in homes where homosexuals are feared and scorned, have this feeling they can always tell who is gay. It inevitably comes as a big shock to discover that you don't know what you thought you knew for sure.

This was one of several issues that I had been worried about. To Roy, my association with what he thought of as liberal politics and my easy relationships in the gay community just didn't mix with the rest of me. As far as he was concerned, I was just the sort of "old-fashioned girl" he wanted, but my politics made me unsuitable in the eyes of many of his friends. Some members of his church were horrified that I had introduced Roy to people they considered to be sinners.

"Listen, honey," I said, "I can't make a choice between you and people I've been friends with for years, who stood by me and helped me when nobody else would. I cannot all of a sudden say to these people, 'I'm marrying this homophobe, so I can't see you anymore.' That would be impossible, Roy. It would be wrong."

The moment when I introduced Roy Ginder to my gay friends in Washington, the warmth of their reception, the sincerity of their joy for us—that was the moment of no return for Roy Ginder.

He asked me to be his wife—and I said yes.

WE WERE married on August 1, 1992.

More than two hundred people came. Family. Old friends and new. For two months I had been taking the shining stones off Andrea's skating outfits—pearls and sequins and aurora beads—and sewing them on my wedding dress.

We held up the ceremony because the car that was bringing Phil and Marlo got lost and made them late. They ended up having to get dressed in a truck stop. The clock ticked; the guests squirmed; my ravishing bridesmaid Andrea gave me that "time to get started, Mom" look. However, I felt like I couldn't get married until Phil and Marlo walked through that door. They were the people who had helped me start over. By introducing me to abilities I never knew I had and helping me build the Ryan White Foundation, Phil had shaped the future.

My wedding to Roy Ginder meant that the future was here.

Chapter 8
Lessons Learned in Rooms Full of Strangers

PEOPLE ask me, "Why don't you just let Ryan die and go on with your life?"

My answer is, for a time there was one person in this country who could really open people's eyes to the dangers of AIDS, and that was Ryan. He's not here anymore, so the next best thing is his mom. I would love not to have to talk about him, not to recall the pain and the horror, to pour my heart out to a room. It would be much easier to quit. But how could I do that to all the wonderful people who helped me who have passed on? If I got out of AIDS education, I'd be letting down a lot of people who had faith in me. If I let Ryan die, I have to let everybody who has this disease die as well. I'm not willing to give up and let these people go.

THE marriage turned out better—and worse—than I could have imagined. Roy and I were ecstatically happy together. Just to look at his face across my morning coffee was enough to bring me a sense of peace and well-being that I hadn't felt ever in my entire adult life.

My big mistake was in thinking I could be the superwoman of stepmothers and change Roy's children. I was sure that Shawn and Adam and Steve would love my orderly, pretty, peaceful house so much that they'd just turn themselves over to me and let me transform them into disciplined, purposeful people. But it didn't work. I couldn't change kids who were already in their teens when I met them, who had already been formed by the pressures of their lives.

Shawn eventually went to live with her mom, then married and had a baby. Adam has moved back and forth between his mom's house and our house. The middle child—Steven—has stayed on with us. I have had to accept his ways, and he has had to accept mine. The biggest part of stepparenting is sometimes accepting what you *cannot* do and then going on from there.

I WONDER sometimes if the photos and memorabilia about Ryan in my house upset Roy's kids. I even wonder if they upset Andrea. Do these children feel they have to compete with a ghost for my affections? Are they sensitive to or intimidated by Ryan's fame, like the boy who threw over his gravestone? It occasionally occurs to me that maybe I should clear the walls of his image, throw out his old stuff. But every time I think that, every time I am tempted to toss out the dead to salve the feelings of the living, I think, No, that would solve nothing.

It is not unhealthy to keep your memories alive. When you let your memories die, you take a lot away from who you are. Sure, it's bad to be obsessed. If I were to go into Ryan's room and cry my eyes out all the time, that would be a mistake, but that is not what happens. The memories come, and they comfort you, and they keep your child with you.

When I'm in the house—which was the house Ryan got for us—and I remember him, I laugh as much as I cry. I feel like his spirit is with me. I like to keep his room the way he had it, with all the cars and action figures and posters and mementos. I remember how he'd like to have his jeans folded just a certain way, and nobody could fold those jeans but him. Sometimes when Andrea and I look at a pair of jeans coming out of the dryer, we'll think about that, the two of us at the same time, and have a laugh. To include your loved ones in your life is really good—provided you include the good times and the laughter and not just the sad times at the end. Dead or alive, your family is your family.

ROY and I have had some incredible times on our travels around this world. Three years ago we went to Alaska (*in February!*), an exciting trip organized by Alaskans Living With AIDS. For two weeks we drove around on the snow-covered roads, listening to the silence of the drifts, loving the calm, the isolation, the peace of the place. One couple in Barrow came over and took us out riding in a dogsled on the ice. The lady lent me a coat because nobody who isn't a native has a coat that's warm enough for Alaska in February. In Anchorage, Roy was thrilled when he saw a moose by the side of the road. He stopped the car and raced out to take its picture. I was afraid the moose would charge, but luckily, it just looked at this guy from Indiana like he was crazy and went on moseying through the frozen forest.

When the Jewish National Fund flew us to Israel, we planted trees in Ryan's memory at the AIDS Memorial Forest, part of the Lahav Forest, near Beersheba. It impressed me enormously to see that desert wasteland growing greener and greener, covered with forests and fields.

A mystery was solved for us in Israel. When we visited the monument to those who had been murdered in the Holocaust, we saw that the memorial markers were heaped with stones, and we realized suddenly that the stones that kept appearing on Ryan's grave at home were not just tossed there, but deliberately put in place by Jewish people as a sign that they had come to pay their respects.

In November 1993 Roy and I went to an event honoring Greg Louganis that was sponsored by the Athletes and Entertainers for Kids. I said a few words and presented Greg with a sculpture of Ryan that Bill Mack had done, and no sooner had I done that than he reached into his pocket and *presented me* with a medal.

Greg told the crowd that our family had been his friends and supporters for many years, that he had learned an enormous amount from Ryan and that he wanted me to have one of the gold medals he had won at the Olympics in Seoul, Korea. He put it around my neck. He had given his Pan American Games medal and a national championship medal to Ryan, but he really wanted me to have a medal all for myself. I was just overwhelmed. I couldn't hold back the tears.

After that, we spent the whole evening together. Greg didn't seem himself. Now that I've had to read so many strange situations, I've gotten really good at sensing a hint of trouble, trusting my instinct that something may be wrong. I said to Roy, "Something is really bothering Greg. I can feel it, like he wants to tell me something." I began to worry.

Concerned about how I would react to the news, Greg didn't tell me he had AIDS. But I kind of suspected. Then in January 1994 he went on Barbara Walters's show, and the truth came out. Thank heaven Greg is still well and strong today. I keep the gold medal in a place of honor among my most precious possessions.

THE Ryan White Foundation—the only national foundation to focus exclusively on HIV/AIDS education—continues to grow. Each year we give Angel Awards to tireless crusaders against AIDS. Generous friends like actresses Lorna Luft and Diana Canova have become our supporters. Christopher Radko, the brilliant glass artist, makes a beautiful Christmas ornament every year to remember the victims of AIDS, and part of the proceeds of the sale of the ornaments goes to our foundation. Great corporations have helped us. The Hyatt Regency has hosted some of our guests. Pizza Hut gave us a large cash gift in honor of Ryan's being named to the National Geographic Kids' Hall of Fame. Phil Donahue and Greg Louganis literally auctioned the shirts off their backs after a benefit polo match one year. Thousands of plain, ordinary people have helped us with donations. They know that the work we do is lifesaving.

Our mandate is to educate youth about the dangers of AIDS. I've tried my best to publicize former Surgeon General C. Everett Koop's advice to young lovers: "Find someone who is worthy of your respect and love, give that person both and stay faithful to him or her. In other words, short of total abstention, the best defense against AIDS is to maintain a faithful monogamous relationship."

But I know that it's often not so simple. One in four new HIV infections occurs in people younger than twenty-two, and young people are having sex earlier than ever. In 1990 the Nebraska Prevention Center for Alcohol and Drug Abuse in Lincoln did a survey that showed that 77 percent of twelfth-grade girls and 66 percent of twelfth-grade boys had had sex in the past year, about 30 percent of each gender with multiple partners. They're not any more liberal in Lincoln than anyplace else.

And that is why education on AIDS is so important in the lives of young people. They are not going to step forward and ask for advice. It has to be given to them in a form in which they will accept it, soon enough to be useful to them and to protect them.

I try to make the kids see that every time they have sex with somebody, they have sex with all the people that person has had sex with. Look how many people a person could have sex with in fifteen years. And think of what it would be like to have to go back and find those people and tell them you've been infected, and then they'd have to go back and tell all the other people they had sex with after you! The numbers are just enormous.

IF YOU raise a child with love and discipline, if you give that child everything you can, then eventually you have to sit back and trust that what you have done is enough and your child will come through okay. That's what happened to me and Andrea.

I had had a lot of trouble with Andrea after Ryan died. She and her brother had been very close. In a hostile world they kept each other going. Even if he was just lying on the couch waiting for her to arrive from school and report on the goings-on in the normal, regular teenage world, such a little presence had given shape to her day. He had been sick so often, and he had always gotten better, and I guess she believed he always would. Now he was gone for good. Just coming home was painful for her because he wasn't there. She started staying out late, not coming through the door until it was time to go to bed. I felt that I was losing my daughter. I was afraid that she was going to get involved with the wrong people, afraid that because she had lost Ryan, she didn't care what happened to herself—as though she wanted to punish herself for being the well child, the one who was still alive.

I simply had to hold my breath and pray that she would come safely through the storms. And she has. Andrea will be twenty-four years old in October 1997. She is finishing up her degree at Indiana University and working as an administrative assistant. She writes a column for our newsletter and volunteers regularly at the foundation office.

I believe that Andrea must have worlds to speak about the terrible problems of the well sibling, but the worlds are silent still. Maybe someday she will understand how important it might be to share her experience with other kids who have wondered why fate has selected them to be okay while a suffering brother or sister slips away. For the time being, she wants her privacy. She wants the past to fade and let her be.

PEOPLE ask me how I feel about being "famous." I don't feel like I'm famous, and I wouldn't want to be—I've seen too much of how the really famous people like Elton and Michael long for a private moment, a moment with family.

No. I want to be a private person, coming and going as I please. If anything, I'd like people to say, "Jeanne White? She was a good mother who had great kids, and she ended up fulfilling one of her lifelong ambitions—she became a teacher."

IN 1995 THE Ryan White CARE Act was in deep jeopardy. A bill to reauthorize it was being sponsored by Senator Kennedy and Senator Nancy Kassebaum of Kansas, and the vast majority of the Congress supported it. However, it was being stymied by Senator Jesse Helms of North Carolina. I thought of his delaying tactics as the "Kokomo offense": Hold things up long enough, and death will come and the whole problem will un-happen.

Senator Helms said he opposed the reauthorization because people with AIDS were sick "as a result of deliberate, disgusting, revolting conduct." He said, "We've got to have some common sense about a disease transmitted by people deliberately engaging in unnatural acts."

The media asked what I thought about what Senator Helms had said. I told them I thought his statements were sad and crazy. AIDS is not a homosexual disease; it is a people disease. Thank heaven the U.S. Congress agreed with me and passed the five-year reauthorization in 1996.

The bill was signed at the White House on May 27, and I was invited. Somebody came over to me and said, "Mrs. White, we'll be taking you into the Oval Office. There you will meet President Clinton. Then we'll go into the Roosevelt Room for the signing. Mr. Clinton always enters the room first. You are to follow him, one step behind and to the right. He will go to his desk and sign the act, and you stand just behind him."

I nodded and smiled politely, but inside, I was frantic. I kept thinking, What is Jeanne White from Kokomo, Indiana, doing here at the White House? This can't be happening!

The Oval Office is a lot bigger than I expected—and President Clinton is a lot better-looking. He told me, "You had a mighty fine son, Mrs. White. He really put a face to this disease and helped educate everybody on AIDS."

Then he started walking, so I walked behind him like I had been told. He turned and gave me this big smile.

I said, "I'm not supposed to be following you yet, am I?"

He laughed. Turned out he was just going to adjust his tie.

Finally they were ready for us. President Clinton gave a wonderful speech. At one point he looked at me and said, "Your fine son became a hero to many of us. He was a brave young man who taught America the truth about AIDS. He helped people all over the world understand that people with AIDS deserve not only the best medical care but also our compassion and our love. And we're eternally grateful for that."

After so much silence, so much ignorance and neglect, it overjoyed me to hear the President of the United States acknowledge the great struggle of those who had suffered with AIDS and those who had struggled to take care of them.

"It's hard to believe, but AIDS has now been with us for nearly two decades," he said. "In that time, more than half a million Americans have been diagnosed; more than three hundred thousand of our fellow citizens have died. At one time, AIDS was thought of as inevitably the end of life, the death of hope. Today there is hope for a cure. But until there is a cure, we cannot and must not rest. Ryan White [has] described himself as 'just another kid from Kokomo.' We know he was much more than that. He taught a nation to care instead of hate, to embrace people living with AIDS as a part of our American family, to extend always the hand of hope."

When the President finished his speech, he sat down to sign the act. I was so overcome with pride and joy and sadness all at the same time that I just reached down and put my hand on his shoulder like I was his mother or something.

His staff people thought that was real funny. "In the entire history of the Republic," they said, laughing, "that has to be the first time anybody has rested a hand on the President's shoulder."

After the ceremony Mr. Clinton turned around and gave me one of the pens used to sign the bill. I thanked him and all the people who had worked on the bill. It was the most glorious moment for me. I just wish Ryan had been there to see how much his life meant to his country.

But on second thought, I guess he *was* there.

WHEN Ryan was ill, I had no time for gardening. Now every single day I work in my yard. I plant tomatoes, blackberries, strawberries, roses and lilies, and all kinds of annuals and perennials. Early in the morning, just at that hour when I used to get up and get my son's medicines ready, I go out there and start up the day. I flip the Japanese beetles off the roses into a jar of water and cooking oil. I feed the two pretty fish in my pond and trim off all the browning leaves and flower heads. The garden has been my therapy. It's my other season besides Christmas. Here among the flowers and the bright fruit, when the light is brand-new and everything is fresh and wet and the leaves are beaded up with dewdrops, I refresh my spirit.

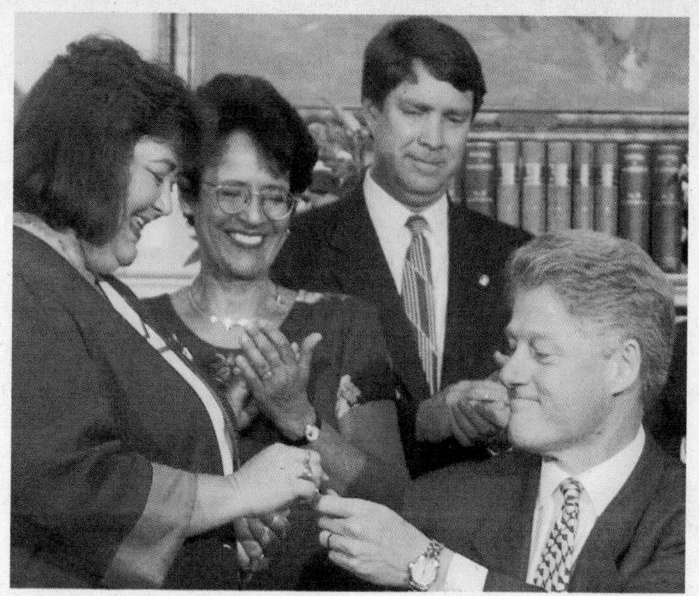

The White House, May 27, 1996. President Clinton presents a pen to me after signing the Ryan White CARE Act reauthorization.

In that lovely garden I know exactly what my dad felt out on the lake under the shooting stars. I am sure, just as he was, that "there's got to be a better Being someplace behind all this." It seems to me that every weed I pull is a bit of grief I am learning to set aside, a tear I've weeded out so that good cheer can grow again.

I see in the faces of the flowers all the friends I have lost; I see my son's face. They are beautiful in the new morning, opening like smiles and shining with hope.

Thank you, Lord, for another day.

INFINITY'S CHILD

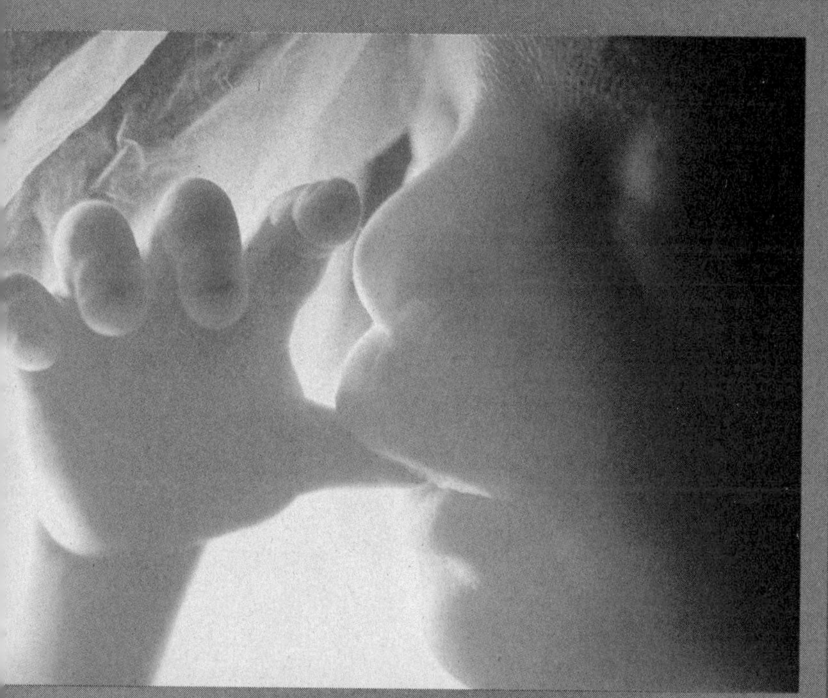

HARRY STEIN

Two scientists stand on the brink of the greatest medical discovery of our time.

To prove their case, all they need is a baby.

But not just any baby.

Her baby. . . .

CHAPTER ONE

SALLY Benedict didn't know how much longer she could keep up appearances. Never much at lighthearted party chatter to begin with, playing hostess this evening for the Edwardstown *Weekly*'s annual Halloween open house left her mouth dry and her head throbbing.

This year there were babies *everywhere.* Where had they all come from? As editor of the *Weekly,* how could she have not known about so dramatic a rise in the local newborn population?

But no, of course it wasn't that. Probably there had been just as many at last year's party. She'd just never noticed before.

The change was in her.

Now, turning the corner on her way to the kitchen for another bottle of cider, she stopped in mid-stride. This one was the most achingly appealing yet. Asleep in his mother's arms, all pink cheeks and blond fuzz, he was a vision out of a Renaissance painting.

"He's two months. This is his very first party," announced the mother, beaming. "His name's Charlie."

"He's beautiful." Though she'd known the woman vaguely since high school, her name always seemed to escape Sally. Tentatively she reached out and brushed the baby's cheek, as always, surprised at the extraordinary softness.

"What about you, Sally? Think you might take the plunge?"

She quickly withdrew her hand. "Uh . . . I can't say."

"Of course," said the mother coolly, defensive. "To each her own, I guess. Not everyone's a baby person."

Jeannie Porter, Sally realized through her pain—that was her name. She'd never much liked her, but she resisted the impulse to answer in kind. After all, the feeling was probably shared by most in the room. Sally Benedict's driving passion was her work; that's what everyone around here thought.

"Does he have a costume?" asked Sally. "I'd love to get a shot of him for the paper."

Generating goodwill for the *Weekly* was, after all, the purpose of this gathering. Kids had been trooping to the makeshift photo studio in the den all evening long to be snapped for the paper's annual "Edwardstown's Kids Do Halloween" feature.

Instantly Jeannie was smiling again. "I tried to make him a pirate, but he wouldn't take the eye patch."

"Next year, then," offered Sally, starting to disengage. "We'll save the front page."

Distractedly greeting people as she went, she made her way through the crowded dining room to what was left of the six-foot-long hero and sliced off a piece.

"You okay?" asked her husband, Mark, appearing beside her.

"I gotta get out of here."

He nodded meaningfully and squeezed her hand. "Don't let Jeannie Porter get to you. She's resented you since high school—ever since you whipped her in the finals of the four forty."

"Thanks, that helps." She gave a wistful smile.

In fact, he'd loved her just as long. Even back then she was more complicated than she showed—a lithe blonde with an athlete's grace, inquisitive and full of humor, her deep brown eyes reflecting her quicksilver moods. Something of a star himself in high school—rhythm guitar in the area's best novice rock band—he recognized Sally Benedict as a supernova, operating at a level of competency and confidence that had nothing to do with normal adolescence.

Already the future she'd been plotting since elementary school seemed to be unfolding. Who else in this rural New Hampshire town had ever won *Mademoiselle* magazine's annual essay contest, with its prize of a summer internship in New York City? Who else had even thought to enter?

Four years ago, when she returned to town after her father's death, it was as a big-deal reporter with the Philadelphia *Inquirer,* while Mark was still going off every day to their former alma mater, teaching science. So he was startled, the first time they ran into one another, by her offer to buy him dinner—and floored by her admission that she'd had a secret crush on him also. Steeling himself for her departure three weeks later, he scarcely dared believe it when she announced her intention to stay.

"What about your job?" was the obvious question.

"My mother needs me a lot more. I hear they're looking for someone to run the *Weekly.*" She paused, then said with conviction, "This is home. This is where I'm happiest."

Even now, just thirty-six, Sally could probably have her pick of high-profile jobs in Boston or New York. But what she wouldn't have was this rambling Victorian with its immense front yard, relatives close at hand, and the ability to bend a work schedule around the demands of motherhood.

To Mark, an easygoing sort, the idea of kids was fine, but not having kids would be okay too. It was this helpless in-between state that was so hard to take, the maelstrom of anxiety and doubt into which Sally had been thrown after more than a year of trying.

"Look," he offered, "why don't you duck out for a while? Your mom and I will handle things here."

She hesitated, then nodded. "Just for a little while."

Slowly she made her way upstairs and into the spare room. She clicked on the TV and collapsed onto the couch. Watching through one heavy-lidded eye, she flashed by the channels.

Abruptly she sat up and flipped back a couple of spots.

Yes, there he was—R. Paul Holland! America's greatest science reporter, a man of unsurpassed integrity and acumen. And the single most cynical person she had ever known. She had last seen him back when they were working together in Philadelphia.

The program was on the cable station CNBC. Holland and another guest flanked the host, who was speaking into the camera.

". . . challenging the belief that aging is inevitable. Could science really make the age-old dream of eternal youth a reality? Our guests: Dr. Jaroslav Dusek, a pioneer in longevity research. And prizewinning reporter R. Paul Holland of the New York *Herald,* who has recently written a series on . . ."

IN THE cozy Fort Lee, New Jersey, studio, R. Paul Holland's adrenaline was already pumping as the host read the last words of his introduction and turned his way.

"So, Mr. Holland, any truth to scientists' claims they're going to stretch the human life-span far beyond present limits?"

"I always like to start with good news." Holland smiled broadly. "What once would have been regarded as close to miraculous is now about to become routine. It looks like millions of us now will live past one hundred."

The host turned to his other guest, an intense, florid-faced man. "Is that a fair estimate, Dr. Dusek?"

"I would go *much* farther," he replied in heavily accented English. "Much. One hundred twenty years will be standard. Some will live to two hundred, even more. There is no limit. These are the findings not just from my own laboratory but of colleagues from around the world."

"That's the bad news," cut in Holland.

The others turned his way. "What?" asked the host.

"The irresponsibility of so many in this field. The extent to which their wild claims prey on people's hope."

"You're saying there's absolutely nothing to all this research we keep hearing about?" asked the host.

Holland hesitated. "Look, this is a booming area. Obviously there's some serious work being done, but you figure the odds. Of the seventy billion or so people who've inhabited the earth since the appearance of Homo sapiens, we know of only two that have made it to even one hundred and twenty—a Japanese man and a Frenchwoman." He paused. "There just are limits to what science can achieve. The human body is a machine; eventually its parts simply wear out."

"This is an incorrect analogy," muttered Dusek.

"No," Holland came back, "it is a very precise analogy. Cells stop reproducing and die. Free radicals—the by-product of breathing and other critical life processes—begin to overwhelm our natural defenses and disrupt cell function. When an autopsy is conducted on an exceptionally old person, they'll often find a seeming irony: everything wrong but nothing in particular. These processes are irreversible. They can't be wished away."

It went on for another fifteen minutes, but for practical purposes it was over.

Afterward Holland shook Dusek's hand and expressed the hope that there were no hard feelings. The host, brimming with good feeling, followed the journalist to the elevator.

"Your series on the antiaging industry has been terrific," he enthused. "You deserve a Pulitzer. But there is something I want to ask you. I didn't think I should say it on the air."

Holland looked at him curiously. "What?"

"It's surprising. You've done all this work in this area, and over and over you find the claims are exaggerated. Yet you keep on. It's like you're on a personal mission of some kind."

Holland's expression betrayed his dismay. "You couldn't give me a higher compliment," he said after a moment. The elevator doors slid open, and he stepped in. "I'm a reporter. With me the truth *is* personal."

SALLY was dead to the world when the phone rang. The room was black; for a moment she was disoriented. Then she realized she'd fallen asleep on the couch, missing the end of her own party! She was still fully dressed, though Mark had removed her shoes before tucking a blanket beneath her chin.

The phone rang again. She reached for the receiver.

"Sally? It's Jack Stebben." The local chief of police. "Don't tell me I woke you."

"Uh-uh," she replied reflexively, glancing at her watch in the dimness. Five forty.

"I'm up here at Grace Church. Got something for you."

Twenty-five minutes later Sally followed the beam of Stebben's flashlight down into the empty pit, then up to the weathered slate slab at the head of the empty grave.

"Who in the world would do something like this?"

"Ah, heck, on Halloween night . . . ?"

In his late fifties, tall and lean, Stebben bore a faint resemblance to the actor Jack Nicholson, and he had the same disconcerting habit of making even chitchat sound insincere.

"You know who was buried here?" she asked, pulling a notebook from the parka she'd thrown on over sweat clothes.

The words on the slate slab had long since been obliterated by weather. "Make up a name. No one'll care." He laughed. "Guess some idiots figured it beat bobbing for apples."

Sally managed a smile. She dealt with Stebben on a regular basis. Putting up with his sense of humor came with the territory. "So there are no suspects in particular?"

"*Suspects?* That's a pretty rough word, missy. We're talking about some local kids pulling a prank."

"You have any actual evidence it was kids?"

"Sure I do. I used to be a teenager around here myself."

"I see." Sally took a deep breath and gazed about her. In northeastern New Hampshire winter comes early, and a few snowflakes drifted lazily down. The churchyard was at the crest of a rise at the far north end of town. Even in the faint light she could make out everything that had long made this community of fifty-five hundred souls so irresistible in postcards: the nineteenth-century buildings of wood and brick along Main Street, the broad porches and steep gables of so many of the houses. Yet all she felt at this moment was the insularity of the place, its astonishing protectiveness of its own.

"You think this is cute, Chief? A law has been broken here. I'd like to know what you plan to do about it."

"Which law is that, exactly, Lois Lane—petty larceny?"

"Worse than that. It's a . . . sacrilege."

"Is that the end of the lecture part of the program? Because I figure I've done my duty by the local press." Turning, he began striding down the hill.

THE deterioration was even worse than the scientists had feared. It was to be expected that after more than two hundred years in the ground in such a climate, there would likely remain no trace of flesh or marrow. What they hadn't anticipated was that the bones themselves would be in such lamentable condition. Most were decalcified—soft and badly eroded.

That noted, they plunged ahead. Time was at a premium. There remained enough funding for only another seven or eight months. And the biotech venture capitalists from whom money would have to be raised were as coolly pragmatic as mob hit men. Impressed as they might be that a pair of unheralded scientists in the wilds of New Hampshire had isolated a protein that helped lab rats live longer, in practical terms the achievement was close to worthless. Lacking persuasive evidence that the remarkable protein also functioned in humans, no one would fork over a dime.

The scientists had no doubt such evidence existed. Their data indicated that the protein was already working its magic in a tiny subset of human beings, encoded in their DNA as the result of a long-ago mutation. The problem was demonstrating it. For the mutation was remarkably elusive, confined to a select few extended families, and even then was not present in all members.

It was this that had led them to the Edwardstown graveyard.

"They did quite a nice job," ventured one of the men. "I understand there's been no outcry in the town at all."

"Not *now,* Lynch," said the other sharply. "Don't talk cops and robbers while we're doing science."

At the rebuke Lynch fell silent. Though he was more physically imposing than his colleague—and, at forty-eight, almost a decade older—five years of working together had left them equals in name only. Lynch was the project's public face, but Foster was its heart and soul. If the younger man was demanding and imperious, Lynch accepted it as part of the price of keeping the project moving forward. With the goal in sight, there was no room for ego.

Now Foster surveyed the several dozen bones and large bone fragments arrayed before them. "We'll start with the right talus," he decided, reaching for the small, intact anklebone.

In theory all it would take was one cell. If they could salvage the DNA from that single cell, they could conclusively establish that this was the family that held the key to the project's success.

The immediate task was locating a pure sample. The genetic material at hand was sure to be randomly mixed with that of worms and moles and other subterranean organisms.

Taking extreme care, Foster worked at the bone with a ball peen hammer; then, when the fragments were small enough, using a mortar and pestle, he reduced them to fine powder. Lynch then placed this in a buffer and bombarded it with ultrasonic waves.

Nothing. The red needle on the spectrophotometer remained resolutely fixed on zero.

They began again, this time with a lumbar vertebra, then tried again. And again. Each such repetition took more than an hour.

It took thirty-two tries. The third day, when they returned to the lab in the early morning, Foster chose a metatarsal bone from the right foot. But this time when Lynch placed the sample in the machine and pressed the button, the needle began to waver; then, after a few seconds, it jumped.

"There it is," enthused Lynch. "We're in business."

But his colleague did not even permit himself a smile. "We're still going to need an intact sample," he said. "*Living* cells."

"I'M REALLY not sure I understand, Sally," said Father Morse, rector of Grace Episcopal Church. "Just between you and me, what difference does it make, anyway?"

Sally and the minister had always enjoyed a pleasant relationship, yet at the moment he represented an aspect of Edwardstown that drove Sally absolutely bonkers: the complacency of the place.

For a moment she just stared at him, dumbfounded. "What difference does it make who was in that grave?"

He smiled. "I don't mean that the way it sounds. But think about it. Is that piece of information going to help anyone?"

"It's a big part of the story, Father—people have a right to know. You're telling me there are no burial records prior to 1815? They've completely disappeared?"

"Now, Sally, don't take that tone." He nodded vaguely at the rectory building behind him. "What I'm telling you is that we haven't been able to locate them just yet. To paraphrase Winston Churchill, Grace Church is a mystery wrapped in a question mark. In the attic alone there are a dozen crawl spaces no one's been in for a century. It would take four or five days to search them all."

"Let me do it."

"Be reasonable. Who's to say those records *ever* existed? This church is over two hundred years old. Surely back then people knew where their loved ones were interred without having to look it up on a chart."

"Let me try."

He hesitated. "Tell me again why the name is so important."

"That poor soul once lived in this town, walked these streets." Sally paused meaningfully. "How do we know? Maybe the family still lives around here. . . ."

SLUMPED in a plastic chair, Mark Bowman flipped through a four-month-old copy of *Ladies' Home Journal.* He paused briefly at an article on Katie Couric's homelife, then tossed it aside.

At her desk across the waiting room in Edwardstown Hospital's department of ob/gyn, Nurse Barbara Walker smiled. "You know, there's probably an *Esquire* at the bottom of the pile."

Mark laughed—which was precisely the point. Having been with Dr. Lee Malen, head of ob/gyn at the hospital, for nearly a decade,

Barbara had a gift for putting people at ease. Mark had been here a quarter hour, waiting for this consultation with Malen, his body language a dead giveaway.

"So," she asked now, "what's keeping Sally?"

"That's what I want to know," echoed Malen, appearing at his office door. In his sixties, he had the look of a faded matinee idol—rugged features set off by a preternatural tan and gray hair.

Mark stiffened. Though the doctor had been among Sally's father's closest friends—and since Paul Benedict's death had shown an almost paternal interest in his wife—Mark had never liked him. Twice married and easily dazzled by wealth and celebrity, Malen had girlfriends, as even Sally joked, younger than some of her clothes.

The feeling was more than returned in kind, the doctor leaving little doubt that he viewed Mark's marriage to Sally as an unfortunate accident—as if vivacious, snappy Murphy Brown had thrown away everything for a New Hampshire version of John Boy Walton. He sometimes treated the younger man with an indifference that bordered on rudeness.

"She said something about stopping by Grace Church," Mark observed now.

"Ah . . ." Malen paused, glancing in annoyance at the clock. "Maybe you ought to remind her to do it on her own time. She's really going way too far with this."

Under other circumstances Mark might have agreed; he too was starting to regard her fixation on the graverobbing as wildly over the top.

Barbara smiled. "Give her a break, Lee. She doesn't find many stories she can sink her teeth into around here."

"No," he agreed curtly. "Not around here."

Mark was at a loss. How to even begin to respond to the insinuation that somehow *he* had derailed Sally's career?

When she arrived, Sally immediately sensed the tension. "Sorry. I got a little hung up."

In her presence, Malen's mood was lighter. "Why don't we get to it?" he said, ushering Sally and Mark into his office.

MALEN LEANED FORWARD. Though both faced him from a pair of leather chairs flanking his desk, he addressed himself to Sally, shooting Mark only an occasional glance. "Sixteen months—that's a long time to have been trying. Still, I really don't think there's any reason to panic. The sperm count and motility are both good. The only obvious problem is the partial blockage in one of the tubes."

Sally's anxiety was not allayed by so casual a reassurance. "That doesn't *sound* minor."

"I doubt it's key. After all, Sally, you got pregnant once before."

From the way Mark's head whipped her way, the doctor abruptly realized she'd never told him.

She hesitated, avoiding her husband's gaze. "That was quite a while ago."

Malen looked from one to the other, quietly relishing the moment. "That's true. You're right. Which of course leads us to the most likely possibility—that it might be age related. There's a clinic down in Manchester that offers an excellent series of diagnostic tests and corrective measures, including in vitro."

"We'll consider it," Mark allowed. "Money might be an issue." Instantly, knowing the remark had been at least partly prompted by his distress over what he'd just learned, he wished he could take it back. "I already looked into this a few months ago," he added quickly, digging himself in even deeper. "Each IV treatment costs roughly ten thousand dollars, and our insurance doesn't cover it."

He could feel Sally's eyes boring into him. "That's our problem," she hissed, defensive and angry. "We'll discuss it later."

AS SOON as they stepped outside, he wheeled on her. "Why didn't you tell me?"

"What's this fuss about money? Money is *not* the issue."

"Why didn't you tell me?"

"If it comes to that, I'll take on freelance work."

He said nothing, just looked at her.

"Mark," she said more softly, "it was a long time ago. I had to tell Malen as part of my medical history."

"That's not an answer."

"Has it occurred to you that maybe it's because I'm ashamed?" She looked away briefly, then back at him. "I miscarried. It was the most miserable part of an awful relationship."

"Right," he said. "I understand." Mark turned away, striding toward his car. He had his answer: Paul Holland.

CHAPTER TWO

SALLY looked up from the proposed editorial written by her managing editor, Florence Davis—a polite appeal to anyone with information on the graverobbing to consider coming forward—and into the woman's hopeful eyes. "Look, Florence," she began, "I'm afraid this needs a lot more muscle. Our concern has to be what the cops are doing to solve this thing—or rather, *not* doing."

Florence looked like she might actually start to cry. In her early sixties, she dated back to the paper's previous regime. "I'm so sorry, Sally," she said softly. "I did my best."

"Of course you did," Sally agreed, "and I appreciate it. We've never had a story like this before. It requires a new set of skills."

Collecting herself, Sally gazed about her sorry excuse for an office: two rooms, four steel-gray desks, two Mac computers, a single light table. She had accepted the job in the optimistic expectation that she would raise the paper to her own high standards of professionalism. But by now, for all the improvements in the paper's style and design, she'd stopped kidding herself. The limitations of budget—and what a small town liked to read about itself—were all but impossible to overcome.

She smiled at the older woman, moving to safer ground. "So what do you see as next week's lead story?"

"The new steamroller?"

"Great. What's our angle?"

"Well, no final decision has been made. The trustees are planning to discuss it again next month."

"So the headline would be something like"—Sally made quote marks with her fingers—" 'New Steamroller *Likely*'?"

The older woman hesitated. "Well, maybe we shouldn't be quite so bold. Perhaps 'New Steamroller *Possible*'?"

"Well, let's look at the issues," Sally said. "How much would a piece of equipment like that cost?"

"I'm not actually working on the story myself." Florence nodded across the room toward the extremely attractive young woman poised before her computer.

"Hey, Lisa!" called Sally. "We're talking steamrollers. How much do those things cost?"

Lisa wheeled in her swivel chair to face her boss. "Figure forty-five thousand, with maybe a ten percent negotiated discount."

"Good. I want that in the first two graphs of your piece."

"I'm way ahead of you. It's already in the lead."

Sally nodded. Lisa, whom she'd hired right out of the University of New Hampshire, at least gave her hope. Raw as she was, she was far more ambitious than any of the reporters Sally had had during her tenure here. "I want to talk about the graverobbing," Sally said.

She caught Florence and Lisa exchanging a glance.

"I don't care how many times I have to repeat this. We're staying with this thing till we get some answers. If people around here have a problem with that, so be it."

"But there's no *news,*" Lisa ventured.

"Maybe we'll luck out and find the church records. Until then we're going to keep pounding away in editorials." Sally paused. "And maybe create some news on our own."

She held up a vintage leather-bound volume, its title, *Rituals of Death in Eighteenth-Century America,* so faded it was barely perceptible. "For starters, did you know that until the nineteenth century almost no one around here was buried in a coffin?"

"Where did you find that book?" said Florence.

"In the library," Sally replied. "There's more. Chief Stebben wants us to believe this is completely harmless. He can't even say for sure that any law's been broken." She opened the book to the page she'd marked. "New Hampshire enacted its first statute pertaining to disinterring the dead in June of 1796, with penalties of up to three years' imprisonment, a thousand-dollar fine, plus a public whipping, and I quote, 'not to exceed thirty-nine stripes.' " Sally tapped the page. "Back then people knew what was what. By the way, that statute is still on the books."

"Who was after those bodies?" asked Lisa, her interest aroused.

"That'll be part two in our series. Often it was medical schools after anatomical samples. They could usually afford to buy off the authorities." She displayed the nineteenth-century lithograph illustrating the point: a pair of shadowy figures going about their grisly work while a policeman stood by, arms folded.

"Will there really be enough for a series?"

"Let's think short term—parts one and two." She snapped the book shut and extended it to Lisa.

The young woman didn't try to hide her excitement. "You want me to write it?"

"It'll look good on your résumé—it shows initiative."

AFTER four afternoons and an entire Saturday morning Sally was almost ready to acknowledge Father Morse might have a point. For all the pristine elegance of Grace Church, with its soaring arches and stunning Tiffany windows, beneath the surface the confusion and disorder was overwhelming.

She found caches of old documents stored in several rooms—more than two dozen wooden boxes in all. All manner of local records were there, seemingly thrown together at random: marriage and baptismal certificates, property taxes and estate settlements, and births dating from the church's earliest years in the mid–eighteenth century to the 1950s, with many gaps in between.

But the record she sought, documenting the early gravesites, was absent—if it had ever existed at all. She discovered only a single document pertaining to the churchyard, and it was useless—a 1738 deed for the original purchase of the land.

As she hurried to her mother's house after this latest futile effort, the heavy early December sky seemed to match her mood. She wanted nothing more than to go to her own house, crawl beneath a soft comforter, and feel sorry for herself. Unfortunately, Saturday afternoons with the family had evolved into a kind of ritual.

"Uh-oh," observed Mark from a living-room chair, catching her look as she walked through the door. "Came up empty?"

Something about the way he said it bugged her, or maybe it was just that he read her so well. Wordlessly, she removed her coat and sat down on the couch opposite him, between her mother and grandmother. "I'm not done," she said. "I'll go back."

Gazing at the three generations of Benedict women—clear-skinned, high-cheekboned, strong-jawed—Mark was reminded of photographs he'd seen of flinty, indomitable pioneer women.

He loved these visits in the house where Mrs. Benedict cared for her own elderly mother. They were his only real family now. His parents' marriage had come apart when he was in college. His father left Edwardstown when the Applejack plant's closing cost him his foreman's job. Within three years his mother and younger sister were also gone, one to southern California, the other to St. Louis.

"Mark been treating you all right, Gram?" asked Sally.

"Not bad."

"He been telling you his jokes?"

"*Repeating* them. They're not exactly new."

Sally laughed. No one who knew them had ever wondered where her wit came from. Though now, at ninety-two, her grandmother was increasingly in and out—talking lucidly one moment, off on some tangent the next—she remained a vital presence.

"I like Mark's jokes," said Mrs. Benedict quickly.

"We all do, Mother. It's just the material gets a little stale. Back in Philly, if there was a big tragedy in the news before lunch, by day's end you'd already heard a dozen jokes about it."

"While out here we clods sat around telling knock-knock jokes."

"She didn't say that, Mark." Mrs. Benedict rose to her feet. "Sally, I can use some help in the kitchen."

"ALL right, Mother, I know it wasn't nice. I've just been a little upset lately."

"Listen to you, Sally. Someone who didn't know you might think you were awfully self-centered."

"Mother, I *am* self-centered."

She considered a moment. "Well, as long as you realize it. . . ." Mrs. Benedict turned away to check the roast in the oven.

"Sit down, Mother. I'll take care of that."

"Just relax. I'm fine."

"Mother, I'm thirty-six years old and healthy as an ox. You're seventy-one with a bad gallbladder."

"Don't concern yourself about that. I don't."

It was an argument they'd had a dozen times before. "Malen's been after you for years to have it taken care of. If it gets infected, it could be dangerous."

"Sally, we're talking about you. Why can't you ever just stop and count your blessings? A wonderful marriage, lots of people who love you, a fine job—"

"I *know,* Mother. I know love makes the world go around. I know good things come in little packages. I know every one of the clichés." She paused and came out with it. "Mark's dragging his feet about seeing a specialist. Maybe he doesn't even *want* a baby."

"Give him time."

"That's what I don't have, Mother!"

"Sally, he's hurting too." She paused. "Why don't you try separating your anger toward him from your anger at yourself?"

Sally avoided her mother's gaze.

"You made choices in your life, Sally. Probably they were the right choices at the time. But you waited a very long time."

"I know that," she conceded softly.

Mrs. Benedict walked across the room and withdrew a small

newspaper clipping from a drawer. "Here," she said, handing it over. "Just to get some perspective."

Sally studied it—a death notice from a local paper in Wilbur, South Carolina: an infant, only five weeks, son of one Charlotte Craig. Born prematurely and still in the hospital, he had been found dead in his crib, apparently a victim of sudden infant death syndrome. She looked at her mother, perplexed.

"Aunt Mary sent it." Her father's Florida-based sister was the family historian. "Charlotte Craig is a distant relative of ours. She's now lost two children this way in two years."

"Oh, how awful."

"Exactly," Mrs. Benedict said. "There are women who have it a lot tougher than you." She paused. "I know you'll get through this all right, Sal. You've always been a fighter."

"Yeah, only it was never my own body I was fighting."

Mrs. Benedict held out her arms, and slowly Sally allowed herself to be drawn in. "Just remember, I was thirty-five when you were born. Gram's mother, my grandmother, was forty-four when she had the last of hers."

"Really?"

"Didn't you know that?" She laughed then, with uncharacteristic pride. "We Benedicts have great genes out the wazoo."

THE invitation to visit the Life Services Institute outside Manchester, New Hampshire, had caught R. Paul Holland by surprise. Given his hostility to nontraditional antiaging research, such institutions rarely courted his journalistic attention.

But the main reason he'd agreed to visit the place was the signature at the bottom of the letter: Clifford Stagg. Responsible for the transcom microchip, wealthy beyond rational measure, Stagg had long ago dropped from sight. Holland hadn't heard his name in years—in fact, he had assumed he was dead.

Rounding a curve in his rented Chrysler, Holland saw the brick rectangle that housed the institute, set back several hundred yards from the road. It was evidently a converted factory of some kind.

At Holland's knock the metal door immediately swung open. Facing him was a tiny, wizened figure well into his eighties.

For a moment the journalist couldn't help but stare. "Would this be the Life Services Institute?"

Squinting, the old man leaned forward slightly, as if trying to make sense of some foreign tongue, but he said nothing.

Another man appeared and touched the old man lightly on the shoulder. When he turned, the younger man said, "Thank you, Clark. I'll see to this," enunciating clearly so he could read his lips.

"Yessir," Clark said, and began shuffling off.

"Mr. Holland," the other man said, addressing the visitor, "my name is Raymond Lynch. I'm chief of research and development here. Please come in. This is a real honor."

Holland stepped into the reception area.

"Come. Mr. Stagg is waiting in the library." Lynch led him down a corridor, stopped at a paneled door, and knocked once. "I'll see you afterward," said Lynch, pushing open the door.

Stepping into the room, fitted with Oriental carpets and Victorian upholstery, Holland was taken aback. The painfully thin old man in the armchair at the far end of the room was draped in an extravagant Hawaiian shirt. A carefully trimmed jet-black beard—an obvious dye job—and the jaunty little sailor cap perched on his head completed the bizarre portrait.

"Come over here and take a load off," he said.

"It's a pleasure, Mr. Stagg," said Holland, heading toward him.

The old man extended a bony hand. In the other hand he held the book he'd been reading.

From the clips Holland knew Stagg to be seventy-six years old, but up close, for all the attention devoted to obscuring the fact, he could have easily passed for ten years older.

"You have an amazing gift, sir," said Stagg.

Holland took a seat in a chair a few feet away. "Thank you. That's nice of you to say. I see that I've interrupted your reading."

"Ah, yes." He held up the book. "Quite a nice little life of George Washington."

"You're interested in history?"

"In the lives of the great, yes, very much so. And lately, of course, in their deaths." Abruptly he shot out his left arm, revealing a shunt—the artery fused with the vein to provide easy access for an outside line. "Chronic kidney failure. I have to undergo dialysis three times a week. I've also had two heart attacks." He paused, then matter-of-factly added, "I'm dying, Mr. Holland. Unfortunately, I won't be able to take advantage of the work that will make mortality obsolete. Soon we'll have so thorough an understanding of the immune system that any chance of breakdown will be eliminated. Imagine a world—can you even conceive of it?—where no one younger than a hundred will be considered mature enough to be a leader."

"I wish I could," Holland answered. "I'm more of a skeptic."

There was a soft knock at the door, and the old man from the front door shuffled into the room with a tray.

"Ah," said Stagg brightly as Clark moved laboriously toward him. "My tea and drug overdose. I'd ask you to join me, but I see Mr. Speedy here's only brought one cup." He laughed. "Don't look so mortified, Mr. Holland. He can't hear anything."

Holland nodded noncommittally.

"I suppose you're thinking I'm no one to talk. But at least I have the excuse of age. Clark's just a kid."

"Excuse me?"

"He's only twenty-two years old, Mr. Holland."

Astonished, Holland turned from the man with the tray to Stagg and back again.

"I'm sure you've heard of adult progeria, Mr. Holland."

"Of course. But never a case so . . . *extreme.*"

Conventional science offers no explanation as to why most human beings move toward old age slowly, their cells replicating themselves fifty or more times, whereas progeria patients rush toward advanced biological age in a mere seven or eight cell generations.

"Well, naturally, the extreme nature of his disease is what aroused interest here."

"He's a research subject?"

Stagg nodded.

"Tell me," Holland asked, "what's been your total investment in the institute?"

"We set aside seventeen million when we began. More since then."

"How much more?"

"I haven't kept track."

Holland said nothing. The figure was far greater than he'd anticipated. Of the many bogus operations he'd looked at, suddenly this one loomed as potentially the most outrageous of all.

"Whatever the sum," the old man picked up, "I consider it a bargain. The work being performed here is revolutionary."

"I'd appreciate the chance to look over the facility."

"Absolutely. How about tomorrow morning?"

"Fine," Holland agreed. "I can't wait to hear more."

"Of course not. You're in the same boat I am."

It took Holland a moment to respond. "How's that?"

"You're dying also, just a little more slowly. You may have—what?—another eight or ten years."

Already the color was going from Holland's face.

"Both your parents died of early onset Alzheimer's, and three of your four grandparents. Isn't that what drew you to this research in the first place?"

Holland was stunned. How could he know?

"Genealogical research is key to what we do here," Stagg said evenly. "If one has the right connections, Mr. Holland, it isn't all that hard to isolate the genetic populations of particular interest."

"I see," Holland managed.

"We're also often able to obtain relevant tissue samples. If you like, I'll have Dr. Lynch take you through the report on yours."

AFTER the working-over Stebben had been getting in the *Weekly,* Sally decided to see him at home on his day off rather than at police headquarters. There was little enough chance he'd come forth with anything useful, none at all if approached in front of his men.

"Want me to wait for you?" asked Lisa hesitantly as they pulled up before the little house in her VW.

"No way," said Sally blithely. She flashed a grin. "It's about time you learned how to deal with guys like this."

As they made their way toward the tidy white clapboard jewel, Sally was struck by how inviting the place looked. Teardrop lights twinkled on the twin fir trees flanking the front porch, brightening this dreary December morning.

They found the chief in back, in the section of garage converted to a makeshift greenhouse. On his hands and knees over a sorry-looking primrose, he glanced up and squinted. "Well, well. My poison-pen pals from the press." He rose to his feet. "I hear you hit a dry well up at the church."

Sally wondered from whom. "I wouldn't say that," she said. "I'm not done yet."

"So I guess you're getting pretty desperate. Hoping against hope I'll give you something to help keep your little story alive."

"What we were hoping, Chief," said Sally with an edge, "was that maybe you were ready to start doing your job."

"Say, Lisa," he replied, "think you can knock it into your boss's thick skull to stop expecting big-city results in a little town?"

Lisa blanched, trying to maintain her composure. "Sally's right," she said. "There's no evidence at all it was kids."

"As a matter of fact, there is." Stebben slowly removed his gardening gloves. "But this has to be totally off the record."

"I can't agree to that sight unseen," Sally said.

He shrugged. "Your call."

For a long moment she stood there mute. Then she nodded. "Okay, off the record. And this better be good."

"Wait here," he said, turning away into the house.

When he reappeared a few minutes later, it was with a large manila envelope. Inside were a number of eight-by-ten black-and-white shots showing the dirt surrounding the empty grave.

"These were taken just afterward." He pointed. "See that?"

Sally looked closely. Footprints could be clearly discerned.

"See these two?" he indicated. "Air Thrill by Nike, almost brand-new. Size nine and a half."

"What about the others?"

"Converse Run 'N Slam, size ten. Both models are real big right now—all the kids are wearing 'em."

"Nice work, Chief," offered Sally pleasantly. "You're right up there with some big-city cops I know."

"Spare me the compliments," he spat, the contempt he'd kept in check finally surging forth. "All I want is for you to leave me alone!"

THE next day Holland asked Lynch, "So what do you want me to see first?"

"The animal lab," said Lynch. "Follow me."

Moments later, turning a corner, Holland picked up the faint, familiar rustle of rodents on newspaper.

It was an impressive facility, long rows of cages stacked floor to ceiling on shelves the length of the room. Lynch proceeded immediately to a large cage and plucked out a white mouse.

"Turn off the lights, will you, Greg?"

Only now, as the room went dark, was Holland aware of a man with a wispy beard watching in the corner.

"Please hold out your hand, Mr. Holland," said Lynch.

Holland played along, but instead of the mouse, he felt in his palm a narrow metal cylinder.

"It's a fluorescent light pen, the kind ophthalmologists use. Turn it on."

He did so, producing a narrow beam of intensely blue light. Lynch slowly lifted the mouse into the beam.

Normally blood-red, the animal's eyes shone bright green!

Momentarily startled, Holland said nothing.

"Hit the lights, please." Lynch stroked the mouse with his index finger. "Aequorin—the same protein that causes jellyfish to glow."

"Ah." Holland nodded, dismissive. "You've injected it into the eyeballs of the mice. A neat little scientific parlor trick."

Lynch glanced at his colleague, then back at Holland. "We're not in show business, Mr. Holland. Our interest is longevity. You recall the Norwegian study on Pacific salmon?"

"Yes," said Holland. "I wrote a piece on it."

"I know," said Lynch dryly. "I read it. I was surprised by your rigidity. My question is this, Mr. Holland. Why even bother studying the ninety-nine point nine percent of cases where salmon die after spawning? What about the tenth of a percent where they don't? That's the question—why is it that a select few members of the species escape what seems a preordained fate? *Why?*"

This actually gave Holland a moment's pause. "There are probably thousands of random genetic tendencies that come together in just the right way to produce exceptional hardiness."

"Why are you so certain? Why couldn't a single genetic mechanism trigger all the biological processes associated with aging?"

"Excuse me." It was the first time Greg Foster had spoken, and they turned to him in surprise. "If I could have a word with you, Dr. Lynch," he asked tentatively. "Just for a moment . . . ?"

"Dammit," said Lynch, throwing up his hands as he started from the room. "Please bear with us, Mr. Holland."

Once they were alone, two doors down, roles abruptly reversed.

"Did I say something wrong?" asked Lynch sheepishly.

"What the hell's the matter with you? Why don't you just bend over and lick his boots?"

"I'm trying to engage him on the issues."

"I'm trying to engage him on the issues," mocked Foster. "We've got him by the short hairs. You'll engage him when you pull!"

From Foster's point of view this had long been the drawback to the operation. Lynch was weak. Only recently, when it became a priority to obtain samples from the newborn in South Carolina, Foster had had to beat back his colleague's squeamishness.

In fact, the South Carolina experience had been a wrenching disappointment. Every scrap of genetic research at their disposal indicated the child should have carried the mutation; indeed, since cells replicate themselves most furiously in infancy, its cells should have expressed the protein in particularly concentrated and accessible form. Yet after all the trouble and risk—the meticulously planned infiltration of the rural hospital, the carefully negotiated arrangement with the local coroner—the autopsy samples had indicated nothing of the sort. They could only surmise that at some point the genetic link must have been severed.

So tantalizingly close to their goal yet more desperate than ever about time and money, they had revised a key element of their strategy. The idea of bringing in a well-connected outsider could no longer be dismissed as unthinkable.

"He is *not* your friend, Lynch," Foster spat now. "So get back in there and close this deal!"

"TAKE a seat, Mr. Holland," said Lynch, back in the lab, indicating the chair before an oversize fluorescent microscope.

Holland did so, sighing, to make clear he was indulging them.

The scientist produced a wooden slide box. "These are tissue samples from one of the aequorin-treated mice." He slid off the top. Each of the thirty or so slides within was neatly labeled: BRAIN, PANCREAS, SPLEEN, LIVER, and so on. "Pick one," he said.

Holland chose the slide labeled LARGE INTESTINE.

"What do you see?" said Lynch, placing it beneath the lens.

Holland peered down. "Specks of green. Thousands of them."

"That's the aequorin. You can pick out any slide, any organ; it will be the same."

The reporter was momentarily confused.

"We didn't *inject* it into the animal's eyes. It's everywhere in its body, in every cell! We've succeeded in packaging the gene responsible for aequorin and transferring it between species."

Holland looked up and stared at him. "To what end? What does that have to do with antiaging research?"

"When it is refined, the same mechanism should allow us to transfer any gene from one living organism to another." He paused meaningfully. "And we have already isolated the gene for the protein that plays the key role in human cellular immortalization."

Holland was stunned. "A protein that allows cells to live forever?"

"Forever's a long time, Mr. Holland. Let's just say we're confident we will shortly have a drug that allows human beings to override their genetic limitations. An antiaging drug, if you will."

Holland had to consider the possibility that these people were mad. Yet, glancing again at the microscope, he couldn't afford to dismiss them out of hand. Could it be? Was it even remotely possible that he'd stumbled onto what he'd been so feverishly seeking all along? A drug that would keep him alive?

He pulled back, looking for maneuvering room. "You've done all this yourself? You two are the only principals?"

"Basic research doesn't have to be as cumbersome as some make it," replied Lynch. "Fleming discovered penicillin in a one-man lab. Einstein developed the special theory of relativity as a clerk in the Swiss patent office."

"That's pretty fast company you put yourself in."

"Not me personally. Dr. Foster is our chief researcher."

Holland turned to Foster in surprise. Scientists with major-league talent often had major-league egos; this guy was so nondescript he all but faded from view. "May I ask your background?"

"Molecular biology," he allowed, though the scrutiny appeared to make him even more uncomfortable. "I'm a biologist."

"Dr. Foster trained at M.I.T. under D. L. Cohen."

"Really?" said Holland. "I interviewed Dr. Cohen after he won his Nobel on the genetic analysis of blood cells."

Lynch eyed him levelly. "That was Dr. Foster's work. He was a postdoc under Cohen. But his name wasn't even listed on the paper as a contributor."

Holland nodded. He knew too much of the cutthroat business of high-stakes science to dismiss the claim out of hand.

"Because he wouldn't go quietly, there wasn't a quality university in the country that would touch him," added Lynch. "He ended up at Barnett College in Salt Lake City. That's where we met and began working together."

"Tell me more about this project of yours," Holland said, his tone carefully neutral. "That's why I'm here."

"Actually, Mr. Holland," said Lynch, "you're here because we told you to be." With a cool smile he turned to Foster. "Greg, Mr. Holland and I need a few minutes alone."

Confident now, Foster quickly walked from the room.

"Dr. Foster doesn't always understand what's necessary to achieve important ends," said Lynch. "We need to raise a great deal of money. Very quickly. We want your help to do it."

"Money?" asked Holland. "What about Stagg?"

"Mr. Stagg is nearly tapped out. If we're careful, we might have enough to see us through another six months."

Holland looked at him. "How much more funding could you possibly require? This seems like a very lean operation."

"Leaner than it was. We've cut way back. A year ago we had seventeen scientists here plus full support staff. Now, besides Dr. Foster and myself, we're down to a secretary-nutritionist and a few others who help keep up appearances. Virtually all resources are now focused on this research. But it is enormously costly."

Holland was silent, waiting for him to elaborate.

"There are quite a number of individuals on the payroll who"—he hesitated—"have no formal affiliation with the institute. People who assist us in various ways."

Holland didn't need to have it spelled out. Clearly they were paying off individuals to supply them with confidential information—as well as, quite possibly, law enforcement, senior medical personnel, and maybe even ordinary citizens.

"You should know," added the scientist suddenly, "that we intend to personally be the first beneficiaries of this work."

Lynch watched the journalist closely. Holland's reaction—suddenly alive, hopeful as a child early Christmas morning—was exactly what Lynch had been looking for.

Twenty feet away, behind a two-way mirror, Foster smiled.

Across the room the door slowly opened. Clark Warren entered with a tray bearing gingersnaps and two cups of tea.

"I understand he is a research subject," said Holland.

The scientist nodded, smiling warmly at Warren. "He's helped establish the overriding importance of our target protein, since skin biopsies indicate its total absence in his cells."

Warren had made it only halfway across the room. As Holland studied him, another question, related but far more troubling, came to mind. "But why only *skin* biopsies?" he asked. "To really nail down the case, wouldn't you need samples from a wide variety of organs? Like with the aequorin-treated mice?"

Lynch paused. "Interesting thought . . ."

By now Clark Warren was beside them, and the scientist took a gingersnap from the plate on the tray. "Thank you, Clark." He mouthed the words. "We're not very hungry right now."

As Warren turned and began moving off, Lynch picked up the phone. Dialing three numbers, he listened for a moment, then nodded. "Get Mr. Van Ost down here, please. Lab three."

The man who entered the room moments later was unlike anyone Holland had ever before encountered in such a facility. Powerfully built, his bulging chest and biceps barely contained by the '50s-era white shirt he wore, he was surely a weight lifter.

"Mr. Van Ost is our director of security. He comes to us from the former South African Bureau of Internal Affairs."

Holland nodded uneasily. "Nice to meet you." If the introduction was intended to intimidate, it had served its purpose.

"The pleasure is entirely mine," Van Ost offered, excessively polite, in an odd, lilting accent the reporter guessed to be Afrikaans.

"It appears Mr. Holland will be working with us."

Holland hoped his smile was ingratiating. "Of course, we still need to talk more about my role. Basically you'll just want me to point you toward some money people?"

"Perhaps a few other small things. This project can make . . . unorthodox demands." He paused, nodded meaningfully at Van Ost. "That's a responsibility we have to share."

In an instant Van Ost had bounded behind Clark Warren and tapped him on the shoulder. "Let me get that for you, Clark," he said gently, easing the tray from his grasp and setting it on a nearby table. As Clark gazed at him, confused, Van Ost placed a comforting hand on his shoulder, then abruptly shifted it to the back of his neck. With a single violent move he jerked Clark's head back. The snap of the cervical vertebrae made no more sound than that produced by a very dry twig when broken.

Holland blanched as Van Ost held up the lifeless form.

"Too bad," offered Van Ost. "He was a sweet fellow. Where would you like him?"

"Ask Mr. Holland. It was his idea."

Light-headed and slightly sick to his stomach, Holland seemed to take the question in stride only by sheer will. "I assume you have a room where you do your cutting."

CHAPTER THREE

ARRIVING at the office before seven thirty, Sally was startled to find the door unlocked. She hesitated before very gently pushing it open and peering inside.

"Hey," Lisa called out from her computer.

Sally strode into the office. "What are you doing here?"

"Trying to get down something Stebben can live with. Suggest that the cops have proof, without violating our agreement."

"I like the instinct," said Sally, "but sorry, forget it."

"You mean because it's off the record?" asked Lisa.

"Because I think Stebben is full of it. Rule one in this business is never trust anyone with an agenda—and his is to get us off his back. If those shots are legit, let him release them."

"He won't do that."

"Why not? It's possible he leaked this to us so we'd embarrass ourselves. What proof do we have they're genuine? I sure didn't notice any prints that night."

Abruptly the phone rang. Sally snatched it up. "Sally Benedict." She listened a moment, then seemed to freeze. "How did you find me here?"

Lisa stared, perplexed. She'd never seen Sally so rattled.

"No," said Sally, "believe it or not, we sometimes put in long days here too."

The call lasted another minute or so, with Sally doing far more listening than talking.

"Who was that?" asked Lisa cheerily when Sally hung up.

"Just someone I used to know. His name is Paul Holland."

"Paul Holland?" Lisa asked, awestruck. "Of the New York *Herald?* It's my dream to work at that place."

Sally turned away to make a notation on her calendar.

"What did he want?"

"To get together. He'll be in the area next week."

FIVE days later Sally emerged from a cold late December afternoon into the Clover Patch, Edwardstown's best bar-café.

Spotting Paul Holland at a corner table, she quickly turned away to hang up her coat. Already she was starting to regret she'd come; indeed, she'd only agreed to the meeting for the most pragmatic of reasons. Prominent and well connected, Holland could help get her the kind of freelance assignments that would make a real dent in the cost of fertility treatments.

By the time she turned back, he was on his feet.

"Sally! You look fabulous."

She was wearing a short black skirt to go with her green form-fitting jacket, the one that so vividly brought out her eyes.

She ignored the compliment. "Hope I didn't keep you waiting."

"No. You know me—compulsively early." He smiled as he pulled out her chair. "All those years of having to make the seven eleven."

"Right. I forgot you live in the suburbs. So how is Elaine?"

"*Used* to live in the burbs. We were divorced last year."

"Sorry to hear it," she said.

"Don't be. It's really for the best. Something to drink, Sally?"

She looked up at the waitress who'd materialized on her left. "Just a coffee, Paula. You, Dick?"

He shot her a look. He detested his never used first name, the short version even more. "I'll have a beer. Any microbreweries around here?"

The waitress looked at him blankly.

"Paula," said Sally dryly, "bring the man a Bud."

"So," she said a moment later, "it still bugs you to be called Dick?"

"It's fine—from you."

"How's Elaine holding up? Not that you care."

He leaned forward earnestly. "It wasn't like what happened between us, Sally. She wanted it over too."

"What happened between us! We had a sleazy affair, that's what happened between us. You cheated on your wife and child, and I was an accomplice. And I felt like dirt every second of every day for a year and a half. And then you dumped me!"

She hadn't planned to sound so bitter, but she couldn't help it. The very sight of this guy pushed her buttons.

"Has it occurred to you that people change?" He tried a smile. "Probably even you've changed a little."

"It's the small-town lifestyle—high on fiber, low on b.s."

"The truth is, a lot of people thought you were crazy for leaving. But personally I admired it. It took guts. Who doesn't dream about dropping out?"

"I haven't dropped out. I like what I'm doing."

"I can see." He reached into his jacket pocket and pulled out a rolled-up newspaper—the *Weekly.* "Very impressive. You can't have very much in the way of resources, but it's a nice little publication. Extremely readable."

"Take some copies home with you. I'm sure it'll impress all your pals at the *Herald.*" She shifted the subject. "You said you were up this way on a story. More on this longevity business?"

"I'm visiting some institute in Manchester," he said, "but it's just spinning my wheels. The whole project's been a bust."

"You've come up with nothing?"

"Not unless you count a lot of frauds and wackos making plans for their three hundredth birthdays." He shrugged.

Sally watched as he picked up his beer. She had never seen him so muted. Stripped of his old cockiness, he seemed to have nothing left but self-absorbed earnestness. All at once she couldn't help wonder how she could ever have been so infatuated with this guy.

"I'm in therapy, you know," he was saying now. "I don't want to keep hurting people I care about—the way I hurt you."

"Forget it. Water under the bridge." She paused. "Look, Dick, it's getting late. I'm due at a party."

"I don't want to forget," he said. "I want to make it up to you."

She hesitated. "Actually, there is something I wanted to tell you. I'm keeping my eyes open for some freelance work. Maybe the *Herald* can use a stringer in this area."

She saw a familiar expression on his face, something between concern and calculation. He looked at her intently. "Sally, can I ask you something? Is this because you're trying to start a family?"

Stunned, for several seconds she said nothing. "Just a lucky guess?" she asked finally.

"Call it a semieducated one. I know you. I kind of expected you'd have kids already."

"It's not always that simple."

He seemed to think it over. "You know, Sally, I'm close to some of the top fertility specialists in the country. I'm talking about the most advanced methods not yet available to the public. Some of these people owe me. I'm sure I can arrange it free of charge."

She hesitated. "That's quite an offer."

"It's nothing—just a small favor. I owe you."

"You're wrong as usual. It's a huge favor." Heart pumping, she pushed her chair from the table. "I'll get back to you."

THE party, at the home of Edwardstown High's principal, was in full swing when Sally walked in. Gazing anxiously about, she spotted Mark in the crowded living room. He had never looked so appealing. She made her way to him and took his hand.

"How'd it go with Holland?" he asked apprehensively.

"Fine." Suddenly she reached out, drew him close, and kissed him. "Mark, don't ever let me forget how much I love you."

He looked startled, then smiled. "Go ahead. See the guy as often as you want."

A slow Johnny Mathis song was playing now, the only kind Mark would agree to dance to, and she led him onto the floor.

"We have to talk," she said, holding him tight. "Something came up with Holland. It changes everything."

EDWARDSTOWN High was closed for Christmas vacation when Lisa's VW bug pulled into the parking lot by the school gym. Three boys in letterman jackets were walking from the building.

What caught the boys' attention first were the long legs in calfskin boots and tight jeans emerging from the car. Lisa actually saw one boy elbow another; then she watched, bemused, as they continued to saunter her way, pretending to be oblivious.

"Excuse me, guys," she called anxiously. "Don't tell me I missed the wrestling team's practice."

The oldest of the three, a tall redhead, looked at her curiously. "It just ended. We get out at noon."

"Oh, no. I thought that's when you started." She shook her head miserably. "My editor's gonna kill me. She wants something about, you know, how dedicated you guys are, working so hard during vacation and all."

Awed by so worldly a creature, the redhead had nothing more to say. "Well, good meeting you. Try again tomorrow."

"Yeah," said the second boy. "Good meeting you."

They began moving on.

"Hey, guys?"

They turned.

She hesitated. "As long as I'm here, something else my editor is making me ask about. It's about some cemetery that got robbed a couple of months ago."

"Oh, right. Grace churchyard."

"Who do you think did it?" She looked back at the first kid.

"How would we know?"

"No one had any ideas? People didn't say stuff . . . ?"

The two older boys exchanged a look. "Sorry," said the leader. "I really don't know what to tell you."

Lisa addressed the smallest of the trio. "How about you? What's your name?"

He reddened slightly but answered boldly, "Brian."

"So, Brian, how about you?" she repeated, lowering her voice conspiratorially. "Heard anything?"

"Oh, you know, nothing special. There were some rumors. . . ."

"That's it? Just a few rumors?" She sighed. "Oh, well, I guess a good rumor's better than nothing. You up for a Coke?"

"WHO else have you seen?"

Lynch hesitated, caught off guard by the question's bluntness. He'd been ushered into the presence of the young husband-wife venture-capitalist team of Craig McIntyre and Melissa Reed only a moment before.

"I really can't get into that," he replied, hoping the discretion would be taken as laudable. "A couple of places."

"Cut the crap, Lynch," McIntyre said. "You've been turned down by *all* the heavyweights, so now you come to us."

"That's not why—"

"Right." Melissa Reed spoke up for the first time. "That's what everyone says." In her early thirties, a few years younger than her husband, she exuded the same confidence. In the increasingly timid world of venture capital, these people were known as riverboat gamblers, always on the lookout for the big score.

"I'm here because, from all I've seen and heard, we'd make a good match."

"And what have you seen and heard?"

"You seem to appreciate that there are new ways to look at old questions. You aren't afraid to make things happen. Fast."

"Which of our deals have you so impressed?" asked McIntyre.

Lynch wondered if they were ever going to ask him to sit down. "Applivax, for one. You obviously saw that their work toward an AIDS vaccine was as exciting as it was risky."

"We're interested in profit, Dr. Lynch," Reed said. "We don't mind helping humanity—it's a nice bonus. But that is not our business."

Lynch nodded. "Also Retinex."

The husband and wife exchanged a quick glance. The company, manufacturer of an experimental antiwrinkle cream, was almost completely unknown. Since the product lacked FDA approval, it was being produced in Matamoros, Mexico, and distributed only in Latin America. But for M & R it was a cash cow.

"Won't you have a seat, Dr. Lynch?" said Reed, ushering him toward the chairs arrayed around a coffee table in the corner.

"Retinex," she picked up with amazing aplomb. "I'm glad you brought that up. This gets us right into the area of equity. On risky enterprises like Retinex our percentage of equity runs in the neighborhood of eighty percent or more."

"That's not a problem," Lynch said, then realized that such ready acquiescence might sound naïve.

"What about Clifford Stagg?" said Reed. "Is he prepared to surrender most of his interest in this venture?"

Lynch nodded. "His interest is in the success of this project. He understands we need more financing to see it through."

"How much financing?"

"A minimum of ten million dollars for each of the next four years. I've brought a proposed funding schedule."

"And at the end of that time you expect to have what, exactly?"

"We expect to all but eliminate Alzheimer's disease."

The reaction was not what he had hoped. Both nodded politely.

"Well then," said McIntyre, "why don't you leave whatever material you have for our science people to look over?"

"Actually," Lynch said hurriedly, "I've brought along a brief presentation. May I use the slide projector?" He was already moving toward it, pulling a plastic box of slides from his briefcase. "This will only take a few minutes."

After a moment Reed rose and killed the lights.

Lynch's first slide showed a human chromosome, its deceptively simple appearance—two *u*'s joined at the base. "Let's start with the basics. What you see here is chromosome number twenty-two. It harbors the gene we are in the process of sequencing. Think of it as the infinity gene."

"The infinity gene?" asked McIntyre.

Instantly Lynch regretted his words. "I realize the term has no scientific credibility. It was dreamed up by the popular-science press to describe an entire constellation of genes."

"No, no," McIntyre cut in, waving away the objection. "That's what makes it appealing. It would make it an easier sell."

"I see what you mean."

The next slide he brought up showed an elderly man, rheumy-eyed and enfeebled. "This is what we see with our eyes," he said.

He brought up another slide, the same chromosome as earlier, but this time with a bright red arrow directing the viewer's attention to one of its four tips. "This is what's happening genetically. The tip of the chromosome is literally falling away. Its genetic blueprint is eroding; vital information is being lost. The result is that the surrounding cell becomes vulnerable to toxins and free radicals that earlier it would have easily defended itself against." He looked at McIntyre. "Are you following?"

"More or less."

"Think of the chromosome as a boxer. At twenty he's fast with his fists and able to absorb a punch; by forty, even under ideal circumstances, his reaction time is slower. By eighty, if he's unlucky, the very memory of what he was once capable of is gone." He paused. "But the protein we've discovered has a dramatic impact on the erosion of genetic information. It actually makes the chromosomes of an old cell resemble those of a young cell."

"Don't tell me," guessed McIntyre. "In mice."

Lynch's silence made clear McIntyre had hit on it.

"Isn't it amazing, Melissa, how many of these brilliant ideas end up helping rodents?"

Reed snapped on the lights. "I don't think there's much demand for a product like that—the *opposite* of a better mousetrap."

"In just a matter of months I'll be able to produce evidence that this protein works in human beings."

"Unfortunately, Dr. Lynch," said Reed with finality, "in this business time really is money."

Lynch's eyes moved from one to the other, calculating. "Will you excuse me for just one moment?"

They were still in place, perplexed, when the scientist hurried back into the room. "I'm not saying your skepticism isn't warranted. But I hope I can offer you at least some reassurance. Have you met Paul Holland?"

Lynch held the door open, and Holland walked in. The effect was everything Lynch could have hoped. Instantly the balance of power in the room was changed.

"You're involved in this project?" asked McIntyre, incredulous.

"On an informal basis. You could call me kind of an adviser."

"Dr. Lynch has made some rather spectacular claims today."

"To my mind he's earned that right. I consider this a breakthrough of almost incalculable significance."

The words hung in the air.

"We have a private dining room downstairs," said Reed. "Any chance we could pick your brain over lunch?"

Holland smiled. "My pleasure."

Taking his arm, Reed looked over at Lynch. "I'll alert our science people. I think it's time to start talking business."

THE following Saturday, in the town of Union, ten minutes down Route 11A from Edwardstown, Lisa stood outside Smart's, the only shoe store of any size in the area. The temperature was brutal, just a few degrees above zero. Peering into the well-lit store, she saw there were no customers. Good.

The weather was a lucky break; she'd have come today anyway. Saturday was the manager's day off, and on an earlier visit she had found him uncooperative. In her pocket was the list she and Sally had compiled over the last month, bearing seven names: kids with a history of antisocial behavior and petty mischief. Each name had surfaced three or four times in a conversation struck up with one of their classmates.

Walking in, she smiled at the one employee, a teenage boy behind the counter.

"Hi," he said matter-of-factly. "Can I help you?"

"I need to get my cousin some sneakers for his birthday."

"Do you know his size?"

"I'm not sure, but I'm pretty sure he shops here." She shook off her coat and, tossing it on a chair, joined him at the counter. "His name's Brian Keane." A nice touch, she thought—the kid on the wrestling team, the first who'd named names.

As the clerk punched the name into his computer, Lisa wandered around the counter to join him. "Oh, that's fantastic!"

"Sorry, you're not allowed back here."

"Oh, c'mon." She gave her most winning smile. Already Brian's sales record had appeared. "I'm curious."

"I can't. It's not authorized."

"I just want to see, you know, the kind of thing he likes."

"I am very sorry, miss," he said, summoning up all the adolescent authority he could muster. "I can give you a printout."

Sighing dramatically, she moved to the other side of the counter. In a moment the machine was churning out a page.

"I can see he prefers Nikes," he said, handing it to her.

She scanned it indifferently. "I want to get an idea of what's available," she said. "How about—I don't know—let me see eight or nine pairs? A variety of makes and styles and colors."

"All in his size? It'll take a little time."

"No problem."

He headed toward the storage room, and in seconds she was behind the counter punching in the first name on her list. Robert Baldwin. Almost instantaneously, there he was. She looked first for the shoe size—nine and a half. Then she searched the sales record. No mention of either Air Thrill or Run 'N Slam.

The next was one David Caine. The shoe size was right, and now her eye began moving down the screen.

"Excuse me?"

Startled, she looked up. The manager!

"What do you think you're doing?"

She shrugged and smiled, hitting the button that cleared the screen. "I'm getting a pair of sneakers for my cousin. I was just looking at his record to see—"

"Wait a minute," he cut her off. "You're the one who was in here before, wanting to look at the records."

She edged away from the counter and picked up her coat. "All right, let's forget it."

"I told you before, young lady, these records are private."

"I'm just trying to do my job."

"Your *job?*"

"I'm a reporter. For the Edwardstown *Weekly*. We've been trying to track down who was responsible for that graverobbing at Grace Church."

"I see," he replied, stone-faced. He reached for the phone. "Well, we'll just see about that."

SALLY'S impulse was to be understanding. After all, it took guts, and at that age she might have done the same thing. "The main thing, Lisa," she offered, "is you've learned your lesson."

"And what lesson is that?" she said, all innocence.

"Simple. You're a journalist, not a con artist. It's never a great idea to get caught rifling the files of a local store."

Lisa nodded. "How about if you *don't* get caught?"

The observation stopped Sally short. "No, Lisa," she said firmly. "There are lines you don't cross. Ever."

"I always thought the bottom line was getting the story." Lisa smiled. "I hear lots of big-time editors are ready to overlook almost anything if you do that."

Sally looked at her closely. "I guess you don't see yourself staying here in Edwardstown very long, do you?"

"Would you if you were me? Yes, I'm trying to make a name for myself. What's wrong with that?"

"What kind of name, Lisa? That matters too."

The phone rang, and Sally took the call. After she hung up, Lisa asked, "So what about the story? What do we do next?"

Sally stared at her a moment, incredulous. "Don't you have any idea what's going on? Stebben had to convince that man personally not to press charges. He has us. We're going to let it slide." Though it was a snap decision, Sally knew it was the right one.

"I can work around him, Sally," said the younger woman, shaking her head adamantly. "Let me stay on it."

Sally was startled by the vehemence. She'd seen that look in the eyes of reporters before—not ones she admired. "You want the best advice I can give you? Trust me. No story's worth even a tiny piece of your soul."

But even as she said it, she knew Lisa wasn't listening.

STEPPING into the Delta lounge at Dallas–Fort Worth International Airport after their flight from Boston, Sally and Mark spotted the limo driver with a placard bearing their names.

Mark approached the man. "For the Keller Clinic?"

The driver nodded and reached for their overnight bags. "Would you like to go there directly, or should I take you to your hotel first?"

"We don't have one. We're thinking *motel.*"

"I have you booked at the Royal."

It took a moment for this to sink in. "The clinic, please," said Sally. "Let's just take it from there."

"DON'T misunderstand," said Mark half an hour later at the clinic, "but we really can't accept all this."

"It's no big deal," said Dr. Carl Keller. He leaned forward, his smile somewhere between solicitous and condescending. "I promised Paul Holland you would be provided with the very best—"

"Forget that," Mark cut him off. "This is none of Holland's business." But he caught himself, knowing that in the impossibly awkward situation in which they'd placed themselves, that's exactly what it was. "Thanks, but we'll take care of our own accommodations."

"Mr. Bowman, this will be a long and arduous process. A little comfort at the end of the day can only help your wife's chances."

Mark considered a long moment. "All right," he conceded, "we'll go to the hotel. But we'll pay for it ourselves."

A FLOOR below, Sally was already on an examining table.

"So," she asked the attractive young black woman conducting the examination, "do they give out medical degrees down here in high school?"

Dr. Carson smiled as she slipped on a pair of latex gloves. "I'm twenty-eight. I was blessed with good genes. You should see my mother." She paused. "All set?"

Sally slipped her bare feet into the stirrups. This preliminary exam was the first of countless procedures she'd be undergoing here in the next ten days. This afternoon she'd be passed on to Keller himself, to begin the real work of high-tech baby making.

"Well," said Sally, pretending to be nonchalant, "if it happens, it happens. My mother would say it's God's will."

"Mine too." Funny, thought Carson, there seems to be a slight bluish discoloration to the cervix. Could that be Chadwick's sign? She'd only read about it in texts.

"But that's her way of protecting herself. This is a woman who was *born* to be a grandmother."

"Uh-huh." She began gently palpating the area with thumb and forefinger. No question about it; there was a softening.

Sally caught her shift in tone. "Something wrong?"

"It's nothing to worry about. It's just . . ." The doctor was suddenly on her feet, reaching for the phone. "This is Dr. Carson in examining room B. Could I get Dr. Keller down here?"

"Doctor, please. I have a right to know!"

But when Dr. Carson turned to face her, Sally was surprised to see the look on her pretty face was one of wonderment. "We'll need a sonogram and a blood test. But you seem to be pregnant."

CHAPTER FOUR

"OH, IT'S such wonderful news!" exclaimed Florence Davis as Sally walked through the door her first morning back.

"Thanks," said Sally, taking off her coat. She smiled with genuine pleasure. "It makes us pretty happy too."

"Now, if you ever need a sitter, you'll know who to call?"

"Don't you think it's kind of early for that sort of talk?"

"Oh, no. You have to start planning now, every detail." Florence threw up her hands in dismay. "The time will *fly* by."

Sally could only nod mutely. Why, she couldn't help wonder, had this woman never gotten nearly so excited over anything that had to do with journalism?

"You hoping for a boy or girl?" called out Ed Keeton, the retired insurance salesman who served part-time as the *Weekly*'s business manager.

"Oh, really, Mr. Keeton," Florence answered for her, "every child's a miracle. The important thing is that it's healthy."

Sally held up her hands. "Look, this is great, but we've got a paper to put out. Unfortunately, this doesn't qualify as news."

"Yes, it does," said Florence. "It's the best kind of news."

"Fine, Florence, but it's not *news* news. Nobody—not even the *Weekly*—runs a pregnancy announcement." This time Sally clapped her hands for emphasis. "All right, let's get to work."

Only Lisa, working away at her computer, had remained aloof from the conversation. Now Sally wandered over to her desk. "No congrats from you, Ace Reporter?"

"Sure. I just can't get into all this goo-goo stuff."

"I hear you—I was the same way." She smiled. "Still am. Mark and I have promised ourselves we won't turn into the sort of parents who run around boring people about our kid."

Just then the phone began jangling. Sally snatched it up. "Sally Benedict." She listened a moment. Speechless, she hung up and looked at the younger woman.

"What's going on?"

"That was Father Morse. There's been another graverobbing!"

THIS time two graves had been violated, and there was no question about the identity of either of the missing bodies.

One of the gravesites, out of view in the back, was marked by an eight-foot obelisk in black marble.

CARLTON L. GILES
APRIL 4, 1911–JULY 12, 1944
WITH THE LOVE OF HIS FAMILY AND
THE GRATITUDE OF HIS COUNTRY

The other was to the left, between the church and the rectory. When Sally came to the simple white stone lying faceup next to the desecrated grave, she let out an involuntary gasp.

MARTHA WHITSON AVERY, 1834–1936

Lisa noticed. "Is something wrong?"

"It's Gram's grandmother," she said softly. "My great-great grandmother. I've heard stories about her all my life."

Chief Stebben, standing on the other side of the hole with another officer, spoke up. "Hey, real sorry about that. My condolences. Or whatever."

Sally looked up at him, stung.

"Well, you didn't *know* the woman, did you?"

"The first question, Chief, is why *you* didn't call us."

"Maybe I learned my lesson the last time." He shot Sally a mirthless smile.

"Question two. When do you expect to make an arrest? Or is that the lesson I should learn from last time—never?"

"We're pretty busy just now, so if you'll kindly excuse us . . ."

"Chief Stebben," Lisa said deferentially, "are you at least able to tell us when you first heard about this?"

"Oh, maybe five a.m. Simmons here called me from the night desk."

"You're saying you knew for over five hours and didn't let us know?" demanded Sally.

Stebben flashed the same smile. "Ooops. Sorry."

Sally turned to the other officer. "How did you learn about it?"

"An anonymous phone call," Simmons said. "The guy didn't say who he was. He just laughed and said I better get my ass down to the cemetery. Like it was a big joke or something."

"How old would you say he sounded?"

"Pretty young."

"How young? Teens? Twenties?"

He shrugged. "Coulda been either."

Stebben held up his hand. "Enough."

"Let's get down to cases," said Sally, ignoring him. "Do you have any witnesses? Anything solid at all?"

"I said that's *all,* ladies. This press conference is *over.*"

"What are you afraid of, Chief? That you'll start looking so incompetent, people won't buy your act anymore?"

He stared at her, the color rising in his cheeks, and jerked his thumb toward the front gate. *"Now."*

Forbidding as he was, she momentarily held her ground. "This isn't just professional, Stebben. I've got a family interest here. You're not going to scare me off this case."

"WONDERFUL!" exclaimed Foster, surveying the corpse laid out on the autopsy table before him, illuminated by a fluorescent lamp. "Now here's something we can work with."

"It was the lead-lined coffin," observed Lynch blandly. "It kept out all the moisture."

"Look at her. She might have died yesterday."

This was an exaggeration, of course. The corpse's face was skeletal, the skin chalky white. Still, the evidence of her life, even her personality, was unmistakable. Her silk dress with delicate pearl buttons up the front was of an age even earlier than the one she'd departed, as was her hair, in a turn-of-the-century knot.

"This will answer most of the questions," observed Foster. "Every organ should be intact."

Lynch nodded. "Let's hope it's enough to satisfy them."

In the ten weeks since the meeting with McIntyre and Reed, the scientists had yet to see even the fifty thousand dollars promised as a good-faith gesture. The hitch seemed to be M & R's chief scientific adviser, who evidently had persuaded his bosses to withhold final approval until the scientists produced clear evidence that the protein in which they placed such hope expressed itself in every part of a subject's body. After all, what would be the use of the liver and spleen remaining robust for two hundred years if the heart gave out after seventy-five?

That's why they'd needed this body.

It was only after Foster had unfastened the first three buttons that it became apparent something might be wrong. There was an ugly gash in the upper chest, and it appeared to have been haphazardly closed by heavy black thread.

"Oh, no," said Foster. "No!" When he hastily undid the last four buttons, all doubt was gone.

"Damn it!" Foster slammed his hand down on the edge of the autopsy table. "She willed her body to science!" For, indeed, the crudeness of the job marked it almost beyond question as a medical-school class dissection. "There's nothing useful *left* in there!"

"There's muscle," observed Lynch. "And tendons. And there's the other specimen."

Foster nodded. Initially, the decision to take a second body had been merely to ensure the appearance of randomness should this latest episode prompt closer scrutiny than the first; they'd come to the idea of locating one that might itself have some research value almost as an afterthought.

But Lynch didn't have to say the obvious: it wouldn't have what they needed. Indeed, they'd been drawn to this subject in hopes of finding evidence that the gene was absent.

There was an unaccustomed edge of desperation in Foster's voice as he handed his colleague a scalpel. "Let's make the best of it. Might as well have a look."

"APPARENTLY that other family—the Gileses—were pretty big stuff around here," Lisa said to Sally at the newspaper office.

"Right. The father was a prominent lawyer."

"I guess the question becomes how to track them down."

Sally looked through some papers on her desk and located one that she handed to Lisa. It bore a name and phone number.

"Wilson Giles," she read, then, looking up at Sally, asked, "Who's this, his son?"

Sally nodded. "The guy's obit—the names of survivors included—is right in our files. After that, all it took was two phone calls. To the Veterans Administration and Pittsburgh information." She picked up the receiver. "Would you like to do the honors?"

Lisa shook her head and handed back the slip of paper. "Show me how it's done."

In thirty seconds Sally had Wilson Giles's secretary on the line. "Yes, I understand he's busy," she was saying, "but I think he'll want this brought to his attention. Tell him I'm calling from Edwardstown, New Hampshire. Tell him it's about his father."

"WHAT is it with you, Dick?" asked Sally mock-conspiratorially, leaning across the table in the Clover Patch. "Keeping tabs on me?" This time he'd shown up in town on only a day's notice.

Sally was surprised the lighthearted remark seemed to leave him momentarily stricken. "No, no. I just wanted to tell you in person how happy I am for you."

Sally could only nod and answer in kind. "Well, believe me, I'm plenty grateful to you. Mark too."

"No, it turns out it was nothing at all."

She smiled blandly. "What can I say? We got real lucky."

"But I also came for another reason. I've got news." He took a sip of beer. "I've lined up something for you at the *Herald*. You'll start on the metro desk, doing features."

"The *Herald?* Listen, Dick, this is real flattering, but . . ."

He looked at her closely. "What's the problem? I thought this is what you were looking for."

"I was looking for *freelance* work. And now I don't even want that." She paused, amazed it even had to be said. "I'm having a *baby,* Dick. My life is here. My mother and grandmother. Mark's job. Even my doctor."

"I've taken care of that. I already have you set up with one of the top obstetricians in town. He's a friend of mine."

"I'm happy with my doctor here. He's a friend of *mine.*"

"Look," he pressed, "what kind of money are you making? The *Herald* will start you at ninety-five."

"Sally!"

She looked up, startled. There stood, of all people, Lee Malen, with an attractive young woman at his side.

"Lee!" She knew she was blushing, as if caught in something illicit. "This is an old friend, Paul Holland."

Now it was Malen who was caught short. "Lee Malen," he said, extending a hand. "I practice medicine here in town. This is Jennifer Downs, a colleague of mine."

Sally had never seen the young woman before. Possibly she was a nurse at the hospital—Malen had dated a number of those.

"So," asked Malen, "what brings you to our little burg?"

"Just happened to be in the area," Holland said.

"Well, anything you want to know about the lay of the land, medically or otherwise, I'm the guy. Right, Sal?"

"That's right, Lee."

He and Jennifer began moving away. "See you around, Sal."

Sally watched as they took a table in the corner. "Well, speak of the devil."

"You mean," Holland said with sudden understanding, "*he's* the one who'll be delivering your baby?"

"Right down the street at Edwardstown Community Hospital. Lee's practice—he and his two predecessors—has been serving this community continuously for more than a hundred years."

"That *is* interesting." He looked at Malen a long moment before turning back her way. "So tell me"—he got right back to it—"what's the real problem? Mark doesn't want to move to the big city? Tell him we have high schools in New York too."

The sneering remark was so unexpected it took her an instant to react. Here, out of the blue, was the old Holland—poisonous, wearing his contempt for others like a badge. "You don't have the faintest idea how you sound, do you?" she said in a quiet rage.

The waitress placed the check before Sally, but Holland grabbed it.

"Look," he tried again, "I'm just asking you to think it over."

"That's what I'm telling you. I *have*." She stood up and snatched the check from his grasp. "Don't worry about it, Holland. You've paid back whatever debt you thought you owed me and then some." She turned away. "So good-bye."

AN HOUR and a half later Holland walked into Lee Malen's waiting room and asked to see the doctor.

"He's with a patient," said Barbara Walker, eyeing him curiously. "Would you like to wait?"

He hesitated, then shook his head. Holland withdrew a business card from his wallet. "Just make sure he gets this."

THE sight of a stretch limo on Main Street this glorious late spring afternoon made people literally stop in their tracks.

Moving slowly past the Independence Pharmacy and Seggerman's Hardware, the black Lincoln drew to a stop outside the two-story brick building at 16 Main. Watching from the window of the *Weekly* office, Sally was struck by the sense of command of the man who emerged from the car. Square-jawed and trim in a tailored pin-striped suit, he was a gracefully aging marine poster boy, in his sixties showing no suggestion of tentativeness.

She opened the door before he reached it. "Mr. Giles, I'm Sally Benedict."

He nodded briskly.

"This is Lisa Mitchell, who's also been working on the story."

"I'd appreciate any details you have."

"Of course." Leading the way into her office, she closed the door behind them. Sally motioned him to the folding chair beside her desk and nodded at her associate. "You're on, Lisa."

Lisa took a deep breath. "The police are working on the premise that it was kids on a lark."

"Why?"

"They claim they have some sneaker prints."

"There was a similar incident a while back," noted Sally.

"*Similar?* I'm told exactly the same thing happened recently in the same cemetery and *nothing* came of it." His hard look moved from one to the other. "I intend to see to it these ghouls are found and prosecuted to the full extent of the law."

Sally nodded. "Just so you know, the *Weekly*'s been trying to get the police to move on this from the beginning."

"All right," he said crisply. "What about these high school kids? Are the police doing everything now that can be done?"

"We feel they could still use some encouragement."

Giles fell silent a moment, gazing out the window at Main Street. "I'd like to visit the cemetery now to see the damage for myself."

"DON'T give me that, Mark. You talk about your students all the time. Sometimes I can't get you to shut up."

"Stop it, Sally! I have an obligation to those kids."

"Not to talk with your wife? It's an innocent enough question. What kind of kids are they?"

"You come to me with a list of names and call it innocent?" He reached into the KFC box for another piece of chicken.

"I'm asking off the record."

"Off the record—so now I'm a *source?* Eat your dinner, Sally."

"Some dinner." She cast a disdainful glance at the mashed potatoes, green peas, and lightly cooked carrots on her plate. "Look, Mark, next week's issue of the paper locks tomorrow at noon, which means I've got less than sixteen hours to decide what to do with the information we've got on those kids."

"What information? You have a list."

"A short one." She pulled it from her pocket and tossed it onto the table, facing Mark. "It's a small town, with a very limited vandal population."

"I thought you were refusing to leap to that conclusion."

"Circumstances change. That's a luxury I can't afford now—not with Giles in the picture."

He looked at her meaningfully. "Fairness is a luxury?"

"The story doesn't have to be airtight; a newspaper's not a courtroom. It's fair to report the police have certain unspecified evidence leading them to suspect certain unnamed minors."

"Sally, you're talking about fifteen- and sixteen-year-olds. You shouldn't even *consider* spreading this kind of maliciousness."

"I don't want to hurt them," she said, "but Giles is out of patience. He's talking about a reward to help things along. Twenty thousand for information leading to capture and conviction."

"Good heavens." Mark just shook his head. In a town where so many were hurting, such a thing could provoke an avalanche of unsubstantiated accusations.

He took a deep breath and let his eye wander to the list. "Robert Butler," he said, referring to the first name. "The kid spray-paints a few walls. So what?"

She poked at her food, averting her eyes. "I hear you."

"And this kid—Garry Apgar. I mean, c'mon."

"How about these?" She pointed at the next pair of names, which Lisa had circled and starred: Pete Boyd and Terry Sutter. "I understand there's a lot more history there. Breaking and entering. Joyriding in a car that happened to belong to someone else."

Mark hesitated. "Look, I've gotten to know Terry pretty well. He's got tremendous potential. Just this semester his grades have started to pick up."

"You're telling me with absolute certainty that they're not capable of something like this?"

He dodged the question. "All I'm saying is don't put them in a box. How'd you like it if someone did that to *our* kid?"

This gave her serious pause. "You're a good guy, Mark."

"Yeah, right."

"Learn to take a compliment." She stopped. "We'll hold the story for a week. After that I can't make any promises."

"I REALLY have to wonder if we should be doing this," said Mark. He read aloud from the consent form. " 'Spontaneous abortion. Vaginal bleeding. Injury to the fetus . . .' "

"I understand how it sounds," said Malen, "but amnio's completely routine." He smiled. "You and I both know lawyers for insurance companies write those things."

Sally looked uncertain. "Still, Lee, it makes it sound like they *expect* a calamity."

The doctor gave her shoulder a reassuring squeeze. "Look, Sally," he said, "if there is a problem, it's best to know and prepare for it—medically as well as emotionally."

Fifteen minutes later Sally was on the examining table, Barbara Walker gently swabbing her midsection with antiseptic.

"Easy as pie," she assured Sally. "Never had the slightest problem. The boys"—she nodded at the austere portraits of Malen's predecessors hanging on the wall—"watch our every move."

Sally barely cracked a smile. "Good."

The door opened, and she was startled to see the young woman with whom she'd seen Malen at the Clover Patch.

"If it's okay with you, I've invited our new anesthesiologist, Dr. Downs, to join us," observed Malen.

Mark nodded.

"Okay," said Malen, "let's get going. Sally, watch that monitor over there."

He switched on the ultrasound machine and began slowly moving the transducer over her belly. Shadowy forms materialized on the screen. The head, the body, the hands were all where they were supposed to be; the tiny heart was pumping.

"Look at that!"

Mark squeezed her hand. "Unbelievable."

"I think we might have some other news here," observed Malen. "Unless you want the sex to be a surprise."

Sally and Mark exchanged a look.

"No," said Sally shakily, "go ahead."

"Barbara, would you like to do the honors?"

The nurse grinned. "Hope you guys like pink."

"Really?"

"A girl!" exclaimed Mark, stroking Sally's hair.

"It's what I was hoping for."

The needle used to withdraw the amniotic fluid from her uterus was fearsome—seven inches long and uncommonly thick.

"Me too," said Malen, who, while Sally was distracted, seized the moment to begin inserting it into her abdomen.

SALLY hadn't known what to expect, but it wasn't this. Located on the far north end of a town of white-picket-fence orderliness, Terry Sutter's home was a ramshackle wooden structure badly in need of a paint job. Finding that the bell didn't work, Sally knocked; then, after a few moments, she knocked again. She was just turning to leave when she heard footfalls on the stairs.

She instantly recognized the boy from the photo she'd found in the yearbook. "Hello, Terry, I'm—"

"I know. You're Mrs. Bowman."

She smiled. No one ever called her that. "Right. I was wondering if we could talk?"

He didn't move from the doorway. "What about?"

"A story I'm working on for the *Weekly.* Can I come in?"

"I guess," he said, and reluctantly let her pass.

The carpet in the entryway was badly stained, and Sally noticed empty soda cans and ashtrays full of cigarette butts in the living room off to the left.

"My mom usually doesn't like people coming over without warning," offered Terry.

"No problem. Maybe we should go to your room."

"All right, come on."

The room was in disarray, the bed unmade, clothes spilling out of half-open dresser drawers. But clearly it was a refuge from the drabness of the rest of the house, a showcase for Terry's private passions, the desk piled high with CDs, the walls adorned by weird phantasmagorical drawings he'd done himself.

Sally turned to the fishtank in the corner. It was an unusual one, octagonal in shape and set in a polished oak stand.

"Impressive. How big is that thing?"

"Fifty-five gallons. It's salt water."

"What kind of fish?"

He pointed at a flat one. "That's a clown anemone, from the Indian Ocean. The long ones are green bird fish. Then I've got a few scissor-tail gobies and a couple of zebra fish."

"Wow." She turned to him. "My husband's right. You're an interesting kid, Terry. Tell me, would you like to go to college?"

"I don't know."

"Well, it's up to you. You're plenty bright enough." She took a seat on the unmade bed. "Which gets to what I want to ask you about. I'm wondering if you might have done something that could screw up your life."

Terry showed nothing. "I don't know what you're talking about."

"Really? I have the idea you do."

He shrugged. "You're gonna believe what you want anyhow. People always do."

"Terry, I'm not here to grill you." Reluctantly she rose to her feet. "Maybe something will occur to you. If you want to reach me, I'm at the *Weekly* office."

"I won't."

But by now, as far as Sally was concerned, it almost didn't matter. Already she'd spotted above the bed the drawing of two spectral figures in black capes, arms spread ominously. Beneath, in ornate letters, were the chilling words she'd only recently stumbled upon in an old book in the course of her research: RESURRECTION MEN—otherwise known as grave robbers.

HOLLAND was struck by the change the instant he entered the room. Stagg looked awful—far worse, even, than he'd expected. Propped up on a gurney, his breathing labored, it was as if the mere act of being awake required Herculean effort.

Located in the institute's basement, the room was a standard operating facility of the sort found in a thousand community hospitals: white tile walls, an operating table, tanks of anesthesia, and an EKG machine. Except there was a piece of equipment the reporter had never seen before: a gleaming silver cylinder, approximately five by eight feet, with a variety of dials and gauges in the front.

A space-age coffin.

Stagg spoke up suddenly in a surprisingly strong voice, pointing a bony finger Holland's way. "Who's this?"

Holland started, then realized that in his surgical mask, gown, and cap, there was no way to know. "Paul Holland."

"Ah, good. Now we can get started."

Holland cast a glance at Lynch across the room, alongside Foster and several men in surgical whites—all, presumably, with experience in the procedure.

"Mr. Holland," confirmed Lynch, "this is Dr. Unger and his team. Dr. Unger is director of Cryolabs in Santa Fe, New Mexico."

"Pretty part of the country," was all Holland could think to say. Based on everything he knew, cryonics—the notion that a body could be frozen and later restored to life—was utterly fraudulent.

"I gather you're pretty dubious about this," snapped Stagg.

Behind his mask Holland bit his lip. This was hardly the time or place for such a conversation. "Frankly," he hedged, "I've had to examine a lot of my preconceptions lately."

"Don't b.s. me, Holland. I've read you on the subject." He gave a thin smile. "Relax. Lynch here agrees with you. So does Foster. They think it's a colossal waste of money."

The scientists, looking on, confirmed the assertion by their silence. Money was tight. No matter the rationale, to them the idea of eating up a big chunk of it on an exercise grounded more in hope than hard science was grossly irresponsible.

"We'll need you on the table now, Mr. Stagg," Unger said. "Would you like some help?"

"I can do it."

They watched the old man slowly drag himself from the gurney onto the adjacent operating table.

Five minutes after administration of the anesthetic the old man appeared to be sleeping peacefully, the EKG machine registering a near-normal heartbeat, his breathing shallow but steady.

Having read up on the procedure, Holland knew exactly what he would see. Still, what he witnessed over the next three and a half hours was riveting as, step by step, the vital figure on the table was reduced to a meticulously frozen mass of meat, his heart steadily slowed and finally stopped altogether, his blood drawn out by pumps and replaced by crystalloid solution.

But what left Holland most shaken at the end was the old man's color. As he was lifted onto the gurney and wheeled to the silver cylinder, his rigid face was the startling white of fresh snow.

CHAPTER FIVE

"WHAT is this?" Lisa wanted to know, entering Sally's tiny office. "I thought this was supposed to be *our* story." She waved the pages she'd just retrieved from her computer.

Sally lowered the newspaper she'd been reading and gazed at her blankly. "It's an *editorial,* Lisa. Last time I looked, I was still top editor around here."

Without citing specifics, the piece implied that evidence existed confirming that local teens bore responsibility for the grave-robbings. The tone was sorrowful, but the message was clear: The time had come for the police to make arrests.

"Dammit, Sally, I've been on this for months!"

"If I may say so, Lisa, your concern's a little misplaced. How about saving some for those boys we're doing in?"

"So why are we running it at all? We had this information months ago, but all I kept hearing was, 'Let's not go overboard.' "

"Circumstances change," Sally said. "That was before Wilson Giles and his money were on the scene. And yes, before I got convinced by my visit to Terry's."

Lisa was momentarily silent.

"You really want the credit for this?" Sally asked.

"I only want what I've earned."

"All right," she decided. "We'll make it a *signed* editorial, both of our names. Will that do it for you?"

"Yes, it will," said Lisa, delighted. "Good. Great!"

Sally smiled wistfully. "Just shut the door behind you."

When she was gone, Sally went back to the paper she'd been reading—the national edition of the New York *Herald.* The lead story in the weekly Science section was bylined R. Paul Holland: NEW ENGLAND LAB IN MAJOR DNA GAIN.

Apparently, if the story was to be believed, scientists at the Life Services Institute down in Manchester had located a gene that showed promise of having a dramatic impact on a wide range of age-related maladies. Never, not in life and certainly not in print, had she seen Paul Holland so enthusiastic about anything.

And after he'd expressed such contempt for this place to her.

What, she couldn't help but wonder, was this all about?

IT WAS Father Morse himself, arriving at the church the morning after Independence Day, who found the cadavers. They had been laid out on the patch of grass by the entrance with care, and on this brilliant summer day they looked almost serene. There was no apparent evidence that either had been defiled. Alongside, in a canvas sack, were the much older bones taken from the first grave.

WILSON Giles returned to Edwardstown two days later for the reinterment of his father, this time accompanied by his wife and grown daughter. Among the dozen or so others who joined them at the brief graveside ceremony were Sally and Lisa.

It was as she walked Giles from the cemetery that Sally decided to broach it. "Are you still planning to offer that reward?"

He looked at her in surprise. "Don't you think I should?"

She hesitated. "You'd probably like to be done with all this."

"I would, yes. But I'm afraid I've got obligations beyond my own preferences. My father was a very special man. I'm not sure *he* would understand."

She nodded. "I know what you're saying. I loved my own father just as dearly. But maybe under these circumstances—"

"He was adopted. Did you know that?"

"Actually, no, I didn't," she answered.

"I've always believed that's why he gave so much to his own children. I was nine when he died. Over the years people have been surprised by my devotion to his memory, but I haven't done a thing he wouldn't have done a thousand times over for me."

"Look," ventured Sally, "from the perspective of the paper a reward would be terrific. It would keep the story alive. But it's clear whoever did it already got the message. I'd hate to see a couple of kids' futures ruined by—"

He cut her off. "Miss Benedict, I expect the details of my offer to be reported in full. Twenty thousand dollars for information leading to the arrest and conviction of the social misfits who perpetrated this monstrosity! If your conscience precludes your doing your job properly, I'm prepared to purchase the back page of your newspaper and print those details myself. Now enough of this!"

He stared at her a moment longer, his eyes bright with anger, awaiting a response. When there was none, he strode out the cemetery gate, trailed by his loved ones.

WITHIN SECONDS OF ENTERING Lynch's office, Foster knew who was on the other end of the line. His colleague's body language and deferential tone were a dead giveaway.

"No, no, no, Ms. Reed, we're absolutely on the same page. I understand your concern. I'm just asking you to understand ours. We'd like to close this deal as soon as possible."

Foster slouched into a chair. "Tell her to go screw herself," he said. "Tell her we don't need this now."

This was a considerable understatement. Although the woman on the other end of the line had no way of knowing it, a problem had arisen that overshadowed even the funding crisis. In Edwardstown the entire operation seemed threatened with exposure.

"You should know, Ms. Reed, we've obtained vital new evidence that we're on the right track—a sample of amniotic fluid proving definitively that the family we're tracking—"

As she cut Lynch off, he was reminded that discussing anything but the bottom line with this woman was useless.

A moment later he slammed down the phone. "They're demanding better terms."

Foster laughed mirthlessly. "They're already looking at eighty percent of the company for their lousy twenty-eight million. Why don't we just sign over the whole thing and be done with it?"

"The problem was not getting what we needed from that last cadaver. It gave them an opening."

"Actually," said Foster, "I've been giving that some thought. There's a chance the organs from that specimen still exist. Have you ever visited the specimen room at Bellevue or Cornell? These places have preserved thousands of organ samples, dating back a hundred years. Anything that seemed of potential value."

"You mean because she lived to be so old," Lynch said with sudden understanding.

"I was thinking that if we could locate those samples . . ."

"It's definitely an avenue to pursue," Lynch said.

Foster nodded. "While we continue to pursue others. The immediate priority is this difficulty in Edwardstown."

"YES?" SAID TERRY SUTTER, surprised to find a stranger at his door late on a suffocatingly muggy summer morning.

"I presume you're Terry Sutter?" The man's voice—lilting, almost soothing—was at odds with his powerful appearance.

"Why? What's this about?"

"I've brought a card."

He handed it to him. Terry looked down at a photograph of the old woman from the grave, then, in horror, at the man.

"I thought that might be familiar," he said, brushing past him. "May I come in?"

"What do you want?" demanded Terry, leaving the door open. "Where did you get that?"

He laughed. "Forgive me for that little maneuver. But we do need to talk." He reached out a meaty hand, and reluctantly Terry shook it. "Herman Van Ost. Please close the door."

"Talk about what?" Terry asked.

"About those favors you and your friend did for Chief Stebben. You see, the chief in turn was doing a favor for us. I'm just here to let you know we're aware how much heat you've been getting. More to the point, we appreciate your standing up to it. And shall continue to make it worth your while. To date you've received seventeen hundred dollars, is that correct?"

"Yeah."

"How does an additional fifteen thousand dollars sound?"

"Just for not saying anything?"

"Just to continue as you've been doing."

The boy laughed. "Sure, I could do that."

"Good. My job will be getting it to you. I'd prefer to pass it along in increments. I understand a young man's temptation to spend large sums in one place, but that could arouse suspicion."

"Not me. The only thing I buy is tropical fish."

He nodded, pleased. "An excellent vice. I shared it at your age. Have you any tangs?"

"I just got a pair of powder blues!"

"Wonderful. But be careful. Watch out for lateral-line disease."

"Do you name them?" asked Van Ost a few minutes later, up in Terry's room. "Foolish, I know, but I always did."

"Just the morays. That's Kurt and that's Hootie."

Already the visitor had the gun out. As the boy pointed, he fired directly into his temple from an inch away.

WHEN she arrived at the Sutter home, Sally's defense mechanism was in overdrive. Opening her notebook, she focused on the details. The stricken young people milling about in the front yard, several of them crying. The psychologist dispatched to the scene by the school district. The coroner's car in the driveway.

Stebben stood off to the side, looking, she thought, almost as shaken as some of the kids. When she approached, notebook open, he acknowledged her with a crisp nod, avoiding her eyes.

"Did he leave a note?" she asked after a moment.

"Did he have to?"

"How's the family taking it?"

"Bad. You'll be a mom soon yourself." He nodded at her bulging midsection. "Maybe then you'll understand."

"Cut me some slack, Stebben," she said. "I was as afraid of something like this as you were. You know I tried to get Giles to back off the reward. How long's the coroner been here?"

"About twenty minutes."

"Have you talked to the other boy?"

Stebben snorted. "*You* try and find him."

"What, he took off?"

"As soon as he heard"—he nodded vaguely at the house—"with a change of clothes and all the cash in his mom's bedroom drawer. He left behind a note stating that he and Terry did it, they're sorry, they didn't mean no harm. Just what you'd think."

"I'd like a copy," said Sally. "We want to get the story right."

"I'll have to see about that."

She nodded. "Gotta run, Chief. Time to bug the coroner."

Still on emotional automatic pilot, Sally breezed past Officer Simmons, manning the door, and into the Sutter home. It wasn't until she was climbing the steps toward Terry's room that she realized the depth of her apprehension.

The boy lay faceup in almost the exact center of the room, eyes wide open. There was very little blood, just a small, sticky pool perhaps six inches in diameter by the exit wound. At first glance he might have been daydreaming while listening to music.

But moving closer, she saw a film had settled over his gray eyes. The gun lay a few inches from his right hand.

He was so young!

"When are you due?"

She looked up at the coroner. "Four months."

"We just had our second." He thrust out his hand. "Ed Clarke."

She nodded. "Sally Benedict. I'm with the Edwardstown *Weekly.* Don't let me interrupt you." She stepped back and watched as he took shots of the body from assorted angles.

"I knew Terry," she observed quietly. "He was quite a kid."

"Yes," he replied. "It's a terrible waste. Teen suicide's become a national epidemic—more than five thousand a year."

She glanced idly around the room. Everything was pretty much as before: the clutter on the desk, the array of posters on the wall, including the one that in her mind had so conclusively linked him to the crimes.

"Oh, my God!"

Only just now had she noticed the shards of glass beneath the fishtank in the corner. The bullet had shattered the heat lamp, leaving the tank dark. Even from here she could see a dozen lifeless forms floating on the surface.

"Yes," he noted, "that's very helpful. It establishes angle and bullet track with absolute certitude."

She nodded. "Have you examined his hand? I understand there's sometimes a bruise from the recoil of the weapon."

"Who told you that?"

"A deputy M.E. in Philadelphia."

"Interesting," he said dismissively. "I'll have to remember that."

Sally glanced down at Terry, almost forgotten in the exchange, and felt a sudden sharp sense of shame. "He was a nice kid," she said.

"I'm sure he was." He clapped his hands together. "I'm just about finished here if you are. I'll have the body removed for autopsy."

"I DON'T want you to beat yourself up over this," said Mark as beside him in the car his wife once again lapsed into sober silence. "It's not your fault."

"Of course it's not," she said, surprised. "I was thinking about that fishtank."

"The fishtank?"

"It just seems to me he would've been more careful."

Mark said nothing, but inwardly he shuddered. What now? For almost ten months they'd lived with this damn story.

"I know it's crazy. . . ." She paused. "But the way he felt about those fish, it doesn't make sense."

"Sally," he said, trying to mute his exasperation, "*suicide* is not a rational act! What in the world are you suggesting?"

"I don't know, it's just a . . . feeling."

This time he couldn't stop himself. "There's a cure for that—*thinking.* The boy's dead; let him rest in peace."

Sally bristled. This was the quality in Mark she'd always found most galling, this smug rationality. Worse, lately she'd detected in him something like condescension, as if her interest in the case, waxing and waning as it did in intensity, was little more than a matter of surging hormones. What he couldn't grasp was that she trusted her instincts. Some things were simply beyond logic.

"I checked with an exotic-fish store down in Manchester," she said. "In all, that kid's setup cost more than fifteen hundred bucks. Where would he have gotten that kind of money?"

He slapped his forehead. "You're making my head spin, you know that? And heaven only knows what it's doing to the baby!"

"Don't you dare bring the baby into this!"

They hit a dip in the road, and the nine-year-old Chevy Impala came down hard.

"When are they going to fix that thing?" exclaimed Mark. "I'm writing a letter tonight to the county public works department."

"You do that, hon," she replied dryly. "You tell them how upsetting their dip is to the Bowman baby."

Even Mark had to smile, realizing that on the subject of the baby's well-being, *he* was the one who'd gone overboard. Though she was just barely into her sixth month, he was already carrying in his wallet the phone numbers of a private ambulance service and the hospital's labor, delivery, and emergency rooms.

The moment seemed to clear the air. He reached over for her hand. "All I mean," he said, "is let's not keep going on about Terry's death. That won't do anyone any good."

"I know that," she conceded. "Maybe you're right. I am feeling guilty. . . ."

"Don't," he said firmly. "It's not your fault."

They drove in silence for a while.

Then Sally asked, "Mark, what's an antigen?"

"An antigen?" Mark looked her way. "Why?"

She slipped her hand into the side pocket of her billowy blue shift and produced a folded newspaper clipping. "This is by Paul Holland. He visited a longevity place down in Manchester, but it sounds like he went to Lourdes."

"Ah," he said noncommittally. "Sal, I really don't think you could be objective about Holland even if you wanted to."

"Please, spare me another critique. This place is in our backyard. I think we should look into it. It's not like Holland to turn himself into a shill for anyone."

Mark sighed. "Antigens are simply proteins that help cells function. Since these people are in antiaging research, they're probably working with declining immune function."

"Good. Thanks." She hesitated. "I've put in a request to visit this place. I'd like you to come."

"Are you kidding me? If you need company, take Lisa."

"I intend to, but that just gives us ignorance squared."

He smiled, knowing it was true.

"C'mon, Mark, I don't know a thing about this stuff." She took his hand and placed it on her belly. "Never mind me. You really gonna let your daughter make a fool of herself in front of those scientists?"

"IT'S not right," said Sally. "I shouldn't leave you alone."

"Please, darling, it's fine. I wouldn't say so otherwise."

"Yes, you would."

Mrs. Benedict smiled faintly, realizing it was true. "Anyway, I won't be alone. Lee Malen will be close by."

Sally nodded uneasily. This dilemma had come at her out of nowhere. She had finally convinced her mother to have the gallbladder surgery, and the date had been set for nearly a month. The call from the Life Services Institute came only yesterday.

"It's just that I'm totally at the mercy of their schedule," Sally explained, mostly to persuade herself. "If we miss this opportunity, there's no telling when we'll get another chance."

"Really, darling, all you'd be doing is sitting in the waiting room twiddling your fingers."

"I guess."

"So it's settled. You can drop me off at the hospital in the morning, do what you have to do, and come back afterward. Drink your milk."

"Drink my milk. Mother, no wonder I still feel like a six-year-old around you." But she picked up the glass and raised it to her lips. "Why can't you worry about yourself for once?"

"Because *you're* having the baby. You'll find out yourself—a mother never *stops* being protective." Mrs. Benedict smiled across the kitchen table.

There was a long silence.

"Sally, just in case—you do remember I want my body to go to medical science?"

"Mother!"

"I don't mean anything by it. But it's foolish not to make arrangements ahead of time. This is what we do in our family."

Sally looked away in consternation, then back across the table into her mother's placid eyes. "It's beyond me how you can be so casual about something like that."

"I'm not eager to die, but there's nothing terrifying about it. I saw my father die very peacefully when I was a little girl. I haven't been scared of it since."

"Well, forgive me, but I am." Sally put down her milk. "Mother, can I ask you something? As long as we're on the big questions? Did you ever want to do other things in your life?"

Mrs. Benedict got a wistful look. "I used to regret that I didn't have more children. But you know something? Now even that regret is gone." She beamed, as radiant as Sally had ever seen her. "Now that you're making me a grandmother."

THEY reported to Edwardstown General a little after seven, three and a half hours before the scheduled surgery. Barbara Walker handled the preliminary screening and blood work. She happily bent the rules, allowing Sally inside the examining room.

"How long will she actually be in the operating room?" Sally asked while her mother changed into a hospital gown.

"Oh, no more than an hour and a quarter."

"I might not make it back in time."

"Don't worry about that. She won't miss you. The anesthetic won't wear off for a few hours more." She smiled.

"You know Dr. Crocker pretty well, I suppose?"

"Sure thing. He's real good in there." She paused meaningfully. "So don't you worry about that bedside manner of his."

She might have been reading Sally's mind. At their preliminary meeting the hospital's young chief of general surgery had been curt, answering their questions with little evident empathy.

At a little after eight Sally made for Lee Malen's office. Her friend was at his desk, a steaming coffee cup before him.

"Lee, I'm thinking maybe I shouldn't leave."

"Sally . . ." His tone was one of almost paternal bemusement. "I promise you I'll stay on top of things." He cupped his hands together. "So go do your number on those longevity guys."

OPENING THE DOOR, RAY Lynch showed his surprise. "Well, I didn't expect quite such a crowd."

"I hope that's not a problem," said Sally, who hadn't forewarned him for precisely that reason.

"Not at all. We're always ready to help out the press."

Initially caught short by her call, Lynch and Foster had quickly decided that denying her request for such a visit could only needlessly invite suspicion. Indeed, given its timing, it might actually be turned into an opportunity. "You're Ms. Benedict?"

"Yes. Lisa here works with me, and I asked Mark along to help us out."

"I'm the interpreter," Mark offered. "The science guy." He nodded at Sally. "I'm also married to the editor."

Lynch smiled, ushering them inside. "Very nice. Keeping it in the family, which is obviously about to get larger. Sorry we had to do this on such short notice."

"Don't be silly. We appreciate your making the time."

He nodded. "Well then, I thought we might start at our operational nerve center." He led them to a flight of stairs.

A LITTLE past eleven Mrs. Benedict was wheeled into the hospital's main operating room. Within minutes Dr. Downs was administering sodium pentothal intravenously to induce unconsciousness. She followed this with an injection of the paralyzing agent pancuronium, to relax the muscles during surgery. A mask was fitted to the sleeping woman's face. Throughout the procedure, in addition to oxygen, this would be a conduit for nitrous oxide and isoflurane to keep her resting comfortably.

Now, scrubbed and prepped, Crocker approached the patient, scalpel in hand. He glanced around at the others in the room—the anesthesiologist, a scrub tech, and Barbara Walker, serving as the circulating nurse. Then, with sudden decisiveness, he made a one-inch incision beneath the belly button.

He inserted a miniature camera, affixed to the end of a rod, through the incision. As he began manipulating it, sharp images appeared on a screen over the patient's shoulder—the liver, the large intestine, the gallbladder, all in extreme close-up.

With the camera guiding the surgeon to ensure he avoided vital organs, he now made three more small cuts. Through these he'd be able to introduce and extricate the camera and assorted instruments.

Everything was going beautifully, the very definition of routine. Less than an hour into the procedure Crocker clipped and secured the cystic artery, then the cystic duct. All that remained now was to sever and cauterize the connection with the liver, and the inflamed gallbladder would be ready for removal.

At this moment, in the recovery room, a vial of bupivacaine was being withdrawn into a syringe. A potent local anesthetic, it would almost surely trigger arrhythmia, leading to cardiac arrest.

The bags of normal saline solution, essential to the maintenance of fluids during the operative and immediate postoperative stages, were kept in a plastic container on a shelf near the bed. It was a simple enough matter, using the "port" at the lower left, to inject the colorless liquid directly into the top bag.

LYNCH led them into a sprawling second-floor lab. Arrayed before them in the center of the room were a pair of machines so intimidatingly complex, Sally was left speechless.

"This is the heart and soul of our operation," said Lynch, smiling. "We're especially proud of our high-pressure liquid-chromatography unit." He nodded at the eight-foot column rising out of the floor. "The design is unique. We're able to isolate the protein fragments we're after with complete precision."

"What about this other one? What does it do?" Mark asked.

"This spectrophotometer determines which wavelengths of light are absorbed by an object and in what quantity."

"Any way you could put that into English?" asked Sally.

"Basically, it reads colors. We use dyes to help us to identify DNA components that wouldn't otherwise be visible."

Assigned the task of taking notes, Lisa piped up, "Should I be writing this down?"

"Go ahead." Lynch smiled at the attractive young woman.

"I'd love to see this machine in action," observed Sally.

"Sure, why not?" Lynch spotted a beer bottle on the desk, then smiled at Lisa. "This part is definitely *off* the record—beer in the lab is a no-no." He poured the dregs into a beaker. "Now, here we have five cc of beer. It's yellow, right? What the spectrophotometer will tell us is *how* yellow. Watch. . . ."

Already Lisa's interest was flagging. Alert for something, anything, that might prove of interest, she allowed her eyes to casually wander from the messy desktop to the bulletin board above it and back again. No good. Everything was in the indecipherable foreign language of advanced scientific calculation.

But now she spotted something scrawled on a yellow legal pad—what appeared to be a list of phone numbers. Immediately one of them leaped out at her. Chief Stebben's office number! It was at the very bottom, accompanied by a notation—"Ck. locally."

Excited but apprehensive, Lisa looked up quickly. Lynch was still busy with his demonstration. "Now look what happens when I place this cuvette in the spectrophotometer."

Hurriedly she began copying the numbers.

There were nine in all. She'd gotten down five when Lynch pushed the START button and the machine started to grind like a kitchen disposal unit. "Now come closer, all of you. Watch what happens to the light spectrum on the screen."

Flipping the page of her notebook, Lisa joined the others.

SALLY didn't make it back to the hospital until past three thirty. As soon as she stepped off the second-floor elevator, she spotted Jennifer Downs heading briskly down the hall.

"Dr. Downs," she called, and the anesthesiologist turned.

"The operation went well? Everything's all right?"

Dr. Downs seemed to hesitate, then nodded. "But you should talk to the surgeon," she said, and continued on her way.

Sally stood there a moment, confused and suddenly uncertain, then heard a familiar voice. "Just get back?"

"She's okay?" she asked, wheeling to face Barbara Walker.

"Perfect. She came through like gangbusters. C'mon. She's still in the recovery room."

"Jeez," muttered Sally as they moved down the hall, "why couldn't Dr. Downs just tell me that?"

Mrs. Benedict lay in bed in the dimly lit room, sleeping peacefully. The only evidence of what she'd just been through was the IV pole hanging over the bed. Sally approached, leaned close, and whispered, "Mother, I'm here."

Mrs. Benedict's eyes fluttered open, and she smiled broadly. "Sally." Then, "I'm so tired," and her eyes closed again.

"You get some sleep now, Mother. I'll be here."

Sally asked the nurse, "I can wait in here with her?"

"Sure. But she might not come to for a while. Just put this on." She offered her a mask from a tray.

"No problem." Sally patted the bag that held her portable computer. "I've got work to do anyway."

As the nurse headed from the room, she glanced up at the bag hanging from the IV pole and noted it was still a third full. "Just ring me when she starts to wake up. She might be in some pain."

Over the next couple of hours Sally managed what would have been a full day's work at the office: editing two pieces and getting six hundred words into a draft on the Life Services Institute.

By the time Mrs. Benedict awoke, the room was getting dark.

"Mother?"

"Sally . . ." she said groggily. "What time is it?"

Sally glanced at her watch. "A quarter of eight. You had a nice long sleep." She kissed her mother on the forehead. "I'll call the nurse. I think she'll give you something to ease the pain."

"That would be nice."

From her mother this was like a primal scream for help.

"So you finally decided to wake up for us," said Nurse Walker, breezing into the room a moment later. She set up a morphine drip on the IV pole, then noticed that the bag of normal saline solution was nearly empty. Plucking up a fresh one from on the shelf, she put that in place first. "Say, miss," she said to Sally, "how long's it been since you ate?"

"A while," she answered vaguely.

"You haven't eaten?" asked her mother with alarm. "Go right now. I won't be able to relax until you do."

Down in the cafeteria, Sally was surprised by the quality of the roast chicken and peas. After a long, anxiety-filled day the interlude was unexpectedly soothing. That could be why, picking at a plate of Jell-O half an hour later, she failed to immediately react when the words came over the loudspeaker: "Emergency team, recovery room—stat! Emergency team, recovery room—stat!"

Only when some doctors across the way leaped to their feet and ran from the room did the realization hit, and then with chilling clarity. She was actually aware of her heart starting to pound as she lurched out the door after them.

CHAPTER SIX

I DON'T know what to say to you, Sally," said Lee Malen. "I don't have the words."

She looked at her friend, outwardly even more shaken than she. Though it had been more than an hour, she hadn't yet cried. Partly it was her innate stoicism, partly her reporter's training. But she also realized that it could be shock.

Arriving on the heels of the emergency team, standing in the doorway as they'd worked frantically over her mother's prostrate form, she'd kept her eyes on the EKG monitor over the bed. Flat line. They were unable to even momentarily reclaim a heartbeat.

"Give me *something,* Lee," she said with intensity. "What do you normally say? How do you help people through it?"

"I tell them not to be afraid to grieve. But I can't pretend this is a normal situation, Sally. I loved her too."

"What about when it happens this way? So unexpectedly? Because I *need* an explanation. I need to know it wasn't a matter of complete randomness." She hesitated. "Or negligence."

"Sally, honey, a woman this age . . ." His voice momentarily trailed off. "She'd just undergone major surgery. It could've been any number of things."

"*What* things? Give me the possibilities!"

"A pulmonary embolism—that's the most likely explanation. Or a stroke. Cardiac arrhythmia's a possibility. She'd been unhooked from the EKG, so that wouldn't have been picked up."

"You're saying this had nothing to do with the operation?"

"The only way to know for sure is if there's an autopsy."

"If?"

"That's your call, Sally. Your mother made quite a point of wishing to donate her organs. You can't have it both ways."

This hadn't occurred to her. "I'll need to discuss it with Mark." She hesitated and suddenly was choking back emotion. "I haven't been able to reach him. He doesn't even know."

Malen took her hands in his. "Unfortunately, you need to decide quickly. Organs for transplant are highly perishable."

She looked at him imploringly.

"You want to know what I would do?"

She nodded. "Please . . ."

"I don't think the details of how it happened would be very important to her; helping others would be."

She looked at him, reassured.

"You know what else? She'd tell us it was God's will."

"Thanks, Lee." She paused only momentarily. "What's the procedure? Are there papers I have to sign?"

OVER two hundred people showed up at the Wednesday morning memorial service in Grace Church—almost everyone, Sally began to think, who had known Helen Benedict. No fewer than a dozen approached her with stories about something her mother had once done for them. Many others wept openly.

Father Morse was never better. Speaking without notes, the very size of the throng lending his words weight, he drew a contrast between this woman's impact on others and that of individuals who, in a status-obsessed culture, are so much more widely celebrated. "When we search for the definition of a successful life," he said softly as Sally's own tears at last began to well, "God help any of us who look to Hollywood or Wall Street or Washington before we think of the woman we honor today."

"YOU okay, Gram?" asked Sally in the back seat of the Impala as they pulled away from the church.

"It was very nice," came the even reply.

"There have been too many terrible events lately," said Sally, looking back toward the cemetery. "Grandmother Avery, Mr. Giles, now Mother."

"Our relations. Our loved ones. . . ."

Sally took the old woman's hand. She couldn't help but worry. Since the tragedy she'd been more disoriented than ever. Sally looked into her watery blue eyes, trying to get her to focus. "Gram, Mark and I would like you to stay with us. In our home."

For a long moment her grandmother continued to stare straight ahead, and Sally wasn't sure she understood.

"Stay with you?" she asked finally.

"Permanently. We'd like that very very much."

Sally was motivated by more than just a sense of obligation. She needed this frail, ninety-two-year-old woman at least as much as the other way around. She was all the family she had left.

"I'll have to think about it," she said, suddenly all there. "I'm a big bother, you know."

"No, you're not." Sally smiled. "Just a small bother."

"I can still take care of myself."

"Gram, I'd like the baby to know you. It's important to me."

"To both of us," Mark spoke up from behind the wheel.

The old woman considered for only a moment. "All right," she decided, and turned to stare out the window.

THE task was more draining than any Foster had ever undertaken—six days of highly technical, demandingly precise grunt work. But finally, by the end, he had what they'd so avidly sought for so long: a skin sample from this latest specimen had yielded the elusive gene's complete sequence, all 4627 letters.

He and Lynch actually allowed themselves a celebratory hour or so, quietly sharing a split of champagne.

But in less than a day that moment of exultation was forgotten, for they discovered that this sample would not yield the other equally vital data they had fully expected: that which would establish that the wondrous protein was active throughout the body.

Bent over the light table, Foster could only stare helplessly at the X ray that told the baffling story.

"It just can't be," said Lynch disconsolately. "We *know* she's got the ability to produce it. Maybe if we run the test again—"

"That's not the problem," snapped Foster. "I've run it half a dozen times already. How long had the subject been dead before we started?"

"She died at about eight thirty in the evening."

"And we didn't get the body till after three in the morning. So these samples were obtained more than six hours postmortem. Think about it, Lynch. Some human proteins are so unstable they break down almost immediately. In less than an hour."

Lynch looked at him hopefully. "You think so?"

"There's only one way to know for sure. How close are we now?"

"Mid-December," Lynch said.

"Talk to our friends on the scene. Maybe we can even help nature expedite the process."

LEE Malen had been in Boston innumerable times, of course, but he'd been in the city's best hotel, the Ritz-Carlton, only once before, and then just for lunch.

Now, wandering through the lobby, all understated elegance, he felt a sudden wistfulness. Though practicing in Edwardstown had its compensations, at certain moments they were easy to forget. He was painfully aware that had he chosen a career in Boston or New York, he'd be a regular at places like this.

He walked to the elevator and rose in silence to the club level on the sixteenth floor. Up here the view of the Commons had to be spectacular. When he knocked, the door swung open immediately.

Extending his hand, Paul Holland smiled. "Right on time. I always appreciate that in a colleague."

FOR nearly six months Sally had made almost no allowances for her condition. She maintained her normal pace, ignoring the morning sickness and creeping fatigue.

But no more, not after all she'd endured lately. For the first time in her life she found herself constantly beat. Owed vacation time, she cut back her office hours to deal with the painful task most immediately at hand: clearing out her mother's home.

A week into the process she maneuvered herself to the top of a stepladder, holding tight to the adjacent bookshelf for support.

"Lucky Mark's not here to see this," she called down to her grandmother, in an armchair across the room. "I hate to see a grown man in hysterics."

"Do be careful, Sally."

She began moving books from the uppermost shelf.

"Hey, look at that." Lying flat on its side was the family Bible. "I haven't seen this since I was a little girl." Gingerly she lifted it—more than a foot across and eighteen inches high, a good four inches thick—and began carefully climbing down.

"It was probably the only spot Mother had where it fit," she mused, moving beside the old woman. "Want to look with me, Gram?"

"Not right now. I'm a little tired. I'll just take my nap now."

As her grandmother got to her feet and shuffled from the room, Sally took her place in the chair and flicked on a reading light.

The volume gave off a musty odor. After studying its black leather cover, Sally carefully opened it. The notations began on the first flyleaf and continued, roughly in chronological order, over the three pages that followed: a record of individuals long gone and otherwise forgotten. Her forebears.

"John Willson," read the very first entry, in a neat, highly formal hand. "Arrived Upon this Earth in Mildenhall Parish, Suffolk, England, 20 May, 1637. Gone to his Glory this Fourth Day of November, 1726, in Edwardstown Village. Amiable, Obliging, and Affectionate. Now he Dwells with Kindred Souls."

Sally had heard of John Willson, of course: her first ancestor in the New World.

Sarah Willson was next. "She Departed this Life on the Ninth Day of August, 1731, olde and full of Dayes."

Now the name Willson disappeared. Only one of John and Sarah's five children—a daughter, Sally, her long-ago namesake—had survived to adulthood. She wed a certain William Hubbard. This was the surname listed most frequently over the next century.

Sally and William also lost most of their children early. These were listed together, without comment.

Jonathan, 1689
Abigail, 1693
Silence and Submit, 1699

Reading down the grim list gave Sally the creeps. She flipped forward and read of an ancestor who'd taken part in the French and Indian War, then ahead to one whose fierce commitment to the antislavery cause had helped make Edwardstown a way station along the underground railroad, then on to her great-great-aunt Susan McKinney, a leading suffragist. The last listing in the book was dated 1936. Her great-great-grandmother, Martha W. Avery.

Sally took a deep breath and sat back in the chair. It would be her job, once she was up to it, to enter the deaths of her parents.

She flipped back to the list of lost children. Immediately following was the entry for their mother.

> Sally Hubbard. November 25, 1654–July 12, 1753 Called to glory in her 100th year. Her Troubles done, She rests in the Farthest corner of our new Churchyard, Gazing for Eternity Upon the Vestry Door.

Sally stared at it, the wheels beginning to turn, rereading the words "the Farthest corner of our new Churchyard." No question the churchyard mentioned was Grace Church; the timing left little room for doubt. And the first pilfered grave was indeed only a short distance from the vestry door. But the farthest corner of the yard? Not a chance. The cemetery extended a good half acre beyond.

Still, before closing the Bible, Sally copied down the entry on a yellow legal pad. She knew herself too well to expect she'd simply leave it at that.

"ALBANY Union Medical College, department of anatomy. To whom may I direct your call?"

Hunched over her desk, Lisa hesitated. She'd had no idea what she'd find on the other end of the line when she dialed the number, the first on the list she'd run across at the Life Services Institute. All she had at this point were intriguing questions: What on earth was the telephone number of Edwardstown's police chief doing in the research laboratory in Manchester? What was the meaning of the cryptic notation that followed?

"I don't have a specific name," she told the operator with calculated chagrin. "I'm with the Life Services Institute in Manchester, New Hampshire . . . ?" She waited an instant, but the name elicited no response. "I'm supposed to get some figures for a colleague who left me your number but neglected to leave a name."

"I'd be unable to direct your call without more information."

Already the young reporter was mentally moving on, eyeing the next number on her list. "I'll get back to you with that."

Department of anatomy. It was a start, even if it didn't obviously compute. Where was the connection with Stebben?

The next area code listed was 718.

"Albert Einstein College of Medicine."

"Give me the department of anatomy."

"Anatomy, Dr. Seidenstein's office."

"I'm with the Life Services Institute. Is he in?"

"No, *she* is not in."

"Actually, I'm just trying to get some information—"

Lisa heard the click before she could complete the sentence. She punched in the next number on her list.

"Yep," answered a youngish male voice after a single ring.

"Is this 212 555-3670?"

"Who wants to know?"

"My name is Lisa Mitchell. I'm trying to reach the department of anatomy."

"You got it, Lisa Mitchell. What can I do for you?"

"And you are?"

"Barry Schneider."

"You're a doctor?"

"That's what my mother likes to tell people. Why, you looking to meet one?"

"Depends," she replied. "I'm twenty-two. How old are you?"

"Twenty-eight. Free for a drink later?"

They both laughed.

"I'm afraid it'll have to be *much* later—I'm three hundred and fifty miles away."

"Oh?" He actually sounded disappointed. "Where's that?"

"Edwardstown, New Hampshire. I'm with a newspaper here. Mind if I ask you something?"

"Shoot."

"What's your connection with the Life Services Institute?"

"With *what?*"

"It's an antiaging research center in Manchester. I'm working on a story. Your number's on a list they've got over there."

"Really?" He paused, intrigued. "Who else is on it?"

"As far as I can tell, it's all medical schools. Departments of anatomy."

"I can't see that anything we're doing would interest anyone in that field."

"How long have you been working there?"

"Here?"

"Right."

He paused. "You don't have any idea *where* I am, do you Lisa Mitchell? You're just winging it, aren't you?"

She smiled. "Hey, sometimes a girl gets lucky."

"I'm at Columbia Presbyterian. We're affiliated with Columbia University."

"Doing what, exactly?"

"There are four of us junior guys in the department who pretty much run the first-year anatomy curriculum. We prepare lectures. Then there's the standard first-year course in gross dissection. I get to do lots of cutting." He laughed. "Of course, I'm also the guy that gets stuck with shipping and handling of the merchandise."

"The dead bodies?"

"Please, *specimens.*"

She jotted this down on a notepad. "What a topic for our first phone date, Dr. Schneider," she said with a laugh.

"Barry. Is that what we're having here, a date?"

"Thanks, Barry. You've really helped me out."

"That's it? We're done?"

"Who knows?" she said coyly. "I might call again."

SALLY'S checkup was every second Tuesday morning at eleven thirty, and she and Malen had turned it into a quasi-social occasion. After he gave her the standard good news—both kid and mom growing normally—they had lunch at the Clover Patch, and after that she sometimes accompanied him back to the office and hung out, reading magazines in his study, so they could chat between patients.

"So," he asked today, "settled on a name yet?"

"Helen. After Mother."

"I was hoping you would!"

"Good, Lee," she joked, genuinely touched. "That was our main consideration." She paused. "I shouldn't tell you this, but you're running pretty strong in the godfather sweepstakes."

Yet just a few minutes later, alone in his study, with *McCall's* open on her lap, she was intensely sober as her thoughts wandered once again to the mysteries of her family's past.

She'd already spent an hour one afternoon wandering around the graveyard trying to pinpoint Sally Hubbard's grave. And just last night she'd had a long talk on the phone with Aunt Mary down in St. Petersburg. As she'd expected, Mary, a genealogy buff on her father's side, had little to add to what Sally already knew of the Hubbard-Avery clan. But toward the end, when Sally casually raised Carlton Giles, expecting her aunt to dismiss out of hand Gram's curious remark after her daughter's memorial service about some kind of family link, there came instead from the other end of the line a long silence. "Yes," Mary said, "I seem to recall something about that. Just a rumor, of course. . . ."

"About his being adopted?"

"About that suffragette great-aunt of your mom's *giving up* a baby."

Now, in Malen's study, it struck her that the proof might be right in front of her. A few years back Malen had shown her the appointment books of his long-ago predecessor, Everett Greiner—a virtually complete record of his nearly forty years serving the Edwardstown area. Leather bound in several volumes, they were in the antique book cabinet just across the room.

In with a patient, Malen would probably be a while. She knew he kept the key to the cabinet in his desk. Surely he wouldn't mind; it would only take a moment. The record was chronological, and she needed to check out only a single date: April 4, 1911—according to Carlton Giles's gravestone, the day he came into the world.

In fact, struggling up from the soft leather couch was more difficult than locating what she wanted—the volume covering 1905–1914. Placing it on the desk, she flipped it open and in seconds found the date in question—the Saturday before Easter.

Nothing. No entry for the day at all. He evidently took it off.

She was about to replace the book when something occurred to her. Back then records tended to be spotty. It was possible that the date of Giles's adoption could have been recorded as his birth date; or even, lacking formal documentation, that someone had simply assigned him a birth date arbitrarily.

To provide for such a possibility, she opened the book to the start of 1911. Most entries listed the names of the parents, the newborn's sex and weight, and a few particulars about the labor or birth. Clearly some of the tales recorded in this emotionless shorthand had been tragic; a number of others made her smile.

But suddenly there it was, or at least *seemed* to be. March 4—a month to the day before the official birth date.

> 4 Mar, '11: Mother: Miss M. Father: unknown. Called to family home appx. 7:30 p.m., Miss M. in E-twn. for confinement. Difficult labor. Healthy boy, 6-14

The evidence was sketchy, but she had no doubt it was Susan McKinney, the suffragist who left Edwardstown for New York. Her great-great aunt. And that baby was Giles!

By the time Malen returned, the book was back in the locked case. Her friend was in good spirits, and the banter between them was as lively as ever, but something—she didn't know what exactly—kept her silent about her discovery. Or maybe she did know and couldn't yet face it: After all that had happened these last months, she was no longer sure she could fully trust *anyone.*

LISA remembered that Tuesday was Stebben's day off. She found the chief in his garden, still gaudy this warm fall day with goldenrod, New England asters, and immense sunflowers.

"Beautiful," she said, coming up behind him.

He turned. "I try. Nice thing about flowers, they never talk back. What can I do you for, little girl?"

She looked at the ground, more nervous than she let on. "What can you tell me about the Life Services Institute?"

He visibly flinched. "The *what?*"

"It's a research place downstate," she said breezily, emboldened by his reaction. "They seemed to know about you."

"Never heard of it."

She showed confused consternation. "Funny, your name was on a list. With your phone number. And the words 'check locally.' What do you suppose that could mean?"

"I can't help you," he said, turning away to examine a cluster of pale blue phlox.

He remembered the call vividly, of course. Lynch had wanted to know if there might be some information somewhere about where old Mrs. Avery's body had been shipped back in the '30s. *How the hell would I know something like that?* he'd told him. *This wasn't part of the deal! You've gotten your stiffs and that should be that!* If he'd come off as harsh, he wasn't sorry. He was still reeling from the death of that poor boy and the disappearance of the boy's friend.

Lisa walked around a huge sunflower to face Stebben. "I was wondering if maybe they had some questions about Sally and me."

"I don't know who they are, and they sure didn't call me. And if they did, I'd have nothing to tell 'em."

She stood there a long moment, not knowing what to say next. "Well then, I guess I'll just have to keep digging."

SALLY had planned to wait till after the birth before making a trip to the county bureau of records, hoping to find more information about her family's history. But after her discovery in Malen's office she felt a new sense of urgency. She made the trip just two days later.

The elderly woman behind the counter seemed delighted to hear that Sally was seeking information on the early days of Grace Church in Edwardstown. She led Sally down a flight of steps and through several aisles. "Now then," the woman said, "this is the general area to begin looking." She indicated the bound volumes, on the shelves in no apparent order. "Fortunately, we were able to transfer many of our records to microfilm." She indicated some filing cabinets. "Do you know how to use microfilm, dear?"

Only since she was eight years old. "Yes, I do, thanks."

Starting with a reel labeled SUSSEX COUNTY, 1670–1700, Sally quickly saw there was little order to the microfilmed material either. A 1693 marriage certificate followed a document recording an unrelated death four years earlier. Then there was a bill of sale for a small farm and the particulars of a lawsuit.

Still, slowly spooling through the reel, Sally found herself transfixed, transported into the daily doings of that lost world. For much of the afternoon she indulged her curiosity, discovering a trove of engaging, amusing, or unexpectedly moving material.

Several times she was caught by surprise at the appearance of one of her own ancestors. According to a bill of sale dated April 17, 1697, John Willson purchased "one milk cowe with the belle on" for three pounds eight shillings. A two-line note to a magistrate recorded the deaths of Silence and Submit Hubbard, and with a shudder Sally grasped that the twins had not been stillborn after all. They died at two, one day apart, of "the pox."

As the day started to slip away, she picked up her pace, now giving most documents only a cursory glance. Suddenly she stopped. On the screen was a bill of sale dated June 7, 1774.

> David Morse, Esq. of Edwardstown, New Hampshire, hereby grants to Grace Episcopal Church of Edwardstown, New Hampshire, in consideration of the sum of Sixty-Seven Pounds, title and rights to the North Meadow of His Farm, said Meadow lying adjacent to the Existing Churchyard. By a survey conducted by Abner Moore, the meadow commences at the stone wall at the edge of the churchyard and runs east 1,120 feet to a Stream, angles north along the Contours of said Stream, and back toward the existing churchyard alongside the property of Mr. John Clark.

Sally read it over twice. This was not a full answer—the land described was on the north side of the church, and it was the south side that interested her. Still, its implications were unmistakable. The original graveyard had been considerably smaller. By this purchase and others, it had *expanded.* Did another bill of sale exist for property on the other side?

But instead, ten minutes later, she found something else: a surveyor's rendering of the original Grace Church property, executed at the time of its purchase in 1738.

Over the past nine months she had walked the cemetery a dozen times, most recently just a few days ago. From the accompanying map she immediately saw how dramatically the cemetery's very shape had changed.

In her notebook she set down the original dimensions. Tomorrow she would again walk the yard, just to be sure. But turning back to the map, she no longer doubted. The first grave violated had indeed once been on the periphery of the yard.

It belonged to her own namesake, Sally Hubbard.

SALLY awoke to find Mark before the bedroom mirror, tying his tie. "Hi," she said groggily. "What time is it?"

"Late—seven twenty. You okay?"

"Just really tired. I'm *so* ready for this to be over."

He grinned. "I wasn't talking to you." He moved to the bed, kissed her forehead, then addressed her belly. "I was talking to *you,* little one. Are *you* okay this morning?"

Sally laughed. "It's like she's the CEO of my body—others do the work; she gets the attention."

"Getting all set to meet Mom and Pop?"

"Enough, Mark. Time to talk grown-up. What've you got going today?"

"Big day—proposals for science-fair projects are due. What about you? Planning a trip back to your place of business?"

"The *Weekly?*" she asked, confused. "Of course."

He grinned. "I meant the cemetery, actually."

"*Not* funny," she said. Every time she tried to talk to him about any of this, the put-downs started flying.

"In poor taste maybe," he said, "but *definitely* funny. Better dress warm. It's supposed to go down to forty today."

WALKING THROUGH THE FRONT door that evening, Mark dropped his briefcase with a bang and flung his coat onto a chair.

"How you doing?" he said to his wife, who was lying on the living-room couch.

"Okay. You?"

"Lousy. I just saw the first batch of proposals for science-fair projects. Not a winner in the bunch. I'm telling you, we could really be embarrassed this year."

He sat down across from her. "I mean, one student actually proposed something on *astrology.* If I teach them nothing else, I want them to learn respect for the scientific process."

Through it all Sally lay there, her arm flung over her face. "You mean respect for logic, don't you?" she said.

Instantly she had his full attention, and he snapped back to this morning's conversation. Only now did he notice the album of vintage family photographs lying open on the floor alongside the couch. "Sally, what is it?"

She didn't reply.

"Please, talk to me."

"You're just going to tell me I'm crazy again," she said.

"You know I don't mean it that way, Sal. I'm just kidding around." He stroked her hair. "Why don't you run through this theory of yours one more time. You were going through the entries in the Bible, and it seems like there's a pattern . . . ?"

She struggled up to a sitting position. "There *is* a pattern. Every other generation lives an incredibly long time. At least a hundred years. That's possible, isn't it? Scientifically, I mean?"

"I suppose it could be genetically programmed," he allowed. "Certain diseases skip a generation. Hemophilia, for instance."

"So it *is* possible?"

"Tell me," he said, trying hard not to sound dismissive, "how large a sample are you basing this on?"

"There're thirteen generations listed."

"That means—since you're taking only every other one—you're dealing with six or seven that are supposedly long-lived?"

"Seven." She hesitated. "Only there are a couple of holes along the way. Two people didn't live out their natural life-spans. One—Josiah Hubbard—died in the Revolutionary War before he was thirty. His granddaughter Priscilla Avery was killed in a carriage accident in her early forties."

"So we're down to *five?*" he said, trying to keep his voice neutral. "Sally, what you've found is interesting, but—please don't take this the wrong way—statistically it's meaningless."

"That's why I need to get more information. I want to find out if the pattern goes back before the family's arrival in America—back to England."

"You'd need, minimum, another six or seven examples. Records probably don't even go back that far."

"There's something else." She hesitated. "Remember what Gram said after Mother's service about Giles being a relative of ours? We *know* Giles was adopted; his own son told me so."

"Sally, you know Gram's in no condition to—"

"I found some old birth records at Malen's. There was a child born out of wedlock around the right date, and there have always been rumors about old Susan McKinney, the suffragist, giving up a child for adoption."

He took a moment before replying. "You're speculating. You're taking fact A and simply assuming it leads to fact B."

"Stop it," she snapped. "I'm not some kid with a science-fair proposal. You want facts? At least two of the bodies taken were in that line of relatives. Maybe even all three."

"And so? That leads you to what conclusion, exactly?"

"I don't *know!* I'm not saying it's rational." She looked into his eyes beseechingly. "But I just keep thinking my mother was in that line. And so's our baby."

"COME into my office," Sally said to Lisa first thing Monday morning. "There's something we have to discuss."

Closing the door behind her, Sally motioned Lisa into the folding chair alongside her desk but remained standing herself.

"Lisa . . ." She stopped, started again. "You know, we're coming up on the anniversary of the first graverobbing. It was Halloween, remember? The night of our party."

"I remember."

"No party this year. I'm just not up to it."

Lisa nodded, waiting.

"I'm thinking we should look at the case again."

"What?"

"I don't like the idea," added Sally quickly. "It's been a nightmare. I think about that poor boy, and I can't help but feel responsible. But I've also run across some new information. It's— I don't know. Mark thinks its meaningless."

"What kind of information?"

She took a deep breath. "I think all three bodies in those graves were relatives of mine."

"All *three?*"

Sally explained about her visit to the bureau of records and her growing suspicions about Giles. She paused, uncertain. "Or maybe I'm just crazy. Tell me honestly, what do you think?"

Lisa hesitated. In fact, what she was thinking was how this might fit in with what *she* had—and how, given half a chance, her boss would again steal the show.

"Honestly? I think your husband's right. The case is *solved;* it's over. It'd be a huge mistake to turn this personal. It would look like some kind of vendetta." Always a lousy liar, Lisa stood and turned to gaze out the window.

Behind her Sally nodded, suddenly feeling foolish for having raised it at all. "You're probably right."

"Anyway, we're too busy. With you in and out it's been hard enough just getting out the paper." Turning to face her, the wheels turning, Lisa smiled, seemingly seized by inspiration. "Hey, if you're not having the party, maybe I'll get away that weekend. I've got a friend from college I've been promising to visit."

"Oh? Where's that?"

"New York City."

THAT AFTERNOON SALLY SHIFTED the phone from one shoulder to the other. "Listen, you're the fourth person I've spoken to at the National Archives in the last twenty minutes. I have what I think is a very simple question: How can I get my hands on *English* records that predate the settlement of this country?"

"I'm sorry, ma'am," said the woman on the other end, with the heartfelt indifference only a bureaucrat can muster. "I wouldn't be able to give you that information over the telephone."

"The National Archives is the chief repository for records in this country, isn't it?"

"Yes, we are, ma'am, but we don't have the answer to every question at our fingertips."

"Don't take this the wrong way," Sally said, trying to pierce the impersonal shield, "but isn't that your job?"

"We do the best we can, ma'am. I suggest that you put your request in writing. We'll get back to you within three weeks."

"Ms. Jacovitz, I don't have that kind of time—"

"How did you know my name?"

"I got it from"—she checked the scrawl on her yellow legal pad—"Mr. Horelick. Who was referred to me by Ms. Conrad. Whose name I got from a Ms. Jamison in your northeast regional office. At least I do seem to be working my way up the food chain."

"I see," she replied, suddenly wary. "Well, as I say, we would prefer that you put your request in writing. But my guess is we won't have what you're looking for."

"Oh?" Sally said. But along with the disappointment there was sudden anger. Why hadn't she simply told her that in the first place?

"We don't have many records from abroad. Probably the only place in this country that would have something like that would be the Family History Library in Salt Lake City. Their collection is remarkably extensive."

Sally jotted the words on a scratch pad as she repeated them. "The Family History Library—Salt Lake City."

"Some of their material's been computerized, but for the real old stuff you'd probably have to go there and poke around."

CHAPTER SEVEN

THE chimpanzee kept a watchful eye on Lynch even as he accepted the paper cup from the scientist's outstretched hand. Uncertain, he lifted it to eye level to examine its contents.

"Go on, Hank," urged Lynch. "It's ninety percent apricot juice. You'll like it."

The chimp's gaze went from the thick orange liquid to Lynch and back again. Tentatively, almost delicately, he took a sip.

"Aaffff!" came the guttural response, his face contorting in rage, his powerful hand crumpling the cup. Already he had rejected the drug in combination with a half-dozen other beverages ranging from Coca-Cola to Gatorade to imported beer.

"Try again," said Foster. "All we have to do is get one good dose into him."

Lynch hesitated. "It won't work. He doesn't trust me." He shook his head. "The best thing is to try again in a few days."

"Dammit," said Foster in exasperation. "What are we supposed to tell McIntyre and Reed when they ask to see new data on oral transfer of the gene? That we've only got one lousy chimp willing to take the stuff?"

Lynch's slow shrug conveyed his own frustration. "Thank goodness for Champagne Charley."

He turned to the chimp in the adjoining cage. Well into middle age at twenty-six, heavier and far more passive, he took his medicine without complaint. Charley had an inordinate fondness for cheap champagne and had guzzled down a large foam cup of André laced with the drug in less than a minute.

"I want to perform a biopsy on him," said Foster sharply.

"Another?" said Lynch in surprise. "This will make four in less than three weeks. The last wound isn't even healed yet."

"We'll do one every day if we have to. I'm not concerned with a chimpanzee's comfort."

As usual Lynch quickly assented. The data indicated they were tantalizingly close now. Where normally a primate's cells, including those of a human being, will survive in a petri dish no longer than ten days, cells taken from capuchin monkeys after oral ingestion were still going strong at nearly three and a half months; and the ones from this chimp, much more closely related to man, showed every sign of doing the same—and after but a single dose!

"Okay, now, Charley," said Lynch, taking the animal in his arms, "we just have to do this one more time."

STARTLED by the good looks of the woman who'd arrived at his office, Dr. Barry Schneider was thrilled to find himself equally drawn by her vivacity and unexpected humor. "I was surprised to hear from you," he said, smiling across his cluttered desk. "I thought you'd moved on to other phone conquests."

Lisa laughed. Skinny and bespectacled, with thinning hair, Schneider wasn't much to look at, but his brains and confidence did lend him a certain appeal. "You make me sound terrible. Don't take it personally. I'm a reporter. It's my job."

"So what do you want with me?" he asked. "Still fishing? Trying to figure out what my number was doing on that list?"

He'd hit it on the head. What she'd picked up so far about the institute in Manchester was at once tantalizing and deeply frustrating. She needed something concrete about Stebben's association with the place or the institute's link to the graverobbings. "Well, can *you* think of why a lab doing antiaging work might be interested in the bodies you work with here?" she asked.

"Beats me."

"They're just used for basic dissection?"

"That's it. Of course, there's been other kinds of research elsewhere in recent years on human remains, but we just—"

"What kind of research?"

"Let me ask you one first, Ms. Reporter. What are your plans for the evening?"

She chuckled. "What is this, a quid pro quo?"

"You don't know me. I'll take any edge I can get."

"Me too—you're on." She paused. "You were saying . . . ?"

"For instance, just recently a group of biblical scholars in Israel were looking into the genetic origin of the ancient Hittites. Were they related to the Israelites, to the Sumerians—*who?* So they extracted DNA from bones found at a Hittite burial site. Fascinating stuff. The genetic markers showed the Hittites weren't Semites at all; they were of Indo-European stock."

"They could do something like that after all this time?"

"The climate left the bones exceptionally well preserved. It's unlikely they could have pulled it off in many other places."

"Like anywhere in the United States," she observed.

"Well, they did dig up Jesse James's body not long ago in Missouri—ran DNA tests to make sure it was really him."

"But that isn't a dry climate, is it?" Lisa asked.

"No. And the body also wasn't five thousand years old. But remember, all these tests are pretty basic. For more meaningful information you really need soft-tissue samples."

She hesitated, thinking back on the conversation with Sally. "What happens to the bodies after you finish with them?"

"If the families are interested, the husks get shipped back home for burial. The organs are usually tossed."

"*Usually?* What happens to the others?"

He looked at her and shook his head. "There's a facility around here. But sorry, you're a civilian; it's probably off limits."

"Oh, come on. . . ."

STARTING with dinner at the River Café and ending with a stroll along windblown South Street Seaport, the evening went better than Schneider had dreamed possible. They moved from small talk to something approaching genuine intimacy.

Around midnight, heading uptown in a cab toward the college friend's apartment where she was to stay, he risked slipping his arm around her and was surprised when she leaned into him and looked up, eyes closed and lips parted for a kiss. Before they'd crossed Fourteenth Street, her kisses became deeper.

"Don't stop," she whispered.

"Let's go to my place," he said.

"First I want to see that place—the one that's off limits."

THE facility was in one of the older buildings at the edge of the med school complex. Flashing his pass at a guard, Schneider led Lisa down a long corridor and through a door marked PRIVATE.

"Hold your nose," he warned, fishing for the key.

She did, but even before he switched on the light, the odor hit her anyway, so powerful her legs nearly buckled. Yet even more overwhelming was what loomed before her: endless rows of glass containers, floor to ceiling on ancient shelves. Every one contained a preserved body part.

Gazing about, she felt a rising wave of nausea. "What *is* this place? These all come from dissections?"

He nodded. "The oldest date from the mid–nineteenth century."

"Why? What good are they?"

"Some represent diseases or deformities that were being studied at a particular moment; some were of interest because of how the patient lived or died. We don't save as many as they used to."

"I've seen plenty. Can we get some fresh air?"

"Right. I can think of lots better things to do myself."

IT WAS almost three a.m. when Schneider fell back against his pillow, spent. "Enough." He smiled. "I've gotta get some sleep."

She laughed. "You okay?"

"Never been better." He kissed her gently. "You?"

"Yeah." She snuggled against him. "I wish all my assignments went this well."

"How about if you stayed here the rest of the weekend?"

"I'd like that. I'll pick up my bag from Janet's in the morning."

They fell silent. Exhausted as she was, her mind was racing.

"Barry, that room with all those body parts—you say it's over a hundred years old?"

"Uhh," he said sleepily, "yeah. . . ."

"Do they have a place like that at Albany Union Medical College too?"

"Actually, yeah, they do."

"How about at Albert Einstein? And Cornell?"

"Uh-huh. I think so."

Could that be it? Were they trying to get their hands on some old body parts, long ago set aside and forgotten? But whose?

The answer that leaped most immediately to mind was unnerving. Was it possible? Could Sally be right? Was her family, with its propensity for exceptional longevity, really targeted for study?

The notion seemed more plausible with the passing minutes. At last, sure Schneider was out, she swung from the bed and tiptoed into the living room. She found her purse and pulled out her address book. Moving into Schneider's tiny kitchen, she opened it to the home listing she'd copied from Sally's Rolodex.

Should she risk calling at this hour? She hesitated, then abruptly dialed. It was too important; it couldn't wait.

Adrenaline pumping, she heard it ring once, twice. Then, not the sleepy, angry voice she was steeled for, but a recording.

"You haven't yet reached R. Paul Holland. But I do check in. Don't be shy."

RISING from the breakfast table Sunday morning, Sally was suddenly so woozy she had to grab a chair for support. "Mark, I don't feel too well."

In a nanosecond he was at her side. "Take it easy, Sal," he soothed, helping her back into her chair.

"My head's spinning!" she said, hands going to her temple.

"I'll call Malen," he said, reaching for the phone.

"Don't bother him, Mark. It's his day off. I'll be okay."

"Drop it, Sal. He'll be furious if we *don't* call."

"The forecast's for snow."

As he dialed, he glanced out the window at the low gray sky; true enough, around here even early season storms could quickly leave the roads impassable. "Then we'd better bring your bag in case you have to stay in the hospital."

"YOU'RE familiar with preeclampsia?" asked Malen after they'd moved from the examining room to his office.

"Oh, my God," exclaimed Mark.

Sally was more shaken by her husband's reaction than by the word itself. "What? Tell me!"

"I don't mean to alarm you. Fortunately, your case appears relatively mild. Your blood pressure is only borderline high, and there's no undue swelling of the hands or ankles." He paused meaningfully. "But this is a warning sign, Sally, and we have to take it seriously. Preeclampsia can lead to oxygen deprivation for the baby, resulting in damage to the nervous system. I want you to shut down. Stay at home until she's born."

"What are you talking about? What about work?"

"Should she stay in bed?" asked Mark.

"For now I don't think that's necessary."

"I say you're *both* overreacting," said Sally, indignant. "I'm fine! I'll just take it a little slower, that's all."

TWO hours later, after he'd taken Sally home, Mark was back.

"What did you tell her?" asked Malen.

"That I needed to run to the hardware store."

"I asked you back," said Malen, "because I'm going to need your help. This condition has to be very closely monitored."

Mark nodded. "I know that."

"I'll be coming by at least every couple of days from now on. But if there's anything unusual—blurred vision, abdominal pain, even excessive irritability—you let me know. Because it's for damn sure she won't."

"I don't think she'd do anything to jeopardize the baby."

"Not intentionally. It's that crazy grin-and-bear-it attitude of hers."

"Trust me. She's not nearly as tough as she seems."

Malen snorted. "You probably never saw her run the four forty back in high school."

"As a matter of fact, I did."

"Sometimes even when she wasn't the fastest, she'd win on pure will. Sally could give lessons in toughness."

Mark's annoyance was rising. Where did Malen come off presuming he knew Sally better than he did? "Speaking of before my time, what's with you and Paul Holland?"

Malen looked like he'd been slapped. "What do you mean?"

"I happened to see you two together. It was the day he made that job offer to Sal. I was driving by the hospital, and you were walking him to his car. Looked pretty chummy. I was surprised. Sally can't stand the guy."

"I hope you didn't tell Sally. It might upset her."

"No. *I* know her well enough to know that."

"He and I might be doing something together. A book on the life of a modern country doctor. But we have to keep it under wraps. You know this town. Even with pseudonyms, how do you think people around here will feel about seeing their medical secrets revealed in print?"

Mark nodded. Though the explanation was plausible enough, it avoided a more central truth. He knew full well that the doctor's real interest in such a project was the possibility it offered of associating with Holland and his big-shot friends. For that he'd betray his neighbors here in Edwardstown.

"Let's be straight with one another," added Malen, as if reading his thoughts. "You don't like me."

"Not much."

"Maybe that's my fault. There was a time I thought Sally would've been happier with some Ivy League type."

"Someone like Paul Holland," Mark spat out.

"Look, what I want to tell you is that I'm sorry. I was wrong."

"Don't try to placate me. I don't want to hear it."

"Mark, I don't care if you like me, but I need your cooperation now. I think we both know Sally hasn't been herself lately."

Mark looked at him in surprise, wondering how much the doctor knew. Was he aware of her growing paranoia? Of her sudden, overwhelming fixation on this library in Salt Lake City?

"So again, I really have to have that promise." Malen extended his hand.

Hesitantly Mark took it. Like it or not, for the moment this guy was his closest ally. "I'll keep you posted," he agreed softly.

SPREAD out on an autopsy table meant for human beings, the old chimp was a heart-wrenching sight.

The scientists still had not determined the precise cause of death; they just knew that once it took hold, it had run its course with remarkable speed. Less than eight hours after Charley refused his morning ration of fruit, he was bleeding profusely from both nostrils. An hour more and he was on the floor of his cage, writhing in agony. By nightfall, curled into a fetal ball, he was no longer fighting it. He died a few minutes before midnight.

Now, scalpel in hand, Lynch leaned in close. To the naked eye all the internal organs appeared healthy, but he quickly located the problem by touch. The small intestine, usually softly pliable, was stiff and unyielding. Slitting the organ open, he found thousands of mushroomlike nodules growing from the inner wall.

"Epithelial hyperplasia," Lynch confirmed.

"That suggests the problem is not with the efficacy of the drug itself, but with the delivery strategy," said Foster.

Indeed, Charley—the only one of twelve chimps to suffer such a fate—was also the only one who'd been dosed with the drug orally.

Lynch nodded uncertainly, peeling off a rubber glove. "Absolutely. This kind of thing happens in the development stage of most successful drugs."

"If anything," added Foster, "we've established that oral administration works *too* well. After all, if a single dose can stimulate such a massive *over*expression of the protein in this organ . . ." His voice trailed off. "Of course, we'll know more when we move up to a human model."

"You plan to run human trials?" Lynch asked in surprise.

"I didn't say that," Foster said, his expression impassive. "At the moment I have just one human subject in mind."

PAUL Holland didn't get home from his weekend place in Amagansett till late Sunday night, and it was only the next morning that he bothered to check his messages.

"Mr. Holland, my name is Lisa Mitchell, and I'm calling at some ungodly hour Saturday night. You don't know me, but I work with a friend of yours, Sally Benedict. By the way, I'm a great admirer of your work. Anyway, I'm calling about the piece you wrote a while back on the Life Services Institute—about certain facts I've discovered. I'm just here in New York for the weekend at 555-5623. This is quite important. I would certainly never bother you otherwise."

Glancing at the bedside clock—8:54—he played the message again. Then he dialed the number. A male voice answered.

"Is there a Lisa Mitchell there?" asked Holland.

"Could be. Who should I tell her is calling?"

"Tell her I'm returning *her* call."

There was a muffled exchange in the background; then the voice from the tape was on the line, only this time more guarded. "This is Lisa Mitchell. Hold on, please."

He heard her say something to her friend; then she was back on. "Why don't I call you back in fifteen minutes?"

"I'M ABOUT ready to kill her," muttered Sally, walking through the *Weekly*'s front door. She stamped the snow off her boots.

Florence, the only other person already in the office, was surprised. An hour before, when she'd reported the crisis to the editor by phone, Sally had seemed to take it in stride.

"What a pain getting here," she explained. "Seven blocks and I got stuck twice. We're definitely due for another editorial on snow removal problems."

"Well," said Florence, "at least it's stopped."

"For now. It's supposed to start again tonight." She paused. "I shouldn't even be here, Florence. Doctor's orders."

"Why? What's wrong?"

"Nothing major. I'm just supposed to ease off for a while." Sighing, she took off her coat and maneuvered herself into Lisa's chair. "All right, tell me about this lurch she left us in."

"It's just that I got in this morning, and there was the message from Lisa. No explanation, no forwarding number, only that she wouldn't be back for a couple more days."

"What's the problem? Isn't this issue about ready to go?"

"I thought so." Florence took a mock-up of the issue's front page from her desk and pointed to a space below the fold. "But this is the slot for Lisa's story. I can't find the file in her computer or any of her notes."

Sally took a deep breath. "Oh, boy."

The article in question was about a new ordinance under consideration by town trustees prohibiting the destruction of trees bordering on village land without specific authorization.

Florence was obviously expecting her to re-report the story over a couple of hours, then dash out the requisite five hundred words. But all at once the prospect seemed overwhelming.

She sat there a moment, unable to focus. Abruptly, from nowhere, the dizziness was back, sending her anxiety level through the roof. Was it the preeclampsia or merely the task before her?

"I'm sorry, Florence. Please forgive me. I've got to get home."

The older woman looked at her in alarm. "Are you okay?"

"Fine." Sally flashed what she hoped was an encouraging smile. "Just do the best you can here."

"MR. HOLLAND?" said Lisa when she called him back. "Sorry to pull the cloak-and-dagger stuff so early in the morning. It's okay; I'm alone now."

"I was surprised to find you at all, Ms. Mitchell. Your message said you'd be leaving town."

"I decided to extend my visit a couple of days."

"That message you left was quite intriguing."

"It was meant to be."

"You say you're a friend of Sally Benedict?"

"A colleague, yes."

"How is she?"

"*Big* is the word that comes to mind. Very pregnant."

"Ah," he said, wondering if there might be more to be gleaned there. "About this matter you mentioned . . ." He paused. "I've got a magazine deadline hanging over me, but we probably should talk. Would you mind coming down here? I'm at 415 East Fiftieth Street. It's a town house just off Beekman Place." Better, he reasoned, not to risk being seen with this girl.

She jotted it down. "When?"

"For lunch—say, around one? I'll order in."

TOWN house. Lisa wasn't at all surprised to hear Holland say he lived in one. The very concept bespoke the dizzying heights of influence and celebrity to which she herself longed to one day ascend.

Her first impression was sharp disappointment. The building was anything but imposing: three narrow nondescript stories in weathered brick. She approached it through a cold, steady drizzle, protected by an umbrella bought on a nearby street corner.

"Well," said Holland, "right on time. I always appreciate that. Come in. Dry off."

"Thanks." She stepped into the entryway. This was more like it: a gleaming black-and-white parquet floor, a small chandelier overhead, an antique mahogany umbrella stand.

"Nice place."

"It is. Unfortunately, I'm only renting." He shook out her umbrella and stuck it in the stand. He was surprised, startled even. The woman before him was drop-dead gorgeous. "Planning to stay?" he asked, indicating the overnight bag slung over her shoulder.

She smiled, flattered. "I'll be heading back to Edwardstown—I was due at work this morning."

"Ah. That's the way all my luck's been running lately."

"SO," HE asked ten minutes later, hoisting a chunk of lemon chicken with his chopsticks, "you enjoy working with Sally?"

"It has its moments." She paused, then impulsively added, "Frankly, I'll never understand how anyone could give up this"—her glance took in not just the apartment but urban life itself—"for *that.*"

He smiled. It was hard not to like this girl. "Is that why you're in town? You're looking for a job?"

"Partly." She flushed slightly at the admission and shifted in her chair, aware he was studying her.

She spoke up to break the silence. "This magazine piece you're writing. Are you allowed to tell me what it's about?"

"Scientific fraud—mainly plagiarism."

"Sounds fascinating."

"Harrowing is what it is—a cancer on the industry. But the sad truth is you find the same kind of thing in every business that attracts talented, highly motivated people, including yours and mine."

Flattered to be seen as a colleague, Lisa nodded soberly.

"One can't afford to get a reputation for sloppiness. In the end, our integrity is all we have. That's why, speaking personally, I'm always grateful to a fellow journalist kind enough to alert me to even minor oversights in my reporting."

"I don't want to give the wrong impression," Lisa said, suddenly fearing she'd be seen as arrogant. "It's just I've run across a couple of things that might be interesting. Not that it means anything. I mean, you wrote so positively about these people. It's hard to believe you might've missed something. . . ."

"For instance?"

She took a deep breath and let it out. "You never mentioned that they might be using human body parts in their research."

"Do you have information they are?" he asked.

"They've been calling university anatomy departments whose collections go back before the turn of the century."

Holland nodded noncommittally. "Well, that is interesting. I never pretended I saw everything. Still, given the nature of their research, that would seem a legitimate course of action."

"But why *old* body parts?"

"You tell me," he said, bemused. "It sounds like you've got some kind of theory brewing."

She hesitated. "I know this sounds crazy. But did you know there've been some graverobbings in our area?"

"In Edwardstown? Yes, I think I did hear something about that. Are you suggesting some kind of link?"

"It's just an idea. But there's evidence that the bodies are all from the same family. Sally's, as a matter of fact."

"That's one helluva charge." He looked incredulous. "We're talking about the scientists from the Life Services Institute?"

"It's just— I don't know. It's a theory," she retreated. "But what's interesting, what got me thinking there could be a connection, is that all those people lived an incredibly long time."

"Didn't they catch the ones who did it? The grave robbers?"

"That's true." She nodded, wondering fleetingly how he knew. "Only, one of them killed himself without ever confessing—no note or anything. And the other one took off." She shrugged. "But couldn't they have done it *for* someone?"

Almost imperceptibly he raised an eyebrow. "I'm sorry, Lisa. I've got to tell you it strikes me as pretty far-fetched."

"I know it sounds crazy," she said, "but I thought maybe *you* might make more of it."

"*Me?* I'm the one who wrote so positively about these guys, remember? If even a tenth of your crazy theory pans out, I'll spend years wiping egg from my face."

"Not if *you* break the story yourself." She paused. "You'll get everything I have. If there's anything to it, you'll reek of integrity."

"And if I don't take the story on, you'll pursue it anyway?"

She looked away a moment, then back at him. "I'm not interested in embarrassing you. But if you were looking for someone to help you out, I'd certainly be open to an arrangement."

"You're suggesting the *Herald* bring you on as a researcher?"

"The title doesn't matter to me. All I'm looking for is a shot."

He leaned back and folded his arms. "Well, you've certainly got persistence and drive. That's a helluva good start."

"So I keep telling people. It's nice to finally be believed."

"All right," he decided with a nod, "but this is my reputation on the line. I need to be absolutely sure I can count on your discretion. Who else knows about this?"

"No one."

"Sally?"

She shook her head. No way was she going to blow it now by mentioning her nemesis had suspicions of her own.

He sat there for a long moment thinking it through. "You're planning to return to Edwardstown this afternoon?"

She nodded. "My car's in a lot around the corner. I'm hoping to make it back by eight thirty or nine tonight."

"Which would put you in Manchester when, around seven?"

She looked stunned. "You want me to stop at the institute?"

"Why not? Let's not pussyfoot around. I want you to ask Dr. Lynch directly if they've graduated to using human tissue in their research. Because this all comes as news to me."

"But, I mean . . ."

He nodded. "I understand. It can be unpleasant when someone objects to the tenor of your questions. But that comes with the territory, Lisa." He smiled, reaching inside his jacket pocket for his address book. "Don't worry. I'll start you off with a safety net."

"Dr. Lynch?" he was saying a moment later, and she noted that his phone voice was as full of easy confidence as Sinatra in his prime. "Paul Holland of the *Herald.* Hope I'm not catching you at a bad time." He waited a couple of beats. "Listen, I'm sending someone to see you. Actually, I think you know her already—Lisa Mitchell, a terrific young reporter in your area."

By the time he hung up, she was already in her coat. He walked her to the door. "Call me as soon as you get back home. Don't worry about the time."

"I will. Thank you."

He gave her arm a squeeze and opened the door.

The rain was coming down harder now. "Oh, my umbrella," she said, and retrieved it before stepping outside.

He watched as she started off, again remarking to himself on how attractive she was. "Hey," he called out, "drive carefully."

THE rain started changing to snow about three hours out of New York, just past Providence. Soon it was coming down hard. By the time she made the Massachusetts–New Hampshire border, Interstate 93 was a broad river of white.

As darkness fell, visibility down to almost nothing, few cars were doing better than twenty. But Lisa's bug managed to maintain a steady forty-five, staying in the left lane behind a monster semi. She was late to the most important appointment of her professional life.

Still, she made it to her exit, just north of Manchester, little more than an hour past her goal. The institute was several miles from the interstate, off a two-lane road. To her surprise and relief, for she was wearing loafers, the long drive leading up to the imposing brick structure had already been plowed, and she was able to pull to within fifteen feet of the front door.

The plow-equipped Range Rover that had done the job stood at the side, idling, set to go again. As she cut her engine, its driver, a short, thick man in a heavy down jacket, came hurrying toward her through the snow, an umbrella tucked under his arm.

Before she'd even gotten out, he'd opened it for her.

"Thanks," she said, and stepped quickly from the car. Only now did she realize how bitter cold it was. "I really wasn't ready for this kind of weather."

"Well, hurry inside. We'll get something nice and warm into you. You're a brave girl to be out alone on a night like this."

"It's no big deal." She smiled. "I've got an appointment with Dr. Lynch. He should be expecting me."

"Oh, surely," he said, nodding to the left.

As she turned in that direction, a rag was suddenly over her mouth and nose, the powerful hand pressing down with incredible force. Startled, for an instant she didn't even react. The odor was intense, sickly sweet, overpowering. Now she began writhing, kicking at him, even as, from some classroom deep in her past, it began to register. Chloroform! But already the world was going dark.

A moment later Van Ost was carrying her down to the basement lab. The silver cylinder was empty, the walls of its inner chamber thickly coated with ice. It was only a couple of hours since the removal of Stagg's body.

"Set her down carefully," instructed Foster.

Beside him Lynch was expressionless. Though he wanted to accept Foster's assurances that Stagg would understand, he couldn't escape the thought they'd violated a sacred trust.

Now, studying the girl, her eyes closed, breathing easily, he observed, "She looks like Sleeping Beauty."

Foster closed the lid. "Try Snow White."

CHAPTER EIGHT

SALLY was alone at the kitchen table, relaxing over toast and jam and tea. When the phone rang, she picked up the receiver.

"Sally Benedict?"

She didn't recognize the voice. "Who's this?"

"My name's Barry Schneider. I'm a friend of Lisa Mitchell."

She tensed. "Do you know where she is?"

"I was hoping you could tell me."

"She hasn't been here in more than a week. The last we knew, she was heading to New York."

"I know. I was with her in New York. In fact, I wouldn't let her out of my sight. She was at my place Monday morning when I left for work. I get back, and there's just a note saying she'll be in touch."

"So you're involved with Lisa romantically?"

"I hope so—with overtones of the professional." He laughed softly. "You've trained her well. She never stopped grilling me."

"Grilling you? About what?"

"You name it—surgery, genetics, creative use of cadavers . . ."

Sally was glad he wasn't there to see her expression. "Genetics! Cadavers!" she wrote on her notepad. "Go on," she said evenly.

"You know her better than I do," he said. "You think she may have just been using me?"

"I don't know. Tell me everything."

LATE that afternoon when Stebben appeared at her front door, Sally wasn't entirely surprised.

"Can I come in?" Stebben's face was pink with cold.

"What for?" she said stiffly.

Though he'd only known since lunchtime, the chief looked like he hadn't slept in days. He'd been so dreading this scene, he very nearly passed on the assignment to Simmons.

"Something's happened," said Sally, not as a question.

He briefly averted his eyes, then looked into hers. "I'm afraid Lisa had an accident. She didn't"—he hesitated—"*survive.*"

For a long moment Sally's expression was blank. No way was she going to give Stebben even a fleeting glimpse of what she was feeling. "What kind of accident?" she asked.

"They found her car on a little side road about forty minutes from here off 113A, half buried in a drift. That little VW of hers. She must've pulled off the highway in the storm and got lost."

Sally nodded. Way out in the middle of nowhere. "Have they determined the cause of death?"

"Exposure. It's not official yet—the body's at the coroner's in Montgomery. It's quite a shock. She was a good kid."

"She froze to death?"

"The storm must've caught her by surprise. All she had with her was lightweight clothes. The temperature was down in the single digits." He paused. "I hope you know how sorry I am."

She nodded. "Someone will have to talk to her family." For the first time her voice wavered slightly. "I'd really rather it not be me, if you don't mind."

"All right."

There was a momentary silence.

"You okay, Sally? Maybe you ought to lie down."

"Don't worry about me."

He nodded and started backing away. "Well, I'd better get on it. But please, anything at all I can do, I want you to—"

But already she had closed the door.

MARK charged through the door half an hour later, calling her name.

"I'm up here."

He bounded up the stairs and stopped at the bedroom door, breathing hard. "Sally, something awful's happened."

"I know," she replied. "Stebben was already here."

Before her on the bed was a pile of laundry that she was methodically sorting, making small, neat stacks.

Mark stood, uncertain for a moment. He noticed beside the laundry pile a half-filled suitcase. "What are you doing?"

"Packing. I'm going to Salt Lake City. I have to know, Mark."

"Know *what?*"

"All those stolen bodies were from my family. Every one! Mother dies suddenly. Now Lisa."

He put his hands on her shoulders and looked into her eyes. "Sally, have you given a single thought to how dangerous this is to the pregnancy . . . to the *baby?*"

"I'm *protecting* the baby!"

"No, Sally—*I* am!" Suddenly, despite himself, he was shouting. "What's wrong with you? You think you're the only one under pressure around here? The only one affected by what's happened?

There is *no* connection between those things! Lisa died of *natural causes,* same as your mom! The graverobbings were *solved!*"

"I'm sorry, Mark. I will *not* just sit around doing nothing," she said, walking past him toward the bathroom. Reappearing a moment later, she flung her prenatal vitamins into the bag.

"Forget it, Sally. I won't allow it. And neither will Malen."

She zipped the bag. "The flight's at six twenty out of Burlington. I'll leave tonight and stay at a motel near the airport."

MALEN must have flown. He was over within a quarter hour of getting Mark's call. He had his bag with him.

"I don't know what to do," Mark told him.

"Where is she?"

"In the bedroom."

The doctor remained unperturbed. "Wait here."

"Well?" said Mark, seizing the doctor's arm when he emerged from the bedroom twenty minutes later.

"I gave her a very mild sedative. We also talked it out."

"She's not going?"

He shook his head. "I made her understand how completely irresponsible that would be from a medical standpoint."

"Thank heavens!" Mark exhaled audibly.

"I promised her I'd get you to go instead."

"What?"

"Just do it and hurry back," Malen said. "Don't worry. She'll be safe in my hands."

MARK got the next shock just past dawn at Burlington International Airport. The ticket Sally had reserved came to $1287—triple what it would have cost had this particular bit of insanity kicked in in time for the supersaver rate.

Exhausted as he was after less than three hours sleep and an hour-and-a-half drive through an icy drizzle, he still couldn't doze off. During the entire first leg of the trip, two and a half hours to Cincinnati, the thought kept rattling around in his consciousness:

almost nine hundred extra bucks pointlessly subtracted from the baby's college fund.

"Is something wrong, sir? You don't seem to have touched your breakfast."

He glanced down at the plastic tray, then up at the stewardess. Darn right something was wrong. Shouldn't all that money buy something more than a granite mini-bagel and lumpy eggs? "Thanks, no. I'm just not very hungry."

"I'M SORRY, sir," said the woman behind the Hertz desk at Salt Lake City International Airport. "There seems to be a problem. I'm showing you've reached your limit on your credit card."

"That's not possible. Can you try it again?"

She did.

"I'm genuinely sorry, sir," she said, seeming to mean it. "Do you have another card you can use?"

Sally must have used it to pay for the ticket!

"I don't," he said. "You don't take checks, do you?"

"No, sir, I'm afraid not."

"Is there a bus that goes into town?"

IT WAS over breakfast with Gram that Sally first felt it, a sensation unlike any she'd ever experienced before.

Even her grandmother noticed. "What's wrong, Sally? Is it time?"

The possibility was too horrible even to contemplate. She still had a month to go. "No, Gram," she said. "Just a touch of gas."

But within half an hour there came faint stirrings of nausea. Though she knew she should call Malen, instead she took a couple of tablespoons of Maalox and returned to bed. Almost immediately she felt better and soon drifted off to sleep.

THE pleasant bespectacled young man beside Mark on the bus seemed to know everything about the Family History Library. Of course he did, he cheerfully offered. He was a Mormon himself, and the purpose of the place was spiritual.

"We do family history research because the church teaches that family life continues beyond the grave. If we the living make covenants on their behalf, even ancestors who've been dead hundreds of years will receive the blessings of eternal family union."

"So the church began accumulating files of genealogical records?"

He nodded. "From all over the world."

Mark sat in silence for a moment, looking out the window. The morning was crisp and incredibly clear. Ahead he could make out the city's skyline and the snowcapped mountains beyond.

The library was in the heart of downtown, part of a vast complex that included the imposing Mormon Tabernacle and the office building that was the church's international headquarters.

Inside, from the high-tech lighting to the microfiche workstations strategically placed at intervals amid the shelves, it was indistinguishable from many other such state-of-the-art research facilities—except for the cadre of young volunteer guides patiently waiting alongside the reception desk.

Within seconds a clean-scrubbed young Oriental man—Korean, Mark guessed—was at his side. "Can I help you?" he asked.

"I'm trying to trace my wife's family. They came here from England."

"You have a name, a date, or place of birth?"

He pulled a sheet of paper from his pocket. "John Willson—with a double *l*. Mildenhall Parish, Suffolk. May twentieth, 1637."

"All right!" the guide exclaimed. "Then we are in business."

He quickly led the visitor down a long corridor, then turned down another. From the place-names affixed to the shelves, Mark realized they were in the section for the British Isles. "For most English counties—shires, they were called—what we have from that period are bound copies of early records," he said.

They stopped, and the young man scanned the shelf. "Here," he announced, standing on tiptoe to withdraw a volume. He led Mark over to a carrel. "These people made it easy. In Church of England records, events are usually listed chronologically. The local minister just wrote them down as they occurred."

With the birth date in hand the volunteer found what Mark was after with astonishing speed. As he read the entry, Mark was surprised to find himself seized by real excitement.

> 20 May, 1637. Born to Richard Willson, farmer, a son, baptized this day John.

"Why isn't the mother listed?"

"That was often the case. To find her name, we should look for the entry recording Richard Willson's marriage."

Less than five minutes later they found it.

> 4 May, 1634. Richard Willson, yeoman, betrothed in this church to Sarah Whitney, daughter of John, yeoman.

"You see?" said the volunteer. "Simple." He nodded and started moving off. "If you need more help, just ask for it."

This was just a start, of course. What Sally was so desperate to know was how long these people had lived. So Mark now jumped back twenty or so years to ferret out Richard's and Sarah's births—1611 and 1616 respectively, as it turned out. Then he moved forward in time, hunting for the record of their deaths.

Already, curiously, he was feeling a kinship with these ancient in-laws, and it was with a certain sorrow that he located the date of Richard's death with ease. He had "dyed accidentally by a blowe to his head," as the notation quaintly had it, at the age of thirty-seven.

But finding Sarah's end proved harder. After a quarter hour trying, Mark decided that in his fatigue he'd inadvertently passed it by. He was about to start over when he turned a page and the name jumped out at him.

> November 17, 1721. Today died Sarah Willson, in the fulleness of her years. 105 years, 7 months, and 12 dayes.

HEARING the doorbell ring while she slept, Sally came to consciousness. She heard her grandmother moving laboriously through the living room with her cane and the sound of the door opening.

Words were exchanged, indistinct but unmistakable. It was Malen.

The knock on her bedroom door came almost immediately. "Sally?" Malen opened it and peered in.

"What's up?" she asked sleepily.

He stepped into the room. "Just checking in. How's it going?"

"I'm fine. Just a little tired."

"Nothing else? No queasiness?"

"I felt a little something before, but it went away."

"What sort of little something?"

"It's nothing, Lee."

"Well, I'd like to take a look, just in case. Why don't you get dressed and I'll run you down to the office."

It was not a request but a statement of an intention.

"I really don't think we have to do that."

He snapped open his bag and took out the blood-pressure cuff. "We'll start here, then," he said.

"C'mon, Lee, I just had a little heartburn. It's gone now."

"You think you could sit up?" He held up the cuff.

Slowly she drew herself up and extended her arm.

"Tell me more about these pains of yours."

"Nothing to tell." But even as she said it, the feeling was suddenly back, only much sharper now. She winced slightly.

On the gauge her blood pressure read one sixty over ninety.

"All right, Sally," he said authoritatively, "we're going to the office. I want to do a pelvic exam. Is your bag packed?"

She nodded, panic-stricken. "Why?"

"Because I think you're in labor."

"Can't we wait for Mark?"

"Sally, get dressed and let's get out of here."

"Who else will be there? At the hospital?"

"Who'll *be* there?" he repeated in exasperation. "I don't know. I don't have a duty roster in my pocket."

"I don't want Dr. Crocker anywhere near me. Or Dr. Downs!"

It took him an instant to understand. Of course, her mother. "I'll try. That's all I can do."

She frantically reviewed her options. Was there another hospital she could get to? Madison was little more than an hour away. If she could just get to a phone, maybe . . .

She heard it before she felt it, a rush of liquid between her legs. "Oh, my God! I think my water broke."

MARK resisted the evidence before him. He'd gone back nearly eleven generations, into the early fifteenth century, moving beyond the Church of England records to the even older ones kept by local landed gentry—and it was nothing short of uncanny. Every second generation was astonishingly long-lived.

Just as Sally had predicted.

Was it possible? Had there really been a genetic mutation that gave this family such fantastic powers of survival?

The very possibility was mind-boggling. Their child would actually be *programmed* for a long and healthy life!

His fatigue was gone now. All that mattered was ferreting out data that would further support or—suddenly he didn't even want to think it—demolish the theory. But he never expected what he found. The mutation's source: Mary Whitby, 1297–1396.

Before her, Mark saw, the pattern did not exist. Within the DNA of this single, unremarkable woman, something astonishing and inexplicable had occurred. Where in other families genetic aberrations would produce centuries of heartbreak, Mary Whitby's heirs hit the jackpot.

"Okay." Mark reined himself in, whispering the words aloud. "Let's see if we can nail this sucker down."

The idea was simplicity itself: If Mary had had other children in addition to Sally's direct ancestor, the mutation should have been passed down in those lines also. Mark began moving forward again, launching this new search in 1297, the year of Mary's birth.

Oddly, the book opened to the page immediately, seemingly of its own volition. He smiled at his luck, then saw it wasn't luck at all. There was a sliver of paper in the crack halfway down.

He flicked it out and moved on.

Yes, indeed, there had been another child—Jane Whitby, born two years after Sally's more direct forebear! Mark located Jane's children, then theirs and the two generations that followed.

It was true. There was no longer the slightest question. This line too had inherited the longevity gene.

Mark sat back in his chair, exhilaration washing over him.

He reached for the huge volume to return it to its shelf and noticed a second sliver of paper. He picked it up, placed it beside the first marker. They were of the same stock.

As he stared at them, a single thought took hold.

Someone had been here before him.

Someone else knew.

Slamming the book shut, Mark was on his feet, briskly walking, then trotting, toward the exit. In the hall, he grabbed the first pay phone in a long bank and dialed collect.

Gram answered on the first ring and readily accepted the call. Thank heavens this was one of her lucid days.

"Listen, Martha, I have to speak to Sally."

"She's not here. I've been waiting all day by the darn phone. She's having the baby."

•

"HOW long do you think it'll be?" asked Sally in the labor room, making the question almost nonchalant.

"Hard to say. You're still only four centimeters dilated," said Malen. "Do I take care of you, or what? Crocker and Downs won't come anywhere near this place." He smiled. "Of course, it helps that they're both off-duty."

She nodded. "It's harder than I thought going through this without Mark."

But she'd forced herself to accept it. Everything will be fine, she kept thinking. I'm safe here. These people are my friends.

She could feel another wave of pain rising, rising till it began to crowd out all else. They were coming regularly now, every five or six minutes. As she gripped the sides of the bed hard beneath the covers, her expression scarcely changed.

After the contraction, Sally's eyes roamed the labor room. It was unlit and dim as the daylight faded between half-drawn curtains. "I'm pretty tired. Think there's a chance I might be able to sleep?"

"*Sleep?* While you're in labor?" Beside Malen, Barbara Walker chuckled. "I guess there's a first for everything."

"It's not a bad idea to try resting," said Malen. "We could be in for a long night." He started from the room. "I'll check back in a while."

Barbara wiped the perspiration from Sally's forehead. "I know this isn't how you imagined it, but don't worry. I'll be here for you."

"Actually, I'd rather be alone awhile. I won't be able to relax."

"Sure thing," the nurse said. "You need me, just holler."

MARK sprinted the block and a half from the library to a taxi stand and headed for the airport. There had to be *something* that would get him home fast.

No good. The woman at the Delta desk told him the only direct connection, leaving in two hours, was a red-eye, and it involved a layover in Cincinnati. It wouldn't have him home before midmorning, but if he hurried, there was a lightly booked flight leaving in twelve minutes. It connected with another that could get him into Boston's Logan around midnight.

He made it onto the plane just before they bolted the door. Taking a third-row seat on the aisle, he snatched up the phone embedded in the seat ahead of him and found his list of key phone numbers in his wallet.

As the plane was ascending, Mark ran his credit card through the slot. Instead of a dial tone he got a recorded advisory to try again. "Oh, no," he muttered, remembering. He tried the card again and got the same recording.

"Excuse me!" Mark said.

Halfway up the aisle, a young male steward wheeled to face him and flashed a programmed smile.

"My credit card's overloaded. Do you know if I can make a collect call? Or charge it to my home number?"

"No, I don't."

"My wife is in labor! I have to reach her."

"I can't help you with that right now, sir. We're very busy."

"Damn it, I need to reach her!"

"I'm sorry, sir," he said, and continued up the aisle.

Instantly Mark was on his feet. "Please, *someone,* I need help!" he shouted. Up and down the aisle, stunned faces turned his way. He whipped off his watch—a cheap Timex. "My wife's in labor. I have to call her. But my card's maxed out."

There was a moment's pause. Then, to his relief, someone was actually waving a card in the air—a middle-aged black woman.

"I've been there. Go ahead, make your call."

With a surging gratitude he offered her the watch.

"That's really not necessary." She smiled and handed the precious bit of plastic to him. "Just call your wife."

THE phone on the stand beside Sally's bed was the kind still found only occasionally in older hotels and hospitals; lacking a dialing apparatus, it allowed patients to place outgoing calls only during certain hours, via an operator. Since she'd already picked up the heavy receiver and found dead air, Sally was startled when it suddenly began jangling. She lifted the receiver to her ear.

"Hello?" came the voice, at once so familiar and a million miles away. "Is someone there?"

"Mark?" she asked with hushed urgency. "Where are you?"

Hunched over in his seat, he spoke softly. "On my way back."

"Really? *When?*"

Her excited relief heightened his anxiety. "It'll be a while. I just left. Are you all right, Sal? Is there a lot of pain?"

"I'm okay," she lied. "Contractions about every four minutes."

"That means you've still got some time. Who's there with you?"

"Right now, no one. I'm in the labor room. Lee Malen and Barbara Walker are outside."

"They taking good care of my girl?"

"Yeah." She paused. "What about the library?"

"I was there all day," he said with all the calm at his command. "You were right. Your family's got some unbelievable genes."

But she knew the nonchalance was a ruse. "What else?"

"That's all I can say for sure."

"Oh, here comes a contraction!"

"Hang on, Sally," he encouraged. "Hang on. . . ."

In response there was only a gasp, followed by the rapid, shallow breathing they called the dog pant.

"That's it, baby," he said soothingly, "just the way we practiced. Short breaths. One two three four, one two three four."

"It's peaked. It's getting a little better."

"Good. Now take a deep cleansing breath."

She exhaled loudly.

"You're doing fine, Sal. You're doing great."

Suddenly she heard approaching footsteps in the hall.

"What do I need to know?" she said hurriedly.

He was confused when he heard her cry of pain. It was too soon for another contraction. Then, in the background, he was aware of a new voice, surprised and questioning.

"It's Mark," he heard Sally gasp. "In Utah. Helping me with my breathing. . . ."

Listening as she went into the dog pant, he understood this was a performance for the benefit of the other person in the room.

"You listening, Sally?" Mark said. "Give me three short breaths if the answer's yes."

Immediately they came.

"I want you to play it safe. Stay alert; don't let them give you anything. Try to hang on as long as you can. I'll make some calls to get someone up there with you."

There was a pause, then the three short breaths.

"This looks like a pretty bad one," came the other voice suddenly, closer now—Barbara Walker. "Is the breathing helping?"

"It's better now," said Sally. "It's fading."

Moving beside her, Walker said gently, "May I speak to him?"

Reluctantly Sally surrendered the receiver.

"Mark, I know your intentions are good, but I think this is pretty stressful for her. Why don't you call Dr. Malen's line and leave a forwarding number? One of us will get back to you."

Before he could answer, the line went dead.

Mark rushed back down the aisle.

"Please," he said, "I need to make a couple more calls."

IN THE room, Sally watched as Barbara pulled the jack from the wall and looped the cord around the phone. "I understand," she said sympathetically, walking toward the door. "But the doctor was very clear. No more disturbances."

CHAPTER NINE

PAUL Holland was with friends for an early dinner that evening at a new Italian place in SoHo. He was in the middle of an amusing story when the pager at his waist began to vibrate. Stopping in midsentence, he glanced down at the display screen. There were but three words: COME TONIGHT. LYNCH.

He rose to his feet. "Sorry. A call I've been expecting."

THE first call from Edwardstown Community Hospital had come in the early afternoon, and there had been updates every twenty minutes or so since. Lynch took the calls at the desk in the library, Foster listening in at an extension. Each message was the same: No problems. Things were proceeding well.

But between calls Lynch stayed on his feet, alternately pacing and standing at the window, staring down the snowy front drive.

"What on earth are you looking at?" demanded Foster. "Holland won't be here till late—if he makes it at all."

"I'm sorry," allowed Lynch. "I guess I'm just a little nervous."

"Don't be." Foster nodded with certainty. "We've waited this long. What's a few more hours?"

CHIEF Stebben zipped his leather jacket up another couple of notches, as high as it would go. A man could freeze out here. What on earth was he doing?

But no, he knew. Though Mark Bowman's call had come at a bad time—fourth quarter of a good game on ESPN—he instantly had Stebben's full attention. The guy was scared—*terrified*—and Stebben didn't feel in any position to reassure him.

Okay, he'd made a few mistakes in his time, maybe looked the other way about things he shouldn't have, but the question now was how to proceed. No way could he march into the hospital. Sally Benedict would start screaming bloody murder.

Then abruptly the idea hit him even before the cruiser was out of the driveway. If there was anything to it, he knew what route they'd take: County Route 112, a little-known shortcut that knocked twenty minutes off the trip from Manchester to Edwardstown.

Why shouldn't he know? He'd sent off a map marking the road himself, just a few days before the first graverobbing.

SHE'D expected the pain, but what Sally hadn't counted on was that the contractions would leave her so spent. Only now did she realize that nature intended that every precious moment between be used to gather up strength for the next onslaught.

But that was impossible now. Even before the last one had fully abated, she was struggling to sit up. Swinging her feet to the floor, she managed to stand. Then, as the room began moving in a slow circle, she had to seize the bed's side rail for balance. Grabbing her robe, she made her way to the door. At best she had three minutes.

Opening it a crack, peering into the well-lit hallway, she saw that the plastic chairs lining the wall opposite were empty. An instant later she knew why: Barbara Walker could be heard at one of the pay phones around the corner, her voice hushed.

Quickly Sally was out of the room and scuttling down the hall in the other direction. She'd been here dozens of times over the years on both professional and personal business and knew exactly where she was going.

Turning a corner past the deserted nurse's station, she glanced at the wall clock. Seven minutes past twelve. It would probably be another six hours before any of the daytime staff returned.

The stairs leading down a flight to the back exit were just around another corner and to the right. If she could make it outside . . . . And then what? Look for a passing car? Give birth in the woods? She hadn't even brought a blanket.

But for now, all that mattered was escape!

Reaching the door, she gently pushed down on the metal bar to open it and was startled when it held fast. She hadn't even considered the possibility. This door was never locked.

"Damn it!" she whispered. She knew by now she had no more than a minute. Quickly she began retracing her steps. Then, at the nurse's station, she stopped. Posted on the bulletin board behind the desk was what looked to be the duty roster.

Suddenly the wave hit, this time without warning. As it peaked, the pain blotted out all else. Fighting it, she seized the desk, then sank into the office chair behind.

A FEW hundred feet away Barbara Walker thought she heard something, but there was nothing to be done. For now, her full focus was on Mark's best friend, Steve Montera.

"Look, this wasn't my idea," Montera was saying. "Frankly, I didn't even enjoy being here all that much when it was *my* kid."

Standing before the open elevator door, blocking his way, Walker smiled. "I remember."

"But when a friend asks you to check up on his wife . . ."

"She's doing fine, Steve. Hanging right in there."

"Can't I see her?"

"You know better than that—the woman's in labor. Now go home and get some sleep. She's doing Mark proud."

THE PAIN HAD LEFT SALLY'S eyes full of tears. She brushed them dry with her arm. It was half a minute before she was able to hoist herself back to her feet and focus on the duty roster.

Young Judith Marsh was supposed to have been on duty tonight, not Barbara Walker! But a line had been drawn through Marsh's name and Barbara's penciled in instead.

Her first reaction was curiously muted. Clearly such switches were routine. It was only after a moment that she understood she was starting to give up. The impulse to denial was overwhelming. Somehow she had to summon up the strength to resist it.

Spotting a tray bearing a roll of gauze and a scalpel, she snatched up the gleaming instrument and stuck it into the pocket of her robe before continuing down the hall.

Reaching the corner, she saw the chairs outside her room were still empty. But now, in the distance, she heard voices.

Could it really be? Montera?

"Help me!" she screamed, starting down the hallway as fast as she could manage. "Please help me!"

As the elevator doors slowly closed, Montera watched the nurse turn away. "Gotta run," she called back coolly. "That's the sound of a woman in heavy labor."

WHEN Mark's flight touched down at Boston's Logan Airport at twenty-five past midnight, he was the first passenger off. Dashing through the near-deserted terminal, he emerged into the frigid night and ran to the taxi stand.

"Where to?" snapped the dispatcher.

"New Hampshire," he managed, breathless. "Near Berlin."

"You gotta be kidding me."

"Please," he called, pulling out his checkbook. "My wife's having a baby."

He waved it at the first driver in line, an Indian or Pakistani. "I'll pay anything!"

"How far is this place?" asked the driver pleasantly.

"I don't know, maybe two and a half hours."

"Try *four* and a half," said the dispatcher acidly. "Straight up 93, then on Route 3 nearly to Canada."

"Get in."

"Thank you so much," said Mark, collapsing into the back seat as the cab pulled away. "I can't tell you what this means to me."

"Indeed you can. I've got seven myself."

There was almost no traffic this time of night, but the roads were still icy. Mark closed his eyes as the car accelerated.

"Do not worry, my friend," was the last thing he heard as he started to drift off. "For sure I will get you there."

STEBBEN knew this desolate road well—two narrow lanes twisting through a heavily wooded pass. Since the storm it was nearly impassable, a solid strip of ice. The chief was certain there'd be no unexpected traffic tonight. He himself had posted signs at both ends warning off intrepid motorists.

Only one driver, he was sure, would ignore them.

Stebben had chosen this spot carefully: a straightaway half a mile long, appearing after a series of harrowingly sharp curves. Parked at the midpoint of the straightaway, the cruiser would stop him cold. There was no way around him. The roadbed was raised here, dropping fifteen feet on either side. Just in case, a .38 Smith & Wesson was in his holster, and the department's Remington .223 rifle was within easy reach on the rack behind him.

Suddenly he heard the sound of the other vehicle approaching. An instant later the Range Rover's distinctive yellow fog lights flashed around a curve in the middle distance.

Less than a mile away, he was coming fast.

Behind the wheel Stebben reached for the rifle. Already the s.o.b. was hitting the last curve before the straightaway. Rifle in hand, heart pounding, Stebben rolled down the window.

Ten seconds more and the Range Rover was on the slick straightaway, doing seventy-five, heedless of what lay ahead.

Stebben flicked on his brights, his siren, and his flasher.

"Oh, no!" shouted Lynch in the passenger seat, shielding his eyes.

Stunned, Van Ost took nearly a full second to react. Though the Range Rover had four-wheel antilocks, at this speed, on this surface, they only helped him hold the road.

Leaning out the window, the rifle against the side-view mirror for support, Stebben watched the distance between them close in mute horror. It wasn't until they were within fifty yards that he fired, the shot crashing through the windshield.

Focused on the obstacle ahead, Van Ost was oblivious. He hit the cruiser just past the driver's side headlight, slamming the smaller car backward over the embankment to the left, where it flipped onto its hood. The Range Rover careened over the embankment opposite, plowing into a massive oak.

Stebben was dead on impact. Lynch, unconscious and bleeding profusely, did not last the hour. Miraculously Van Ost had suffered only a concussion and several broken ribs. But he was pinned inside the vehicle and, with the windshield gone, exposed to the elements. No one would come upon the wreck for hours.

USHERED into the institute's spacious library, Holland realized it was the first time he'd been in this room since the day he met Stagg. He was surprised to find Foster sitting in the old man's chair.

Foster checked his watch. "One ten. You made good time."

"I caught the last flight out of La Guardia. Where's Dr. Lynch? He wanted me up here immediately. Tonight."

"Asleep. He asked me to wait up for you." Foster stood up. "Do you drink champagne?" he asked.

"Is there something to celebrate?"

"Come with me."

Holland followed as Foster briskly led him from the room down a corridor to a lab Holland had never seen before.

"This is where we've done some of our best work," said Foster, walking into an adjacent storage area. Holland heard the opening and closing of a refrigerator door, and the scientist returned with a pair of slides. These he placed side by side in microscopes on a lab table and invited the journalist to examine them.

"Biopsy samples?" asked Holland, peering at the first. It showed healthy cells growing in a regular, mosaic-like pattern, the dark nucleus within each a near-perfect oval.

"Very good, Mr. Holland. You really do know your stuff."

"Human?"

"Close—chimpanzee."

Holland moved on to the second sample. Here there was mayhem. The cells were irregular in shape, their nuclei disintegrating.

"One of your chimps has about had it," he remarked.

Foster nodded. "You're right. The sample reflects extremely advanced age."

"And the other is younger?"

Foster looked at him meaningfully. "No, Mr. Holland. It's the same animal. The healthy sample was obtained two months after the first, following a single treatment with the drug."

It took Holland an instant to fully grasp the meaning. "You've nailed it?"

Foster allowed himself a small smile. "No one else knows yet. We're calling it Terminase."

Holland looked like he was about to hug him. "If I were you, I'd be bouncing off the walls. Congratulations."

"So . . . champagne?"

"Absolutely!"

Foster again disappeared into the back room, this time returning with a bottle of André.

"It's not exactly my usual brand," laughed the journalist.

"It's a private joke, actually. It's what we used to slip the drug to the chimp." He paused. "Of course, you're free to take it straight, as both Dr. Lynch and I did."

Only now did he see that in his other hand the scientist held a vial of colorless liquid. "You've tested the drug on *yourselves?*"

"And you'll be the third. As promised." He held aloft the vial. "Twenty milliliters. When it's marketed, a dose like this will cost upwards of twenty-five thousand dollars."

"Tonight?" asked Holland in a sudden panic. *"Now?"*

"The truth is, I envy you. Given your condition, your results will constitute the real breakthrough. We fully expect that whatever damage has already been done to your nervous system will be reversed in a matter of months."

Always a coward, Holland felt faint, but he couldn't allow himself to hesitate. Never again would he be handed so stunning an opportunity. "I'll take it with the champagne," he said, and watched as Foster carefully mixed the liquids in a plastic cup.

THE contractions were coming on top of each other now, and this was the worst one yet. Sally breathed rapidly, her cheeks puffing with every exhalation until, at the peak of the contraction, she clutched the bedsheets and cried out against the white-hot pain.

Watching, the nurse stood over her, arms folded.

"That was a bad one," said Sally a moment later, her face bright with perspiration. "Hold my hand, Barbara. Please."

"You're doing just fine," she said, taking it, but there wasn't even the pretense of warmth.

It had been nearly five hours since the nurse had caught her out of bed. Irate, Walker had not even responded to Sally's frantic claim that she'd just been trying to go to the bathroom, and she hadn't let her out of sight since.

"I think it's about time to get the doctor now," she said.

Already the next wave was upon Sally. "No," she managed with a ludicrous try at nonchalance. "I'm sure it'll still be a while."

Walker moved to the door and flung it open. "Dr. Malen!"

In seconds Malen was in the room.

Walker drew him to the side. "It looks like she's in transition. Contractions are strong and lasting more than a minute."

The doctor watched Sally struggling against this latest contraction. "You're pretty far along now, Sal." She grimaced, biting her lower lip, unhearing, as he said to the nurse, "Let's get her into the delivery room."

Only now, the pain abating, did she focus on his words. "Not yet! I'm not ready!"

"But the baby is. You're fully effaced and nine centimeters dilated."

"She's resisted every step of the way," said Walker, unclamping the front locks that transformed the labor bed into a gurney.

"Well, now it's zero hour," said Malen, positioning himself at the front of the bed. He nodded at Walker, behind. "Let's do it."

They'd moved the gurney out the door and into the hallway when Walker cried out, "Watch it!"

Wheeling, Malen saw the nurse was flat against the wall as Sally, still on her back, slashed at her with a scalpel. "Just keep away from me," she said with the remorseless determination of the truly mad.

"Put that down, Sally! You're going to hurt yourself."

"I swear, Lee, don't come any closer!" Her face bright red, her features twisted, she seemed utterly possessed.

"What should we do, Doctor?"

"Just wait." For he could see that even now a new contraction was taking hold. "All right, Sally," he said with quiet authority, "give me the scalpel." In no time he'd grabbed her wrist and was working the scalpel free. "Quick," he shouted at the nurse. "Get her in four-point restraints, and let's do what we have to do!"

"I'll cooperate, Lee," Sally gasped. "I promise."

Another minute and she was on the delivery-room table, her feet in the stirrups. She gazed around, wild-eyed, at the various monitors and the crash cart loaded with emergency drugs. Focusing on the wall clock, she saw it showed five thirty-two.

"Now *push,* Sally," ordered Malen with the onset of the next contraction. "I want you to *stop* fighting it."

Sally ostentatiously gritted her teeth and made grunting noises.

"She's still holding back," noted Walker.

He glared at her. "Dammit, Sally, do what I tell you! Don't you know you're putting your baby at risk?"

She made no reply. Already the next wave was starting to build, but his terrifying warning cut right through the pain.

"Should we put her out, Doctor?"

He hesitated, then nodded. "Get a syringe ready. Succinylcholine."

As the contraction eased, Sally saw that Walker already held the syringe at the ready.

"I don't want to do this," Malen was saying, "but you're leaving me no choice."

"Are we doing a C-section, Doctor?" Walker asked.

Malen hesitated, unsure. "I don't know. Maybe it won't be necessary." He leaned close to Sally. "Like it or not, this baby's *coming.*"

"All right," she said wearily, "I'll do what you want."

The next contraction was so intense that, closing her eyes, she could actually see the pain, kaleidoscopic, changing shape and color. It was like she was being slowly ripped in two.

"Push, Sally," urged Malen. "Only you can make it stop."

It only took another five minutes.

"There it is," she dimly heard Malen, exultant. "There's the head! C'mon, Sally, push! Just a couple more."

FOR an instant she felt only the wondrous absence of pain.

Now, cutting through the fog, came Malen's familiar laugh. "See that, Sal, nothing to it. You've got a beautiful little girl."

He gently lifted her for her mother to see. Tiny and hairless, she was remarkably unperturbed; indeed, she seemed to gaze about at this new world with genuine curiosity.

Sally reached out for her, the powerful, contradictory emotions surging—ecstasy and uncertainty, a growing sense of relief warring with deep mistrust and suspicion. "Let me hold her."

"Whoa. Mind if we cut the umbilical cord first?"

"Please! My baby!"

With practiced efficiency Malen double-clamped the cord and snipped it. "Now then," he said, smiling into the newborn's eyes, "let's spruce you up to meet this crazy mommy of yours."

"Give me my baby!"

"Okay, okay," he said, "we'll towel her off later."

He handed her over, and Sally clutched her close, arms around her defensively, shielding her from the others' view.

"Barbara," asked Malen, "did you catch the exact time of birth?"

"Five forty-six."

He looked up at the clock, which showed five forty-nine. "Why don't you fill out the form while we take care of the afterbirth?"

"What about clearing the child's ears and nasal passages?"

"No!" interjected Sally. "She stays with me."

"No problem," agreed Malen. "That can wait."

"Doctor, you know it's standard operating procedure."

"I won't tell if you don't, Barbara. We haven't gone by the book on anything else tonight."

Sally watched in tense silence as the nurse left the room.

Malen turned back to her. "Now, think you have one more good push in you?"

Sally kept a protective arm over the baby as Malen moved to the table and placed his hands on her abdomen. Gently he began applying pressure, helping her expel the afterbirth.

"Well," he said, smiling, as he heard the door open behind him, "at least *that* part was uneventful. But we still have a lot of work to do on your attitude—don't you think, Barbara?"

But the figure who entered the room, gowned and masked, wearing a surgical cap and gloves, was unrecognizable.

"Excuse me, Doctor . . . ?" asked Malen, confused.

"I'd like to examine the child if I could," he said.

"No!" shouted Sally.

"And you would be . . . ?"

"My name's McCall. I'm from Madison General. We got a call from the father asking that someone look in on this child."

"It's okay now," said Sally. "Everything's fine." Already she was edging off the table, the baby in her arms.

"You're frightening her, Doctor," said Malen curtly. "I really must ask you to leave."

"I have a job to do. I've come quite a ways."

Her soreness and exhaustion abruptly gone, in seconds Sally was in the far corner of the room with her child. "Keep him away!"

Eyes on Sally, the stranger continued slowly forward. "It will only take a minute."

Malen stepped in front of him, blocking his path. "Thank you, Doctor, but these are my patients. *Both* of them."

"No, Doctor," the man said, and from within his gown he produced a gun. "Stand back," he snapped. "This isn't a joke."

"A twenty-two?" said Malen. "It sure looks like one."

The gunman himself seemed startled by the crack of the gun. He looked on in silence as Malen sank to the floor.

The bullet had shattered his clavicle and collapsed a lung. As he lay there laboring to breathe, Sally made a sudden move for the door. But recovering quickly, the gunman stepped over the prostrate form and cut off her angle.

Suddenly the baby started to howl.

"I promise I won't hurt her," he said, edging closer.

Sally moved around the table, using it as a buffer. He circled around, stalking, as if they were children playing indoor tag. Suddenly her legs started to buckle, and she had to reach for the end of the table, the baby nearly slipping from her grasp. "Keep away!"

The man stopped, terrified by what he'd just seen. "Careful!"

Sally instantly picked up the fear. "Keep away," she said again, and now backed away toward the window ledge.

"Just hand me the child," he urged, following, his tone almost seductive, "and it will all be over."

She reached the ledge and grasped it for support, starting to swoon. "Please," she said faintly, "just leave us alone."

"It's going to be all right," he said soothingly, inching forward. "No one's going to hurt the child."

She started to totter, her hand slipping from the ledge.

Rushing forward, lunging for the baby, the man never saw the syringe flashing upward from waist level. It entered his abdomen beneath his rib cage and slightly to the left, the drug shooting directly into the left ventricle of his heart.

For an instant Foster was disoriented, then saw the words on the label of the syringe embedded in his chest, SUCCINYLCHOLINE, 20 MG, and understood. He looked at her with pained surprise as the color drained from his face and he toppled to the floor.

Sally watched in mute horror, the adrenaline pumping so hard she was unaware of the sound she'd been awaiting so long: the ding of the elevator.

Mark heard a baby crying as he bolted from the elevator and down the hall. The first thing he saw on flinging open the door was Foster, faceup and glassy-eyed on the floor, a tiny bloodstain on his gown by the syringe. Then he saw his wife slumped on the table with their howling child still in her arms.

"Sally!" he gasped.

"We're all right," she said. "Help Lee."

Across the room Malen managed to slowly raise himself up on one elbow.

Mark rushed to his side. "What happened here?"

"A tough delivery." Though Malen's breathing was labored, his smile was intact. "But we got through it."

IN HER first party dress and a headband festooned with fairy roses, two-month-old Helen stared wide-eyed at the throng as her father cruised through the living room with her in his arms.

"Quite the little party animal, aren't you?" cooed Steve Montera, following with a camcorder.

Lee Malen, his arm in a sling, smiled at them from the couch. "Just tell her not to forget who this party's for."

Montera turned the camera his way. "Ooops, sounds like the doc wants to remind us again of his heroism. Then again, if you're gonna get shot, a hospital *is* the place to do it."

"The battling co-godfathers!" observed Sally, setting down a plate of hot hors d'oeuvres. "I hope this isn't a preview of the next twenty years. Actually, Lee, we're celebrating lots of things."

In fact, though they'd delayed it until Malen was out of the hospital, the party's timing seemed perfect, for only now was the town itself beginning to recover from the gruesome episode.

To the rest of the world the story was a two-day wonder. Few news outlets even bothered to follow up that the renovated factory building on the outskirts of Manchester, formerly home to the Life

Services Institute, was now on the block. Only Sally seemed to notice that Paul Holland suffered no repercussions for having missed the story of the institute's secret project. The august *Herald* continued to feature his byline as prominently as ever.

But the night's terrible events shook this small town to its very foundations. Few in Edwardstown were startled to learn of the naked amorality of Lynch and Foster. It was understood that in other places the ruthlessly ambitious did horrible things almost as a matter of course, but Barbara Walker was one of their own. At one time or another almost everyone in town had been in her care. Even though she was caught that night on the Massachusetts Turnpike after an APB, some refused to believe she was involved at all until she pleaded guilty to attempted kidnapping.

Malen, at least, helped redeem the town's sense of itself—along, of course, with the late Chief Stebben. And if some harbored suspicions about Stebben's role in events leading to that night, no one was inclined to voice them now.

"Hey," called Sally, "how about getting a shot of the god*mother* for posterity?"

"Oh, really, no," demurred Florence, hand to her face as the camcorder turned her way. "I always get so tongue-tied."

"Right. And you told me you couldn't run the paper either."

Florence shrugged this away. "That's different. I'm just keeping the job warm for you."

"Uh-uh. I've never been happier, having only a weekly column to worry about." Sally looked around, her eyes finding her daughter. "And plenty of material to fill it."

"How about a toast?" Mark chimed in. "Everybody get some champagne!"

THOUGH this early February afternoon was nearly as cold in New York as in Edwardstown, the heat in Paul Holland's East Side home was turned way down. Holland always worked best this way; it helped him think. Supposedly fiction, the work in progress was actually a thinly veiled account of his own involvement with the project, and he fully expected it to make him more money than he' earned in twenty years of journalism.

Today, though, the writing was going badly. Awakening with severe stomach cramps, he'd had to drag himself to his computer. Hard as he tried to focus, the words just wouldn't come. In over four hours he'd managed only a few paragraphs.

Turning back to the screen, he reread them yet again, reaching for a glass of seltzer water. Suddenly he froze.

There was a drop of blood on his keyboard.

Now, as he watched, there came another. Touching his face, he felt it coming from both nostrils. He ran to the bathroom. The blood was pouring out, uncontrollable.

In horror, a washcloth to his face, he retreated to his bed and called his doctor but got only the service.

Now, all at once, the abdominal pains grew so severe he reflexively grabbed a pillow and clutched it hard against his midsection, drawing himself into a fetal position.

Lying there softly moaning, he was a pitiable sight—if there had been anyone else to see it.

"WELL," said Sally, eyes glowing as she gazed around the room at her friends, "I guess it's my turn." She paused. "What can I say? I've done lots of things in my life people consider incredibly interesting and exciting." She held up her glass and smiled. "To our Helen. Who would've guessed that having a child would be the greatest adventure of all?"

THE AUTHORS

MICHAEL CRICHTON

A knack for turning today's hot issues into megahit books and movies has made Michael Crichton better known than most movie stars. The former medical doctor has tackled such topical subjects as lethal viruses (*The Andromeda Strain*), the panic over Japanese investment (*Rising Sun*), the dangers of meddling with DNA (*Jurassic Park*), and sexual politics in the workplace (*Disclosure*). A planned big-budget movie of *Airframe* is likely to spread his fame even further.

DIANE CHAMBERLAIN

Diane Chamberlain first got the idea for *The Escape Artist* when she bought a secondhand computer. "Someone left some files on it," she says, "and I thought, What if they had left something incriminating? What would I do?" A former social worker who specialized in treating adolescents, she has written eight novels. Chamberlain lives in Vienna, Virginia, with her husband, David. Her two loyal companions in the photograph are Chapel and Ben.

PHOTO: DAVID HEAGY